DIRTY NASTY FREAKS
Copyright © 2018 Callie Hart

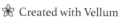 Created with Vellum

1

SERA

LIBERTY FIELDS

"Ma'am, I don't give a fuck what your GPS is telling you to do. The road's closed. We have power lines down all over the goddamn place and water up to our necks. Now turn around go back the way you came before I have your car towed."

The man wearing the high visibility vest, leaning in through the window of my rental, looked like he was about to burst a blood vessel. His name was Officer Grunstadt, and he'd eaten curry for dinner; I knew this because he'd been blasting me with his spicy breath while I'd been arguing with him about the state of the road up ahead for the last ten minutes. The twitch in his left eye was a recent display of his frustration. The rain had fogged up his glasses, and large, fat water droplets coursed down his face as he, once again, pointed back in the direction I'd just come from. "Liberty Fields is only thirty miles away. There are two motels there and a bed and breakfast, though I think the bed and breakfast was already fully booked the last I heard. You can figure out what you want to do tomorrow, once the storm's died down."

"I can't go back to Liberty Fields. I have to get to Fairhope, Alabama, in two days, or I'm going to miss my sister's wedding."

"I don't know what to tell you, sweetheart. Catch a flight."

"Every flight out of Rawlins and Laramie is canceled until further notice. I need to keep driving, officer. You have to understand, I—"

"I do understand, miss. I understand perfectly well. You're a pretty young millennial with a bad case of 'I always get my way.' You're not used to being told no, and you want me to break the rules. Unfortunately, I have a twenty-one year old daughter, and I'm used to all this..." He reaches out his hand, gesturing at my face, "...*nonsense*," he finishes.

Asshole. Rude, small town punk asshole. "Firstly, sir, please do not gesticulate in my general direction like I'm a piece of trash you found at the side of the road. Secondly, I am *not* a millennial. I'm twenty-eight years old. I'm a successful business owner. The reason why I'm successful is because I've worked my ass off, not because I've pouted, sulked, or convinced anyone to break rules for me. I know the storm's bad, but the winds are calming down, and Waze does say the road is open and clear just another mile up ahead. You have no idea what stresses I'm dealing with, or the consequences I'll have to face if I don't make it to this wedding on time. *So just let me through the damn blockade.*"

Officer Grunstadt gave me a tight-lipped smile and pointed through my car, out the passenger window, to the other side of the road, where an overweight guy in a yellow plastic rain jacket was eating a sodden Subway foot-long. "See Jo over there? Jo gets four hundred dollars from the state to tow cars. That's why he comes and stands out here on nights like tonight, come hell or high water. If I wave Jo over here, it's gon' cost ya an extra two-fifty on top of that four hundred to get your car outta his lot, and that's after the twenty-four hour holding time is up. So, Miss...?"

"Lafferty," I said, sighing heavily.

"So, Miss Lafferty. Is sitting here, arguing with me worth six hundred and fifty dollars to you? Or would you rather just turn back, get dry, get a good night's sleep, and hope the fallen power lines have been dealt with by the time you wake up?"

God, this guy was a real piece of work. I forged a smile, digging my fingernails into the rental's steering wheel, begging myself not to say anything that would get me into trouble. It had happened before. "You're right, Officer Grunstadt. A night in a shitty motel does sound perfect right now. Thanks *so* much for your assistance."

The road back to Liberty Fields was narrow and winding, turning back on itself a hundred times before I even saw another car. The whole world seemed deserted. I'd tried to convince Grunstadt the wind was dying down a little, but the truth was it buffeted and rocked the car like crazy as I drove through the hammering rain; I had to focus to keep the thing from careening off the road and into the dark line of trees that bordered either side of the single-lane highway.

"Should never have left Seattle," I grumbled to myself. "Should have just stayed home and watched Shark Tank, for fuck's sake. Wyoming is the worst."

My sister and I had always wanted to road trip across country. Sixsmith, my father, had forbidden us from doing it, which made sense. Sixsmith hadn't wanted us driving off, because he'd known full well we'd never have come back. He would have had no one to torture and manipulate. He'd have had no one to cook his meals and clean his house. He'd have had no one to beat on when he came home drunk and bored.

So I'd waited. I'd waited until Amy was eighteen, a legal adult, before I'd packed up our bags, stole Sixsmith's red Chevrolet Beretta, and got us both the fuck out of Montmorenci, South Carolina, for good. We'd worked in bars and as temps in offices, scraping enough money together to go to community college. Amy had studied languages, and I'd studied business management. Once we'd completed our degrees, unbelievably, Amy had moved out to South Carolina with her boyfriend, Ben, and I'd relocated to Seattle with dreams of creating my own consulting firm. It hadn't been easy. There'd been many months when I couldn't make rent, and many months when I'd thought about giving it all up, becoming a waitress, and living from pay check to pay check. I'd thought about that a lot, but I'd stayed the course. My persistence had finally paid off six years ago, when I'd landed a huge corporate account with a private lender. After that, I'd had more clients than I knew what to do with.

I'd had to take on three new members of staff just to cover the workload.

My H.R. department—namely a perma-harrassed woman in her late forties called Sandra—had insisted I take time off to drive to Amy's wedding. If only I could wrap my hands around Sandra's neck right now, I'd throttle her. It would have taken six hours to fly to Alabama. Maybe a couple of hours in a car on top of that to reach Fairhope. But now, here I was, after three days on the road, stuck in the middle of the biggest flash flooding the state of Wyoming had ever witnessed, instead of being tucked up, comfortable and warm in a fancy hotel.

Goddamnit.

As I pulled up outside the Liberty Fields Guest House and Artisan Art Gallery, I mourned the fact that the place certainly did *not* appear to be a fancy hotel. Fat lot of good my Hilton Rewards points were going to do me out here. The guesthouse looked like a derelict, abandoned farmhouse, perched on the side of the highway embankment as I pulled into the packed parking lot. My teeth rattled together as I traveled over a series of giant potholes, invisible in the near perfect darkness, and I swore colorfully under my breath. I didn't want to be here. I didn't want to be dealing with any of this. It didn't seem to matter what I wanted, though. The car rocked from side to side as I slid my arms into my thick winter jacket, preparing myself to face the weather. Through the windshield, the trees on the other side of the parking lot were bowed, their branches waving like outstretched arms, reaching for help. God, it looked fucking miserable out there.

Opening the car door, I swung my legs out, and my feet disappeared up to my ankles in frigid, inky black water. "Ffffffff—" I stopped myself from swearing. This night just couldn't get any better. Seriously.

There were so many cars parked haphazardly in the lot that I had to walk a solid hundred and fifty feet to reach the dimly lit entrance to the guesthouse. The rain seemed to come down harder as I half ran toward the building, my teeth grinding together. I had no idea rain could actually be this cold. Shit, I needed to get inside. I needed to get inside. The rust-flecked handle on the front door of the motel threatened to fall off in my hand as I yanked on it. A blast of heat hit me in the face as I hurried through the entranceway, and strains of Jonny Cash's 'I Walk The Line' flooded my ears. The left hand side of the lobby wall was fitted out with a stand—the same kind of stand you'd find in any normal hotel, where local businesses and tourist attractions advertise themselves—but the slots on this stand were all notably, depressingly empty. Liberty Fields was a black hole in the center of the State of Wyoming, zip code: nowhere.

The motel lobby smelled like damp and mildew. A puddle the size of Lake Michigan had collected in front of the rickety looking front desk; it was impossible to avoid the vast body of water as I made my way to the counter to ring the brass bell. Not that it mattered, of course. My feet were already soaking wet, right along with the rest of me. I hit the top of the bell for service, and nothing happened. No sound. No cheerful, inviting, *I-need-help* chime. Nothing.

"For fuck's sake." I looked around, searching for the night manager, but no one was to be seen. I leaned over the counter, hunting, hoping and praying for a savior to come along and tell me they had a secret, exclusive retreat out back that I hadn't noticed on my way in, but all I found were stacks of rotting newspapers, a metal dog bowl with food encrusted around its rim, and a mouse trap butted up against the wall. Very encouraging indeed.

On the other side of the lobby, I spied a public payphone. Pulling a handful of quarters out of my jeans pocket, I took advantage of the opportunity and I called Amy.

"God, Sera. It's nearly two in the morning," she groaned when she picked up.

"I know, I know, I'm sorry. I just—fuck—I'm still stuck in the middle of nowhere. I have another twenty-four hours to drive, and it looks like tomorrow's going to be a complete wash out. I don't know if I'm going to make it." In my experience, it was better to rip the Band-Aid off as quickly as possible, especially with Amy. She was hardly a no-nonsense woman, but if you strung things out with her, she tended to get a little hysterical.

"What do you mean, you don't know if you're going to make it?" Her voice was a little groggy when she picked up a second ago, but now it was sharp with accusation and worry.

"There's a huge storm, Amy. The roads are all closed. I'm stranded in Liberty Fields."

"Liberty Fields? Where the fuck is *Liberty Fields*?"

"I—god, *I* don't know. It sucks, though. I can tell you that much."

Behind me, the guesthouse door chimed, and a loud groan drowned out Johnny Cash for a second. I glanced over my shoulder, hopeful that it was the night manager entering the building, but when I saw the guy who stooped through the doorway to enter the place, I immediately knew he didn't work here.

A creature like that simply didn't exist in a place like this. Tall. Square jaw, lined with a swathe of black stubble. Bright, intelligent eyes—so damn pale, like quicksilver—traveled over me as the newcomer took in the lobby. The black suitcase in his hand appeared to be designer. Definitely not something a night manager would be carrying around with him. He looked like a character right out of Reservoir Dogs. Our eyes met, and there was absolutely nothing. No greeting smile from a fellow, weary traveler. No relief at finding someone else waiting in the lobby. Absolutely no flicker of emotion whatsoever.

"*Sera.* You do know what'll happen to you if you're not here on Saturday, right? I will disown you and never speak to you again." Amy's voice rattled down the phone. I turned back around, pressing the receiver harder against my ear.

"Yes, yes. Disowning. Eternal silence. I'll do everything in my power to make it, I promise."

"Don't promise me you're going to try! Promise me you're going to be here!"

"*Okay!* I promise. If I have to get up in two hours and break through the road cordons, I'll make sure I get there. How's Ben?"

"I don't know. Drunk?" Amy said pathetically. "Who has their bachelor party two nights before the wedding?"

"Hmm. I'm sure he's fine," I replied. I wasn't really paying attention, though. The guy who'd just entered the guesthouse was standing at the front desk, and he was about to ring the bell.

"It doesn't work," I told him.

His back was to me; he didn't turn around.

"Sera, we can push the ceremony back to later in the afternoon, but that's it. The weather's not going to hold into the evening. We have to make sure we're inside by five."

"I know." I pinched my brows, trying not to groan. "Everything will be perfect. Please don't stress."

I recognized the manic edge to my sister's voice. The vein in her temple would be visibly pulsing right now. "Oh, okay. My maid of honor's telling me she might not make my wedding, but I shouldn't get stressed. I'll just start popping those Valium Ben's dad pre—" The line crackled, and I couldn't hear Amy anymore. Static flooded down the line.

"Amy? Hey, Aim?" Nothing. The static grew louder, roaring, drowning out the thunderous rain hammering against the lobby windows. I pressed my forehead against the side of the payphone, slowly closing my eyes. Perfect. She was gone. No surprise, with the weather being what it was. I must have seen four or five downed telephone poles on the way into Liberty Fields. It was a miracle I'd even managed to make the call in the first place. God...

She was going to be freaking out so hard.

I turned away from the payphone, resting my back against the wall. The guy with the suitcase had moved away from the front desk and was stabbing at his cell like he was trying to force it into cooperating by sheer force of will alone. "Good luck," I muttered under my breath. "I had service until I turned around on the highway, then...*poof!* Gone."

The guy glanced at me sideways, and once again I was startled by the intensity of his pale blue, silvery eyes. His mouth lifted up at the corner into half a caustic smile. "You don't say?" His voice was the snarl of a chainsaw: rumbling, low and raw. He'd probably smoked a pack a day for fifteen years to get a voice like that.

If I hadn't already been frozen solid, I would have melted from the wave of heat that exploded across my cheeks. Turned out Mr. Black (as I'd named him in my head) wasn't so friendly. He slid his phone into his pocket, straightened his spine, allowed his head to tip back, and then cracked his neck.

He looked like he was about to say something else, then apparently thought better of it. He rubbed his hand through his dark, wet hair, sending a shower of water droplets up into the air. He was dressed head-to-heel in black, nothing too out there or ostentatious, but it was clear the plain shirt and the plain pants were brand name. His shirt was soaked at the shoulders, and his leather shoes were splattered with mud, but other than that he was very well turned out. His facial stubble wasn't due to neglect. It was the perfect length— not too long, and not too short. His neck and his throat were trimmed neatly, too, showing that he obviously took care of his scruff on a daily basis.

The men in my line of business were a little more showy with their wealth, their clothing, and their personal hygiene. A couple of the guys at the law firm opposite my offices had even started wearing makeup, believe it or not. I certainly had *not* believed it when Sandra told me she'd found a guy touching up his eyeliner in the elevator mirror one morning. It had taken seeing the exact same guy, doing the exact same thing, a couple of weeks later for the idea to really take root in my mind.

Mr. Black definitely wasn't wearing any eyeliner. His eyelashes were dark enough already, inky against the paleness of his skin. Perfect, really. The kind of eyelashes a woman would lynch a sales rep at Sephora for. I quickly glanced away when he turned to face me. Had he noticed me looking? Fuck, I hoped not. That really would have been the perfect way to end an already shitty day: busted checking out a particularly cold, frosty character in a crappy motel lobby.

"You're in the doghouse, then," the guy said. Once again, his unique, devastatingly deep voice caused a relay of electricity to run up and down my spine, lighting up my nerve endings.

"I beg your pardon?"

He pointed an accusatory finger at the payphone.

"Oh. Oh, right. Yeah. My sister. Her big day's on Saturday."

"And you're stranded in the middle of nowhere, in the middle of a giant rain storm."

"Yeah. Bad luck, I know."

He shrugged, scratching at his jaw. "Or bad planning."

I'd been told in the past that my death stare could literally eviscerate a man at twenty yards. Mr. Black didn't wither and die under the weight of my cold look, though. If anything, he seemed to be enjoying the attention. I buttoned my lip, choosing to ignore his barb. Yeah, sure, I could have made better arrangements. I could have checked the weather ahead of time. I could have used common sense and caught a goddamn plane, and yada yada yada. Just because he was right and I did land myself in this particular predicament through my own lack of foresight, didn't mean he got to chide me like I was a complete moron. But I could take the high road. I could be the bigger person and not sink to bickering with a stranger.

"You're upset," he offered.

I flared my nostrils, exhaling slowly down my nose. "I'm fine. I just want to get a room, get some sleep, and get out of this shit hole. Just like you, I'm sure."

Mr. Black laughed silently, propping his black suitcase up against the threadbare, heavily stained couch that had been positioned beneath the large picture windows by the front door.

"Not at all. *I* plan things very well," he informed me. "I'm right where I need to be."

"You came here *on purpose*?"

I was met with stony silence and a flat, indecipherable stare. "Liberty Fields is an historical landmark. Why not?"

I'd been out of the habit of rolling my eyes for well over a decade, but I felt prompted to give the ceiling tiles a once over in this instance. This guy was something else. He was baiting me, being difficult on purpose, and it didn't look like he was going to quit any time soon. "All right, buddy. Well, I hope you have a stellar Hicksville vacation."

"I'm here for work, actually."

If this conversation had been a text message, I'd have given him the big blue thumbs up by now. Being passive aggressive was a nuanced art, and far easier via emoji, especially when you didn't *actually* want to start a fight with someone. Mr. Black didn't seem to care that he was being kind of hostile, though, so why the hell should I? "Let me guess. Playing in an emo 80's cover band? Vampire coven gathering? Tarantino cos-play convention?"

Mr. Black's smile was cool and unruffled, though he seemed to be spitting sparks of ice from his eyes. His irises were the color of winter. The color of early morning skies in February. They reminded me of being very, very small. Smoke on my breath and stiff, unresponsive fingers. Stomping my thick rubber soled boots against hard-packed snow, trying to regain feeling in my toes.

It was amazing how visual or auditory cues affected me sometimes. I could be waiting in line to buy popcorn at the movies, and then the next second I was being dragged backward through time, to fifteen years earlier, when my very first boyfriend tried to make me touch his dick in the back of his pick-up truck.

Every time I saw the ocean in person or even on TV, I immediately smelled the peachy, light, fragrant scent of my mother's perfume, instead of the briny, salty sharpness of the water. My mind played tricks on me all the time.

"I'm a hitman. I took a job here in town," Mr. Black said nonchalantly. He ducked down, unzipping his suitcase, and pulled out an iPad, which he turned on. The white flare of the screen as it powered up briefly lit up his face before it dimmed. I jabbed my fingernail into the rubbery seam that ran down the side of the public payphone, considering his last statement.

"I hear it pays well. Being a hitman."

"It does." He was distracted, not really paying attention.

"So, you roll up on a dark and stormy night. You secure a base for yourself. Then you sneak across town while the place is in chaos, and you..." I made a gun out of my hand, pretending to take aim, "...*pull the trigger.*"

"Pretty much. Something like that. Though, I'm going to wait until morning. Roads aren't safe right now. Wouldn't want to end up being responsible for an accident or something."

That made me snort. "So you're going to kill someone, but heaven forbid you cause an accident while you're at it."

"If I'm gonna kill someone, it's because I'm being paid to do it. Not because the roads are treacherous and I can't control my vehicle."

Wow. This guy was good. He didn't even flinch as he spoke of murder. Most people wouldn't have been able to keep up the pretense. They would have laughed, or winked, or pulled a face, but not this guy. He lied as if he was speaking the truth. Looked like he believed it one hundred percent.

The lobby entryway opened, and a blast of wind howled through the door, pelting the couch and the small, peeling veneer coffee table with rainwater. A short, rotund, sour looking man wearing a cheap, plastic waterproof poncho bustled inside, swaying a little as he fought to get the door closed behind him. Mr. Black didn't help him, but then neither did I. We both just watched as the strange, oddly shaped figure belted the bottom of the door with his booted foot, slapping his palms against the doorframe, as if he were trying to reshape the woodwork with his bare hands.

"*Stupid...fucking...motherfucking...*"

The door closed, and the man stopped swearing. He turned around, panting, his wide frame shuddering as he looked from me to Mr. Black and back again. His eyes were a watery blue—inconsistent and weak—and his cheeks were marked with a spider web of ruptured blood vessels and thread veins. "You're outta luck," he said, slurring a little. Shoving away from the entrance door, he pushed himself forward toward the front desk, as if he needed the momentum to help get himself there. "No more rooms!" he cried. Instead of raising the hatch in the counter, walking through and lowering it behind himself again, he ducked down and scurried underneath it, growling unhappily as he struggled to heave himself upright on the other side. I crossed the lobby and leaned against the desk, being very careful not to raise my voice.

"I'm sorry. There *are* rooms available. Your vacancy sign's lit up in the parking lot."

"So what? Sign's always lit up, no matter what." The man, in his late fifties and reeking like a stale bar rag, flashed me a yellow smile rotten enough to turn my stomach. "Besides, I ain't had no time to turn the damn thing off. I been run off my feet, checking you people in and out all over the place. Don't know if you're comin' or goin', none of you."

Mr. Black appeared beside me and leaned across the counter, taking something from the night manager's hand: a long, scuffed, brass fob attached to a dangling key. On the brass fob: the number twenty-seven. "So you *do* have a room," Mr. Black said, holding up the fob.

The night manager tore the cheap plastic poncho over his head, exposing a broad section of dimpled belly fat as his shirt rose up; he growled under his breath as he wadded up the waterproof poncho and tossed it into the overflowing trashcan behind him. Above his left shirt pocket, the name 'Harold' had been stitched in black thread.

Harold staggered a little as he turned to face Mr. Black. "I ain't checked that key back into the system. So, no. It ain't free." He lunged to snatch the key back, but drunk as he was, he ended up grasping at thin air and nearly hitting the counter face-first. Mr. Black cleared his throat, flipping the key over in his hand.

"How much to expedite the process of securing this room from you, Harold?"

"Hey! I was here first. If anyone's gonna bribe him for the room, it's going to be *me*." I was far more successful in wrenching the key from Mr. Black's hand. The handsome stranger standing next to me didn't see me coming, or maybe he didn't expect me to hurl myself at him. Either way, I yanked the key from his grip and shoved it into my pocket, hurling a vicious look at him, just in case he was thinking about trying to get it back.

With the strangest expression on his face, he whispered a word that made my blood run hot and cold at the same time. "*Hellcat.*" His entire body pivoted to one side, away from me, as he curled a finger, motioning for Harold to lean in and speak with him. "I probably have way more money than her. What's it gonna be, cowboy?"

Harold, clearly a little discombobulated, just frowned. "The room's forty-nine ninety-nine for the night."

Mr. Black smirked. "Yeah. But if you give it to me, I'll pay you two hundred."

God, what a bastard. "I'll give you three hundred, Harold."

Mr. Black huffed down his nose, his smirk now a full-blown smile. "Five hundred, Harold. And a box of Cuban cigars. The good kind, not the cheap shit you can buy at customs."

Harold's eyes had glazed over a while back. He didn't seem to be taking any of this in. I grabbed hold of Mr. Black by the arm and tugged him forcefully away from the check in desk. "Look. You heard me on the phone just now. I have to get to my sister's wedding in Fairhope by Saturday. If I let her down, I'll break her damned heart. I'm the only member of family she'll have at this stupid fucking ceremony. Now, please... I need to drive out of this dump first thing in the morning, and to do that I need to fucking sleep. Please! Just let me have the fucking room!"

"You know you say fuck a lot?" he whispered, leaning into me, as if imparting a piece of information I might not yet be aware of. His snowstorm eyes flashed at me, filled with amusement.

"Lady, what's your name?" To my left, Harold scratched at his temple with the chewed end of a ballpoint pen. Oh, thank god. The guy had seen reason. I'd been the first person waiting for a room, so therefore I got it. Fair was fair. I breathed a sigh of relief, releasing my grip on Mr. Black's arm.

"It's Sera. Sera Lafferty.

Harold stuck out his tongue, his brow furrowing as his hand weaved toward what looked like a guest ledger. I risked a victorious sidelong smirk at Mr. Black, but I wasn't rewarded by a look of dismay plastered across his face. The bastard was still smirking, himself.

"And you. What...?" Harold hiccupped. "What's *your* name?"

"Felix Marcosa."

Of course his name was fucking Felix Marcosa. It suited him down to the ground. What an asshole. Harold obviously agreed with me. He groaned, shook his head, and then scribbled something sideways in the ledger. "I entered you into our state-of-the-art database as Mr. and Mrs...." Hiccup, "...*Jones*. Twenty-seven's got two beds. Figure it out. Now..." He squinted at me and then at Felix, narrowing his eyes. "What did we agree? Three hundred from *you*," he said, pointed at me. "And five hundred from *you*. Plus...a box of Cuban cigars."

Felix Marcosa wasn't smiling anymore.

But then again, neither was I.

2

FIX

HOW PEDESTRIAN

a person's hands tell most of their stories. You can learn a lot about someone by simply studying the wear and tear to their hands. As Sera Lafferty lugged her bag down the flooded walkway toward room number twenty-seven, her knuckles were blanched. I noticed the two deep, perpendicular scars that ran across the back of her right hand, silvery and smooth under the bright, white security lights. The scars were defensive wounds. Would have bled a lot. There was every chance her tendons had been severed given the placement of the scars, which would have meant months of excruciating, time consuming physical therapy. She'd been lucky she hadn't completely lost the use of her hand altogether.

What did Sera's scars tell me about her, other than the fact that she'd been assaulted at some point? They told me she was a fighter. They told me she was fierce. I made a number of deductions as I followed close behind her toward the room, my shoulders hunched up around my ears against the rain.

One: Sera Lafferty's attacker was someone very close to her. Someone she knew very, very well.

Two: Ever since she'd been attacked, she'd spiraled out of control, allowing herself to stumble blindly from one dangerous situation to another.

Three: If I wanted to, I could fuck her and slit her throat tonight, and she probably wouldn't even care.

Not that I'd do that, though. I didn't rape women.

When we reached the green-painted door with the gold two and seven etched onto it, Sera slid the key into the lock and tossed an irritated look at me over her shoulder. "Guess you're not as good at planning as you thought you were," she snapped. "You'd have booked a room ahead of time if you were."

"I'm right where I'm meant to be," I said, echoing my words from before, back in the lobby. If only she knew...

Sera didn't notice my repetition. Or, if she did, she didn't say anything about it. Most women in her position would have screamed and pleaded with Harold at the front desk, begging to be allocated the room on their own. If that hadn't worked, other women would have cursed me out, thrown up their hands and gone and slept in their car for the night. A car was a safe, metal box, studded with locks. A car was easily defensible. It had a loud alarm and flashing lights. But Sera simply scowled at me, shrugged, handed over three hundred dollars to Harold, then hurried out to her car to collect her bags.

The inside of room twenty-seven was pretty goddamn miserable. There were two beds, just as Harold had claimed, but they were clearly about thirty years old and heavily sunken in the middle. Both of them were as bad as each other. The walls used to be white at some point. Or maybe...peach? Now they were a scuzzy nicotine-stained yellow, and the air buzzed with the stench of old cigarettes. In the corner, an old television with a dial to change the channels sat on top of an old, scratched dresser, the top drawer of which was missing.

Sera didn't seem to notice any of it. "I'm taking the bed closer to the door," she announced. "If you don't like it, you can go ask for your money back and sleep on that couch in the lobby."

"The other bed's fine." I hefted my suitcase up and slung it onto the mattress, surprised when the whole bed didn't collapse under the weight of the bag.

"Jesus, what have you got in there?" Sera mumbled. "Bricks?"

"Guns," I corrected. "Lots and lots of guns." Being honest was one of my favorite games. It was far more entertaining to tell someone the truth and let them make of it whatever they chose than to fabricate some boring, fake life. Sera, like most people I told the truth, thought I was being ridiculous and decided to mock me for it.

"Oh, right. Because you're a hitman, and you have to kill someone in town tomorrow. Silly me. How could I forget?"

She was beautiful. Beautiful in an unconventional way that didn't meet any of my usual requirements. For me to find a woman attractive, she usually had to be short and petite. She had to have long hair, either red or blonde, and blue eyes. She had to be submissive and pretty damn quiet, too, unless we were in bed. In that case, she could be as loud as she damn well pleased.

Sera was a brunette, her hair cropped into an edgy, shoulder-length style that was longer at the front than it was at the back. Her eyes were dark, dark brown, filled with intelligence and suspicion. She was close to five-nine, though in her heeled leather boots, she nearly stood as tall as me at six-one, and as far as the submissive thing went...I could already tell there was no hope of that ever happening. She was forged in the fire, this one. There wouldn't be any cooling her or calming her down. If she were one of my grandfather's horses back on his farm, he would have eyed her for a second or two, paced around her, looking her up and down, and then declared she needed cutting loose. He wouldn't have even bothered wasting his time trying to tame her.

"I'd appreciate it if you didn't turn the television on," she said, unzipping her own bag. "I'm a light sleeper."

"Naturally. And I'd appreciate it if you didn't get your makeup all over every single towel in the bathroom. I'm allergic to all the weird crap they put in that stuff."

Sera huffed as she pulled a blow dryer out of her bag, winding the cable around its handle. "Fair enough. But there's no weird crap in makeup. You don't need to be an ass just because I asked you not to do something."

"Bird shit."

"What did you just say?"

I pulled back the sheets on my bed, inspecting them for any suspect stains. So far, all was clear. "Bird shit. They put that in some makeups and moisturizers. As well as snail secretions. And baby foreskins."

Sera dropped her blow dryer onto her pillow, rounding on me, hands on her hips. "What the *fuck* are you talking about?"

"Look it up. All those magical creams, powders and potions you smear onto your skin every day? They're fucking gross. But who cares, so long as they hide the cracks, right?"

Her face darkened to the point where I could almost see the thundercloud hovering over her head. "I don't have any 'cracks.' And also, they do *not* put baby foreskins in makeup."

"All right. If you say so." I took a shirt out of my bag, then removed my shoes and began picking at the mud that was crusted around the sole. How long was it going to take her to react? Three minutes? Five? 'All right. If you say so,' was probably the most incendiary thing a man could say to a woman. They couldn't fucking stand it. With her fiery temper, it wouldn't be long now before Sera was ripping her own shoes from her feet and throwing them at me.

Instead, as if she knew what I expected her to do and was determined to prove me wrong, she sat slowly in a chair and began humming softly.

I grabbed my wash bag, a set of clean, dry clothes, and headed into the bathroom.

"What are you doing?"

I glanced back at her over my shoulder. "Showering." I smiled my most inviting smile. The one I used to coerce women into my bed. The one that never failed to work. "Care to join me?"

Sera pulled a disgusted face, apparently immune to the smile, right along with the disreputable glint in my eyes. "I'm not in the business of showering with perfect strangers."

"This place is probably running on a generator. Who knows when the hot water's going to run out," I countered.

"I'll take my chances."

"Suit yourself." I closed the bathroom door and locked it behind me. Of course she wasn't going to shower with me. It was fun fucking with such an uptight person, though. Sera carried herself with confidence. She knew she was attractive, and there was nothing wrong with that. First meetings with women like her, sexual or otherwise, were always a power struggle, however. She wanted to assert her dominance over me, and I was damned if I was going to let her. The moment I gave in and bowed down to her, worshipping her for the goddess she was, she'd no longer respect me. Or the idea of me. Whenever a man and a woman met for the first time, it was human nature for both of them to imagine some reality in which they were fucking, regardless of their marital status, desires or inclinations. If you showed me a person who claimed otherwise, I'd show you a liar. I wasn't having her imagining she could dominate me in the bedroom. So baiting her, refusing to be the simpering, weak gentleman she's probably used to, was just par for the course.

I turned on the shower, wrestling out of my wet clothes, and then, naked, I studied my face in the mirror, rubbing my hand across my jaw to see if I needed a shave yet. I usually avoided mirrors at all costs; I had my father's eyes—hard to fucking miss—and my mother's nose. My mouth was my father's, too. What would they both think of me now? The life I'd chosen for myself. The steeply inclined, slippery as fuck path I'd begun descending straight down into hell.

Thankfully, I'd never know their shallow opinion of me. The priest and his obedient homemaker wife were both long gone. St. Peter must have alerted the media the moment my parents arrived at the pearly gates, shortly after plowing into the back of an articulated truck one frosty, dark October night in Upstate New York. If anyone had been guaranteed VIP entry into Heaven, it was those two. They'd been poster children for the Catholic Faith their entire lives. And I was their biggest disappointment.

I scowled at the pieces of Eric and Louisa Marcosa staring back at me in the mirror, defying them in the only way I still had left available to me. My image slowly disappeared, eaten up by the steam from the hot shower that gradually fogged the glass, and the ghosts fled the bathroom, leaving me standing stripped bare and very much alone.

I showered, thinking hard. I had two jobs on my books, and neither one of them was going to be pretty. Tomorrow's job was gonna be really shitty. I'd already accepted the payment, so I couldn't back out of the job, but the more and more I thought about it, the less and less I wanted to dirty my hands with the work.

The guy, Franz Halford, owned an auto mechanics' shop on the other side of Liberty Fields—had inherited it from his grandfather about twenty years ago. No wife. No children. Just a pile of bad debt and a racist streak a mile wide. I always made a point of investigating why my clients wanted their targets dead—due diligence was important. Crucial in my line of work—and this instance had been no exception. When I'd reviewed Franz Halford's file, going over the paperwork that had been supplied to me, explaining why the world would be a better place without Franz Halford in it, it had been a pretty clear cut case, as far as I could see. Franz had raped a young woman. A twenty-year-old college student by the name of Holly Shoji. And he hadn't raped her because he thought she was attractive (though she was), or because she blew him off in a bar one night when he was drunk and making a fool of himself. He'd done it because she was Japanese, and Franz Halford didn't like Japanese people. He didn't like anyone unless they were white.

My own skin was pretty damn Caucasian, but I had Spanish heritage. My great-grandparents on my father's side were both from Altea, a tiny coastal town in the south of Spain, but they'd come over to America just before the start of the Second World War in search of a new life. Ridiculously, I'd had issues with people in the past. When they heard my family name—usually the only clue that I wasn't pure as the driven snow—they'd cast a derisive glance over me, looking for the tell: the set of my features, or my height, or an accent that would set me apart from them, marking me as different. I despised the motherfuckers who looked at me like that. I usually wanted to cleave their head from the base of their neck, which was why accepting a racist as a mark was a horrific idea. I'd been heavily involved in this line of work for the past five years. The only time I'd ever come close to being caught by the authorities was in a situation very similar to this one; a young girl had been kidnapped by a group of Clan members in the middle of bum fuck nowhere, Tennessee. I'd laid the place to waste, taking my time torturing each and every one of those sick pieces of shit for the brutal acts they'd committed to that fifteen-year-old girl's body. I'd broken my own rules and stayed in that dingy, dirty rat-infested warehouse too long, and when I burned out of there in one of their stolen cars, I'd barely missed the fleet of cop cars that rolled up on the place only moments later.

God only knows what they had made of the chaos and destruction they found when they threw up those roller shutters and saw what was inside. They probably still had nightmares about it.

The shower water was scalding, but that didn't seem to have helped the temperature inside the bathroom when I stepped out of the tiled cubicle. The air was frigid, biting at my skin, and I hurried to get dry as quickly as possible. While the rest of my body was suffering from borderline hypothermia, my dick didn't seem to have noticed the cold. I had a raging hard-on that was becoming difficult to ignore. I glanced down at it, contemplating stroking it for just a second, but then I decided against it. There was no such thing as just a second when it came to jerking off—I either completed the task at hand, or I didn't start it in the first place—and I didn't have time to be touching my cock. Not with Sera sitting on the other side of the bathroom door. She was the reason I had a fucking erection in the first place. She seemed smart as well as beautiful, and it wouldn't take much for her to figure out what the hell I was doing in here if I didn't come out fairly soon.

Once dressed, I left the bathroom, rubbing at my damp hair with a towel. Sera pursed her lips as she looked up at me over the top of a book. She'd moved from the chair and was now lying on her bed, propped up against a stack of lumpy looking pillows. "Your cell phone's been blowing up," she said, curving a dark eyebrow at me. "Who, or what, is a 'Fix'?"

Well, well, well. She'd looked at my phone? I curved an eyebrow right back at her. "Naughty girl. You make a habit of invading the privacy of total strangers?"

"I did no such thing. Harold from the front desk called while you were primping and preening in there. He asked me to give you a message. He said, a woman called Monica called, and said..." Sera cleared her throat, closing her book and laying it on top of her chest. "'*Fuck you, Fix. You're already late. If you don't come home soon, I'm coming to find you.*"

Urgh. Monica. What the hell was she doing, calling the motel? I'd only told her where I was so she'd quit calling me every five seconds. Now she had the name of the place I was staying, I'd simply given her another avenue through which to harass me, apparently. And Harold shouldn't have given a message meant for me to another guest, but then again Harold was fucking useless and didn't know his ass from his elbow, so...

I collected my cell from the night stand beside my bed, and sure enough I had six missed calls from Monica, alongside a collection of colorfully worded text messages that would have made a sailor blush.

"You still haven't answered my question," Sera said loftily.

"Hmm?"

"Fix?"

I laughed, sliding my phone into my back pocket. "Felix. Fix. I'm Fix. That's what some people call me." If they knew I murdered people for a living, that's what they called me, anyway. Five years ago, I'd made a decision. I'd stood in a hospital, covered in blood, hands sticky with it, and I'd decided that there was no justice in the world. I'd decided to rectify the situation. I'd set Felix aside, and I'd become Fix.

Since that night, I'd spend every waking moment searching for the bastard who'd hurt the woman under my care. I hadn't found him yet, but I had a long fucking memory. I wasn't about to give up any time soon.

"A verb as a nickname. How pedestrian," Sera mused, lifting a glass to her lips. Her tone was a little mocking, but I could see she was intrigued. She probably wanted to know who Monica was. She probably wanted to know what I was eight days late for. Shame I wasn't going to tell her. The amber liquid in her glass caught the light as Sera tipped it back, taking a healthy swig.

"That's a healthy pour. You plan on driving with a hangover tomorrow?" I said.

She laughed softly, shaking her head. The glass was now empty. "I learned how to throw back tequila when I was fourteen-years-old. I can drink most people under the table. Haven't had a hangover in years."

God. If I were any kind of asshole, which I was, this was the moment I'd offer to test out that theory. I wasn't about to fulfill whatever expectations she'd clearly formed of me, though. Sera and I were still playing our little game of *who's in control here?* And I didn't lose that motherfucking game. Ever.

"I can leave the room if you need to return all those phone calls," Sera said. Her voice was interesting—a little huskier than most women, which was a nice change. I'd had enough of nasal, high pitched, whiny girls to last me a lifetime. The tequila had probably set a rough edge to her tone, but I wasn't complaining; it was sexy as fuck.

"Thanks. I'm good."

"Ah. So you're a player. You're going to keep little Miss Monica waiting."

Ha! Keeping Monica waiting? That was a fucking riot. I smirked, laying down on my bed. "You want to know if I'm fucking her."

A scandalized look flashed across Sera's face. She had a faint scar running along her jawline that I hadn't noticed before. The silvery line of healed tissue was narrow, no wider than the blade of a knife, and must have been expertly stitched, because it was barely visible. I probably wouldn't have noticed it had she not dramatically reacted to my statement.

"I don't want to know that. I don't want to know anything. I'm merely making an observation."

I assessed her scar surreptitiously, only allowing my eyes to skate over it one more time before I raised my gaze to hers. You didn't get a scar like that accidentally. It was too long and straight and perfect to have been caused by anything other than a weapon. So Sera was interesting, after all. She wasn't just a prissy princess with a bad attitude. She had stories of her own to tell. Not that I was going to ask her to spill. That would make things complicated. That would be a point to Sera, and I was still keeping a weather eye on the leader board. "You're judging me," I said. "You're trying to figure out who I am."

A long pause followed, a small, shallow line forming between Sera's perfectly manicured brows. "*And*?" She sounded frustrated. "That's what people do when they meet other people. They form opinions of them. They try and decide if they like the other person or not."

"What does it matter if you like me or not? Why would it matter if I was the biggest asshole on the face of the planet? We're here for one night. Once tomorrow morning arrives, you're going your way and I'm going mine. You'll never see me again, and you'll have wasted all that precious time making *decisions* about me."

I could play this game forever. Sera stared at me for a drawn out second. All my life, I'd been told over and over again how confronting my eyes were. Too blue. Too cold. Too paralyzing. Too piercing. When Sera turned her warm, chocolate eyes on me, I finally began to understand what people were talking about. It wasn't that they were out of the ordinary, or even that remarkable for that matter, but the intelligence that existed in her eyes, shining out from her intricately painted irises, was enough to pin me to the mattress. Looking directly at her was like looking directly into the eyes of a tiger. There was so much happening behind the look, so much going on inside her head, and yet she managed to conceal it all so well. Still, I knew she was sizing me up. Trying to decide if she could take me on, one way or another.

Inhaling sharply, she sat up, breaking off our weird little staring contest. "You're right," she said, reaching for her purse. "I won't waste my time making any more decisions." Out of her bag came a bottle of Clase Azul Reposado tequila, which she set down on top of her comforter, leaning it against her leg so she could unscrew the top. Another considerable amount of the golden liquid went into her glass. She didn't ask if I wanted a drink. She just grabbed the other glass sitting on her nightstand and poured. "Here. Take it. It really *is* unimportant if I like you, but we do have to spend the next few hours holed up in this room together. We might as well attempt to make them as bearable as possible."

A series of potential outcomes flashed before my eyes as I reached over and accepted the glass of tequila: I drank with her, got wasted, and I woke up to an empty motel room, with all my hardware stolen; I drank with her, got wasted, woke up feeling shitty, and I allowed Franz Halford to get the jump on me when I paid him a visit at his auto-mechanics' tomorrow; and, my personal favorite, I drank with her, got wasted, and ended up fucking Sera's brains out.

This trip was a job, I reminded myself. I was here to take care of business. But how long had it been since I'd fucked anyone? At least three months. I was an attractive guy. No, fuck that, I was *hot*. Girls stopped their conversations when I passed them in the street. I was followed by double takes and open stares everywhere I went. I was a bad call. I was dangerous. I was a risk that should never be taken. I was the devil, and I wasn't even in disguise, but it didn't stop women from wanting to take the chance. I was selective, though. I didn't just sink my dick into the first available and willing, wet pussy, just because I could.

I took a sip of the tequila, relishing the burn that spread down my throat and into my chest, warming me from the inside. "This is nice. Expensive." Sera might have learned how to drink at a young age, but I'd had my fair share of tequila, too. This wasn't cheap and nasty; it was top shelf liquor.

"It was a gift for my sister," Sera said, considering the contents of her own glass. "We were supposed to drink it tomorrow night when I arrived, to celebrate her wedding. But since it looks like I'm going to be missing the ceremony altogether, I thought fuck it. Be a shame not to enjoy it."

"Sounds like you two are close."

She shrugged. She was tall, her frame strong, but the act of shrugging made her look small and fragile. "Sometimes you end up close to someone because you have no other choice. I used to take care of her, once upon a time."

Did she mean to let these small snippets of information slip? I was learning a lot about her just by sitting here, watching her, but her words told me even more about her past. The scar on her jaw was an act of violence. Her defensive attitude said she was used to protecting herself. And now she was telling me, perhaps inadvertently, that the childhood she'd shared with her sister was fraught with discord. I tossed back another mouthful of the tequila, and my phone buzzed in my pocket again. Damn it, Monica was on a mission tonight. I'd have to call her tomorrow or she really would set out to track me down. That would not end well, for me or for her.

Sera's mouth turned up at the corners, forming a half amused smile. "You think an awful lot for a pretty boy."

"*Pretty boy?*" I'd just met her. Most girls weren't comfortable teasing me about my looks until at least the fourth or fifth drink. Then again, I didn't usually find myself locked inside a seedy motel room with many women until long after that, and look at where we found ourselves now. "Am I not allowed to think?"

"It's been my experience that good looks aren't often married to intellect," she said.

"Great. We're making sweeping generalizations. I fucking love those. I guess you have an IQ of fifty-three, then. And you're a woman, so you're probably horrible at putting flat-pack furniture together. And you're a bad driver. And you love to shop and waste all your money on manicures and frivolous, sparkly shit. You probably have a wardrobe full of purses and shoes, and you take four hours in the morning to apply your makeup and straighten your hair."

She scowled. Drank. Scowled some more. "You know none of that is true. You wouldn't have said it otherwise."

"Maybe."

"You're the one with the designer suitcase, not me."

"I stole that off a dead man."

Her scathing expression said she didn't believe me for a second. "Come on. You're probably some sort of investment banker or something. Or a military brat. Although your haircut's too fancy for that."

"Thanks. Your hair looks like you've had rats nesting in it." I'd never been told I looked like an investment banker before. Someone claimed I looked like a mortician once, and even that was less offensive than *investment banker*. I came to Liberty Fields straight from another job, one where I had to look the part, so I could understand Sera making a few assumptions. The old adage, 'never judge a book by its cover', was so pointless. People *always* judged a book by its cover, and the cover Sera saw when I walked into that lobby earlier tonight was a polished, well turned out, very stylish cover. If she'd met me last week, when I was sporting a full beard and covered in dirt, head to toe in camo gear, she would have formed a very different opinion of me. She probably would have thought I was a survivalist nut with a nuclear bunker full of supplies underneath my house. She would never have agreed to share this room with me, that was for fucking sure.

Sera cocked her head to one side, her eyes narrowing into slits. She probably wanted to come across as assessing and severe, but that wasn't the outcome she achieved. Instead, she looked like a little girl who couldn't make up her mind. "I'm gonna go to sleep soon. Don't even think about trying to climb into bed with me. It's a sure fire way of getting yourself castrated."

"*Please*. You know you want to sleep with me, Sera Lafferty. You wanted to sleep with me the moment you set eyes on me."

A slow, frankly unnerving smile spread across her face. She was beginning to look like a woman who really *would* tear a guy's dick off for climbing into bed with her. "You have a very high opinion of yourself, *Fix*."

I grinned back at her, flashing her my teeth. "Of course I do. I'm really fucking awesome."

3

SERA

BAD ANGEL

"Just admit it. Admit it to yourself. What harm will it do? You saw me, you thought I was hot, and you wanted to fuck me."

Where did this guy get off? How could he be so arrogant and brash, without even a glimmer of humility? He was probably the hottest guy I'd ever crossed paths with, hotter than my ex, Gareth, by strides, but with great looks came great responsibility. He should have been humble about his appearance, but instead it seemed as though he'd never even heard of the term.

"Oh, come on. Don't look so pissy. I shoot from the hip," he said, grinning. "There's nothing wrong with taking what you want every once in a while."

"I want tequila," I told him, hefting the half-empty bottle in the air. "I want this stupid storm to end so I can get out of here. I do *not* want to fuck you." I wondered if that little speech had convinced him. I was fist pumping inside, because to my own ears I'd sounded like I meant it. For all intents and purposes, it *was* true. Fair enough, I couldn't keep my eyes off Fix. It was all fun and games, imagining what his hands would feel like all over my body, but I wasn't dumb enough to act on those thoughts. Fix grunted. Kneeling on the floor at the foot of my bed, his elbows resting on the edge of my mattress, he looked like he was about to climb up onto the damn thing and prowl toward me like a stalking panther.

"Where are you from?" he asked. The question was out of the blue.

"South Carolina. A tiny place called Montmorenci." I took a swig directly out of the tequila bottle.

"Did you hate it there?" he probed.

"Yes."

"Why?"

I hit the bottle again, then offered it to him. "What does it matter? I was born there. I left there. Now I live in Seattle. Where are you from?"

"Upstate New York. I live in Brooklyn now."

For some odd, unknown reason, it was a relief to know that Fix lived just about as far away from me as he possibly could. He drank, and I watched the muscles in his throat work as he swallowed. Damn, that was diverting. I had no business being turned on by such a simple action.

When he lowered the bottle from his lips, he asked, "What do your parents do?"

"I haven't spoken to my father in nearly ten years. My mother's dead. She used to work for a little insurance company. A little mom 'n' pop place. Dealt mostly with life insurance and agricultural liability."

"Sounds like a thrill a second."

Melancholy washed over me. I didn't think about Mom very often. She'd died when I was eight, so it seemed that the few memories I had of her faded more and more as I grew older. It seemed to me that one day I'd wake up and I wouldn't remember what her face had looked like at all. That eventuality was the saddest thing in the world to me.

Fix didn't seem perturbed by my somber admission. "How'd she die?"

"God, you ask a lot of personal questions. What about *your* parents? What do they do?"

"Both dead," he answered. "Car accident seven years ago. Happened the day before my thirtieth birthday." Not a twinkle of emotion. It was weird, as if he were completely shut off from what must have been a very traumatic event. Either that, or he just didn't care.

"Fair enough." I sighed. "Two dead parents trumps one dead parent. My mom had an aneurism. She was fine one minute, watering the garden. Yelling at me and my sister to come in for dinner. Next thing I knew, she'd keeled over in the grass, dead. When they completed the autopsy, the doctors said hers was the largest aneurism they'd ever seen, the size of Texas. Completely inoperable. They said she'd probably had it for years and never known. Walking around every day, oblivious, with a huge bomb waiting to go off in her head."

"Better that way." Fix said this as if it were a matter of fact. "She lived her life without worrying every time she needed to sneeze."

I'd spent a long time wondering if it was better that she hadn't known. Would Mom have done things a little differently if she'd been aware her time was limited? She might have pulled us from school, taken us on vacation, spent as much time with me and Amy as possible. She could have sent us to live with her friend Natalie in Utah. She used to talk to Natalie on the phone every day. Sixsmith liked to blame my mother's death for his raging alcoholism, but the reality was he'd started hitting the bottle a little harder then he should have a couple of years before Mom went. I liked to think Mom would have taken us away from him if she'd known the truth of what was going on inside her brain.

"Hmm. Well, it's all said and done now. That was a long time ago." I didn't want to think about Mom. I sure as fuck didn't want to think about Sixsmith.

I took another drink from the bottle, and my head started to buzz. I needed to be careful. I could drink people under the table, but I wasn't immune to hangovers. Tequila hangovers were the absolute worst.

Fix didn't say anything as he stood up, kicked his shoes off, and threw himself down next to me on my bed. I quirked an eyebrow at him. "Uh...what do you think you're doing?"

"I'm sure you like your guys servile and meek, Sera, but I'm not kneeling on the floor forever."

"Then go and lie on *your* bed."

He propped himself up on his elbow and leaned across my body, reaching for the tequila bottle—a pretty bold move for a guy who'd been more than a little frosty toward me in the lobby not that long ago. "How are we meant to pass back and forth if I'm all the way over there?" he said. His feral smile made him look particularly wolfish. This close, I could see the fine details of his face...and they really were fine. Strong jaw line; high cheekbones; long, curled eyelashes. He was the epitome of tall, dark and handsome, and he smelled heavenly. I wracked my brain, trying to pin down the scent to a single origin, but I couldn't do it. He smelled like winter mornings, and wet grass after rain, and clean sheets drying on a line. His breath smelled a little of the tequila we were drinking, but there was an underlying hint of mint. He'd probably brushed his teeth after his shower.

"You're staring," Fix rumbled.

"I don't have much choice. You're hovering over me so closely, you're filling my entire field of vision."

"Fair point. Can I kiss you now?"

"*WHAT*?" If he'd tried to kiss me without warning, I would have kneed him in the balls so hard he'd never be able to have children. Since he'd *asked*, though, I settled on sending him a look so scathing that it was a miracle he didn't flee the motel room and sleep on that couch in the lobby after all. "Why the hell would I let you kiss me? From the moment we met, you've been an asshole. We're complete strangers. We have nothing in common. You're just bored and looking for a way to pass the time. I'm not going to be your entertainment, okay? Guys like you are unbelievable."

"You've never met a guy like me before," Fix said, tilting his head a fraction to the left. "I'm unique. And who said anything about me using you for my entertainment? I'd rather you used *me* for *your* entertainment."

Seriously, this guy. He was striking, there was no denying that, but his arrogance knew no bounds. Unique? His eyes made him one of a kind, but the fact that he thought he could have me swooning over him because he got up close and personal with me made him just like every other guy I'd ever met. "Just...forget it, Felix Marcosa. I'll drink with you. I'll share this room with you. But that's it."

Fix sank back down onto the mattress, sighing. "My dick's pretty fucking phenomenal. You should see it. Grown women have been known to weep when they behold it." He drank from the bottle, long and deep, which was a blessing. Gave me a second to recover myself after that dick comment. I supposed a part of me was curious. He was a giant. His hands were like shovels—strong, powerful and calloused. Hands that had been used to build, create and destroy. What would they feel like on my body? Would their roughness be too much for my skin, or would it make my nerve endings sing with pleasure.

The last person I'd slept with was my ex, Gareth, close to six months ago now. Gareth's hands had looked nothing like Fix's. They'd been soft and well manicured—the hands of a pampered, spoiled rich boy who'd never done a hard day's work in his life. He hadn't known how to touch me. I'd faked an orgasm nearly every time we got into bed together. The times I hadn't faked an orgasm were the nights I'd simply been too tired to even pretend.

"I'm sure your dick is magnificent," I said, groaning under my breath. "I'm sure women across the country have carved wooden replicas of it that they worship daily. It's probably the most stunning cock to have ever gotten a boner. But I'm gonna pass this time."

Fix cracked his neck; the action made the muscles in his throat and in his left shoulder stand out. His shirt was tight enough that his chest muscles were straining against the material, too. The guy had muscles fucking everywhere. Maybe he was a professional athlete or something. A football or a hockey player. That would explain the attitude, if he had hoards of adoring fans chasing him down the street twenty-four seven.

He didn't seem fazed by the fact that I'd turned down his junk. Flopping back down beside me, he pressed the rim of the tequila bottle to his oh-so-perfect lips, up-ended it, and drank. "I think we should shoot the rest of this and kill it. We're already halfway through."

This was really irresponsible behavior. This was flirting with disaster in the biggest way. "Fine." I took the bottle and chugged.

The next hour passed by in a blur. At some point, I started feeling good. Really good. And then I just started to feel drunk, and missed the feeling good part.

My conscience kept whispering in my ear that I should get some sleep, that tomorrow was going to be a long day, but in the end even she began to slur her words and said what the hell. I never cut loose anymore. I was Little Miss Sensible, getting to sleep at a reasonable time, working after hours on my projects, cooking my own meals, and looking forward to Sundays, so I could clean and fold all my laundry.

Where had fun-loving Sera disappeared to? She'd gone out on the weekends with Sadie and gotten rip-roaring drunk, weaving arm-in-arm with her friend through the streets of Seattle, singing bawdy songs at the top of her lungs. She'd gone on adventures for the sheer hell of it. She'd gone kite surfing. She'd seen a guy she'd liked in a bar and made the first move, because she was confident and sexy, and she could be anyone she wanted to be, and do anything she wanted to do.

Now I searched myself, hunting high and low, and found no trace of that Sera left behind. She'd vanished, and no one had bothered to put up missing posters or tried to hunt her down, least of all me. "How old are you?" I asked Fix, peering at him over the top of the pillow I was now hugging to my chest.

"Thirty-seven," he replied. "You're..." He half-closed one eye, studying me. "You're twenty-eight."

"Yeah. Wow. I am. Most guys guess four or five years younger than they really think a woman is, just to stroke her ego. Does that mean you think I look thirty-three?"

"No. You look twenty-eight. I don't play stupid games."

"Pfffttt. Yeah, right."

"I don't."

"What was all that stupid, 'wanna see my cock' bullshit, then?

That was a game if ever I saw one."

"I beg to differ."

"You were trying to fluster me. Make me all embarrassed and shy or some shit. Guys think women faint whenever they mention their dicks. It's hilarious."

"I said it because I meant it. I'll happily prove it."

I raised the nearly empty tequila bottle, tipping it in his direction. *"Be my guest."* He wasn't going to just whip his dick out right here and now. Even a smooth-talking, macho, big talker like him wouldn't just take down his pants and get his cock out. He didn't take those pale eyes off me as he unfastened his belt, though. Continued to stare at me as he unzipped his fly. And he maintained eye contact every second as he pushed his boxers down over his hips, and his cock sprang free.

Oh...my...*god.*

I'd asked for that one.

I wasn't looking. Hadn't dared look down to see what he was doing with his hands and his dick. I just held Fix's intimidating gaze, doing my damnedest not to react like a prudish little schoolgirl. "You're an asshole," I informed him. "You can put it away now."

"But you haven't even looked. I'll be offended if you don't take a quick peek." His grin was fiendish to say the least.

"Whatever." I gripped onto the tequila bottle so tightly that I suspected I wasn't far away from shattering the glass neck. I looked down, trying to act nonchalant, but I felt my cheeks explode with color the moment I saw what Fix was doing. Not only was he big, but both his hands were wrapped around the shaft of his cock, and he was slowly working them up and down. His dick really was stunning. I was sure plenty of women had swooned at the sight of it, because I was feeling rather impressed, and I didn't typically care what a guy's junk looked like, so long as he knew how to use it.

From the dark, sexual glimmer in Fix's eyes, I could tell he knew *exactly* how to use that thing.

"You really have no shame, do you?" I said, drinking to hide the blush that had stained my cheeks.

Fix looked down at himself; he sucked his bottom lip into his mouth and bit down on it, pulling it through his own teeth, groaning a little. He squeezed his dick in his hands, then let his head fall back onto the pillows. "*Shame?*" He laughed. "I know all about shame. I used to wrestle with that bastard every hour of the waking day. Now I don't have the time."

"Jerking off too much?"

Fix hissed out a breath of amused laughter. "Life's just too short for that kind of bullshit. I like being real. I like being honest, as much as I can be, especially with myself. Are you honest with yourself, Sera?"

"Yes."

"Then tell me...is watching me touch myself turning you on?"

I balked at the question. He really had no right asking me personal shit like that, but then again he didn't exactly have the right to be stroking his dick in front of me, either. I'd pretty much invited him to do that. I stole a glance down, my heart stalling for a couple of beats as I watched Fix tease the end of his cock. He was so fucking hard. He must have been hard even before he'd undone his pants and gotten his cock out. He twitched a little as he pumped his hand up and down, and a wall of heat slammed into me, stealing my breath. He *was* turning me on.

Watching him do this felt...wrong. Dirty. Immoral. But I couldn't tear my eyes away from him. I set my jaw, channeling a defiant streak a mile wide, as I said as evenly as I could, "Yeah. It's turning me on. You know it is."

Fix made an appreciative humming sound, low and gruff, as if it originated in his boots. He seemed pretty damn pleased with my response. "Are you wet right now?"

I downed another mouthful of tequila, grimacing as the bitter flavor bit at either side of my tongue, searing a burning pathway down the back of my throat. "Yes. I'm wet. It doesn't change anything, though. Things turn me on all the time. I don't give in to every single desire and whim that presents itself to me."

"Slide your hand down your pants, Sera. Touch yourself. Show me how wet you are."

Was he for real? I mean, there was no way I was going to do that. I'd never touched myself in front of anyone before. Never. "You can forget it, Fix."

"Why?" I wouldn't have thought it possible, but lust had made the timbre of his voice even deeper. He had the sexiest voice when he was talking normally. Now, visibly turned on and out of breath, the basement register of his voice made my head tilt and spin. If I wasn't careful, I was going to tumble off the bed.

"We're strangers," I said, clearing my throat. "I'm not some outrageous exhibitionist. I don't just start masturbating in front of a guy I only met a few hours ago."

"You should try it. It's fun," Fix growled. "I won't touch you, Sera. Not if you don't want me to. But that doesn't mean you shouldn't do it yourself. You should enjoy yourself. You should do whatever the fuck you want to do."

"Oh, and you get absolutely nothing out of me lying next to you, fingering myself?" I scoffed. Shit, even saying that out loud made heat pool between my legs. I was beginning to ache in a way I hadn't ached for a very long time. It was inappropriate. It wasn't right that my body should be responding to him the way it was, but I couldn't control it.

"I'd get a lot out of it," he admitted. "I'd benefit immensely from watching you slide your fingers over your wet pussy. It would drive me insane. Especially if you hitched your shirt up and pulled down your bra so your tits were exposed."

"Haha! You're getting greedy." I laughed, but I was getting more and more turned around by the second. Fix was just using his right hand on himself now, and I was losing my battle with impropriety, struggling and failing to look away. Fuck, he really was something to behold. His shaft was well over eight inches, but he was thick, too. Fix's middle finger and thumb didn't meet around the circumference of his hard-on as he tightened his grip and increased the speed with which he moved his hand up and down.

Gareth had never wanted to have sex with the lights on, which was weird given the amount of time he'd spend flexing and posing in front of the full length mirrors in my bedroom. Fix was unabashed and unaffected by what he was doing, which somehow made the whole thing even hotter.

"Sera. Being greedy is great. Be greedy. Be demanding. Be fucking hungry. Take whatever you want. If you want to touch your pussy and make yourself feel good, then do it. If you want to touch me, if you want to stroke my cock and make me so hard that I can't stop myself from fucking your hand, then do it. If you want me to hold you down and bury my tongue between your legs, to lick at you and tease you until you're begging me to let you come, then let's make it happen. If all you want is for me to stop being such a fuck up and jerking off right next to you, then tell me and I'll stop immediately. Whatever you want, just *claim* it. Let yourself go. Or tell me to fuck off. But be *honest*."

"I—" My first instinct had been to tell him to put his dick away and go to sleep, but I stopped myself. Maybe...fuck, maybe he was right. I hadn't had a single sexual experience that I'd enjoyed in so long. Where was the harm in doing something if I was going to enjoy it? And...perhaps the fact that Fix and I were strangers was a good thing. He lived in New York. I lived in Seattle. It wasn't as though I was going to have to deal with seeing him walking through my city every other night of the week. He'd go his way, and tomorrow, as soon as the roads were clear, I'd be speeding toward Amy's wedding. My ears were buzzing as I put down the bottle of tequila, exhaling a deep, slow breath.

I was going to regret this. I knew I was. But tomorrow was future Sera's problem, and right now, I was drunk, frustrated and, thanks to the fact that Fix had his dick in his hand and was pumping it up and down with intent, I was getting increasingly turned on.

I didn't say anything. Instead, I unbuttoned my jeans and slid them down my legs, steeling myself, begging my hands not to shake as I ran them up the insides of my thighs.

I typically touched myself every day. It was just part of my shower routine. Being watched made the process far more intense, though. Fix's chest began to rise and fall a little quicker, his eyelids lowering, desire pouring off him as he watched me pull my panties to the side and tentatively rub myself.

"Fuck, Sera. Your pussy is incredible. You're soaking wet." He loosed a sound that resembled a savage growl, and goose bumps erupted all over my skin. This was so weird. It was strange, and it was hot, and it was going to make me wish I'd never been born tomorrow, but the look on Fix's face made me want to continue. He was observing me like I was the hottest thing he'd ever seen, and it made me feel like I was damn well glowing.

"Show me, Sera," he whispered. "Let me look at you." He got to his knees, positioning himself at the end of the bed, and a brief moment of panic clawed at me. I didn't know this guy. He could be capable of anything, and I was trapped in a room with him, and there was a storm raging outside. No one would hear me if I cried out for help. Over the howling wind and rain, my voice would be drowned out and lost. Did I think he was going to hurt me, though? I looked up at Fix, where he was now kneeling in between my legs, and I only saw desire on his face. His cock was standing proud, and I wanted it. I finally admitted it to myself. I wanted to feel it in my hands. I wanted it in my mouth. And yeah, I wanted him inside me, too. I just didn't know if I was going to be brave enough...

I sucked in a deep breath, and closed my eyes, the tips of my fingers working in small circles over my clit.

"Shit, Sera. You're fucking beautiful."

"What...what do you want me to do?" I asked, swallowing down the lump that had risen to my throat.

"This isn't about me," Fix answered. "This is about what *you* want. If you want me to watch you, if you want me to fuck you, if you want me to leave you alone. Just say the word."

Every time I looked at him, I was taken by surprise all over again. He wasn't just good looking. There was something about him that made me feel very small. He was raw, untapped power, a storm trapped inside a bottle, and I got the feeling he raged day and night, no matter what. It felt unsafe being so close to him, like I was being drawn closer and closer against my will, and no matter how hard I tried to resist him, I just couldn't. Moving slowly, I unclipped my bra at the front, underneath my shirt, and then I slipped the remainder of my clothes over my head, tossing them onto the floor beside me.

"Fuck," Fix snarled. "Your breasts are just..." He raised a hand, then immediately withdrew it. "They're fucking phenomenal, Sera."

"You want to touch them," I said quietly.

He didn't even blink. "Yes. But I'm not going to. Not until you tell me you want me to."

"I do. Want you to. I want you to suck and bite on my nipples." I didn't know where that had come from, but the moment the words were out of my mouth, I realized they were true. My breasts were swollen and full, my nipples throbbing along with the crazed tattoo of my heartbeat. Fix remained absolutely still for a moment, as if waiting for me to change my mind. When I arched my back away from the bed, allowing my eyes to shutter closed, he swore violently under his breath and moved. He cupped both of my breasts, testing the weight and the fullness of them, and then he squeezed and kneaded my flesh, a pained groan slipping free from his mouth.

"You'd look so good covered in my come." His words sounded like metal grinding on metal. "Your body is fucking flawless."

I knew that wasn't true. I had plenty of scars and marks all over me from years of fielding Sixsmith's attentions, so I was far from perfect. None of that mattered when Fix soothed me, running his hands over my skin, though. It was freeing to let someone touch me and appreciate me the way he was doing. He dipped down, and I gasped as he took my left nipple into his mouth, lightly grazing it with his teeth before he sucked.

"I want..." I stammered over the words, not sure how to just spit them out. "I want to go down on you." I instantly regretted saying that, but it was too late to take it back now. Fix leaned back, tracing his fingers down my cheek, over my jaw and down the length of my neck, his fingers pausing over my collarbone.

"You don't sound so sure."

"I am."

"You want me to slide my dick past your lips, down deep into your throat, Sera?"

"*Yes.*"

"You want to feel me getting harder and harder as you suck on me? You want to taste me?"

"*Yes!*" Fuck me sideways. He was good with words. Good at making me want him more than ever, even though I was shot through with nerves.

Fix leaned down, so that his mouth was hovering mere inches away from mine. He lowered his voice, and I couldn't help but shiver when he said, "You want to take my come, Sera? You want it in your mouth? You want to swallow me?"

"Fuck...*yes!*"

"Good. Good girl."

I opened my eyes as Fix shifted up my body, kneeling on either side of my head. His cock filled my vision, which made me second-guess myself for a moment. He was huge. I was going to choke on that thing, and Fix was going to love it. Still, my pussy was crazy wet as I parted my lips and Fix pushed himself into my mouth. I was right: I could barely fit *half* of his length inside.

Fix moved slowly, gently rocking himself in and out, making strained, frustrated sounds and as I sucked and licked at his cock. He tasted kind of sweet—a completely unexpected, vaguely pleasant flavor that wasn't anywhere near as salty as I'd imagined it would be. Angling his body forward, Fix planted his hands against the walls, supporting himself, and began to thrust harder. I couldn't even swallow my own saliva around the girth of him, but Fix didn't seem to mind. I panted down my nose, growing braver and braver every time he pushed himself inside my mouth and I realized how hard he was getting. He was *so* fucking turned on.

"Your lips look amazing wrapped around my dick," he growled. "I'm gonna be having wet dreams about this for fucking years."

I wasn't going to be forgetting it any time soon either. I grasped hold of the base of his cock, applying pressure there, rubbing my hand up and down as I sucked, and Fix's entire body shuddered. "If you keep doing that, you're going to make me come, Sera."

It was a warning in more ways than one: he was letting me know to expect a mouthful of come any second if I continued down this path, but also that he wouldn't be able to do anything else if he finished. Did I want him to fuck me? Did I really, truly want him inside me? The answer, despite the remaining shred of common sense I still possessed post half a bottle of tequila, was yes, I did. Pushing him back, I gasped for breath, still running my hand up and down Fix's cock.

"I want you inside me," I told him. "I want you to fuck me. I want you to make me come."

Fix bared his teeth, palming my breast, pinching my nipple so hard that I yelped. "How do you want me to fuck you? Be specific."

"From behind. I want you to fuck me as hard as you can," I said. "I want you to make me see stars."

"*Oh,...I can do that.*" It took less than a second for him to rip his shirt over his head, and then he was naked. His chest and stomach were...I literally had nothing even close to compare them to. He was so unbelievably perfect; he looked like he had been conjured out of someone's dream, not born of reality. His skin was a light golden color, a sun-kissed tan that probably came from weeks spent out in the sunshine. I wanted to run my hands over him, to explore and appreciate every curve and defined line of muscle, but Fix had other ideas.

"Get on your stomach and get that ass in the air," he commanded roughly. "Make sure you're spread wide for me."

Thank god my blood was mostly alcohol right now. I'd have died of embarrassment if someone spoke to me like that while I was sober. I rolled onto my front and obeyed him, though, lifting my ass up in the air for him to inspect.

He showed his appreciation by slapping my ass cheek, not hard enough to hurt, but hard enough to leave a stinging hand print.

"*Ahhh!* Shit!"

"You wanted it rough," Fix reminded me. "Tell me if you change your mind." The sound he made when he rubbed the tip of his dick over my pussy and my ass sent shivers skating all over my skin. He sounded just as turned on as me, if not more. When he pushed himself inside me, I stifled a moan into the pillows.

"Fuck. Oh, fuck. That...that's too much!"

Fix curved his body over me, his chest to my back, and his warm breath danced over my skin as he whispered into my ear. "Breathe. Your body will work it out. Just give it a second."

So I breathed. Three long, deep breaths, then another, and then another. Little by little, I realized Fix was right. I was relaxing, stretching to accommodate him inside me, and it was beginning to feel good. I whimpered as Fix began thrusting himself inside me, rocking himself forward, holding me by the hips as he gently pushed deeper. God, it was incredible how wet I was. By the time Fix really began to fuck me, I was ready for him and begging him silently to take me.

My pride wouldn't allow me to beg him out loud, but in the end I didn't need to. Fix was in tune with me, reading my body and responding accordingly. I'd never been one of those women who screamed the house down during sex, but I couldn't stop myself from moaning and crying out every time Fix's cock slammed into my pussy. It felt...*shit*, it felt so fucking amazing. Especially when Fix reached around my body and began to rub my clit at the same time. He was talented with his fingers, and he was definitely talented with his cock.

"Jesus. You're...that's going to make me come," I panted.

He didn't reply. He grabbed a handful of my hair and pulled back on it as he fucked me faster, hissing between his teeth.

"*Fuck. I'm—I'm going to—I can't stop it. I'm—*" I ran out of words and oxygen at the same time, as Fix railed into me, his fingers digging into my skin. My climax was a thousand fireworks igniting inside my head, and I couldn't see or move or feel my way around it. I could only go with it, allowing the spikes and waves of pleasure to course over and through me as I came. It was fucking spectacular.

"My turn now," Fix rumbled into my ear. "Do you *want* me to come?"

"Yes." I exhaled the word on an exhausted breath.

"*Where* do you want me to come?"

"Inside me," I told him. "I'm on birth control." The prospect of him coming inside me turned me on more than anything ever had. I'd never let Gareth come inside me, even though I received the contraceptive injection every three months. I'd just never wanted to be that intimate with him. But with Fix, a man I didn't even know, and never would, I wanted it so bad I could think of nothing else.

"All right. I'm gonna let myself loose," Fix spoke into my ear. "I'm not going to hold back. You still want this?"

"Yes! Fuck yes, Fix. Make me come again."

From behind, Fix wound his hand around my body, his fingers closing lightly around my throat. His lips brushed my ear as he spoke. "Oh, I intend on it. Get ready, Angel."

And he fucked me. He rocked against me, slamming himself home, making me scream every time he pushed himself inside me as deep as he could. It felt so good. More than good. It felt fucking amazing.

When he came inside me, I called out, my own orgasm ripping through me at the same time, and Fix clung to my body, holding me tight, locking me in place as he pumped me full of his come. I was bone tired and weary when he spun me over and laid me out on the mattress.

"See? Being greedy is pretty fucking awesome," he said quietly. His hand slipped down, between my legs, and my eyes rolled back into my head as he dipped his fingers into my pussy. They were sticky and covered in his come when he held them up a second later. I was too tired to ask him what he was doing as he used his fingertips to paint around my areolas and the tightened buds of my nipples. He painted a line down my belly, and then proceeded to rub his semen all over the insides of my thighs and my hips. He smirked like the devil himself when he rubbed his fingers against my lips, and I used the tip of my tongue to taste him.

"*Bad* Angel," he whispered, smiling as if to himself. "Close your eyes now. It's time to get some rest."

4

SERA

DEBT

*H*ow could it *still* be raining? Water droplets pelted at the windows, the sound of fingers insistently drumming against a table top, and weak, greyed morning light eked through the yellowed net curtains that had been hung from a cheap length of plastic coated wire, suspended haphazardly from hooks screwed directly into the ceiling. I closed my eyes, groaning internally. What time was it? I'd been getting up early my whole life—my internal body clock typically woke me at around six in the morning. Judging by the sun's anemic attempt at dawn, today was no different. I reached out for my phone, patting my hand against the surface of the nightstand before locating the device and dragging it underneath the covers with me. Cracking just one eye, I inspected the screen, already prepared to be angry at whatever was displayed there. The clock read twelve minutes past six. Great. There were two text messages from Amy, asking me to call and let her know what was happening as soon as I could, and three missed calls from Ben, who was probably having an apoplectic fit by now. No messages from the office, though. None from Colby, my dog sitter, and none from Sadie.

I threw back the covers, resisting the urge to nurse my skull. It was my own fault that my head was pounding. That's what happened when you smashed a whole bottle of tequila. Only...

Oh shit.

I hadn't finished that bottle alone. I'd shared it with a dirty mouthed ingrate named Fix, and...*oh my god*. I'd fucked the bastard.

I laid as still as I could for a second, figuring out my options. The mattress next to me was cold, which meant he hadn't slept beside me. That was a relief. But it was early—he was probably still crashed out in the other bed. *Fuck.*

This was so, so typical. I was my own worst enemy; without fail, I was blessed with the uncanny ability of taking a bad situation and making it even fucking worse. Time to get all my crap back into the rental and get the fuck out of here. And before my ass hat roommate woke up, too. Only, when I spun around, ready to sneak into the bathroom to quickly brush my teeth before heading out, Fix was nowhere to be seen. His bed was untouched, his sheets only rumpled a little from where he'd placed his bag on it last night. The bag which was now gone. Turning over, I saw the indention in the pillow next to me, the comforter thrown back on the other side of the bed, and I growled to myself. He *had* slept in the bed with me. He'd just gotten up and disappeared already. I didn't know why, but it irked me that he'd managed to leave before me. It would have been far more gratifying to have been the one to sneak out on him, not the other way around.

I got dressed, treated myself to a two-minute shower, and dashed to the car, swearing loudly at the fact that I was, yet again, getting drenched by rain. It took thirty seconds to toss my bags into the trunk of the rental. I hadn't eaten last night and my stomach was grumbling loudly. The Liberty Fields Guest House sign outside the building claimed the motel offered a continental breakfast between the hours of seven and nine, but I wasn't going to hang around to check out whatever paltry offering was going to be laid out in the lobby. Hell no. I'd grab something on the road, once I'd left Liberty Fields far behind, and the nightmarish place had disappeared from my rearview mirror altogether.

Twenty-two hours and seventeen minutes: the amount of time it was now going to take me to get to Fairhope, when I plugged the location of the church into the navigation app on my phone. The ceremony was a late one—two pm—and last night Aims had said she could push back the ceremony a little to accommodate my tardiness if she needed to. So there was time. Against all the odds, I was going to make it. Thank fuck for that.

I started the engine, spun the wheel, hit the accelerator, and a loud, offensive grinding sound assaulted my ears. What the hell was *that*? The car lurched forward, but it felt uneven. Wrong. Oh, no. Oh, *no*. This wasn't happening. Was. Not. Happening.

I sat very still for a moment, staring straight ahead out of the car, my hands gripping hold of the steering wheel, while my mind did back flips. I didn't know a thing about cars. I didn't have a clue what was wrong with the vehicle, but it didn't sound good. It certainly didn't sound like something that was going to go away all on its own. The world outside was a blur of grey, and blue and brown as sheets of water streamed down the windshield. I had Triple A. I could call them and someone would come and resolve the issue for me for free, but how long would it take them to arrive? In this weather, with so many people struggling to get from A to B, it would be hours, and I didn't have hours.

A knock on my window startled me, disturbing my downward descent into despair. I nearly screamed with frustration at the dark, distorted figure standing next to my car, but instead I growled under my breath, slapping my palm against the center console of the rental. A gust of wind blew into the car when I buzzed down the window, and the freezing cold blast of rainwater hit me square in the face. It was Fix. Of course it was Fix. He was wearing a black t-shirt and shorts, and both items of clothing were water logged, plastered to his body. He was covered in mud, his sneakers so badly caked in the stuff that I couldn't even see what color they were, and his bare calves looked like they'd been sprayed down with dirt. His face was blank as he ducked down, resting his forearms against the driver's side door of the car.

"What have you been doing?" I hissed at him.

"What does it look like? I went for a run." His hair was spiky with water, the longer strands on top of his head slicked back out of his face. It was ridiculously unfair: he'd been too sexy to resist last night, and now, looking like he'd just completed an assault course, soaked to the skin, he was even sexier. Dark, brooding, and delicious. I railed against the way my heart rattled at the bars of my ribcage, letting me know exactly what it thought about Felix Marcosa, post run. I was doing my best to master my features into an expression void of any emotion, but I was giving too much away, I could tell.

"Who goes for a run in this kind of—ugh, never mind." I shook my head, slapping my palm against the steering wheel. "My car's broken."

"Not your car. Your wheels. You have a flat."

"Oh. Is that it?" That was a relief. A flat was easy. A flat was actually something I could take care of myself. "I have a spare in the trunk."

"One isn't gonna cut it," Fix said casually, tapping his fingernail against the lip of the window. "You have *three* flats."

"What? *Three*? How can you tell?"

Fix looked down, a ghost of a smile lifting at the corners of his wretched, perfect, talented mouth. Lord, the man was divine. "Well. You're sitting on the rims. But it was the huge, 6-inch gashes in the rubber that really gave it away."

"That is *not* possible." I unfastened my seatbelt and scrambled out of the car, gasping when I saw the state of my tires. They were completely deflated on this side, and just as Fix had said, there were huge, deep tears in the rubber. "*How?*" I squatted down, sticking my finger directly into the tire, through the gaping hole. "There's no way a rock did this."

Fix leaned his ass against the hood of the rental, folding his arms across his chest. "Yeah. You can safely rule out accident on this one."

"You mean someone did this *on purpose*?" As soon as the words left my lips, I rocketed to my feet, my mouth hanging open like a

Venus flytrap, waiting to catch its dinner. "*You!*" I jabbed him in the chest with my index finger, rage spilling out of me. "*You* did this!"

Fix let out a rumble of laughter, his head tipping back as he roared. "Why the fuck would I do that? I like my balls hanging right here between my legs, Angel."

"Gross. Don't talk about your balls."

"Why not?" He practically purred the words. "You seemed to appreciate them plenty last night when they were slapping your pussy as I fucked you from behind."

"*Holy...*" He was such a pig. I shook my head, then cocked it to one side. "What the fuck is *wrong* with you? Just...*stop*. Don't bring up last night again. There's no need for us to rehash my drunken stupidity."

"But I'd love to rehash it." He was leonine. A consummate predator. I didn't stand a chance against him—not with his soaking clothes displaying every outrageous curve and line of his muscular chest.

"Just quit it. You're the only person here who'd slash my tires!" I cried. It had to be him. It had to be.

"Last night was pretty fucking phenomenal, Sera. I very much appreciated your incredible body, not to mention your talented mouth. As of right now, I'd say I'm probably the only person in Liberty Fields who *wouldn't* want to slash your tires."

I set my jaw, glaring at him with the force of a thousand volatile suns. "I thought we just agreed we weren't going to talk about last night."

Droplets of water coursed down Fix's face. He licked his wet lips, and my mind transported me back to his naked form last night, and the way he'd run his hand up and down his hard-on, looking like he wanted to sink his teeth into me. Oh, for crying out loud...

He smirked, as if he knew exactly what I was thinking about. "Maybe you should just be less rude to people you meet in the middle of a storm."

"This isn't funny, Fix! My sister's going to kill me. I swore I wouldn't let her down, and now I'm going to do exactly that. I'm the only person she's ever been able to rely on. I'm the *only* person in her whole entire life that hasn't continually dropped the ball. And now I'm going to break a promise I made to her, and it's all your fault."

Fix held his hands aloft in the air, pushing away from the car. "This has nothing to do with me. I swear it. I did *not* touch your car."

The worst part was that he really did look like he was telling the truth. It would have been far more convenient for me to blame him, because he was standing right in front of me. I could have taken my anger and frustration out on him, and I might have felt a little better at least. But with him apparently innocent of the crime... I dragged my hands back through my hair, fighting back tears. How many more things could possibly go wrong on this trip? It didn't even bear thinking about.

"All right." I scrutinized his stupid, handsome face out of the corner of my eye. "If you're so good at fixing things, Felix, fix this." My voice was small and pleading. "Please. I really need some help right now, or I'm going to lose my mind."

The smile on Fix's face slipped a little. His shoulders dropped at least three inches, and a strange look formed on his face. A look that resembled quiet surprise. "I have an appointment to keep this morning," he replied slowly. "An appointment I can't break."

"Then go! Take care of your appointment, and I'll meet you in Liberty Fields. I just need a ride to the next town over. The next place I can rent another car. Anywhere. Please! Just get me back to civilization. I'll forever be in your debt."

Fix seemed to think this through. For a second, I was sure he was going to say no, and my eyes began to sting like the miserable traitors that they were. Eventually, he said, "I gave you the best fucking of your life last night, Sera Lafferty. You're *already* in my debt. But I'll give you *another* ride," he said, mischief and arrogance flashing in his eyes. "And you'll owe me a favor, to be repaid at a later date. Do we have an accord?"

"You sound like a pirate," I grumbled.

"*Sera...*"

"Yes, yes, fine. I'll owe you a favor. I don't see how you're gonna cash it in when we live on opposite sides of the country, but whatever. You have yourself a deal."

5

FIX

ALL AMERICAN SCRAMBLER

*I*f she hadn't been so obviously distressed and sorry for herself in the parking lot, I wouldn't have agreed to drive her anywhere. But when Sera looked at me like I was her only hope, and she'd asked me for *help*, I'd fucking caved. Hopeless. I shouldn't have still been hanging around Liberty Fields. It was a miracle that two jobs had converged, miraculously right on top of one another. I should have completed both of them already and been on my way back to New York, but...

I was distracted.

Sera had thoroughly distracted me, and I wasn't ready to give her up just yet. That made me cruel, and wicked, and evil, and a thousand other things including stupid, but I'd never faltered before. I'd never dropped the ball. I wasn't going to now. I was entitled to a little fun, though.

That was what I told myself.

A long time ago, people used to ask me for help all the livelong day. It had been my job to help people, and I used to like doing it. A lot had changed since then. I'd lost myself, not to mention my soul, on the road about ten thousand miles ago, and I'd never turned back to find either. I should have gotten into my truck and driven away from Sera and her destroyed car just now, but...I just couldn't. I'd liked the way my name sounded on her lips. It had been hotter than fuck hearing her panting it over and over into my ear last night. And so what if I wanted to hear her say it a couple more times before I ended this? She was different. I got the sneaking suspicion that she was more than a little broken inside. She'd obviously been through hell at some point, but the flames had forged her, not burned her to ash. In a lot of ways, she reminded me of Monica.

I hadn't slashed her tires. I had no idea who the fuck had done it, but I wanted to pat them on the back and also shove a whittled down toothbrush through each of their eyeballs for creating this situation, that was already seriously complicated enough.

I'd changed out of my wet running gear and dressed in something a little more murder-appropriate—black pants, black shirt, black leather driving gloves and a ball cap—before heading out to Franz Halford's auto mechanic's shop. As I piloted my way through a network of roads that bore a closer resemblance to swamps than highways, kind of enjoying the huge spray that went up from both front tires whenever I went through a particularly deep patch of standing water, I counted no less than three overturned vehicles, sitting on their roofs, waiting to be hauled out of ditches and away from the medians.

At the turn off I needed to take in order to reach the auto shop, a row of power lines had collapsed, and a confusion of cables, tangled and sparking, were causing havoc for passing drivers, who couldn't quite figure out how to circumnavigate them without electrocuting themselves and dying horribly. A large woman with a tabby cat tucked under her arm, wearing a bright yellow waterproof jacket, seemed to be trying to direct the traffic, but she didn't seem to know what she was doing either, so I wheeled around her and the fast growing line of cars and made the turn regardless.

Idiots.

I'd allowed my phone to go dead last night—there was nothing more distracting than an irate woman sending you a thousand text messages when you were trying to fucking come—but I'd plugged it in to charge when I climbed into the truck. The screen finally lit up as I took a left and pulled into the cluttered parking lot of Halford's Family Auto and Lube, and I braced myself for a litany of messages from Monica. Nothing came through, though. Nothing at all. That was fucking weird. She'd said she needed me to call her immediately, and when Monica said immediately, she meant *yesterday.* Her patience was wearing thin with me, I knew that, but fuck me if she didn't make my life harder. I was used to having her around now. I was used to her panicked outbursts, and her need for me to check in every day. I should probably have cut her loose by now, but it wasn't that easy. I didn't really have the right to do that to her, either.

The rusting, spray-painted roller shutters that fronted Halford's Family Auto & Lube were still firmly shut and very locked, and a huge, fat, tarnished padlock was glinting in the weak early morning light. Didn't look like Franz was an early riser. Didn't look like anyone was at the shop at all, though it was really fucking hard to tell with all the decrepit vehicles that were sitting in the parking lot. Given all of the dirt, corrosion, smashed glass and bald tires, it was hard to imagine any of the cars were running, but who fucking knew...

Across the street, the neon 'open' sign of a dingy looking café flickered to life, causing a red glow to be reflected across the surface of the family-sized swimming pool that had formed in the café's parking lot. *Hot Donuts! Fresh coffee! All American Scrambler Breakfast!* I read the sign in the window, not really paying much attention. The food would be shit. The coffee would be shit. Their donuts had probably been gathering dust and rat crap sprinkles for days, but I still got out of the truck, popped the collar of my jacket, shoved my hands in my pockets and ran across the now empty road. My socks were soaked in less than a second.

From inside the diner, I had a perfect view of the auto shop; there'd be no chance I'd miss the comings and goings of one Franz Halford from the booth I selected right in the window, so I sat my ass down on the cracked and peeling faux leather seat and pretended to read the sticky laminated menu that was propped between the salt and pepper shakers on the table in front of me. The garish, very badly taken, very unappealing photos of limp toast and rubbery eggs did nothing to inspire hunger in me. Committing homicide was usually something I liked to do on an empty stomach—things had a way of getting really fucking messy, after all. People shit themselves. They vomited. They bled all over the goddamn place. I'd learned my lesson in the past: food was never a good idea when the potential for bodily fluids was so high. I ordered a black coffee from a pimple-faced waiter when he finally decided to come over and check on me, and that was it. The poor bastard seemed disappointed.

An hour passed, and the caffeine in my veins began to make me antsy. Normally, patience was one of my strong points. I mean, the last job I'd done required me to hunker down for five hours in a forest, amongst the leaf litter and dead tree branches for my quarry to come along, and that hadn't fazed me one bit. Waiting for Franz Halford this morning was hell on earth, though, and I knew why. It was her fault. Sera's. God, her mouth really had been so fucking perfect, pouting, wrapped around my hard dick. And when she'd turned over and presented her ass to me, I'd known I was in fucking trouble. My job was now almost impossible, because I'd been stupid enough to think with my dick. Sera oozed sex appeal from every pore of her beautifully crafted, stunning fucking body. She welcomed a good fucking with every sideways glance she sent you, but she did so unintentionally, without expectation or any true knowledge that she was even doing it. Basically, she was the living embodiment of every-thing that turned me on. And I was *still* fucking turned on. My dick hadn't stopped raging since last night—it had still been hard enough to crack concrete this morning when I'd woke up. I'd had to run in the pissing rain just to stop myself from sliding my fingers inside her while she slept. Even now, sitting in the booth, being handed luke-warm, disgusting coffee in a very dirty cup by a teenager who looked like he might not be all that clean himself, my cock was throbbing like a pulsing beacon.

The way she'd hesitantly wrapped her hand around me...

The way her eyes had flashed when she'd squeezed and felt how thick and ready I was...

The way she'd inadvertently wet her bottom lip with the pink tip of that delicate little tongue of hers...

Shit. I needed to go jerk off in the bathroom. These kinds of thoughts would do nothing but claw at my mind, demanding my attention, distracting me from the task at hand, and this wasn't a line of work you could bumble your way through. I needed to be sharp. Focused. Single minded. So long as Sera Lafferty's pretty pink pussy was fogging my brain, I'd never be able to get anything done.

Getting up, I rearranged my cock in my pants to avoid any embarrassment, and then made my way into the restrooms. They were clean, at least, and smelled faintly like lemon. Plenty of paper towels. I grabbed a couple and locked myself into a stall, dropping my pants and pressing a hand against the back wall. I could make myself come in less than a minute if I wanted to. The memory of last night, of Sera looking so perfect and frankly fucking edible, deserved more respect than that, though. I worked my hand up and down the shaft of my cock slowly at first, relishing the pressure and the buzz of pleasure that began to tingle at the base of my dick. Fuck, that felt good. Not as good as Sera's mouth, but still...

I stroked faster, sucking in a deep breath and holding it inside my chest. She looked so fucking hot this morning, her hair damp and curling at the ends, her dark eyes flashing with rage as she realized what someone had done to her car. Her shirt had been tight and a little wet from the rain; the very first thing I'd noticed when she'd lowered her window to scowl at me was her tight nipples, poking out of the material at me. I'd taken them into my mouth last night. I'd licked and I'd sucked them. I'd pinched and rolled them, knowing all too well that Sera would enjoy the frisson of pain racing between her breasts and her cunt.

God, she'd opened up so nicely for me. She'd smelled so fucking good. Her pussy juice had coated more than just my cock; I'd reveled in the silky feeling of her excitement between the pad of my thumb and my index finger. Next time, I was going to lap at her like a hungry dog, and I was going to go back for seconds.

I sucked in a fresh lungful of oxygen, holding that one in my chest, too. My mind transported me back to the moment when I was about to thrust into Sera for the first time, and my balls tightened, my cock pulsing in my hand. The tip glistened with pre-cum, and I couldn't help it. I imagined her on her knees, her hands wrapped around my shaft, the tip of her tongue darting between her lips as she gently licked the clear fluid from me, and my legs threatened to bail on me.

Fuck, it was wrong of me, but I wanted her again. Last night should never have happened, but it did, and now? Urgh. I was never going to stop wanting her. I should complete my work and go. I should just do what I came here to do and get the fuck out of here, but that was the thing about *should*, though. People rarely ever paid any heed to something they *should* do. Should was rear-view mirror knowledge, a right hand turn that you could still see over your shoulder if you turned around far enough to catch it out of the corner of your eye. The turning was still there. You could still make it, if you performed an emergency one-eighty and headed back in the opposite direction. But somehow your foot always stayed on the gas, pressing you toward disaster, and there was nothing you could do about it.

I wasn't going to leave Sera here in Liberty Fields today. I was going to collect her from the motel as soon as my task was complete, and then it was inevitable. I was going to fuck her again. I was going to charm the ever-loving shit out of her, and she was going to be laid flat on the back seat of the truck, panting, digging her fingernails into my back all over again. And I was going to love every second of it.

God, it was so wrong...

I screwed my eyes shut, changing out my breath again, biting down on the inside of my cheek as I felt myself slipping and sliding toward oblivion. My hand was coated with pre-cum now, slick with the viscous fluid, which made running my hand up and down all the more enjoyable. It was easy to pretend that I was fucking her. It was easy to imagine I was pushing myself into her hot, wet, slick pussy. Too easy. I tipped my head back, straining as I teetered on the brink of coming, holding it back for as long as I could.

Her eyes, though...

Her mouth.

Her hands.

Her breasts.

Her spread thighs, and the fragile, pale pink between her legs, redder and darker where I slid myself inside of her...

Fuck...

Oh, *fuck*...

No way I was going to be able to hold it back. I opened my mouth and blasted out the air inside my lungs, making sure the roar that escaped me was a silent, wordless one. My cock throbbed once, twice, three times as I came, sending out jets of hot, white ejaculate that hit the wall behind the toilet. My vision danced. I'd come hard last night, I'd expected it then, but now, jerking off? It shouldn't have felt that fucking good. It shouldn't have felt so fucking incredible that I lost control and blew my load all over a motherfucking breezeblock wall. What the fuck *was* that?

I felt a little unsteady as I wiped myself off and put my dick away. My legs were jelly, and the back of my neck was burning, hotter than usual, the tips of my ears prickling with pins and needles. For a second I considered leaving my come running down the wall, but then I thought better of it. Leaving considerable deposits of DNA lying around was one thing, but when you were about to commit a crime directly across the street? Yeah, that wouldn't have been the smartest move on my part. Took me a minute to do away with my mess, and another thirty seconds to wash my hands, straighten up my hair and my jacket, and then I exited the bathroom and went to locate my coffee.

Sitting opposite my booth, another customer had come in while I was busy in the back cleaning my rifle. I recognized him the moment I laid eyes on him, but my expression and my body language didn't change. The world had shifted, but to the acne ridden server and the balding, overweight guy sitting at the bar, squinting at a menu, every-thing appeared completely normal.

"I'll take the pancakes, Jason. And make sure Herb doesn't skimp on the syrup this time. Last time I ordered 'em, they came out drier'n my grand mammy's cooter."

Jason blanched a little—probably was a good church-going boy. Probably only heard words like cooter and references to them being dry when he was here, working in this shithole. Franz Halford didn't seem to realize he'd made the boy uncomfortable, though. He dropped the menu down on the counter and pulled a tin of tobacco, popping the lid and thumbing a small amount of its contents underneath his top lip. Why was I not surprised the guy dipped? Such a gross, nasty habit. I enjoyed a cigarette more often than I should, but shoving that shit directly into your mouth made me want to gag.

I'd been careful not to make eye contact with Franz as I sat down and settled myself back in the booth, picking up my coffee mug and taking a sip. I was a fucking professional, for god's sake. I'd given him absolutely no reason to talk to me whatsoever, but when Jason, the server, turned around and went to hand in Franz's order to the kitchen, the miserable fucker turned around on his stool and grinned at me, a flash of brown liquid running over his teeth as he did so.

"How you enjoyin' this here weather?" he asked. Then he did something I just could not fathom. He turned his head and he spat on the floor. I'd just been flinging my come around in the bathroom like a deranged monkey that couldn't stop touching its own junk, but this was far, far worse. This was fucking unforgiveable.

I hid my disdain. I hid my violence—the violence that lived under my skin at all times, begging to be unleashed. I hid the fact that I wanted to pull out the gun I had resting in a holster in the small of my back at that very same moment we sat there. I plastered a broad smile on my face that said, *Hey! I'm utterly enamored by your authentic Southern charm and I am abso-fucking-lutely thrilled that you decided to talk to me, kind sir.* "We sure as hell don't get rain like this where I'm from," I announced. To a trained ear, the laughter I forced out of me next might possibly have sounded a little manic and unhinged, but Franz didn't bat an eyelid. He pointed to the bench opposite me in the booth, waggling his bushy eyebrows up and down.

"You want some company while you have your mornin' Joe, or

you wanna be left alone? I don't mind either way. I just thought you might like to enjoy some of the local color, seein' as how y'ain't from 'round here and all."

I gestured to the seat opposite and shrugged a shoulder, shaking my head. "Please. Be my guest."

Halford slid from his stool, hiking his baggy, stained jeans up on one side, though the action was pointless. His belly was sticking out from beneath the hem of his Budweiser t-shirt, and hanging over his waistband at the same time—no matter how many times he pulled his pants up, there was no way his considerable belly was going to allow them to stay up. The man grunted like a walrus as he lowered himself down into the seat, then removed his sweat-rimmed baseball cap and wiped his forehead with the back of his hand, before returning the cap to the crown of his head.

"I gotta say, people tell me I'm pretty good at figurin' where people are from, sir. I can identify an accent from the other side of a crowded room, and I'm pretty sure I got you pegged. I'd be willing to bet good money that you're from Minnesota or the like." Franz's eyebrows were more than bushy. They were like furry caterpillars that had crawled up onto his forehead and had the misfortune to get stuck there. I couldn't stop staring at them—mostly grey, with a stripe of ginger in the center of each. Weird.

"I *am* from Minnesota! That's really damn impressive," I told him, taking another mouthful of coffee. Fuck knows who'd said he was good with accents, but they were dead fucking wrong. The Minnesotan accent bore absolutely no resemblance to the thick Chicago accent I was putting on just for him. Screw it. Let him believe what he wanted to believe. From the powerful waves of Jack Daniels that were wafting across the table, and the loose, watery grin on Franz's face, there was a high probability that the guy was still drunk from last night. It was best not to antagonize half-drunk people by disagreeing with them.

"You were in the army, weren't you?" Franz says, his eyes glazing over a little. "You got that look about you."

"And what look would that be?" I say, smiling easily: a lie, a trick, a trap. A spider weaving his web with practice and ease.

"Back's too straight for a civilian. And your eyes are quick," he told me, scratching at the red scruff on his chin. "You're looking at everything here, figuring it all out."

I lowered my head—a show of deference—laughing a little under my breath. "Sad to say, I've never served. Wish I had, though. I'd probably have gotten a lot out of it when I was younger."

Franz nodded enthusiastically, then spat on the floor again. Urgh. Bastard. "I was in the army for fifteen years," he said. "Best years of my life, too. Protected the freedom of my fellow American citizens. Got to see the world. And got my dick sucked more times'n I can count!" He slapped the table, eyes disappearing into slits as he burst out laughing, his belly spilling over onto the table.

This was getting worse and worse by the second. Things would have been far simpler if I'd run into Franz over at the auto shop; now the piece of shit was ordering breakfast, and I was going to have to sit here with him until he fucking finished.

No.

Just no.

Completely ignoring his last statement, I stabbed a finger out of the window at the shop across the street, frowning slightly. "Hey, friend? I don't suppose you know if that auto place is gonna open today? My truck's making a rattling noise. I'm a little worried about driving it in this weather without getting it checked out first."

Franz sat back in his seat, puffing his chest out with an unreasonable amount of pride. "That place most definitely *is* going to open up today. I'm Franz Halford. I own the place." He thrust out his hand toward me, waiting for me to shake it, face split open with a grin, like he'd just surprised me with the biggest secret known to man or something. I shook, unhappy about the contact, feigning amusement to rival Franz's.

"That's well met, then. I'm lucky to have run into you. All the other places in town are closed."

Franz pulled a face, waving me off with an unsteady flick of his wrist. "Those motherfuckers over at Dimson's are criminals, man. Fucking immigrants. Don't speak a word of English between 'em. They ain't ever open before midday, and when you do catch 'em open, they'll over change you by a couple'a hundred bucks every single goddamn time. It's unchristian is what it is."

A shiver of annoyance raced down my spine, but once again I managed to hide my reaction to the grotesque human being in front of me. "Then I really will consider myself lucky. Listen," I said, making a show of looking down to glance at my watch. "I heard you ordering breakfast and all, but I was wondering...I'm in a serious hurry. If I picked up your tab here and shot you an extra hundred bucks for accommodating me, would you get your food to go and come cast an eye over my engine for a second? It's probably nothing, I'm probably being overly cautious, but I just wanna make sure..."

Franz narrowed his eyes at me, looking me up and down. "A hundred bucks and you pay for my breakfast, *on top* of the assessment fee for looking at your vehicle?" He pronounced the H in vehicle— one of my pet peeves. I nodded, though, continuing to smile.

"Yes, sir."

"Well, alright then. I ain't gonna argue with you, mister. What's your name again?"

"Ray. Ray Sheraton."

"Ohh, like them there hotels? You own any'a those things? *Jason! Put my damn pancakes in a box! We're leaving!*" He lost half the sodden tobacco from his mouth when he pivoted toward the counter, suddenly yelling at the server, who I'd decided I now felt sorry for. Jason didn't know which way to turn first as he hurried from one end of the diner to the other, first collecting Franz's food from the service hatch, and then up and down as he clearly scrambled to locate a to-go box.

I paid the kid, Franz took his pancakes and a two-liter bottle of coke, and we headed over to the auto shop. I saw more than a couple of inches of Franz's ass crack as he stooped to unlock the roller shutters. Once we were inside and Franz had opened the side door to the shop, he hiked up his pants again, hawking to clear his throat, and he pointed out into the parking lot, in the direction of my truck. "Shall we take a look at it, then?"

"Actually, I wanted to ask you a question first, if that's okay?"

"Sure thing, Ray. Ask away."

"Does the name Holly Shoji mean anything to you?" I watched as Franz's expression transformed itself into something wary at first, and then something hard and unfeeling.

"I'm sorry, boss. Doesn't ring a bell." The lie was as obvious as the broken capillaries at the end of his nose. He wasn't even trying to convince me he didn't know Holly's name. There was disgust in his eyes as he started to shuffle past me out of the garage. "I have a busy morning, too. If you want me to look at your truck, let's get on with it. If not, I'm afraid we're gonna have to save the chit chat for another day."

Sidestepping, I blocked his path, preventing him from walking outside. It took all of a second to lean over to the wall and hit the switch on the wall—the switch that lowered the roller shutters back down again. Franz studied me with ice in his eyes, assessing me from head to toe.

"You sure you wasn't in the military?" he asked, taking a step back.

"Nope. I never joined up. I thought about it, like I said, but my father had other ideas. He wanted me to follow in his footsteps."

"And what did he do?" Franz muttered in an airy tone. It was funny how many times people did this—acted like nothing untoward was happening, when something clearly *was* happening. As if, should he keep his voice free from aggression and hostility or panic, I would be held at bay, unaware that a situation was developing, and he would somehow be able to distract me while he escaped. There would be no distracting me, though. No escape, either. I watched calmly as Franz fumbled with his left hand, reaching out for a tire iron that was sitting on top of a messy workbench.

"He was a priest," I said, glancing down lazily to inspect my fingernails.

Franz nearly tripped over his own feet as he tried to back away from me. "So you're Catholic, then. Like me."

"Oh, we're nothing alike, Franz. We're not even the same species. See, I did follow in my father's footsteps. I studied. I became a priest, just like my father wanted me to, and I learned many things. I learned that the Catholic Church doesn't believe in brutally raping people just because they don't share your skin color, or your belief system."

Franz's eyes were wide now. His fear was plain to see, but there was something else there, too: hatred. So much anger and hatred. He didn't agree with what I was saying. Didn't care for it one little bit.

"If you're a priest, then what are you doing here, Ray? Shouldn't you be tending to your flock?"

I smirked, reaching not for the gun in the holster at my back, but for something a little more fun. Something a little sharper. Something a little more...*wicked*.

"I *was* a priest," I said, flipping over the heavy, serrated combat knife I was now holding. "I was a priest for quite a while. And then I realized something. Wanna know what I realized?"

Franz shook his head, his jowls wobbling all over the place. "No, man. No. Just go. Get the fuck out of my shop. That filthy little whore deserved everything she got. She didn't belong here. She was taking money from the government to study. And when she finished that course, what then? She was gonna take a job that belonged to a fucking American, man! We're just lettin' 'em waltz in here and take everything from us. I showed that bitch we weren't all gonna take it lying down. That *she* was gonna have to take something lying down, too, if—"

I tilted the blade from left to right in my hand, peering into the highly reflective surface of the weapon as if mesmerized by its beauty. "I realized I wasn't really helping anyone by spritzing them with holy water and shoving bread into their mouths every Sunday. I realized... I didn't believe anymore. I realized there were better ways to help save people, so I picked up this knife, and I decided to take matters into my own hands. Just like I'm about to do right now."

6

SERA

CONVINCE ME

I wouldn't have known it was Fix's truck if I hadn't seen him get in it and drive off earlier. After sitting around in the motel lobby for hours, waiting for him to come back, I grew anxious and begged a ride into Liberty Fields off another woman who was checking out of her room and leaving. I'd hoped I might find a gift store where I could grab another wedding gift for Amy, since I'd demolished the tequila last night. Instead, I spotted Fix's truck and asked to be dropped off in the parking lot of a very run down, sketchy looking auto shop.

The front roller shutters were down, but the side door to the building was open. Inside: Darkness. The smell of oil, grease, and unwashed male. I hovered just inside the door, trying to decide if I ought to go in or not. Sixsmith used to cart me around a lot when I was really small. He used to take me to dark, strange, unfamiliar places like this, and there would always be trouble. Someone would be drinking. Someone would be cooking meth. Someone would be fucking loudly in the back. There would be things young eyes weren't meant to see. And, by the time we left, there would usually be blood.

I could just wait outside for Fix. There was no reason to barge into the shop and start yelling at him for taking too long, when he promised me he'd only be gone an hour or so. I could do that in the truck, once the dark-haired bastard emerged and saw me leaning against his murdered-out ride, waiting for him.

I walked over to the truck and tried the handle to the passenger seat, but it was locked. I checked my phone—another missed call from Ben, but nothing from Amy—and then slid it back into my pocket, trying not to scowl. Things were so much simpler before cell phones. If you didn't want to be harassed by anyone, all you had to do was leave the house, walk away, and not look back. I'd gotten my first phone when I was sixteen, bought and paid for with money I'd earned waiting tables in a diner, and I'd been so excited; everyone else in school had had one for a couple of years, and I'd finally got to play catch up. Now, there were days I wished I could just throw all of my devices in the trash and never purchase another one again.

The rain had eased slightly since I'd left the motel, but it was picking up again. Heavy, fat beads of water thumped against the hood of Fix's truck, falling from the branches of a huge live oak that loomed over the parking lot like a grim sentinel. The tree was bare of leaves, and its considerable, crooked limbs raked upward toward the overcast sky like the fingers of a twisted, grasping hand.

I raised the hood of my jacket, shivering when the already damp fabric brushed against the back of my neck. I couldn't wait to get the fuck out of this town. It was dreary, cold, and far too wet. Seattle was world-renowned for it's miserable weather and grey skies, but at least it had life to it. A lot of life. Music. Great food. Art. Culture. Business and industry. Liberty Fields was an unmarked town on the map that no one visited on purpose, and no one really cared about, apart from the three hundred worn down people who lived here.

I waited for Fix, picking at my fingernails inside my pockets, breathing deeply. He'd come out soon and drive me somewhere I could get another car, and then everything would be okay. I tried not to let my mind wander. When I did, I ended up replaying the events of last night and driving myself a little crazy. Fix must have thought I was used to sleeping with random strangers hours after I'd just met them. He had to believe that, since that's exactly what I did with him. The truth was I'd been more than a little intimidated by him last night. His looks were enough to make my cheeks color whenever he turned his attention to me—skin golden, like he spent a good amount of time out in the sun. His face was all angular lines, sharp enough to cut. His eyes were both exquisite and frightening. It wasn't just their color that froze me to my core. Whenever he looked at me, a very real chill skated over my body, as if his frosty expressions produced their own wintry breeze that bit at my skin. He was an enigma—closed off and secretive. He didn't want to share with me what he did for a living, and that was fine. Annoying, but understandable. Sometimes people wanted to keep things private, or they just didn't realize they were being rude. There'd been plenty of times *I'd* forgotten the subtle nuances of social etiquette—etiquette I'd had to learn through studying other people at an early age, since my father hadn't been too concerned with teaching me anything at all—and I'd been cold to the point of rudeness. My slashed tires proved that well enough. That traffic cop had probably seen my car parked there last night and decided to teach me a lesson in Southern manners.

A sudden blast of wind pummeled me, hurling cold rainwater into my face, and I bit back the urge to scream. Okay, this wasn't working. If I had to change my clothes one more time, I really was going to scream, and what manners I had left were going right out of the window. Wrapping my jacket tighter around my body, I hurried back across the parking lot and darted into the auto shop through the side door, grinding my teeth together. So freaking cold... I couldn't remember ever being so cold in my entire life. My eyes took a second to adjust to the darkness inside the building. Another second to take in the stacks of molding newspapers that were piled up against the walls, and the numerous, rusting tools that were discarded all over the place. To my left, a tiny office, with nothing more than a small desk and a heavily stained chair inside sat abandoned. The air was stale and reeked of old cigarette smoke, coupled with the sour tang of rotting food—probably emanating from the large, dented metal trashcan that was bursting with old takeout wrappers in the corner of the room. I was about to head further into the darkness, when the low, gruff timbre of Fix's voice reached my ears.

"—*so I picked up this knife, and I decided to take matters into my own hands. Just like I'm about to do right now.*"

Huh. He was talking to someone...and it didn't sound like a particularly nice conversation. From around the corner, in what I presumed was the main floor of the auto shop, another voice cut through the air, loud and edged with something like anger.

"You can go ahead and put that down now, motherfucker. You think I haven't been threatened before? You think this is the first time someone's come in here and tried to act tough with me? I ain't some dumb piece of shit that don't know how to protect hisself. I've killed men before. I doubt you've ever had the fucking stones."

There was a long, pregnant pause, and something changed as the silence thickened—some tense, darkness seemed to develop, that spread from one side of the building to the other, poisoning the air from corner to corner.

"All right," the other voice said quietly. "Maybe you *have* killed before. So what makes you any different to me, *Ray*? What gives you the right to judge me, when you've committed the same sins?"

"I've never *raped* anyone," Fix growled. "And I've never killed anyone who didn't deserve it. I'm very selective about the jobs I take. A set of criteria has to be met before I'll consider taking another person's life."

"Criteria?" There's a loud hawking sound, and then the wet splatter of something hitting the floor. "Sounds like excuses to me. What criteria cursed *me* to die?"

"You're corrupt. You're irredeemable. You feel no remorse over the pain and suffering you inflicted on that poor girl. You don't regret your actions, and you'll more than likely repeat those actions again in the future."

"Fuck you, man. You can't tell me what I do or don't feel bad about. You can't tell me what I will or wont do in the future."

"You're saying you won't hurt anyone ever again?"

"Yeah, what if I am? Would that change your mind?" The other man's voice was hard and aggressive, filled with defiance. He didn't sound sincere in the slightest.

My heart was thundering like a freight train in my chest. I had no idea what I was hearing, couldn't really make sense of any of it, but my blood had turned to ice in my veins all the same. Fix had told me back in the motel that he was an assassin. He'd told me he killed people for money, but I'd brushed it off as nonsense. Now, listening to the tense exchange that was taking place between him and this other man, it sounded like he'd *actually* been telling the truth. But there was no way. It simply couldn't be true.

"Changing my mind isn't easy," Fix rumbled. His voice was filled with enough gravel to set my teeth on edge. I'd never heard the promise of such violence in anyone's words before; it made me want to back up, to clap my hands over my ears, to quietly tiptoe my way back outside and run for my goddamn life. I couldn't do it, though. I couldn't make a single one of my muscles move as I stood there, listening to the men talk.

"Convince me that you'll never attack another human being for their differences. Convince me you'll never raise your hand in anger, or take something from someone weaker and more vulnerable than you, simply because they aren't white. If you can do that, I'll let you live."

"All right, then. You have my word as a good Catholic. I won't never do that shit again."

I'd heard that same haughty, smug tone before, the night I'd held a knife of my own up to my father's throat. He'd sworn he'd never touch me again. He'd sworn he'd never touch Amy again, and I'd known he was just telling me what I'd wanted to hear. I'd heard the lie in his voice. I'd witnessed it in his eyes, that had been conniving and glinting with the revenge he was already planning against me. I was sure the same look of contempt and disgust would be on the face of the man Fix was talking to, and that made my heart stop beating altogether.

God, he was going to hurt this guy. Fix was *seriously* going to injure him. I couldn't understand why, but I found myself propelled forward, toward the sound of their voices. I didn't want to see... I didn't want to watch what was going to happen next, but a part of me felt obliged to stop it, to prevent whatever was about to take place. I didn't know how I was going to accomplish that, but...

My body was numb as I moved. I didn't feel a thing. My lungs quit working as I found myself standing in a doorway. Fix stood with his back to me, and in his hand...

In his hand: the cruelest, sharpest knife I'd ever seen.

The man opposite him was shorter than Fix, soft around his midsection, his face crumpled into a mask of hate and fury. Despite the faint lighting, I could make out the dark splatter across the shoulders of his tired, worn jacket that the rain must have created when they were outside. His jeans were streaked with grease, and frayed at the hems. The baseball cap he was wearing was so worn that the material had split over the brim. Strange that I should notice such fine details, when I should have been charging forward, shouting, demanding that Fix leave the guy alone.

"You aren't going to change," Fix said softly. "The way you hurt that girl... you zip-tied her hands, and you pinned her down. You kept her in your basement for days. You forced yourself inside her time and time again, and you laughed as she begged and pleaded with you for her life—"

"I *didn't* kill her," the other man protested. It was then I saw the tire iron he was holding in his hand. "I didn't take her life."

"You might as well have done," Fix countered. "What kind of an existence do you think you left her with? Do you think she'll ever be able to sleep again? Do you think she'll be able to go back to her daily routine and forget about everything you did to her? Normal doesn't exist for Holly anymore. She'll never be able to have the normal life she deserved. She'll never be able to form a connection with a man. She won't be able to fall in love, get married and have children. Every time a guy looks at her in the street, every time someone smiles at her and admires her, she'll never be able to smile back. She'll see you. Your hideous face looming over her. You, palming your disgusting dick as you prepare to shove it inside her one more time. She'll remember every single terrible thing you did to her, and she'll die just a little more inside. You robbed her of everything good."

The other man's scowl deepened in the flash of an eye; he'd heard the finality in Fix's tone, the same way I'd heard it, and he knew he was never going to be able to trick Fix into believing him. "That little fucking cunt didn't deserve *anything*. She deserved exactly what I gave to her. I should have slit her fucking throat. You're right. I didn't stop hurting her when she begged. It made my dick hard. I loved fucking the shit out of her. I fucking loved hurting her. I'd do it all again if I had the chance." When he launched himself forward, I didn't see it coming. He was slow and sloppy, hefting the tire iron over his head, bringing it swinging down in a savage arc aimed directly at Fix's head. Fix sidestepped out of the way with apparent ease; he didn't even raise a hand to defend himself. He simply moved out of the way, tutting under his breath. The other man stumbled, carried forward by his own momentum, and that's when Fix reacted. He flipped the knife over in his hand and angled his wrist, darting it out to the right—a casual, fluid movement that looked like it cost him nothing at all. The tip of the knife plunged into the other guy's side, and time stopped. The other man looked up at Fix, his eyes wide with surprise, and a long, wet gasp hissed out of his mouth.

"You...fucking asshole," he wheezed. "You fucking piece of fucking..." The tire iron moved again, flying toward Fix's shoulder, but Fix reached up and took hold of the man by the wrist, halting his attack in midair. He was so calm. So collected. With his back still to me, I couldn't see his face, but there was a serenity that poured off him, loosening his shoulders. It was over quickly, but the scene would play out in my mind until the day I died: Fix slowly, carefully withdrew the knife from the man's side, and he raised it to his throat.

"I won't *let* you hurt anyone else," he whispered. "You're done, Franz. It's over. I'll make it quick."

There was resignation in Franz's eyes. He knew Fix was telling the truth, and a part of him looked like it had accepted it. He was welling up, tears threatening to spill down his face as Fix stepped closer to him, holding him tightly by the arm. Franz swallowed, a flicker of pain passing over his face. "You...you're a priest," he gasped. His face had gone white, turned to the color of ash, and tiny spots of blood flecked his lips and his chin. "Absolve me. Free me of my sins."

Fix swiveled his body, the sound of his boots grinding against the concrete underfoot filling the air. "I *used* to be a priest. I can't help you. And even if I could, I wouldn't. You have to actual repent to be absolved. And I don't take confession anymore." In one swift, predatory movement, Fix slashed out with his arm, and the knife sang through the air. I watched, horrified, as the wicked edge of his serrated blade cut across Franz's throat. Then the blood came. A gushing spurt of crimson that sprayed all over Fix, and up over his head, hitting the wall right beside me.

Franz gurgled and choked as he died. He was unable to scream, which might have been a blessing had he not been trying very hard to do just that. A further jet of blood spouted from the jagged tear in his neck, and he grasped at Fix, hands clawing at him as he tried to remain upright. It was useless, though. Completely futile. The light faded from his eyes in a matter of seconds, and then he was slipping, sliding, hands releasing Fix as he sagged to the ground.

I still couldn't move. My nerve endings weren't responding, even though I was hollering at them to obey. I could have snuck away and hid before being discovered, but the shock of what I'd just seen had me rooted permanently to the spot. As Fix slowly turned around, I knew with every fiber of my being that I was about to die. I'd seen what he'd done. I'd witnessed the whole thing. There was no way I'd be allowed to live to tell the tale. The coppery taste of metal and fear flooded my mouth, so thick and overwhelming that I almost gagged on it.

Fix saw me immediately. He was a vision of terror—face and hands covered with blood, jacket doused and drenched in red. He was the stuff of nightmares, and I was locked in his gaze, unable to run. He didn't look shocked to see me standing there in the doorway.

He didn't look surprised at all. There was a darkness shrouding him as he took a step toward me, wiping his face with the back of his hand, smearing the blood like it was war paint.

"I didn't think you'd stay to watch, Sera. I didn't think you'd have the stomach for it."

7

FIX

JUSTICE

I'd known the moment she'd entered the auto shop. Her perfume had given her away—sweet, soft, floral and delicious, the same smell that had been haunting my senses ever since I'd fucked her last night—and I'd waited, figuring out how I was going to handle the situation. She'd stop me. She'd come running in and save Franz. She'd call the police. She'd have me arrested if I laid one finger on the guy. Those were the things I'd been expecting her to say and do, only she didn't.

She'd remained hidden in the shadows, observing silently, and I'd realized exactly how fucked I was. If I let Franz go, he'd try and come after me. That wouldn't go well for him, naturally, but it was inconvenient. And then what? If he took his anger at being confronted out on another unsuspecting girl? If he raped someone else? There was just no way...

I stepped carefully, making sure Sera could see me clearly as I approached her. No sudden movements. No surprises that might have her screaming. She looked like a frightened deer, trapped in the headlights of an oncoming vehicle that she could plainly see but do absolutely nothing to avoid.

"You killed him," she breathed, her eyes skating to the dead body on the ground behind me. "You...you took that knife and you killed him."

"I did."

She looked at me like I'd just denied my actions instead of admitting to them. "You *killed* him."

"I know."

"Wh—" She shook her head, grasping for the wall, trying to steady herself as she swayed. "*Why*? What the..."

"He hurt a girl. I was hired to make the situation right," I said, keeping my voice even. In the years I'd been doing this kind of work, no one had ever stumbled upon me in the act. I'd never been so obviously caught red handed. My mind was reeling. I wanted to pick Sera up, sling her over my shoulder and get the fuck out of there, but that would be risky. If I didn't handle *this* situation right, and she was bawling and crying as I dragged her through the parking lot, someone was bound to see us. The moment Franz was found dead, it would be easy enough for someone to report what they'd seen and the cops would be on my tail in no time. It was bad enough that the waiter in the diner had seen me with Franz as it was, but the kid had barely looked twice in my direction. There had been no cameras in the diner, the place was far too low rent for any kind of security measures, so the police were going to have to go off a very vague description as it was. But if Sera lost her shit and was hysterical as I bundled her into the back of the truck, that would complicate things immensely.

"He—how is this making the situation *right*?" Sera had lost all color to her face, and she kept swallowing. Her gag reflex was probably working overtime. I remembered the first time I'd seen someone murdered, and while I hadn't flipped out the way I suspected she was about to, I'd definitely parted company with my lunch once I found myself alone in a bathroom.

"The cops around here would never have pressed charges against him," I said, cautiously wiping my palms against my pants. "And even if they did, the girl's too scared to press charges. So I took the job. If I thought the justice system would have taken care of this, I would have left the whole thing well alone."

Sera sniffed, then covered her mouth with her hand, cringing. "God, the smell..."

The thing about dead people was that, when they were on their way to dying, they often lost control over their bowels. It was more common than not. Combined with the thick scent of blood in the air, the odor of death was already developing from faint to pungent.

"Fuck. I think I'm going to throw up." Sera staggered back, bending over at the waist, but I rushed forward and took hold of her, pinning her in my arms.

"Do *not* throw up in here. If you're gonna puke, do it outside. Preferably seven or eight miles away from here."

She groaned, a look of panic forming as she took in the way I was holding her. She was going to lose it. Any second now, she was going to have a meltdown, and I was going to have to take measures to calm her. I didn't want to have to knock her out, but I would if I had to. Her body shook, one violent shudder, and she tried to lift her hand to her face again, but she noticed the blood on her jacket and her skin—the blood she had just put her hand in when she tried to steady herself against the wall—and that was it.

Her eyes rolled back into her head, and she fainted.

～

S tep one: Get Sera into the truck.
    Step two: Calmly drive back to the motel.
Step three: Strip out of my blood soaked clothes and change in the truck.

Step four: Collect Sera's bags from the lobby.

Step five: Get the hell out of dodge.

I completed steps one through five mechanically, not really thinking about anything. There would be time for thinking later. Now was a time for action, and I'd been over scenarios like this enough times in my head that I knew exactly what I had to do. Okay, so maybe not scenarios exactly like this, but similar enough. For some reason, I'd never considered there might be a time that I'd have to lay an unconscious woman down on the backseat of my vehicle and hightail it away from a murder scene. The faintest possibility that something like this could happen just never fucking occurred to me.

So fucking stupid.

We were back on the road before Sera woke up, which was concerning since, as far as I knew, people who fainted generally woke up quickly, but she'd obviously suffered quite a shock. Her body, her mind, must have needed a little time to reset itself. I heard her stir, and then within a second she was scrambling at the door handle, trying to open the motherfucking door. Thankfully, I'd taken precautions to lock them all before I'd started driving again.

"We're doing eighty. Wouldn't recommend a tuck and roll right now."

"Let me out of the car, Fix. Stop the car right now and let me go." She was frightened, and I couldn't really blame her for it. The last thing we needed was her losing her shit while we were moving, though. I pulled over to the side of the road, hitting the hazards, and I snatched up the brown file that I'd placed on the passenger seat, ready for this moment. Opening it up, I grabbed the first photo from within the file and thrust it over my shoulder, snarling under my breath. It was Holly, the girl Franz had so brutally assaulted, covered in bruises, her mouth split open in so many places that her lips resembled mangled meat from a deli counter. She was naked in the picture, and the bite marks and burns all over her skin, her breasts, her thighs, and her stomach were livid and purple. Horrific to behold.

"This is what he did," I snapped. "This is how he left her, when he finally released her. Seventy-two hours, he kept her in that basement, Sera. Seventy-two hours, where he tortured her, and raped her, and sank his teeth into her skin. He gave her hepatitis, for fuck's sake."

Sera didn't take the photo from me. She stared at it, shaking, her eyes filling with tears. A car burned past us on the road, way faster than the speed limit, and the truck rocked from side to side in its wake. Sera just sat there, staring at the picture of Holly, unmoving. I tossed the photo into her lap and grabbed another from the file: an image of Holly's buttocks, which were flayed raw and covered in blood. I tossed that one into Sera's lap, then followed it with another, and then another, each one worse than the one before. "If you're gonna try and tell me that sick bastard didn't get what he deserved, then you're going to have a very difficult time."

Quietly, Sera began to cry. "I don't...I don't know what to think. I just...please. Please don't kill me."

I'd already figured she would think that—that I was going to kill her. Her desperate plea still made me feel sick to my stomach, though. "I'm not going to kill you, Sera. Why the fuck would I kill you? You've done nothing wrong." My stomach tied itself in a knot.

She stopped crying, her body going still. She raised her head, looking me in the eye for the first time since she'd awoken. "Then... what are you going to do with me. Why won't you let me go?"

"I need to know you're not gonna call the cops. I need to know, the moment I let you go, you're not going to send the authorities after me."

With fumbling hands, Sera gathered the photos of Holly's battered and broken body and threw them at me, sending them falling into the foot well. "Do you think I'm stupid? I wouldn't breathe a word of this to anyone, Fix. I fought long and hard for the life I have right now. I wouldn't risk it by snitching on a clearly very fucking deranged and dangerous man."

Ouch. The dangerous part I could handle. Deranged, though? That was uncalled for. I turned around, gripping hold of the steering wheel, sucking in a deep breath through my nose. "I'm sorry if I don't believe you right now, but it's been my experience that people will tell you anything when they're scared for their lives. You heard Franz, right?"

Silence.

I blew out my breath, huffing. This wasn't going well. None of it was. I'd formulated a plan in my mind. It was fucking nuts, completely against what I was supposed to do. I already knew Sera was going to balk at it, but fuck. I couldn't handle the alternative. If she didn't like it...

"Just let me go, Fix. Please. I don't need this, and neither do you. All I wanted to do was get to my sister's wedding. After that, I wanted to go back to Seattle and get back to work. This doesn't change any of that."

She sounded sincere, and honestly I was inclined to believe her. "I'll take you to your sister's wedding," I said evenly, restarting the truck's engine. "Then I'll go with you back to Seattle, and everything will be normal again. So long as you keep your mouth shut and say nothing of what you saw this morning, everything will be fine. Do you understand?"

I pulled back out onto the road, waiting to see what she would say. I didn't have to wait very long.

"You're holding me hostage?" she asked quietly.

"No. I'm not holding you hostage. I'm going to monitor the situation, until I'm certain you won't bring the sky crashing down on my head. That's different."

"You're *insane.*" I could hear the panic in her voice, but it wasn't as bad as before. She was gradually regaining control over herself, believed I wasn't planning on murdering her to tidy up my loose ends, and that was progress. "You're going to drive me to Alabama, and then what? You're going to watch me like a hawk? Pretend to be a waiter at my sister's fucking wedding? Keep tabs on me, and take me out if it looks like I'm losing my cool?"

"Why the fuck would I pretend to be a waiter, Sera? Jesus. It's a wedding. You have a plus one, right?" I glanced in the rearview mirror to look at her, and the expression on her face was more than a little incredulous.

"My plus one? You want to be my plus one? You just killed a rapist, slit his throat from ear to ear, and now you want to be *my date to a fucking wedding*? I can't...I just can't make any sense of what's happening right now. I feel like I'm having a bad trip or something. The worst trip in the history of drug abuse."

"Don't be so melodramatic."

"Melodramatic? You think this is melodrama? You kill people for money, Fix. You stab them, and you shoot them, and you...you do god knows what else to them. I saw you do it with my own two eyes, and I'm being melodramatic when I don't want to spend time with you at my sister's wedding. You have *got* to be kidding!"

"A couple of days. All you have to do is make me believe I'm not gonna find myself in handcuffs, and I'll let you go. It's easy, really. If you hadn't come investigating like fucking Columbo, then we wouldn't be in this position in the first place."

She laughed a cold, hard, derisive laugh. "If you hadn't killed Franz, we wouldn't be in this position. *I think that trumps the fact that I walked into a building, looking for* you."

"Hadn't you better be texting your sister right now, instead of yelling at me? She's gonna want to know you need someone added next to you on her seating plan."

"Fuck, Fix! You're just as bad as Franz was if you think it's okay to keep me with you against my will."

I sent her a sharp, narrow-eyed glare behind me, trying to tamp down my rising temper. She was the fucking crazy one if she was comparing this to what Franz had done to Holly. I saw the moment in the rearview that she realized how wrong her statement was. She didn't take it back, though. She set her jaw, lifting her chin in defiance, and slumped back into her chair.

"All right. Fine. You can come with me to the stupid wedding. You can escort me back to Seattle like the naughty little girl that I am. But the second it looks like you're going to hurt me, or do something I wouldn't like, then I'm going to start screaming. And trust me...I can scream really fucking loud."

I breathed a sigh of relief. I'd just bought us *both* some time.

8

SERA

LOLLIPOP

Amy: Who is he? And why are you just telling me about him now?
I asked you months ago if you were seeing anybody, and you
said no.

Me: I'm sorry. I'm telling you about him right now, though. It's
nothing serious. I didn't think he was going to be able to make the
date, so I didn't mention anything. He called this morning and
told me he was going to come and pick me up, so there we have it.
Look, if it's a problem and you'd prefer him not to be there, then I
understand. Just let me know.

*I*t was probably a bad idea to tell Amy she could veto Fix's
impromptu attendance at her wedding. She was far more
polite than I was, however, and barely argued with me over the
matter.

Amy: If you're here on time and everything goes according to
plan, then I don't care who you bring. So long as he doesn't fuck
up my big day.

So long as he didn't fuck up her big day? God, that was a riot. There were a thousand and one ways Fix could fuck up Amy's big day, which included, but were not limited to, murdering one of the guests. My sister's friends were all assholes as far as I was concerned, but Amy was fond of them for some reason, so she probably wouldn't take too kindly to having any of them killed. My ex-boyfriend, Gareth, was going to be there. Things between us had hardly been serious, but when he'd cheated on me and totaled my car, I'd sworn I'd remove his balls if I ever saw his miserable face again. Amy had warned me he was going to be in attendance—as Ben's oldest friend, he'd been assigned best man duties—and she'd begged me not to cause a scene. I'd been dreading setting eyes on Gareth again, but now he was the least of my worries. Fix was going to turn heads. There would be questions. Lots of them. And when someone asked my plus one what he did for a living, what the fuck was he going to say? "Oh, I kill people for money?" He hadn't even blinked when he'd told me that in the motel lobby last night. His comment had washed over me, but if he said that to Amy? God, there would be fireworks. Fourth of July fireworks. The kind of fireworks that could be seen three counties over and would permanently burn the retinas of anyone unfortunate enough to catch sight of them.

"You're grinding your teeth." Fix hadn't said much in the past few hours, and neither had I. I'd been staring at the back of his neck from the back seat, wondering how easy it would be to choke him out and escape without him crashing the car during my attack. I'd decided the chances of him driving head-on into a barrier, or veering off the road altogether, were far too high, and I'd shelved the idea, but that didn't stop me from imagining how satisfying it would be to wrap my hands around his neck and to squeeze as hard as I could.

"I tend to do that when I'm stressed," I answered him. "And, as you can probably tell, I'm really stressed right now."

"This isn't exactly how I'd planned on spending my week either, Angel."

"Oh? And how exactly *did* you plan on spending your week?" This was going to be good. He probably had another four or five hits lined up or something. I had no idea what his quota was, but he seemed like an industrious guy. Didn't seem like the type to be taking time off to sip whiskey in front of a roaring fire while reading a good book.

His eyes darted to the rear view mirror. I pretended not to see him look back at me. "I had responsibilities back in New York that are going to have to wait now. Believe me, this is highly inconvenient."

"Responsibilities?" A number of possibilities occurred to me: what if he had a wife and a family back home that were waiting for his return? He fucked me last night, but so what? A guy who ended people's lives on a regular basis was hardly going to flinch at cheating. What if he had an ailing grandmother in a care home that he usually had coffee with every Wednesday? Would she know all about his extra-curricular activities? It was then that I remembered the woman who'd been trying to get hold of him so desperately. "Do your responsibilities involve Monica? Does she know who you are, Fix? Does she know what you do whenever you leave the state?"

A ghost of a smile twitched at the corners of his mouth, before it vanished. "Monica isn't my responsibility. But yes, she does know who I am. She's probably the only person in the world who *does* know me. And yes, she knows exactly what I do whenever I leave the state." The tone in his voice hid a shadow of amusement. There was a story behind his relationship with this woman, Monica, but he didn't seem like he was going to share it. I sure as hell wasn't going to ask him about it.

I turned to stare out of the window, leaning my forehead against the cold glass. Wyoming whipped by in flashes of green, blue, grey, brown and white. Columns of smoke poured from the chimneys of homes set back from the road. There were people inside those houses, preparing lunch for their families. Planning the rest of their day. Cleaning and cooking. Paying their bills. Watching television. How could life carry on so normally, so blindly, for some people, when my whole world had been turned upside down in the space of a couple of hours? I closed my eyes, and all I saw was blood pooling on the floor of that auto shop. The body of that rapist lying there on the frozen concrete, rapidly cooling, his eyes open, staring at me, frightened, as if he were pleading with me to help him, even in death. "How many people have you killed, Fix?" I asked quietly.

Silence filled the truck, and I began to think he wasn't going to answer. Then he cleared his throat, and spoke. "Does it matter? Doesn't the death of one person at my hands damn me to hell either way?"

"I don't believe in hell."

Again, another cursory, if a little intrigued backward glance from Fix in the mirror. "So you're an atheist, then."

"I'm someone who believes you shouldn't kill people, even if there is no higher power monitoring our behavior up in the clouds, chalking up points for or against us."

He smirked. The truck was filled with the scent of fresh, cold air and pine needles. It would forever be a smell that reminded me of this moment. If I were destined to have any more moments, that was. Fix's ice blue eyes returned to the road, scanning the horizon, and I caught myself staring at the line of his jaw; his facial hair had grown noticeably overnight, and now he was sporting a healthy five o'clock shadow. I hated myself for it, but once again I found myself stunned by how absolutely, ridiculously attractive he was. He was beyond dangerous, and I was beyond stupid to be thinking such things about him at a time like this, but I'd known it for a long time now: there was something fundamentally fucked up inside me. I'd been in too many messed up situations already to react the way any sane person might when locked in the back of a moving truck with a potential mass murder. And he really was pretty.

"Are you hungry?" he asked. His voice was deep and penetrating —the sound of rumbling thunder. I tightened my grasp around my cell phone, holding onto it for dear life; it was a miracle he'd let me keep it, really. Fix was a smart man, that much was desperately obvious. So there had to be a reason he hadn't confiscated my only current means of contact with the outside world. From the backseat, I could easily send a text, pleading for help, and Fix knew that.

"No. I'm fine," I answered him.

"Okay," he responded flatly. But another five miles down the road saw him pulling off our course and onto the forecourt of a gas station.

"I told you I wasn't hungry."

"And I said okay. But, with all the grumbling and rumbling coming from your stomach for the last hour, I knew you were lying. Also, this truck doesn't run on thin air. If we're going to make it to Alabama, then we're actually going to have to stop for gas every once in a while." He paused while he killed the engine, then turned in his seat and pulled a face that must have matched my own pretty closely. "I know. The laws of potential energy and physics in general are fucking stupid, right?"

The ease of his smile struck me as odd. But then, Fix had had a long time to come to terms with the fact that he was a killer. It was old news to him. I'd had less than a few hours to wrap my head around his entire existence, and it was taking me a hot minute to figure out what the fuck was going on. "I'll have a bottle of water and a bag of chips," I said. "Plain. No cheesy shit."

According to Amy, I had a look that withered men's balls and had them retracting inside their bodies, never to be seen again. I was giving Felix that look now, but he seemed utterly impervious to it. Didn't even bat an eyelash. In fact, he laughed under his breath as he opened up the driver's door and hopped out of the cab, moving with the ease of someone very comfortable inside their own skin. I hissed under my breath when, instead of filling up the car and heading inside the gas station, Fix tugged open the back passenger door—*my* door—and gestured rather bluntly for me to get out.

"I head inside that building, I'll come out to find my truck gone," he said, smiling from ear to ear. "You think I'm that dumb?"

"I wasn't going to steal your truck, Fix. You took the keys with you, for god's sake."

"You look like a girl who knows how to rig a hot wire. Now come on. And play nice. The guys in these rural rest stops usually have about fifteen weapons strapped to their bodies, they're bored, and they have itchy trigger fingers. One doe-eyed, please-help-me-kind-sir look from you, and they'll be pumping me full of buckshot."

I felt a little unsteady as I slid out of the truck, straight into Fix's arms. His fingers curved around my sides, pressing lightly into my ribs, and I could feel the warmth of his body radiating right through my jacket. "I don't need help, thank you," I hissed, trying to wriggle free of his grasp. He shoved me, stepping forward at the same time, so that my back was butted up against the side of the truck and his chest was flush against mine, my body pinned between the vehicle and his solid, strong, muscle-packed form. I gasped, trying to catch my breath. Trying to figure out which was stronger—Felix Marcosa, or the Ford I was leaning up against.

"Are you listening?" he growled, leaning in so that our faces were mere inches apart.

"And why would I care if you're riddled with buckshot?"

"Because. You don't hate me. You're trying to avoid the thought altogether, but you actually quite like me, Sera. And you're not at all sorry about the guy I left on the ground back there in Liberty Fields. You know you're not. He was a rapist and likely a murderer, too. He was a violent man, who reveled in the misery and the suffering of others, and I can tell...you've seen your fair share of people like him." He reached up and slowly ran his fingers along the edge of my jaw, along the slightly puckered line of my scar, and a jolt of ice rushed through my veins. I whipped my head to the side, removing myself from his touch, shuddering at the very idea that someone, anyone, had just dared to touch such a secret, hidden, vulnerable part of me with their fingertips *and* their words.

"You have no fucking idea what you're talking about," I snapped, slamming my palms flat against his chest, pushing him firmly enough that he had to take a step back. "You don't know me. You don't know anything about me, my past, what I'm thinking or what I like. You're grasping at straws, trying to convince yourself that I'm safe. That I'm not going to tell anyone what you did. And if that's what needs to happen in order for you to let me go, then I'm all for it. But please... please don't try and convince *me* of anything. I'm not that simple to figure out, Fix. You'll never see inside me. You'll never piece the fractured pieces of *me* back together long enough to make a whole picture, so don't even try."

My heart was galloping away from me as I slid around him and made my way across the forecourt. I didn't look back. Underfoot, the ground was buckled and broken, huge ruptures in the concrete creating a giant spider's web of cracks. Weeds had shot up from the earth beneath, ankle high, knee high in places, and I couldn't help thinking it: Amy and I were so similar to those weeds. We'd been born beneath a pile of shit so high that it seemed impossible we'd ever make anything of ourselves, but somehow, between the cracks, we'd managed to push our way through, fighting, and we'd survived. We were still weeds, though. We'd never be anything more.

"Can I help you, miss?" The guy behind the counter, armed to the teeth as Fix predicted, was actually an old woman. Her weapon of choice were a pair of knitting needles. She was probably someone's grandma, and she smelled of talcum powder and gentle, sickly sweet smell of someone who might just die any moment now. Her cardigan was three sizes too big for her. I could see the balled up wad of tissue stuffed up her right sleeve a mile away. Why did the elderly always insist on keeping tissue to hand at all times? And why was a pocket or a bag not good enough? Why did it have to be up the sleeve?

"I'm just gonna look around for a second, if that's okay?" I said softly. My temper was still flying high, but there was no sense in lashing out at the poor old girl behind the counter, knitting what looked like baby clothes. I paced up and down the aisles, eyes scanning over the products stacked on the shelves but not really seeing anything. The strip lighting overhead hummed and spat, the light itself flaring and dimming, flickering epileptically—the first signal in any bad horror movie that things were about to get fucked up. I picked up a can of Pringles, wondering how I'd use the tube of chips as a means of self-defense, and that's when the door opened and Fix sauntered in, flicking his hair back out of his face like some sort of goddamned demi god. The old woman behind the counter stilled, her needles ceasing their rapid-fire clack, clack, clacking, and she just stared at him like she couldn't believe her eyes. Truly, I felt sorry for her. Her accent was thick and local. She'd probably never left this shitty, dull, backwater, and she'd almost certainly never seen a man like Fix before. Not in the flesh, at least. The men around here were beer swilling, overweight, and belligerent, no doubt—of the opinion that brushing their hair or their teeth would make them a 'pansy' and half a man in the eyes of his guffawing peers. Gross.

Fix, on the other hand, looked like he'd just stepped out of a TV screen and accidentally stumbled inside the gas station while trying to find his way back to the Oscars. "Good...good evening?" the old woman said. She sounded confused, as if she didn't really know what time of day it was anymore, or if the evening *was* any good.

Fix flashed her a smile that could easily have stopped the old woman's heart; miraculously, she survived the experience. "I'd like to pay for pump number four, please," he purred. "And whatever my friend has decided she'd like."

I slapped the can of Pringles and a bottle of water down on the counter, arching an eyebrow at Fix. "*Friend?*"

He gave me a rueful smile, then shrugged his right shoulder before wrapping his arm around me. "You're right. Sorry, Angel." He gave the old woman a conspiratorial flash of his teeth, his eyes wrinkling ever so slightly at the corners. "She's my girlfriend. We're going to a wedding, y'know. I'm meeting the family for the first time."

"Oh, well don't you be nervous," she said, wagging her finger at him. "Manners. That's all you need to make a good impression. You seem like a charming young man, and you, my dear, seem like a lovely young lady, as well. I'm sure your folks are going to be thrilled to meet your new beau." She poked her tongue out in a really weird and awkward way, winking at me, and I couldn't rein in the cringe that bunched my brow. If she saw my expression, she didn't react to it, though. She accepted Fix's cash, giggling like a little girl when he changed his mind at the last minute and decided to buy a lollipop. He tore the wrapper right off the candy and shoved it into his mouth there and then at the counter.

Two identical pink dots of embarrassment blossomed high on the old woman's cheeks, and a fiendish smile tore across Fix's own face.

There appeared to be life in the old girl yet. Fix knew the sight of him sucking on that thing was having an effect on the cashier, and he was delighting in the attention. I mean, I couldn't deny it—there was something damned distracting about a grown man sucking on a lollipop. Fix's mouth was sheer perfection. His lips were full, and fuck me if they weren't perfectly bitable. I'd learned that last night, when I'd fallen into bed with him without a clue who he really was. It was a good thing he didn't cast me a sideways glance; he undoubtedly would have found identical flushed cheeks on me, too.

Grabbing the bag the old woman had placed my items into, I stormed out of the gas station, kicking myself for reacting. I'd made a host of remarkably stupid decisions in my life, but allowing Felix Marcosa to crawl his way under my skin wasn't going to be one of them.

Back in the car, I climbed into the front seat of the truck instead of the back. Sitting next to Fix wasn't high on my list of priorities, but at least I could watch him properly from the passenger seat. And if he tried anything, I had a better chance of seeing it coming.

Fix started the engine, then made a soft humming sound, pushing the lollipop into the side of his cheek. "You're going to have to stop scowling at some point, Sera."

"I'll stop scowling when you get in this truck and drive off without me."

He laughed, as if this amused him greatly. "Then you're gonna develop some deep lines on that pretty forehead of yours, Angel."

He tore out of the parking lot like the cops were already on our tail.

9

SERA

SIXSMITH

"*This place is a fucking shit hole, girl. What have you been doing all day?*"

I tried not to tremble. Sixsmith didn't like it when we showed fear. He also didn't like it when we showed any form of confidence, arrogance or defiance, so I trained my face into the blankest expression I could and rose from the chair where I'd been sitting at the scuffed dining table.

The kitchen wasn't a mess. I'd spent three hours cleaning it, until the counter tops, regardless of the cracked and chipped tiles, were sparkling. The floor didn't have a mark on it. The trash was empty. There wasn't a dirty cup, plate, or bowl in sight, and yet I'd known it wouldn't matter to my father. He always did this—came home steaming drunk in the middle of the night, when Cressida, the bar tender at the dive bar my father frequented every night, finally cut him off and refused to serve him anymore. He'd be pissed that he hadn't been able to get that final beer he'd whined and pleaded for, and he'd come home and take it out on my sister and me. Tonight, I'd helped Amy with her homework and made sure she'd gone to bed early, though. Someone had to wait up to serve Sixsmith his dinner. That someone would bear the full brunt of his wrath, and it served no purpose for Sixsmith's anger to fall on Amy's shoulders, when mine were broad enough to take it, and had done so many times before.

My father stalked around the kitchen, his shoulder-length hair stringy with sweat, his eyes bloodshot and roving; he was searching for something. Something to punish me for. Yanking open the fridge door, he bent over, inspecting the contents inside.

"There's no beer in here," he snarled, straightening, then slamming the door closed. "I thought I told you to make sure this thing was fully stocked by the time I got back?" His mouth was twisted into an ugly sneer as he turned to look at me.

"I bought groceries. I got everything I could. I tried to buy the beer, but the guy at the store asked me for ID. He said he knew I was only thirteen."

The disgust that rippled off my father was a tangible thing, and made the hairs on the back of my neck stand to attention. "Don't sass me, you little bitch. You should have convinced him you were old enough."

I'd done my best to persuade the store clerk that he was mistaken, that I was in fact out of high school and almost finished at college now, but he hadn't believed me for a second. Still, I'd tried again and again, until the gnarled guy behind the till had threatened to call the cops if I didn't scat. "His daughter's in my year," I said quietly. "He said he'd seen me at school, and he knew I was lying. There was nothing I could do."

"Bullshit!" My father spat the word, and flecks of saliva flew from his mouth. I tried not to stare at the fine rope of spittle hanging down from the corner of his mouth. "You're a dumb little slut, Sera. You know exactly how to get a man to do what you want. I've seen the way you look at that boy down the street. You push your tits out to try and get his attention. You could have just smiled at that prick and made him harder than concrete. He'd have given you anything you wanted."

This wasn't going well at all. Cressida must have served a little longer than usual, or perhaps Sixsmith had scraped some cash together and managed to fill his hip flask with cheap whiskey on his way to the bar. Either way, he was much drunker than usual, and he was humming with a new kind of rage, even more volatile and unpredictable than usual. His hands were balled up into fists as he stepped toward me, and a bolt of ice-cold fear chased down my spine. The door to the living room was behind Sixsmith, and there was no way I'd be able to make it to the door on my right, the back door leading out into the garden, without him grabbing hold of me first. I swallowed, forcing my body to remain absolutely still.

"I don't know how to flirt with men," I said evenly. "I can't do th—"

Lightning fast, Sixsmith lunged for me and grabbed hold of the first thing he could: my hair. Pain ripped across my scalp—it felt like he was tearing every strand out by the root—but I didn't scream. Screaming did something to Sixsmith that I couldn't comprehend. It made his breathing hard, and lit a wild fire in his eyes that terrified the ever-loving shit out of me. "Don't lie to me," he hissed. "You're lucky I don't take you over my knee and tan your ass raw. I know you've given it up to half the boys in town. You're a whore. You're worse than a whore. At least hookers get paid for opening their legs. You've been letting people ride the shit out of you for fun."

I hadn't let anyone ride me for fun. I hadn't let anyone ride me at all. Brody, a jock in the year above me, had tried to hold my hand last semester, but when I'd attempted to claw his eyes out of his head, screaming at the top of my lungs, hysterical and uncontrollable, he'd shoved me so hard that I'd fallen onto my ass in front of the entire canteen. After that, I'd been branded frigid. Crazy. Retarded. Not a single boy had looked at me since. I sure as hell hadn't been pushing my tits out to get anyone's attention. I'd been strapping them down for the last year or so, desperately trying to disguise the fact that I was developing a woman's body, but eventually I'd had to give up. It was impossible to hide anymore.

Sixsmith jerked my head, and I bit the inside of my cheek; I wanted to fight back. I wanted to defend myself, but I'd been here before. Once my father's temper reached this stage, there was nothing to be done. If I lashed out, pushed him away, or tried to escape, things would be so much worse for me. I formed the shape of a gun inside my head, and I imagined what it would be like to grasp hold of it by its cold metal handle, to slide my finger up against the trigger. To aim the weapon at my father, and pull...

"Now that I come to think about it, maybe I've been lookin' at this all wrong," Sixsmith said, wiping his mouth with the back of his tattooed hand. "Maybe you'd like selling your ass for money. I'm sure you'd be good at it."

My eyes were stinging, filling with tears, but I didn't say anything.

Arguing was a bad idea. Moving was a bad idea. Even breathing was a bad idea. Sixsmith let go of my hair and slid his hand down, across my face, over my cheek, cupping my head beneath my chin, forcing me to stand up straight and look at him. He was like a deranged dog. Looking him in the eye was never an option, far too dangerous, so I focused on the end of his nose, praying this would be over quickly. Sometimes it was over quickly. There were nights when he came home and he was so unbalanced by the alcohol in his system that he'd only hit me once or twice, and then he'd stagger into the living room and slump down into his recliner, snoring almost immediately. It was a futile hope, though. Tonight, Sixsmith was fired up. He was probably going to drag this out as long as he could. He was probably going to make it hurt.

Leaning in close, he whispered to me, "You think you're so much better than me, don't you?" His breath reeked of rotten teeth and stale booze, a smell I'd grown so accustomed to that I didn't even flinch at it anymore. "ANSWER ME, BITCH!"

A couple of years ago, Sixsmith hadn't paid the rent on the tiny, dingy apartment we'd been living in, and we'd been kicked out. The three of us, Sixsmith, Amy, and me, had all gone to live at my grandfather's house for a while, until Sixsmith 'got back on his feet'. It'd taken a long time for Sixsmith to get money together for a new place, and so there had been a period of time when things had gotten better. Sixsmith hated his father, but he'd never raise his voice or his fists to us when we were under the old man's roof. My grandfather was an ex-military man, a hard ass that never smiled, rarely spoke, and glowered at Amy and me whenever we were in the room. He would never have tolerated Sixsmith treating us badly, though. He had that one thing going for him.

I found myself wishing we were back there, in that stuffy, silent, mausoleum of a house, under the watchful eye of the General, as the hate beaming out of my father's face flickered, transitioning into something else altogether. The sneer disappeared, replaced by a vacant, loose smile. "I bet Jacob would give me money for you," he said. "That pervy bastard's been sending looks your way for a couple of years now."

Oh god. My heart rate soared through the roof, and I couldn't do it any more. I couldn't live inside calm, flat, lifeless Sera anymore. I became scared, angry, panicked Sera, exploding into action, trying to rip myself free from Sixsmith's grasp. He had hold of me by the throat now, though. And he wasn't letting go. "Sixsmith, please..." I croaked, as his grip tightened around my esophagus, crushing, preventing me from drawing in breath. Was there a way out of this situation right now? I couldn't think. Couldn't decide what to do. Couldn't fathom a way to make him release me so that I could bolt to freedom. A long, torturous second passed, and I watched as a spark of excitement flared inside Sixsmith.

"I bet Sam Harrodan would clear all that money I owe him if I let him sink his dick inside that pretty little mouth of yours, too. The girls he has hanging around his place are always young. Fucker's always acting so goddamn high and mighty, but I know. I know what a piece of shit he is."

"Sixsmith, please! I'm sorry. I'll get the beer next time, I promise." I couldn't think of anything else to say. The inside of Sixsmith's head was a labyrinth of bizarre and confusing pathways that made no sense to me. Trying to figure out exactly what to say to him and when had always completely escaped me, and now, with his hand blocking off oxygen, starving me, I had no clue how to appease him. He was cold, and he was evil, and whenever he got an idea he thought might benefit him, he grabbed hold of it with both hands. There was a chance he was drunk enough that he wouldn't remember this in the morning, but the prospect that he would remember it, that he'd be calling on his friends to see if they wanted to use and abuse my body in lieu of his debts, made my entire being sing in terror.

My father smiled, flashing me broken, crooked teeth, discolored from the cigarettes he chain-smoked every waking hour of the day. "Yeah, Sera. That pleading tone... They'd probably like that. They'd probably like it if you put up a bit of a fight."

Pure instinct clawed at me, demanding I react. I had to get out of the kitchen. I had to get out of the house altogether. But how? Sixsmith wasn't a big guy. He used to be fairly fit, back when Mom was still alive, but over the years since he'd let himself waste. His midsection was bloated and strained against his t-shirt, and his arms were wiry, barely strong at all anymore. None of that changed the fact that he was nearly two feet taller than me and a man, while I was a slender thirteen-year-old girl. I couldn't over-power him, there was no chance of that, so I did the only thing I could think of to break free. I scrambled, trying to steady myself, and then I drew my leg back and I swung...

My knee found its mark a second later, and Sixsmith's eyes widened. There was a moment when I thought the blow I'd dealt him to his balls had had no effect whatsoever, and then Sixsmith's hand fell from my throat. He crumpled forward, groaning, a pained exhalation escaping his lungs as he clutched at his stomach and between his legs.

"You...stupid...cunt," he wheezed. "You stupid fucking cunt. You shouldn't have done that."

A second later, I was running. I smashed my hip against the corner of the table in my haste to reach the back door, and I sucked in a gasp of air, forcing the pain away as I took hold of the door handle and twisted. The door opened, and a surge of relief washed over me. Sixsmith was still bent double, trying to regain himself. He wasn't following after me. I was fast when I needed to be, I could put a considerable distance between us if I pushed myself as hard as I could—

Amy.

My fractured thoughts came to a screeching halt. Oh my god. My sister. She was two years younger than me, but in her head she was much younger still. Her body was still that of a child. If I ran now, if I left this stinking, miserable house, filled with so many terrible, bitter memories, I'd be leaving Amy behind. And Sixsmith...there was no telling what Sixsmith would do to her. If I left, he might use her in my place. She might be the one he tried to barter to clear his debts and earn some extra cash.

My hand stilled on the door handle. My feet were still trying to move forward and carry me away from this god-awful place, but it was as if a solid, crushing weight was suddenly fixing me to the spot. I couldn't do it. I couldn't go and leave her behind. I'd never be able to forgive myself.

My bones were steel. My skin was dread. My heart was fear. My soul was...gone. I turned back around, and I faced my father.

Sixsmith roared as he grabbed the kitchen knife I'd left in the drying rack earlier. I saw the flash of the blade as he hurtled toward me, and I felt my fear leave me. He was going to kill me. After all this. After the beatings, and the abuse, and the screaming, and constantly walking on eggshells every day for as long as I could remember, he was finally going to kill me.

I'd denied myself the freedom that leaving would grant me just now, but this was an escape outside of my control. I wouldn't be able to stop him.

"I'm gonna make you beg for your fucking life," Sixsmith growled. Advancing, he held the knife aloft, and my heart stopped. The blade seemed to take forever to reach me. I thought he would plunge it straight into my chest, but he didn't. He held it to my neck, baring his teeth. "Beg, Sera. Beg me not to fucking kill you."

I wanted to. Begging wasn't beneath me. If it would save my life, and save Amy from future misery, too, then I would do it. It was a small price to pay. But when I attempted to push the words out of my mouth, they wouldn't come. My voice had fled me. Everything had fled me. I sighed, letting go of the breath I'd been holding, and I felt strangely light. As if I'd been relieved of a burden I'd been carrying around with me for so long that I had forgotten all about it until now.

Sixsmith pressed the blade harder against my skin, and I didn't move. I didn't blink. My father's eyes were a void, black and bottomless, merciless and cruel. "Beg," he hissed.

When I did nothing, Sixsmith's face contorted into a rictus of pure, uninhibited fury. I waited for the piercing, burning agony that would accompany having my throat slit from ear to ear, but it never came. Instead, pain flared along my jawline, as Sixsmith slashed to the right with the blade. A moment of shock claimed me; he'd cut my face?

The knife clattered to the floor, and then Sixsmith's hands were tearing at me, ripping at my clothes. The NASA t-shirt I was wearing ripped, the sound filling the kitchen, and then he was tugging at my bra.

I thought I'd known fear before. There had been countless moments in my life when I'd been so claimed by my own fear that I thought I'd never be able to surface from it again. At least not whole. But now, with Sixsmith greedily staring down at my exposed body, I experienced a level of fear I hadn't even known possible.

The smell of copper flooded my nose. Something wet and warm was flowing down my neck, but it wasn't until I caught sight of the bright crimson droplets hitting my bare breasts that I realized I was bleeding so badly. Sixsmith lifted his right hand, and it was shaking. I was never going to forget how terribly his hand shook as he reached out and tentatively cupped my breast. I was marble, solid and immoveable. What was he doing? What...how could he... why? My skin was crawling, a thousand insects burrowing into my pores, as Sixsmith sucked his bottom lip into his mouth. He wasn't shouting anymore. His anger had evaporated, leaving behind a strange, rotting silence that coated me like grease. Sixsmith stared. Not at my face, but at my chest. I needed to cover myself up, hide myself away from him. He shouldn't be looking at me the way he was looking at me. It wasn't right. It wasn't right at all.

My father was no longer standing in the kitchen with me. He'd gone somewhere far away, withdrawn into himself, and all he seemed to register now was the fact that he was holding my breast in his cupped hand. Slowly, he moved his fingers, and he rolled my nipple between them.

My mind was fragile. It was going to snap in two. I couldn't...I couldn't even...

"Daddy?"

Amy stood in the doorway to the living room. Her pajama bottoms were twisted around her body, as if she'd been tossing and turning in her sleep again. She'd never been a very good sleeper. Her eyes were wide, her face ashen, drained of all its usual color. There were tears streaming down her cheeks—silver ribbons of abject grief and horror.

"Daddy, what are you doing?" she whispered.

Sixsmith recoiled like he'd been stung, his hand pulling back from my skin. The anger returned in a flash, contorting his face once more. I hiccupped—the strangest reaction to what had just taken place—then I was grappling with the torn material of my shirt, trying to cover myself, hands frantic and trembling.

"What the fuck are you doing?" Sixsmith spat between gritted teeth. "You're meant to be asleep." Rounding on me, he lifted his hand and whipped it out, striking me so hard across the face that I stumbled, my legs giving out underneath me. "Get her to bed. And get this mess cleaned up. You're a fucking disgrace."

The mess, of course, was my own blood. Large, round, fat spatters of red stained the floor, and a good amount of it had run down the length of my body and pooled at my bare feet, collecting between my toes. I *hiccupped again, pressing my palm to my burning cheek, biting the urge to burst into tears myself.*

The back door opened.

The back door closed.

Sixsmith was gone.

10

FIX

ROADTRIP

*S*era slept. Dreaming. Twitching in her seat as I drove. She clearly hadn't meant to fall asleep, but about a hundred miles past Wichita her exhaustion had claimed her, and her eyelids had fallen shut. I'd thought about turning on the radio, but then decided against it. I wasn't planning on stopping at all until we reached our destination, so this was probably going to be the only rest she got. Disturbing her, on top of frightening the shit out of her, kidnapping her and forcing her to be my unwilling co-pilot, seemed a little unfair.

I'd stuck to the speed limit and observed the road rules as we'd traveled for hours, the sky turning from overcast and grey, to clear blue, to bruised orange, then red, and then dipping into darkness. The roads were quiet. Barely more than a handful of vehicles passed us as I headed east. Eventually, we hit Memphis, and on and on I kept driving.

At around one in the morning, my cell phone, clipped into the mount on the dash, lit up, signaling an incoming call. Even the rapid, bright flashing of Monica's name on the screen seemed angry. Great. I shouldn't answer it. She was bound to yell at me, and even on the other end of the telephone line that was bound to be loud enough to wake Sera. Monica had a set of lungs on her to rival a UFC announcer. How long could I keep avoiding the woman, though? Time was running out. She'd sworn she'd come and find me if she had to, and I wasn't about to put it past her. She'd done crazier things in the past.

One-handed, I connected headphones into the cell, stuffed the buds in my ears, and hit the green answer button.

"Yeah?"

There was silence for a second, then Monica replied. "Yeah? *Yeah?* That's how you answer your phone to me?"

Oh boy. "I'm driving, Monica. Is this important, or can it wait?"

"No, it cannot wait. My god, what the hell's gotten into you, Fix? We're working on a deadline here, and you've just...I don't even know what you're doing. You've gone rogue!"

"How the fuck have I gone rogue?"

"Language," she chided, tutting under her breath. "If you listened to my voicemails, or actually picked up your phone every once in a while, you'd know this *is* important. You dealt with the Halford issue, correct?"

"Yeah." I wasn't about to explain to her what had happened right after Franz had fallen down dead, or where I was headed now. That was just an invitation for an ear chewing.

"Our other client wants to know if we've completed work and we're ready to accept the rest of our donation."

"Just tell him we need a little more time."

"Forty grand, Fix. We already took half. He's getting impatient. Making noises about getting a refund and taking his money elsewhere."

I whistled quietly through my teeth. "It doesn't work like that. We're not J.C. fucking Penny. He can't just get a refund."

"Then you'd better do the work, Fix!" Monica's frustration traveled down the phone very clearly.

Monica and I had never discussed the fact that we shouldn't talk about accepting money for killing people over the phone; it was just common sense. Our client's fees were tailored to match the level of danger and risk the job entailed. Fifty grand for a low risk mark. Seventy for low rent gangbangers and criminals. Ninety for well protected, violent and hazardous individuals. Monica assessed each mark carefully and quoted a price based off the information she gathered, so for her to have assigned a forty thousand dollar price tag to my outstanding job clearly indicated how quickly she intended me to take care of it. I had the other manila envelope in the glove box, waiting to be assessed. I couldn't do it now, though. I just couldn't.

"I'm on the road for the next few days," I said quietly, cracking my knuckles. "I can get to it in a week. Maybe ten days."

"No can do, Fix. This matter's time sensitive for the client."

"I'm sure you'll handle him for me, Monica. You always do. I'll call again in twenty-four hours."

"Fix! Twenty-four hours is—"

"Twenty-four hours is the best I can do," I snapped, grinding the words out. Monica knew my moods. She'd witnessed first hand how quickly I could snap if pushed too far. Even I knew I was frightening to be around once the darkness grappled hold of me. I usually did whatever I could to avoid sinking into that pit of anger and turmoil, but the last day and a half had tried my patience beyond measure. "Be careful," I warned. "Give me a day. Also, give me a fucking break. Don't text or call me again. I need time to work this out. I'll be in touch."

"*Fix—*"

I hung up the phone, stabbing at the cell phone screen so hard I nearly knocked the damn thing out of its cradle on the dashboard. Motherfucker. Working alone would have been much, much easier than having to deal with Monica. She was hyper emotional, stubborn as an ox, and demanding as fuck. God, it would have been great never to have to argue with her again, or field her constant, prying questioning. But then again it *was* better to keep the admin and the muscle separate. People were twitchy around me. It had nothing to do with who I was as a person, what I looked like, how I acted or behaved in front of them. Most people had a crisis of conscience when they looked the man they'd asked to murder someone in the eye. They expected judgment from me. Their own guilt convinced them that they saw it written all over me, and they couldn't deal. When they met with Monica, they were faced with a sympathetic, understanding, kind middleman. There was a safe, reassuring code in place during all conversations. There was usually a safe, friendly place to meet. There was usually a glass or two of whiskey to calm the nerves. Monica was a disconnect between action and consequence, and that suited most folks down to the ground. Typically, they didn't want to have any idea who would be committing the act. They just wanted to get it done and move on with their lives, while someone else, somewhere else, lost the privilege of living theirs. So Monica was a necessary, annoying evil. I was stuck with her.

Beside me, Sera's legs tensed, locking out in front of her. Her body went rigid, her back curling away from the seat beneath her, and her fingers twitched violently. Fuck. Had she heard the phone conversation? No. No, when she whimpered, I knew she was still dreaming. Worse. By the looks of things, she was drowning in the depths of a nightmare.

It was one thing allowing her to sleep, to rest and recuperate, but letting her suffer through something harsh enough to make her body twist and contort while she was unconscious was something else entirely. I shouldn't have cared. I shouldn't have given a fuck, but...

I turned on the radio, swiftly adjusting the volume control so that the sound of some rocky, upbeat hipster song filled the cab of the truck. It was enough to draw her from her sleep. Her body bowed, flexing, before she blinked blearily, turning her head as she took in her surroundings, no doubt remembering where she was. Her expression was hard as flint when she pushed herself up in her seat, blowing out a long, unsteady breath down her nose.

"Where are we?" Her voice was softened by sleep, but there was an edge to her words that said she was still very unhappy to be locked in a moving vehicle with me.

"Just passed Meridian."

"How long until we get to Fairhope?"

"Another few hours. We'll get there just after dawn. You'll probably have enough time to pass out for a couple of hours before your sister needs you."

Sera's relief was obvious. Her hair fell in soft waves around her face, framing it perfectly. I'd been with many attractive women before, but there was something different about her. Something that made my chest feel tight. Her features were fine and delicate, and at first glance gave her the look of someone who needed protecting from the world. But the sharp, intelligent, piercing way she looked at me altered all of that. She didn't need protecting. She was capable of taking care of herself, and was ready and able to do so at a moment's notice. Perhaps that's why I found myself drawn to her so much; she was uncontainable, raw, and bold, and she wasn't afraid of me in the slightest. Silly, silly girl. If she'd had any idea what was good for her, she would have been terrified.

"Don't look at me like that," she murmured, angling her body away from me.

"Like what?"

"Don't play games, Fix."

"I'm not playing anything."

She tutted, shaking her head. "You were looking at me the same way you looked at me the other night."

"You mean, right before I sank my cock inside you?"

Most girls would be embarrassed or annoyed at my directness. They'd shy away from the mere mention of what took place between us. I was kind of looking forward to a coy reaction from Sera, but I was shit out of luck. She eyed me fiercely, setting her jaw, her gaze unwavering. "Yeah. Right before you sank your cock inside me," she confirmed. "Right before he fucked me senseless, made me come harder than I ever have in my life, and turned my whole fucking world upside down."

Ha. So much for *me* being direct. Looked like Sera was the queen of direct. "I can't help it," I told her, alternating my attention between her and the road. "I was fascinated by you. I still am."

"Well, don't be. You lost the right to make eyes at me the moment I walked into that building and watched you kill that guy."

"What you saw doesn't change anything, Angel. You were attracted to me back in that motel room. I saw it on your face. I smelled it on your body. I felt it when I slid my hand down the front of your panties and discovered how wet that beautiful pussy of yours was. An attraction like that doesn't just go away."

Her lips parted into a half-snarl. "You can't be serious. Of course it does! I'm not insane. The moment I saw what you did, any and all attraction I felt for you went up in smoke."

"False. You still can't stop looking at me, thinking about what happened between us, and you hate yourself for it. You don't *want* to want me. You don't want to know that I've been inside you, and that when you close your eyes you can still feel me inside you, but it's the truth. Deny it all you want. I know it's true. You hate me, hate who I am, but there's a very large part of you that wants me to fuck you again, Sera. My dick's the best you've ever had."

Her eyes were the size of silver dollars as she stared at me, her face growing paler and paler by the second. "You really think you're untouchable, don't you? You think no one can resist you, regardless of the fact that you're a monster."

"No. I don't think that. I think most women would have killed themselves trying to get away from me by now, no matter how great the sex was. You haven't tried to get away, Sera. You've thought about it. I've seen the look on your face. I let you keep that phone in your pocket just to see what you'd do, and you haven't tried to ask anyone for help. The truth of the matter is that you're not horrified by what I've done. You don't care that I'm punishing the bad guys, even though you know you should. And you can't tamp down the need you feel every time you fucking look at me, because I can read it all over your body. Look at your hands right now, pressed flat against your thighs. You're palms are sweating, and all we're doing is talking about sex."

"Well...I don't want to talk about sex anymore."

"Why not?"

"Because! Because it's fucking pointless!" She was flustered. Her cheeks were scarlet, and her eyes were shining a little too brightly.

"Okay, okay. No sex. What do you want to talk about instead?" I asked her, trying to bite back a smile. This was more fun that it should be, but it was her own fault. She presented herself in such a tough light. Unbreakable Sera. If she wasn't so determined to maintain her cool, then it would be far less fun watching her lose it.

"I don't care. Anything," she said, folding her arms across her chest.

"All right. Tell me what were you dreaming about just now."

Silence.

I knew I'd asked the wrong thing the moment the words left my lips, but it was too late to drag the question back and reclaim it now. The truck was already swamped with tension. Sera looked straight ahead out of the windshield, and for a long, long time she held her tongue. Whatever she'd been dreaming about, it must have been terrible for her to shut down so abruptly. It was done, though. There was no going back. I could practically hear her grinding her teeth together again.

"How about we don't talk at all?" she murmured.

And so that was that. The remainder of the journey to Fairhope took place in silence.

11

SERA

DON'T GET ANY IDEAS

*T*he chapel was iconic. White. Tiny. Cute as fuck. The kind of chapel that went on the top of a wedding cake. It was visible from the bottom of the long, winding, sweeping road that led up to Easterleigh Estates, the venue Ben's parents had paid fifteen thousand dollars to secure for their big day. Madness.

Fix made a clipped, clicking sound as we wound our way up the road toward the main hotel, where the bridal party were undoubtedly still fast asleep. "This place looks like hell on earth," he muttered under his breath. They were the first words he'd parted with since he'd asked me about my nightmare—the same reoccurring nightmare that plagued me so regularly—and they were a mirror to my own thoughts.

"My sister likes pretty things," was all I offered in response.

"And you? You don't like all this...pomp and ceremony?" He wrinkled his nose. "You wouldn't have all the bells and whistles if you got married?"

"I'd never get married in the first place."

He grunted. "You know we're going to have to share a room again, right?"

My nostrils flared, a cold finger stroking its way down my back. I'd already realized we'd have to share a bed again. The hotel was at capacity, filled with Amy's other numerous guests, and on top of that my sister would have questions if the man I brought as my date to her wedding was sleeping in another room. The fact that I'd realized this didn't make the idea of sharing a room with Fix any more comfortable, however. Fix pulled up outside the large, colonial building, lit up by columns of bright light, and I struggled to swallow down the lump that had risen in my throat.

"You can sleep on the couch." I got out of the truck as soon as the engine died, and Fix was hot on my heels. He collected our bags, and I was hit by the strangest sensation: how normal this all could have been. Me, bringing a date to the wedding. Him being a gentleman and collecting our things, before we headed inside together.

"Fair enough," he said airily. "I've slept in worse places."

He'd probably slept inside a dead animal or something, trapped out in the wilderness while he was stalking one of his prey. I could see him doing that so clearly in my mind that a shudder traveled down the length of my body, settling at the base of my skull. "My sister's going to see right through this bullshit. You know that, right?" I said, hurrying up the steps that lead inside the hotel. Fix kept stride beside me, taking three steps at a time.

"She's not going to be investigating the veracity of our relationship. She's getting married. She's going to be focused on her dress looking just right and her flowers arriving on time."

"You don't know my sister." Amy might have fussed and preened over lace and silk, silver and gold, ever the magpie, but her mind wasn't always fixed on the trivial. She saw things, noticed the subtle undertones and subtexts of people's speech and their behavior. Fix was right in that she would be worried about everything going smoothly later on today, but there was no doubt in my mind that she'd sense something was up.

The inside of the hotel was plush and decadent: soft, thick, cream carpet underfoot; warmed light dripping from sconces on the walls and grand chandeliers suspended from the high ceiling; heavy, embroidered curtains hanging at the eight foot high windows; a counter of white marble, shot through with dove grey and gold veins, running the length of the right hand wall. In short, it was absolutely stunning. Ben came from old money, I'd known that for a long time, but this was the first time I saw the luxury and comfort that old money could buy. This was the life he could afford to give Amy, and for one very short moment I forgot everything that had happened in the past thirty-six hours. I was glad, instead. Relieved, in a way. I'd been taking care of my sister for so long that it seemed as though I would always be doing it. I'd never resented the fact that she needed watching out for, but now, with Ben in her life, someone else had taken that burden from me and discharged me of the crushing responsibility once and for all.

Fix dealt with the concierge, explaining who we were: Amy's devoted sister, Sera, and her loving boyfriend, Felix. He took the keys and thanked the guy behind the counter, and as we climbed the sweeping staircase up to the first floor where our room was located, I noticed that the sky was lightening in the east, day just about to break over the canopy of trees stretching off into the distance for as far as the eye could see.

Not long now. Not long until the hustle and bustle that would arrive with the morning. There would be makeup and hair, and squeezing into the ridiculous bride's maid's dress my sister had picked out for me—the dress I hadn't even seen yet. And there would be painfully polite chatter and niceties, and meeting Ben's family members who'd traveled from all over the country to be there for his wedding. I would do what was expected of me, smiling and hugging and shaking hands. It would be a bitch of a day, but I would get it done. And the whole time, I would try to not think about the man standing next to me, and what he had done. More importantly, I would try not to think about his hands on my body or his mouth on my own. Those thoughts were far too dangerous to even comprehend.

When we entered the room, suffice it to say, there was no couch. That was just fucking perfect. I made sure my voice was firm as I rounded on Fix, arms folded across my chest. "I don't care. You're not sleeping in the bed."

"Come on. That thing's big enough for four people."

"Don't get any ideas."

Fix's head lowered, his chin almost meeting his chest as he prowled toward me. His lips curved up on the right hand side—the most salacious suggestion of a smile. "What? You wouldn't like sharing a bed with four people?" he mused. "You wouldn't like three pairs of hands on you, touching you, caressing and kissing your body?"

"No! God! Jesus!"

"Mary? You're missing a few family members."

"I'm sure you'd just love three women in a bed with you," I snapped, snatching my bag from his hand. "I'm sure you've had plenty of crazy, ridiculous experiences with multiple women. But not everyone is as depraved as you."

His mouth curved even higher, and his left eyebrow hitched up to his hairline. "Yes. I have. But who said anything about women joining us? You don't think you'd be able to handle three men at once, Sera? Three guys, all stroking..." He took a step forward, his shoulders rolling in the most sensual way as his muscles shifted beneath his black button-down shirt. "Licking... Kissing... Biting... Sucking..." With every word, he took another step, closing the gap between us until he was standing right in front of me. "Three cocks, Sera? One in your mouth. One in your pussy. One in your ass. Imagine what that would feel like."

Holy shit. He was unhinged. Absolutely insane. How did he even have the balls to say shit like that to me? If he expected me to laugh at his words, to shrug them off, or worse, to actually consider them, then he had another thing coming. I moved quickly, planting my palms against his chest and shoving him as hard as I possibly could. I'd used all my strength, but the bastard had barely moved an inch.

"You're a pig, Felix," I growled.

"Ohhh. Felix. Full-name treatment. I must have been a very bad boy."

"As if you'd fuck a girl with two other guys, anyway. Men are always too concerned about who has the biggest dick."

Fix inhaled, rolling his eyes slowly up to the ceiling, his head slowly angling backward. He hadn't shaved in two days, and the sight of the exposed column of his throat, marked with thick stubble, did something strange to me. Polluted with me with thoughts and feelings that I didn't want to own. "Sera. You've seen me naked. You've seen my cock. You've held it. You've stroked it. You've taken it in your mouth, and your pussy. You really think I would have anything to worry about on that front? You really think I'd care what another guy had going on in his pants? And, in the unlikely event that another guy's dick was bigger than mine, it wouldn't fucking matter and you know it. I've already explored your body. I've already made you quake and shiver. I've already painted my come all over your skin, and you've loved every single second of it." He reached out, his hand slowly rising up to my face, his fingers uncurling until the tips of them were grazing my bottom lip.

I'd stopped breathing a full thirty seconds ago, and my head was starting to spin a little. God, he was so fucking hot. I hated him for it. I hated myself for noticing, over and over and over again. This shouldn't be happening. He shouldn't be able to affect me this way, and have my heart thundering beneath my ribcage. My body, my mind and my heart should all be on the same page—the Felix-Marcosa-is-too-dangerous-to-be-sexy page—but none of them were in alignment. My head knew what was up at least, but my body was overheating like crazy, and my heart had just plain flipped the fuck out.

"I know how to fuck. I know how to make you come. I know what makes your eyes roll back into your head, and I know how to tip you over the edge. I wouldn't give a shit about other guys sharing a bed with us, because I'd know none of them would make you feel as good as I do."

There were no words to describe his arrogance. And even if there were, I wouldn't have been able to form them right now, because my mouth felt like it was lined with sandpaper. Fix leaned in closer, so close that I could see the fine, delicate slashes of silver that threaded their way through his irises. His eyes were truly beautiful. So unbelievably unique. I'd never seen eyes like his before, and I knew I was unlikely to ever see similar again. They sparked with an intense amusement as he tipped his head to the side and lowered his mouth —now barely an inch away from my own.

"You said it yourself, Sera. You're an atheist. You believe you only get one life...*so why haven't you been living it?*" So slowly, Fix's lips parted, and I watched as the tip of his tongue slid past his teeth. He flicked it, swiftly licking my upper lip, and I gasped, stepping back out of his reach. Asshole. Complete, irredeemable, undeniable asshole. Wiping my mouth with the back of my hand, I tried to rein in the wild response that his one, brief action had created in me, but it was harder than I'd expected. My mouth was burning, my lips throbbing. My throat was on fire.

"Don't do that again. Don't touch me without my permission. You'll regret it."

Fix didn't look so sure. "Would I? How would you make me regret it? Would you kick and scream? Would you use your teeth on me? Would you hurt me? Do you want to hurt me, Sera?"

"You're goddamn right I do! You're...you're fucking *impossible*! You act like you're just some guy who's interested in showing me a good time. Have you forgotten about what happened? I saw you kill someone. I witnessed you murder someone. Am I just supposed to wipe that memory from my mind? Pretend like it didn't happen? Pretend like your actions haven't scared the shit out of me? And while we're at it, am I supposed to overlook the fact that you shoved me in the back of your car and took off with me without my consent? I'm not some airhead bimbo who's going to fall in love with you, just because you have a pretty face, y'know. Lines have been crossed. Massive, irrevocable lines. Once this wedding is over, I'm going to go back to Seattle, and I'm going to force myself to eradicate you from my mind. I'm going to move on, and I'm going to black out this entire week. It's the only way I won't be permanently traumatized by what you've put me through."

Fix shrugged. It was a calm, carefree response to my heated rant —a shrug that told me he was cold and dead inside. He didn't care about me, or what I saw. He was going to follow through with this ridiculous farce of a plan, and he wasn't going to give two shits if it worked out or not. He didn't care about the consequences if this charade failed. All he cared about was making sure I kept my mouth shut. And if he wasn't sure I was going to keep his secrets, then...then I didn't doubt he would take measures to ensure I kept my mouth shut for good.

"Have it your way, Angel. Fool yourself if you like. Tell yourself whatever you need to in order to get yourself through this. I can get on board with that. I'll play my part. Just make sure you play yours."

12

FIX

PLEASED TO MEET YOU

"*B*less me father, for I have sinned. I...I touched myself three times this week. Between...between my legs. I couldn't help it. I knew it was wrong, but..."

The soft, female voice on the other side of the confessional grill paused, and I could hear the woman sitting in the darkened, cramped space breathing heavily. Days like this, I was sure none of my congregation were getting laid. I knew the woman's voice—it was Yvonne Prescott, a young, pretty woman in her late twenties who'd married a guy called Gus last winter. Gus was one of those preppy motherfuckers who pretended like he had his shit together, like he was one of the sainted few who never put a foot wrong. Worked in the community, was the first to stick his hand up when there was volunteer work that needed doing at the church or in the community. He'd been in here twice this week, crying his eyes out, though, sobbing over the fact that he'd jerked off to porn on his computer repeatedly in the past week. He didn't just like watching porn. He had an addiction, and it wasn't the vanilla, everyday shit he was watching. He liked to watch gang bang porn—skinny Czech girls laid flat on their back, while a line of over thirty guys in masks waited for their turn to shove their cocks inside them. He liked to watch groups of guys thrust their dicks into a vulnerable girl's mouth and her ass, to use and abuse her like she was a toy. It was more normal than people realized: repressed guys liked to see a woman defiled in the basest of ways.

I rubbed at my temple, trying to ease the headache that was lurking behind my eyes, threatening to make an appearance. "Have you spoken to your husband about your urges, child?" I asked. If Yvonne was honest with Gus and revealed herself to be a sexual creature with the same desires, wants and needs that most women had, perhaps Gus could lay off his dick and actually satisfy his wife for once. I already knew what she was going to say, though.

"I—I can't," she whispered. "He's devout, Father. He tries to lead a holy life. If he knew the feelings that overcome me sometimes..." She started to cry. "He deserves a holy wife. I want to be pure for him. Clean. And if he found out that I was driven to such wanton acts...he wouldn't...he couldn't love me anymore."

For fuck's sake. Did these people not talk to one another? Were they so closeted and shut down that they truly didn't realize that they were all as horny and fucked up as the rest of the human race? "Don't cry, child. In the grand scheme of things, masturbation isn't the end of the world. Say three Hail Mary's and get back to baking those cupcakes."

"Cupcakes?" Something thudded on the floor. Sounded like she'd just dropped her bible. "You...you know who I am, don't you?"

I huffed out a breath, pinching the bridge of my nose. "Of course I do, Yvonne. Only twenty-six people come to this church."

She whimpered. "Oh. Right. Aren't you supposed to tell to me refrain from doing it again, though?"

Fuck. Seriously? "Yeah. You should stop touching yourself, Yvonne. It leads down a dark and scary path. Now, if we're finished here..."

"I don't think you're taking this seriously, Father Marcosa. Your father would have given me a proper lecture on the dangers of..." She launched into a tirade about the Father Marcosa who had preceded me, and I ceased to listen. It made sense that people compared me to my father. We shared the same name, for fuck's sake. And I looked like the man, there was no denying that. He'd been dead for well over two years, though, and I was sick to death of people holding me up to the light, comparing the two of us. I

was nothing like my old man. I was never going to be anything like that dour, miserable, tyrannical piece of shit.

"All right, all right, Yvonne. You want to feel absolved of your sins. I understand. For your penance, say twenty Hail Mary's, three Glory Bes, and three Our Fathers. Hopefully that will make you feel better. Now, I've really got to prepare the homily for Sunday. If you don't have anything else you'd like to discuss, then..."

Yvonne had shut up when I'd interrupted her. She remained quiet for a moment, before saying, "Twenty Hail Mary's, Father? That seems...a little..."

"Twenty Hail Mary's," I said firmly. The three I'd prescribed a moment ago were obviously too low to make her feel like her slate was being wiped clean. Now, twenty made her feel like she was being unreasonably punished. Well, fucking guess what, Yvonne? You can't have it both ways. "I'll see you at Mass," I said, getting to my feet. I was meant to wait until Yvonne had vacated the confessional and had a chance to get the hell out of dodge, but my patience was non-existent, and I really did have to write the damn homily. My hand rested on the edge of the thick, black curtain that covered the entry to the confessional; I was about to pull it aside, when a high pitched wail of terror sliced through the air. It was a woman's voice, and it wasn't just a cry of pain. It was also a cry of abject terror.

"Lord!" Yvonne hissed. "What was that?"

"Stay here, Yvonne. Don't come out until I tell you it's safe." I carefully, quickly slid the curtain aside, scanning up and down the length of the church, searching for the source of the cry. At the far end of the building, the door to the rectory was cracked open; strange, since it was usually kept locked. Only two people had a key to open that door: myself and the sister on shift, charged to welcome congregation members, maintain the church and keep everything clean and tidy throughout the day. I wracked my brain, trying to remember who the sister on duty was today, but I drew a blank. I'd been stranded in my office all morning; I hadn't seen or spoken to anyone before I stepped into the confessional booth. The sisters never typically needed to enter the rectory, though. And there was certainly no reason the door should be open like that, either.

My cossack billowed around me as I hurried down the aisle, checking the pews as I went, making sure there were no other people sitting there who might have come in to pray. The place was empty. Hurrying through the apse, my footfall rang out, echoing off the high stone walls, reverberating around the church, emphasizing just how abandoned the place truly was. When I navigated my way around the lectern, reaching for the handle of the rectory door, seconds from pushing it open all the way, that's when I noticed the crumpled five-dollar bill on the floor.

It was covered in blood.

Shit. What the hell was going on here? Once, when I was thirteen, a drunk, homeless guy had walked into the church one night and demanded that my father hand over all of the donation money from that evening's service. I'd been tidying away the hymnbooks, and I'd watched on in horror as the man had staggered toward my father, a knife thrust out in front of him. I'd expected my father to swing for the man, to knock the weapon from his hands, to beat him black and blue for trying to steal the church's charitable donations. When my father had handed over the money without so much as a second thought, I'd been wracked with shame. My father had been a coward. He'd turned over the money instead of defending it. The man had left, reeking of alcohol and soiled clothes, and I'd turned on my father, admonishing him for not standing up to the man.

The words he'd said to me then were still with me today. "Felix, what do we use that money for?"

"For helping people. For clothing and feeding the poor," I'd snapped.

"Okay. Well, then. That money went exactly where it was meant to go."

As I stared down at the blood-flecked bill lying at my feet, I realized, once again, that my father was a better man that I was. Because I wasn't just going to let someone walk in off the street and rob my fucking church. It was wrong of me, I knew it was, but I was going to find whoever had broken in here, and I was going to knock their fucking teeth out.

I stepped into the rectory, and...

...the world....

...oh, god...

I threw out a hand, steadying myself against the wall, trying not to fall down.

Blood.

There was so much blood.

It was sprayed up the walls, had drenched the curtains at the window, and had formed a ruby red pool on the floor, that had seeped into the waxed canvas material of the backpack I'd left on the ground earlier when I came back from my morning run. The air smelled sour, contaminated, with a chemical edge to it that made my nostrils burn.

I found her in the hallway, sprawled out on the polished wooden floorboards. Her wimple was gone, her head uncovered entirely, and her bright blonde hair, almost white, spread out around her head like spilled milk. She was face down, one arm thrust out, as if she were trying to reach for something. There was blood all over her hands, along with the simple white shirt she was wearing. Her black skirt wasn't where it was meant to be. It had been hitched up around her waist, and her bare buttocks were exposed...also covered in blood.

She wasn't moving.

A consuming rage swept over me, and for a second I could do nothing with it. I couldn't claim it. I couldn't push it away. I stood there, hating the scene before me, unable to look away, my blood seething through my veins.

One of the sister's shoes was missing. A sensible black shoe with a very small heel, barely a heel at all. Gone. Her stockings were ripped and torn, bunched up around her ankles. Where...?

I looked around the entrance to my living quarters, frowning, not breathing, not understanding.

Where had her other shoe gone?

"Oh my god!"

I didn't turn around. I wanted, no, I needed to process what had taken place in here, and I needed for it to make sense. Yvonne obviously hadn't listened to me, and had followed me in here. She was behind me, whimpering under her breath, low and quiet. She sounded winded and numb. Shortly, the shock she was experiencing would wear off and she'd become hysterical, no doubt. I had to get my shit together before that happened.

"That...is that Sister Rayburn?" Yvonne sobbed.

"Rayburn?" My voice was flat. Emotionless. I didn't know the name.

"She just moved here from Canada. She came as part of the Young Missionary program. She's...god, she's only twenty-two."

Oh. Fuck. All the churches in our archdiocese had been enrolled in the program—I'd been told to expect someone this week, but I hadn't realized she was already here. I had no fucking idea she'd been carrying duties right under my nose.

"We need...we need to call the police," Yvonne stammered.

I should have replied. I should have done as she suggested and called the cops. I should have done something. Anything. But I was still rooted to the spot, staring at the bloodied, mangled body that had been left in such an undignified, degrading way, like so much trash, discarded by the side of the road.

I did nothing.

I did nothing, until...

A twitch.

Yvonne screamed, grabbing hold of my arm, digging her finger nails into my skin through my cossack. "Oh my god! Oh my god, her foot moved. Did you see that?" Yvonne wailed. "God, she's still alive!"

Then I was running, charging toward the broken body on the floor, slipping and sliding in the blood as I tried to stop myself next to her. I lost my balance, toppling on my ass, but it didn't matter. I didn't feel the pain shooting up my spine, or recoil in horror as I put my hand down in a puddle of cooling blood. My only concern was the girl. She was alive, and I was determined to make sure she stayed that way until help arrived.

"Call an ambulance," I hollered. Gingerly, I slid my hand underneath the woman's body, applying as little pressure as I could, turning her. Aside from the worrying amount of blood that had marked her buttocks, there hadn't been any visible sign of injury when she'd been lying face down. It was another story now, though: five deep, vicious looking stab wounds, all to the stomach, had rented the material of the woman's shirt open, and blood was flowing freely from the yawning mouths in her skin where the knife had obviously gone in.

"Fuck." I held the back of my hand to my mouth, swallowing, trying to think. Pressure. I need to apply pressure, to stem the bleeding.

"Please...help me. I don't..."

Shock seized me once more. I'd purposefully avoided looking at the woman's face, hadn't thought I'd be able to handle it yet, but when she *spoke to me, I had no choice but to look her in the eye. She was very young —barely more than a child. If she actually was twenty-two, I'd have been surprised. Her tawny brown eyes were locked onto me, burning with a fever so intense that it brought tears to my own eyes.*

"I don't...want...to die. Not yet," she wheezed. Her breathing sounded wet, rattling, like there was fluid in her lungs.

I grabbed her skirts and yanked them down, covering her body, then I scooped her up in my arms, drawing her to me. Moving her was probably a bad idea—I'd seen enough movies to know you were never supposed to move the injured person—but honestly? She looked like she was running out of time. And no one, absolutely no one, deserved to die alone and scared. Despite how futile it seemed, I pressed my hands over the woman's stomach, maintaining pressure. She blinked up at me, splotches of blood all over her face, covering her skin like red freckles.

"The EMTs are on their way," Yvonne said. She was clutching her cell phone in her hands so hard that her knuckles had gone white. "I—I think I'm going to throw up." She groaned, folding at the waist, then bracing herself against the windowsill.

"Go outside," I commanded, "Wait for the ambulance. When the paramedics arrive, bring them straight here."

Relief flashed over Yvonne's face; she didn't really want to stick around and witness this. I got that, understood how rattled she probably was, but it also made me hate her a little bit. Where was her fucking compassion?

In my arms, the woman stirred, her head angled back, lips a deathly shade of purple. From the look of my living quarters, she'd lost a lot of blood. She moaned, her brow furrowing as she clearly tried to focus her eyes. "I was meant to make...a good impression," she whispered. "How's this for a first day?"

I forged a dead smile; it was all I could manage. "I certainly won't be forgetting it any time soon. Who did this to you?"

Her eyelids fluttered. "A man. A man with a scarred...face," she panted. "He had paint all over his hands. He was...he was so...angry."

"Did he want money?"

"N—No."

"Then what?"

Shame colored her cheeks, despite the fact that most of the blood had left her body. She closed her eyes, her throat bobbing, and I suddenly realized what she was having such a hard time saying to me. Why her buttocks were covered in blood.

Oh, no. God, no. Please.

"Shhh. Shhh, it's okay," I said softly, rocking her in my arms.

"They told me you were handsome," she wheezed. "All the...girls were... gossiping about you. They were...so...jealous...when I got...sent here."

"Shhh, it's okay, Sister. You don't need to speak. Help will be here soon. Just relax, okay?"

She reached up with a shaking hand, and her weak fingers curled around my wrist. A shuddering sigh escaped her. "Please...call me by my name. If I'm going to die...then I want to feel like at least one person...knew who I...was here."

My eyes were filling with tears, but I was damned if I was going to cry in front of her. I needed to stay strong. I needed her to stay strong, just long enough for the ambulance to arrive. "Sure. My name is Felix," I told her, hugging her to me.

She gave me an uneven smile, her breath growing shallower by the second. "Great...Felix. My name is...Monica. It's very...nice to meet you."

13

SERA

ARIANNA

*A*fter my slip-up in the car, I told myself there'd be no way I'd pass out in the bed. I needed to keep my guard up, needed to make sure Fix didn't try and smother me with a pillow while I was unconscious. But when he laid down on the blanket and cushion set-up he'd arranged for himself, promptly passing the fuck out like he'd been hit upside the head with a hammer, I couldn't help it. My eyelids were like lead weights. It occurred to me, as I found myself relinquishing control over my body, that now was a prime opportunity to escape Fix once and for all. It would have been as simple as getting up, tiptoeing silently across the room, opening the door, hurtling down the hallway as fast as I could, and then demanding the concierge call the police.

If the cops turned up, sirens wailing, tires spinning, on Amy's wedding day, though...she'd never forgive me. She'd be horrified that I'd been through such a traumatic experience, sure. She'd probably hug me as if my life depended on it, crying and thanking god that I was okay. But inside, she'd be seething. I knew her. She'd spent close to a year designing the floral arrangements for this event. If her magnificently coiffured hair, the delectable vol-au-vents, and her perfect princess dress weren't the first things people thought of when they remembered the wedding of Amy Lafferty and Ben Stewart, then she would carry this secret kernel of hatred toward me around with her for the rest of her days. She was horrible at hiding things like that.

It was the dumbest thing I'd ever done, but I didn't creep out of the room and high tail it down to the lobby. I turned on my side, gripping the hotel pen tightly in my hand, ballpoint end facing down, just in case I needed to stab Fix in the neck with it, and I succumbed to an exhausted sleep.

~

"*I* think if you curl it the other...yeah, that's it. I know, it's weird, right? But...I guess someone told me that if you hold the wand upside and kept it really loose in your hand it would seal the cuticle, and make your hair really shiny."

"Wow! You're right! That's a great tip!"

I recognized the sound of Arianna's voice with a sense of dread and irritation. Only daring to open one eye, I scanned the unfamiliar room, processing and remembering everything with a sense of disbelief. That's right: I'd seen a man murdered, I'd been kidnapped by a guy I'd had the most incredible sex of my life with, and now he was in our hotel room, giving hair styling advice to my sister's prissy best friend. In his underwear.

I sat up. I stood up. I straightened my shirt, flattening down my mussed hair with one hand.

Hmm. Well wasn't this an interesting development.

I quickly decided not to warn Arianna to get away from Fix; she looked like she was about to drop to her knees and start licking his abs, but the red-haired witch had fucked Gareth the moment she'd found out we were no longer together, and as a result I was feeling a little disinclined to look out for welfare. If she wanted to giggle and flirt with a guy who could exsanguinate someone without even a flicker of remorse, then she could go to town.

"Arianna. What a surprise. I didn't think I'd see you until we were called down to get dressed." I shouldn't have been so happy about the fact that she'd put on a little weight, but let's be honest. I was smirking beneath the cordial, friendly mask I'd just donned.

Arianna blinked, as if she'd forgotten altogether that she'd come into *my* hotel room with my supposed boyfriend while I was still sleeping in the bed. "Oh, hey, Sera! It's so nice to see you!" She put down my curling iron and hurried across the room, throwing her arms around my neck. I didn't want to hug her. I didn't want to be near her. I didn't want anything to do with the girl. Her perfume was utterly overpowering—whatever she was wearing, it was too sharp, too chemically, and she'd bathed herself in it without any idea that it made her smell like she cleaned toilets for a living. "I'm sorry, the stylist's curling iron keeps blowing the fuse in the makeup studio downstairs. Amy sent me to come and borrow yours. When Felix opened the door, here, I thought I'd come to the wrong place." The way she tittered nervously, her cheeks rosy and pink, practically glowing, told me enough: Arianna had a crush on yet another of my boyfriends. Didn't matter that Fix was a fake boyfriend. Didn't matter that I had absolutely no claim over him whatsoever. It was just fucking typical that this little viper would be trying to snake her way into Fix's Georgio Armani shorts right underneath my nose.

"Of course. Take the curling iron," I said, pressing my lips together into a thin smile. "What time is it?"

"Eleven thirty," Arianna told me. "We're going to be dressing in an hour. Your hair and makeup are at one. You're last. Amy knew you'd be tired. You could probably rest for another hour or so, if you wanted. You have the most *terrible* circles under your eyes." She feigned concern, pouting and frowning as she ran the pad of her index finger under my left eye, as if she could brush away said circles with the slightest touch of her hand. I considered grabbing her by the wrist, wrenching her arm behind her back, immobilizing her, and then breaking every single one of her fingers, but I refrained. It was a goddamn Christmas miracle.

"I know. This one's been keeping me up all night," I told her, jerking my head in Fix's direction. I smiled conspiratorially, as if sharing a secret with a girlfriend. "He's very skilled with his hands. And his tongue. No concept of time, though."

Fix leaned back against the armoire, folding his arms across his chest, a crooked smile on his face. His arms were ridiculous. So was his stomach. He must have spent years in the gym perfecting a body like that. I'd already seen him naked before, so I'd had a chance to come to terms with just how fucking sexy he was. Arianna, on the other hand...

Her cheeks were flushed, her general demeanor that of a dazed high school student meeting their boy band crush in real life. She couldn't seem to focus on anything but Fix's abs. It was getting a little embarrassing. Guiding her to the door, I shoved my curling iron at her and smiled through gritted teeth. "I'll be on time for my turn with the stylist. I doubt he's going to let me go back to sleep now, but I'll try and do something about the bags under my eyes."

I swung the door closed, pushing it with the very tips of my fingers until it clicked. I'd wanted to slam the door so hard it made the very foundations of the hotel shake, but instead I went the other way, being incredibly gentle as I shut her out of the room.

"Good with my tongue, huh?"

My body locked up as I felt hands on me—Fix's hands, skating over my hips, sliding over the massive t-shirt I'd worn to bed last night. The back of my neck prickled in response to his warm breath caressing my skin.

Shit.

Shit, shit, shit.

His chest pressed up against my back, and...something else... brushing up against my ass. God, he had an erection. He was hard as hell, and he wasn't making any efforts to hide the fact as he lowered his mouth into the crook of my neck, brushing my skin with his lips.

I froze.

Jesus...

How were good girls supposed to stay good when bad boys like Fix made it so ease to sin? How the fuck were smart girls supposed to retain their sanity, not to mention their heads, when they had Felix

Marcosa's hands roaming all over their body? It just...it wasn't fucking possible. It wasn't fucking fair. Fix's voice sent a chill charging through my veins, rocking me to my core.

"I thought you said you didn't like playing games," he whispered.

"*I don't.*"

"Then why did you just play that girl so hard, she didn't know what fucking day of the week it was?"

With every word, his lips grazed my neck, and a volley of anticipation, mixed with fear burned over my skin. "She's not as oblivious as she makes out to be. She plays the simpering idiot, but she knows exactly what she's doing. There's no such thing as innocent flirtation with Arianna Foster. So what if I fucked with her a little?"

"Mmmm..." Fix's hands moved up my body, stroking over my stomach and then back down my thighs again. A heady wave of pleasure flowed through me, and my eyes rolled back in my head. Thank god he couldn't see. If he knew the effect he was having on me...

"I know I'm good with my tongue, by the way. I know I'm good with my hands. It's nice to hear you admit it out loud, though, Angel. I could always treat you to round two, if you'd like? I could lick and suck and tease your clit. I could lave at it until you came, and then I could lick you some more. I could slide my fingers inside your pussy and tease that little spot you like. The one that has you bucking against me, screaming my fucking name. And when you're done coming, when you're boneless and half blind from the orgasms I've given you, I could lick you clean."

Oh... Shit...

"As for the way you handled the redhead. I enjoyed the show, Sera," he murmured. "You're full of piss and vinegar when you're defending what's yours."

That was it. That was enough to snap me out of my moment of stupidity. I stepped out of his arms, shaking off the desire that had, for a second, made me forget who Fix Marcosa really was. My face was trained into a deadpan, flat void when I spun around and locked eyes with him. "You're *not* mine, Fix. *We're* not...this isn't a thing. You're a *bad* person. You do know that, don't you?"

The charming, devil-may-care grin that was plastered all over Fix's face didn't slip, but there was a flash of something akin to pain that shone out of his strange, pale blue eyes. It was only there for a split second, but I saw it. I saw how badly I'd hurt him.

"Yep. You have me dead to rights, Lafferty." Inhaling, he looked around the room, stretching that breathtaking body of his like a cat lounging out in the sun. "Since you're awake now and there are no more bridesmaids to coo over me, I guess I'd better go and find myself a suit."

Urgh. Of course he didn't have a suit. "How the hell are you going to find a suit in a hotel in the middle of nowhere?"

My stomach did something strange as Fix slid his arms into a t-shirt and threw the thin black material over his head. He looked so good in a tee. Shit, the man looked good in absolutely anything he put on his body. He'd be able to make a trash bag look amazing, for fuck's sake. I turned away, refusing to allow myself to watch him as he kicked his feet into a pair of dark grey jeans, torn and ripped at the knees.

"I'll find a way, Lafferty," he said, his voice thick with amusement. "I always do. I'm a very resourceful guy."

14

FIX

BAD PERSON

*M*y dick was as hard as a concrete post, and there was nothing I could fucking do about it. I could have slipped into a bathroom and jerked off, but where was the fun in that? It would get the job done, relieving some of the pressure that had been building up in my pants, but fuck...

I didn't want my own hands on my cock. I didn't even want that redhead's hands on my cock, even though she had been fairly pretty and her mouth looked like it was used to being wrapped about a boner. I wanted Sera's hands on me, and if I couldn't have her, then I didn't want anyone else.

How the fuck had this happened? How had I decided somewhere along the way that I wanted her? Like, really wanted her? Not just for a night, but for longer. She was literally the worst person to pursue, and I knew myself. That was probably the exact reason why I'd formed such an obsessive attraction to her over the past few days. It was as if my dick enjoyed setting me up for failure and catastrophe. I had to keep reminding it that we were on the same team, but it didn't appear to be listening. Bastard.

Okay. A suit. I needed to find a suit.

The concierge would probably have one. People left clothes in hotels all the time. They hung them up in the closet and forget all about them. I didn't want someone's misplaced second hand shit, though. Just because I was crashing this wedding didn't mean I couldn't look sharp.

There were people wandering around in the lobby, drinking mimosas, wearing robes or their pajamas, chatting politely with one another. Obviously they weren't dressed or ready for the ceremony yet, but the lure of alcohol in the lobby had been too much for them. Drinkers. My favorite. A million years ago, a different lifetime ago, in fact, I used to warn people of the dangers of imbibing too much alcohol from a pulpit. Then, after everyone had left, their faith and their good intentions reinvigorated after my stirring speech, I'd get so fucked up that I couldn't walk straight.

People probably assumed I drank the communion wine. Fuck that, though. Communion wine was nothing better than watered down piss. Gentleman Jack had been my tipple of choice. It still was, when I didn't need a clear head to get shit done. I felt Jack calling to me as I scanned the crowd meandering around the lobby—it would be easy enough to order a drink from the small bar that had been set up in the corner of the hotel's plush entryway—but now wasn't the time. I needed to be bright eyed and bushy tailed, just in case Sera decided to do something stupid. Also, if I was being honest, I wanted to make a good impression today. I wasn't blind to the trauma Sera had been dealing with. I knew she was more shaken than she was letting on.

You're a bad person. You know that, right?

She'd lashed out with her words without even thinking, which made her statement even more caustic. She'd meant it. She'd really meant it, and I'd seen as much on her face. I was a killer. I ended people's lives for money. I got that. But in some warped, fucked up corner of my head, I still thought of myself as a good guy. Hilarious. It had been years since I'd done anything truly good. Carrying Monica out of that church, stowing her in the back of the ambulance, sitting with her for days, listening to her confession over and over again, reading her last rites on more than one terrifying, hair-raising occasion...

That was the last good thing I did.

Seeing her like that had done something to me. I'd lost all hope. I'd lost what little faith I had. And I'd lost any desire to continue on acting out the charade that I'd only undertaken in the first place to keep my parents happy. They were dead, and it didn't matter anymore. There were people out there with the blackest hearts, capable of raping and torturing and maiming people more vulnerable and fragile than they were. They didn't believe in any god. There was no moral compass guiding them, leading them away from the darkness. So I put away God, and I put away my compass, and I walked into the dark with a single, defining purpose: to find and punish the man who hurt Monica. To hurt him, the way he hurt her.

I didn't know if there would be any justice in the afterlife for men like the guy who'd attacked Monica, and I couldn't fucking bear it. Couldn't let it fucking stand. If there was accountability after death, then great. He would pay eternally for the pain and suffering he'd caused. But, just in case there *was* no accountability, I was going to make him, and other men like him, fucking bleed in this life too.

"Can I help you, sir?"

A short, middle-aged man in a suit stood beside me, holding out a polished silver tray loaded up with cucumber sandwiches. The crusts had been cut off, and I grimaced down at the food. "Are there any guys my size staying in the hotel?" I asked.

He looked confused, but, ever the consummate professional, didn't question me. Eying me up and down, he arched an eyebrow. "Oh, I shouldn't think so, sir. You're quite tall, and very broad. The only guest who might be close to you in stature would be Master Gareth, there. Might I ask why, sir?"

I glanced in the direction he pointed, taking in the guy standing on the opposite side of the lobby—slicked back blond hair, sparkling blue eyes. Unlike everyone else sipping from their flutes of champagne and nibbling delicately on the de-crusted sandwiches, he'd made the effort to get dressed before coming downstairs. His beige chinos had been pressed so violently that there was a knife-edge crease down the front of them, and his dusky pink button down shirt looked like it had come straight out of the packaging. He was wearing a fucking Aran-knit sweater over his shoulders, the arms of which were tied loosely around his neck. I immediately hated the prick. He was a mirror of so many guys I'd gone to college with; he came from money, that was clear enough. And from the way he tipped his head back and laughed loudly, seeking attention, he was used to people fawning over him in public.

"Never mind," I said, still staring at the stranger. "You're right. I don't think he's broad enough. Not by a long chalk." My parents had had money. Plenty of it. They'd packed me off to receive the best education money could buy, and when I'd agreed to undertake my seminary training, they'd insisted on putting me up in an exorbitantly expensive hotel instead of allowing me to room with another student at the church facility. Their wealth had set me apart from the crowd. I wasn't like this Gareth asshole, though. I'd never flaunted the healthy state of my bank account by wearing expensive clothes or sporting three hundred dollar hair cuts. I'd worn the cheapest shit I could find, stocking my wardrobe by shopping at thrift stores. And when the time had come, when both my parents died, I'd tied up every single penny they'd left to me in trusts and bonds, making sure I couldn't even see the disgusting amount of cash that had fallen into my lap anymore.

Next to Gareth, a flash of red caught my attention, and I realized the person Gareth was laughing so boisterously with was Arianna, the woman who'd been flirting with me back in the room only fifteen minutes ago. Her hand was resting lightly, possessively, on Gareth's arm—a clear sign to the other tittering women hovering around him that he was already taken. So...Arianna was the jealous type. But also the type to flutter her eyelashes at other men whenever the fuck she felt like it. Sounded about right.

I was about to slip down the remaining stairs and sidle my way out of the lobby, when Arianna looked up, her gaze settling on me. Gareth looked up at the same time, frowned, then whispered something into Arianna's ear. Her cheeks were stained with color as she replied to him, nodded, then waved me over.

Under no circumstances did I want to go and join them. I'd suffered through root canal surgery before without anesthetic, and even that sounded more pleasant that being introduced to this fucking jack-hole. Still...this was Sera's sister's wedding. I had to keep reminding myself of that. Sera thought I was the shittiest human being to ever draw breath, but I could at least prove her wrong in this. I could at least make sure today was nothing but smooth sailing.

"There we are, darling," Arianna said breezily, as I arrived at their group. "I told you he was part of the wedding party. Felix Marcosa, meet my boyfriend, Gareth Douvillier. Gareth was just saying that you looked like you were about to perform at a rock concert, not attend a wedding."

"Actually, I didn't," Gareth said tightly. His eyes were bland and uninteresting. Untrustworthy. "I said he looked like an underpaid roadie, who should be lugging DJ equipment through the service entrance at the rear of the hotel, not lurking in the lobby during a wine mixer."

Well, well, well. Gareth had a sharp tongue in his head. He wanted to look down at me, I could tell. Trouble was, I was about six inches taller than him, and I wasn't wearing lifts in my shoes like he was. Arianna laughed, high pitched and nervous, playfully slapping Gareth's arm. "I'm sorry, Felix. Gareth's always a little testy at these things. People ask him so many questions, y'know? He's very successful at what he does, and everyone wants to know his secrets."

"Oh. That's great. I'm pretty fucking successful at what I do, too."

Arianna's mouth gaped open the moment I swore. Gareth didn't seem to care, though. "Oh? And what might that be?" he drawled.

"Who knows?" I slapped him on the shoulder. Hard. "Maybe one day you'll find out first hand."

He bared his teeth at me. It was supposed to be a smile, but good ol' Gareth was transparent as fuck. He didn't like me, and he wasn't doing a very good job of concealing his emotions. "Whatever she's told you, it's not true, you know," he said. "None of it. She's a fucking liar."

"I'm sorry? I don't follow."

"Sera. I never cheated on her with Arianna. We'd already broken up when I got with her."

I stifled a laugh. "Sera? Sera was with *you*?"

Gareth was indignation personified. "Don't give me that shit. There's no way she didn't tell you about me. She lost her freaking mind when we split."

God. So I wasn't just crashing a wedding. I was neck deep in ex-drama, too. That was just fucking perfect. I folded my arms across my chest, making sure to flex my muscles a little. "I don't know what to tell you, man. She's never mentioned your name before. She can't have been that distraught. Good on you, though. Sera's a catch. You're a lucky man to have spent any time with her at all." Gone was my smile. And gone was the arrogant glint in Gareth's eye.

"She's a head case, man. You've got your hands full with all the luggage that bitch carries around with her. I mean, why the fuck would you want to involve yourself with damaged goods like that? Her own father fucked around with her."

I'd been planning on walking away from this conversation without being a cunt. There were times when it was appropriate to smash your fist into someone's jaw in the middle of a crowded room, and there were times when it was smarter to send a parting shot across the bow and walk the fuck away. Gareth was a needy piece of shit who didn't like the idea that there were people out there in the world who'd witnessed his ugly side. I'd handled scores of guys just like him, and I'd learned how to cut them down and move on without breaking a sweat. But to call her a bitch? To speak openly to someone you don't know about her being *sexually assaulted*? I'd have to unpack that one and deal with it later, but for now...

Nope. No fucking way.

I was itching to lay the bastard out. Fair enough, I knew very little about Sera, had no right to feel protective over her, but none of that mattered. Slating your ex to the man who was now dating her (as far as he knew) was a classless act, but resorting to name calling was just fucking horseshit. I played out what it would feel like to knock the motherfucker out right here and now. The bright snap of pain as my knuckles connected with his jaw. The vivid, bright red of the blood he would shed. The satisfying thud his skull would make as it bounced off the floor. It was all going so well in my head, until I imagined the look of horror on everyone else's faces, and the shit Sera would have to field as a result of my rash actions.

Fuck.

The sense of gratification that had been welling up inside of me vanished. I couldn't do it to her. "You don't need to worry about me," I said. The vein in my temple was pounding like a demented drum. "Sera's baggage is nothing compared to *mine*. And besides. I work out. I'm perfectly capable of carrying whatever pain and heartbreak she's been through *for* her. Not that I need to, of course. Sera's a wildfire. A lot of guys aren't capable of caring for a woman who's been brave enough to fight her way through dark times. Don't worry. I get it. Their strength can be intimidating."

Gareth's mouth was yawning open, moments away from spewing out even more bullshit. A right hook would have been impeccably timed right now, but instead I turned around and walked away. I knew exactly what I was doing; men like Gareth were used to being listened to. They believed everything they said and did was of great import to others. For someone to belittle them, cut them off, turn their back on them and walk away? That was fucking crushing to a puffed up, egotistical degenerate like him.

As I casually strolled out of the lobby, I grabbed a bellboy by the arm, jerking my head back over my shoulder in Gareth's direction. "Hey, that blond guy over there with the redhead? What's he driving? Tell me and this is yours." I showed him the hundred-dollar bill I'd taken out of my pocket.

The bellboy squinted at Gareth, then back at the hundred-dollar bill again. "The red Lamborghini out back. The brand new one with the black leather interior."

"I'll give you another hundred if you loan me the keys for ten minutes."

"Why? You're not going to do anything bad to it, are you?"

"Oh, god, no. I'd never do damage to someone's ride. I just have a gift for him is all."

By the time I was done pissing in the front seat of Gareth's stupidly ostentatious vehicle, the pounding in my temples had eased. I wasn't done with that motherfucker, though. Not even close to done. My boots bit into the gravel on the way back across the parking lot. Fuck it. I wasn't going to bother finding a suit for this ludicrous event. I'd skip the ceremony, and then hang out at the reception once the photos were out of the way. And once night fell and ever—

"Father? Father Marcosa?"

My boots stopped. My heart stopped. The world stopped.

Who?

Who would know to call me that out here, in the middle of nowhere? The chances were non-existent. My mind went blank as I turned around...and looked into the face of a man I never thought I would see again.

15

SERA

INTERFERENCE

*A*my was crying, make up streaming down her face when I entered the beautifully lit, luxurious reception room where I was supposed to be having my makeup and hair done. She looked up, blinking like crazy through her tears, and let out a loud, heartbroken sob when she recognized me.

"Sera, oh god…"

"What is it? What's wrong?" I was used to Amy's fits of hysterics, but her temper tantrums were typically accompanied by screaming and breakable objects being thrown. Today, she was curled in on herself, shoulders rounded, the strap of the nude slip she was wearing falling off her right shoulder. She looked like a broken little girl, like she was physically hurt in some way, and my heart rose up into my throat. She hiccupped as she buried her face in her hands, hiding herself away.

"God, I didn't know, I swear," she moaned.

I crouched down in front of her, trying to gently prize her hands away from her face. "Didn't know what?"

"This—this is such—a mess," she whispered. "I don't want to do this now. I just want to go home."

"*You don't want to get married*?" If she really didn't want to tie the knot today, I'd help her plot a plan of escape out of the hotel without a second thought, but Jesus... After everything I'd been through in order to get here, I had to fight down the urge to slap her.

"No, of course I want to get married. I love Ben. But..."

"But?"

I managed to peel back one of her hands. She allowed the other to fall, revealing bloodshot eyes and smudged lipstick. She was a mess, but I did everything I could to keep my dismay from showing. That wouldn't help at all. Pulling in a deep breath, she picked at a hanging thread on the hem of her slip, her fingers tugging at it nervously.

"They thought they were doing the right thing, Sera. I swear. They would never have invited him if they knew..."

"Amy, take a deep breath. I can barely understand a word you're saying. Start from the beginning. Who thought they were doing the right thing? Who did they invite?"

The second Amy exhaled, shivering from cold, and then looked up at me, a sinking, dreadful weight pulled at my insides. No... no, god, no one would have invited *him* here. They wouldn't be that cruel. Amy wasn't shaking from the cold; she was shaking from *fear*. My hands dropped to my sides. Strangely, I couldn't feel my body anymore. I was numb from the hairline down. The only way I knew my heart was racing out of control was because of the dizziness that had washed over me.

"Who invited him?" I asked breathlessly.

Amy hiccupped again, wiping her nose on the back of her hand. "Ben's parents. I told them he used to be abusive. I told them about the alcohol and the drugs. I explained how we hadn't been in contact for many years. I just...couldn't...tell them about..."

She trailed off as a fresh wave of tears took her over. I kept my face trained into a blank, expressionless mask. If I allowed myself to react, I was going to fall apart. There was no way I'd be able to hold myself together, and, just like always, Amy needed me to be strong for her. So I did my best.

"You don't understand people like Ben's parents," Amy said, sniffing. "Family is so important to them. They couldn't bear the thought of me getting married without my father present, so they reached out to him. They...god, they went to see him, Sera. They said he'd turned himself around, was doing really well for himself, and that he'd...he'd cried when they told him about me getting married to Ben. They asked him to come. It was meant to be a surprise, but Ben let it slip this morning. Said he didn't want me to be blindsided when I saw him sitting there on the front row."

Blindsided. That was such an appropriate term. Who the fuck went and invited someone's father to their wedding without their consent? Amy had planned this whole thing down to the last letter. Her attention to detail was meticulous. Her failure to invite Sixsmith to her wedding hadn't been an oversight. There was a damn good reason why she'd left him off the guest list, so why in the name of fuck would Ben's parents have pried and interfered so badly?

I wasn't surprised Sixsmith had convinced them he was a reformed character. When most people thought of an alcoholic, they imagined a person living in squalor, dirty and unkempt, broke and unemployed. Our father's addiction wasn't an obvious thing. He was obsessively clean, managed to get himself to and from work every day, dressed himself nicely for the most part, and always made sure he had a few dollars in his pocket.

When he wasn't drinking, he was the epitome of charming. The one and only time I ever breathed a word of what was happening at home to an adult, I'd shown my sixth grade teacher the bruises that covered my upper arms, thighs, stomach and buttocks, and she'd stormed over to my house to confront Sixsmith. By the time she left an hour later, Sixsmith had managed to convince her that I'd lied, that I'd been acting out of late, vying for attention because Amy had been sick and taking up everybody's time, and that he was so, so sorry for the time my teacher had wasted. I'd listened to their conversation from the top step of the stairs, hugging my knees to my chest, eyes screwed tightly shut, and I remembered being so sure that Miss Harriet was going to see straight through Sixsmith's ruse. It was so clear to me. So easy to detect the subtle edge to his tone that revealed how angry he was that he'd been found out. But it was as though Sixsmith was a blind spot for most people. They'd try and fail to see an entire picture of him. Miss Harriet had believed him, and when I returned to school the next Monday, after a weekend of severe beatings, being locked in Sixsmith's bedroom and forced to sleep naked under his bed, she'd told me to cover up my bruises, and that if I showed anyone else I would be sent to the principal's office.

"Please, Sera. Don't...don't cause a scene. I just...I don't know what to do." Amy was rocking back and forth; she grabbed my hands in her own, alternating between squeezing way too hard and shaking like a leaf. "I didn't even tell Ben," she said sorrowfully. "The man I love. The man I'm meant to be marrying in less than three hours. I couldn't bring myself to face the truth, and telling Ben about Sixsmith just...just made it all seem so real. If I hadn't been such a coward, he would have known that bringing him here was a terrible idea. He could have stopped his parents from ever going to see him."

"Has he arrived yet?" I asked stiffly.

Amy shook her head, fresh waves tumbling into her face. "I don't know. I don't think so."

"All right. It's okay. I'll deal with it."

Amy stopped shaking. A moment later, she stopped crying. "How?"

"I'll find him. I'll make sure he doesn't stay. Don't worry. Just get into your dress and have them fix your makeup. Everything will be fine. I promise."

～

*E*verything was *not* fine. I didn't think I was going to make it to the bathroom before I threw up, but I proved myself wrong. I slung the door closed, dropped to my knees and leaned forward just in time to get most of my vomit in the toilet bowl.

My mind was spinning as I sagged back against the door, legs tangled up beneath me, my throat burning. Ben's parents were meddling assholes. When I figured out what they looked like and tracked them down, they were going to wish they'd never stuck their noses into Lafferty business.

My father.

My father, here, in the same place as Amy and me.

After eight years...

I bowed over the toilet and puked again, so hard and so violently that it felt like I was tearing muscle. I'd suffered through all those nightmares, year after year. I'd told myself they were nothing, just bad dreams, and I could handle them, because I'd never have to see Sixsmith again in the flesh. The version of him that lived inside my subconscious could taunt and harass me until the end of time, because I'd never have to stand in front of him and allow him to harm me in real life ever again. Except now here we were...

I could do it. When Amy and I had finally escaped Montmorenci, I'd told Sixsmith I'd gut him like a fish if I ever saw or heard from him again. For my troubles, he'd punched me so hard I thought my eye socket had caved in, but we'd still gotten up and walked out of that place. If I'd been able to do that back then, I could tell the piece of shit to get the fuck out of our lives a second time around. He couldn't be allowed to ruin this for Amy. Ben was about as engaging as a wet paper bag, and as far as his physique went, he had just about as much chance of fighting his way out of one, but he made my sister smile. He made her forget her past, and that was the most important thing in the world. I wasn't going to let that sick fuck stroll back into her life and screw everything up for her. It just wasn't going to happen. I'd do anything in my power to prevent that. It didn't matter that seeing Sixsmith would be traumatic for *me*. I could reinforce the Band-Aids that were currently holding me together later, when all was said and done. But, in between now and then, I had to face the man the demon who stalked my sleep, and I had to be fucking brave.

I found Fix, still in his t-shirt and ripped jeans, talking to an old man outside a door labeled, 'Reading Room.' On either side of the old man's head, perched just above his ears, were two tufts of thin white hair, like little puffy clouds of smoke. His face was a riot of wrinkles, a roadmap of years that seemed to have taken a harsh toll on him. His eyes were alert, sharp and bright, though. When he spotted me over Fix's shoulder, he broke into a smile.

"Well, there's no mistaking you, then," he said. "You're Sera, Amy's sister. I'd recognize that chin anywhere."

"Haha, yeah. The old Lafferty chin. It's a pleasure to make your acquaintance." I had no idea who I was meeting, since the old guy failed to supply me with his name. Fix rocked uncomfortably on his heels, his hands shoved deep in his pockets. Even with everything that was going on, my insides reeled whenever I looked at him. He was so...*Fix*. A creature made out of shadows and light. A dream, and a nightmare rolled into one. He was both sides of a coin toss, consequence and reward. I wanted to kiss him so badly right then that my lips ached. I wanted to run away from him, screaming, just as badly. It was my duty to warn everyone that a wolf had snuck in amongst the flock of sheep, and was likely to start feeding any second, but I found myself standing there, pretending like nothing was wrong.

"I was wondering if I could talk to you for a second?" I said. Then to the old man, "I'm sorry. I don't mean to interrupt your conversation. This will only take a second."

"Oh, that's quite all right. Felix and I were just reminiscing about the good old days when I taught him at seminary. We can pick up where we left off later. That is, if I haven't dropped down dead by then, naturally. When you get to my age, every passing minute is somewhat a surprise, to be honest." His laugh was raucous; he might well have been in his late eighties, but his constitution seemed strong. I wasn't paying too much attention to the old guy's mirth, though. I'd caught and stuck on a word he'd just said: seminary.

Seminary?

It wasn't a word you heard often these days, but I knew what it was. Fix had been in seminary? That image just would not compute. I frowned at him as he placed his hand into the small of my back and guided me away from the old man.

"Who *was* that?" I hissed.

"Father Gregory Richards. He's officiating your sister's wedding."

"And you *know* him?"

"Barely." Fix shrugged, navigating his way out the front of the building, pushing me in front of him. As soon as we were outside, I dug my heels into the gravel, refusing to take another step.

"You went to seminary, Fix? What the fuck were you doing in seminary school?"

"Learning, mostly. Getting an education."

"A Catholic education? In order to become a *priest*?"

"I thought you knew," he said quietly. "You heard the conversation I had with Franz in the auto shop before..."

"Before you killed him? Yeah, I heard what you both said. I thought it was code or something. I didn't think he meant...I didn't think you meant...Oh, fuck. So... *Great*. You're a kidnapper. You're a murderer. And now you're a fucking priest."

"I'm not a priest anymore." Usually pale as ice, his eyes had darkened and taken on a stormy, malevolent edge.

"Why didn't you tell me?"

"You didn't ask."

"*Fix!*"

"I'm sorry. It just didn't seem like pertinent information."

"I don't—" I shook my head. "God, I just don't understand you!"

"Are you supposed to? Is understanding me gonna make any of this easier?"

He was so fucking infuriating. He had a point, though. Knowing a detailed history of his life wasn't going to change anything. It was just...really? *He went to seminary school?* "How long were you a priest? Did you have a parish? Were you always this..."

"Fucked up?" The sun lanced down through the trees, hitting him from behind, and there was a moment when his dark hair turned to burnished copper. His broad shoulders were tensed; his whole body seemed to be tensed, actually, though I couldn't figure out why.

"Yeah," I snapped. "Have you always been this fucked up? How did you end up transitioning from weekly bake offs and charity drives to killing people, for fuck's sake? I mean, it doesn't make any sense. You're a walking dichotomy."

"I was never a very good priest," he said softly. "I wanted to be good at it for a while there. Helping people gave me a purpose and a direction I hadn't experienced before. But in the end, that collar I wore around my neck every day ended up strangling the life out of me. Something happened, and I left. In the end, it wouldn't have mattered, though. I would have gone eventually. It just wasn't who I was."

It was so strange to hear him speak this way. I'd gotten used to the idea that he was an evil, mindless psychopath, but the mental image of him that had just conjured itself inside my head conflicted with all of that.

"Don't," Fix growled under his breath. "Your thoughts are written all over your face. You're wondering if this is all a phase. If I'm going to wake up one day and want to be holy, righteous, pious Father Marcosa again. I *know* you're wondering that. Don't waste your time. I'm never going back, Sera. This is who I am now. Who I'm always going to be. I won't change for you. I won't be redeemed. Nothing on this earth would make me tuck my tail between my legs and run back to be forgiven. I don't want it. And let's face it. At the end of the day, I don't deserve it."

I stared at him, trying to read him. It was impossible. He was an expert at shielding his emotions, secreting them away, hiding them from the outside world. I knew so little about him, really, but I knew this for sure: it would take a crowbar and a lifetime of effort to get this man to open up. Things had gotten so confusing. I still didn't know if I should have been afraid for my life or not, and there I was, trying to decide if I wanted to own up to the perplexing feelings I was rapidly developing for this man.

"I don't care if you change your mind about your path or if you don't, Fix. I just need to know one thing." I held my breath, waiting for him to answer.

Fix took a step forward, bowing his head so that he didn't tower over me quite so badly. "Like I said. Ask away."

Here went nothing.

"Where do you keep your guns?"

16

FIX

CRACK PIPE

I hadn't heard her right. I couldn't have. She wasn't asking to borrow a gun, because that would have been absolute insanity. Sera stood her ground, gaze steady, fixed on me, unwavering. For someone who was fucking around, she sure was starting to look pretty damn serious.

"It doesn't have to be loaded," she explained. "I just need it to scare someone."

"You know pointing a gun at someone is still a criminal offence, even if it isn't loaded?"

"Like you care about the law!" She laughed, hard laughter, full of anxiety and worry, devoid of any humor. "Just give me a gun, Fix. I'll give it back to you in a couple of hours, I swear."

"I don't want a weapon handed back to me after it's been used to commit a felony. I'd rather you threw it into a lake or a quarry, like every other half-witted would-be murderer in this country."

"Whatever! I won't give it back, then. I'll get rid of it. Just...give me the damn gun, Fix!"

"Do you even know how to *hold* a gun?"

She rolled her eyes. "It's got a handle and a trigger. I think I'll figure it out."

"Why don't you tell me what's going on instead? Maybe I can help."

"If, by help, you mean put a bullet in the back of someone's head for me, then yeah. Maybe you *can* help." She said this flippantly—an off-the-cuff remark that didn't mean anything to her. She wasn't serious in the slightest. If only she knew...

Sera's eyes unfocused, her body stiffening as she looked out of the window over my shoulder. I followed her gaze; an old red Chevy was pulling up the driveway, rust pockmarking the paintwork, and a considerable dent in the driver's side door panel. The car had seen better days, and so had its driver. A guy in his mid-fifties sat behind the wheel, his dark hair slicked back, thinning on top badly enough that the top of his shiny head was easily visible. When he got out of the car, handing his keys off to the valet slash bellboy with a flourish, as if his ride was a brand new Tesla, I made a quick assessment of him. Scuffed brown leather shoes. Yellowing shirt underneath a faded blue suit that looked like it last saw the light of day in the seventies. The man, of course, was Sixsmith Lafferty, Sera's father. I knew as much, but I kept my mouth shut.

Sera had turned a deathly pale white, her face bleached of all color. "*Shit.*" She took a step back away from the window and nearly knocked over a small walnut side table that was laden with flowers and a large bowl, containing chocolates wrapped in gold foil. I grabbed hold of her by the arm, steadying her.

"Time to tell me what the fuck's going on," I said. "Does that man mean something to you? Is he the reason you want a gun?"

Sera looked like she'd shrunk to about half her regular size. There was so much fight and fire in her when she was confronting me, but right now, she looked like she wanted the ground to open up and swallow her. Gareth had said Sera's father had touched her. The slice on her jaw wasn't confirmation of that, but it was almost certainly confirmation that he'd been violent with her. I had to turn myself to stone as Sera let out a ragged breath, scanning the hallway from left to right; it looked like she was searching for an escape route.

"That's Sixsmith," she said, her voice three octaves higher than normal. "He's my father. We don't...we don't see eye-to-eye."

From what I knew of Sixsmith Lafferty, he didn't see eye to eye with many people. He was the lowest of the low. Scum of the earth. A worthless, violent, disgusting piece of trash that needed putting down. "You're sweating, Sera." I reached out and touched her fore-head, contemplating the wet pads of my fingers before I carefully slid them into my mouth.

"God, now really isn't the time, Fix," Sera panted.

I angled my head to one side, studying her. "I've tasted your ecstasy. I've tasted your anger. I wanted to know what your fear tasted like."

"I'm not afraid."

"Then why are you shaking?"

Sera opened her mouth. She had something to say, but...nothing came out. I wanted to scoop her into my arms and press her into me. I wanted to hold her so her tight, she didn't need to breathe anymore. I wanted to protect her, even when protecting her would only cause more hurt and anguish. "If you really want a gun, I'll give you one," I whispered. "But you threatening him...do you really think you could do it?"

Sera's expression hardened, turning to molten steel. "You don't know what I'm capable of."

"I can guess. But, when you take on that kind of violence... it taints you. It transforms you. You think you'll just point a gun at him and he'll go away? That's not how men like him work. They love confrontation. They love seeing the terror in their victim's eyes. They're excited by it. Violence begets violence, Sera. If you're not willing to actually follow through and pull that trigger, to make him go away for real, he'll know. He'll see it in your eyes."

"Then...urgh! *WhatamIsupposedtodo*?" Her words ran into each other, frustration and panic rearing their ugly heads. Her chest was rising and falling too rapidly; she was on the brink of an anxiety attack, and it was within my power to stop it. I didn't need to hand her a weapon and allow her to face Sixsmith alone. I could take care of him for her easily enough, but then there'd be no closure for Sera. The whole thing was complicated, and growing more and more complicated by the day. If I were smart, I would take the bastard out to the small copse of trees at the rear of the hotel, and I'd dig my thumbs into his eye sockets until he was dead. No noisy gunshots to alert the hotel patrons of something untoward. No real mess. There'd be a bit of blood, but not as much as there had been with Franz back in Liberty Fields. Killing Sixsmith with my bare hands would feel like justice. It would be a brutal death, and yet it would still be far kinder than that sick, depraved motherfucker deserved.

"Just...let me take care of him, Sera. You don't want him here? Fine. I'll make him leave. You should go and get ready. The ceremony's going to start soon, right?"

Sera inhaled sharply, her eyebrows rising up her forehead. She hadn't expected me to make an offer like that. Making a joke out of me killing her dad was one thing, but apparently the concept that I might handle the situation in another way hadn't occurred to her.

"You can't," she whispered. "I couldn't ask you to do that."

"Why not?" I smirked. "Haven't I made your life miserable since we met? Don't I owe you a favor or two?"

Suspicion flared in Sera's eyes, but the tension that had been radiating off her dissipated a little. "You think telling my father to leave a party will absolve you of your guilt, then fine...go ahead. Make him leave. But..."

"But I'm still an evil piece of shit, and you're never going to trust or forgive me. Don't worry. I got it."

Her smile was wobbly as I left her standing there by the window. Lafferty had probably entered the building by now. The valet had immediately moved his car from outside the hotel, probably so no one would see the broken down beater, so he'd been free to enter and make himself comfortable. Only, when I lapped the lobby, squeezing through the crowd, handing out tight-lipped smiles to everyone who tried to say hello or stop me, I couldn't find Sera's father anywhere.

I slipped out the front, searching for him, but he was nowhere to be see—

Wait.

There.

To my right, camouflaged in the bushes at the side of the sweeping driveway leading up to the hotel, I spotted Lafferty's busted up brown leather shoes. The guy nearly shit himself as I yanked back a thick branch of foliage, exposing him. "What the fuck man! Can't a guy take a leak in peace around here?"

There was nothing of Sera in him. Rather, there was nothing of him in Sera. She must have had her mother's eyes, and her mother's chin, and her mother's cheekbones. Sixsmith Lafferty's face was little more than paper-thin skin wrapped around a gaunt skull. His eyes were brown, dull and cruel. The deep wrinkles that bracketed his mouth had nothing to do with laughter. They were the result of a permanent sneer the man seemed to have perfected and was sending in my direction this very second.

"Funny. I didn't know you could piss and hit a crack pipe at the same time. You're very multitalented," I shot back.

Sixsmith had dropped his hands down when I'd pulled back the branch, but not quick enough. I'd seen the glass pipe held up at his lips, and the curl of acrid smoke escaping down his nostrils right now was pretty damning.

Sixsmith's sneer deepened. "You a cop?"

"No."

"Then it's none of your fucking business, is it?" He turned his back on me, which was his first mistake. There was a vast anger inside me. A lake of it. No, more than a lake. There was a *sea* of anger inside me, and the only thing holding it back was the high dam wall I'd constructed in my mind. The dam was high, and it was thick, and it had held back my anger for years. The dam was weakening with every second I spent in Sixsmith Lafferty's presence, though. Cracks were forming, deep and jagged, and I had no idea how long the wall was going to stand. Sixsmith put the glass pipe to his mouth, holding a lighter to the bulb at its end, then drew in a stream of pure white smoke.

He didn't hear me approaching. And he didn't make a peep when

I drew back my fist and slammed it into the base of his skull as hard as I fucking could. Sixsmith's neck made a sickening crunching sound, and the guy crumpled into the leaf litter like his legs had just been taken out from underneath him. *That's right, asshole. Knocked the fuck out.*

He wasn't dead. I could easily have killed him with a punch like that if I'd really wanted to. All it would have taken was a little more strength and a little determination. I didn't want Sixsmith dead, though. Not yet, anyway. He wouldn't even be paralyzed when he woke up from his momentary nap. He'd have a raging headache, but aside from that he'd be fine.

I didn't have much time. There were people at all the windows, now dressed for the wedding in their finest suits and dresses. I'd be noticed if I dragged Sixsmith's lifeless body across the gravel turning circle that fanned out in front of the hotel entrance. I was going to have to drag him through the trees, around the side of the building, and then around the multitude of cars that had been parked as close as possible to the building. From there, I should be safe to sit down with Sixsmith and have a little, friendly chat with him. It wouldn't take long.

Dragging Sixsmith's limp, unresponsive body to his car, parked in the furthest spot possible from the hotel, was no fun whatsoever. Sixsmith looked like he weighed a buck sixty, but his bones must have been made out of surgical steel or something. He was a dead weight. I wasn't exactly careful with him as I lugged him toward my destination; he'd be black and blue in a couple of days, and it'd take a solid week for his headache to disappear.

Sixsmith didn't wake up when I dumped him next to his Chevy. He didn't wake up when I kicked him with the toe of my boot, either. It took a firm backhander across the face to rouse him, and when he did wake up, he peered up at me, brows banked together, confusion swamping him.

"What the...fuck? You fucking hit me?"

"Yeah, I fucking hit you. And if you don't keep your tongue in your head, I'll do it again, bitch."

Sixsmith slowly closed his eyes, manic laughter bubbling out of him, growing louder and louder. "You're a fucking dead man," he wheezed. "I'm gonna fucking kill you. This is my daughter's wedding. I was invited here, you little shit."

"Amy didn't invite you. Amy doesn't want you here. Neither does Sera."

Sixsmith stopped laughing at the mention of Sera's name. He adopted a blank, void stare, laced with...desire? A chill ran down my spine. It *was* desire. Not a sexual kind of attraction, but one of dominance. "Sera's here, too?" he rasped out.

"You're not going to see either of them. You're going to get in your car and drive away. Right now."

"Like hell I am. I drove five hours to be here for this thing. I have every fucking right to see my kids. Who are you to tell me to fuck off, huh?"

"I'm Sera's guest."

"Ha. Her *guest*? Not her usual type, I gotta say. She normally likes her guys a little...*older*."

I dropped into a crouch in front of him, resting my elbows on my knees, lacing my fingers together. "Can I ask you something?" I said softly. Sixsmith just frowned. He must have been thrown by the change in my tone of voice. "Do you *want* to die? Because I'm getting the feeling that you don't care about your life very much."

"What the fuck are you talking about?" Sixsmith snapped.

"If you did value your life," I continued, "then you'd take one look at my face and know better than to utter Sera's name ever again. You wouldn't even think about her. You sure as fuck wouldn't make another derogatory remark about her choice in sexual partners, because I can guarantee you that will lead you to a very bad place. Do you understand me, asshole?"

God, how much would I have loved to smash his face into the concrete, until there was nothing left but mangled meat and shards of bone? The dam inside my head had crumbled a little further, and my wrath was spilling forth. There was nothing I could do about it now. It was too late to try and ignore it. I had to be strong, though. I had no other choice. If I lost myself and killed Sixsmith here, there would be no escaping the consequences. My name was on the hotel's guest register. I'd given them a copy of my driver's license for their records. The place was steeped in Southern charm, and bygone hospitality was still a very real concern here, but they weren't operating in the dark ages. I'd noticed at least three cameras in the lobby, not to mention the two I'd spied in the hallway this morning on our way up to the room.

So they had my ID. They had me on camera. They knew what I looked like, and they had plenty of footage to evidence that I was here today. Therefore, today could not be the last day anyone saw Sixsmith Lafferty.

"Tell them to come out here and make me leave," Sixsmith said breathlessly. "Tell them...if they come out here and tell me they don't want me here, I'll go."

"This isn't a negotiation. We're not having a conversation here. I'm telling you that you need to leave. You're going to hear me and oblige me, or you're going to end up in a shitload of pain. Your call."

Sixsmith's lips peeled back. His teeth were a fucking mess. He spat on the ground next to him, wincing as he slowly turned and got onto his knees, then stood up. "What's your name?" he asked quietly, shooting daggers at me out of the corner of his eye. "If you're such a bad ass, you won't mind telling me."

Shit. I knew why he wanted the information. "My name's Fix. But you won't find any information on me when you go snooping around in my shit, old man."

Narrowed eyes. Humiliation and fury boiling in his veins. "And why's that, *Fix*?"

"Because I'm smart. I don't leave cookie crumbs lying around for idiots like you to follow. And let's face it. You're fucking dumb. Forget the needle. You couldn't find a piece of hay in a haystack." Sixsmith growled under his breath. He pushed back his worn blue suit jacket and made a point of showing me the wicked-looking knife he had clipped to his belt. I just shrugged. "Go ahead. Pull it on me. See what happens."

He didn't pull it. He tilted his head back, setting his jaw, posturing, as he walked to his Chevy and got in. I stood back and watched him with my arms folded across my chest. Sixsmith was in the car and the engine was running when I remembered something I was supposed to do. Shit. I grappled with my cell phone, tugging it out of my pocket, flicking up the bottom tool bar and hitting the camera icon.

"Hey, Sixsmith. Say 'America's Most Wanted.'"

Sixsmith turned on me, nostrils flared, cheeks stained red, his brow marked with sweat. I took his picture, and I watched as a stone cold, deadly, flat kind of calm overtook him. "Next time I see you, I'll return the favor," he said. "I'll be the one with the camera in my hand. And you'll be the one lying on the floor, dead, with your own severed pecker shoved down your throat."

"Ouch. Quite the visual. I doubt I could take my own dick in my mouth, though. I'm a big boy." I doubled over, bracing, hands resting on my knees, at eye level with him now. "Maybe you could give me some pointers. I bet you got good at swallowing cock when you were locked up in that control unit down in Eddyville."

"Sera told you I was locked up in Kentucky?" he asked, ignoring my barb.

I just smiled at him. We both knew Sera couldn't have told me her father had just been released after completing a four-year sentence in Eddyville. They hadn't communicated in the past nine and a half years, so how could she possibly have known that? I slapped my palm against the roof of his shitty car, then gave him a passive aggressive wave. "Safe journey back to hell, Sixsmith. I'll be coming to pay you a visit shortly."

17

SERA

TOXIC

The ceremony was kind of fucked up. Amy walked down the aisle to a David Bowie song—Starman—that had absolutely nothing to do with love, commitment or the beauty of everlasting companionship. Must have been some sort of private joke between her and Ben, who was struck with nervous laughter just as Father Richards began the service. One of the flower girls threw up as the bride and groom were taking their vows, and Ben's grandfather, Jerry, who'd apparently escaped the Nazis in a muck cart in occupied France right at the end of the Second World War, had an angina attack, and everybody thought he was about to die. I wasn't counting the growing list of individual disasters that were tarnishing Amy's day, however, because none of it mattered. Sixsmith wasn't here. And if Sixsmith wasn't here, then everything else was going to be perfect no matter what.

As maid of honor, I stood up at the front in the hideous peach dress Amy had picked out for me, and I held Amy's bouquet for her when Ben slid the wedding ring onto her finger. Father Richards droned on and on about the sanctity of marriage, loyalty and obedience for a little too long, during which time I scanned the people parked in the pews, searching for Fix. He wasn't there.

A range of emotions took their turn at confusing the fuck out of me as Father Richards told Ben he could now kiss the bride. Worry came first. Had everything gone smoothly with Sixsmith? Had my father attacked Fix or something? Sixsmith was unpredictable and insane, totally capable of launching himself at a guy twice the height and size of him if he felt like it.

Annoyance came next. Fix insisted on coming with me to Fairhope. He'd sworn up and down he wasn't going to let me out of his sight, and then...what? He'd just fucking vanished? Great.

The last emotion to hit me, as I finally spotted the man in question out of a window to my right, was desire—the most confusing emotion of all. Fix was outside, leaning against the wall of what looked like a small guest cottage, one leg bent, the sole of his boot resting against the wall, and there was a cigarette in his hand. Tendrils of smoke snaked their way from his nostrils, rising around his face, and my stomach turned over on itself.

The man in black. I'd only ever seen him wear black. Did that have something to do with his days spent as a priest, drowning in his cossack, or was it just a reflection of who he was, devoid of light? I didn't want to wonder about him. It was foolish to allow my mind to wander onto such treacherous ground, but...I couldn't help it. Fix had done something I couldn't understand or move past. But then again, he'd kept his word, and he hadn't harmed me. Quite the opposite, really. He'd prevented Sixsmith from destroying what was supposed to be the happiest day of my sister's life.

Some of the people in the chapel had noticed Fix waiting outside, too. They muttered under their breath, whispering behind their hands to one another, sending scathing glances in his direction. What did they see when they looked at him? A guy smoking a cigarette, dressed in black, wearing torn jeans. It was obvious; they saw someone who wasn't a part of their crowd. He wasn't a banker, or a lawyer, or a doctor. His face wasn't clean-shaven, and his hair was a little too long to satisfy their tastes.

I wasn't a member of their little clique either, though. I'd come from a base stock, working class family, and so had Amy. They'd overlooked our weak breeding because we were young, and we were pretty enough, and we'd done our best to lift ourselves out from underneath the poverty we were born into. It had never sat right with me, how Ben had tried to change Amy. Had thrown out her old wardrobe and told her how pretty she was in the clothes *he* had bought for her. I'd never have imagined Amy wearing a string of pearls when we fled Montmorenci and moved to Seattle. She'd liked to listen to the Ramones and dye her hair black. She'd liked to walk a fine line between madness and sanity—after escaping Sixsmith, I think we'd *both* felt that way—but these days all she cared about was improving her credit rating and making sure she got to bed by eight thirty.

These people were toxic.

When *I* looked at Fix out through those windows, I didn't know what I saw. He was an enigma. When I'd hidden in that auto shop and seen what he'd done, I'd been scared. I'd wanted to run from him and never look back. But...things weren't so clear anymore. I was never going to be able to say I agreed with what he did for a living, but the photos he'd shown me of the poor girl Franz had tortured and abused...

I still saw those images every time I closed my eyes. They were going to be seared into my retinas for the rest of my life. And...and how many times, when I was younger, had I wished for someone like Fix to come along and put an end to Sixsmith once and for good? If I'd had the money back then, wouldn't I have hired someone just like Fix to protect me?

Fix flicked his cigarette, and the butt flew in an arc before hitting the ground, sending up sparks from the cherry. I hadn't noticed that Amy and Ben had already walked down the aisle, and were almost outside. Everyone was on their feet, backs to me, shoving out of the pews, trying to get by one another in their efforts to hurry outside first. Father Richards cleared his throat, nodding out of the window. "Felix's father was a priest, too, you know?" he said.

"Really? I didn't think priests were allowed to get married and have families?" Which Fix's father obviously must have done.

Father Richards sighed. "Well. Things are a little laxer now. But back then, in the late seventies, when Felix's father decided to follow his calling, he was already married to Louisa, and Felix was...*hmm*. Two years old, I believe? If you were already married and you wanted to become a priest, exceptions were often made. If you were single before you were ordained, however, then you could expect to be celibate for the rest of your life."

"Sounds miserable."

"Actually, I'd say I've enjoyed my bachelor status. It's been rather...*peaceful*." Father Richards smiled sadly, his eyes taking on a distant stare. "I heard about what happened at Felix's church," he said quietly. "It was a horrific thing. When such terrible atrocities are committed in our communities, we feel responsible. We are protectors and shepherds, and when one of our flock is hurt, we feel the pain deeply.

"I didn't think Felix would leave us forever, though. He always was a wild child, but...I don't know. Maybe I'm wrong. Maybe I'm being selfish. The church is full of dusty, crabby old men, so blinded by years of routine and regulation that they can't find their own joy anymore. I suppose I just hoped Felix would come back to us, because....well, he was what *we* needed. More rebels to shake our foundations."

Father Richards left me standing there, staring out of the window, wondering what the hell he was talking about. Fix stared back at me, hands in his pockets, his face awash with pain, as if *he* knew what Father Richards had just said to me, and he really was still crippled by some unknown grief. I couldn't look away. Fix was broken and undone. He was light *and* he was darkness. And despite every warning bell in my mind that said otherwise, I couldn't shake the feeling that, while I knew he was danger personified...he might, just *might*, also be my safety, too.

18

SERA

SCANDAL

"*Y*ou look like..." Fix stepped back, scanning me from head to toe. He grimaced. "I don't like the color. I don't like the dress. Fuck. I don't like any of it. Only thing I like about it is the fact that it's so sheer."

"Why's that appealing? You can't see through it." Still, I curved my shoulders, rounding them in, just in case I was wrong and my boobs were currently on show for everyone to see.

"I like the fact that it's so thin, because I know you're not wearing any underwear. There'd be...*lines* or something. I'd be able to see your panties, and I don't see panties. Which means your pussy's completely naked under that thing right now and it's making me fucking hard."

Jesus wept. At least he was consistent. He hadn't let up since we'd met, using every opportunity he could to slide in an innuendo or a sexual pun into our conversations. But this...this was a little more direct. "My pussy's none of your business, Fix. Don't talk about it. Don't even think about it."

He'd found me back in our hotel room, where I'd briefly returned to plug in my cell phone. Fix was a leaner. Guaranteed, anything he could use to prop himself up with was going to be leaned against.

Right now, he was leaning against the TV cabinet, hands in his pockets, watching me as I rifled through my bag, looking for a charger.

"Aren't you going to ask me?" he said.

"Ask you what?"

"How it went with your father."

My hands stilled inside my purse. I'd known what he was referring to, but even mentioning that man's existence caused palpitations in my chest. "Did he leave?" I asked.

"Yes."

"Did he hurt you?"

Fix snorted. "*Please.*"

"Did *you* hurt *him*?"

"Uhhhh..."

"That's all I need to know." I pulled the cable out of my bag and plugged it into the wall. "We should go downstairs. Amy wants me in the photos."

"I'll get changed. I have a shirt I can wear—"

"Don't. You don't need to get changed."

A small, entertained smile. "You really don't want me in these photos, huh?"

"You're going to be gone from my life in a couple of days, Fix. Why *would* I want you in my sister's wedding photos? They're gonna be hanging over her gaudy ass fireplace for the rest of time. That's not the reason why I don't want you to change, though. I don't want you to change, because these people are all assholes, and I don't give a fuck what any of them think. Amy won't care what you're wearing. It's only Ben and his stuck up relatives, who can frankly go fuck themselves. Screw it." I'd been boiling over since the chapel, getting madder and madder about Ben's parents interfering, nearly ruining Amy's day by inviting Sixsmith here. They were snooty, miserable, belittling motherfuckers, and I wasn't going to bow and scrape in order to make a good impression with them. I loved Amy with all my heart, but I wouldn't change myself for her, or for anyone else.

Fix was right. The dress I was wearing *was* fucking hideous; I looked like a goddamn macaroon. Snatching some clean clothes, I headed for the bathroom.

"Don't lock yourself away in there on my account," Fix called after me. "I swear I won't peek."

"Yeah. Right. There's no way in hell I'm getting changed in front of you," I retorted. "I'm *not* wearing any underwear, after all." I really wasn't. He'd been perfectly right in his assumption, and the knowledge he was turned on by the idea of me in nothing but this monstrosity of a dress had affected me more than I thought it would. I slammed the bathroom door, tearing the dress over my head, and tried not to gasp in horror when I realized just how wet I was between my legs. Goddamnit. I wasn't ready to find myself embroiled in an attraction with another human being. A normal human being, who had a steady job, hobbies, was good to his family and friends. How the fuck had I found myself in this situation, becoming more and more attracted a guy who was never going to spell anything but trouble for me? Fix might not have been a priest anymore, but he was still in possession of the holy trinity: a killer smile; an ass you could bounce a quarter off; and a set of abs so perfectly defined that gazing upon them made you want to weep.

He wasn't just a man. He wasn't even of this planet, as far as I was concerned. He was either an alien, crash landed here from some distant galaxy, where *everyone* was unbelievably attractive, or he really was an angel, who, having fallen from grace and tumbled from heaven, was now living amongst us mere mortals, confusing us all with his surreal, otherworldly hyper-masculine beauty, and generally causing chaos and disruption wherever the fuck he went.

If I valued my sanity, I would get through this next few days, and I'd walk away from him. There was no future for us. I had to go back to work in Seattle, and Fix was constantly on the road, taking jobs, doing things that made my hair stand on end. I'd realized something, as Father Richards had been talking to me just now. I *wasn't* horrified by what I'd seen in that auto shop anymore. Yeah, I could have done without the imagery inside my head, but... Franz hadn't been sick. He hadn't acted out of some mental health issue that drove him to behave in depraved, cruel ways. He was just a fucked up, evil piece of shit that had liked hurting people. That was the end of it. Franz would never have stopped. He wouldn't have reformed, or suddenly not wanted to rape and torture young girls. I was never going to agree with what Fix had done, but...

He was right.

I wasn't afraid of him.

Not anymore.

I pulled on my own ripped jeans, shoved my feet inside my tan ankle boots, slid the black, silk cami over my head, and ruffled my hair out, ridding myself of all the pins and clips that the stylist had shoved in there. Looking in the mirror, I felt much better. I was me again. Weirdly, I realized I'd actually learned something from Fix. He was far from perfect—like a galaxy away from perfect—but he owned himself. He owned his actions. He didn't hide himself away. I'd been hiding myself away for so long now, trying to be something I wasn't, that I barely even recognized myself anymore.

How long had it been since I was happy? How long had it been since I'd felt comfortable in my own skin?

I blinked at the woman staring back at me in the bathroom mirror, and felt kind of sorry for her. She'd been lied to. She'd been promised that making a lot of money, and winning high profile clients would enrich her life. She'd been sold an idea—the idea of happiness—and that idea wasn't something that could be bought, or faked until it came to pass.

Happiness was a byproduct of embracing your own flaws, your insecurities, and your desires. I wasn't sure how to accomplish that, but it seemed, against all the odds, that Fix had.

~

*A*my didn't say a word about my change of clothes. She was probably so relieved that I'd taken care of the Sixsmith business that I could have come to the wedding reception wearing a hessian sack and she wouldn't have given a shit. The other members of the wedding party traded some pointed looks and raised eyebrows, though. I was uncomfortable for all of three seconds, thinking about rushing upstairs and getting changed back into the dress, but then I watched Fix grab a glass of champagne from a passing waitress and down the bubbling golden liquid, and I shed my nerves. It didn't matter what anyone else thought of me. It sure as fuck didn't matter what anyone else thought of Fix. I snagged my own glass of champagne, downed it, and shot Fix a grin.

"If we have to do this, we might as well get fucked up, right?"

He didn't give me his usual, wolfish smile, but I could see the wicked delight lurking behinds those silvery blue eyes of his. "I knew you were hot as fuck. I didn't know you were *fun*, Sera."

"Don't get carried away." I took another glass from a short, balding waiter, who grunted at me disapprovingly when I thanked him. "I just use alcohol as a crutch when I'm stressed or nervous."

"Can I get a Jack on the rocks please? A double?" Fix didn't even look at the waiter. He remained focused on me, the tip of his tongue running along his top row of teeth—the actions of a hungry man. Fuck, he looked like he was starving, and I knew he wasn't interested in the hors d'oeuvres that were floating around on trays. He was hungry for *me*.

"Why are you bothering with this?" I murmured.

"What do you mean?"

"Why are you bothering with any of this. You believed me when I said I'd keep my mouth shut about Franz. You *did*. So why bother driving me all the way out here? And why...why bother with the constant flirting? You're attractive, and you know it. You could have any woman who catches your eye. So why keep trying to wear *me* down?"

"You don't think you're worth my attention?" A muscle jumped in his jaw, and I couldn't stop staring at it. I'd tried to avoid looking at him for too long up until recently. If I did, I found myself transfixed on some small detail of him—the three, faint freckles under his jaw; the large, worn-smooth callouses on his palms, at the base of each of his fingers; the dark, short hair that twisted into a tiny whorl at the base of his neck—and I couldn't look away.

"This isn't about what I think. It's about what *you're* thinking, Fix. What's motivating you at this point? Because I've tried, and I can't figure you out. Not even a little."

Fix accepted the glass that was proffered to him by the waiter, drank some of the burnt amber liquid in the bottom of the highball, took a step toward me and lowered his head. "You're right. I know how I look. I've used my appearance to take whatever I've wanted, whenever I've wanted, for a long time now. But you're selling yourself short, Angel. You're fucking beautiful. Your body is so fucking distracting, I can't look at you without forcing myself not to stare at your tits. They're fucking perfection. Your nipples are..." His eyes rolled back into his head. "God, they're fucking amazing. I can't stop thinking about licking them. Teasing them between my teeth. Your ass is a goddamn gift from heaven. Doesn't matter what you're wearing. Jeans, a skirt, sweats...whatever. I'm constantly imagining that I'm behind you, in between your legs, holding you by the hips while I rail you from behind. Watching your ass bounce while I was fucking you like that was one of the most amazing, erotic, sexiest things I've ever fucking seen.

"Your eyes are full of fire," he continued. "They're clear and commanding. Every time you turn those things in my direction, it feels like I'm being speared to the floor. Normal people look *at* me. They see the surface of me, the appealing outer shell. They never delve any deeper. But you...your eyes probe and they search. It feels fucking *real* when you look at me. After thirty-seven years of being admired and coveted because of the way my genetics predetermined what my features would look like, it's refreshing to be fucking *seen*, Sera.

"I'm not stupid. I know you. You're not shallow enough to be won over by a good-looking guy with freaky eyes. I'm drawn to you, because you're brave. Your courage and spirit burn through you, even when you're scared. You don't back down. You were terrified of seeing your father today, but you didn't respond by running and hiding. You asked me for a gun, so you could threaten that motherfucker. That's not how normal people react. You want to know why I keep hitting on you, even though I know you're too smart to fall for my shit? It's because I think you're courageous, and unique in all the world. That's worth more than anything to me. I think you're remarkable, Sera."

My body had turned against me, and my palms had started to sweat. I'd expected him to...*shit*, I didn't know what I'd expected him to say. Maybe spin me some self-deprecating line about how he wasn't that good looking, or that he'd never do something so morally corrupt as use his looks to his own advantage. But he hadn't done that. Not even close. He'd told the truth, and then he'd said a number of things about my anatomy that made my cheeks burn with embarrassment. Could he really be so enthralled by my sheer stubbornness, and my refusal to let my fears overtake me, though? Could I really wrap my head around that?

Fix took another step toward me, stooping low over me, bending so that he didn't tower over me quite so badly. "There's something else..." he whispered. "One more reason why I'm so addicted to you, Sera Lafferty."

He could have used those eyes of his to hypnotize people. "What?" I said breathlessly.

"Your cunt, Sera. Your cunt is fucking magnificent."

Three feet away, an old woman dropped the side plate she'd been holding to the floor, sending a helping of shrimp cocktail flying in all directions. She gasped, hand pressed to her chest in horror, her mouth hanging open so wide that her jaw was almost resting on her voluptuous chest. She'd heard what Fix had said. Of course she had, because he hadn't lowered his voice in any way when he told me how great he thought my vagina was. He'd raised his voice, in fact, to the point where anyone within a ten feet radius of us heard his words with perfect clarity.

He was positively beaming with glee as he continued. "Your cunt is the prettiest thing I've ever seen. I love how you taste when you're wet. I love burying my face in between your legs and fucking devouring you. I love how pink and fucking delicious you are. I can't wait to slide my tongue inside you later. I'm going to fuck you with my tongue until I break you. You're going to be *begging* for my cock by the time I'm done with you."

Everyone had stopped talking. *Everyone.* Silence reigned supreme as I stood stock still, stunned, trying to comprehend what had just happened. Was he...? Did he really just...? *Oh...my...god.*

"I have never heard anything so disgraceful in all my life," the woman who'd dropped her plate muttered. She did exactly as Fix had, raising her voice, making sure she could be heard.

My immediate response was to bow my head and hide my shame. That's what I would have done a month ago. Fuck, it was what I would have done a week ago. But when I saw the challenge in Fix's eyes, I knew all too well that he was playing games with me. Issuing me with a challenge. Daring me to be as brave as he believed I was.

No one had moved. Everyone was still staring. Still horrified. I'd hoped at least one person would have started laughing, brushing it off as a joke, but it appeared I was out of luck. The judgmental bastards were all sneering down their noses at us, disapproving and disgusted.

Fuck 'em.

I tossed back the remainder of my champagne, and then I set the glass down on the table next to me. "Thank you, Felix. That's incredibly sweet. I'm one lucky, lucky girl. The way you eat my pussy makes me lose my freaking mind. It's a miracle I'm even capable of speech. But, honestly, all I want to do is tie you to the bed and fuck you with my tits. I love oiling them up and sliding your cock between them until you come. It's so fucking hot."

A waitress entered the room, carrying yet another tray filled with food. She stumbled to a halt when she saw the stunned looks on everyone's faces. I reached out and picked up a mini kabob, taking a bite out of it. I chewed a couple of times and swallowed. "You have no idea how insane it drives me, using both my hands on your huge cock, Felix. You get so fucking hard. And when I dip down and tease the tip with my tongue..."

I held out the kabob to Felix, flashing him a triumphant smile. I'd won. I'd accepted his challenge, and I'd beaten him. "Want some?" I asked.

He slowly shook his head, a dark, highly sexual energy vibrating from his body. He didn't need to speak; I knew I'd pleased him by playing along with his game. "No thank you, Sera," he said calmly. "The only finger food *I* want to eat tonight will be sucked clean from these,"—he held up his right hand, wiggling his fingers—"after I've made you come with them."

"Goodness! What on *earth* do you two think you're doing?" A tall man with tiny, round spectacles perched on the end of his nose shoved through the crowd, throwing down his napkin onto the drink's cart. He reminded me, weirdly, of Larry David. "Are you both sick or something? This is a Catholic wedding, not a...a...debauched night of sin at some sort of a...a...*sex club!*"

I burst out laughing. He'd put such a weird inflection on the words 'sex club.' His face had turned purple, and his cheeks were shaking with every word he spat out. I'd remembered who he was—Ben's old college professor—and the ridiculousness of the entire situation suddenly seemed hysterical to me. A number of scandalized hisses traveled through the reception party, but I didn't bother to seek out their outraged expressions. I was trapped, laughing so hard my stomach was hurting, and there was nothing I could do to stop myself. I was never going to stop laughing.

At least, I thought that was the case until...

*"WHO THE **FUCK** PISSED IN MY LAMBOGHINI?!"*

I stopped laughing, swiveling my head toward the entrance of the reception ballroom, and there, hands balled into fists at his side, cardigan half slipping off his shoulders, hair in disarray and sticking up in five different directions, stood Gareth Douvillier. I hadn't looked for him during the ceremony. I hadn't even thought about him. I'd been dreading seeing him here for weeks and weeks, and then, ironically, I'd forgotten all about him. He was fuming, his whole body visibly shaking, the tips of his ears bright crimson. Arianna tottered over to him in six-inch heels, cooing and murmuring, trying to soothe him, but Gareth pushed her away, grinding his teeth together. "I know it was you, you fucking prick. Marcosa! Where the *fuck* are you?!"

Marcosa? Gareth was accusing Fix of pissing in his car? Gareth had met Fix? I had no idea when that had taken place—Fix hadn't breathed a word about it—but clearly he'd made a lasting impression.

"Did you piss in Gareth's car?" I whispered, looking at Fix out of the corner of my eye.

"Yeah," he whispered back. "I kinda did. Maybe we should get out of here."

19

FIX

TEASE

*M*y phone was ringing. I was running, though, so I didn't have time to answer it. I held onto Sera's hand as we tore through the garden behind the hotel, breathing hard between bouts of laughter and trying to scream at one another. "You're fucking insane!" Sera yelled. "Why did you do that? Gareth's richer than god. He's going to press charges if you don't apologize."

"I'm not fucking apologizing to that prick. He deserved far worse, believe me."

"Why? What did he do?"

Ah, shit. I'd decided I wasn't going to tell her what Gareth had said this morning. I was going to keep the whole thing to myself. "He wasn't very nice. That's all."

"Fix." Sera stopped running and pulled her hand out of mine. "What did he say?"

"He said something about not cheating on you with Arianna. And that you had a lot of baggage."

"And what else? I know him. He wouldn't have stopped there."

"He said your father interfered with you when you were a kid."

"Wow." Sera's brows shot up in unison. "Don't sugar coat it, will you?"

"How else am I meant to say that?" I shrugged. "Would you prefer it if I hugged you? Stroked your hair and danced around it, cooing in your ear until I finally spat it out? *Sera, I'm so sorry... He said you and your father... Well...and I don't want to offend you, but... Everything's okay, I promise... This is a safe space, but... Gareth said your father might have...*" I took out my pack of smokes and lit one. "Which version's better?" I asked, gripping the cigarette between my teeth as I slid the pack into my back pocket.

Sera held out her hand. "Give me one of those."

"Why? You smoke all of a sudden?"

"Just give me one, asshole."

I gave her the cigarette I'd already lit. There was something so fucking sexy about watching her put her lips around the filter. Highly sexual. Sera exhaled a cloud of smoke, scowling at me. "Fair enough. You're right. I'd fucking hate it if you tried to baby me. I guess I'm just not used to people spitting it out like that."

I didn't ask her the question that was burning in the back of my mind: did her father actually do it? If she wanted to tell me, she'd tell me in her own time. Sera hadn't really offered up much about herself to me at all, and I wasn't one to wheedle information out of people unless they were willing to give it. I could blame hours spent sitting in a confessional booth for that. "Shoot from the hip, remember," I said, extending my fingers, gesturing that I wanted the smoke back. She returned it.

"Yeah. I should never be surprised by anything that comes out of your mouth, should I? Nothing's off limits. Nothing is sacred."

"That's not true. Plenty of things are sacred."

"Like my cunt?" She arched an eyebrow, and I couldn't stop myself; I laughed, blowing smoke down my nose.

"Yes. Your cunt is very sacred to me. If you'd only let me worship it some more, you'd make me a very happy man."

"Bullshit. You said all of that for show back there."

I grabbed her hand and walked her through a gap in a fence that looked like it marked the perimeter of the hotel gardens. The sun was still hanging above the horizon, about half an hour from setting, and it cast long fingers of burning golden light over the tall grasses that spread out like a thick carpet before us. A huge live oak to our right was the only tree for about a mile; in the distance, the forest that surrounded the hotel thrust up toward the sky—a loom of a thousand different greens, ranging from verdant and bright spring jade, to rich flashes of deep, Irish emerald. It was the first time I'd caught myself stopping to admire the beauty of nature in a very, *very* long time. The kind of people I dealt with on the regular made the world seem like a dark, corrupt, shitty place. I hadn't wanted to believe in beauty, hadn't wanted to see it, for the longest time, because it made all of the vile, awful things that happened out there behind closed doors, down badly lit side streets, and under railway passes all the more ugly. But with Sera standing next to me, in that moment, I couldn't deny how breathtaking the view was.

"I didn't say anything for show," I told her quietly. "It was all true. Now I'm going to take you over to that tree, Sera, and I'm going to make you ride my face until you come in my mouth. Any objections?"

"*Jesus.*" She flicked the cigarette, dropping it to the ground, grinding the butt beneath her heel. "You're never going to stop, are you?"

"No. Never. You were right. I did believe you when you said you'd keep my secrets. I knew it was doomed, that there was no chance we were going to go anywhere, but I was curious about you, Sera Lafferty. I wanted more time with you. It was fucked up and selfish, I know that. But I'm a fucked up, selfish guy. You've probably already figured that out. So, I won't keep you hostage anymore. You can let me drive you back to Seattle, and you can let all of this sink in a little. Or you can tell me to go fuck myself and I'll leave right now. Tonight. You won't ever see me again. It's all up to you, Sera. I'll abide by your wishes. But..." I turned, cupping her chin in my hand, lifting her head so that she was looking up at me. Her gaze was intense, stripping me bare. "I still want you to ride my fucking face," I growled. "I need to make you come one more time. I know you want me just as much as I want you. It's eating you alive inside. It's consuming you piece by piece. I'm your addiction, just as much as you're mine. I'm toxic for you. I know that. If I were a better man, I'd let you go. But I'm not. I'm fallen, lost, driven by revenge and hatred. I'll do whatever I can to keep you with me, and that includes fucking the sense right out of you until you can't think straight."

I waited for her to answer. If she looked away from me, I would know. The moment she sighed, or folded her arms across her body, or took a step away from me, she would have already told me what she wanted. But she didn't do any of those things. Her eyes were bright and conflicted. If she were anyone else, I'd take her, lift her into my arms, and I'd carry her over to that tree and fuck the shit out of her. She wasn't someone else, though. She was the woman with the defensive wounds on her hands. The jagged, deep line of purple scar tissue along her jaw. She was the warrior woman with the dents in her armor, her battles still raging, pain in her eyes, and I wouldn't make assumptions with her. I would wait. I would kneel at her goddamn feet until she told me she wanted me, and I wouldn't move an inch until then, regardless of how badly I wanted to claim her.

"You just told me you'd never baby me," she said softly. "I can see what you're thinking. I'm not broken. I'm not a bird with an injured wing. I have a past, and it's tricky, and it often visits me in my dreams, but I'm still kicking ass, Fix. So...if you want me, try and take me. I'll kick your ass if I don't want your hands on me."

"It'd be much easier if you just said yes," I rumbled.

She cocked her head to one side, her full lips bowing into a broad smile. "Would finding out for yourself not be worth a potential kick to the balls?" She was so damn sweet when she said it, but I could see it in her eyes—she'd knee me in the balls for sure, and wouldn't think twice about it.

My answer to her question was to bring my mouth crashing down on hers. I couldn't bear it anymore. Whatever happened, I needed to taste her. I needed to feel her tits crushed up against my chest. I needed her tongue in my mouth, and I needed her to make those panting, desperate little whimpering sounds when I slide my hand down inside her jeans and I rubbed my fingers over her clit in tight little circles.

Gathering her loose, wavy hair in my hands, I dug my fingers into the thickness of it, groaning. Sera froze for a moment. Time stretched out, driving me to madness as I waited to see what she would do. The moment she tried to shove me away, I would remove myself from her. I'd bind my own hands behind my back with sheer force of will alone, and I wouldn't touch her anymore. I was ready, willing and prepared to do that. Dipping my tongue into her mouth, Sera's lips parted a little wider, and then...

Fuck...

And then she was winding her arms around me, her hands sliding up my back, fingernails digging into my shoulder blades through my t-shirt. She kissed me back, her mouth pressing against mine, the sweet taste of her filling my senses, and a fire erupted inside me, raging through my veins. I'd done some stupid, messed up things as a teenager. I'd done equally stupid, reckless things after I'd thrown down my collar and walked right out of St. Luke's, but nothing in my life had ever gotten me as high as Sera Lafferty. She was the light that flowed in my veins. She was the oxygen in my lungs. She was the fuel that fired my heart.

I'd only been in her presence for forty-eight hours, but I'd known, the very first time I'd seen her...

Fuck.

It was too early to tell her how alive she made me feel, so I nursed the words I might have said to her in my chest, harboring them there, keeping them safe. There would come a time when I could part with them, but for now I was going to take her out of herself. I'd use every part of me to make *her* come alive, and when she was done screaming my fucking name, I'd thrust my cock into her and make her do it all over again. I wasn't going to hold back now. I wasn't going to handle her with kid gloves.

It was harder than it should have been to rip my mouth from hers and hurry her over to the oak. The tree's trunk was broad and thick, too wide for three people to link hands and wrap their arms around in a circle. I guided Sera so that her back was up against the tree, and then I slid down her body. She didn't move as I unfastened her jeans and tore them down her legs.

"God, Fix! Someone's going to see us!"

I looked up her body, a deep, animal need searing at me from the inside. "Do you really care?" I asked. "If those stuffy bastards catch sight of us, it'll probably be the most exciting thing that's happened to any of them in decades."

"Amy's going to kill me," she groaned, allowing her head to roll back to rest against the tree, too. I tugged her boots off her feet and threw them over my shoulders into the grass, one at a time, then removed her jeans entirely. Her panties were black silk, classy yet sexy. At either side, by her hips, I hooked my fingers beneath the sheer, sleek material, and I slowly shimmied them down her long, toned, beautiful legs.

"Fuck. Sera...if I'd met you five years ago...*shit*."

"You were...still a priest then," she panted.

"I was. And I would have broken every vow I'd made for you. I would have cast every belief I had aside. I would have abandoned my calling and run with you as far as I fucking could, and I never would have looked back. Not once. You're the ultimate game changer."

Sera parted her legs. She wasn't a shy little kitten anymore. She'd grown brave; she was a lioness now, giving demands, and I fucking loved it. Her pussy was smooth bar a thin strip of hair. I loved that, too. A shaved pussy was one of my biggest turn-ons, but not completely hair-free. That felt wrong, like I was sleeping with a prepubescent kid, and I was going to get sprung for statutory rape. Sera was all woman, though. She wasn't perfect. Her skin bore scars. Lots of them. Some were deep, and some shallow—mere hints at a history that intrigued and saddened me. In her flawed state, she *was* perfection, though. I didn't want a bubblegum princess who spent two hours every day curling her hair and was afraid of getting some fucking dirt under her nails. I wanted a woman who wasn't afraid to fight for what she wanted. I wanted a rough and tumble woman who wouldn't freeze if she felt threatened. I wanted strength, and I wanted fire, and I wanted passion, and Sera possessed all three in spades.

Dipping my head, I stroked my tongue over her bare pussy, and Sera shuddered. Her breathing was quickening by the second. She was sweet, and slick, and the moment I tasted her, I wanted to unbutton my own fly and start palming my cock, but my pants remained buttoned up. Didn't stop my dick from straining against the denim, demanding a way out. It wanted to be squeezed and sucked. It wanted to be pushed down Sera's throat, and holding back was going to cost me. *Holy fuck, down boy.* I bit back a frustrated groan, working my magic on Sera's clit, relishing how fucking wet she was, and how she shuddered every time I flicked her with the end of my tongue.

Her breathing was fast and uneven. Music to my fucking ears. Meant I was doing my job right, and she was starting to loosen up. Her hips rocked forward, legs parting even wider, giving me greater access to her, and I lost my shit.

Wrapping my arms around her, I grabbed her ass from behind and pulled her to me. Her pussy was mine. Every inch of her was mine. I wanted to inhale and consume every part of her, until she had no comprehension of what was real and what wasn't anymore.

Sera panted, winding her fingers into my hair.

Yes.

Fucking yes.

So. Fucking. Hot.

When she started pulling and tugging on my hair, I nearly swept her off her feet and slammed her into the grass there and then, so I could thrust myself inside her.

Innocent girls were all well and good. Sometimes, dominating a woman in bed felt great, and was the only way I could fucking come, but not with Sera. I didn't want to dominate her. I wanted to be her equal. I wanted her to let me know what she wanted. When she tightened her grip on my hair, rocking her hips against my mouth, I took the hint: she wanted more.

So I fucking gave her more.

I gave her my tongue inside her pussy. I licked and laved at her expertly, and I didn't stop when she began to shiver with the beginnings of an orgasm. I gave her my fingers, pumping them inside her, teasing her g-spot as I sucked gently at her clit, and when her knees buckled out from underneath her and she couldn't stand upright anymore, I gave her three seconds to recover herself before I laid her down and started all over again.

"Jesus, Fix! Oh my god!' Her eyelids fluttered like crazy as she rocked herself against my face. "You're...you're going to make me come," she gasped.

Was I ready for her to come? Nope. No fucking way. Just as she was about to tumble over the edge, her fingers clawing at my back, scratching the material of my t-shirt, I stopped.

"Oh my god," Sera hissed. Her back was arched, head tilted back, her tits straining against the ACDC shirt she was wearing—easily the most arousing thing I'd ever seen. I prowled up the length of her body slowly, enjoying the view as she writhed and twisted beneath me. My dick was throbbing in my pants, almost painful now. I was so fucking hard. Sera wasn't going to know what the fuck had hit her when I finally unleashed myself on her.

"Open your eyes," I commanded. Using my right hand, I held her lightly at the base of her throat—I wasn't going to cut off her air supply. That would be fucking stupid, considering she was a likely victim of abuse, so I just held my hand there, waiting for her to respond. She obeyed my command, her eyelids flickering open to reveal those, warm, deep eyes that I'd become so besotted with.

"*Tease*," she whispered. Her lips were plump and swollen, a darker, more sensual red than normal. I took her bottom lip between my teeth and I tugged, pulling at it, just enough that the pressure would sting a little.

"I haven't even shown you the meaning of the word. I will, though, Sera. You don't need to worry about that. I'm going to drive you to insanity. First, I need you naked. I need your skin on my skin, and I need it fucking now." I grabbed the hem of her shirt, pulling it up over her head. Her bra—pretty, lacey, also black—went next.

The moment her bare tits were exposed, bouncing as I tore away her clothes, all common sense vanished. My ears started buzzing, high-pitched like tinnitus. "*Jesus...fucking...wept, Sera.*"

Even lying on her back, her breasts were perky and full, her skin pale and creamy, like fine porcelain. My hands literally hurt—the prospect of *not* touching them was so traumatic that my skin buzzed with anticipation. Cupping her in both hands, I had to breathe deeply for a second. Control. I needed control. Fuck, no amount of will power in the world was going to hold me back now.

"I'm gonna get naked now, Sera," I gritted out through my teeth. "I'm gonna do all the things I've been fantasizing about doing to you, and I swear to everything holy that you're gonna fucking like it. You're gonna come all over my cock. You're gonna shake and moan, and your head's gonna fucking spin, and I'm going to fucking adore it. Are you ready?"

She trembled, like her whole world was already shaking, being turned upside down, but her eyes were clear when she met my gaze and said, "Yes, Fix. I'm ready for you."

～

SERA

I'd never been so wet in my entire life. Everywhere Fix touched me, his fingers and his mouth left a trail of fire in their wake. I'd given up reminding myself how stupid this was, and I'd succumbed to inevitability. That's what this had been, from the beginning: inevitable. The draw between Fix and I was wild and confusing. I was never going to understand why I couldn't seem to shake myself of this need for him, so... what was the point in even trying? I'd known for a while I was going to end up back here with him, entwined with him, losing myself in him again, and it felt divine. I'd surrendered myself to him, and the relief I experienced when I had done so was monumental.

"Yes, Fix. I'm ready for you." I breathed the words out, and I realized that I didn't just mean right now, here, naked in this field. I meant that I was *ready* for him. All of him. His wicked tongue. His quicksilver eyes. His dark past. He was Pandora's box, and I knew opening him was a bad idea. I wanted to know his secrets, though. I wanted to learn everything about him. I was willing to accept the risk that getting to know him properly would inexorably pose.

What kind of person took stock of a person like Fix and decided they wanted them in their lives? Who was I becoming? I didn't know anymore, and that scared the shit out of me. All I knew was that Fix stirred such powerful, demanding desires within me, and I was helpless to fight them. We were a catastrophe waiting to happen, and I was walking into it with my eyes open. To hell with the consequences.

Fix had been hovering over me, picking me apart with forensic intensity. The muscles in his shoulders and his arms strained as he rocked himself backward, sitting on his heels first, and then rising to his feet. "Look at me," he commanded. "Look at my body. Look how much I fucking want you, Sera." His t-shirt came off first, swiftly followed by his shoes, socks and jeans. He didn't have to remove his boxers, because he wasn't wearing any. His cock sprang free, and I did as I was told—I witnessed just how badly Fix wanted to be inside me. He was rock solid and swollen. Fucking magnificent. Shit.

Shit, shit, shit!

I really must have drunk a lot the other night in the motel; the tequila sloshing around my system must have dulled my reaction when I'd seen Fix's cock for the first time, but now I was clearheaded, and my immediate response was to close my legs. He was fucking *huge*. Not just in length, but in girth, too. Penises weren't attractive to me in an aesthetic way, but Fix was kind of astonishing. If he put that thing inside me...

If he was rough with me, he was going to split me in two.

"Don't look so frightened," Fix murmured. He took his dick in his hand, squeezing the end, but he didn't move his fist up and down his length. "I know what I'm doing. I made you feel fucking amazing last time, didn't I?"

Swallowing, I nodded. "Yeah. But...*fuck*, Fix..."

A ruinous, wretched smile transformed his face. God, he was so sexy when he was so obviously thinking sordid thoughts. "Fuck is right," he said. "Don't move. Don't breathe. Just get on your knees and open your goddamn mouth."

My pussy tightened, an unbelievable wave of pleasure, feather-light, skating its way up my spine. I didn't even know my body could react like that to mere words. It seemed Fix's dirty mouth had a way of coaxing the darkness out in me. I got up onto my knees, my heart skipping all over the place like a needle jumping over a broken record. His cock was going in my mouth. He'd driven me to the edge of distraction with his tongue, and now it was my turn to return the favor. More than anything, I wanted to make him feel good. I wanted to make him quake and shiver, and to bring him to *his* fucking knees.

I'd do it. I'd make him fucking sweat.

I opened my mouth and Fix gathered my hair, sweeping it back over one shoulder. He cupped my face in his hand, stroking the pad of his thumb over the line of my cheekbone. "You're fucking *mine*," he groaned. "You don't need to worry anymore. You're safe. I won't let anyone hurt you. I'll fucking flay the skin off anyone who tries to lay a finger on you."

It made no sense, but his words made me feel secure. Protected. Relieved. Fuck, how long had I felt like I was still running from something? I'd left Sixsmith in my rear-view nearly a decade ago, but there had always been an ominous dark cloud hanging over me. Fix blew that cloud right out of the sky.

He squeezed his dick, his hand slipping around to the base of my neck, guiding my head forward. I closed my mouth around the end of his cock, blowing a deep breath down my nose, and then slid him inside...

"*Holy fucking shit!*"

Looking up, I saw Fix's head fall back, every single muscle in his chest, his stomach, his arms and his neck straining. He was indescribable. I just...I couldn't even find the words to do him justice. His body was packed muscle, not a scrap of fat on him. I couldn't take my eyes off him.

I teased my tongue around the head of his cock, sucking, sliding him further and further into my mouth, and Fix let out a deep, agonized, rumble. "Sera... Sera, shit! Your mouth... *Fuck!*"

I'd done my fair share of writhing and cursing under Fix's ministrations, so to hear him do the same was rewarding. He reached down, palming one of my breasts, rolling my nipple, pinching it hard enough to make me whimper, and my reaction seemed to send him barreling toward the gates of madness.

"Fuck! Open your mouth, Sera. Take all of it. Take me deep. I want to feel the back of your throat while I fuck your mouth."

I could barely breathe as he slid himself further past my lips. His hands were in my hair, tugging, not hard enough to cause pain, but hard enough to let me know he was in charge right now. I closed my eyes, wrapping my hand around his shaft, applying pressure to the base of his cock, too, and Fix roared. The sound echoed across the field, startling birds from their trees in the distant forest.

"Get on your back," Fix ordered. "Open your legs for me. Show me your pussy. Show me your ass. I want to see it all." He withdrew his cock from my mouth, and when I looked up, I saw the molten mercury of his eyes had hardened to sharp-edged steel. He was already imagining what it was going to feel like to fuck me. There was no doubting him, or how badly he needed me, but when I sank back into the grass, spreading my legs for him just as he'd told me to, he didn't fall on top of me and take me right away. He sat back, hands by his sides, chest heaving, his cock still wet and glistening from my mouth, staring down at me with a level of appreciation that made me want to run and hide.

"You're not real," he whispered. "You can't be."

"I'm as real as you," I answered breathlessly.

Fix swallowed. Carefully, he reached out, stroking his fingers over my pussy, sliding his index and his middle finger inside me. "If that's the case, then fine. Neither one of us is real. Let's be fucking make-believe together."

He pumped his fingers inside me, slowly at first, as he positioned himself over me, supporting himself on just one hand. His mouth was on mine, his dark hair falling into my face as he kissed me, claiming me with his tongue, probing and exploring. He quickened his pace, then, working his fingers faster, grunting as I bucked and arched against him.

"You gonna come all over my fingers, Sera?" he growled into my ears.

"Ahh! Shit! Yes! Yes, I'm going to come!"

My vision turned white. Completely and utterly white, which was strange since I had my eyes closed. The muscles in my calves cramped like crazy as my climax tore through me like an unstoppable freight train.

"Yeah. Yeah, that's it." Fix held onto me, kissing my neck, my collarbone, my shoulder... He kissed me everywhere as I came, still thrusting his fingers inside me, until eventually I fell slack on the ground.

I was boneless and limp as Fix sat up, running a finger down my body, between my breasts, between my legs, making my skin break out into the goose bumps.

"I meant it, Angel," he said slowly, his voice thick with lust. "The only finger food I wanted today..." Oh, god. I'd offered him a bite of that stupid kabob back in the ballroom, and he'd made a comment about licking his fingers clean after I'd come all over them. I couldn't find my voice quick enough to object as Fix slid his fingers into his mouth, sucking on them.

Oh...my...god...

He was so fucking hot, I just couldn't handle it anymore. "Please... Fix, *please*. I need you to fuck me. I want to feel you inside me. I want your cock." I'd never pleaded with anyone before. I sure as shit hadn't begged anyone for their *dick*, but Fix had a weird, profound, irrefutable effect on me; I did it without thinking.

A merciless, knowing laugh teased at my ear; Fix shoved my legs apart again, sinking between them. "Hold onto me, then," he whispered. "Don't let go. I'm about to give you what you need."

And he did. I gasped as he drove himself into me, digging my fingers into his back. I couldn't cry out. I couldn't even breathe. For a second, all I could do was lie absolutely still as Felix Marcosa thrust his cock inside me. I was so full. His body, so much bigger than mine, enveloped me, and I was lost. With his arms around me, his mouth pressing down on mine, my breath mixing with his, hot and insistent, I ceased to exist. I broke apart, down to what felt like a molecular level, ready to drift away on the slight breeze that caressed our naked bodies.

This was so different to the motel room back in Liberty Fields. It was so much *more*. There was still so much for us to learn from one another, but this felt honest. Raw. Perfect. I clung to Fix as he fucked me, and I melted into him. His cock grew harder and harder every time he rocked his hips, driving himself deep inside me, and soon I was drowning in him, my senses overloaded, my heart racing away from me, my head spinning on its axis.

"Fix, I'm...I'm going to come. Oh, god..."

"Do it," he snarled. "I want to feel it coursing through your body. I want to feel your pussy tighten around my cock when it takes you. Come for me, Sera. Come right now."

I didn't need a second invitation. The orgasm was an explosion; it went off inside my head and between my legs at the same time. I clawed at Fix's shoulders, desperate to get closer to him as an incomprehensible surge of pure ecstasy swept through every cell in my body. "Fuck! Oh, fuck!"

Fix buried his face into the crook of my neck, groaning deeply, fighting with his breath as he slammed himself into me, over and over again. He came just as hard as me.

And when he came, the sound of his savage cry echoed so loudly that even the stars, tiny pinpricks of flickering light, just beginning to appear in the darkening sky overhead, seemed to tremble and shake.

20

SERA

CRIMINAL MISCHIEF IN THE THIRD DEGREE

*I*t was inexplicable, really. I'd been dreading this wedding for months, and yet, through a series of weird, fucked up, very disturbing events, I'd ended up actually enjoying some of it.

Gareth was still prowling around the lobby, searching for Fix, when we snuck back into the hotel. We slipped in through an open side door, hoping to avoid the reception, which was still in full swing, if you could call dull conversation over quiet classical music full swing. Gareth spied us, bee-lining straight for us, his index finger already extended in a very accusatory manner, mouth pulled down at the corners in a furious grimace.

We fast-walked in the direction of the stairs, but he intercepted us, cutting us off at the pass. "Do you have any idea what kind of penalty willful destruction of property carries in this state, asshole?" he snapped at Fix.

Fix grinned at him. "Nope. Don't care."

"It's classified as criminal mischief in the third degree, you fucker."

"Sounds scary."

"You're going to jail for six months at least!" Gareth spat the words, a giant vein throbbing in his neck, his face a frightening shade of crimson, and I couldn't leash the surge of laughter that burst out of my mouth.

"Do you have any proof that Fix pissed in your car, Gareth?"

"I don't need proof. The bastard hasn't denied it!"

I turned to Fix. "Felix, did you urinate in this fine gentleman's vehicle?"

"Me? Lord, no. I'd never do such a thing."

Somehow, both of us had adopted British accents, which made absolutely no sense, and only made it harder to keep a straight face.

"You think this is funny? You're going to regret fucking with me, Marcosa. I promise you that. And you!" Gareth stabbed his index finger into my shoulder. "You're fucking *insane*. I shouldn't be surprised that you'd bring a guy like this to Amy's wedding. You're damaged goods. I dodged a fucking bullet when I—" He was moving to jab me with his finger again, but Fix moved like lightning, snatching hold of his index, stepping between us.

"Should I let him apologize?" Fix ground out. His voice was layered with anger, so deep it made my heart stutter.

"Gareth never was very good at apologies," I said softly. It was the truth. Even after I'd walked in on him fucking that blond in his office, he hadn't once said he was sorry. He'd blamed me for not holding his attention. He'd said it was my fault for not making an effort to be more interesting.

"Got it." Fix's hand snapped back in a flash, and something else snapped right along with it...

Gareth's finger.

His howl tore through the hotel lobby, yet no one came running to find out what was wrong. Not even Arianna. "You ever touch her again, I won't just break your remaining fingers. I'll break your fucking dick in two, and I'll feed it to the dogs. Now disappear. Right fucking now."

Gareth's anger shone out of his eyes like twin beams of pure hatred. "You're gonna—"

Fix took another step forward, and Gareth shut the hell up. He held his hand to his chest, clutching at it, backing away. He turned and stormed back into the wedding reception, hollering for Arianna at the top of his lungs, and I watched him go without the slightest flicker of remorse. Fix wouldn't have done a thing if I'd asked him to stand down, but the humiliation and the embarrassment Gareth had put me through last year, not to mention the heartache...

I'd thought I loved him. I'd thought he and I were going to be together forever. I shivered out of that thought, thanking my lucky stars. Whatever Gareth said, it was *me* who'd actually dodged the bullet. "We'd better get the hell out of here," I said. "Amy's probably drunk by now. I don't want her to try and murder me the next time I see her, though."

"I haven't even met her yet," Fix mused.

"You can come to her second wedding in a couple of years," I told him. "This one's bound to fail." I attempted to head up the stairs, but Fix took hold of me by the wrist. He pressed something into my hand: a crumpled yellow valet ticket.

"Why don't you give this to the bellman and have him get the truck? I can grab our bags and be down here in a couple of minutes."

"Sure." I'd already tidied my stuff away into my rolling suitcase this morning, so there was nothing laying out that he'd have to tidy away for me. Fix took the stairs three at a time, disappearing around the sweeping staircase. Moments later, I was sitting in the passenger seat of Fix's truck, battling with my conscience. I couldn't just leave without saying anything to Amy. She'd be hurt. Worse, she'd be angry, which was understandable given that Fix and I had distressed a number of her wedding guests with our profane conversation, Fix had potentially ruined some leather car interior, we'd vanished to fuck in a field, and then Fix had broken someone's finger.

When I thought about it, Amy was going to be furious no matter what. But if I didn't even leave her a note or something before bailing? God, she'd skin me alive. I needed a pen and paper. I could go back into the lobby, but then I risked seeing Gareth again, and that wasn't something I could deal with. Fix probably had something I could write on. There was bound to be some paper in here somewhere. I tried the glove box, expecting it to be locked, but the drawer dropped down, and I was rewarded with a multitude of papers and receipts stuffed inside. Perfect. Better to use an empty envelope. Those things always ended up floating around people's cars for ages before they got thrown out. Grabbing the first envelope I laid my hand on, I went about searching for a pen, but couldn't—

Wait.

I cocked my head, looking down at the brown envelope that was now resting in my lap. It had been folded in two to fit inside the glove box, but it had opened out once I'd removed it. There, on the front of the envelope, written in thick, black sharpie, was a name.

My name.

Sera Lafferty.

Why was my name written on the envelope? What...what possible reason could Fix have for keeping an envelope with my name on it in his glove box? A thousand frantic thoughts collided in my head at once.

Oh...

Oh, *shit*.

These were the contingency plans he'd made after I'd watched him kill Franz? It was the only thing that made sense. He'd created a dossier on me in case he thought I'd changed my mind and I was going to go to the police. My blood was like ice, pumping slowly through my heart, gradually freezing me bit by bit. With shaking, unsteady hands, I untucked the envelope's flap and I took out the papers inside.

My brain ceased to function.

What was I looking at? It made no sense. These weren't contingency plans at all. At least not contingency plans made because of what I'd seen go down in that auto shop. There were photos of me, at least eight of them, none of them really recent. Candid stills of me getting into my car, leaving the office. Me, out running through the park three blocks from my apartment. Me, out to lunch with my Sadie. More and more of them, all taken without my knowledge. What did this mean? Why the hell would Fix have shots of me like this lying around in his car? My panic levels rose dramatically as I put the photos aside and picked up a sheaf of paper. On it, a complete breakdown of my daily routine back in Seattle. The following sheet was a copy of the detailed itinerary I'd created for my road trip to the wedding—the one I'd emailed to Amy, letting her know exactly how long I'd be on the road, where I'd be stopping, and for how long.

The very last sheet of paper was a photocopy of a yellowed document marked with a coffee ring. My birth certificate, bearing my full name: *Seraphim Alicia Rose Lafferty*. A shockwave detonated in my head as I scanned the document; ever since I'd run into Fix, he'd used a pet name with me. He'd called me Angel, over and over again, and it had seemed like a coincidence. Such a weird, fluke of a thing. My mother hadn't been religious, but she'd liked the idea of guardian angels, watching over us, keeping us all safe. She'd called me Seraphim because she'd thought it sounded pretty, but I'd hated it. I'd shortened it as soon as I could legally fill out the paperwork, and all of my ID, my credit cards, everything...it had all been changed to Sera.

It was all so clear now. His nickname for me hadn't been a coincidence at all. *This* was why Fix had started calling me Angel. Because he'd done his research on me, just like he'd done his research on Franz Halford. The photos Fix had shown me of Franz's victim had come straight out of a brown envelope, identical to the one I was holding in my hands.

God.

Oh...oh my god.

My pulse was a raging, demented, thundering drumbeat. My vision had tilted, and I could no longer see straight. I knew what this meant now. I knew, and I was too surprised to run. I was too surprised to do anything but sit there with the evidence all over my lap as I tried not to pass out. I knew the driver's side door opened, and I knew Fix climbed into the car, but I was too numb to process the information. I just...*what?* What the fuck had just happened?

I turned, swiveling the entire top half of my body so that I was facing Fix. I held up one of the photos—a particularly nice shot of me laughing, walking with Sadie down a busy street—and the smile slipped from Fix's face. His whole demeanor changed in the blink of an eye.

"Who?" I demanded. "You owe me that much at least." My voice was rough, broken, shattered... and my entire world right along with it.

I could tell by the expression on his face.

It was real.

It was true.

It was more than I could bear.

"Who the fuck hired you to kill me, Fix?!"

PROLOGUE

SERA

"*I'm not interested in excuses. I'm not interested in playing games. I'm only interested in your pussy. Now pull down your panties for me, Angel. I'm gonna make you fucking come.*"

I gasped as Fix slipped his hand up my skirt and took hold of my underwear, tugging on them insistently. He didn't give me the opportunity to obey him. The sound of ripping lace filled the car, alongside Fix's ragged, lust-filled breathing.

His hands were all over me. Pulled over at the side of the road, the truck was alone in the darkness. We'd been driving for hours, the journey made that much longer by the fact that we'd been stopping every hundred miles or so to claim each other, our mouths hot and demanding on each other's skin, our nails digging into each other's skin, our bodies permanently soaked in a thin layer of sweat and sex.

"I'm going to stick my cock inside this tight little pussy, Sera." Fix groaned into my mouth, and I saw stars. Fuck. It was never meant to be like this. Sex was designed for enjoyment, the ultimate, most intimate plea-

sure that could be shared between two people. But this was more than sex. This was an unfathomable need that broke boundaries and smashed through walls, and I was incapable of walking away from it. I kept drinking Fix in, drinking long and drinking deep, but I could never slake my body's constant thirst for him. And from the way he couldn't bear to remove his hands from my skin, always stroking and caressing, touching and teasing, it was clear he felt the same way about me.

The cab of the truck was spacious—enough room for me to angle my body toward Fix. He grabbed me by the hips, hands working quickly, and he lifted me up from the seat, then he was shoving my skirt up over my hips and tearing at the sheer, ruined fabric of my panties. He held the scrap of lace up to his nose and breathed in deep. "Fuck, you smell so good," he groaned. "I want to eat your cunt. I want to lick you every goddamn hour of the day. I want to live off your come and your sweat, Sera. Give it to me. I want to coat my tongue with you."

It was a miracle I was even able to sweat at all at this point. We'd stopped for food and huge bottles of water, trying to fuel ourselves and rehydrate, but an hour later, panting and breathless, we were both exhausted, ravenous and thirsty again. I bit down on my bottom lip, my hands working at the buttons on my shirt.

"You're taking way too long." Fix took hold of the shirt and ripped it open, sending buttons flying.

"Hey!"

"You really give a shit about your shirt right now?" he snarled. "I won't wait. I'm going to have you. Right fucking now. And if I destroy every single item of clothing you own before we arrive in Virginia, then I won't be sorry. I'll be fucking glad. I'm going to keep you naked for the rest of fucking time," he said, his voice colored with impatience. He tore the shirt from me, and then he yanked down the cups of my bra, exposing my breasts. "My dick just went from wood to fucking steel, Sera. Your nipples are mind-blowing." He dipped down, planting a hand on the seat beside me to support himself. With his other hand, he cupped and kneaded at my bare breast, digging his fingers into my flesh. "You want me to suck them?" he whispered. It wasn't a real question. He knew I wanted his mouth on my breasts. He knew how the searing, wet heat of his tongue circling and *flicking at the tightened, swollen bud of my nipples sent me certifiably insane. He wanted me to pant for him, though. He wanted my pussy wet. He wanted me clawing at the upholstery inside the truck, begging him to satisfy me.*

"Yes." *My voice cracked as I made my confession.* "I want it. I want you to bite them. Please." *I gasped, crying out as he fell upon me, his teeth grazing the soft, sensitive fullness of my breasts. He was so good at that—a master manipulator with his tongue. He had me quaking and shaking instantaneously, my whole body coming apart beneath his highly talented mouth.*

He was so much to handle. So much to take in. Pure fucking sex. His dark hair was ruffled, standing up at all angles as I grabbed hold of it, winding my fingers through it, and I held him against me, whispering into the crown of his head. "Harder. Bite harder."

He gave me what I wanted. He gave me what my body was crying out for, and I couldn't fucking take it. The pain when he bit down on my nipple was heady and blinding. Heat blossomed between my legs, slow burning and penetrating, and I could feel the slickness there, pooling between my thighs. I wasn't just wet; I was soaking. Fix moved to the other breast, lavishing the same attention on my other nipple, and I all but screamed as another frisson of sharp pain fired in a relay around my body.

"Please! Please! Fix. Oh my god."

"Please what, Angel?" *he asked.* "Please rub your clit with my fingers? Please make you come? Make you squirt? Make you feel like you're about to explode?"

"Yes! Yes! Fuck."

Fix's mouth tilted up at one side—a trademark dash of arrogance that I was growing more and more accustomed to. Every time his lips curved up like that, the deep dimple forming in his cheek, my body responded in kind, as if I'd been conditioned to crumble and surrender myself to him whenever I saw the expression. My eyes rolled back into my head as he stooped down and he kissed my neck. His dark, rough stubble scraped lightly at my skin, and I couldn't suppress the breathless moan that escaped my lips.

"Or please take your clothes off, Fix?" *he purred.* "Please let me see you?

Please let me take you in my mouth? Please make my cunt ache with need as you fill me with your cock?"

With each dirty, nasty word that came out of his mouth, I felt myself succumbing to him. I'd tried to resist. I'd done everything I could to hold myself back, to be as cautious as possible. But it would only be so long, before I was irrevocably, undeniably his.

I couldn't even form the shape of words in my mouth.

"Don't hold it in," Fix growled, as he pushed his fingers inside me. "I want to hear you, Angel. I want to hear every last little whimper and moan as you tighten around me." He pumped his fingers, stroking them inside me, hitting my pleasure center with ease. No guy had ever hit my g-spot before. Gareth had firmly argued that the female g-spot didn't even exist. But Fix knew exactly where mine was, and he was determined to put it to good use.

"That's it. That's it, beautiful girl." He held me tightly in place with his free arm as he used his other hand to coax me into madness. "Come for me. That's it. Good girl. Good girl."

When I came, unspeakable ecstasy rushing in at me from all sides, claiming the attention of every nerve ending in my body, I didn't hold back the cry that built up at the back of my throat. I released it, and my climax soared, lifting me, lifting me out of my body, higher, higher, higher...

Fix unbuckled his belt with one hand, and then unfastened his jeans. His jaw was set, his eyes flashing like molten steel as he continued to work his fingers slowly, deliciously inside me. "I'm going to take you. You're mine. You're fucking mine, do you hear me?"

"Yes. I'm yours. I am. I—"

My eyes snapped open, and the sudden, unexpected motion of the truck made me grab hold of the seat beneath me. My heart was racing. My brow was damp. The shirt that Fix had just ripped off me was back on my body, right along with my skirt and my panties. And Fix wasn't kneeling over me, massaging me as I rode out the final waves of my orgasm. He was in the driver's seat, his hands firmly grasped on the steering wheel. He hadn't noticed me waking. Or if he had, he was pretending that he hadn't.

Fuck.

Fuck.

I closed my eyes, slowing my breathing, my fingers digging into the leather seat underneath me. What the fuck was *that*?

The hottest dream I'd ever had? The most confusing, hurtful dream? The past few days came rushing back at me with the most frightening urgency, and a kernel of fear sprouted in the pit of my stomach. I'd just had a sex dream. About the man sitting beside me. The man who'd been paid to kill me, and who might be driving me to my death even now.

I shouldn't have been surprised. I knew I was kind of fucked up. This wasn't the first time I'd found myself trouble. There had been plenty of other terrible, dangerous situations—situations most normal people would never understand, because they'd never had to go through it. I'd been beaten and abused, and I'd been robbed of all that was good in me. And here I was, yet again, neck deep in the shit, but this time it didn't seem as though there would be a way out.

I hated myself for the images that had just bullied their way into my subconscious. But a part of me—the largest, smartest part—knew the truth. Those images hadn't forced their way into my subconscious. They'd forced their way *out*. Fix was ingrained inside me, down to the very roots, and it didn't matter that he had been given money to take my life from me. It didn't matter that he was a murderer and had the blood of countless people on his hands.

I'd wanted him.

I still wanted him.

I was the most foolish girl in the world.

21

FIX

BUTCHER'S MOUNTAIN

*T*here were stars piercing through the windshield, brilliant and blinding. The glass was dirty, streaked with mud and a thick layer of burned yellow pollen that had gathered overnight while the truck had been parked underneath a bank of trees. The windshield wipers groaned as they went to work, swinging maniacally back and forth, but they had little to no effect. If anything, they smeared the glass even further, making it almost impossible to see the pot-holed road that stretched out ahead of the truck, winding up the side of the mountain like the looped coils of a snake.

Butcher's Mountain: that was the name of the giant, vertical shadow that loomed in the darkness up ahead. It was owned by the Pamunkey Indians, but even they didn't come up here. The place was either considered sacred or haunted, I couldn't remember which. All I knew was that the lone mountain, punching upward beyond a curve in the broad Pamunkey River, was deserted, and there was no chance of being disturbed. The night had closed in three hours ago, and Sera hadn't said a word. Her face was pale, her hands gathered in her lap, underneath which sat a brown envelope containing the case information Monica had sent through to me—information about Sera. I should have thrown out the envelope. It had only been a matter of time before Sera found it and freaked out, and that's exactly what had happened. She'd wheeled on me in that parking lot in Alabama, demanded to know who had hired me to kill her, and when I'd refused to answer her, telling her we needed to sit down and discuss it like level-headed adults, she'd clamped her mouth shut and hadn't said a word to me since.

That was ten hours ago. More like a lifetime ago. My mind had run a marathon since then, and I still couldn't stop it from racing. Sera hadn't even tried to escape the truck. She'd been so still for so long now, that I kept wondering if she was still breathing. She barely blinked.

I'd used the cabin at the summit of Butcher's Mountain a couple of times before when I'd driven cross-country. It had been left to the church back when my father had still been priest at St. Luke's, by a member of the congregation who had passed away. The woman (whose grandfather had been gifted the cabin and surrounding woodland on the side of the mountain by the Pamunkey Indians in 1897) had no family to speak of, and so she had bequeathed her holdings and possessions to St. Luke's.

The church had tried to sell the land. However, since it was surrounded by Pamunkey land, planning permits were impossible to come by and new structures couldn't be built, and the Pamunkey weren't too happy about the idea of the mountain being disturbed. Whenever a real estate agent came out to the property to place a 'for sale' sign, the board was gone by the time they'd reached the bottom of the mountain. Not that anybody would have ever seen it.

It was too far from New York to use as a retreat base for youth camps, and far too small besides, so it had been forgotten about. *I* hadn't forgotten the place, though. When I left the church, I'd made sure to grab the paperwork for the cabin, as well as the key, and that was that. As far as anyone else was concerned, this place didn't exist. It was a handy base whenever I was on the road. I came out here to clear my head on occasion, mostly after a messy job set my mind reeling. I liked the solitude.

Thirty minutes passed by, and I drove through the darkness,

chewing on the inside of my cheek. This was fucked. This was so, so fucked. When I eventually reached the narrow dirt track that signaled the turn off to the cabin, I was ready to start fucking smashing my fist into things.

Sera didn't react at all as I pulled up in front of the small, run down log cabin and I shut off power to the truck. I knew what she was thinking. What she'd been thinking ever since I locked the truck doors and we sped away from that hotel in Fairhope. She thought I was going to complete the job I'd accepted, and I was going to kill her. I could have told her that her worries were unfounded, but she wouldn't have listened to me. Not right now. There were too many worries spiraling around inside her head, and she couldn't be blamed for that. It was selfish of me to refuse to talk to her about this until we stopped for the night. I knew that. But if I had to be selfish, then so fucking be it. I needed her to be calm, and I needed her to look me in the eye, and I needed her to *hear* me.

"Do I have to carry you inside?" I finally growled. "Because I will."

A sharp look formed on Sera's face, her eyes narrowing—the first emotion she'd shown in hours. I was glad of the display, even if it was anger. "You won't. You won't touch me. You won't come near me, Felix Marcosa. You do *not* have my permission."

"Okay. Then I'll see you inside when you're ready." I took the keys out of the ignition, and I climbed out of the car, slamming the door behind me. Sera's door opened just as I fished the key for the cabin out of the rusting metal pale that sat on the top step of the porch.

"Aren't you worried I'll run? If you leave me out here, I could just head back to the road and wait for someone to pick me up, y'know. I'm not afraid of the dark."

I sighed, rubbing at the pockmarked steel key with the pad of my thumb. "You could do that, yeah. But you're too smart for that. You know exactly how far it is back to the road, and you know exactly how many cars we passed on the way up here. That being none. If you did manage to find your way back to the road, you'd have to walk all the way back down the mountain. That's four long, winding miles. And once you're down, you'd have to walk another fifteen miles to reach a road where you might come across another car. You're wearing Chuck Taylors on your feet, and you don't have a jacket. In case that doesn't sound unpleasant enough, you should know that this is Indian land. The Pamunkey hunt here," I lied. "And so do plenty of mountain lions and cougars." That part *wasn't* a lie. I shot her an incorrigible smile. "So...if you're determined to go wandering off in search of a rescue, then please be my guest. On the other hand, if you'd like to come inside and have a proper conversation with me, difficult and shitty though it may be, then I'll have a fire going in a minute. I'm also pretty sure there's a bottle of whiskey stashed under the floor boards in the bedroom."

Sera's scowl was Olympic gold medal-worthy. "Fuck you, Fix."

It took every ounce of strength I had to bite back the retort that was dancing on the tip of my tongue. "Your choice. Sleeping in the truck isn't all that comfortable, but I've done it before. It wouldn't be the end of the world." I let myself into the cabin, stamping the dirt off my boots as I stepped over the threshold. Inside, the air was stale and stuffy, the tang of damp wood permeating the small, partitioned living space. There was a breaker box on the outside of the building, but it would be quicker to light the storm lanterns that I knew were scattered around the place. How long exactly had it been since I'd made my way up here? A year? Eighteen months? The batteries in the lanterns would still be good. I found the first lantern sitting on the low coffee table in front of the fire, and it was a moment's work to turn it on. A circle of dim white light flickered into life, illuminating a three-foot radius around me; from there, it was simple to locate the other lanterns and turn them on one by one.

The cabin was comprised of two main rooms—a bedroom to the back, and a living room with kitchenette along the right-hand wall—as well as a bathroom on the other side of the bedroom. Stuffed animal heads hung from the walls, along with dried furs and skins, and a number of rusting bear traps that were so old they likely didn't even close shut anymore. Their jagged teeth protruded from hooks in the timber like the gaping, snarling mouths of long-dead sharks. Everything was covered in a thick layer of dust. The throw rug that rested over the back of the three-seater sofa was so moth-eaten that its numerous holes were beginning to form some sort of a crochet pattern.

Underfoot, the floorboards were splintered and worn but swept clean. I tucked the truck and the cabin keys into my jeans pocket, and I went about loading some of the chopped, dry wood into the fireplace, counting inside my head.

Fifteen. Sixteen. Seventeen. Eighteen. Nineteen. Twenty. Twenty-one...

I'd reached twenty-eight and just about finished constructing the base of the fire when the cabin door creaked open and Sera slipped inside. I didn't look back over my shoulder. I used my lighter to ignite some balled-up newspaper, and I slid it in between the logs, blowing lightly until the flames caught and strengthened.

"Well, this is homey," Sera muttered. "Nothing screams '*I'm not planning on killing you*' like an array of spiked traps and murdered animals hanging all over the walls."

"This place used to be a hunter's lodge. People who hunt tend to collect spiky traps and dead creatures. That's the whole point." I straightened, brushing my hands off on my jeans, then I grabbed a flash light from one of the drawers beneath the kitchen counter, heading back toward the door.

"Why are you being like this?" Sera hissed.

I stopped, turned and faced her properly. "Being like what?"

"Like..." She threw her hands up in the air, huffing loudly. "Like everything's normal. Like we're just crashing here for the night, and everything is totally fine."

"How *should* I act? Should I make you sit in the cold? Tape you to a chair?" I stepped toward her, cracking my knuckles. "Should I take you out back, put a shovel in your hand, and tell you to start digging, Sera? Is that what you want?"

"Don't be fucking stupid," she snarled. Her fury was tinged with fear as she backed away. "Of course that's not what I want."

"Then sit down. I'll go turn the power on, and when I come back, we'll start this thing from the beginning."

The exterior of the cabin was a latticework of vines and kudzu; I had to rip at it with my bare hands in order to get to the breaker box. Once I'd turned the power on, I grabbed our bags from the truck on the way back inside the cabin, dumping them on the floor by a rickety old bookcase that was overloaded with rotten old copies of National Geographic and agricultural almanacs. Sera had her back to me as she stared directly into the fire that had properly taken hold while I was outside.

She was in silhouette, beautiful and closed off, her back ramrod straight. Any other woman would be cowering in a corner right now, but not Sera. She stood there, bravely awaiting her fate, ready to face whatever was about to come next, and she was doing it with a level of defiance that made me want to tear the clothes off her perfect fucking body and devour her. I couldn't do that, though. She was never going to let me do that again. Not after what she'd found in that fucking envelope in my glove box.

God, moments like this were going to be few. She was going to slip through my fingers like smoke, and I was going to let it happen, because she deserved an uncomplicated life. She deserved far more than I could give her and that was a fact. I stood as still as I could, watching her, drinking her in—the way the amber and gold glow of the fire lit her hair, as if she too were ablaze, a creature born of fire. I was a creature of ice. That hadn't always been the case. Once upon a time, I'd been warm and carefree, quick to laugh. My father had soon seen to that, and my time studying at seminary finished me off. Unlike my father, who had already been married with a child before he joined the priesthood, I'd been young and single, like most men who donned the collar. I'd never truly wanted to dedicate myself to the church, but it had seemed that my path was already set before me, and nothing I could do or say was going to change that fact. So I'd accepted that I was going to be alone forever, and I'd made whatever peace I could with that knowledge. I let my heart frost over, allowed my blood to cool, to form shards of ice within it, and after a while I didn't even notice the chill as it flowed through my veins.

When I walked away from the church, it didn't even occur to me that I might want to thaw myself out. I'd left for a reason, and that reason was to bring punishment down upon the heads of the wicked and the cruel. That kind of mission didn't leave room for softness, or kindness, or emotion of any kind. Sure, there had been women along the way. Many women. But I'd never stood still like this and looked at any of them, my chest aching like someone had taken a pickaxe to it, because I suspected I'd never see them again. This was entirely new and different, and I did not like it. Not one fucking bit.

Still, I knew myself. I wasn't going to be able to change the dull, thumping pain that spiraled through me every time that cursed, damage fist of muscle squeezed beneath my ribcage. Better to accept the reality of the situation, bite down on the pain, hold my breath and wait it out until it hopefully passed. I'd probably be in fucking Mexico, wrist deep in a cartel boss' chest cavity, by the time I managed to shake this feeling.

"*Speak,*" Sera whispered. She knew I was standing behind her, but she hadn't turned away from the fire. Her steel-edged command ripped me from my thoughts and dragged me back to the cabin, and back to the things I needed to tell her. Fuck, this was going to be tricky. I sat myself down on the sofa, cleared my throat, and then I began.

"Monica handles the clients and the money. She called me a month ago and told me she'd accepted an unusual job. A job we didn't normally touch. I've only ever killed one woman before, and she'd purposefully set fire to her sister's house with her three young children inside, while they were screaming, trying to get out..." I paused, taking a breath. That had been a shitty job. Remembering it, remembering the photos...it took me to a severely dark, fucked up place. "When Monica sent through your file, I couldn't see the reasoning behind her accepting your case. There didn't appear to be anything untoward. You weren't a murderer. You hadn't committed any atrocities, as far as I could tell. I called Monica, and she said she hadn't met with the client in person. That they'd contacted her via email, and they'd spun some story about you killing your mother. They said you were slowly poisoning your sister, trying to kill her, too.

"I asked Monica for the evidence, and she sent me a toxin report, showing high arsenic and mercury levels in your mother's bloodstream. The test had been conducted during her autopsy—"

Sera slowly pivoted around, her arms hugging her own body, her face a picture of pure shock and rage. My first response was to go to her, pick her up and hold her to me. I couldn't, though. I just... couldn't.

"I told you my mother had an aneurysm. She was fine, and then, one day, she just dropped down dead. How the hell can you say she was *poisoned*, Fix? How the hell can you say that *I* poisoned her? *I was just a kid!* I would never...I would *never* have hurt her. She was my entire fucking world. And *Amy?* I'm meant to be trying to kill Amy now, too? What you're saying doesn't make any sense."

"The report looked legitimate. I checked the paperwork myself. The autopsy was filed on county clerk's paper. Stamped. Didn't look like it had been fabricated. Monica wouldn't just accept a job based on unfounded claims, so I trusted that she'd done her due diligence. I went to Seattle. To find you. To kill you. But when I got there, I saw you, saw how young you were, and how normal you were, and I began to doubt. I stayed to watch you, to see how the fuck it might be possible that you were planning on killing your sister, and all I witnessed was a woman going about her daily life, working, meeting her friend for coffee. It made no sense to me, either. So I stayed longer. I stayed for two full weeks, to try and *force* it to make sense in my head. But..."

"But you realized it was a load of horse shit. And you still followed me to Liberty Fields. You were still going to kill me, Fix." Her voice was laced with accusation and hurt. She was well within her right to feel hurt. Every mile that had brought me closer to her in Wyoming had felt like a noose getting tighter and tighter around my neck. I hadn't just watched her Seattle. I'd followed her every movement. She'd become more than a job. For those fourteen days, she'd consumed my every waking moment. She was so damn beautiful, and so damn complicated, and, more often than not, so damn alone. I began to find myself dreaming of her, for fuck's sake, and I couldn't get her out of my head.

"The job in Liberty Fields was a fluke," I said softly. "I asked Monica if there were any jobs in Wyoming to buy myself some time. I knew you were heading that way. I thought with a couple more days I might see something in you that justified such an extreme course of action. You weren't even supposed to be stopping in Liberty Fields. If that storm hadn't been so bad, you'd have kept on driving and I would have caught up with you in a completely different state. I was going to watch you at Amy's wedding. I was going to see if you tried to hurt her. When I walked into that motel lobby and saw you on the phone, I damn near died, Sera. I had to turn my back to you, so I could figure my shit out before I faced you. When I spoke to you that first time, when I saw how worried you were about reaching Alabama and being there for Amy on her wedding day, I knew you'd never hurt her."

My heart was fumbling drunkenly in my chest. It couldn't seem to find its footing, and with every beat I was sure it was going to fail. Sera's expression was stony to say the least. She was having a hard time taking all this in. I knew she would, which was why I wanted to speak to her like this, privately, quietly, and alone. I needed her to believe me, and there was still a lot I had to say. Her mind must have been racing, too, though. I bit the inside of my lip, and I waited for her to spill the words burning in the back of her throat.

"*You fucked me,*" she ground out. "You came to my city. You were there for two weeks. Someone paid you to kill me, and you waltzed into that motel room like you didn't have a care in the world. You... you *fucked* me, Fix. You were inside me, and the whole time, you must have been planning how you were going to end my life." Her voice rose, bouncing off the walls, growing angrier and angrier with each word. She took a step forward, and then another. Soon she was standing in front of me, the toes of her Chucks little more than an inch from the toes of my boots.

"Did you plan on shooting me as soon as you'd had your fill of me, Fix? Is that it?" I saw her hand coming. I did nothing to block the strike. Her palm connected with my cheek, and the sting was bright enough to make my eyes water. I held my words inside me, though. Kept my hands resting on top of my knees. She slapped me again, this time even harder, and a ragged sob slipped from her lips. "Funny, huh? Get drunk with me. Seduce me. Fuck me. Use me for your pleasure, then snuff me out when I was no longer entertaining to you."

She closed her hand into a fist, and I raised my jaw to meet her blow. I deserved it. She had every right. My head rocked back with the impact—she had one hell of a right hook. The taste of copper filled my mouth, and my jaw barked with pain. Slowly, I opened my mouth and slid my tongue between my lips, tasting the blood that she'd drawn. She'd split my bottom lip wide open.

Sucking in an uneven breath, Sera staggered backward. She sobbed once more, looked down at her hand, and then sank into a heap on the floor. Her tears came quick and fast, and still I didn't move. If I so much as twitched right now, there would be no going back. She'd launch herself at me, or she'd run, and neither of those options lead anywhere good. I'd end up hurting her if I had to restrain her, and she'd end up breaking her fucking neck careening through the forest in the pitch black. So I remained seated on the sofa, my hands glued to my kneecaps, and I allowed myself to bleed.

"I already told you," I said softly, "I knew the moment I heard you on the phone that you'd done nothing wrong. Sera..."

She covered her face with her hands, choking on her own tears.

"*Sera*. Look at me."

"*No!*"

"Sera. I need you to take a deep breath, and I need you to look at me. Right now."

She tore her hands away, her eyes flickering with fury. "I don't give a shit what you need," she snapped. Her rage was unadulterated and cut deep, but at least she was looking at me. Glaring, to be more precise.

"I should never have touched you. I know that. It was fucked up, and I had no right. I don't blame you for hating me. I won't blame you if you can't forgive me for it. But I was never using you, Sera. I didn't fuck you because I considered you sport. You have to believe that."

"Then why? Why would you bother? You could have any woman you wanted," she gasped through her labored breath. "You had no reason to screw me, unless you wanted to demean me before you put me down."

"*I fucked you because I care about you!*" I roared. "I spent two weeks watching you, every single hour of every single day. When you slept, I slept. *Barely.* When you ate, I ate. *Barely.* While you worked, I sat there and I memorized the shape of your face. The way you would stretch at your desk. The way you would constantly tap a pen against your leg whenever you were on the phone. The way you would force a smile at that fat woman who brought you a coffee every morning at eleven. The way your eyes were always so utterly distant and unfocused while you listened to your friends talk. The way you looked so withdrawn and removed from nearly every aspect of your life. I saw how fucking haunted you were. And I saw how absolutely fucking breathtaking you were. How your smile, rare though it was, completely transformed your face. That smile..." I swallowed, trying to rein myself in. It was a fool's errand, though. There was no marshaling myself now. I'd opened my stupid fucking mouth, and the words just kept on spewing out of it.

"The first time I saw you smile, I forgot how to fucking breathe. You were talking to someone on the street, some guy with a shaved head, and he gave you something. You looked down at whatever he'd placed in your hand, and you laughed. And I...I couldn't fucking move. It was as if I'd stepped outside of my body and lost complete control over myself. I sat there at the table in a coffee shop across the street from you, and I was filled with this incomprehensible rage. I was furious at that guy with the shaved head. I fucking hated him, because he was on the receiving end of that smile, and not me.

"I'm the boy who fell for you from afar, Sera. I should have done the right thing and walked away. I've never had a problem walking away from anything in my whole damn life, but I was weak. I could *not* walk away from *you*. I don't know how I thought this was going to all pan out. It was fucking crazy of me to believe anything real could come of this. But there was a moment in that motel room, a moment when you looked at me and I could see that you were attracted to me. I could tell by the way you were watching me drink from that bottle, how blown your pupils were, how restless you were, and I fucking caved. I was going to stay my hand. I was going to get up in the morning and I was going to leave you far, far behind. But the chance to be the guy that made you smile? That made you purr and shake? To make you come undone? Just once? I couldn't stop myself. And then, your tires were slashed, and you pleaded for my help, and..." I finally moved my hands from my knees, turning them over and splaying my fingers. "Here we are."

Sera had stopped crying. She was a statue of a woman, sitting on the floor in front of the fire, her eyes wide and round. Her throat worked, as if she was trying to swallow unsuccessfully. "You didn't know me. You didn't know anything about me. You barely know me now. How can you say you care about me?"

"Because," I said, sighing. "I know myself. I know I've never been so fucking obliterated by a woman before. I know you and I are *something*, Sera. I don't know what, or why, but I know it down to the very marrow of my fucking bones. If that's not good enough for you, I can accept that. I can disappear, and you'd never see me again even if you came looking. But it's the truth, and I'm willing to put up a goddamn fight to prove it."

She looked stunned. Fuck, *I* was stunned. I had no business saying this stuff to her, but in the moment, it felt right. It felt honest, and that's what I wanted to be with her from here on out. I had no idea how to try and pursue a relationship with a woman, especially one who thought I was trying to kill her, but it was what I wanted. Come hell or high water.

Sera wiped her tears away with the back of her hand. "I don't—"

"Don't say anything. I don't want you to. For now, let's sleep. I'll take the couch. In the morning, you can tell me where you want to go, and I'll make it happen. I'm sure you need time to process all of this."

Her face was a mask of incredulity. Yeah, there probably wasn't enough time in the world to process this mess. "I *will* stay here tonight. I will try and get some sleep," she said. "And I will think this whole thing through, Fix. But I want two things from you before I walk into that bedroom."

"Tell me."

She narrowed her eyes at me, tilting her head to one side. "I want to know who hired you to kill me. *Now*. And I want a fucking gun."

22

SERA

THE TRUTH

J waited to see what he'd do. If he gave me both weapons—the truth and the gun—I'd know his story, or at least part of it, was genuine. If he refused, I'd know he was bullshitting me, and I'd have to try and find a way out of here as soon as dawn broke.

Fix didn't even flinch. He reached back, lifting his shirt, and he pulled a matte black handgun from the waistband of his jeans. He held it out to me with a steady hand. "Do you know how to take the safety off?" he asked, his voice rich, deep, and penetrating.

My hand wasn't as steady as his as I took the gun, staring down at it. "Yes," I answered.

"Do it. Show me," Fix commanded.

I held the gun aloft, releasing the small safety catch by the trigger so he could see what I was doing.

"Good. Now point it at me."

"What? Why?"

The growl that issued from his throat was frustrated. "You want the gun to protect yourself. *From me.* So show me how you'd aim it, if you were going to kill me."

"Don't be fucking stup—"

He grabbed me by the wrist, jerking out my arm and pulling the weapon forward so that the muzzle was butted up against his chest, directly over his heart. "Like this, Sera," he snarled. "Keep your arm locked at the elbow. This is a big gun. It has a wicked kick. You need a stable base in order to hit your mark."

"Felix, let go of me."

"When you pull the trigger, don't just jerk at it. You have to breathe out. You have to exhale and *squeeze*..."

I couldn't fucking breathe out. I couldn't fucking squeeze. I couldn't do anything as he held his hand over mine, pressing the gun up against his chest. "Is it loaded?"

Slowly, carefully, he nodded. "Helps to keep your gun loaded if you're planning on using it at some point."

God. He was showing me how to kill him. And he was doing it with a loaded gun, forcing me to hold the damn thing over his heart. Guns went off accidentally all the time. I was shaking so badly, I felt like I was going to slip up and shoot him. A part of me felt like it wouldn't be such a bad thing. Fix was dangerous. *So* fucking danger-ous. Not just because he was a killer, which was clearly a huge prob-lem, but because...his eyes were capable of stripping me bare. The casual uplift of his sensual, full mouth was capable of setting my heart racing. His muscled, powerful body made me want to throw myself at his feet. When he wrapped his arms around me, and held me in his calloused, strong hands, it felt like the world stood still. And the words that just came out of his mouth, words that told a story that was frightening and hard to hear, also struck something deep inside me that made me feel warm, safe, and thrilled me more than I was willing to admit.

God, how was I going to make sense of any of this?

I'd never found myself in such peril. I'd never found myself tightrope walking over such a precarious, deadly fall, knowing I was going to lose my balance at any second, and being oddly okay with the consequences.

Fix calmly removed the gun from my hand, placing it down on the floor beside me. His eyes were quicksilver again, flashing with so much energy and...something else. Something like trepidation, mixed with determination. "As for your second request, are you sure you want to know, Sera?"

He was talking about my murderer. The person who wanted me dead. He wanted to know if I was ready and willing to accept the truth in all its terrible glory. I answered him by straightening my back and staring him directly in the eye. "You don't need to dance around it. We both know who hired you. The only person who would do such a thing. Just spit out his name and I'll be able to breathe again."

Felix's eyes shone a little brighter, as if they were illuminated from within. They really were something else, those eyes of his. I could feel them on my skin at all times, even when he appeared to be looking elsewhere—an equally comforting and disturbing sensation. "What if your assumptions are incorrect? What if you're wrong?" he asked

"How could I be?" A knot of dread tightened in the pit of my stomach, though. He'd spoken softly and slowly, adopting a gentleness that didn't marry up with the gruff, gravely timbre of his voice, and his cautiousness made me panic.

"Sera." He looked down at his hands. "Sixsmith is a piece of shit. He's incapable of loving another living human being. I wouldn't put something like this past him, but...paying to have someone killed costs money. A fuck load of money. Where do you think your father would have come by forty grand?"

I nearly bit off my own tongue. "Forty grand? *Jesus Christ!*" I had assumed Sixsmith, whatever his perverted reasoning might be, was responsible for this completely fucked up nightmare. But Fix was right: I hadn't considered where my father would have gotten the money to set a ball this size in motion. He wasn't below begging and scraping for money, but there was no way he'd saved forty thousand dollars. And none of his worthless, shit-eating loan shark friends would be dumb enough to loan him such an exorbitant amount of money. They'd loaned him plenty before, and *I'd* been the one to pay it back, one way or another. "If it wasn't Sixsmith, then who was it, Fix? I'm so tired of all these games. Just fucking spit it out!"

Fix blew out a long breath down his nose, rocking his head to the side until his neck cracked loudly. He liked doing that—cracking his bones. I wanted to crack his neck myself at this point. "As I said, Monica never met the client who hired us to take care of you," he said. "But the person who emailed referred to themselves as a man. *'I'm not a patient man,'* were his exact words. And the email came from a business account. Mpc@gerrityholdings.com. Does that ring a bell with you?"

MPC? Gerrity Holdings? I allowed my gaze to drift as I considered the email address. Was MPC short for something? A position within a firm? I couldn't think of a job title that shortened down to that acronym. Someone's initials, then. It had to be someone's name. I didn't know anyone with those initials, though. Not that I could recall off the top of my head. And I'd never heard of Gerrity Holdings before. A holding company was typically a puppeteer, pulling the strings on another larger company. In business, they were a great way to hide your true identity if you didn't want your competition to know you were trying to strike a deal, strengthen your footing in the marketplace. For the most part, holding companies had to be legally registered with the state, the business owner's details documented as a matter of public record, but something told me I wouldn't find anything if I looked up this particular organization.

"I take it from the baffled look on your face that you have no idea who that might be?" Fix continued.

"No. None. Are you telling me *you* don't know who hired you, Fix? Because I will literally—"

"I have a name. I have a physical address. We searched the user's IP." He reached into his pocket and pulled out his wallet, retrieving a folded-up piece of paper from inside and then holding it out to me. I took it, and my mouth was suddenly drier than the Sahara. Everything was going to change, the moment I unfolded the paper and saw what was written on it. My life was never going to be the same again. I pressed my tongue against the roof of my mouth to stop my teeth from chattering together nervously as I flattened out the paper.

In blocky, scrawled, undeniably male handwriting:

ARVER

62634 Wood Street, Centralia, PA 00000.

frowned at the paper. "Pennsylvania? I've never even been to Pennsylvania. And I don't know anyone called Carver."

"It's probably not a real name. The address is probably fake, too."

"Great. Fucking *perfect*. So someone wants me dead, and it could be fucking anybody. You really *don't* know who hired you." I screwed up the paper and threw it at the couch, snarling at the back of my throat. I wasn't prepared for this. I'd been so sure in my head that Sixsmith was responsible, but there was just no way. Aside from the financial unlikelihood, my father was hopeless with computers. Couldn't even log onto Google to look something up, let alone operate an email account. There was just no way in hell he'd had the foresight to set up a limited liability partnership to hide behind, and the man sure as fuck didn't have the common sense to come up with an alias. Whoever this Carver person was, it wasn't my father.

"We need to go to there. To Pennsylvania," I announced, jerking my chin toward the balled-up paper now nestled into the pancake-flat cushions on the couch. "We need to go to that address. Even if it's fake, we need to go and check."

Fix leaned back into his seat. His body looked stiff, which was unusual; he was always so fluid and comfortable inside his own skin, but there was something off about the way he was moving now. "So... you don't want me to take you back to Seattle?" he asked slowly.

Of course. He'd assumed I'd never want to see him again, and he was right. Or he *had* been right until he'd spilled his guts to me and placed a gun in my hand. I believed him now—that he didn't want to kill me. I was yet to wrap my head around the fact that Fix had already developed some weird attraction toward me before he'd even opened his mouth to speak to me in person, but...

"No. I don't want you to take me home. Not yet. I want to find this asshole and ask him why he's doing this to me. I want to fucking know what I've done to deserve this. And when I've confronted him and gotten the answers I need...I want you to kill *him*."

I was aware of how crazy I sounded. Hypocritical. I'd given Fix endless shit about what he did for a living. I'd told him he was a bad person. I'd been scared and intimidated by him, amongst other things, and now here I was telling him I wanted him to do the very thing that I abhorred. Amazing how everything changed the moment I found out I was his primary target and the blood in my veins turned to molten lava. My life certainly hadn't started out great. To an outsider, the small, secure, comfortable existence I'd built for myself in Seattle might not have been that impressive, but I'd worked hard for what I had, and I'd be damned if I was going to let anyone take it away from me.

Fuck that. And fuck them for trying.

Fix pressed his fingers to his forehead, closing his eyes for a second. "Let me get this straight. You want me to figure out who this Carver guy is, take you to him, and then you want me to kill him."

"Yes."

"I'm having a hard time figuring out how you think any of that is a good idea, Sera."

"None of it's a good idea. I know it's a bad fucking plan. But it's what I want, Fix, and you're going to do it for me because you owe me that much. And when it's over..." The sentence died on my lips. When this was over, I didn't know what would come next. I literally couldn't imagine what would happen once I'd dived into this world of chaos and crime with Felix Marcosa, but I was willing to bet it would be messed up and out of the ordinary. I'd have to go back to Seattle. My business was waiting for me, as were my clients. My dog, was there. My apartment, with its shabby chic décor and the mountainous stacks of books I still was yet to read. My favorite coffee shop, and Sadie, and the best clam chowder money could buy. There was no doubt in my mind I'd be returning back to Seattle, but...

There were other thoughts inside my head. Thoughts that made me uncomfortable, down to the very roots of my soul. I couldn't even allow them to form properly, but they lingered like a permeating smoke, weaving themselves through my synapses, digging in deep. No less than an hour ago, I'd been convinced Fix was still on a mission to murder me. His confession, though worrying, had changed things. I didn't know how, and to what extent I was going to allow it to affect me, but it was undeniable: it *had* affected me.

Proceed with caution. Do not *do anything stupid, Sera.* The voice in the back of my head, which had always lead me to be careful and kept me out of harm's way, was now screaming at me to be smart. And I was listening. "I'm going to sleep now. And this gun is going to be glued to my hand until I feel like I'm safe. Do you understand?"

A ruinous smirk spread across Fix's face. He really was magnificent, damn him. "Fine by me. There's nothing sexier than a woman with a weapon in her hand. Just be careful you don't shoot yourself, Angel."

Angel. The nickname both set my teeth on edge and made my body stand to attention at the same time. I fought against the shiver that pressed against my spine. "Don't call me that. And don't worry. The only person in any danger of being shot is you, Marcosa. You should get some sleep, too. We have a long drive in the morning. Centralia, Pennsylvania, is a long fucking way away."

23

SERA

CENTRALIA

I supposed I would have known the mess I was walking into if I'd bothered to Google Centralia. Never having been to Pennsylvania, I'd assumed the small town was going to be exactly that: a small, unremarkable town, populated by hard working, everyday people, doing normal, everyday things. There would be grocery stores, and hardware stores, and people mowing their lawns. Kids playing in the streets. However, as we approached our destination, it became increasingly apparent that all was not well in Centralia. There was nothing normal about the place, and there were plenty of signs to prove it. Not metaphorical signs. Real, physical ones that started to pop up at the side of the road, about five miles from the town limits.

**WALKING OR DRIVING IN THIS AREA COULD RESULT
IN SERIOUS INJURY OR DEATH.
DANGEROUS GASES PRESENT.
GROUND PRONE TO SUDDEN COLLAPSE.**

Area subject to mine subsidence and toxic gas emissions.

SILENT HILL, PA.

*F*ix's face said it all: he hadn't known about Centralia's mine fire either. As we crossed into the town proper, the cracks in the highway's blacktop evolved from considerable to catastrophic. Eventually, a crack wide enough to swallow the truck whole put a stop to our journey, and we had to get out and head toward the rundown, ramshackle buildings in the distance on foot.

"Place is fucking deserted," Fix murmured.

He was right. The closer we got, the more obvious the neglect and decay became. The only cars in sight were those abandoned at the side of the road, rusting, at least twenty years old and sprouting long grasses and saplings through the rents in their warped metal shells. Smoke rose in great plumes from the hillside that buttressed the town, presumably escaping up from the ground.

"Those signs were decades old," I said. "There's no way there should still be smoke, right?"

Fix considered the dirty grey columns that listed on the breeze, scratching at the back of his neck. "Who knows? The town's sitting right on top of a coal mine. If a fire caught down there, there's no saying how long it would burn for. It'd explain the smell."

The air was acrid and tainted by the bite of chemicals. Not enough that it made breathing difficult, or enough that it felt like your lungs were bleeding, but enough to know that every inhalation was shaving a minute off your life. We walked further down the highway until the buildings grew closer and the blacktop buckled altogether, split into two right down the median and yawning open like a mouth that lead directly into hell.

The asphalt was no longer a dull industrial grey. It was every faded color of the rainbow, a carpet of chalk graffiti stretching out before us, every available square inch of the ground covered in messily scrawled handwriting and spray-painted images. Turtles.

Cheshire cats. Men, hanging themselves. Love hearts. People fucking. And, naturally, about a thousand crudely drawn dicks.

"Why do guys always draw dicks on everything?" I sighed, stepping over a large chunk of debris in the road. Out of the corner of my eye, Fix grinned, his eyes flashing with mischief.

"How do you know it was guys? I'm sure a chick drew one or two. Look. That one." He pointed. "That one's got a foreskin and veins. And the balls aren't massively oversized. A chick definitely drew that one. Far too realistic to have been a guy."

"I s'pose you're right. Guys do always like to think their balls are way bigger than they are."

As we passed a dilapidated gas station, covered in red spray paint, my nerves jangled like a set of keys. The town was a ruin. It was highly unlikely that the person who hired Fix to kill me actually lived here, but there was a chance. Maybe some of the derelict, crumbling buildings that lined the main street of the town—the ones that were still standing—*were* occupied, and the piece of crap who contacted Monica had chosen to hide himself away here.

Carver. Even the name sent chills up and down my spine. It placed images inside my head. Very disturbing images of flesh being sliced and gouged. Of bone being whittled, and of sinew being severed.

A stifling silence hung thickly in the air like a blanket, covering Centralia. People obviously came here—someone had to have drawn all of the graffiti—but as far as I could see the rubberneckers and tourists who arrived armed with paint cans and sticks of chalk showed up infrequently. Nothing moved here. Nothing really lived. Even the grass and trees that covered the hillside and pushed their way up through the concrete looked yellowed, sour, and sick.

"You're very quiet," Fix said. "Sure you don't want to go back and wait in the truck?"

I stuffed my hands into my pockets, setting my jaw. "No. I already told you. I want to look this fucker in the eye. I want him to tell me why he did this. And then I want to watch you make him bleed."

"You're not going to watch me kill him." Fix's tone brooked no argument.

"I *will*, Fix. You can't stop me."

"Wasn't planning on it," he retorted. "But the last time you watched me hurt someone, you passed the fuck out. You don't have the stomach for that level of violence."

"If you think for one second I won't watch you punish the person who intended to cause me harm and fucking crow with delight while you're doing it, then you don't know me at all."

A thoughtful frown flickered at his brow. "Perhaps you don't know yourself. Murder's never easy. No matter who it is, whether they deserve it or not, witnessing someone losing the only thing they really, *truly* possess, is always going to stick in your throat. If a person can watch another die and feel nothing but self-righteous satisfaction, then that person's probably a fucking sociopath."

There was no judgment in his voice, but I could hear the reprimand there just fine: *you don't know what you're talking about. You have no idea what it means to kill a man. You're in way over your head, Lafferty.*

Each of those statements were correct. I had no experience in this arena, and I sure as hell didn't know what the fuck I was doing, but, sociopath or not, for better or for worse, I knew what I was capable of. And in this instance, I was going to tamp down the bile at the back of my throat, and I was going to set aside the panic that had been crippling me of late, and I was going to make sure justice was done.

We kept walking. It seemed as though Fix knew where he was going, despite the complete lack of street signs to demark what was left of Centralia. The tourists had likely stolen them all. Fix grunted next to me, then pointed to our right. A squat, single story building with a spackled, dingy fascia crouched on the other side of what had once been a parking lot but was now a shopping cart graveyard. The sign above the building read:

*C*entralia Luxury Suites. Rooms available!

"*L*ooks like our kind of motel. Wanna check and see if they're lying about those rooms?"

I scanned his face and immediately regretted it. Every time I looked at him, my stomach managed to coil itself into another knot; at this rate I was never going to untangle my insides. He was so breathtakingly handsome. Rugged, yet edged with a subtle softness that took me unawares every single time. The sinful smirk that appeared to have taken up permanent residence on his face, regardless of all the crap that had happened in the past week, made me feel so conflicted that I didn't know what was right or wrong anymore. "I'd rather saw off my own right arm than spend another night in a shitty motel with you."

"Brava. You almost sounded convincing there."

"It's the truth."

"Nope. You just told a big, fat fucking lie."

"Really. And how do you presume to know when I'm lying, Fix?"

His eyes sparked with amusement. "I used to sit confession. I've had upward of a thousand experiences where people told me half-truths or blatant falsehoods. It was amazing how people would still try to convince me, *and themselves*, that they'd done nothing wrong, when the sole purpose of sitting in that booth was to absolve themselves and clear their consciences. Also, my dick is an excellent lie detector."

My cheeks exploded with warmth. "Let's keep your dick out of this, Marcosa."

He laughed. "That's the problem. You don't want to keep my dick out of this. You want my dick in this. In *you,* specifically. It can hear the need in your voice, and my dick wants you to know that it's more than happy to oblige."

"If you say one more word about your penis, Father Marcosa, I'm going to tear the damn thing off."

The smile on Fix's face faltered, then slowly faded, right along with the mirth that had been dancing in his eyes. There had been a carefree bounce in his step, too, probably because he knew just as well as I did that this trip had been a complete waste of time and nothing bad was going to happen, but now it seemed as though he were suddenly having trouble lifting his feet from the ground. I'd said the wrong thing. And it wasn't the threat to his manhood that had soured his mood. It was the fact that I'd called him Father Marcosa.

"This way," he said, taking a right down an unmarked side street. As soon as we rounded the corner, we both stopped dead, though. There was...nothing. No houses remained on the street. Not even the foundations were visible amongst the fractured concrete, the tires discarded amongst the grass, or the heaped mounds of dirt. If there had ever been any buildings here, they were long gone now.

Fix scowled at the scene before us, his eyes assessing everything with an analytical professionalism that probably came in handy when he was working a job. "There," he said, heading over to the other side of the road. I followed after him, peering around him to see what he'd discovered. Using the toe of his boot, Fix pushed a tuft of grass out of the way, revealing a length of concrete curb behind it, painted with numbers. Six-two-six-two-zero. That was what it looked like anyway; the third number in the sequence was mostly missing, the concrete having crumbled away. It could have been an eight, maybe. Or even a zero.

"House number," Fix announced. "This *was* a residential street at some point. I guess that confirms it, then. The IP address Carver's email came from might have been routed here somehow, but Carver himself sure as shit ain't here."

I shouldn't have been disappointed or mad, but I was both. I wanted to take action, and I wanted to make this guy pay for what he'd set in motion. I knew how reactive I was being. A few more days on the road would probably give me more time to think this through reasonably, and I would feel relieved not to have found Carver.

Standing here surveying the empty street, however, I felt bitterly cheated.

"What now?" I asked. "He's not here. So how do we find this guy?"

Fix carried on down the street, searching up and down the concealed curb, deep furrows creasing his brow. "We go back to Seattle. You go back to work, and you forget this ever happened. I'll find this guy on my own and make sure he never bothers you again, Sera."

"No!" My shout rang out, cutting through the still afternoon air. A cat streaked across the road ahead, darting into the grass, nothing more than a flash of white and orange. Fix stopped what he was doing, straightening up, and then turned to face me. He was wearing a black t-shirt under a black leather jacket. His jeans might have been black once upon a time, but they were more of a faded, washed out grey now. There was a darkness to him that had nothing to do with his clothes, though. The darkness that radiated from him on occasion, sinking through my skin and into my bones, turning me inside out, resided in his eyes, and it was a frightening, terrible thing to behold when that darkness was turned on you without warning.

"*Enough*," Fix growled. "We're done with this nonsense. I know I owe you. I know you have the right to feel angry, and hurt, and scared, Sera. I know you want revenge—"

"I don't want *revenge*. I want—"

"I *know* you want revenge for what this guy was planning to have done to you but involving yourself beyond this point is sheer recklessness and stupidity. That's not how this thing gets done. You can't go blindly charging after this guy without any forethought. You'll end up getting hurt. And I won't be party to anything that will risk your safety. It's just not gonna fucking happen. So get used to it."

My mouth hung open. I'd been so angry with him over the past few days as we'd driven here, and he'd played along so well—the remorseful little boy with his tail between his legs—that I'd almost forgotten that wasn't who he was. He'd been repentant and patient, carefully considering his words (for the most part) whenever he spoke to me; he'd slept on the couch or on the floor without complaint, and besides a few tongue-in-cheek comments like the one he'd made just now about that motel, he hadn't made a single move toward me.

But none of that was him. Not truly.

This was the real Fix, and he was a force to be reckoned with.

"You can't just blow into my life like a goddamn storm, turn everything upside down, and then expect me to walk away from something like this," I ground out.

He narrowed those beautiful pale eyes of his. "If you were smart, that's exactly what you'd do."

"I've been in the business of protecting myself and those dear to me my entire life. And I'm not going to quit now. If that makes me stupid, then I'll gladly accept the title. *With pride.*"

Fix clenched his jaw. He folded his arms across his chest, rocking back, sizing me up. His lips parted. I knew I wasn't going to like the next words out of his mouth. I was already ramping up for the fight that was brewing, but when he inhaled, about to speak, whatever he had been going to say never made it out. His dark brows banked together, his gaze drifting over my shoulder. "What the fuck is that?"

I turned. I frowned, too, hunting for the source of his confusion. And there it was, on the other side of the road, almost invisible amongst the long, dried out grass. A hatch, steel, industrial and heavy looking, two feet across and sunken into the ground.

"What house number's in front of that?" Fix asked, already walking over to investigate. He got there before me, answering his own question as he stooped down and uncovered the numbers six-two-six-three-four in dull white paint on the broken piece of curb that he overturned. "This is it," he said. "This is the address the IP was registered to." He was already eyeing the hatch with intent. I stepped right up to it, immediately noting how shiny and new the metal seemed. There was no visible lock. Nothing to prevent anyone from coming along and raising the slab of steel to see what was inside.

Blowing a hard breath out down my nose, I shook my head, backing away. "If there really is a fire burning beneath this entire town, the very last thing we should be doing is lowering ourselves into a hole in the ground."

"Looks like a bunker or something. Probably has concrete walls three-feet thick. Where's the harm in opening it up and looking inside?"

"If you want to burn your face off, be my guest. I'll be ready to call 911."

Fix didn't flinch, but something about him hardened. "It's gonna be fine. But...never call 911, Sera. No matter what. Ever. Under any circumstances. What do you think would happen if I were ever taken to a hospital?"

I shrugged. "I don't know. They'd patch you up, and you'd be on your way. You have insurance, don't you?"

"Paper trails are bad, Sera," was all he said. He turned his attention toward the hatch at his feet, considering it intensely, like it was a coiled snake that was rearing back, preparing to strike. "If I do get my face burned off, just shoot me in the back of the head and leave me for the crows."

"Gross."

"What? Birds love barbeque." He took hold of the thick handle on the hatch, wrenching it upwards. There was no squeal of metal on metal, or shower of rust erupting from the hinges. Whoever had put the hatch here had done it pretty recently, it would seem. It yawned open, revealing a pitch-black darkness beneath it.

"No flames," I observed.

"Nope. Doesn't look very hellish."

"You'd know, given your history with the devil."

"I prefer to think my history was with the other guy. He's undoubtedly not speaking to me anymore, though, so you're probably right."

For the first time, I found myself wondering whether Fix still spoke to his god. It seemed unreasonable to think that a person would devote their lives to their religion for years, and then turn their backs on it so irrevocably. I didn't plan on asking him about his faith;

it was too personal a line of questioning, but I was pretty damn curious.

Fix swung his legs over the side of the hatch, peering into the darkness, and a jolt of panic swept through me. He didn't know how far the fall was below, and he hadn't bothered to check. He was just going to slide himse—

He disappeared before I could even finish the thought, and my heart leapt up into my throat. *Oh god. Oh god. Oh god...*

A soft thudding sound reached my ears, along with an *umpphh*—the air leaving Fix's lungs. I hurried to the hatch, dropping to my knees, leaning over to look over the side. The day was bright, which made it hard to make out anything in the hole at first. And then, gradually, my eyes adjusted, and I could make out dim shadows below, one of which was moving.

"Didn't break both your legs, then?" I asked.

"Apparently not," came a reply. "It was only eight or nine feet. Drop your phone down."

He had his own phone, but I didn't bother asking why he didn't have it on him. At all times, the man seemed to be doing his solid best to leave it anywhere but on his person. Grumbling, I took my cell out of my back pocket, holding it down into the dark, and my breath caught when Fix's fingers brushed against mine. It was the first physical contact we'd had since I found that envelope in his truck, and I wasn't expecting the instant reaction the gentle brush of his fingers had on me.

In the field, back at the hotel, Fix had held onto me so tight. His hands had explored every inch of my body. His mouth had possessed me in the most intimate of ways. It had been dizzying and heady, every last second of it, but the short second that our fingers grazed now was filled with so much electricity that the oxygen rushed out of my lungs and left me spinning. How could I still feel this way about him? How could I still keep losing myself every time I found myself watching him out of the corner of my eye? There was no reason I should still be so winded by his very presence, his very touch, but there was no escaping it.

Fix was bad news, the kind that would be plastered across the front pages of newspapers all over the world if people knew a man like him existed, but I couldn't rid myself of the thoughts of him that constantly plagued my mind, or the raw, wild, living energy that burst into flame whenever he captured me in his silver-blue eyes.

Light bloomed down in the hole. Fix had activated the flashlight feature on my phone, and he was casting it around, shifting about. His investigation stopped just as quickly as it had started.

"*Fuck.*" His one-word statement mirrored my own thoughts when I saw what he'd found down there. The space was cramped and small, the walls barely more than ten feet apart. A small desk sat against one of the walls, completely bare of any papers, trash or computer equipment. Against the opposite wall was a small cot, and on the cot lay a body. A man. His plaid shirt strained against his bloated belly, and the fingers on his meaty hands were twisted and contorted, as if they were reaching out and trying to grapple hold of something that wasn't there. Cloudy brown eyes stared straight up at me out of what, indeed, appeared to be a bunker. His mouth was stretched open, and something fat and purple protruded out between his teeth. It took me half a heartbeat to realize that the mangled piece of flesh was his tongue.

Shit! *Shit, shit, shit!*

I toppled back, kicking and groping in the grass, scrambling to get away from the hatch. God...he was dead. He was fucking dead, and he was staring right at me. Holy fucking shit. My stomach clenched, and then unclenched. A loud, high-pitched sound pierced my mind, deafening me, making it impossible to hear anything over it. What the *fuck?*

I couldn't get up. My arms and legs failed to respond as I begged them to move me further away from the fucked up scene I'd just witnessed. A million thoughts raced through my head, whirling, spinning, spiraling, tumbling.

I was back in that auto body shop, watching Franz bleed out on the ground. I was looking at the blood on my hands, and my stomach was lurching. Except this time there was no blood. From the brief snapshot I'd witnessed of the dead man lying on his back on that cot, I hadn't seen any visible sign of injury or trauma. The veil of death that hung over him had been obvious, though, like a direct hit to the face.

Fix was next to me, then, his hands grasping at my arms, trying to pull me to him. I fought against him, trying to get away, but he was too strong. His arms closed around me like a vise, and the smell of him flooded my senses. "Sera. Sera! Fuck! It's okay. It's okay. I've got you." His mouth was pressed up against my ear. I could hear what he was saying, but his words only seemed to make my panic worse.

"How? How is it *okay*? That guy! That guy was fucking *dead*."

"I know. I know. I've got you. Shhhh. Breathe. Take a deep breath for me, Angel. Come on."

I inhaled, not because he'd told me to, but because it felt like I was going to pass out. "What the fuck, Fix? Why...why are there dead people everywhere you go?"

He made a tight, low, growling sound that vibrated in my ear, and he pressed my head against his chest. I was still thrashing and flailing, but he didn't release me. He didn't let me go.

"I'm sorry," he breathed. "I'm sorry. I'm sorry." Over and over again, he chanted his apology, the beat of the words like a metronome. I railed against him, clawed at his leather jacket and his shirt, trying to free myself of him, but it was useless. Eventually, the adrenalin that had flooded me dissipated, and a tidal wave of exhaustion hit me like a wall. I fell slack in his arms, muscle by muscle relaxing until I felt myself go limp against him.

Fix pressed his lips against my temple, holding them there in a drawn-out kiss that was designed to comfort. His breath, pulling in and out down his nose, rushed over my forehead and my cheeks. "You're right," he murmured. "There are always dead bodies wherever I go. This is what happens, though. This is what happens when you go looking for death instead of running in the opposite direction. You find it. Or, inevitably, it finds you."

24

FIX

DRAWN

I left Sera huddled up, perched on the curb, her arms wrapped around her legs, her knees drawn up under her chin. She was shaking like crazy. I didn't want to leave her on her own, but I needed to get a look at the guy in the bunker. I'd used the ladder I'd found propped up against the wall, almost directly underneath the hatch, to climb my way out and I'd gone to her the second I'd heard her flip out, so I hadn't had chance to investigate. Now, I needed to know who the guy was that was lying down there, and how the fuck he'd died.

I couldn't count how many dead bodies I'd seen in my lifetime. There were always vigils being held for the deceased at the St. Luke's when I was a kid. And I was a nosy, inquisitive kid, so I'd snooped nearly every single time I'd learned there was going to be a funeral. Then, giving people their last rites in hospice or at home, in their beds, I'd been present countless times as men, woman and, unfortunately, children had passed on from this life. Ironically, I saw less dead people now that I was an assassin than I had in my previous life. I knew death. I knew what it looked like. Felt like. Smelled like. And the guy in the bunker... he wasn't behaving like your typical dead person.

There'd been absolutely no smell when I'd opened up the hatch. It was really uncommon for tongue protrusion to occur, but when it did it usually happened because the body had been exposed to fire either before or after death. The body hadn't looked burned. But...

But.

Could the underground heat have caused the guy's tongue to do that? The bunker was hotter than hades. It was possible. I wasn't a doctor. I wasn't even fucking close to being a doctor. I wasn't going to have answers on that front until I managed to sit down in front of a computer and did some research. As I dropped back down into the bunker, Sera called out. "Be careful. Just...*Fix*. Please. Be careful."

Care wasn't something I often afforded myself. Care was a precaution undertaken by a person who loved their life, treasured and valued it, and it had been a long time since I'd given two shits about myself. But now that Sera was here...things were different. I could see myself caring, and that scared the living shit out of me. I didn't have time to think about that now, though. There were more pressing matters to attend to.

From the bloating, it looked as if the body had been down here for at least two days. Rigor Mortis hadn't passed yet, which meant it certainly hadn't been more than three or four days. I closed the guy's eyes; that had always been the first thing I'd done when I'd been called out to a body when I worked for the church, and old habits died hard. Then, it was about preserving the deceased's dignity. This time, it was because the dead guy's stunned, accusatory gaze was creeping me the fuck out. The guy's skin felt waxy and weird as I touched his face. I cringed, resisting the urge to scrub my hands on my jeans—there was no point trying to clean myself yet. I still had to go through the guy's pockets.

I found nothing in the breast pocket of his shirt. A branded book of matches—*Crazy Girls' exotic dance club and men's revue!* —and a pouch of rolling tobacco were in the left-hand side pocket of his stained cargo pants. A set of keys in the right-hand side pocket. Who the fuck wore cargo pants anymore? I held my breath as I rifled through the numerous pockets down each of his legs, but I didn't find anything else.

No wallet. That was weird, but perhaps it explained a few things. Maybe this guy ended up dead because he'd been mugged, in which case it made sense that he had no wallet. Something told me he hadn't been robbed, however. In a bunker, in a deserted town? Highly unlikely, unless his attacker had known about this place and had come here with him. More likely, if someone *had* come here with him, that they'd taken his wallet so he couldn't be identified, not because they wanted to steal his money.

There was a pair of shoes tucked neatly underneath the cot. Black. Simple. Leather. They were polished to a high shine, not a scratch or scuff mark on them. I cocked my head, studying them for a moment, before I came to a number of conclusions. These shoes did not belong to the dead man. They were at least two sizes too big, for starters. And they hardly went with plaid and cargo pants. They were dress shoes, the kind worn with a high-end suit or a tuxedo. From the dirt underneath Dead Guy's fingernails, he wasn't the kind of person to be wearing a suit or a tuxedo.

There were no other shoes inside the bunker, which begged the question: where had Dead Guy's shoes disappeared to? He hadn't arrived here barefoot. The holey socks on his feet were dirty, but not dirty enough to suggest he'd been padding around in them up there on the graffiti highway.

It was growing hotter and hotter. Stifling, even though the hatch was still wide open. Time to go. I placed my foot on the bottom rung of the ladder and stepped—

Wait.

What was *that*?

There was something underneath the desk. I crouched down, squinting, shining the phone's flashlight under the desk, and saw what looked like a small black bag sitting there on the concrete. There was no chair at the desk, which was strange. Why bother having a desk but no way of sitting at it? I stooped down and retrieved the bag—small, canvas, with looped handles—and then I surveyed the room to see if I'd missed anything else. There was nothing obvious, so I climbed up the ladder and got the fuck out of there.

Sera had stopped shivering, but her face was pale as I sat down next to her on the curb. She looked askance, her lips drawn into a tight smile. "Figure out who did it, Sherlock?"

I held up the bag for her to see. "There's very little to go on down there. I found this, though."

Sera eyed it as if it were about to blow up any second. It was too light to contain anything too sinister, though. "What's inside?" she asked.

"Let's open it up and find out."

She paled even further, her skin turning a sickly shade of green. "That's what you said about the bunker, Fix, and the surprise waiting for us down there was pretty crappy. You'll forgive me if I don't want to stick my hand inside that thing and pull out a mangled human heart or something."

I arched an eyebrow at her. "For someone who wants to get their hands dirty, you're very unwilling to *actually* get your hands dirty."

"*You* open it and see what's inside," she said. "Establish that it's not a biohazard or toxic in any way, then show me."

"Suit yourself." I unzipped the bag, opening it wide, and I took a look inside.

No human heart. No vials of deadly pathogens. No weird voodoo bones, or dead babies in jars. Just a stack of papers. Papers were great. Papers were fucking amazing when it came to gathering information. I tipped the bag upside down, shaking it so the contents slid out and landed on the ground between my feet.

The first page I toed with my boot revealed a drawing. Hand sketched, rough and messy, but it actually captured the likeness of its subject with surprising accuracy. It was Sera. Just her face. Beautiful, the rendition of her eyes almost perfect, staring out of the paper. I hissed between my teeth, picking the piece of paper up, holding it gingerly between my thumb and index finger. Sera glanced at it and started shaking all over again.

The second piece of paper was another drawing. Another image of Sera. As was the third, and the fourth, and the fifth. The sixth drawing was of her naked, her full breasts and the smooth slope of her stomach drawn with far more care than the other images.

"Oh my god," Sera whispered, covering her mouth with the back of her hand. "What the fuck *is* this?" Her eyes flitted from one picture to the next, as she slowly shook her head. I leafed through the remaining pieces of paper, my blood turning cold as each drawing grew more and more pornographic in nature.

Sera, touching herself, her fingers dipping between her legs.

Sera's mouth wrapped around a cock.

Sera, on her back, legs spread, her pussy on display.

Sera on her hands and knees, looking up, lips parted, an expression of ecstasy on her face.

A sob slipped out of Sera's mouth. "That's not me. That is *not* me. I never posed for any of these. I would never..."

A dark, poisonous, toxic anger spread its way through my body. "I know. I know you didn't do any of this." The author of these works had nailed her face, but I'd seen Sera naked. I knew her body, her breasts, her legs, her ass... Whoever had drawn these pictures hadn't known her the way I knew her. He'd made an educated guess as to what she would look like if she submitted herself to him, and the details were frightening in nature.

These were dreams.

Fantasies.

I closed my hand around the drawing I was holding, grinding my teeth together so hard I felt my jaw crack. "Whoever that guy was," I snarled, hurling the balled-up paper into the street, "I swear to god, if he drew these, it's a good job he's already fucking dead."

～

The fire crackled and spat cheerfully as I fed it the drawings one by one. We'd driven twenty minutes down the road to the town of Lavelle, where I'd found and booked us into a decent hotel and told Sera to wait in our room while I disposed of the black bag and its contents. Once the last drawing was gone, eaten by the flames, I doused the fire I'd set in a ditch off the highway and I made my way back to the hotel.

When I entered the room, Sera was sitting in the exact same position she'd been in when I left her, perched on the edge of the bed with her arms wrapped around her body. She gave me a sidelong glance, every part of her screaming with panic. "You were gone so long," she said softly. "I didn't think you were coming back."

"You think I'd just leave you here?" I sat down beside her, then fell back so I was lying on the bed.

Touch her.

Hold her.

Kiss her.

I put a stop to the urgent voice in my head immediately. She wasn't ready for any of that. Didn't want it. I was a piece of shit, but I wasn't going to try and comfort a woman who didn't want to be comforted, just because it hurt *me* to see her so freaked out.

"I haven't been able to stop thinking," she said slowly. "The things that guy drew..."

Graphic.

Demeaning.

Terrible.

"He wanted to do those things to me," she continued. "He wanted...*me*. Why would he hire you to murder me if he was so..."

"In love with you?" I bit the end of my tongue. Why the fuck couldn't I keep my goddamn mouth shut?

She grimaced, sucking in an uneven breath. "Why would he want me dead, if he was so into me?" The question cost her dearly, I could tell. She was frightened and ready to bolt, and saying things like that clearly made her skin crawl.

"I have no idea," I told her. I didn't tell her what I suspected: that there had probably been another man down in that bunker at some point. That there was every chance those drawings *hadn't* been inked by the dead man on the cot. I huffed, closing my eyes. "Lie down, Sera."

"I don't want to lie down."

"Just fucking do it."

She sat there for a moment. I knew her well enough to know she was trying to think of a colorful way to tell me to go fuck myself. But then she sank back beside me, her hair spilling around her head like a halo of jet-black ink against the pure white of the bed sheets. "This is a bad dream," she said. "I keep waiting to wake up, but the seconds keep on ticking by and I'm still stuck here, wondering when the fuck it's all going to end."

"It *will* end," I told her. "Everything's going to be fine."

"How do you know?" She turned her head so that she was facing me, her question mirrored in the troubled expression on her face. "You can't know that, Fix."

Fuck, she was beautiful. I curled my hands into fists, pressing them down into the comforter. "I do know it, because I'm here with you. And if you're with me, nothing bad's going to happen to you. I won't allow it."

Her mouth turned up into a tight, unhappy smile. "You're gonna protect me if someone comes after me?"

"I'll fucking destroy anyone who dares to try. I won't take you back to Seattle, if that's truly what you want, but you have to promise me something. You have to promise you're not going to go off the deep end and do anything stupid in order to find this guy. I'm going to make sure you're safe at all times. You're my only priority. My entire focus is on you and keeping you alive. But *you* have to keep you alive, too."

"I do know some Muay Thai. I can protect myself if I need to." She smiled a woefully sad smile. "I *will* protect myself. My life's been so normal for a long time now. I just don't know what the fuck I'm supposed to do through any of this. I want to bury my head in the sand and move on, pretend like none of it's happening, but I can't. If I do that, I'm always going to be looking over my shoulder, wondering if the guy behind me in Starbucks is going to grab me and throw me into the back of his dirty rape van. That's no life, Fix. I feel like I've been violated. Those drawings were so specific. I mean, who does that? Who'd draw a woman they didn't know in a bunch of porn positions, just to get off?"

"You'd be surprised. Guys can be fucking disgusting."

"You followed me. You watched me in Seattle, and now you say you're attracted to me. How am I supposed to know..." She swallowed. "How am I supposed to know that you're not like that, too?"

Her question was the hard-soled heel of a boot pressing down against my neck. God. She was fucking right. Whoever drew those pictures of her was obsessed with her in a very dangerous, fucked up way. I'd crossed a line when I was in Seattle. I'd allowed myself to do it, not believing that I'd ever even come face to face with her, but I had been wrong. Telling her that I was attracted to her back in the cabin on Butcher's Mountain, explaining that I had been for some time, had been really fucking hard. In my head, I'd convinced myself I'd never have to tell her that. But I needed for her to believe I meant her no ill will, and in order to do that I'd had to tell her the truth.

Now, here was a guy who'd also developed a crush on her from afar, and had been drawing sick, evil pictures of her while he no doubt jerked off, who was also probably the guy who'd paid to have her killed in the first place, and I was expecting her to be able to tell the difference between me and him.

The comparison made me sick to my stomach, but I understood how she felt. I didn't blame her for questioning absolutely everything. It simply made her smart. I was going to show her that there was a difference between me and this fucking guy, though. I was going to make it so damned obvious that she would never doubt me or my intentions again.

Rolling onto my side, I flared my nostrils, staring into her eyes. I reached into my pocket, and I pulled out her phone. I hadn't given it back to her after we'd discovered the body. I typed three numbers into the keypad and I handed it back to her now. She looked down at it and frowned.

"You want me to call 911?"

"You can if you want to. I won't stop you. I won't run. You can tell the cops everything."

Her hands shook as she held her phone. "They'll arrest you. You'll go to prison, Fix. You'll never see the light of day again."

"I'd rather die in fucking jail than have you think I was some monster who pursued you because he was sick in the head."

She looked at me, and then looked down at the three digits blazing on the screen of her phone. Her finger hovered over the green 'send call' button. "You're not serious?" she said.

"This is it, Sera. I care about you, and I fucking want you more than I've fucking wanted anything in my life. But I've put you through hell since I walked into that motel in Wyoming. I know that. You don't know me as well as I know you. I *did* have the benefit of watching you in Seattle, and you haven't had the same opportunity, so I get it. The events of the past week are all you have to go off. I'd be thinking the same things you're thinking, too, if I were in your shoes. I want you to know, though…there's the man you think I am, and the real me. I'm a killer. When it comes to putting a bullet in the skull of a man who has raped and hurt and caused pain since the moment he was old enough to make his own decisions, you should know…I won't fucking hesitate. But when it comes to you, I'm a breach wall. I'm the thing that stands between you and the dark. I will always be standing there, bracing for the shit storm, ready to fucking defend and protect you, if that's what you want, because you're the most important, pivotal, vital thing that's ever happened to me. You'll never find me sitting in a bunker, plotting and planning how to capture you behind closed doors. You'll find me with a knife in my hand, ready to sink it into the throat of the first person who dares to look at you fucking sideways. That's the truth. That's fucking *real*. That's the man you see lying on this bed with you right now. And if you doubt it, if you doubt me, even for a second…hit that call button, and I'll be gone in the most permanent way possible."

My heart was fucking racing. She could do so much damage with just one phone call, but I'd never been more serious, or meant anything so much before. My future was in her hands. Literally. And I was willing the face the music and fucking dance.

Sera's throat worked. Her pulse was racing and skipping just below the line of her jaw. She didn't know what to do, and who could blame her. Time stretched out endlessly as she speared me through with those demanding eyes. Prison wouldn't be a walk in the park. She didn't realize it, but the chances of me living out a long life in jail were slim to none. The crimes I'd committed, spread out across the breadth and width of the country, were heinous and violent enough to earn me a one-way trip to the electric chair. Or to a table with a needle in my arm, depending on which state fought for me the hardest. But let her envision me trapped behind bars, living out a long, miserable life if it made this easier for her. I wasn't going to weight her decision by letting her know that her next move might end up signing my death warrant.

She sucked her bottom lip into her mouth. I wanted to close my eyes; the waiting was like a knife inching closer and closer to my heart with each passing second, but I wasn't going to shut her out. She needed to be able to look into me. She needed to see the truth that was burning me up inside.

Sera exhaled, and then... the phone dropped from her hands onto the bed. She closed *her* eyes, and a fat, heavy tear chased its way across the bridge of her nose, streaking across her cheek, falling onto the mattress alongside the phone.

"I don't want you to go to prison," she whispered. "I believe you. I shouldn't. But I do. And now, I don't know what to do, because..." Her voice caught in her throat. She paused. Regained control over herself. "Sixsmith used to beat me. He beat Amy, too. And he...he did much, *much* worse. When I left South Carolina, I vowed that violent men were never going to play a leading role in my life again, Fix. The violence that lives inside you petrifies me. It fucking *terrifies* me. I can see it sometimes, a dark, cold, inexplicable thing that forces its way out of you, and I want to run. But I never do. You just gave me my phone and told me to call the cops, but the truth is you've never cut me off from the world. You never took my phone away from me and forbade me from screaming for help. And I think...that fact alone is what's kept me here with you. A part of me's *always* known you're not like that guy in the bunker. A part of me is stupid, and reckless, and it's been playing Russian roulette with my life since the moment I realized I was free of my father, because that part of me was used to feeling like I could die at any moment, and it missed...it missed the threat. That's...god, that's *so fucked up*."

Another tear fell, and then another. She was crying, and I'd made her do it, and it made me fucking hate myself. It also made me sing with fucking relief, because she wasn't going to end this. Dying didn't scare me as much as being without her. *That* was *really* fucked up, but it was the truth. I reached out and I stroked my fingers lightly down her cheek. She could pull back at any moment, and I was ready for that. I'd accept it. But the brief moment of contact was worth the possibility of rejection, and I was used to playing Russian roulette, too.

"You're a weapon, Sera. You were forged in fire. When you remove a weapon from the flames, it becomes even stronger. Sharper. A hundred times more lethal than it ever was before. And it misses the burn. You're not fucked up for inviting danger into your life. You're just trying to prove that you're still strong."

She didn't flinch away from me; her eyelids flickered, and then she opened them. Slowly, tentatively, she raised her hand to touch mine, threading her fingers through my own. "I'm not going to ask you to collar the monster inside you, because I already know it, and it's a part of you," she said. "I'll allow your demons to protect me, and I'll use mine to defend you, too. Stupid though that is. However fucking dangerous and unbelievably idiotic though that is. But I'm keeping the gun, Fix. And I will use it the moment your demons look like they're turning on me."

Holy. Fucking. Shit.

This woman.

She was miraculous.

She was beautiful.

She was strong.

She was everything.

Grinning, I rolled myself over, straddling her body, supporting myself over her. Gradually, I began to lower myself.

"Sera Lafferty...I wouldn't expect anything less."

25

SERA

TUG OF WAR

*I*f I were home and telling Sadie about what I was about to do, she'd call St. Peter's Hospital and have me fucking committed. Unlike me, Sadie was sensible. She was steadfast and reliable. When she saw an accident on the side of the road, she didn't lean her head out of the fucking window and wind up crashing her car, too. She'd been brought up by college professors. Parents who hadn't gone ahead and died on her, or raised their fists to her, or sold her to the highest bidder. She hadn't had to worry about anyone creeping into her bedroom late at night when the rest of the world was sleeping. When I'd first moved to Seattle, I'd used Sadie as a touchstone for sanity, watching how she reacted to situations and experiences to see how a *normal* person might respond. After a while the constant editing taking place in my head became exhausting, though, and I gave up.

Sadie was the only person who knew me well enough to call me out when she thought I might be teetering on the edge of stupidity, but she wasn't here right now. I was alone with Fix, and I was about to do something remarkably stupid.

I. Did. Not. Care.

His mouth was getting closer and closer, and the smell of him was filling my head—a fresh, masculine, indefinable scent that made my back arch up off the bed. I wanted him. I wanted him on top of me, his entire weight pressing down on me, making me feel safe. I wanted his hands tearing at my clothes, his tongue in my mouth, his cock pushing inside me, and I was going to have it all.

Fix's wicked eyes, brimming over with lust, promised as much if I wanted it. They promised ecstasy, and pleasure, and release. They promised that he was going to steal my breath away, and my soul, too, if I allowed it. I slid my hands up over his back, digging my fingernails into his skin through his t-shirt, and the demanding, breathtaking man on top of me growled so low that a thrill of anticipation shot through me, rocking me to my core.

"*Bad Angel*," Fix murmured against my lips. He was moments away from kissing me, and I could barely hold myself still long enough for his mouth to meet mine. My need filled me like there was a dam wall holding it in place, but the wall was buckling. The pressure was too great. Too intense. If I'd been with anybody else, I would have reined in that need, forced it into submission so that cooler heads could prevail, but this was different. My need for Fix washed away the worry, the pain, and the fear that I'd been wrestling all day. My desire muted anything and everything else so efficiently that I knew it was going to become a problem. An addiction, like a drug. Every hit of Felix Marcosa that I took left me higher than I'd ever been before, and the come down, though considerable, was completely worth it.

The muscles in Fix's shoulders strained as he lowered himself down yet another inch, and I couldn't do it. Couldn't hold myself back anymore. I reached up to meet him, and when our lips crashed together it felt like I'd just jumped from a high board into a deep, bottomless pool, my body rocking from the impact. Fix groaned as I opened my mouth and allowed him to slide his tongue inside. I was cocooned in him. Surrounded by him. Enveloped in him. I forgot to breathe, forgot why I even *needed* to breathe as Fix lowered himself down on top of me, bracing part of his weight on one elbow, as he used his free hand to cup and knead at my breasts. I was drowning in him. I was meters down, and I couldn't tell which way was up, and I had no hope of surfacing any time soon. To do so, I would have to tear myself away from him, and that just wasn't going to happen.

Fix pushed one of his knees between my legs and roughly shoved them apart. At the same time, he squeezed my nipple between his thumb and finger, pinching, and a sharp pain volleyed between my breasts and my pussy, making me gasp against his mouth. A perilous smile spread across his face as he settled himself between my legs. "Can you feel it?" he rumbled.

"Feel...what?" I was feeling everything all at once, and the over-load of stimuli was threatening to turn me inside out.

"*This.*" Fix rocked his hips up and forward so that the hard length of his cock pressed up against my pussy.

Oh...my...*god.*

I sucked in a breath, trying not to moan, to let him know how badly that one small movement on his part affected me, but it was impossible to hold it back. I shook as Fix repeated the movement, grinding his hips up against me, so that the length of his erection rubbed upward over my pussy, and he laughed darkly into the hollow at the base of my neck.

His teeth nipped at my too-sensitive skin, and I shuddered, my eyes rolling back into my head. He'd barely touched me, barely kissed me, and yet I was already prepared for him, burning between my legs, my nipples peaked and throbbing. I was considering tearing his fucking clothes off with my goddamn teeth.

"Yes, I feel it," I panted. "I can feel your cock. You're so fucking hard."

In one swift movement, he grabbed hold of my wrists, tugging my arms up over my head, pinning them there. I was immobile. Trapped. "Good," he ground out. "I could make you come like this alone. I could make your body sing so prettily for me like this, Sera. But I won't. I want your naked body on mine. I want to watch your tits bounce as I thrust my dick inside you. And..." His raised his mouth to whisper to me, his lips gently grazing the shell of my ear. His hot breath sent a barrage of sensation needling all over my body. "I want to feel how wet your cunt is, Sera." He spoke the words reverently, like he was professing his sins. "I want to slide my fingers inside you, and I want to feel your pussy tighten as I fuck you with them, Angel. And when you're close, when you're so close to coming that you're completely out of control, I want to slide my fingers back, and I want to tease your ass with your own come, Sera. I want to dip my fingers inside you, and I want to feel you pulse and throb as you tumble over the edge. Have you ever had someone finger your ass while you come?" he growled.

He held both my wrists in his left hand, and with his right, he traced his fingers down my body, his touch lighting me on fire, blazing a pathway between my breasts, over my stomach, until he reached the waistband of my jeans, where he halted.

"No, I've never... No one's ever..." I stammered. It had felt like Gareth's life mission was to stick things into my ass. He'd wanted to do anal so badly that he ended up calling me a prude every time I refused him. Gareth had never asked, though. He'd simply tried to (roughly) shove his dick into my ass at every available opportunity, to the point where I wouldn't let him fuck me from behind anymore, because he kept 'accidentally slipping.'

Gareth was a bully. He'd wanted to fuck me in the ass because it inflated his ego and empowered him. He'd intended it as an act of dominance designed to demean me, and even though I'd convinced myself I was in love with him, I'd still had enough dignity to tell him to go and get fucked.

The way Fix was talking about this now was a completely different experience. He didn't want to degrade or debase me. He wanted to incite pleasure, to make me feel good, and the fire that was burning in his mercurial eyes made me want to give in to him without a second thought.

"I want to use my tongue on you there," he rumbled. "My fingers. My cock. I want to fuck your pussy with my fingers while my dick is in your ass. I want to make you come so fucking hard. You'll scream for me, and you'll beg, and you'll love every second of it. I promise you."

He released me without warning, sitting up on the bed. Rising from the mattress, he got to his feet, and disappointment gnawed at me. He wasn't going to fuck me? That searing kiss and his raging hard-on, which was still visible, straining at his jeans, had suggested otherwise, but...

Fix pulled out the chair that was pushed underneath the desk by the window; he picked it up with ease, and then placed it three feet from the bed, facing me. He toed off his shoes, and then sat down on the chair.

"Come and undress me," he commanded.

I'd tugged a guy's clothes off before, hands scrambling to strip the guy I was about to tumble into bed with, but Fix made this sound like a formal event. I sat up, then slowly slid off the bed, feeling slightly unsteady on my feet. He had such a mind-bending effect on me. I wasn't a shy, retiring wallflower, though. I wasn't going to wilt before the very first challenge he placed in front of me. I'd do as he asked of me, and I'd make him fucking proud.

Fix watched me, his eyes tracking me as I shifted to stand in front of him. I mustered every last scrap of confidence I possessed, and I reached out, cupping my hand to his face. He was a deity amongst mere mortal men. Every line of him was carved out with precision and purpose—the embodiment of perfection. His stubble bit at my palm, rough to the touch, as I stroked the pad of my thumb over the rugged line of his cheekbone. Fix hummed—an amused, deep sound that vibrated in the air.

"It's yours," he murmured. "My face. My mouth. My hands. My body. My cock. All of it. If you want it, it's all yours. Feel free to use the fuck out of me."

Dear Lord. Thank you so much for your depraved servant, Felix. Those poor women back in New York who'd had to look at Father Marcosa every Sunday. Married or single, he must have been the wickedest temptation. At least they'd never known what they were *truly* missing. The things this man could do to make a woman feel good. The words that could slide so easily from his tongue and melt a woman in an instant. I doubted very much that he'd ever looked at any of his female congregation the way he was looking at me now—pure sex. Pure carnal lust. It would have driven them insane with the unfairness of it all. It was the height of irony that a man like him had once been a proponent for virtue, obedience, restraint and morality, when he was precisely none of those things.

He called me Angel, but the truth was *he* was the angel. An angel who had fallen so hard and so dramatically that neither one of us knew whether he stood for right or wrong anymore.

I pressed my hand to his chest, sliding it down over the hard, packed muscle that made up his torso. When I reached the hem of his t-shirt, I didn't hesitate. I gathered the material in both my hands, and I pulled it upwards over his head.

It was difficult not to stare at him. His broad shoulders; the smooth, tan lines of his chest; his abs, which were frankly ridiculous: he was magnificent, every inch of him flawless, and from the cocky, tilted smile he was wearing, he fucking knew it. I assessed him coolly, moving to stand between his legs.

His belt buckle was easy to unfasten. I yanked on the length of leather, freeing it from his jeans.

"You going to put me over your knee and spank me with that?" Fix asked, his smile spreading even further across his face. He was joking—the tone of his voice told me as much—but still, my cheeks burned with a heat I had no hope of mastering. He was such a bastard. He knew exactly how a question like that would affect me, and yet he still asked it. He liked to see me squirm.

"You're too big," I answered. "And besides...we both know you're the one who wants to spank *me*."

His laugh was more of a snarl. "You have no fucking idea. I'd love to spank you. I'd love to see that amazing ass of yours all pink and covered in my handprints."

I dropped the belt, and it clattered to the floor. Fix followed me with his eyes as I dropped to my knees, and I deftly unfastened the button of his jeans. "*Up*," I told him.

This was entertaining the shit out of him. He grunted, licking his lower lip, and then he got to his feet. With quick, determined movements I pulled his jeans down over his hips—and then his cock was there, right in front of me, level with my mouth, so damned hard and so damned perfect. Fix's eyes glittered as he looked down at me, on my knees, before him. "Do you know how good it feels to push my dick into your warm mouth, Sera?" he asked, his voice rough, edged with need. "When you use your tongue on the tip? When you take all of me in and you *suck*?"

The last word was emphasized plainly enough that I knew it was what he wanted. I wasn't going to give him everything on a platter that easily, though. I jerked his jeans from his body, discarding them, enjoying the view as I looked up at his naked form. God...I didn't have words for how he made me feel. I was so drawn to him, compelled to him like a supercharged magnet, tearing through whatever obstacle stood in between us in order to reach him. I hadn't been very honest with myself recently, but it felt safe to be honest now. He consumed my every thought. His smile. The arrogant tilt of his jaw. The outrageous things that came out of his mouth.

I'd never been so turned on by someone before. *Ever*. I knew with a certainty that I could sleep with another hundred men, attractive men who were all seriously talented in the bedroom, but I would never be so attracted to anyone else for as long as I lived. It wasn't just his body. It was the way he spoke, and his fierce protectiveness, and his surprising sense of humor, and the way he looked at me, like I was the only thing that existed in his world. It was the way he made me come alive in every imaginable way. There were countless factors that drew me to him, and I knew as I ran my hands along the outside of his toned, muscled thighs that I was well and truly fucked. Somewhere along the way, I'd given too much of myself over to him. It had happened so gradually that the concessions and allowances I'd made for myself when it came to Fix had seemed small and unimportant on their own.

But just now, on the bed, when he'd handed me that phone, and said all of those frightening, beautiful things to me, I'd handed over the very last piece of myself before I'd realized what was happening. And the scariest part, that would haunt me for the rest of eternity, was that I *wasn't* scared at all.

"You think you're hot shit, don't you?" I said, smirking up at him.

He nodded. "Yeah. Because I am."

"You think your dick's the most incredible thing to happen to woman kind." I studied the appendage in question as I spoke, and Fix had the audacity to make the damn thing twitch.

"Not to woman kind. Just you, Sera."

"You are *so* arrogant. You make a lot of assumptions."

"I assume nothing. I *know* I'm good in bed. I *know* I can make you come, and I take great fucking pleasure in doing it. You're the only woman I'm interested in pleasing, Sera, which means my attention, and my dick, are solely devoted to giving you the most earth shattering orgasms possible. That makes you a lucky girl." Fix reached out and stroked his hand over my hair, tipping his head to one side. "I *am* an arrogant piece of shit, but I know just how fucking lucky *I* am, too. You take my breath away. Your body is exquisite. Your cunt feels fucking phenomenal when I push myself inside you, and when you make me come, I lose my goddamn mind. I can't see straight. I can't hear properly. You set fire to me whenever we come into contact, and I fucking *burn*. You have license to be just as smug as I am."

I'd felt how hard he came when he was with me back in that field at the wedding, and the way he'd cried out, crushing me to him when he climaxed, told me he'd enjoyed the encounter just as much I had. But it was very gratifying to hear him say it. "Sit down," I told him.

"You realize one of these days one of us is going to have to submit," Fix said. "You allow me a little leash. I allow you a little." He sat down tauntingly slowly. "One of these days, one of us will have to acknowledge the other is in full control."

"You just did," I answered. "You put me in charge of your future just now when you gave me that phone. You told me you cared about me. You've shown your hand."

Laughing gently, he ran his tongue over his bottom lip. "Oh, Angel. Don't be fooled. Just because I'm capable of dispelling the idea that I'm a heartless, emotionally stunted caveman who can't ever share what he's thinking or feeling, doesn't mean I'm weak. I'm strong enough to fight for you. Strong enough to tell the truth. Strong enough to command you. And I'm strong enough to bend your will to me."

"Bend? Not break?"

He leaned back in the chair, stretching out his body. So fucking handsome. Beyond handsome. They hadn't created a word that would do him justice yet; I was left wanting when I tried to pinpoint a satisfactory adjective to describe him. I nearly had to sit back down on the bed when he took his cock in his hand, and he began to stroke it—smooth, fluid movements of his wrist that damn near mesmerized me. "No, not break," he said, his voice gruff. "I will never break you, Sera Lafferty. What would be the point? That fiery defiance that burns inside you? I am drawn to it like a moth to a flame. I adore it. I worship it. Why would I want to extinguish it?"

My mouth was dry as sandpaper. I wanted him. God, I wanted him so badly, and he knew it. Fix squeezed the end of his cock, staring right into me. His lips parted, pleasure etched into the lines of his face. "Take off your clothes," he said softly. "Get undressed and lie down on the bed."

My blood thundered in my ears as I stripped. I laid down and waited for him to come and join me, but he didn't. I propped myself up on one elbow, arching a questioning eyebrow at him. "Are you going to make me wait, Fix Marcosa?"

"*Touch yourself.*" His order filled the silent room.

"You...want me to masturbate?"

"I want you to make yourself come. I want to watch how you make yourself feel good. Make yourself pant. Make yourself moan for me, Sera."

"And you're going to be...?"

"I'm going to be doing the exact same thing. Feel free to observe." As if in response, he pumped his hand up and down his cock a little faster. He hissed quietly, and heat danced over my lips, making them tingle. I wanted him in my mouth.

So. Fucking. Badly.

He was beyond turned on, that much was clear, and watching his hand work up and down the length of his erection was beginning to have the same effect on me. Rejecting the nerves that fluttered in my stomach, I spread my legs open, and I slid my hand down, until the very tips of my fingers met with the wet, slick apex at the top of my thighs. Fix's eyes shuttered, taking on a glazed, distant look, and my skin erupted into goosebumps. His hunger was a tangible thing. He watched with rapt fascination as I worked my fingers in small, tight circles over my clit.

"Fuck, Sera. You have the prettiest pussy. You're a fucking goddess," he groaned. Faster still, Fix's hand pumped harder, and a small bead of pre-cum gathered at the tip of his cock. I wanted to lick it from him. To taste him. To swallow him down. I couldn't move from the bed, though. I was trembling too hard, so much adrenalin flooding my system, and my clit was growing more and more sensitive with every light rub of my fingers.

"Slide one inside," Fix instructed. "Fuck yourself for me."

I gave him what he wanted. My breath caught in my throat when I dipped my fingers down, slipping two of them inside myself. "Oh, god. Fix, I need you so bad. *Please.*"

He remained on the chair, his eyes locked on me, sweeping over me, devouring my breasts, and my legs, and my fingers, as I thrust them inside and withdrew again and again. A rough, frustrated sound, half growl, half groan, came from his lips. "Soon, Angel. Soon."

Shit, this felt so fucking good. I used my other hand to rub my clit at the same time, and soon I found myself getting close. It had taken no time at all. It wasn't the way I was touching myself that was going to make me come. It was the fact that Fix was watching me, and the fierce intensity in his eyes as he jerked his hand up and down even faster. The muscles in his arm and his neck strained as he looked up at me, and I saw his own urgency—he was about to come, too. I moaned, strained and breathless, a sound I'd never heard myself make before, and my legs locked up.

There was no need to tell him what was about to happen. He knew. He must have been able to see the tension in my body. My back arched away from the mattress, and Fix swore savagely.

"Fuck, Sera. Fucking do it."

I stopped breathing. A brilliant, blazing explosion erupted between my thighs, quickly spreading outward, traveling over my buttocks, down the backs of my legs, prickling at the soles of my feet. The tingling sensation in my nipples, over my chest and pooling at the base of my throat and the back of my neck bordered on painful.

I almost closed my eyes, wanting to lean into the shockwave that threatened to rip me apart, but I saw the expression on Fix's face, and I couldn't look away. He was magnificent. Glorious and terrifying. His eyes were spearing into me, flaring with desire, and the muscle in his jaw was popping as he ground his teeth together. His head rocked back, the tendons and muscles in the column of his neck straining too, now, and Fix let out a violent snarl as he released. I couldn't look away as his shoulders rolled back and jets of fluid arced from his cock, landing on his chest and his stomach.

We both slowed, both gripped in a post-orgasmic daze, and Fix rolled his head forward again so he was looking at me.

"You're the most amazing thing I've ever seen," he said hoarsely. "I couldn't fucking stop myself."

My legs were unsteady beneath me as I pushed myself off the bed and went to stand, naked, before him. He'd slid down the chair when he was coming, and now his back was curved, his abs bunched together and glistening with his come. He was a sight to behold—so fucking hot, I didn't quite believe that he really existed. He scrutinized me with quick, sharp eyes, his pupils so blown they were almost obscuring the silver that ringed them.

"Thirty seconds," he said.

I angled my head to one side, marveling at how absolutely breathtaking he was. At how ridiculously sexy it was that he was covered in his own come. "Until what?" I whispered.

A dark, treacherous kind of mischief shone in his eyes. "Until I'm fully recovered," he answered. "You have thirty seconds until I fuck the living daylights out of you. I hope you're fucking ready."

It was only twenty-seven seconds later when he had his tongue in my mouth, my legs wrapped around his waist, and he was driving his rock-solid cock into me, making me scream out his name.

26

FIX

COFFEE AND TOAST

*M*y feet pounded out a rhythm like a drum as I ran through the rain. There were no cars out on the road of Lavelle yet, and the streetlights were still on, but the sky was already light enough to see by. It was going to be a perfectly miserable day. Other men were climbing out of their beds, grumbling under their breath, hating the fact that they had to leave the warmth and comfort of their slumber behind and head out into the wet and the wind in order to get to their shitty day jobs. I, on the other hand, felt like it was Christmas fucking morning.

Sera was mine.

Sera was mine.

Sera was mine.

Sera was mine.

The thought played on a loop through my head as I pushed myself harder, sprinting through the abandoned streets, not caring when my feet ended up submerged in deep, freezing cold puddles. Sera was fucking *mine*.

I'd always loved running in the rain. I'd started doing it in high school, when I ran track for the state. I'd quickly realized that besides keeping me fit, running also cleared my head, swept away the cobwebs, and made me feel absolutely incredible. The rain? The rain was an added bonus. It kept my mind from wandering.

Three miles to go, and I could go back to the hotel, take a shower, climb back into bed and make Sera come all over my dick again. It was amazing how an incentive like that could make me fucking fly. My lungs were aching, and my legs felt like lead by the time I neared the hotel, but my mood was soaring.

To my right, a small diner had opened while I'd been gone, and the faded red sign glowed in the washed-out morning light. The hotel definitely had room service, but the moment I walked into that room and saw Sera still peacefully sleeping in that bed, the very last thing I was going to want was someone hammering on the door and disturbing us. It would only take a few minutes to stop in at the diner and grab some coffees to go. Totally worth it. I swung a left, slowing to a walk as I approached the diner, calming my breath so I wasn't panting like some kind of animal when I stepped inside.

Surprisingly, there were three people already sitting at the counter with steaming mugs in their hands—two rough-edged men who might have been brothers, and a woman with blonde hair so pale that it almost looked silver. By the looks of things, they'd come together for their morning injection of caffeine, and their conversation, loud and boisterous, halted when they heard the door swing closed behind me. The woman, who was well kept and maybe in her late forties, jerked her chin at me, and said, "Morning. Sally's in the back. She won't be a minute."

"Thank you." I smiled at her, then scrubbed my hand through my hair, sending a shower of rain drops scattering into the air. I made a show of fussing over how wet I was while I tried to figure out if it was a good idea to stay.

The moment that woman had looked in my direction, I'd known she was law enforcement. The other two guys with her were, too. They were either finishing a shift or about to start one. Their jackets, hanging on the backs of their chairs, were turned inside out. Some counties were really strict when it came to cops and members of the other emergency services sitting down to eat or drink in their uniforms; it looked like Lavelle was situated within the limits of one of those counties.

There was no need to panic. Not yet anyway. I had a really fucking smart mouth sometimes, but I knew when to shut the fuck up and keep it closed. I also knew how to play the polite, respectful, law-abiding member of the community. I'd lost count of how many sticky situations I'd talked my way out of. Leaning against the counter, seven seats down from the officers, I took my cell phone out of my pocket and stared industriously at the screen, pretending to look busy. Phones were great for that. A man lost in his phone was unapproachable, and the rest of the world generally left him alone.

Monica had texted me.

*M*onica: Lafferty job is off. Cease and desist.

*Y*eah, no shit the Lafferty job was off. I'd decided that before I'd even met Sera, but Monica wasn't to know. It was a good job she hadn't known more of what had been going on in Wyoming and Alabama. She would have flipped her shit so epically, her meltdown would have been visible from outer space.

I typed back.

*M*e: Consider it called off. Why?

*A*lmost immediately, Monica began to type out a response.

*M*onica: Our friend Carver decided to go with another option. Said our services were unreliable. I think he was right. Something's wrong with you, and I'm losing patience. I know you're in Pennsylvania. Tell me what's going, or I'm jumping on a plane. I'm not kidding!

*S*hit. I'd kept Monica at bay for much longer than I'd thought I would be able to, but this was eleventh hour talk from her. She really would come and find me, and soon. We had contingencies in place. If I went missing, or I got myself into trouble, Monica was able to track me via my cell phone, and given that she knew I was in Pennsylvania, she'd done just that. If I switched off the 'find my iPhone' feature on my cell, she'd panic and be flying out of the door before she had time to even pack a bag. I needed to figure out what to tell her, and I needed to do it fast.

I was worried about that for sure, but I was more worried about the fact that our 'friend' Carver had decided to hire someone else to complete the job. Another paid killer was on his way to find Sera. Another trained professional, who wouldn't think twice about shooting Sera the moment he had her in his sights.

"Kinda blustery out there this morning, huh?"

My head snapped up. The woman sitting at the other end of the counter was smiling at me in that small town, friendly way that usually meant she wanted to engage in conversation. I cursed silently, flashing her another smile of my own.

"Yeah, it's a little wild. Nothing I'm not used to, though."

The woman turned her coffee mug around, so she could pick it up by the handle with her other hand. "You staying at The Orroton?"

She knew I wasn't a local. Places like this, the local police knew everyone and all of their personal business inside out. "Yeah. My wife and I are traveling to see her mom in Kansas City. We're gonna be hitting the road in a couple of hours."

"Kansas City's a long old stretch. I'm not surprised you wanted to squeeze in a run. My back and my legs ache something chronic when I drive for more than an hour at a time."

"Yeah." I gave her a bland laugh. "Me, too."

The double doors that presumably led into the kitchen swung open, then, and a small, pixie-like woman with a mass of brown curls appeared, stuffing a notepad into the front pocket of her black apron. She looked startled when she caught sight of me. Startled, and then a little flustered. "Oh. I'm sorry, sir. Damn bell on the door fell off last week. I didn't hear you come in. Is there something I can get for you?"

"Just a couple of coffees, please," I told her. "And some croissants if you have them."

"Sorry. Best I can do is toast and preserves. Don't get much call for croissants, I'm afraid."

"Sure, that'll be great, thanks. To go." My head was doing somersaults. There was every chance someone was on their way to Sera's apartment in Seattle, hunting for her. They wouldn't find her there, but that was neither here nor there. I was good at finding people. Really fucking good at it. Credit card charges, a cell phone, emails— there were plenty of resources available to someone equipped with a little determination when they wanted to track someone down. And it was unlikely Carver would have hired someone who didn't have a clue how to locate their target.

The waitress—Sally, the cop had called her—put in the order for the toast and coffee, then poured the drinks, placing them on the counter in front of me. She rung me up, I paid, and then I stood there, waiting for the toast, considering just bailing on the food and rushing back to the hotel. Sera's phone needed to go. I needed to make sure she didn't tell anyone where we were. I needed to cut up her fucking bankcards. We needed to get somewhere safe and fucking fast.

Sally eyed me like she was thinking about talking to me, but I saw the moment she decided against it. I'd spent years honing my leave-me-the-fuck-alone face, and I'd donned it the second I'd taken my change from her and stuffed it into my pocket. She went and stood by the cops, propping herself up next to a glass cabinet that showcased a number of stale, dry looking dishes of food. "So, they identified that body?" she said in a brazen tone. She'd intended for me to hear, probably so I'd get pulled into conversation without her having to approach me directly. It was human nature. People were nosy as fuck. If they heard a dead body being discussed, they naturally wanted to know the details.

I remained glued to the spot, facing straight ahead, though. One of the male cops tutted under his breath, tapping a finger against the counter. "You know we can't tell you anything, Sal."

"She shouldn't even know about that. You been running your mouth, Tyrone?" the guy next to him chided.

"No bickering over breakfast," the blonde said. "*I* told Sally. She only knows what the morning papers are going to be reporting by now anyway, so no harm done."

"Come on, Moira," Sally pleaded. "Just tell me. Was it Anderson? No one's seen him for days. His car was towed from outside the fire station yesterday, and when have you ever known that man to leave that car of his somewhere he can't see it?"

I felt more eyes on me, but still I did nothing. Didn't move an inch. Didn't show the slightest bit of interest in what they were talking about.

"If you must know, then yes. It *was* Anderson," the woman, Moira, replied.

"That nut job's been causing problems since he showed up here in two thousand and six," Tyrone mused. "Ain't no wonder he ended up dead in a hole in the ground."

"But why was he over in Centralia? He never even drove by there if he could avoid it. Said those *methane gases* were giving everyone brain tumors." Sally said 'methane gases' like someone else might have said UFO, as if she didn't believe methane really existed.

"Who knows?" I watched Moira set her coffee mug down on the counter and slide it toward Sally in my peripherals. "Fill that up, would you, sweetheart? Today's gonna be a long ass day."

Sally picked up the coffee mug, but she didn't budge from her spot next to the glass cabinet. "Have you found any evidence down there? Any weapons or such? Hairs, or boot prints, or anything? I've been watching CSI: Miami a lot recently. It's amazing what you can figure out with the smallest little thing."

"Only a couple of fingerprints," Moira said. "Sent 'em off to the crime lab in Bethlehem this morning. We don't have access to the database out here, but apparently those Bethlehem guys have found at least one match. The files are waiting for us back at the station."

Shiiiiiiiiiiiiiiiiiiit.

They were talking about the same body Sera and I had discovered, that much was blatantly obvious. I'd been down in that hole. I'd touched this Anderson guy's body, whoever he was, and I'd also touched the desk. I was normally so careful about cleaning up after myself, but Sera had been distraught yesterday. It had been hot and airless, and I wanted to get the fuck out of there. I hadn't wiped down a fucking thing. My fingerprints were in plenty of police databases. If the cops had a file waiting for them back at the station, there was every chance it would be *my* file. And my photo would be plastered all over the fucking thing. These bastards would take one look at it and be hurtling out of the door, coming straight to The Orroton to find me.

Fuck.

Fuck!

How the hell had they even discovered the body?

We had to get the fuck out of Lavelle. We had to get out of Pennsylvania.

We had to leave.

Now.

27

SERA

MILKSHAKE

BEFORE

"*Did you brush your teeth?*"

I pinched the inside of my arm with as much force as I could muster, refusing to let my eyes fall shut. If I closed them, tried to block out my fear, Sixsmith would beat the living shit out of me. It wouldn't matter if he took his belt to me. It was the end of July, and we were still three weeks away from going back to school. I'd be all healed up by the time anyone of any importance would see me. "Yes, I brushed them," I answered quietly.

"And your hair?" Sixsmith's face twisted into an angry sneer. "You ain't brushed that."

"I'm sorry. I'll do it now." Meek. Docile. Eyes on the floor. Shoulders slouched. At first, I'd fought back against my father, but the more I'd refused to comply with his demands, the more I'd kicked and screamed, scratched and bitten at him, the more Amy had paid for my insolence. Sixsmith had finally figured me out. Last week, he'd given my sister a black eye because I hadn't washed out his favorite coffee mug. And only days before that, I had *jumped, startled by the sound of a door slamming, and I'd dropped one of his whiskey glasses. He hadn't allowed me to sweep up the shards before he'd made Amy walk barefoot in laps around the kitchen table. He finally had me on a very tight leash. Sixsmith knew I wouldn't be submissive for my own sake, but for Amy, to save her pain and suffering, I would be the very picture of obedience.*

My father rubbed his palms against the thighs of his filthy jeans, then scratched at his nose. "And between your legs. Go upstairs and wash yourself," he commanded.

I was stupid. For a moment, I forgot myself. "What? Why?"

Sixsmith snarled, lashing out at me with a steel-toe-capped boot. I made myself stand still to receive the blow—it would be ten times worse if I tried to avoid it—but Sixsmith was already drunk. He missed me entirely. "You're fifteen years old," he hissed. "Couple'a hundred years ago, you'd have been married off and probably have two kids by now. And guess what? I would have chosen who you fucking married. You wouldn't have had a single word to say on the matter. Now get upstairs and wash your fucking cunt before I knock every single one of your teeth out of your damn head."

I wanted to move. I knew I had to get the hell out of the kitchen and up the stairs, but my feet were like blocks of iron. I couldn't even muster the strength to lift them, let alone move them one in front of the other. Sixsmith rubbed a dirty finger at his stubble, his head slowly falling back until it was resting against the back of the chair. "If you don't get out of my sight, I'll drag you up there and I'll do it," he said quietly. "I'll take the wash cloth, and I'll rip down your clothes, and I will clean your pussy myself."

My disgust was a living, breathing thing inside me. His threat made me rally; I spun on my heel, hurrying out of the kitchen, and I raced up the stairs, mindful not to slam the bathroom door behind me once I'd run inside.

He didn't need an excuse. He would have done it. My father had been crossing more lines of late, and I could see the change in him. There was a shadow over him that hadn't been there before. Since that night in the kitchen when I'd kicked him in the balls and he'd torn my shirt, his hands cautiously cupping at my breasts, his fingers pressing down on my nipple, that shadow had been showing up regularly. I'd be completing my chores, humming quietly, thinking myself alone in an empty house, but when I turned around, there would be Sixsmith, watching me, pupils darker than midnight, sweat beading on his brow, his long, thin hair plastered to his skull and down his neck in the afternoon heat. Often, his hands would be in his pockets, but that did nothing to hide the fact that he was hard between his legs.

I unbuttoned my jeans and kicked my way out of them, and then I removed my shirt, every part of me shaking. I'd been waiting for this day to arrive for weeks. Sixsmith had threatened and warned, and threatened some more, made out as if it wouldn't happen if I behaved myself, but this morning he'd burst into my bedroom, almost ripping the door off its hinges, and he'd told me what was going to happen today in no uncertain terms.

"Sam Halloran's coming over here at midday. You're to be clean and dressed and waiting for him on the front porch. You're gonna go with him, and you're gonna do whatever he tells you to do. And if he comes back here and tells me you gave him any sass, I will strip your goddamn hide. Do you hear me?"

I'd just laid there, staring up at him, my heart thundering like a herd of wild horses. My mouth moved entirely of its own accord. "Yes, Sixsmith."

"Good. And don't you fucking cry, Sera. You fucking cry, and you won't even recognize the world of shit you find yourself in."

I reached for my wash cloth, and I caught sight of myself in the mirror over the sink. I looked older than I had just a couple of weeks ago, even I could see that. When school was in, things were a little more bearable. Amy and I were out of the house before Sixsmith dragged his lazy, hungover carcass out of bed, and he was still at work for three hours once we got home, so there were moments of peace. There were stolen moments when I could relax and read a book or watch Friends reruns on the static-filled TV in the living room, or just sit on the porch and do my homework with Amy in the waning sunlight, listening to the cicadas roaring in the fields.

I hated summer break. With school out, and with Sixsmith not getting much work recently, Amy and I had been at his mercy day and night. He hadn't had the money to go drinking at the bar like he usually did, and so he'd been buying the cheapest beer he could, sprawling out on the couch and drinking it at the house instead. If we made a noise, if we were under foot, if *we were an inconvenience in any way, then Sixsmith was tearing his belt from his pants and wailing on us with every last ounce of his strength.*

I barely recognized the face that stared back at me now, as I wriggled out of my panties and cleaned myself as I had been instructed.

I didn't allow my mind to wander. No good would come of it, and I needed to remain strong. Sam Halloran was a loan shark Sixsmith owed money to. Sam had come to call in his debts last week, and my father had cried poor. This was obviously the arrangement they had come to in lieu of the money Sixsmith owed, and I was being sold off like a slab of meat. I was collateral, and it didn't matter that I hated Sam Halloran almost as much as I hated Sixsmith. I was my father's property, and I wasn't entitled to a say in the matter.

Suffice it to say, I was terrified.

Once I was finished washing, I got dressed, but then I couldn't bring myself to leave the bathroom. Instead, I continued to stare at myself in the mirror, trying to talk myself through what was about to happen.

I was going to lose my virginity.

I was going to have a strange old man's hands all over my body.

I was going to have his tongue in my mouth.

I was going to have to remove my clothes for him, and I was going to have to keep quiet while he fucked me.

I couldn't react. I couldn't try to run. There was no option for me, other than to do as Sixsmith had bade me. He would be here, after all, back in the house, effectively holding Amy hostage until I got back, and Sam gave me a shining report.

I lifted my chin, shoving down the bile that was trying to rise in the back of my throat. I could do this. I had to do this. It was only a couple of hours. It was only my body. I'd learned the hard way already that a person could cause you pain and physically hurt you, but so long as you stayed strong inside, they could never break you. This encounter with Sam would be just like that. He would use my body and take whatever he wanted from it, but I would retreat into my mind, strengthening the walls there that protected me. I would get through it, and one day...one fucking day, I would repay Sixsmith for all that he had put me through.

No matter how long I had to wait, it would be worth it.

Steeling myself, I turned and opened the bathroom door, just as Sixsmith yelled out my name. "Sera! Get the fuck down here. Your ride's waiting out front!"

Ice filled my veins. I took one step down the stairs, and then there was Amy, tiptoe-running toward me down the hallway. She was still in her pajamas, and her hair was a mess. The shadows under her eyes were soft purple—the color of a bruise just as it starts to develop.

"Sera." She hurled herself at me, throwing her arms around my waist. "Are you okay?" she whispered. "What is he making you do?" She was old enough to know what a grown man could want from a young girl in order to settle a debt. I tucked her hair back behind her ear, squeezing her arm lightly. The smile I gave her cost me dearly, but it looked genuine enough.

"Don't fret, Aim. Sam and I are going to watch a movie, then afterwards he's going to take me for a milkshake at Remmy's. Should be fun."

She looked doubtful as she frowned up at me. "Tell him you don't want to go. Or tell Sixsmith you want me to go, too."

Sixsmith would probably delight in selling both of his daughters off. Twice the money? Even more than double the money probably, since Amy was not only still so young, but also so unbelievably innocent and sweet. I shook my head firmly, chucking her under the chin.

"It's okay, I promise. It'll be nice to get out of the house for the afternoon. Just keep out of Sixsmith's way. Stay in your room. Don't make a lot of noise or anything, and when I come back we can hang out, okay?"

"What movie are you going to see?" she asked, pouting.

"I'm not sure yet. I don't know what's playing."

"Will you bring me back a milkshake?"

God. I was going to throw up. I managed to nod, drawing in a deep breath. "Yeah, of course I will."

"You promise?"

"Promise. What flavor do you want?"

She grinned at me. "Chocolate, stupid."

"All right, stupid. Chocolate it is. Now I gotta go."

~

*T*he SUV was black and sleek, unlike any other vehicle you might see driving around the streets of Montmorenci. Inside the back seat, the air was blasting, freezing cold. It was ninety degrees out, so I hadn't brought a jacket, and I had to wrap my arms around myself to stop from shivering. The man sitting opposite me in the black suit held out an open bag of peanut M & Ms, offering me some of the candy.

I shook my head. "No thank you, Mr. Halloran."

Sam Halloran used to be a body builder back in the eighties. He had framed photographs of himself all over the bar he owned on the other side of town—pictures of him half-naked, wearing a thong, lubed up with fake tan and baby oil, in a multitude of poses that showed off his bulging muscles. I'd seen the photos myself, when Sixsmith had taken me with him to the bar when I was younger, back before Sixsmith had borrowed money from Sam and my father still felt comfortable drinking in his bar. Sam no longer looked like the man in those photos. He was only in his late forties, but he'd quit working out many years ago, and all of that muscle he'd been carrying around with him had since turned to fat.

His hair was still shockingly dark and thick, though there were touches of salt and pepper at his temples. His blue eyes were small and beady in his heavily jowled face, and his lips were thin—two mean looking slashes across the great expanse of his face. His eyebrows seemed to have fallen out for some reason, and all he had left were two small, round patches of black hair, no bigger than dimes, right above each of his eyes. He looked like a hard man. An unhappy man. The kind of man that enjoyed the suffering of others.

"You look just like your mother, y'know," he said, observing me coolly. "Beautiful woman. I asked her out before Sixsmith, but she turned me down. I could never figure out why she chose that drunken piece of shit over me."

I kept quiet, my hands gathered in my lap, my back pressed as far into my seat as possible. His leg kept touching mine, but there was no room to move away. He snorted, stuffing his hand into the bag of M & Ms. "I could have been your father. Kind of ironic that I'm here with you now, don't you think? I got the younger, prettier, sexier version of your mother in the end."

"I wish you had been my father," I murmured under my breath.

"I'm sorry?" There was a sharp edge to Sam's voice.

"I wish you had been my father," I repeated. "If you had been my father, I probably wouldn't find myself in this position. Unless you're the kind of man to touch his own children, of course." God, I was playing with fire. I was alone with this man. Alone, and completely at his mercy. I had no idea where Sam was taking me, but I knew without a shadow of a doubt that once we arrived there, I would be on my own. There would be no one there to protect me or intervene if things got out of hand. Sam could slit my throat if he wanted to. There were any number of fucked up, depraved things Sam could do to me, and I wouldn't be able to do a thing about it. So baiting and offending him? Sassing him, and being sarcastic? That wasn't a good idea. I knew it, and yet I couldn't stop myself. He was scum. A vile monster loosely dressed in a once powerful man's skin, and he had traded non-consensual sex with a minor in payment for money owed. Sam laughed, his cheeks shaking.

"You got spirit. I like that, Seraphim. Your mother was a bit of a hell raiser, too. Got her into all kinds of trouble when she was a teenager."

This piece of information surprised me; the woman I remembered from my childhood hadn't been fiery at all. She'd been calm and quiet, her voice the most soothing sound I could have possibly imagined at the time. Her touch had always been gentle, soft and kind. I didn't like that this miserable old fucker had known my mother since she was a teenager. I'd only known her for eleven years before she'd passed away, whereas Sam had known her for closer to twenty-five. That didn't seem fair at all.

Sam's smile was jagged and unfriendly. "Just for the record, I'm not a child molester. I do have a daughter. She's a year older than you, and I adore her more than life itself. I'd never lay a finger on her. I'm not a child molester."

I didn't flinch. I stayed very, very still. "Am I not a child?" I asked slowly.

Sam's eyes narrowed into slits. "In the state of South Carolina, you can legally consent to have sex at sixteen."

"I'm not sixteen. I'm fifteen. And I didn't consent to this."

A ripple of anger flared in Sam's eyes. "Your father told me you were old enough," he hissed. *He didn't mention anything about the fact that I'd just told him I hadn't given my consent, though. Convenient.*

"Sixsmith lies about things. He's an addict. I'm guessing you deal with addicts on a daily basis. You should know they can't be trusted," I said.

A thick red stripe had developed across Sam's cheeks. He looked as if he were about to swell up and explode all over the inside of his shockingly expensive SUV. "No one can find out about this, Sera. Do you understand what will happen if you breathe a word of this to someone at school? Your father will pay the price. We'll hurt him. We'll hurt him real fucking bad."

He really had no idea if he thought he could use Sixsmith's safety as a bargaining chip for my silence. A surge of excitement hit me as I considered the idea: I told the first person I came across what happened here with Sam. And as a result, Halloran would pay for what he was about to do, and Sixsmith would end up dead in a ditch somewhere, the birds eating out his eyeballs before his mangled body was discovered.

It would solve all of our problems. It would be better without Sixsmith, even if Amy and I ended up in the foster care system. But then, would she and I be placed in a home together? We were both teenagers now. A family wasn't likely to take both of us on. And what would happen to her in a stranger's home, if I wasn't there to protect her? I turned away from Sam, looking out of the window, watching the town fly past as we traveled through familiar streets and suburbs.

Sam didn't speak to me again, but his gaze was crawling all over my skin like a thousand fire ants. Soon, we reached his bar. The place was known around town as The Bar. The establishment had been known as The Dutchman once upon a time, probably as a tip of the cap to Sam's Dutch roots, but the locals hadn't called it that in years.

Sam got out of the car, and I saw his driver for the first time—a young guy I recognized from high school. Peter Fairley. He'd graduated last year and told everyone he was going to move out to California, but here he was, playing chauffeur to the sketchiest thug in Montmorenci. His eyes met mine, and the guilt I saw there told me enough: he recognized me, and I recognized him. He knew perfectly well what was about to happen, and he wasn't going to do a damn thing to stop it.

Sam didn't take me into the bar through the front door. He took me in through the back, leading me up a flight of rickety, steep steps; he grunted and heaved as he dragged himself up behind me, blocking my way, just in case I decided I wanted to turn tail and flee.

The residence above the bar was small but plush and decorated in dark hues of crimson and grey. It smelled alien and musky—a masculine, faintly unclean smell that itched at the back of my nose. Not a pleasant smell at all.

"Go and wait for me in the living room," Sam ordered Peter. "And you," he told me, placing his hand in the small of my back. "We're going to the end room there."

I'd hoped he would leave me for a moment, so I could get myself together, but he followed directly behind me, his hand forcefully moving me forward. We passed a room to our right, and a pair of wide, brown eyes met mine—a young girl with dark hair, sitting on an overstuffed couch with a book in her hand. She jumped when she saw me, leaning forward, as if she were stunned to see another young woman inside the apartment. Must be the daughter Sam had mentioned back in the car, I reasoned. All thoughts of her vanished when Sam shoved me non-too-gently into the room at the end of the hallway, and I saw the huge, king sized bed inside.

My heart turned to lead, sinking inside my chest. On top of the sheets: a pair of handcuffs and a red rubber ball attached to a length of black webbing. Sam closed the door behind us. He saw me staring at the cuffs and the ball, and he tutted under his breath. "You know what that is?" he asked, gesturing to the red ball.

"No." My voice was a whisper.

He chuckled. "Such innocence. I love it. That is a ball gag." He picked it up from the bed and held it up in his hands. "Here. Open your mouth."

Panic sang through me, loud and urgent. "I—No. I don't want—"

"Open your fucking mouth," Sam snarled. "If you know what's good for you, you'll do as you're told."

God. Why hadn't I secreted a knife into my pocket before I left the house? I knew where Sixsmith kept his small weapons stash. He'd threatened me with a flick knife before that I would easily have been able to keep hidden. I hadn't been thinking straight, though. I eyed the ball gag, my heartbeat frantically thumping all over my body. I had to do it. I just had to. Closing my eyes, I opened my mouth. My jaw almost popped out of its socket as Sam jammed the large rubber ball into my mouth, past my teeth, and I whimpered, trying to force it back out again.

Sam hissed as he held the ball in place, wrapping the webbing around my head, and fastening it tightly. He leaned into my face, and I could see the faint, spidery blood shot veins in the yellowed whites of his eyes. "Now we won't have to worry about you screaming."

I could barely breathe. The ball in my mouth made it hard to swallow, too, which made my ever-increasing fear even worse.

"The handcuffs are just in case," he told me, leering as he looked down at my chest. "If you're a good girl, and you don't fight me, I won't use them. But if you give me any trouble, I won't hesitate to restrain you. Do you understand?"

Tears were welling in my eyes. I could do nothing but nod.

He took hold of my shirt, and he tore it over my head, then, his breath quickening as he surveyed my bra, and my breasts within. I'd promised myself I wouldn't cry. I'd convinced myself that it would be easy to disassociate myself from my body as Sam Halloran took his fill of it. But as he stripped me bare, and he started to touch and grope me, I couldn't help it. I cried. Silently. Pitifully. I hated myself for my weakness, but over the next three hours, as Sam got naked and forced himself on me, hitting and slapping at me when I didn't obey him immediately, I wept uncontrollably.

At one point, I tried to hold back the pathetic sobs that escaped down my nose, worrying that Sam might grow angry with me, but he gripped my face in his hands, grinding his forehead against mine, and he said, "Don't stop on my account, sweet girl. Your tears are better than Viagra. My dick hasn't been this hard in years."

So he touched me. He took the most precious thing I possessed from me. For hours, he shoved his way inside me, and I bore it because I had no other choice. When he was finally spent, he rolled off me and unfastened the ball gag, then flopped back onto the bed, panting and groaning like he was about to have a heart attack. "Go and get dressed, then get the fuck out of here. I don't want to look at you anymore,"

I'd been dismissed. I gathered up my clothes and fled the room, not caring that I was still naked, or that Sam's come was running down the insides of my thighs. As soon as I'd located the bathroom, I bent over the toilet and my body locked in a spasm as I violently threw up the contents of my stomach into the bowl. I wanted a shower. I needed to scrub the top five layers of my skin from my body, but I didn't have time. I washed myself between my legs for the second time today, extra thoroughly this time, and when I dumped the fluffy grey towel on the floor that I'd used to dry myself, I was startled by the amount of blood that marked the material.

So much blood.

I got dressed, and I ran out of the apartment, my body burning, aching, trembling, shaking. I could barely remain upright as I charged down the flight of stairs at the back of the building. There was a shout behind me, a male voice. I turned around, my heart beating out of my chest, and I didn't see Peter, standing at the top of the stairs, asking me if I wanted a ride home. I saw the face of a young girl, peering out of a window, her large brown eyes filled with horror.

The walk home should have taken thirty minutes. It took closer to an hour, though, primarily because I was in so much pain. No matter how hard Sixsmith hurt me, the pain had never come close to this. The raw, sharp ache inside my body was mingled with shame, and had wrapped itself around my very bones, until it felt like the agony and the humiliation were going to be a part of me forever.

At Remmy's, I used the single five-dollar bill in my pocket to buy Amy a chocolate milkshake.

It had melted by the time I walked through the front door.

28

FIX

ON THE LAM

I nearly yanked the door out of its frame in my haste to get it open. Sera was exactly where I expected to find her, curled up in bed on her side, her dark hair messy and tangled around her head. She looked so peaceful that it was almost a shame to wake her. There was no time to admire her, though. No time for the coffees and toast I'd had to calmly carry out of the diner like nothing was wrong. I'd felt that female cop's eyes on me as I walked up the road toward the hotel. All I'd wanted to do was sprint back, but I'd had to keep my shoulders loose, my back straight, my head held high, as if I were taking everything in with interest, an out-of-town guy inspecting his surroundings.

Sera jumped when I closed the door, her legs jolting beneath the covers. She looked back at me, blinking furiously. "Fix?"

"Get up. We're leaving."

I hurled the toast in the trash can, snatched up our bags, placing them on the desk, and then began shoving our belongings inside them, not paying attention to who's stuff was going into which bag.

"Why are you stealing my panties?" Sera asked, her voice still thick with sleep.

"Get out of bed," I commanded. "Get dressed. We have to get out of here. The cops found the dead guy in the bunker, and they have fingerprints."

Sera sat bolt upright, eyes wide, now very alert. "You didn't kill him, Fix. You have nothing to worry about."

"Are you kidding me? If those prints are mine, they won't look any further for their killer."

Sera swung her legs out of the bed—long, beautiful and toned, her skin begging to be touched. It had felt so fucking amazing to have those legs wrapped around me last night. Even with this urgent need to get into the truck and burn rubber out of Lavelle, I could still appreciate how fucking perfect she was. "Have you really been that sloppy in the past?" she asked. "How would they have your prints on record? From other...*incidents*?" She didn't like referencing the fact that I'd murdered many other people. Didn't want to say the words out loud. It was obvious.

"I'll explain everything in the car. Now please. I'm about to pick you up and physically fucking move you myself. I'm assuming you don't want that."

Her eyes flashed, her back stiffening. "It'd be the last thing you ever did," she replied. But she moved. She got her ass up, and she moved.

Eight minutes later, we were in the car and hurtling down the freeway at breakneck speeds. Sera didn't ask questions until we were thirty minutes out of Lavelle.

"I'm really worried, Fix. Should I be really worried?"

"No. Yes. Probably."

I explained what had occurred in the diner, and I didn't spare the details. Sera paled when I told her what Monica had said. "So this isn't over. There's still someone trying to kill me, and that guy back in the bunker wasn't Carver."

"The cops said his name was Anderson. Carver might have been his last name, but..." My gut was telling me it wasn't. I didn't want to scare her. Didn't want her to panic. But there had been enough secrets and half-truths already. Keeping this from her wouldn't do either of us any favors, and she needed to be careful. I was going to be watching her like a hawk from here on out, but she had to be equally as vigilant. "You see anything you think looks suspicious, you tell me. Anyone looking at you, following you. You get a strange feeling about anything, and you let me know immediately. Do you understand?"

She just stared ahead out of the windshield.

"*Sera*! This is fucking important."

"Yes! Yes, okay. I'll tell you. God, Fix."

"When are you expected back at work?" I asked.

"Two days from now. I took three weeks off for the road trip and for Amy's wedding."

"Email them right now and tell them you'll be back in the office next Monday. Tell them you're taking some time to relax when you get back to Seattle. Tell them you'll be back in town tomorrow night."

"Is that smart? I mean—"

"And that brunette? The friend you hang out with all the time?"

"Sadie?"

"Text her and ask to meet for coffee or lunch or something this weekend. Tell her you had a great time at the wedding, but you're excited to be coming home."

"Fix, I don't understand why you want me to do that. Going back to Seattle is the last thing we should be doing."

I gripped the steering wheel tighter, pressing my foot down on the gas pedal. This was fucked. This was all *so* fucked. "I know. Which is why we're not going anywhere near Seattle," I ground out. "We're going to New York."

29

SERA

EDDISON GAS & ELECTRICAL WORKS

*T*hree and a half hours. That's how long it took to travel from Pennsylvania to New York. Few words were exchanged on the drive, and Fix emitted fury and aggression the entire way. I wasn't exactly calm myself. My heart rate kept spiking all over the place. I'd wrestle with the adrenalin pumping around my body for thirty minutes, finally be able to convince myself that everything was going to be okay, only to have a wave of dread slam into me, sending me spiraling back down into the depths of despair.

Who was this fucking Carver guy? And why the fuck did he want me dead so badly? I had no answers. None whatsoever. And since our trip to Centralia had done nothing but get us into even more trouble, we had no clues to go on, and no way of figuring this thing out. We were flying blind, and I didn't like it. I could tell Fix detested it, too. He was probably used to being in control, calling the shots, and right now he was completely powerless.

As the city approached on the skyline, tall high-rise buildings reaching upward into the sky like pillars of shining glass, and metal and concrete, I bit down the urge to have Fix pull over so I could throw up. I'd never been to New York before. Never had the opportunity. I'd always wanted to, but work had consumed so much of my life recently. I'd been telling myself for the last eighteen months that I'd come visit soon, go do the tourist thing and check out the Empire State Building, go see The Lion King on Broadway. I hadn't for one second envisioned my first trip to the Big Apple would be a flight to safety, because my very existence was in danger.

I watched the city explode up around the truck with a tight knot of fear sitting heavy in the pit of my stomach. Restaurants; bars; high-end clothes shops; souvenir stands; hot dog stands; bodegas; parks. There was so much going on, and so, so many people. Everything, everywhere. People hurrying, talking into cell phones, gathered in groups on street corners, gesticulating to one another like maniacs, waving their arms in the air.

Eventually, Fix spoke. "The Manhattan Bridge is coming up. Then we'll be entering Brooklyn. We're close." There was a relieved softness to his voice, which had an immediate effect on me. Fix knew Brooklyn well. He lived here, so it stood to reason that he'd be much more confident on home ground. He probably had an arsenal of weapons at his place, and he knew how to get in and out of the city as quickly as possible.

Next thing I knew, we were on the bridge. I'd driven across the Golden Gate Bridge before, so I was used to the overwhelming depth and scale of such a massive structure, but the Golden Gate Bridge was outside of the city, spanning a vast stretch of water. This bridge was monstrously huge, but it was right in the middle of everything, connecting two metropolitan hubs, and the sheer size of the tangle of steel struts and supports momentarily overwhelmed me.

Traffic sucked. The vehicles in front of us crawled forward at a snail's pace, and I slid my hands underneath my legs, sitting on them, trying to stop myself from shaking. Or, rather, trying to hide the fact that I was shaking from Fix.

Didn't seem to be doing a very good job, though. "Everything's going to be okay, Angel," he said softly. I looked at him, and his ghostly eyes were burning with such intensity. "I won't let anybody hurt you. I won't let anybody fucking touch you. I *promise* you that."

"I know. I..." I didn't know. I didn't know anything, but weirdly I trusted him. I knew he was going to do everything in his power to fix this situation. That's what he did, after all. He fixed things. I looked out of the window to the right, across the expanse of gunmetal grey water, and I swallowed hard.

"The bridge's safe, Sera," Fix said. "It's solid as fuck. And we're almost at the other side."

"Yeah. I just..." How could I explain all of the thoughts churning in my head right now? I'd lost the ability to communicate effectively. I was trapped inside my own skull with so much negativity and fear, so many potential threats presenting themselves to me, one after the other, that even breathing felt dangerous. I'd feel better once we were off the bridge. I'd feel even better once we were out of the truck, locked behind closed doors, and I could get the gun Fix had given to me out of my bag. He hadn't even given me a chance to retrieve it before we'd set off earlier. Said I didn't have need of it, not yet, but having it on my person would make me feel a little better, I was sure.

Soon, we were back amongst streets, immersed in the crawling madness that was Brooklyn. Seattle was a big city, but it was nothing like this. Didn't even come close. Twenty minutes after that, Fix was turning the truck off the road, down a narrow side street that terminated almost immediately. A tall, old brick wall towered in front of us, trapping us, covered in torn, tattered, faded posters and a large white and red sign that read:

EDDISON GAS & ELECTRICAL WORKS
Keep out.

*F*ix grunted as he climbed out of the truck and slammed the door closed behind himself. He navigated his way around the truck and opened my door, gesturing for me to get out, too.

"Through there," he said, pointing to a rusting steel doorway in the building to our right, about ten feet from where the truck was parked. "The code is 3887. Go up to the top floor. I'll be right behind you."

I didn't want to head into the building alone. Telling Fix that felt like an admission of weakness, though, so I walked to the door, punched in the code, and entered, breathing deeply through my nose. There was no elevator beyond, just a bare concrete stairwell that led up and up forever. My Converse scraped against the steps as I ascended, my palms sweating like crazy.

Life was so fucking strange sometimes. Three weeks ago, I'd been packing my rental, about to set off on what was supposed to have been an enjoyable, exciting trip across the country. I'd been planning on doing some sightseeing, relaxing, but instead I'd been met with hurdle after hurdle on my way to Alabama. I'd found myself stuck in a motel room in the middle of a storm with a complete stranger, and now here I was in New York City, and there were dead bodies everywhere I damn well looked, and I was sleeping with the most dangerous man I'd ever met. The most dangerous man *anyone* had met.

By the fourth floor, I was beginning to think the stairs were never going to end. Thankfully, one more floor up and I found I'd come as far as I could go. I could hear Fix below, banging about, stomping up the stairs behind me. There was only one door in front of me, as there had only been one door to exit the stairwell on each of the floors below. I tried the handle, expecting to find it locked, but it turned and opened without protest. On the other side: a long narrow hallway, lit by small cut glass chandeliers suspended from the unbelievably high ceiling. The walls were a flat, slate grey color, and the floor was a much darker grey polished concrete, flecked with gold. Understated. Masculine. Tasteful. Somehow, I knew Fix was responsible for the appearance of this hallway, and I almost burst out laughing. Fix, painting and decorating? Picking out gold flecked concrete? It was a ridiculous vision that just refused to make sense in my mind. God knows what the rest of his apartment was going to look like. I'd given absolutely no thought to where he might live. What his space would look like. For the short time I'd known him, Fix had been a drifting entity comprised of violence and mayhem. Now that it appeared he had roots, a real home of his own, I supposed that altered my perception of him a little. Made him more...human.

There was only one door here in the hallway, too. Fix owned the whole floor by the looks of things. I didn't know much about property prices in Brooklyn, but I did know that New York was one of the most expensive places to live in the country. Space was at a premium. To be able to afford an entire penthouse apartment, Fix's bank account must have been really healthy. I guessed being a hitman did have its perks.

I turned back, about to go back into the stairwell to see what was taking Fix so long, when the heavy, hardwood door to his apartment swung open. My heart did a backflip, and then another. I stepped back, my body telling me to run like hell, but—

A nun.

There was a *nun* standing in the doorway.

White shirt.

Long black skirt.

Black and white wimple.

Small golden cross hanging on a chain around her neck.

She was young.

Pretty.

Blonde.

And she looked like she was about to fucking kill me.

Fix chose that specific moment to appear through the other doorway behind me, and an instant electrical charge flooded the hallway. He glared at the nun, the woman, whoever she was, his expression thunderous.

"What the fuck, Monica?"

~

*M*onica was a nun.

Twelve minutes had passed since she'd opened the door to Fix's apartment, and I still hadn't been able to wrap my head around the concept that Monica was a nun. Monica, who worked with Fix. Who fielded emails from psychopaths who wanted to pay to have their wives, and their bosses, and their next-door neighbors killed. She was the one who assessed Carver's reasoning for wanting me dead. She was the one who'd decided I had what was coming to me, had accepted the down payment, and sent Fix off on his merry way with a gun in his hand.

She was a fucking *nun*.

Even more shocking was the colorful language that kept spewing forth from her mouth, as she reamed out Fix in the middle of his penthouse. Her face had gone a strained shade of purple.

"Are you fucking insane, Felix?" Monica stabbed a finger in my direction, violently shaking her head. "*That's* the reason you've been in the wind the past week?"

"Uhhh..." I held up my hand, the base of my neck growing hot. "I am a person. 'She' isn't great, but it's definitely more flattering than '*that*.'"

Monica didn't look at me. Didn't correct herself or apologize. She flared her nostrils, shooting daggers at Fix. "Please explain what this is. Please convince me that you haven't lost your motherfucking mind. Because right now it looks like you've been traipsing around the country with a...a *person of interest*..." She trailed off, her eyes growing wide. She looked Fix up and down carefully, then snarled. "Shit. Felix. You've been fucking her, haven't you? You bailed on a job to get your dick wet. I thought you were smarter than that. What in god's name are you going to do with her when she finds out what you do, huh? She's going to run as fast and as far as she can, and you'll have compromised us for a quick, cheap lay."

Uhhhh......

Nope. No way. Not a chance. The tips of my ears were on fire now, which always happened when I was about to lose my temper in a very big way. Fix's jaw was clenched so hard, I suspected it was going to be difficult for him to open it again. I stepped in front of him, rolling back my shoulders, and Monica gaped.

"Are you guys married?" I fired at her.

"Just stay out of this. You don't know what you've walked into right now."

"I'm pretty sure I do. I know you're not Fix's wife. I know you're not his mother. Which means you have no reason to be so angry at him right now."

Monica let out a scathing laugh. "If you had any idea—"

"I don't need an idea. I have *facts*. Fix was sent to kill me. He takes on jobs that *you* send to him. He hunts people, tracks them down, finds them, and then he kills them. For money. That's what he does. I already know everything there is to know, so you can quit being so outraged and fucking crazy, and you can calm the fuck down. I'm not going to report him to the cops. And I hate to disappoint you, but I'm not running anywhere either."

The anger that had been erupting from the woman like lava from a volcano sputtered out. Looked like it had been replaced with disbelief. "You...told her? Everything?"

Fix nodded slowly. He folded his arms across his chest, and for a moment I felt sorry for Monica. I'd never seen Fix look so damn angry. I was really glad I wasn't on the receiving end of the scathing look he was sending her way. "Couldn't have given me five minutes to sit down and fucking breathe, could you, Mon. How long have you known me? If I've been in a tight spot, I've asked for help. If I've needed you, I've reached out."

"And? I could tell something was wrong, so I checked in. Simple. And I had every right to be worried." She glanced from Fix to me, her mouth open, her hands raised in the air. "I've never known you to be so reckless, Felix. Since we started this thing, you've been the overly cautious one. You've never risked our safety like this before."

"Your safety? You're not at risk," Fix volleyed back.

"Of course I am! I'm the one people meet with. I'm their first point of contact when something goes wrong. Do you think this Carver guy's just been sitting happily on the sidelines, waiting for an update? No, he fucking hasn't. He's been hounding me day and night. He threatened to show up here two days ago. You have *no* idea what I've been dealing with."

Fix's head hung forward, his chin almost touching his chest. He sighed heavily. "Okay. You're right. I should have considered that, and I'm sorry. I should have kept you in the loop. Sera and I are going to stay here for a couple of days. We're going to figure out where to go from here, and how we're going to proceed. In the meantime, we need to decompress. Why don't I come by later, and we'll go through everything then?" It may have been worded as a question but Fix clearly meant it as a statement. He wasn't going to stand here and be chided by her.

Monica was not happy. "All right. Fine. I'll go. But bear in mind... this is not like you, Fix. You're acting completely out of character, and I'm the only one who appears to be concerned by this."

"*Goodbye, Monica.*" Fix didn't look up at her. She remained there, staring at him for a moment. Finally, she huffed, snatching up a black jacket and a purse that was sitting on Fix's table, and she stormed out of the apartment, slamming the door so hard behind her that the windows rattled.

Fix looked at me out of the corner of his eye. "Sorry?"

I didn't know whether to laugh or cry. "It's fine. But I think you'd better tell me how the hell you two started working together, because honestly? I am so confused right now."

30

SERA

HOOKERS AND BLOW DON'T COME CHEAP

"*M*onica overstepped. She treated you like shit. Not to mention the fact that she scolded me like a little boy caught playing with his dick. Not gonna fly. I'm going to have to have a serious fucking talk with her."

I sat down at the table, lacing my fingers together, looking up at Fix expectantly. His nerves were frayed—didn't seem like he was used to dealing with hysterical women. "How did an ex-priest and a nun fall into this, anyway?" I asked. "Does she have feelings for you or something? Because that? To me? It all looked a little jealous."

Fix rubbed at his jaw, huffing as he sat down opposite me. "No. She's not jealous. She's just...protective. Five years ago, she was attacked in the rectory of my church. I found her. She'd been brutally beaten. Raped. *Repeatedly*. The man who assaulted her did as he pleased with her, and then, when he was done, he stabbed her over and over again. She should have died. I didn't think for a second she was going to survive. I held onto her while we waited for the ambulance, and she'd looked up at me, and I'd seen it in her eyes. She'd believed she was going to die, too, and there had been so much *courage* in her eyes. She hadn't been afraid. Not really. She was in the hospital for a month. Underwent a total of eleven surgeries to repair the damage to her internal organs. She came through each and every one of them fighting. But when she was finally strong enough to leave the hospital, they'd forgotten to repair one final injury. She was broken in her soul. And I guess I was, too. The cops weren't doing anything. They shelved Monica's case, because a string of kids had just been kidnapped in Red Hook, so they just closed her file down like she didn't matter anymore.

"We started looking for the guy. That's how all this started. And the more we looked, the more fucked up, depraved, shitty, sick people we found. The more broken, traumatized people we found. The more people we found who wanted to hire someone to make things right."

"So you decided to quit being a priest, because you realized you could make money solving people's problems?" I'd never suspected the money was a drawing factor to Fix. Not until he'd just spoken those words.

"No. That wasn't it. One day, a woman came to me. She'd heard I was trying to find criminals, to have them convicted of their crimes. She showed me pictures of her eight-year-old son—what had been done to him. The pictures showed a small child, face-down in an alleyway. He was naked. He'd been raped. His neck had been snapped. The woman had given him five dollars and told him to walk to the shop three doors down from her building to pick up some milk. She'd been cooking, so she hadn't wanted to step away from the stove. Everything would have burned. Her son was taken right outside and dragged across the street. Three people on the street heard him screaming for his mom, screaming for help, but no one went to him. He'd died alone, terrified and in pain. His mother was planning on killing herself. Something inside me just snapped."

Fix looked at me steadily, his eyes unblinking, but reliving this memory was affecting him. I could tell. He was filled with a deep, bottomless, fathomless rage. "I told the woman to wait. I told her I wasn't going to be able to take her pain away, but that I was going to try and ease it some. That night, I went out and I found two people who both said they'd seen the same man with the young boy, dragging him by the collar of his t-shirt across the road. Both of them gave the same name. It was *easy* to gather that information, which just made me madder that the cops hadn't done their jobs properly. I asked around some more, and I figured out where this guy lived.

"When I knocked on his door and asked the man who opened it if he had killed the little boy, he'd spat at my feet and said, yeah, so what if he had? What was a priest going to do about it? I ripped my collar off, and I took out the serrated knife I'd put into my pocket, and I said, 'I don't know what a priest could do. But *I'm* going to make things right.'

"I took that bastard's balls back to the woman in an old Slurpee cup I found on the floor of his apartment. And I wasn't sorry for what I'd done. She asked me if he was dead, and I told her he was. She cried. She wept with relief, because, for her, in some small way, it felt like it was over. And then she tried to give me three thousand dollars. I refused to accept it. I quit my position the next day. I walked away, so I could devote myself to finding the man who attacked Monica, but it wasn't long before people were contacting me, searching for justice. They'd heard rumors about what I'd done and they wanted to pay me for my services. I didn't take a single one of those jobs, it would have been too dangerous, but it got me to thinking. If people did want to hire me, then why not? Everything I'd believed in was a fucking lie. My life had been a farce. And the cash would come in handy while I was looking for Monica's attacker."

I picked at my nail, studying it fiercely, eyes down on the table. "So...you keep the money?"

"Hookers and blow don't come cheap," he replied.

There was no resisting a statement like that. I glanced up at him, frowning deeply. "Seriously? That's what you spend your money on?"

He cocked his head to one side. "What do you think?"

"I think this place must have cost a fortune, and your truck is top of the line, and your money has to come from somewhere."

Fix huffed lightly down his nose. It kept catching me off guard, and at the most inopportune of moments: the man sitting across the table from me was *real*. He was so utterly dysfunctional, and so unquestionably bad, and so undeniably dangerous, but he was also sexy, and fierce, and loyal, and fucking *fascinating*. I didn't want to keep staring at him like a complete freak, especially given the content of our conversation, but I couldn't seem to help myself. "My mother came from old money," he said softly. "They left everything to me when they died. I didn't want it back then, but when I left the church, I decided it wasn't doing anyone any good tied up in trusts and funds. So I bought this place outright. And I dip into it here and there whenever I need to. Yes, we do charge the people who hire me, Sera, but I don't touch a cent of it. Monica handles all of that. She uses it for good."

I wasn't happy about how my first meeting with Monica had gone down. She'd been more than a little aggressive and hostile. Downright unpleasant and rude, really. But now, knowing a little more of her story, how she'd been viciously attacked in the most horrific of ways, my anger toward her had dissipated a little. Still, I couldn't help but ask. "How can you know she's not lining her pockets with all that money?"

Fix shrugged—a carefree, nonchalant jerk of his left shoulder. "I *don't* know. But I trust her. And, honestly, it wouldn't matter if she was skimming the money, or keeping it. She can have it. All I know is *I* don't want it."

~

I hadn't paid much attention to the penthouse when Fix and I had entered. I'd been a little more concerned about the crazy woman screaming at us to take in our surroundings, but as Fix moved to the kitchen, saying he was going to make something for us to eat, I allowed myself the time to explore a little. The living space was massive and open plan, with large floor-to-ceiling windows that looked back over toward the bridge we'd crossed earlier, and the steepled columns of countless Lower Manhattan high-rises. The city looked like it had been constructed out of Lego from this distance— so many blocks and bricks, all jumbled together to create something oddly magnificent.

The immense windows flooded the apartment with the afternoon light, which I loved. The furniture in the penthouse was sparse, practical, but beautiful: A brushed copper lamp that swept upwards gracefully from its stand on the floor like the graceful, arched neck of a swan; the light fitting hovering over the roughhewn dining table; a battered leather three-seater couch that looked wildly comfortable; stacks and stacks of books on shelves; understated trinkets hidden in corners, and striking, bold, dark artwork that covered the walls. The same gold flecked, polished concrete spanned the length of the living room, and caught the light so well that it looked like it was burning in places.

It was so, so quiet. Sadie had told me she hated New York because of the sirens and car horns blaring twenty-four hours a day, audible even inside your building, but Fix must have soundproofed this place, because I couldn't hear a goddamn thing. It was lovely and peaceful, and I felt very at home, even though I had absolutely no right to do so.

I sat at the dining table and methodically emptied my wallet, cutting up one bankcard after another, four in total, just as Fix had asked me to. Having no access to my own money was worrying, but the alternative was flat out terrifying. I used a card to pay for something, and Fix's replacement would be able to pinpoint my location no problem at all. Just because it turned out Fix had money, and plenty of it, didn't mean I was going to rely on him for everything though. I was going to keep a track of my expenses, anything and everything he bought or paid for on my behalf, and the moment this was done I was paying him back every last dime. That was, if this thing was *ever* done.

When I picked up my cell phone, I texted Amy first. The weird, terrible things Fix had said to me back in that cabin on the mountain had made me so freaking angry. They'd also scared the shit out of me.

Was Amy actually sick? She'd seemed as though she were in peak physical fitness at the wedding, but Fix had mentioned a toxin report. I knew Aim. If she was ill, if there was absolutely anything wrong with her, she would have told me already. But the short message I sent her, asking her if everything was okay, would confirm either way.

I emailed work, and I texted Sadie. Jasmine, who'd been taking care of my client list while I was away, didn't blink when I told her I wasn't going to be back until next week. Sadie agreed to lunch at our favorite Italian spot, and wanted to know all about Amy's wedding. Life for everyone else was skipping forward without a care but making these fake plans with my colleagues and my friends only served to highlight how dramatically it had screeched to a halt for me. Even if we managed to find Carver and resolve the fact that he wanted me dead, how was I just supposed to go back to waking up, hitting the office, working out, drinking the odd glass of wine, paying my bills, and keeping my apartment tidy? So much had changed. So much was going to change.

I made my way into the kitchen, planning on offering to help Fix with whatever he was doing, but when I entered the light, bright, open space, the delicious scent of cooking garlic and onions hit me, and I closed my mouth. Fix's back was to me as he worked at the stove. His head was bowed, his shoulder blades and his muscled back perfectly defined through the t-shirt he was wearing. I'd assumed he was capable of whipping up something easy for us to eat, but watching him now, it turned out he was very proficient in the kitchen.

Who knew he was so accomplished. His dating profile would have been fucking stellar:

Felix Marcosa.
     Handsome.
Charming.
Funny.
Safe driver.
Culinary genius.

Murderer by trade.

Cunnilingus level: *expert.*

"*Y*ou gonna stand there, staring at my ass, or are you going to help?" Fix asked. He hadn't turned around, but he was permanently aware of his surroundings. I'd noticed that back at the hotel—how his eyes scanned over things so quickly that it barely looked like he was paying attention, but I'd known he was cataloguing and recording everything, stowing the information away just in case he needed it. To have known I'd silently approached him now meant that he probably had eyes in the back of his head, though.

"Looks like you've got this covered," I said, moving to stand behind him. "How very modern of you. What makes you think I was staring at your ass?"

"Because you were standing behind me, and it would have been impossible not to stare. My ass looks damn fine in these jeans."

Good god. The man was incorrigible. He never fucking stopped. He thought so damned highly of himself, it was borderline infuriating. If he hadn't been right most of the time, I wouldn't have been able to stand it. "They are nice jeans," I said, sighing. "You probably stole them from a dead man, right?"

Fix looked back over his shoulder, an incredulous look plastered all over his face. "No. What the fuck? I wouldn't steal a dead man's jeans. I sure as hell wouldn't *wear* a dead man's jeans."

"Oh. Right. So it's just luggage and electronics you steal from the dead, then," I observed.

"And Vinyl. And sometimes cars."

"Got it." I gave him a tight-lipped smile, slapping him lightly on the back. "How can I be of service?"

"Too late now, Lafferty," he informed me. "I'm almost finished. You're going to owe me for this."

"I didn't realize I was getting myself into debt."

Fix's eyes were filled with trouble as he shot me a sidelong look. "Anal. I want anal."

My face was blooming with heat. "I'm beginning to think you might be a little obsessed with *my* ass," I fired back.

"Damn right I am. I've seen plenty of assholes, and yours is by far the loveliest. You know it's going to happen." There was no humor in his voice. No edge of sarcasm. His expression was void. I didn't know another person on the face of the planet who could tell someone in all earnestness that they had a lovely asshole and be completely serious about it. Fix was a law unto himself. He was never ashamed or embarrassed by the things that came out of his mouth, and that made the content of his shocking statements somehow seem...okay? I hadn't made my mind up yet.

"Maybe we shouldn't be talking about you fucking me in the ass while you prepare food," I said, laughing. *When in doubt: make a joke out of everything.*

Fix stirred the creamy sauce he had bubbling away on the gas ring, his expression one of concentration. "You're afraid too much," he said. "You let words make you feel uncomfortable."

"And why shouldn't I? Words are powerful things. They make normal people feel things."

He grunted, as if he were conceding to this. His voice was so deep and low, it sounded like a rockslide. "Still. You shouldn't let a remark cause you to retreat. You're stronger than that, Angel. You should tell me to go fuck myself if you don't like what I'm saying."

"If you'll recall, I *do* tell you to go fuck yourself. Regularly."

"When you're mad, maybe. But when you feel uncomfortable, you laugh. You make it okay for me to tease the shit out of you when you laugh. You're saying, 'I find that funny.'"

"Maybe I do find it funny."

Fix dropped the black spatula he was using to stir the sauce into the pan. He whipped around so quickly, I didn't even have time to react as he rushed me, placing his hands on the counter, trapping me between his arms. He leaned in close, so close that I could see the filaments of silver and amber that twined together in his eyes. His mouth was barely an inch away from mine. The tip of his nose grazed my own, and my breath hitched at the back of my throat.

"You think it would be funny if I were to lick you right now, Sera? Would it be funny if I used my dick to rub your pussy until you screamed from the anticipation? Would you be laughing if I bent you over this counter, and I tore your panties from your body, and I spread your legs as wide as they would go? Would it be hilarious if I knotted your hair around my hand, so I could jerk your head back as I fucked the shit out of you?"

His voice was like coarse silk, spilling from his lips. Lips I badly wanted to suck into my mouth and bite right now. I'd been kind of nervous a moment ago, on the back foot because of the way he was speaking so casually. But his tone was far from casual now. It was loaded, and it was tense, and it was turning me on more than I cared to admit.

"No. That wouldn't be funny," I breathed. "Not even a little bit."

He growled, and the sound that came out of him sent a penetrating shiver chasing down my spine. His gaze was alive and searching; for such impossibly cool, frosty colored eyes, they burned rather impressively. I felt naked, as if he'd just torn every scrap of material from my body and left me standing bare and vulnerable in front of him.

"I'm not going to fuck you now," he informed me. "You need to eat. But later...once your appetite's been assuaged...I'm going to take care of *mine*."

Oh. God. The tip of his tongue was gripped between his teeth. I couldn't tear my eyes away from him, not even for a second. I didn't know what to do with myself. "Sounds like you're very hungry," I said.

A twisted smile quirked his mouth up to one side. "You have no idea, Sera. I'm fucking *ravenous*." He leaned in a fraction closer. He was going to kiss me. He was going to kiss me. My breath caught. His lips were a millimeter away from mine when he pulled back, leaving behind a vacuum where he'd been standing only seconds ago. What the...?

My head was spinning as I righted myself against the counter, straightening out my shirt. Damn him. Damn him and his ability to turn me into a nervous teenager. He didn't even need to try. There was something so sexual about him. One second, he was admonishing me for letting him make me feel uncomfortable. The next, he was looming over, pressing his body up against mine, making me see stars.

"There are bowls in that cupboard," Fix directed, pointing to a cupboard on the other side of the kitchen. "Grab two. The food's just about ready."

As I took the bowls out of the cupboard and placed them down on the dark grey marble countertop, it felt like my heart was working overtime, trying and failing to keep up with Fix's erratic mood. He'd been so worried on the drive here, as had I. And then he'd been angry because of Monica. And now, he seemed entirely focused on making me blush.

My blushing days were behind me, though. A woman didn't have room for such frivolous things as blushing when her life was being threatened and the man she was currently fucking might just be insane. At least that's what I was telling myself, in order to convince myself that the heat in my cheeks wasn't rising.

I watched Fix as he went back to tending the food. He was unknowable in nearly every way—a different, inhuman kind of creature that I couldn't pretend to understand. He was dark, and tortured, and beautiful, and more than a little fucked up. He was the very study of villainy. But where did that leave me? What was my role in this fucked up fairytale. Was I meant to play the simpering damsel in distress, or was I going to pick up a gun and start shooting? The thought that I might have to do just that was paralyzing. It was empowering at the same time, though. I had a gun. I knew how to shoot it. I was forewarned and forearmed, and I wasn't going to back down without a fight. This situation was not going to break me. No way, no how.

Fix served up the food and handed me the bowls, which I carried through to the dining table. He sat down opposite me, stuck his fork, loaded with food, into his mouth, and he grinned at me. I followed suit, taking a bite of the beef stroganoff he'd somehow miraculously put together in a little over half an hour, and my eyes rolled back into my head. "Oh my god," I groaned. "This is delicious."

My compliment earned me a salacious wink. "I know," Fix said loftily. He bit down on the tines of his fork. "I'm basically a fucking genius."

31

FIX

DUE DILIGENCE

$\mathscr{I}$ knew New York like the back of my hand. If you wanted a fake ID, you needed to head to Lower Manhattan. If you wanted guns, typically you'd need to head out to The Bronx. Staten Island harbored some of the most violent, skilled, and dangerous thugs in the continental U.S. But if you wanted to employ the services of someone skilled in the art of hacking and data infraction, you needn't go much further than Brooklyn. Handy, since Monica's apartment wasn't very far, and I had to go collect her laptop. Sera had fallen asleep on the couch an hour after we'd eaten, so I left her a note on the table and crept out of the penthouse, stuffing a vile-looking knife into its sheath and hooking it onto the back of my belt as I jogged down the stairs.

Outside, the sun was blazing. So much had happened already today; it was hard to believe it was only one in the afternoon. If I could get Monica's laptop and head over to Williamsburg in the next hour or so, there was a chance I could drop off the computer and head back before Sera even woke up from her nap.

I stopped and bought a slice of pizza and a bottle of Snapple at the seven eleven two blocks from Monica's place. The doorman of

The Oakwood Suites—an older guy with a rust colored moustache and a network of scars rick-racked across his throat, saw me as I hurried toward the building, and his back straightened like a rod. I'd made it very clear to the owners of The Oakwood that it would make me very happy if Gil were to secure a permanent position as doorman here. The twenty thousand dollar 'gift' I'd slid in front of the strata manager had eased things along. I'd first met Gil years ago at an underground cage fight, where he'd been in the process of breaking both the arms of a guy who had been trying to assault one of the female bartenders in the bathrooms. The guy hadn't flinched as he'd grappled with the guy, snapping his forearms like they were twigs. He was huge, built like a brick shit house, but he was also very fast, didn't care for the authorities much, and gave precisely zero fucks about hurting people when the need arose. I'd wanted to make sure Monica was safe in her apartment, and so Gil had been watching over her, making sure no nefarious types gained access to the building, for the past three years.

"Mr. Marcosa," he said stiffly, thrusting out a shovel of a hand for me to shake. "Been a while. I didn't know you were back in town."

"Got back today. I'm assuming Monica came back here a couple of hours ago?"

"Flew in with a face like thunder. I didn't ask what was wrong," he answered.

He might have been big, and he might have been tough as nails, but Gil was also smart; asking Monica what was wrong when she was mid-meltdown was never a good idea. She'd claw a guy's eyes out just for making the mistake of looking in her general direction. I gave a dry, rueful bark of a laugh. "If I'm not back down in thirty minutes, call an ambulance."

Gil flashed a jumble of crooked teeth at me, wheezing—presumably an attempt at a laugh. I clapped him on the shoulder as I entered the building.

If you were rich enough to live on one of the top floors of The Oakwood, you were given a special key that had to be inserted in order to reach your floor—a nice little extra to ensure the riff raff wouldn't be wondering your halls. If you'd bought out the entire top floor of the building, however, you were given an embossed, chipped security key, and you had your own private entryway to a dedicated elevator that other residents would likely be shot if they were caught even looking at.

I prowled through the lobby, scanning the area as I always did. The plush carpets; the thick, luxurious curtains; countless vases dripping with flowers, cluttering up every available surface; the heavily flocked, gold foiled wallpaper: there were other residences in Brooklyn far more expensive and exclusive than The Oakwood, but this place had somehow maintained a glimmer of old New York. There was a faded, decayed, rat pack extravagance to the place, and Monica liked it. She'd chosen The Oakwood when it had come to finding her a place of her own to live, and I'd signed off on the location because it was defensible. Unlike in my building, there were no easily accessible stairways. The exits on each floor only unlocked and opened in the event of a fire, so there was no real way for someone to sneak in unless they came in through the front door, past Gil, and they somehow managed to bust their way into the correct elevator and rig it so that it would go up to the penthouse. And it was highly unlikely that that was ever going to happen.

My ears popped like a bitch as the elevator hurtled up to the twenty-seventh floor. Manhattan buildings went way higher, but here in Brooklyn, twenty-seven floors was nothing to be sniffed at. When the elevator doors rolled back, I was greeted by a wall of ear-splitting noise.

Huh. Uncanny. Sounded just like Pantera.

Monica's apartment was turned upside down. Empty Chinese takeout boxes were discarded all over the floor, chopsticks abandoned and kicked underneath the stools at the island counter. Monica always said the huge expanse of glass at my place made her feel dizzy. She'd opted for somewhere with normal windows—windows that were now shuttered, blinds drawn everywhere, blocking out most of the daylight and the impressive vista of Governor's Island in the distance. Clothes were draped over the backs of chairs and piled in heaps on the floor. A candle had toppled over on the small table in front of the white leather couch, and a puddle of bright red wax had oozed all over the glass top. From the finger marks, streaks and smears that ran through the wax, it looked as if Monica had tried to clean up the mess, but she'd obviously given up halfway and abandoned the task.

I stalked my way through the apartment, fuming as I went from room to room, searching for the woman. I found her in the bedroom, sprawled out on top of the bed, her stockinged feet dangling over the end. The wimple she'd been wearing earlier was laying on the floor, next to a pile of magazines and a bong shaped like a chimpanzee.

She didn't rouse when I entered the room. It took me clearing my throat to bring her to life, at which point she sat bolt upright, her eyes flashing, chest rising and falling rapidly as she blinked blearily at me with bloodshot eyes.

"I thought we agreed you weren't going to get high anymore," I said.

She glared at me—the kind of glare that would send most men running in fear for their lives. "Urgh!" Flopping back down on the bed, Monica closed her eyes, turned on to her side, away from me, and curled herself into a ball.

"You could have knocked," she said flatly. "You could have called and told me you were coming over. Oh, wait. You don't believe in phone calls anymore, right?"

"You have a really short memory. You let yourself into my place less than three hours ago," I shot back. "And I told you I was coming over. Get up, Monica."

She groaned. Curled herself up tighter.

"Get the fuck up now, or I'm going to drag your ass into the bathroom and I'm gonna toss you into a cold shower."

She flipped over, anger radiating off her in waves. "I'm not *that* high," she snarled. "And you have no right to come in here, making me feel like shit, when you're the one pulling all the crazy, stupid, reckless stunts."

"My actions have no bearing on how you choose to conduct yourself. Why the fuck are you wearing that again, Monica? Go and get changed, for fuck's sake."

With the wimple gone, her long, blonde hair was unbound and hanging almost down to her waist, but she was still wearing the rest of her habit. "I can wear whatever I want," she hissed. "I don't see why you can dress however the hell you please, but I'm expected to cater to your tastes."

"You *can* wear whatever you want. You always do. But this is crossing a line, don't you think?"

She turned back over, looking down at herself. "I wore this thing for years, Felix. What's your problem? They're just clothes."

"My problem is that you wearing a fucking habit out on the streets of New York, when you haven't been a member of the church now for years, is asking for trouble. It draws too much attention, and for what? You're not a novice anymore, Mon. You gave all that up a long time ago. Just like I did."

"You're wrong. This *doesn't* attract attention. Men don't look at me when I wear this," she replied. "Their eyes skate over me like I don't even exist. When I wear this, I'm a ghost. A nobody. Some days, that's better than being picked apart by every hungry, sex-mad moron wandering around this city with their dicks raging in their pants."

Monica had tried to stick with her calling after the accident. For a full year after she was discharged from hospital, she'd remained a servant of the Catholic church, eating and sleeping at the convent three blocks over from St. Luke's, praying, repenting, and searching for meaning. She'd insisted there was some kind of meaning to be found, some sort of lesson that she was meant to learn in the wake of what had happened to her. I'd admired her courage and determination at first, but in the end, I wasn't surprised when she'd turned up on my doorstep one evening, wearing a pair of jeans and a yellow and red branded Denny's shirt, saying that she'd had enough and that God was dead.

Ever since that day, she'd dressed herself in the weirdest combination of clothes—a Fedex delivery uniform; NYFD overalls; nursing scrubs. I'd never asked her why she dressed that way. It was obvious. Monica had lost her sense of identity when she gave up the church. She'd lost a huge chunk of her heart and her soul, and afterward she hadn't known who she was anymore. She'd needed something to define herself by. Something to make her feel like she still belonged to something. Normal, everyday clothes were too ambiguous, and so the uniforms made her feel safe.

"I need your laptop," I clipped out, storming into the room, and up to the bed. Thrusting out the pizza slice toward her, I also dumped the Snapple onto the bed beside her, and Monica flushed. She took the slice from my hands, her expression turning to one of uncertainty. It had been a long-running ritual now—me bringing her pizza and something sweet to drink whenever I came here. Monica didn't look up at me when she took the food and the drink from me. Biting the piece of pizza, she wiped her mouth with the back of her hand, then she scooted herself to the edge of the bed and got up.

Her mouth was full of dough and cheese when she said, "Why? What do you need it for?"

"Because I need to track down this Carver guy once and for all. The IP address from the message he sent was a dud, but your laptop's encrypted. There might be a way for Rabbit to backtrack the data and sever the dummy IP if he has access. He might be able to figure out the location and true identity of this Carver guy before he can cause any more problems for us."

Monica snorted. "You mean, cause any more problems for you," she corrected. "Or any more problems for that woman."

"Her name is Sera. Use it."

Monica leaned forward, aggressively tearing off another bite of her pizza. "She should be dead by now Fix. Dead. You do understand that, right?"

"We only accept jobs that deal with murderers, dictators, cartel bosses and rapists. Sera doesn't fit into any of these categories, so why the fuck would we take her on as a mark? It makes no sense. The money wasn't even good, Mon. What happened to your due diligence? What happened to making sure the people I bumped off really fucking deserved it?"

Monica stopped chewing. She lay the pizza down on her bed, wiping her hands off on the hem of her skirt. "I read the email. Saw the sister's medical reports—"

"Her mom's medical reports. When you saw her *mom's* medical reports."

"No. When I saw the *sister's* medical reports. What was her name? Amanda?"

"Amy."

"Yeah. Whatever. Amy. When I saw *her* medical reports, in conjunction with her mother's medical reports, it seemed as though they were both being poisoned by the same person. And since their father no longer has any contact with either of the girls, the only common denominator in both scenarios was Sera. There were no family friends still on the scene. No boyfriends, or neighbors. No one else that was around for both Mrs. Lafferty's death and Amy's worsening sickness. Ergo," she said, widening her eyes at me meaningfully, "Sera was responsible for her mother's death. And she's responsible for poisoning her sister, too."

"How could that even be possible? Before the road trip she went on to the wedding, Sera hadn't left Seattle in eighteen months. She couldn't have done anything to poison Amy."

Monica regarded me as if my IQ had just dropped dramatically. "She could have easily poisoned her without leaving Seattle. Use a little imagination, Fix. Fuck. She could have sent her something in the mail. Something she could have inhaled. Perfume. Plenty of toxins can be breathed in and have dramatic consequences. Or she could have applied something to paper. Three seconds' contact with bare skin would be enough to make someone terminally ill, if the toxin was potent enough."

I shook my head, staring up at the ceiling. "Sera loves Amy. There's absolutely no fucking way she would try and kill her. She's the only family she has left."

"Wrong. She has her father."

"Sixsmith's a deadbeat piece of shit that can't keep himself straight for more than twenty-four hours. Sera wouldn't have anything to do with him if you paid her."

"Does she have a lot of money, Fix?"

"What?"

"Sera. Does she have a lot of money?"

"I don't think she's struggling."

"Well, she'll certainly have a lot of money when Amy shuffles loose the mortal coil."

"What are you talking about?"

"Amy has a life insurance policy. A big, fat, prize turkey of a life insurance policy. If and when she dies, a grand total of three point one million dollars gets paid out to Sera."

I blinked at that. I was still processing the news that Amy was sick. She hadn't seemed ill in any way at the wedding. I hadn't really met her, but she'd seemed in perfect health from a distance. But a life insurance policy? With such an unbelievably high payout? That was concerning news. "If the policy's new, her husband's probably the one making her sick," I said. "Now that they're married, he's her next of kin. He'd be the recipient of any pay out, not Sera.

"It's *not* a new policy. It's been in effect since the day Amy was born. Some small, Podunk company that got bought out a decade ago. They're honoring the old policies, which cannot be amended by the way. It doesn't matter who Amy's married to. If she dies, the policy states her sister will receive the money no matter what. And besides, I looked into the husband. His family has lots of money. Old oil money. Three point one million is a drop in the ocean to them. The guy looked like a total asshole, but it's highly unlikely he'd commit murder for what would be such a meaningless amount to him."

I scoured Monica's face, hunting for the slightest hint that she wasn't being honest with me. There was no sign of hyperbole or deception playing across her features, though. Monica had told me plenty of lies over the years, and I'd gotten really fucking good at catching her out. I rarely confronted her about the mistruths, it generally served no purpose, but if she was fucking lying about this...

"I know Sera," I growled. "She loves her sister. She wouldn't try and kill her," I repeated. "Not for any amount of money. Now give me the laptop, Monica."

"You know her, do you? During the short time you tailed her across the country, you figured out everything there is to know about her. You didn't even *speak* to her until recently. You're fucking crazy if you expect me to believe that you know her. You know *me*. And when have I ever gotten something like this wrong?"

Something rankled inside me, something nasty and uncomfortable. I shoved the feeling aside, inhaling deeply through my nose. "I don't have to answer to you, Monica. I never have, and I never will. I don't need to justify a single thing to you."

She rocked back an inch, pain flickering in her eyes. "You're going to regret this madness," she said softly. "You're going to get locked up or wind up dead. Just cut ties with the girl. Take her to the airport, kiss her goodbye, and move on to the next job. It's for the best."

I thrust my hands into my pockets, digging my fingernails into my palms. There had been times when Monica and I had failed to see eye to eye. More times than I could count, actually. But this was different. This time, she was really worried, and I knew exactly why. If I was locked up, or dead...then Monica would be on her own. Truly on her own, for the very first time since she was attacked. My old friend guilt tried to whisper in my ear, but I clenched my teeth together and banished the motherfucker. There was no room in my life for guilt. Guilt was the most hazardous thing in the world to a man like me.

I just stared at her.

Monica returned my gaze, her eyes pleading. When I didn't move, speak or breathe, she loosed an uneven, ragged sigh and turned away from me, leaving the room. When she returned, she had a silver MacBook in her hands. She thrust the laptop into my chest, and I had just enough time to grab hold of it before she let go.

"Rabbit's hosting a party tonight. He's not going to be back at the warehouse until later." She went to her bedside table and retrieved a small envelope, which she then thrust at me, too. The envelope had been opened, though the word Fix had been messily scrawled onto the front of the card. Monica had opened it? *Monica had lost her goddamn mind.* "If you go tonight, I'd think long and hard before taking Sera as your plus one. Rabbit's mad at you. He's *really* fucking mad, and he doesn't take kindly to strangers. Even pretty ones with great tits. Don't say I didn't warn you."

32

SERA

DIMPLE

The silence woke me. A thick, stifling, roaring silence that jolted me from my dreams as effectively as a klaxon blaring right next to my ear. I sat up on the couch, my head reeling, and for a second I couldn't remember where I was, or who I was, or what the fuck was going on.

It all came back to me in the time it would take to click your fingers. I was Sera Lafferty, and I was in New York. And Fix Marcosa was...Fix Marcosa was nowhere to be seen?

The penthouse was almost dark, the waning light of the day turned deep purple and blue, and shadows had grown in the corners of the huge, sprawling living room; they resembled masked figures, lurking, ready to jump out of the half-light, preparing to attack. I got up and hit the lights by the entranceway, casting the shadows away, and the apartment suddenly felt much friendlier, if not entirely safe.

Where the fuck was Fix?

I got my answer when I came across the note he'd left for me on the dining table.

*A*ngel,

I was fucking you in your sleep.

You were moaning and panting, and I know only my dick can make you squirm like that. Probably the hottest thing I've ever seen.

I'll come back and give you the real thing soon, I promise.

Gone to see a man about a dog.

F

I frowned at the note, trying to figure out through the haze of sleep what the hell he was talking about. He was getting a dog?

Damn, I was getting a headache. I need pain killers.

There were no medical supplies in the kitchen. Was Fix even the kind of guy to keep a medical kit? Of course he was. He was in a high-risk line of work. He probably had a full operating room set up in the penthouse somewhere, just in case he got shot and needed immediate surgery.

I found the bathroom and proceeded to rifle through the drawers and cupboards there, trying not to drool over the huge copper claw foot tub that sat pride of place in the middle of the room. Goddamn, that was an amazing bath. Could easily fit three of four people it. The thought immediately made me feel queasy. Fix probably *had* fit three or four people in there. Not a pleasant thought. I'd always had a vivid imagination. Looking at the tub now, I could picture three naked women, covered in soap bubbles, all stroking him, making out with him, rubbing themselves all over him.

I was a fucking grown up. I could handle the fact that the guy I was sleeping with had a past. Everyone had a past. Fix's past was probably just a little more colorful than most, though, and the prospect that he'd had such scandalous adventures twisted my stomach a little. I was jealous, of all things, and I'd been convinced the man had wanted to kill me two days ago. What the fuck was wrong with me?

I opened up Fix's medicine cabinet and right away I found a bottle of Tylenol. There was only one small blue pill left inside, so I tossed it back and stooped to chase it down with some water from the faucet. Closing the cabinet, I surveyed myself in the mirror, pulling a face at myself. My hair was a rat's nest, and my eyes were puffy from sleep. I'd hardly been rocking a tan of late, but my skin seemed paler than usual. The truth was, I was washed out, and the shadows under my eyes made me look exhausted, even though I'd just woken up from what I'd thought had been a sound sleep.

Fix said I was moaning and panting. I couldn't remember if I'd been dreaming. If I had, I sure as fuck would have remembered having a sex dream. I remembered the one I'd had on the way to the cabin vividly. I splashed my face with water, but it didn't really help. Now I just looked tired and wet. Slowly, I shucked my clothes off, stretching my body as I got undressed. It would take a year to fill the tub with water, and after the mental images I'd just tortured myself with, I didn't really feel like soaking in it anymore, so I got into the huge glass walled shower and turned the water up as hot as it would go.

Heaven.

Nirvana.

Sheer bliss.

As the scalding water poured over my body, I felt the muscles in my neck, my shoulders, and my back relax, and I near melted from the ecstasy of it. It felt so good. Once I felt a little more mentally alert, I began to investigate the bottles of shampoo and body wash sitting on the recessed, tiled shelf in the wall, sniffing each one.

Leather. Citrus. Dark roast coffee, and oak. None of the scents here were *Fix*, though. His smell was something else entirely, and I highly doubted I'd find it in a bottle. I got cleaned up, turned the shower off, located a towel and dried off as quickly as I could.

Clothes. I needed clean clothes. I'd passed out on the couch, so I didn't know where the bedroom was, but I assumed that was where Fix had deposited our bags. The penthouse was bigger than I'd thought. I opened and closed five doors before I stumbled upon what was unmistakably Fix's bedroom. The room was dominated by a huge four poster bed that sat in the middle of the far wall. It was higher than any bed I'd ever slept on and stacked so high with pillows that it seemed as though a person would struggle to actually climb into the thing. Everything was slate grey, simple, but cleanly designed and tasteful. There were no curtains at the windows, nor were there any blinds. The building next to the Eddison Gas and Electrical Works was much lower and looked like it might have been abandoned for the last few decades, so it wasn't as if anyone could see into the penthouse, but still... Normal people didn't want to wake with the dawn. The penthouse was eastward facing, so it would be blasted by the sun the moment it rose up over the jigsaw puzzle of high rises on the horizon. Maybe Fix just never slept. He'd driven for such insanely long stretches and had shown absolutely no sign of tiring. And when we'd stayed at a hotel, or at the cabin on Butcher's Mountain, he'd been awake, showered, dressed and with a mug of coffee in his hand before I'd even opened my eyes. And I was *not* a late riser.

For an assassin, sleep probably didn't come easily. The mental images alone must have been enough to deprive him of rest. There were also undoubtedly occasions when things didn't go smoothly. When someone ended up pissed off and looking for retribution, Fix must have been constantly on his toes, just waiting for someone to kick the door in and try to slit his throat while he slumbered. He'd probably become accustomed to functioning on three hours' sleep or less.

There were matching dressers at either side of the room—the most beautiful mango wood, with hints of grey, and ash, and subtle green. The floor was the same polished concrete, but a huge dark grey rug covered most of it. The pile was thick and plush, and felt amazing when I dug my toes into it. The furniture all screamed '*Fix!*'

but the real reason I knew this was Fix's bedroom was the fact that there was a semi-automatic weapon propped up against the wall by the door to the walk-in closet.

So unbelievable. Who just left an assault rifle lying around in their bedroom? Normal people slept with a baseball bat beside their bed. Was this Fix's version of home invasion protection? Lord have mercy on the soul of the unwitting idiot who tried to break in here.

Everything was so much more extreme with Fix. He couldn't just be well-off. He had to be stinking rich. He couldn't just be a hot guy who liked me. He had to be a goddamn paid assassin/ex priest with a truckload of baggage, who, as far as I could tell, was a little obsessed with me. The world couldn't just be in turmoil; it had to be crashing and burning, engulfed in flames and about to explode.

I tightened the towel around my body, stepping into Fix's room, trying to find more of him here. There had to be some sort of personal items in here, though there were no knick-knacks or framed photos, or trophies on top of the dressers, or hanging from the walls. Just like the rest of the apartment, the room was meticulously clean and tidy, however it was sparse. Sparse as a monk's cell.

Oh....

It hit me, then.

A monk's cell. Fix had been a priest for a considerable amount of time. He'd probably had to live on site, close to the church. And he probably hadn't been encouraged to collect and display many personal items there. After so many years engaged in such a life of simplicity, he probably didn't have the capacity for luxurious living now.

I stared at his bed and wondered what his sheets would feel like on my skin. If the material would smell of him. If he'd allowed many other women to sleep next to him in there.

"You can get in if you like."

I nearly dropped my towel, my heart rocketing up into my throat. Oh god. *Oh my god.* Fix was standing behind me. I hadn't heard him enter. He hadn't made a sound as he'd sneaked up on me. He'd completely caught me off-guard. His eyes shone wickedly, as if he was enjoying the fact that I'd just had the ever-loving daylights scared out of me. Asshole.

"I haven't slept here in three months," he said, prowling into the room. His leather jacket was hanging over his arm, and he was holding a laptop in his hands. He placed both the jacket and the laptop down onto the bed, and then he turned and sat down on the edge of the mattress, a slow, suggestive smile spreading across his face like warm honey. "Drop the towel, Angel."

I angled my chin up, narrowing my eyes at him. "I don't think so. I'm jumpy as fuck, in a strange apartment, alone, and you snuck up on me. What the fuck is wrong with you?"

"I was hoping I'd catch you touching your pussy," he purred.

"And if I had been? You'd have burst in here and embarrassed me?"

Fix's moonlight eyes flashed with interest. "I would have cracked the door and watched with my dick in my hand. Spying on you while you were fingering your own pussy would be the highlight of my entire life, Sera. I'd have wet dreams about it until the day I die."

"You already watched me at the hotel last night."

"Not the same." Fix shook his head. "You *knew* I was watching. But if you thought you were alone...if you didn't know I was there..." He groaned, and a wave of heat rolled through me.

"Well, then. I'm sorry to disappoint." Part of me wished he had caught me. The look on his face, and the timbre of his deep, gravelly voice was more than a little flustering. God, the way this man made me feel. He was very skilled at making me squirm, fully dressed or otherwise. Which reminded me. "Where are my clothes, Fix?"

He pouted, and the shadow of a dimple formed in his cheek. Perfect.

Just...

Fucking...

Perfect.

He was already striking to look at. His bone structure was flawless —the cut of his jaw, and the line of his brow, and the high, etched lines of his cheekbones. His chin was defined and strong. And now here he was, showing up with a motherfucking dimple? Come on! Was there no justice in the world? If there was, Fix would have had some sort of visible fault. A third nipple. A weird birthmark. A mole on his back. Webbed fucking toes. Every part of the man was perfect, though. Even his teeth were glowing white and in regimented alignment. Every time I looked at him, I wanted to bury my face into his messy, dark, sexy hair, and just breathe him in. I was so beyond fucked.

"Your clothes are in the walk-in," he said, as if it should have been obvious. "Your shoes are in there, too. I put your make up bag and your toiletries in the en suite, just over there."

I glanced in the direction he was pointing, but I saw no door. Just plain, unadorned, slate-grey wall. Fix must have seen my frown.

"You push on it, and a panel door comes out. Looks a little tidier."

"You have a secret door in your bedroom? I always wanted a secret door in my room when I was a kid."

"Why?"

"Don't most kids want a secret door?" I paced over to the wall, running my hands over its smooth surface, trying to locate the spot where the door popped out. Took me thirty seconds to track down an almost indiscernible seam. Pushing down gingerly, I grinned to myself as a panel did indeed pop out, and the skinny door slid open without a sound. Beyond, in the bathroom on the other side of the door, yet another bathtub sat in the middle of the room, but this one was far more modest than the copper claw footed tub. It was simple and looked like it had been designed to accommodate just one person this time. How refreshing. The white subway tiles gleamed so bright, they were almost blinding. There was no polished concrete in here; the floor was made up of...*pennies*? Hundreds and hundreds of shiny copper pennies, under a thick layer of polyurethane. I sucked in a breath through my teeth, bending down to take a closer look. It was beautiful.

"They're all from nineteen eighty," he said behind me.

"The year you were born."

"Did you wish you had a secret room in your bedroom, so you could hide from Sixsmith?"

I froze, my palm planted firmly against the floor. I didn't think about Sixsmith. I didn't think about what he did to me when I was a teenager. I didn't think about what he allowed numerous other men to do to me. I didn't allow my father to pervade my thoughts, or my dreams, because he was insidious. If I dropped my guard down long enough to think of Sixsmith, the man poisoned me from the inside out. He took root in my mind, and he tangled himself up in every good, happy thing I had worked so hard for. I couldn't talk about Sixsmith. I didn't want to even form the shape of his name inside my head. It would only lead to heartache. Slowly, I straightened up, turning to look at Fix. I smiled, and said, "No. Not really. I just always wanted a secret library or a den. A place I could hang out."

Fix nodded, smiling too. "Bullshit. You're a horrible liar."

"What?"

"You're lying out of that fine ass of yours. You don't need to tell me the truth if you don't want to. You're entitled to your secrets. But, just so you know, you fucking suck at lying."

"No, I don't!"

"That smile that you've plastered all over your face? It's the fakest smile I've ever seen. Do you have any idea how fake the smiles are in a Catholic church on a Sunday, Sera? I used to stand in front of a sea of people all smiling so hard, it looked like they were trying not to collectively shit themselves. Yours is worse than that."

"Oh, gee. Thanks so much. So full of compliments."

"I could compliment you all day," he replied. Reaching up, he took hold of a strand of my wet hair and held it up, studying it intensely. "There are a thousand things I could say to flatter you...but you don't want that. You want someone real, and I'm about as real as it fucking gets. Want to know what *I* want? I want to know everything about you, Sera Lafferty. I'm not just here to whisper sugar and honey into your ears. I want your dark and ugly, as well as your beautiful and bright. Maybe one day I'll make you comfortable enough that

that won't be such a frightening prospect. Until then, know that every time you give me that bullshit smile, I'll know you're lying to me."

God. If he were any sort of gentleman, he wouldn't have called me out like that. He would have seen through my shitty smile and would have pretended like he'd believed me, and we would have moved on. But no. Fix had to be a contrarian. Fix had to open his mouth and say things that made me feel like I wanted to crawl out of my own skin. Fix had to put me on the spot and make me feel uncertain of myself.

"I'll never give you my dark and ugly," I said tightly. "You should count yourself lucky that you *might* just get the beautiful and bright."

A soft, muted sadness glittered off the ice of Fix's eyes. "Believe me, I do. But...there aren't many men out there like me. I've seen shit that would make most men soil their underwear. I've heard things that would give guys like your ex night terrors. There isn't a thing that you could tell me that I can't handle. There isn't a thing you could share with me that would come close to breaking me. I'd never judge you. I'd never pity you. I'd never feel sorry for you—"

"*That's* a lie," I snapped. My vision was see-sawing. If he kept talking about this, I wasn't going to be able to help myself. I was going to snap, and I was going to launch myself at him. He did *not* understand. Couldn't. "Everyone tries to hide it, but I can always see the pity, Felix. Everyone feels sorry."

"Why the fuck would I feel sorry for you?" he said, shrugging. "You're not a weak person. Whatever happened to you hasn't broken you, Sera. You're a force to be reckoned with. Whatever shitty, hellish experiences you've had in the past have forged you into this relentless, empowered, fierce individual. You're unstoppable."

I met his gaze, and his eyes were crystal clear, lancing into me. Who did he see when he looked at me like that? When I looked at myself in the mirror, I didn't think I saw the same person he'd just described. I saw someone who was hiding, who had been hiding for some time now, and was very used to living behind the safety of a very thick, very high shield wall. That woman wasn't brave. She wasn't empowered or fierce. She was a goddamn *coward*. If I were the person Fix thought I was, I wouldn't have just withheld the truth about my childhood from him. I would have taken a deep breath and told him everything, regardless of whether it made me uncomfortable or not. It didn't help matters that I was currently wearing nothing but a towel. I was incredibly vulnerable, and in more ways than one. "Can we just...*not* do this right now, please? I—" I stopped talking. A loud alarm had begun to pulse, the throbbing sound echoing throughout the penthouse like a frantic, loud, uneven heartbeat. My eyes went wide as I stared at Fix, lips pressed together, not daring to breathe. "What the fuck is *that*?"

"The doorbell," he answered. So fucking cool. So fucking calm. I wanted to kick him in the balls. Who had a doorbell like that? It was worse than that wailing, haunting siren from fucking Silent Hill. "Don't be shitty with me, but I got you something," Fix said, as he exited his bedroom and headed toward the front door. I followed behind him, clamping my towel tightly under my arm to prevent it from falling.

"Something? What kind of something?"

"A dress. A few dresses. We have an event to attend this evening, and I've seen every single item of clothing you brought with you on this trip. I love the jeans and t-shirts, Sera, but tonight requires something a little more...*elegant*."

We were going out? And Fix had bought dresses for me? The headache that had been threatening to split my skull open when I woke up earlier was now gone thanks to the Tylenol. I was feeling better, but it would have been nice to have been asked before Fix started organizing things for us to do. "Hey! What if I don't want to go out, huh?"

Fix planted his palm on the security pad beside the door to the penthouse. He turned his attention to me, cocking his head to one side. "If you don't want to come, you can stay here. You can go sightseeing. You can do whatever the hell you like. But I'm going to be gone for hours, and it would reassure me to know that you weren't having sheets of skin peeled from your body by Carver's new hitman while I was out, drinking champagne and shoving hors d'oeuvres into my face. But like I said, it's entirely up to you."

Well. When he put it like that...

Fix winked at me, then pulled open the door, revealing not one but two women standing out in the hallway. Maybe in their mid-twenties, both of them were beautiful with dark, raven-black hair that was pulled back tightly into neat buns, not a strand out of place. Their eyes were dark, smoky and heavily kohled, their full mouths were slashes of bright crimson lipstick. They wore plain black dresses that emphasized every line and curve of their willowy frames. In each of their hands, they held at least three hangers, hooked over their fingers, and the items on those hangers were covered with plastic garment bags.

Fix didn't say a word to them. He stepped to one side, and the women entered the penthouse, strutting in on perilously high heels, the light bouncing from the toes of their superbly shiny patent pumps.

They moved rigidly, their eyes slipping coolly over me as they passed me by, heading down the hallway and into the bathroom.

"Robots," I whispered over my shoulder. "They look like robots."

"Either that, or Robert Palmer finally released the extras from the 'Simply Irresistible' video shoot."

I hid the fact that I was smirking as I followed after Fix's guests. In the bathroom, the two women had already removed the garment bags from the dresses, and they were hanging them up on a rail by the window.

I gasped as I surveyed the different materials—black, red, gold, all glimmering and shimmering under the light. Some of the dresses were understated and classy, while a couple of them looked like burlesque outfits, barely anything to them, and covered with sequins and sparkling stones. I'd never seen anything like it. I balked when one of the women selected a particularly scandalous gold number, holding it aloft in my direction, squinting at me.

"Oh no. Sorry. That thing is way too short. I'm not leaving this penthouse with my ass hanging out," I said.

The women wrinkled their noses in unison. "So crass," the woman holding the gold dress said. Her accent was thick; at first I thought she was Spanish, but when she spoke again, I realized she was, in fact, Italian. "You don't need to worry, miss. No one will see something they are not supposed to see," she reassured me.

"This dress is long enough to cover everything that matters," the other woman said. Their English was colored by their heritage, but it was also perfect. Soft, melodic, and lilting. It sounded like music. I pulled a face.

"Very pretty, but it's a no from me."

The woman on the right turned to the woman on the left, frowning. "Does she get a choice?" she hissed.

I stepped forward, frowning. "I'm sorry? What did you just say?"

Coolly, the Italians arched their sculpted brows at me. The slightly taller one said, "My sister was just asking if you were allowed a choice in what you wear tonight. Typically, the women we deal with..." She trailed off, her voice rising at the end.

"Shhh, Sofia. Maybe we're not supposed to talk to her," the other girl hissed.

I planted my hands on my hips, my mouth hanging open as I looked between the two women.

"Listen...Sofia, right?" I said to the tall one. "And you? What's your name?"

The shorter woman pursed her lips in a tight, unfriendly line. "My name is Martina. But you don't need to know who we—"

"Sofia. Martina. I'm not sure who you normally dress in this city, but I can assure you, I am not someone's property. I do *not* belong to that man out there. I'm not a mannikin to be decorated without my consent. There's no fucking way you're forcing me to wear something I don't want to wear, and if you try, you're seriously going to regret it. Do you understand me?"

The sisters reeled back, their feathers most certainly ruffled. I pitied the women they usually came to assist. They were either so meek and retiring that they never said a word as they were poked and prodded at. Or, conversely, perhaps their clients were too scared for their lives to object as they were stuffed inside dresses, their feet jammed into shoes, and they were painted up like pretty, docile dolls.

Sofia was the first to loosen, the rigidity in her back relaxing as she slowly smiled at me. "We apologize, miss. We deal with all kinds of situations. Sometimes, it's difficult to know which rules apply."

My stomach rolled. Were there times when Sofia and Martina turned up to a residence in the evening, and they tended to a woman who was being held there against her will? It was possible. It sounded like it was more often than not the case. Sofia and Martina were young. They were a part of a generation where women stood together, fought alongside one another, demanded equal rights and equal pay. They were part of a sisterhood, whether they liked it or not, and they were betraying that sisterhood.

If I showed up to carry out a job I'd been hired to do, it wouldn't matter to me. Wouldn't matter if it was a woman, or a man, young or old. If I was faced with someone who was being held against their will, I would not be party to it. I'd probably get myself into serious shit trying to *free* them.

I was tempted to ream Sofia and Martina out for being such vapid, spineless bitches. But if I did that, I would only be extending this weird, awkward situation longer than it needed to be. I just wanted this to be over, and for them to leave as quickly as possible.

"I'll take that long black one." I pointed at the dress on the end of the rack.

Sofia and Martina looked at me, looked at each other, and then looked at the dress in question. "That dress is not for you," Sofia said flatly.

"Why not?" It was simple and far less flashy than the other options. The neckline was low enough to emphasize my boobs, but not low enough to suggest that my services were available by the hour. There was a small beaded detail just underneath the bust—black beads that glinted and shone but weren't massively over the top like the brocading and sequins on some of the other pieces.

Martina took hold of the dress and flared it out, revealing the split in the skirt of the material. "Goes all the way up to here," she said, stabbing herself with her finger, right on her hip bone. "You cannot wear panties with this dress. And *you*..." She wrinkled her nose again. "You complained about the gold one. This one shows way more skin."

It certainly was one hell of a split. And to go out not wearing panties? I eyed the other dresses, assessing each of them one at a time. Some of them were almost acceptable, but then I'd notice something about them that wasn't going to work. A see-thru panel; a garish fake flower; way too many blingy crystals and stones. I pointed to the black dress, gesturing with my hand.

"Just give it to me. I'll try it on. See how bad it is."

Sofia smiled tautly, collecting the dress and holding it up in front of me. "Well done, miss. Very brave. You're going to make your friend very happy indeed."

33

FIX

THROAT PUNCH

*R*abbit wasn't happy with me. That's what Monica had said. Why the fuck wasn't Rabbit happy with me? I sent the bastard work every damn day of the week. I paid him three times the amount anyone else did when they hired him. I didn't owe him anything—it was a point of principle that I never owed *anyone* anything—so what could Rabbit possibly be shitty about? The guy was unassuming. Five foot nine. Quiet. A nerd, there was no denying it, but he wasn't your archetypal geek with glasses, braces, bad skin and greasy hair. He worked out. He wasn't going to be winning any body building contests any time soon, but he kept himself in relative shape. He wore expensive button-down shirts, and even more expensive Amiri jeans, and he held these little mixer parties every once in a while, just to remind people how important and awesome he was.

He knew a lot of people, and therefore he knew a lot of people's secrets. When you were wrist deep in someone's data on their laptop, it was hard not to accidentally notice something damning, illegal, or just plain fucked up. The things he found on some computers had people screaming and begging for him not to go to the cops. He never went to the authorities. He played it cagey, though, acting up enough that, when he asked for a hefty increase in his fee for extra 'parts and labor,' not a one of those rich motherfuckers ever made a peep.

It had been a while since I'd been to one of Rabbit's parties, but I knew what to expect. It would be an even split: a group of twenty-something-year-old kids, high as fuck and out of their goddamn minds, dancing like *they* were the ones who discovered expression through goddamn movement or some other bullshit. And at the bar and sitting in dark corners, a bunch of older, stuck up well-to-dos with their hands in their pockets, all talking in code, hating each other. The air would be thick with jealousy, pride, arrogance, and deafeningly bad EDM music. I had to hand it to Rabbit, though. He blew an inconceivable amount of money on his parties, so there was always enough booze. And party favors, if that was your thing. Usually there'd be a group of girls fingering each other in the pool by the end of the night.

Monica was right. Taking Sera along to this thing was a bad fucking idea. Rabbit was as paranoid as they came and was constantly accusing people of being cops. He'd done an array of questionable things on the dark web. Had been involved in an underground supply and demand site that had catered to just about every messed up, dark, deviant desire known to man, and the administrator of that site had been arrested just under a year ago. His ass was still rotting in jail, awaiting trial, and Rabbit was convinced his old boss was going to start spilling people's real names and addresses to the authorities in order to reduce his own sentence. There was a very real chance he was right, and the cops were going to smash his door in any day now. I didn't point that out to Rabbit, though. Fucker was already difficult to be around as it was, without stoking the flames of his distrust. Sera's presence this evening might be tricky. I was going to have to work out what Rabbit's issue was with me, and I was going to have to smooth over the fact that I'd brought a guest with me. And once I'd accomplished that, I had to get him to take Monica's laptop off my hands, so he could figure out who the fuck Carver was, and hopefully be able to pinpoint his actual location for me.

All in a night's work.

I showered quickly and then got dressed in my bedroom, trying to ignore the fact that my dick was still raging hard. Coming home to find Sera wandering around in a towel, her hair wet and plastered to her head, beads of water rolling down between her pronounced shoulder blades... My reaction had been instant and demanding. She was so fucking beautiful. She had no idea just how beautiful she was. Her wet, naked body, barely concealed beneath that towel, had made it very difficult not to fucking take her. I'd considered it. Had wanted to. Had wanted her to unfasten my fly and to take my swollen cock into that pert, pretty little mouth of hers. But then Sofia and Martina had shown up and spirited her away, and I was left to only imagine what it would have felt like.

There was later, of course. After the party. There would be plenty of time to strip Sera bare and fuck her in as many holes as she would allow. I slid my arms inside the jacket of the suit I'd picked out for the evening—jet black, pristine, specifically tailored to my body, so that it fit me like a second skin. It was a thing of true beauty. I'd only worn it once before, many years ago, but the moment I saw it sitting there in the closet, I'd known tonight was the night I was meant to wear it again.

Sofia and Martina were still busy working on Sera by the time I made my way to the kitchen and poured myself a large measure of scotch over a single ice cube. I'd met the sisters before, had run into them all over the city, in various situations, most of which involved the mafia in one way or another. I'd been hired by the mob before. I'd also had to take care of a few higher up members of The Family, which had been really fucking stressful. The Italians were proud people. They believed in honor and respect. Forgiveness? Not so much. They all professed to be Catholic and went to church every Sunday without fail, but fuck me sideways if they didn't know how to hold a grudge. I was lucky that I was so good at what I did. If I'd been careless or sloppy and the cops had somehow tied me to any of those murders, then it wouldn't have mattered if I were in police custody or not. I'd have been eighty-sixed within a matter of hours. And the mob had so much money, pull and influence, that it wouldn't have even been the other inmates I would have had to worry about. It would have the prison guards and the cops themselves that put the bullet in the back of my brainpan.

I sipped the scotch, relishing the burn as it slipped down the back of my throat. The sky outside was a deep royal blue, smattered with a handful of white pinpricks—the only stars visible beyond the light pollution of the blazing, burning city at night. I stood at the window, sipping the scotch, watching the ferries slowly shuttle out across the water toward Lower Manhattan, and the whole time my ears were trained on the low hum of conversation that was coming from the bathroom. Was she all right in there?

Maybe Sofia and Martina were a bad idea. Some women felt threatened by others, especially if they were attractive. The sisters were definitely attractive, but I'd never touched either of them. Never done more than grunted an acknowledgement in their general direction whenever I'd found myself in their presence. It was one thing, offing the occasional made man in Hell's Kitchen. It was another thing altogether sticking my dick inside one of their daughters. I wasn't that fucking dumb. And besides how absolutely crazy I would have needed to be to involve myself in that kind of trouble, I'd never had any real desire to fuck either of them. They were vapid, dull women without an ounce of personality between them. They were too obedient and well trained for my tastes. I always wanted a girl who would pull at the leash. And now I had a woman who refused to wear one altogether. She was fucking perfect.

I was already thinking this when I saw Sera's reflection in the window. When I spun around to look at her properly, though, my breath left my body all at once.

Holy...fucking...*shit.*

She was stunning. Her dark hair had been curled into loose waves, and her makeup was immaculate. It barely looked like she was wearing anything at all, but as I grew closer, the distance between us vanishing, I could see that I was wrong. Her eyes were smoky, just like the sisters' eyes, but it was subtler. Less obvious. Her lips were a fresh, neutral pink-peach color, and slightly glossy. God, I wanted to bite those lips between my teeth. I wanted to see them parted open and swollen, while she panted out my name, begging me to come inside her. I wanted those lips wrapped around my cock...

Fuck, I wanted all of it. And I wanted it right now.

The dress she'd selected was exquisite. Her tits were on display in the very best way, and the black, silken material of the slim-fitting, floor-length gown, hugged her curves perfectly. When she took a step toward me, I groaned out loud as the material of the skirt parted, revealing the entire length of Sera's toned, golden, impeccable leg. From ankle to hip, she was perfection. And that wasn't all. She halted in front of me, a small smile playing on her face, and when she turned...

The dress was backless. Completely backless. The material scooped dramatically, plunging all the way down, so that even the very lowest point of her back was on show.

Magnificent.

She was absolutely magnificent.

I pointed to the door, trying to keep my temperature down as I slowly opened my mouth and spoke. "Ladies. You can leave. Now."

The smile on Sera's face grew wider.

"You're pleased with our work?" Martina asked. "Our uncle will be very unhappy if you're not satisfied."

"I'm very satisfied. But I would have been just as happy without the dress, or the makeup, or the hair. She's perfect just the way she is."

The sisters left without another word—a good thing, since I was about ready to pick them up and forcibly remove them from the penthouse. Once we were alone, I discarded my empty scotch glass on the coffee table, and I rushed Sera, sweeping her up into my arms. "Fuck. You have no idea how badly I want to thrust myself inside you right now. You're fucking breathtaking. I want your cunt on my mouth. I need you to ride the fuck out of my face or I'm going to fucking die."

She laughed, the sound peeling through the penthouse like the ringing of a bell. I'd never heard her make that sound before. Not once. To hear it now, with her in my arms, looking so spectacular, her hands pressed up against my chest, her eyes revealing her reluctant amusement, was the most amazing moment I'd experienced in well over a decade.

"I don't think there's time for any face-riding," she murmured. "Unless showing up fashionably late to this party is an option, that is."

Fuck. It *wasn't* an option. Rabbit's parties were notorious for being impossible to get into. Even if you had an invite like the one sitting in my pocket right now, the same invitation Monica had opened without my consent, there was still a fifty/fifty chance you wouldn't be admitted. If you weren't dressed well enough? If you seemed even slightly drunk? You weren't getting inside. The invite clearly stated admittance was between eight and nine pm, and they weren't fucking around either. I'd seen it happen plenty of times—people, showing up to party five minutes after nine, and that was it. There was no bending or breaking the rules, no matter who you were. Rabbit's rules were steadfast and concrete. There was no circumnavigating or cheating them. It didn't matter who the fuck you were.

I lowered my mouth slowly, until Sera understood that I wanted to kiss her. She tipped her head back, exposing the pure, alabaster, creamy skin of her throat, and I was tempted to dip my head down and bite her there. It would be a sinful pleasure to sink my teeth into her skin. To feel her flesh yield to me beneath the pressure. I would save it for later, though. I'd only end up marking her, and how would that look, walking into a packed party, if she had a huge welt on her neck? It was hard, though. Shit. So fucking hard. And I wasn't just talking about my dick.

My lips touched hers, and I stifled yet another groan as I tasted her mouth—she was so fucking sweet. She was timid with her tongue as she licked and laved at me. I took great fucking pleasure in the knowledge that I wasn't going to be timid with my tongue later. I was going to use it to make her buck, and scream, and writhe.

Sera's breath started to quicken, as I slid my hands down her body, grabbing hold of her ass. "Your body melts beneath my hands whenever I touch you," I growled into her mouth. "I love making you melt."

"I can't...seem to stop myself," she admitted. "You have this crazy effect on me. I don't understand it. It takes me by surprise every single time. All it takes is one look from you..."

I ground my teeth together, resisting the urge to tear her out of her dress right here and now.

I was strong. I could defy my own urges. My cock was going to be throbbing painfully all damn night, but I could restrain myself. If it meant I was able to leave the laptop with Rabbit, able to track down this phantom client who'd introduced himself as Carver, then it would be more than worth it.

Fastening my bottom lip between my teeth, I cursed the world for demanding we show up and play a part in it this evening. "Come on, Angel," I murmured, breathing in the fresh, floral scent of her hair. "It's time to go to church."

34

FIX

YVONNE

FIVE YEARS AGO

*M*y feet were killing me. They felt weird in the sneakers I'd put on my feet—too new, not broken in, and strange. I'd worn leather shoes for years now. Simple, smart, respectable dress shoes that went unnoticed beneath a cassock. The sneakers were cushioned, nothing fancy in themselves, but...they were too comfortable. A strange issue, but after so long feeling every crack in the ground underfoot through the dress shoes, the fact that I couldn't feel the streets of New York beneath my feet now was unsettling.

I'd been walking for hours. Six hours to be precise. I'd needed to clear my head, to get out of the penthouse that I was also still so unused to sleeping in, but I found that even now I couldn't stop my mind from racing.

Everything had changed. Nothing was the same. I felt uneasy in my skin, as if I'd donned a suit that belonged to someone else and was completely unrecognizable to me. I was wearing someone else's skin. Ever since I'd left seminary, I'd been Father Marcosa. I'd had responsibilities and a set list of rules that were to be adhered to on a daily basis. I'd known *exactly what was expected of me, and I'd known exactly how to behave. Today, I'd shrugged out of Father Marcosa's skin, along with his cassock and his familiar, thin-soled shoes, and I'd become someone else entirely.*

I'd never felt at home being a priest. I'd always railed against those rules, the expectations, and the responsibilities that had felt stifling to me. I'd wanted to free myself of that life a thousand times since I'd made my vows, but I'd given no thought to who I would be afterwards. I'd certainly never thought I'd be a fucking murderer. There were new rules to follow now, new responsibilities that had to be undertaken, and I couldn't seem to wrap my head around any of it.

I tightened my jacket around me, trying to ward off the bitter cold that had all but numbed me to the core, and I continued on down the street.

One mile followed the other, followed the other. At some point, the pregnant, grey clouds overhead gave way and it started to snow, though I didn't register when. It wasn't until I looked up, realizing that I'd somehow found my way back to St. Luke's, that I noticed the great stone lintel above the entranceway to the church was dusted with white flakes.

I stood and stared up the building, limned in silver, and I found that my feet suddenly didn't know which way to go.

"Father?"

I followed the sound of the voice and found a familiar face looking up at me. Yvonne Prescott, who had been in confession with me the day I'd found Monica half dead in the rectory, bathed in a sea of her own blood. Yvonne was slim and pretty in her own way. Mousy. I'd always thought her eyes were too big for her face. She hadn't been to church since the day Monica was attacked, and so I hadn't seen her. I'd forgotten all about her until I found myself looking down at her now.

"Yvonne. Hi." I didn't know what else to say.

She looked at me, at my civilian clothes—the thick, grey felt jacket with the collar popped against the weather, and the black jeans, and the new shoes, and a frown wrinkled her brow. "I'd heard you'd left," she said softly. "I didn't believe it until yesterday. The new priest is a woman. The first in our district. Did you know that?"

My face felt like it was made out of Play-Doh, as I trained my features into what I hoped looked like pleasant surprise. "Oh? No. I didn't know."

I didn't fucking care. The Pope himself could have replaced me at St. Luke's and it wouldn't have made the slightest bit of difference to me. I was still struggling to understand why I'd even found my way here in the first place. I hadn't homed in on the church because it was a place of sanctuary to me, that was for sure.

"I—I'm sorry," Yvonne mumbled, glancing down at her feet. "I'm sorry I didn't come back while you were still here. I just..." She sighed, pursing her lips. "I was ashamed. Of how useless I was that day, when..."

She didn't continue, and I didn't need her to. She'd fallen apart when she'd seen Monica lying on the floor. Most people would have done the same. The fact that she hadn't rallied and kept her head about her must have been making her feel guilty, though. "It's okay," I said. "Monica's okay now. She's doing much better."

"Yeah. They said she's out of hospital," Yvonne said, her voice brightening. "She'll be able to go back to Canada soon, right? Back to her family and her friends."

I almost laughed out loud. Monica would be doing no such thing. She'd made it perfectly clear that she was staying in New York, legally or otherwise, until we'd found the bastard responsible for her attack, and we'd dealt with the situation.

"What about you?" Yvonne hiked her purse strap higher onto her shoulder. The end of her petite, up-turned nose had turned red from the cold. I couldn't stop fucking staring at it. "What are you going to do, now that you're not at St. Luke's?" She made it sound like I'd merely worked at the church. I'd been there every day for years, barely leaving the confines of the building unless charity work or home visits had required it. I hadn't just stopped working at St. Luke's. I'd left behind an entire way of life.

What am I going to do, Yvonne? What the fuck am I going to do? I'm going to be a killer. I've been murdering people all over the fucking place, and I'm not going to stop any time soon.

I shot Yvonne a smile. A shitty, disingenuous smile that made my face hurt. "I'm not sure. Macramé? Maybe I'll become a professional tennis player. I used to have a mean backhand in high school."

The tentative smile on her face faltered. Her eyes fell back down to her shoes. "I'm sorry. That was a stupid question. I—"

I cut her off. "Come and get a drink with me." It wasn't a question. It was a command, and one Yvonne hadn't been expecting, from the way her eyes bugged out of her head. Honestly, I'd surprised myself by saying it.

"A drink?"

"Yeah. My shout. What do you drink? Wine? Beer? Tequila?"

Yvonne's head swiveled up and down the street, and then her gaze settled on the building in front of her, her cheeks flushing with color. It was as if God Himself had leaned over her shoulder and whispered into her ear, telling her not to do it. "It's three p.m. on a Monday. I don't think I'm meant to be drinking, Father."

"Felix."

"I'm sorry?"

"Felix. My name's Felix. Does it really matter what day it is?"

"Uh...not...not really. I suppose," she stammered.

"Good." I grabbed hold of her, taking her hand. Five minutes later we were sitting at a bar and I was ordering two whiskeys.

"Have you stopped touching yourself, then?" I demanded, as she took her first sip. She almost spat the amber liquid all over the bar.

"I beg your pardon?!"

"You don't need to beg for my pardon anymore. I can't forgive you for shit."

Yvonne slid the ice from one side of her glass to the other. "Perhaps this was a bad idea. I don't think...I told you those things in confidence. They were part of my confession. I never thought—"

I tossed back my whiskey, placing the high ball down onto the bar with exaggerated care, then I pierced her through with my eyes. "You used to sit on the front pew every week and stare at me, Yvonne. I noticed. Your husband sat there because he cared what people thought, wanted them to believe he was fucking perfect. The most pious. The most devout. But you sat there, with your skirt hitched up just a few inches too high, your knees pressed together like you were pinching a hundred-dollar bill between them, because you liked the idea of me seeing you." I gestured to the bartender, motioning for a refill. Meanwhile, Yvonne's face had turned so red, she'd started to look like a beet. "You used to run your hands up and down your thighs. You wanted me to notice you," I murmured. "You sat there on the front row, and you used to imagine what it would be like to have my head between your legs. My tongue buried in your pussy. And when you went home, when you touched yourself, you'd imagine what it would be like for me to thrust my cock inside you until you screamed. And then, you'd come to me to confess and flagellate yourself over it. And being in that tiny little box, all hot and bothered under the collar, listening to my voice, hearing me breathe...that made you want to go home and do it all over again, didn't it?"

Her hand shook as she slowly put down her glass. "I think I ought to be going now, Felix."

"Don't be such a fucking coward," I growled. "Don't you see, this is all bullshit? We're all animals. We have base needs that drive us. There's nothing we can do about it. Life is only fucking bearable if we recognize that and we're fucking honest. Even if it's only with ourselves."

The bartender placed another glass of whiskey on the bar, and then he held out his balled-up fist to me. "Amen, brother."

I bumped it without even looking at him; so what if he was eavesdropping. "Life is short, Yvonne. If touching your pussy makes you feel good, then so be it. If touching your pussy and thinking about me makes you feel good, then that's even fucking better. You have my permission to go to fucking town. I'm not gonna be upset."

Poor Yvonne. Her horror was written all over her. But her pupils were wide, like she'd just snorted an entire gram of coke, and her lips were wet and parted. She was turned on just as much as she was embarrassed. I leaned an inch closer to her. "You can politely excuse yourself and run back to fucking Gus. You can go home and scrub yourself until you feel clean again after bad, bad Felix made you feel dirty," I whisper. "Or, you can come with me into the bathroom back there, and I can show you what it feels like to have my tongue on your clit. I'll show you what it feels like to have my hard cock inside you, and then, when I've made you come, you can go home feeling like a woman. A woman who took what she wanted."

This was wrong. This was really bad. But fuck it. I was fucking done being good. Yvonne didn't take her eyes off me. She was panting, her breath coming in short, panicked little gasps. "I can't do that. I love my husband."

"No, you don't." I laughed into my whiskey glass as I held it up to my mouth. "You love that he makes six figures. You love that you looked perfect

together in your wedding photos, like a perfect goddamn American dream come true. You love how jealous people are when they look at Mr. and Mrs. Prescott, and they imagine how wonderful your fairytale life is. But you know the truth, and so do I. You hate Gus."

Indignation flashed in her eyes. "You shouldn't say things like that. It's not...it's not right."

I smiled at her, the first real smile I'd given anyone in a long time. "All right. Then run along home. I'm sorry to have upset you."

I flagged the bartender again, pointing at my empty glass. Yvonne looked boneless as she slid off her stool, slowly collecting her purse and her coat. She didn't say anything as she slowly, mechanically turned around and walked out of the bar.

"That was impressive," the bartender said. "Here. A double, on the house. You got stones the size of fucking bowling balls. Shame she didn't pick up what you were putting down."

I watched him pour until the whiskey was almost level with the lip of the glass.

I didn't say a word.

One... Two...Three... Four...Five... Six... Seven...

The door to the bar swung open, and Yvonne hurried back inside. Her coat and her purse were still in her hands. She kept her head down as she continued past me, her eyes barely flickering toward me, as she made a beeline for the bathrooms at the rear of the bar.

I picked up the whiskey, tipped back the glass and I drained the thing in one.

I got up.

The bartender's mouth was hanging open. "Holy shit, dude."

I still didn't say anything as I followed Yvonne into the bathroom.

35

SERA

GUEST LIST

*L*ights.

A million lights.

Small flicking flames, scores of them guttering and dancing in the dark like blades of grass in an endless field. They covered every available surface as Fix guided me through the ancient graveyard, lining the cracked, jumbled flagstone path before us, and perched on the tops of headstones, so close that the wax pillars had merged and melted together to form drunken, lopsided structures.

The headstones themselves looked like the nubs of decaying, broken teeth, protruding from the ground. So old. Beyond old. I caught sight of a couple of the dates inscribed into them as Fix wrapped his arm around my shoulders, pressing me to him: eighteen ninety-three; Seventeen ninety-one; Eighteen fifty-six. Arthur; Gerald; Beatrice; Agatha: the names inscribed into the aged stonework were from another time. Another world. The New York they'd known must have been very different to the metropolitan hub that flexed and breathed and seethed today, never pausing, never sleeping.

"How does this guy host parties inside a church?" I asked, my voice hushed. Seemed rude to speak loudly amongst the dead.

"The building was damaged in a fire fifty years ago. The parish-
ioners couldn't afford to repair it, and the arch-diocese wanted to build
a more modern, contemporary church close by, so this place just sat
here for years. Rabbit bought the land, thinking he could tear down the
building, but the ground's still consecrated. You can't legally disrupt
consecrated ground, so he said fuck it and renovated instead. I've seen
old photos. It looks exactly the same as it did before the fire now."

"He lives here?"

"Yeah. Along with a handful of body guards and a Rottweiler
named Jaws."

I crinkled my nose, studying the building that was growing larger
by the second, emerging out of the darkness like a monolith. "Seems
like bad luck to live in a church?"

Fix's fingers dug lightly into my side. "You're superstitious now?"

I ignored him. "Aren't you outraged that someone would turn a
sacred space into their party den?"

"They could turn the place into a fucking brothel for all I care."
His expression was hard. Stony. Devoid of any emotion. "It's just a
building, Sera. It's older than most, and the windows are pretty. That's
all there is to it."

"You really don't care?"

He turned and looked at me. The light from the countless candles
played across his skin, casting him in both inky black shadows and a
subtle golden warmth. He looked timeless: his suit was classically cut,
and his eyes seemed ancient, as if they'd witnessed innumerous
generations rise and fall and fade away. As if he, himself, were
peering at me through a porthole in time, back from a long-forgotten
age. "I don't," he confirmed. And he didn't expand further on the
matter. I could have probed, prodded and pushed for more of an
explanation, but the set of his jaw spoke volumes. He didn't want to
talk about it.

The church would have been the perfect set for a horror movie. It
was beautiful in its way, but the gothic tower with its high steeple was
hardly welcoming, and the gargoyles crouched on the parapets,

snarling and bearing their teeth, their tongues unfurled like banners, were unfriendly to the eye.

The windows Fix had just mentioned were the prettiest thing about the building. I couldn't tell what the stained-glass scenes depicted from our vantage point, but the colors—red, gold, orange—backlit from the light inside the church, burned like flames.

At the door, two large guys in suits with shaved heads and wrap-around sunglasses—Ridiculous. It was so dark, I could barely see three feet in front of me—stood with menacing authority, awaiting our arrival. There were no other people outside, and weirdly I couldn't hear any sounds coming from within.

It had taken time, but I'd grown accustomed to Fix's moods. I was able to read him more and more as the days passed. He was always watching. Always assessing. His quicksilver eyes always picking apart the scene before him. He listened with deep intent whenever someone spoke, analyzing and processing every word. I knew, whenever I opened my mouth, I was being catalogued, saved, committed firmly to memory. More often than not, the man was silent, his fathomless attention to detail occupying the larger part of his mind, but there were different qualities to his silences. His expression could barely change, but I could *feel* when he was angry. When he was amused, or when he was worried. It was easy to recognize when he was turned on now, too, though he hadn't been doing much to hide those moments.

Having spent so much time learning Fix's tells and tics, the shift that occurred in him as we approached the church was now obvious. The grim set to his mouth didn't alter. The flint in his eyes didn't harden further. The set of his broad, strong shoulders remained confident and self-possessed, and the swagger in his step was the same as always, but *something* changed. I couldn't tell what exactly, but Fix was...nervous?

His teeth flashed in predatory warning as we arrived in front of the doormen. "We're expected." Producing a slim card from his pocket, Fix handed it to one of the heavies and made to push past him. The guy slapped a huge hand against Fix's chest, stopping him in his tracks. Dull brown eyes studied me, traveling from my feet to the crown of my head.

"She hasn't been vetted. You know the rules," he rumbled.

With slow, drawn out movements, Fix took hold of the doorman by the wrist and removed the hand from his chest. "I don't bring trouble here. I never have. Now get the fuck out of the way."

The other doorman snarled, his lip curling. "You can go inside. *She* has to disappear."

Fix's face was a mask of nonchalance, but fury burned behind the ice in his eyes. "I've had a particularly shitty week, friend. I haven't been able to vent my frustration quite as thoroughly as I might have liked. It'll bring me great pleasure to throat punch you so hard you'll need feeding through a tube for the rest of your life. So please. Continue standing in my way. *See what fucking happens.*"

Both men grew taller at the threat, puffing out their chests. They were like silverback gorillas, with the mean set to their faces, their sloped brows, and their over-the-top posturing. They were putting on a show of dominance. I tried not to laugh under my breath. I succeeded, but my mouth still developed a small, entertained quirk.

The doorman on the right, the one who had stopped Fix in the first place—narrowed his eyes at me, his nostrils flaring. "If you think anything about this situation is funny, then your asshole boyfriend did you a disservice. He should have explained this wasn't the kind of place to bring a date. Time to run along home now and wait for him there like a good little girl."

Fix was taut as a bowstring. I sensed him gathering himself, ready to launch at the guy, but I squeezed his hand, shooting him a sly side-long smile. "He's not my boyfriend," I said. "But I do enjoy it when he fucks the shit out of me." I turned my gaze back to the doorman. I hadn't had reason to load my tone with such hatred since I'd abandoned Montmorenci and left Sixsmith in my rearview, screaming and shouting, and purple in the face as he chased the car I'd just stolen from him down the road.

"Just so you know, I'm *not* a good little girl," I informed the doorman. "I'm probably what you two idiots would refer to as a *bitch*. I don't like being spoken to like I'm a mindless, worthless pussy with legs. And I take offense when Neanderthal bouncers are disrespectful and overstep."

Fix chuckled under his breath. He hadn't moved an inch. Unlike the two bruisers barring our way, he hadn't pulled himself up to his full height, or swollen himself up to make himself look more threatening. To an outside observer, he appeared loose and relaxed, entirely at ease.

Only I knew better.

The bouncer to the right took a step forward—toward me, not toward Fix. He leaned down, his face filling my view. "You're right. You are a bitch," he snarled. "A mouthy one, who needs to learn her pl—"

He didn't finish the insult. The other doorman had been watching Fix, waiting for him to fly at his companion in defense of my honor. Neither of them had expected Fix to stand utterly still as I drew my hand back, knuckles extended, and I drove my fist into the asshole's neck.

The flare of pain in my hand was worth it; the doorman staggered back, clutching his throat, tongue sticking out as he tried to drag in a breath, his eyes bulging out of his head. He wheezed and hacked, but he couldn't seem to draw any oxygen into his lungs.

"*You dumb...fucking...slut!*"

"Shouldn't have done that," the other doorman growled, skulking forward. "You don't just hit a guy like Cruise. Your man hasn't taught you any manners. Looks like we're going to have to do it for him."

"You good, Angel?" Fix asked casually. He slid his hands in his pockets, shifting his body to rest his weight on one leg—not the stance of a man about to jump in and protect his woman. Not even close.

"I'm fine. I've got this covered."

"That's my girl."

Wide-eyed, the doorman glowered at Fix. "You're seriously going to stand there and let your girl get knocked out?"

Fix just shrugged. "We both know you're not going to knock her out."

"Oh? And how's that?"

"Because. She just winded your buddy there. Made him look like a grade-A dick. Embarrassed the fuck out of him. Now you're wondering if she's capable of doing the same to you. You're waiting on me to intervene. Getting your ass kicked by me isn't embarrassing. Getting your ass kicked by me is a badge of honor. It's expected. Getting your ass kicked by a woman is something else entirely. No offense, Angel," he said quickly, gracing me with a devastating grin that made his whole face shine with pleasure. "I know you're a badass."

"Oh, none taken."

The guy I'd struck in the throat had recovered himself now and was loosening the collar of his black shirt. His hate-filled glare was aimed directly at Fix. "I'm not going to knock her out. I'm gonna take your whore around back and hold her down while I show her how a woman should behave in front of a real man. When she's bleeding out of her mouth, and her ass, and her cunt, you're only gonna have yourself to blame."

The playful light dancing in Fix's eyes guttered and went out in a heartbeat. Again, something about him changed. His smirk was still there, and his head was still cocked at a jaunty angle, but a darkness lit him up from the inside. He was done playing around. He was ready to murder this guy, and he was going to fucking enjoy it. The door to the church swung open just as the doorman I'd throat punched reached inside his suit jacket and pulled out a knife.

"*CRUISE!*" A tall, gangly man emerged, holding a can of beer in his hand. Brown, shaggy hair, jeans, a t-shirt, a worn bomber jacket with a red collar, and a smattering of freckles across the bridge of his nose. He *was* a man, but barely. Maybe twenty-three years old. And he looked like he was about to go nuclear.

"Cruise, what the *fuck* do you think you're doing with that knife in your hand? Did I just hear you threaten to ass-rape someone?"

A flash of silver and Cruise's knife disappeared back into his jacket pocket. "We told this guy he couldn't bring the girl inside. He was being a dick about it. And she... She..."

The guy, who must have been Rabbit, cast me a throwaway glance. I doubted he even registered my existence. "She what?" he demanded.

Cruise's cheeks colored. "She was causing trouble. Sometimes you need to school people, boss. That's what we're here for, right?"

"No." Rabbit took a swig out of his beer can, shaking his head from side to side as he did so. He peered down into the can once he'd lowered it, as if hoping to find more beer there, even though he'd just drained it. "You're here to make sure everyone who shows up has an invitation. Does Fix have an invitation?"

"*Fix?*" Cruise stiffened. He looked back over his shoulder at us. "The invitation said Felix."

"Fix. Felix. What the fuck does it matter. He had an invitation. Did it say 'plus guest' on the back of the invitation, Gary?" he said, firing the question at the other doorman.

"All of them say 'plus guest' on the back," Gary replied sullenly.

"Well then, why are you threatening to stab people, Cruise? More importantly, why are you threatening to stab people with your cock? In the ass?"

Cruise was glowing red by this point. "You told us not to let anyone suspicious—"

"Suspicious? That beautiful woman, wearing the sexiest dress I have ever seen? *She* looks suspicious to you?" Rabbit crushed the beer can, tossing it over his shoulder with complete disregard. "This isn't a James Bond movie. She isn't a Russian spy, come to murder us all with the garrote she has stuffed down her cleavage. This isn't the cold war, Gary. She's a fucking *guest*. Have some manners." He paused, then said, "It's not as if she's going to *attack* either of you."

Cruise opened his mouth. Closed it. Opened it again. Nothing came out.

Rabbit gave Fix a curt nod of his head, pointing a thumb over his shoulder. "Come on. I need another beer, and it's getting cold out here. Plus I'm dying to meet your lovely friend."

He headed back inside the church. We followed him inside, and my heart was beating out of my chest. Not because I was nervous. Not because Cruise had threatened me in a very violent way. But because Felix Marcosa was standing beside me, the most attractive man I'd ever seen, and he had quietly, easily, taken hold of my hand.

36

FIX

THE CRYPT

*T*he inside of the church was a tomb. Leaves were gathered in burned orange piles against the rotten pews, and the wind groaned through the gaps in the stonework. Sera looked around, examining the interior of the building with confusion.

"I thought there was a party here," she hissed under her breath.

"There is a party," Rabbit called back to us. "Downstairs. Not enough room up here. Besides, the basement's far more exciting. Fun stuff always happens in the crypt, right, Fix?"

"I wouldn't know," I rumbled. "The church I served in didn't have one."

"Pity. Fiddling with the choir boys must have been much more difficult above ground."

Rabbit always pushed boundaries and my buttons right alongside them. Insinuating that I used to corrupt little boys was a sure-fire way of getting my heckles up and the bastard knew it. I grinned tightly, squeezing Sera's hand. "Again. Wouldn't know. Choir boys were never my thing."

Rabbit laughed, loud and obnoxious, like a goddamn hyena. "I thought all priests dipped their proverbial wicks. You weren't allowed to fuck the nuns, right? How old were you when you lost your virginity anyway? Thirty-three? Thirty-four?"

The cheeky fucker was about two seconds away from getting his neck snapped. He deserved it. But at the moment, Rabbit was the only hacker in New York I knew capable of lifting the data that I needed from the laptop. At least, he was the only hacker I trusted not to tell anyone what I'd come to him for. He was an arrogant little shit, and he loved to incite war, but he knew how to keep a secret. "Your balls must have been blue by the time you found somewhere to sink your dick, Marcosa," he added.

"I'm touched over your concern about my balls, Rabbit. But you can rest assured they were taken care of."

He snickered as he led the way down the abandoned aisle, rapping his knuckles against the backs of the pews as he passed them. "Yeah. I'm sure you worked your dick five times a day to compensate for the lack of pussy. *Very* boring."

"Very," I agreed.

Rabbit grumbled something under his breath, presumably annoyed that I wasn't taking the bait he was casting. We reached the back of the church, and he slid a key card into a small, silver panel on the wall. The door—it looked like any other, regular wooden door—released a hushed hissing sound as it slid to one side, allowing us access into what had once been the crypts. Sera tucked herself into my side. Was she holding her breath as she peered down into the long, narrow stairway that descended into darkness on the other side? It seemed as though she might have been. Loud music with a demented, heavy, growling bassline floated up to us, along with the sound of many people talking and laughing. Rabbit had sound-proofed this place to perfection. Before he'd opened the security door, I hadn't been able to hear a damn thing.

"We need Jell-O shots," Rabbit announced, as he headed down the stairs into the loud, thumping chaos below.

Jell-O shots? Fucking child. I rolled my eyes at the red neon sign hanging on the wall as we descended: *Welcome to Hell.* Rabbit was a fan of irony. He presumably thought it was ironic to name the place

Hell, when the church was meant to be a direct link to heaven. So fucking tacky.

I watched the top of Sera's head as she walked in front of me. Her body really was fucking perfection in that dress. The slit up to her hip was so sexy, but it was the back that was making my dick harder than reinforced concrete. Her shoulder blades and the fine muscles in her back shifted beautifully as she moved. And the way the material barely covered the very top of her ass... *Shit.* She was fucking stunning. I wanted to run my hands and my mouth all over her. It had taken a fucking feat of strength to stop myself from claiming her in the car over here. The scent of her skin... dizzying. The dark eyeshadow she was wearing made her look exotic, as if she were from a foreign land. She was rare and fine, a thing of true beauty. And god help the first guy to look sideways at her, because I was feeling about as territorial and protective as any man could. I'd draw blood and plenty of it before I allowed anyone else to appreciate her the way I was right now.

The church crypt was bigger than most. It was comprised of many small, vaulted rooms, carved from stone, and even older than the building above ground. Thick velvet curtains hung at the entryways to a number of the vaulted nooks, and some of those curtains were already closed. The lighting was dim and had a suggestive red hue to it, illuminating people's faces. The low ceilings were barely half a foot overhead, and made the space feel incredibly tight—a sensation that was emphasized by the multitude of bodies tightly packed from wall to wall. They undulated and swayed, dancing together, making out, hands fumbling all over each other, their eyes glazed and distant. Some of Rabbit's revelers weren't as high as kites, but these guys, grinding and licking at each other's bodies, were definitely gripped in a drugged frenzy. Seemed like they were having a great fucking time.

Rabbit guided us down a walkway to the right, and a guy standing in front of a red velvet rope unfastened it and allowed us by. Beyond: a much darker, quieter room with a separate bar. The female bartender standing behind the bar was wearing a black button-down shirt with the top three buttons undone, her considerable cleavage straining against the material. She smiled and waved as Rabbit gestured to a booth at the very back of the room.

Sera's face blanched when she looked up and saw that the rear wall of the booth was constructed out of human skulls. Rabbit noted her wide-eyed expression and smirked like some sort of fucked up magician who'd just unveiled his magnum opus. "Yeah. Catacombs aren't very common in this country. There are a few, though. I was so stoked when I came down here and found these guys." He made it sound like the fifteen or so dead people that he was currently using as a back rest were his long-lost friends.

Sera eyed the wall of the dead with obvious distaste. "Weird, don't you think? These people were put down here to rest."

Rabbit pulled a scathing face. "I'm sorry. Fix hasn't been polite enough to introduce us." He held out his hand. "Your name?"

"Sera. Sera Lafferty."

"Sera. With an E? Unusual. I like it." He beamed at the bartender, his eyes locked on her tits as she bent down extra low in front of him to place his beer in front of him. She gave both Sera and I the same treatment as she placed flutes of champagne in front of us. She stalked off wearing a pout when neither of us paid her chest the same attention Rabbit had.

"These guys behind me are dead. You think a single one of them gives a shit that I'm sitting here with you in front of their stripped skulls, enjoying a drink?" Rabbit said.

"No. I don't think they do. But still. Feels a little disrespectful all the same."

"I'll tell you something about disrespect," Rabbit said slowly. "Your friend Felix here is the most disrespectful person I know. He invited me for coffee two months ago, and then he never showed up."

Fuck's sake. I invited him for coffee? What the fuck was he—

Oh.

He had to be fucking joking. Three months ago, before I even knew Sera existed, I'd come to Rabbit to ask him for a favor. I'd needed some information on the mark I was about to take care of, and I'd needed it quickly. Rabbit had hacked into a server and downloaded some emails for me while I'd waited. I'd thanked him, told him I owed him one, even though I'd paid him a ridiculous amount of money for the work, and the kid had said, "Buy me a coffee next week and we'll call it even."

It had been a throwaway remark. I'd laughed and said sure, and then I'd promptly forgotten all about it. I squinted at him, now, biting the tip of my tongue. Rabbit was a little unhinged. Too many drugs. Too much money. Too many fingers in too many counterfeit pies. He'd started coming apart at the seams six months back, but I hadn't realized he would take something so stupid as a personal slight.

"*That's* why you're mad at me?"

Rabbit flicked the edge of his fingernail against the lip of his beer can. The guy could have been drinking vats of Moet every night, and yet he insisted on drinking cheap beer out of cans. Said he preferred the taste, but I knew the truth. His paranoia had reached such a degree that he didn't trust anyone to open and pour drinks for him. Not even Tits McGee behind the bar. A sealed can of beer couldn't be tampered with if he opened it himself. "You think because I'm young that I'm beneath you," he said, his voice flat, echoing around the booth. "I waited all week for you to call, and you didn't. You came and got what you needed from me, and then you put me out of your mind. You *used* me, Fix."

Sera tilted her champagne glass to her lips, her throat working gently as she took one, two, three mouthfuls from the flute. Glancing at me out of the corner of her eye, I could see what she was thinking: *is this guy fucking crazy?*

The answer was yes.

"I didn't use you," I countered. "I hired you to perform a service, which I paid you for. That's how business deals are carried out. Supply and demand."

Rabbit ignored me. "And now," he said, still addressing Sera, "he's come back here while I'm trying to host a party, while I'm trying to spend time with my real friends, because he wants to use me again."

Ahhh, Jesus. He was behaving like a petulant child. It'd only take a second to lean across the table, grab the little shit by the shirt, and slam his face down onto the table. I envisioned doing it in my head, and it felt good. Really fucking good. Sera cleared her throat.

"I think maybe Fix didn't realize you'd made solid plans. I'm sure he didn't mean anything by it. And...Fix hasn't come here tonight to use you, Rabbit. He came here because he's trying to help *me*. I'm sorry if we've offended you." She gave him a winning smile, and Rabbit drummed his fingers against the table.

"I know why he came here. And I'm sorry, but I wasn't very honest just now. I did know who you were, Sera. Monica's been very upset with Fix recently, too. She explained his little predicament to me this afternoon." Finally, the little fuck turned to look at me. "Not smart, Fix. Not smart at all. Falling in love with the girl you've been paid to kill. That's got to be the most ironic slash tragic thing I've ever heard. Only you would be stupid enough to do something like that. You wanna know what I think about this whole mess?"

I pinched the bridge of my nose, blasting out a loud sigh. This was fucking ridiculous. "No. Not really."

"You're a horrible hitman. Paid assassins are good at their jobs because, typically, they're all sociopaths. They have no empathy. If you aren't empathetic, you can't feel sorry for the dumb schmuck you're about to stab, or shoot, or poison, or however you choose to fucking do it. But you, Fix...you're *not* a sociopath. You have too much empathy. Too much heart. You like to put on a show, pretend you're hardened to the world, but then along comes a beautiful flower..." He reached out, slowly tracing his fingers along the line of Sera's jaw, teasing a lock of her hair around his finger. "And you can't fucking help yourself. You just have to stick your nose inside that flower and *smell*."

Nope.

My blood pounded inside my ears, drowning out the thumping bass of the music.

No fucking way.

He had no right to touch her.

No right whatsoever.

I couldn't fucking see straight.

My body was vibrating as I lunged across the table, grabbing hold of Rabbit by the wrist, wrenching his hand away from Sera. Two seconds later, the punk was face down on the table, his arm twisted high up behind his back, and I was leaning my elbow into the base of his neck, applying enough pressure to make him gasp out loud in pain. "It's rude to try and smell someone else's flowers," I snarled into his ear. "You're right. I'm not a sociopath. But I'm fucking good at my job. I can kill a man in any one of a thousand different ways, and I've tried them all. If you touch her again, if you so much as *think* about touching her, I will force a fucking pipe down your throat, and I will pump you full of formaldehyde. *Do. You. Fucking. Hear. Me?*"

Mere seconds had passed. Enough time for the bartender to raise the alarm and summon help, though. Three huge guys with guns barreled into the room, their weapons primed and aimed directly at my head.

"Fix!" Sera's voice rose to a shout. "Fix! Let him go. You're going to get yourself killed."

I'd been shot before, in the shoulder. It had sucked, hurt like a motherfucker, but I'd happily endure the pain again if it meant I was able to defend what was fucking *mine*. "Do you understand?" I growled into his ear.

Rabbit thrust out a hand, halting the men who were approaching. A loud, manic sound slipped out of him, and it took me a second to realize he was laughing, gurgling like a goddamn drain. "Wait! Wait-waitwait," Rabbit wheezed. "Don't shoot him. It's okay. It's okay. Everything's fine."

"But boss!" I recognized the voice. It was Gary from upstairs. He must have been itching to pull the trigger after our little run-in just now.

"Stand down. Everything's fine. Just...go back upstairs," Rabbit panted. "*Now!*"

I hadn't let him go. Wasn't planning on it. But then Sera's hand was on mine, pale and slender, and she squeezed. I took my eyes off Rabbit, turning to look at her instead. She was worried. A little frightened. "*Please*," she whispered.

And that was it. With that one word, she doused the raging inferno that had gripped me. I reeled back, releasing Rabbit, swallowing down the remaining burning embers of my fury. Rabbit stayed down, sprawled across the table, still laughing like a fucking madman. "See," he said. "You care about things too much. But...I like that about you, Felix. You're a walking contradiction. The most interesting paradox I've come across yet. And I've studied quite a few."

I sank back down into my seat, straightening my shirt. Behind me, grumbling, the guys who had burst in to help Rabbit left one at a time. "Just shut the fuck up, Rabbit. If Monica told you why we were coming here, then quit fucking around and tell me. Can you figure out where the emails came from? Can you help us find this Carver guy or not?"

Rabbit slid off the table, slouching into his own seat, a reckless, annoying smile plastered all over his freckled face. "Of course I can."

"Great. How long will it take?"

His shit-eating grin spread even wider. "A day. Maybe two. But the cost's gonna be much higher this time, Fix."

Surprise, surprise. "Fine. Tell me how much. You'll have the money in your account tomorrow morning."

Rabbit slowly shook his head. "Not that easy, I'm afraid. I don't want your money. I want something else."

I gunned him down with a sharp glare. So fucking typical. Nothing was ever easy with this little shit. "What do you want?"

He splayed his fingers, holding his hands palms up. "An item was stolen from me. An extremely important item. I want it back."

"Jesus Christ. I'm not your fucking errand boy. You have plenty of guys who can go retrieve shit for you. Ask fucking Cruise and Gary."

"The person who has this item isn't easy to reach. He has a series of safeguards in place."

"What kind of safeguards?"

Rabbit shrugged, looking off, over my shoulder. "Oh, nothing for you to worry about. There are fifteen of them, but you've already compl—"

Oh no. No fucking way.'

I shoved my chair back, getting to my feet. My chest was suddenly unbearably tight. Rabbit had stopped talking, but I didn't need him to say anything else. I knew who had taken this item of his now, and I knew all too well the safeguards he'd just mentioned. "You can forget it. Name another price."

"Don't be such a baby, Fix. You're already an alumni of The Barrows. If I sent Gary and Cruise over there, they'd die before they made it to the third floor. You know that. All I need is for you to show up, retrieve the thumb drive Oscar took from me, and leave. Simple."

When he put it that way, it did sound simple. He knew it wouldn't be, though. He *knew* I'd probably end up dead if I stepped foot on Oscar Finch's turf. "Name another price," I repeated.

"There is no other price. You either get the thumb drive for me from Oscar, or you don't get the information. Sorry."

I ground my teeth together, scowling at him with the burning intensity of a volatile sun. He wasn't going to give in, I could tell. If I took him, chained him up in my penthouse, and I tortured the shit out him, there was a chance, a slim, *slim* chance, he'd break and figure out where Carver was for me. Rabbit was stubborn as fuck, though. He'd probably hold out for days, by which time whoever Carver had hired to replace me could easily have located where Sera was, who she was with, and things could get seriously fucking nasty.

Relenting to such a ridiculous request was undoubtedly only setting myself up for even more outlandish demands in the future. But Sera wasn't safe. Sera was all that mattered, and that's all there was to it. "Fine. I'll go see Oscar for you. I'll get your stupid thumb drive back."

"It'll have to be tonight," Rabbit added. "The Barrows won't be opening its doors again until next month, and we both know a month would be too long to wait."

Great. This just got worse and worse. He was right, though. It would have to be tonight, or not at all.

Sera glanced between the two of us. "What are The Barrows?" she asked.

I shot Rabbit a warning glare—*don't you dare open your fucking mouth.* "It's kind of like a gentlemen's club house," I answered quickly. "It's well protected. Difficult to get inside. I'm already a member, or I was a couple of years back. I'm sure I'll be allowed back in, though." Her frown lessened but it didn't disappear altogether. She believed me. Partly. Understandable, since I was only partly telling her the truth. Thank god she couldn't see the doubtful, annoying smirk on Rabbit's face as he raised his eyebrows at me. "Don't worry, Angel. I'll be in, out, and back before you know it."

The small glimmer of worry in her eyes waned, gradually fading until it was gone. "Okay," she answered.

She wouldn't be saying that if she knew anything about Oscar Finch. And she sure as fuck wouldn't be saying 'okay' if she knew that the last time I was at The Barrows, I'd sealed the doors with a heavy steel chain, padlocked that fucker, and I'd set the place on fire.

37

SERA

YOU WANT MORE?

*F*ix watched me like a hawk as he made arrangements with Rabbit. I felt his eyes on me, boring into me as we climbed the stairs out of Hell and we left the church behind us. He didn't speak, and neither did I. It wasn't until we were back at the penthouse and the door had slammed shut behind us that Fix cupped my face in his hands and he kissed me deeply.

He leaned his forehead against mine. "I've been dying to do that all fucking night."

"You have?" God, I literally purred the words. I was so high on him most of the time that I could see nothing but clouds. "Should have kissed me earlier then."

Fix pressed the pad of his thumb to my mouth, sucking his own bottom lip into his mouth and biting down on it. So. Fucking. Hot. "If I'd kissed you," he said softly, "I would have done more. I would have put the spectacular split in this dress to good use. I would have pulled the material apart, laid you on a table in those stupid fucking crypts, and I would have fucked the shit out of you in front of everyone."

"Mmm. I don't think I would have minded."

Fix's expression transformed to one of inquisitiveness. "Is that so,

Miss Lafferty. Have you had sex in public before? A crowded room full of people, no less?"

"No. But I'm assuming you have."

He stroked his thumb down, over my chin, staring at my mouth thoughtfully. "Maybe. Once or twice. I'd never do that with you, though, Angel." His pale, moonlit eyes carefully observed me. It was at times like these that he was so unknowable to me. I had no idea what was going on inside his head. No way of knowing what he was thinking or feeling. I'd been so convinced earlier that I'd started to figure him out, but right now he was a complete and utter enigma. Twin spots of heat burned high in my cheeks.

"Am I not adventurous enough to take on that kind of sexcapade? Or am I just not pretty enough. Would I need to look like a porn star for you t—"

His thumb moved back to my mouth, gently sealing my lips, preventing me from speaking. Fix's eyes seemed to thaw, taking on a rare, unusual warmth. "No, silly girl. I'd never do that with you, because I care about you too much. In the past, sex has just been a physical action. A way to scratch an itch. It didn't matter if twenty people were sipping cocktails, sitting on sofas, jerking off or fucking while they watched me screw back then. It wasn't important. It didn't mean anything. Sex with you is..." He huffed down his nose, irritation lining his face. "Sex with you is a holy act. I can't think of a better word, Sera, but that's what it is to me. It's a communion between our bodies and our souls. It's certainly not meant to titillate random strangers just for the hell of it."

I closed my eyes, bowing my head. Shit. He really knew how to completely throw me for a loop. I'd gotten angry so fast, ready to assume he didn't think I was worthy of him, and then in a heartbeat he'd turned everything upside down. He didn't think I was unworthy. He considered me precious, something to be treasured, and he didn't want to share.

"I'm sorry," I whispered.

"What for?"

"For all of this. Having to run me all over the country. Having to try and find this Carver guy. Having to try and keep me safe. I *know* it's fucked up, apologizing to you for that, but...I don't know. I just don't want you to think I'm a terrible person, because someone wants me dead this badly."

His mouth twitched. Just a little. "I murder people. A lot. And you're worried about what *I* think of *you*?"

"This isn't funny, Fix."

"I'm not laughing."

He wasn't, but I knew he wanted to. "Tell me what you're thinking right now," I demanded.

"Why are you so panicked about what I'm thinking?"

"Because. I have no control over anything anymore. I'm lost. I'm freaking out. I don't have a fucking clue what's going on, and—"

"I'm thinking about how beautiful you are," Fix said, cutting in. "I'm watching you climb the walls, and I'm thinking about how absolutely stunning you are, and how fucking lucky I am to get to be the guy who *didn't* kill you."

I stopped pacing. "You are *so* weird."

"Weird is good. Weird's okay with me."

Exhaustion crept out of nowhere, sinking its claws into me. I closed my eyes, letting my arms fall limp. "I'm glad you're the guy who didn't kill me, too," I whispered. "You could have been some fat, hairy guy from Michigan named Calvin. At least you're pretty."

He snorted. "Correct me if I'm wrong, but I think this might be the most romantic moment ever documented between an assassin and his victim."

A bark of laughter burst out of my mouth. "This is all so...unbelievably, categorically *fucked up*. Please. Just tell me life is going to go back to normal soon. I don't think I can take one more second of this."

A shadow fell across his face. "If normal is what you want, then I promise you'll have it really soon. In the meantime, take off that dress."

"What?"

"Take. Off. That. Dress."

"Why?" I knew perfectly well why.

"You need a good fucking, Sera. You need my cock inside you right now."

"Actually, I need a Valium, and I need to call the cops. Plus, you need to get to this Barrows place to get that thumb drive for Rabbit."

"I have plenty of time."

He was so serious; he looked down at me like a predator, assessing its prey, and my pulse leapt into overdrive. Fuck. He meant it. He wanted me to strip, and from the set, determined look on his face, he wasn't going to take no for an answer. "I did my best, Sera," he rumbled. "I behaved myself, and I held myself back. Now it's time for you to take off the damn dress."

"I don't know. I'm feeling..."

"Vulnerable?" Fix finished for me. "Unsafe? Alone? Heartbroken?"

"Yes." I clenched down on my jaw, flaring my nostrils. I didn't like hearing those words come out of his mouth. He was right, but admitting I felt all of those things felt pathetic somehow.

"When you're with me, you're not vulnerable. When you're with me, you are safe. When you're with me, you will never be alone. And as for your heart, Sera, I'll make sure it's beating too fast for you to ever feel it ache again."

I couldn't locate the part of me that drew taut and snapped. All I knew was that I'd been having trouble scrambling to keep all of the broken pieces that comprised me in place, and then suddenly I just...*stopped*. I suddenly didn't need to fight so hard anymore. It felt like all of the things Fix had just said to me were true, and I was finally realizing it for the first time. He hadn't left my side. He hadn't abandoned me to my fate when things had become severely complicated. Not for one second had I felt like he was going to hand me my bag and pack me off back to Seattle without him. I wasn't alone. He was going to fight for me, and protect me, even when I thought I didn't need it.

So fine.

I would do it.

I would lose the goddamn dress and to hell with the consequences.

The world was still and impatient as I reached to my side and slowly unzipped myself. There weren't any straps to hold it up; the material slid from my body and pooled at my feet, and then I was bare, standing before him in nothing but a pair of ostentatiously high heels.

Fix's eyes skimmed over my body, devouring every inch of me, observing every curve, dip and line, and I held my head high as he feasted. I wasn't ashamed. I didn't try to hide myself. I gloried in the fact that the sexiest, rawest, most powerful man to ever draw breath was looking at me like I was the sun and he had been locked in the dark for years. It felt fucking incredible.

"Make my heart beat then, Fix. Make it race. Make me lose myself. I want to forget." If only for a minute, if I could lose myself in *him*, my life wouldn't feel like it was hanging by a fragile thread. My anger would wash away. My fear wouldn't cripple me. Fix was my anchor to sanity, to safety, and to my very self. A dark, sinister smile etched itself into his face, and I braced myself for what was to come. He stepped around me, and I closed my eyes as he stroked a finger down the length of my spine.

"Your skin is like warm silk." His warm breath skated over the back of my neck, and I embraced the cool shiver that chased its way after his finger, down my back. "Like smooth, perfect silk. Flawless. So fucking beautiful. Your ass is divine." He cupped my right buttock as he spoke, squeezing it hard. "Your tits..." He moved closer, his chest brushing up against my back, and I felt his full, sensuous lips move as he spoke into my hair. "I think about your tits all the time, Sera. I imagine my dick between them. I think about grinding my hips, thrusting my cock up between them, very slowly, and your tongue...*fuck*. I think about that perfect little tongue of yours licking at the tip of my cock as I do it." He slipped his hands between my ribcage and my arms, reaching around my body, so that he was cupping my breasts, and I fought to stay upright as he pinched and rolled my already stiffened, sensitive nipples.

He was hard. Really fucking hard. His cock butted up against my behind through his pants as he tilted his hips forward. He was showing me what lay in store for me, reminding me, and the deluge of images, sensation and desire that swept over me made me cry out.

His hands traveled down, over my torso, over my stomach, and then Fix was dipping his fingers even lower, between my legs. "I think about this most of all," he growled into my ear. "Your pretty pink cunt. Your delicate pussy lips. The bud of your swollen clit. How wet you get. How wet *I* make you. It drives me to fucking distraction."

I gasped as he curled his fingers upward, sliding them inside me. Not very deep. Just deep enough that I began to pant. Rhythmically, he pumped his fingers in and out, teasing me, and I couldn't keep myself still anymore. I rocked myself against his hand, panting out shallow breaths.

"You want more?" Fix murmured. His voice was laden with his own lust, the burning need roughening his tone as he slowly licked at my neck. God. It felt so good being in his arms, having him holding me, tasting me, teasing me with the tips of his fingers.

"Yes," I answered. "I want...more."

"So greedy. So eager. Your body's mine to direct. Mine to conduct. Mine to pleasure. Mine to possess. Agreed?"

"Yes."

"Always?"

"Fuck. Yes, Fix. Always."

"Then get on your hands and knees."

I dropped to the floor like a stone, without even the faintest question or afterthought.

"Ass in the air for me, Angel," Fix rumbled. "Show me. I want to see."

For such a long time, sex had been taboo to me. It had taken years for me to overcome the fucked up things that had happened to me in my youth. A lot of people in my position might never have been able to even have sex again, but I'd railed against that notion. If I'd refrained from sex, I would have been denying myself my own right to pleasure, and I had refused to do that. I would have been giving power to those who had sought to steal it from me forever. When I'd moved to Seattle, I'd met guys and I'd taken them home. *I'd* fucked *them.* I'd demanded control, respect and submission from them, to prove to myself that I was the one with all the power. Gareth had enjoyed the novelty of being owned by a woman at first, but the shine had soon worn off. He'd tried to force *me* into submission, and it hadn't gone well for either of us.

This, with Fix, though? This was different. Everything was different with him. We were constantly warring with each other for dominance, but when I handed myself over to him, it didn't feel like I was losing anything. It felt like I was gaining something: the ability to trust. And being able to trust him was far more precious to me than my need to feel like I was his master.

I spread my legs for him, and his tortured groan sent sparks of heat hurtling through me like the beginnings of a wild fire.

"Fuck, Sera. I can't wait to sink my dick inside you. I'm going to make you scream first, though. I want to feel your pussy tighten around my fingers. I want to feel your body shake."

He was between my legs before I could pant out a response. His tongue was hot and insistent as he laved at me from behind, his fingers teasing and stroking at me. I tensed as he gently rubbed at my ass.

"You think I'm going to hurt you?" he rasped.

"No. I just..." I didn't know how to explain myself to him. If he knew how violently I'd had to fight to prevent anyone from ever taking me there, he'd avoid the area like it was radioactive. But I didn't want that. I wanted the pleasure and the enjoyment he'd promised when he'd spoken about ass play before. And, beyond that, I didn't want him treating me as if I was a breakable, fragile thing that needed to be handled with extreme caution.

"Relax, Sera," he murmured, stroking his tongue over my core again. "You have nothing to fear from me. I'll claim you. I'll explore every single inch of your body, but I will *never* do anything to hurt you."

He was telling the truth; his honesty resounded in the depths of his words like a struck bell. I believed him. And, more importantly, I wanted to give him all of my fear, my doubts and my shame. He was capable of eradicating it, cleansing me and washing me clean, until there was nothing left but want and desire.

He was the architect of my ecstasy...and if I didn't give him the permission he needed to build on that, I was only limiting myself. It took effort, but I wrestled my body into a calm, peaceful place, and slowly my muscles unknotted themselves.

"Good girl. That's fucking perfect," he said, running his hand slowly over the curve of my ass cheek. He rubbed in circles, until I felt myself soothed, melting under his touch. "That's my good girl," he breathed. "Such a good girl."

Soon, I was rocking my hips again, struggling to keep myself from falling apart as he worked at me with his mouth and his hands. I sucked in a surprised breath as he licked upwards, over my ass, but I didn't shy from the contact this time. I reveled in the heat and the undeniable pleasure as he flicked his tongue. My clit throbbed as he slowly pushed his fingers inside me.

"You smell so good," Fix groaned. "You're so damn wet. I want to lick every part of you. I want you to come all over my tongue so I can swallow you down, Angel. I want you all over my mouth. All over my fingers. All over my cock. Lose yourself for me, Seraphim. Can you step away from the controls, so I can make you feel good? I promise it will be worth it."

My mouth was filled with cotton wool. My head was filled with shifting sand. Every grain was a thought, an idea, or want or a warning. Try as I might, I couldn't grasp hold of a single one of those grains as I ground my pussy against Fix's face "Yes. I...I can. Take it. Take it all."

I nearly exploded when the pressure from Fix's fingers against my ass increased. He wasn't just rubbing me now. He was gently sliding the tip of his finger inside me. The pain was momentary and negligible, over in a matter of seconds, replaced by a burning warmth that quickly traveled down the backs of my legs, my calves, and bit at the soles of my feet. It was strange—an unexpected sensation that had me gasping out loud.

"Shit. You've soaked my fingers. You want me, Angel," Fix groaned. "You fucking need me." His fingers dipped a little deeper, and the flash of pain returned, only to vanish a moment later, deepening the searing burn that was spreading underneath my skin, moving up my back, now, sparking between my shoulder blades.

"Oh...*god*." I huffed out a breath, allowing my head to fall slack. "That feels...fuck, it feels really good."

"Close your eyes," Fix commanded. "Just feel. My tongue. My lips. My fingers. Feel where I touch you, Sera. Don't think. Just fucking *feel* me."

His tongue moved to my ass again, his finger still working inside me, and I tumbled over the edge of a high precipice, my ears roaring as he pushed himself deeper.

"Show me. Show me how much you want. Show me where to stop." His voice was savage. Wild. So deep that the hairs on the back of my arms and my neck stood to attention. Oh my god. Oh my god, he was fucking incredible. I pushed back against his hand, and his finger slid deeper. I moaned, not in pain, but because it felt...so...good.

"Oh my fucking god. Felix! *FIX!*"

I didn't see it coming. One moment, I was rolling my hips, working him inside me, and then next, I was being tumbled and pitched by the powerful climax that roared through me, lighting me up like a goddamn bonfire.

Fix grabbed at my hip and encouraged me to move deeper as I came. "That's it. Good girl. So fucking good. Come for me, Angel. You come so beautifully."

I felt like I was sinking down, down, down, lost beneath the waves of a storm-tossed ocean, and there was no light, and there was no sound. There was only Fix, coaxing me and stroking me as I shattered and fell apart.

He drew back the moment I fell slack, and I heard him stripping out of his clothes. When I turned around, he was naked, his body a towering wall of effortless muscle. Fuck, he was beyond sexy. Fix fully dressed was a sight to behold. Fix naked was an altar to be worshipped at. He was more than just a man. He was a god, a deity in his own right. And I was devout as I revered him.

He was so fucking hard. Taking his cock in his hand, he worked it up and down, and I realized that I was staring. Couldn't take my eyes off him, as he squeezed the end of his dick, making himself shudder. He laid down on the floor next to me, his pale, startling eyes flashing with lust, and then he was grabbing me, pulling me on top of him. I glanced down at his erection, the solid length of it brushing up against my pussy, and Fix made a deep humming, growling sound.

"Ride it," he commanded. "Fuck it. I want to watch your tits bounce."

When I slid him inside me, it felt as though I was shifting, expanding to accommodate the sheer size of him.

"Oh, shit. Fuck. Fix!"

His fierce, ruthless smile would haunt my dreams and make me sweat until the day I died. "You feel it?" he whispered. "You know how good it's gonna make you come?"

"Yes. Fuck yes."

I rocked myself forward, sliding up and down his cock, and Fix bared his teeth. "Damn it, Angel," he hissed. "You have no idea how fucking incredible you look right now." His hands found my hips, and then he was helping me, guiding me, directing me to set a fast, heady pace as he pushed himself up to meet me. He touched and stroked me as I rode him, his hands moving to cup my breasts. He pinched my nipples, sending an explosion of heat down, in between my legs. His stomach muscles flexed and contracted as our bodies swayed together, two parts of one whole, coming together at last.

He rubbed my clit, the pad of his thumb working in small, tight circles, and before long I was scrambling, desperately clinging to that ledge again.

"Don't fight it," he commanded. "Come on my cock. I want you so fucking wet that I can't take it anymore. *Fucking do it.*"

My back arched as my orgasm ripped through me. His hands

were everywhere. He sat up, his hand pressing into my lower back as he moved my legs so I could wrap them around him, and then he was biting down and sucking on my nipples as wave after wave of pleasure took me from my body and lifted me higher, higher, higher...

"Hold on, Sera," he whispered into my breasts. "I'm going to fucking come inside you." He crushed me to him as he came, his teeth grinding into my neck. He didn't hold back. I felt my skin break, and the pain was the sweetest, most dizzying thing I'd ever experienced. A secondary climax tugged at me, stealing my senses as I came with him, and Fix's roughened cry destroyed what was left of my sanity. I dug my fingernails into his back, and he drew a sharp breath. "*Fuuuuck, Sera*. Holy shit."

When he leaned away, he was wearing a serious, intense expression that stopped my heart dead in my chest. "We both marked each other. I didn't just claim you. You claimed me, too." Dipping his head down, he licked at my neck, and when he buried his hands in my hair, kissing me deeply, I could taste my blood on his tongue.

38

FIX

THE BARROWS

*S*era slept. She was so fucking beautiful when she slept. She was *always* beautiful, but there was just something about her when she was lost in unconsciousness. After we'd climbed into bed, I'd held her in my arms properly for the very first time, and a piece of me that had been broken and in pain for a very long time seemed to breathe a sigh of relief.

It had freaked me the fuck out.

There was every chance this wasn't going to work out. I'd met Sera under extremely fucked up circumstances, and we were both more than a little broken, that much was obvious. If we'd met at a coffee shop and we'd started flirting, maybe asked one another out on a date, we'd still have been facing a monumentally steep uphill climb toward the realms of a normal relationship. Her past with her father hung over her like a thunderhead, black and angry, ready to break into a fully-fledged hurricane at any moment. I could see that a mile off, even though she tried to keep it from me. And my own demons were constantly on the prowl, demanding attention, determined to shred apart whatever ounce of happiness we might be able to forge. We were dancing with disaster, and if I couldn't find this Carver guy before his new assassin found us, then god only knew what would become of us.

It fucking killed me to climb out of bed and leave Sera behind. I had work to do, though. I had somewhere I needed to be, and it was somewhere I couldn't take her.

The Barrows wasn't safe. Wasn't safe for me, let alone a woman. Sera could throw a mean right hook but otherwise she was defenseless. Maybe in time she could be trained, honed into a lethal weapon capable of facing down the dark tide that promised to wash over us, but until that day...

I gathered up the items I needed—gun, an extra clip, throwing knife, duct tape—and I packed them all into a backpack. Outside, the night air was muggy and oppressively humid, causing a layer of sweat to break out across my back as I hurried to the truck, got in and started the engine. As I drove across the Manhattan Bridge, I prepared myself for what was to come.

The Barrows was dangerous any night of the week, but tonight was First Night, the first Friday of the month. If a fighter wanted to be able to compete for the rest of the month, he at least had to show up tonight and lose a match in order to return. If he missed fighting First Night, then that fighter would have to wait until the first Friday of the following month to try his luck again.

New York City's most deadly and deranged would be out on the prowl, ready to claim as many victories and as much money and weapons as possible. The arrogant, the hard up, the ambitious, and the raving mad would be braving the fifteen-story building on the outskirts of the Bronx tonight, each of them hoping to reach the rooftop—to as much tequila as they could drink, and as much pussy as they could fuck. And overseeing the whole clusterfuck, the man in charge, the most soulless, morally corrupt, evil piece of shit crime boss there ever was: Oscar Finch.

I detested the man more than any other living soul, but I was going to have to learn how to maintain a civil tongue in my head if I wanted to get Rabbit's fucking thumb drive back. It had been a long time since I'd felt nervous about anything, but I was nervous right now.

The city whipped by in a blur. I had to calm my shit before I reached my destination, otherwise all would be lost. The men I was about to face were like blood hounds; if they scented fear on you, even the faintest whiff of it, they'd rally together like pack animals and tear you apart until there was nothing left behind but a handful of teeth floating in a pool of blood and viscera.

I'd broken out in a cold sweat by the time I reached The Barrows. The building was a monstrosity, the exterior once grand and impressive, but now the heavy stonework was cracked, the mortar crumbling, the windows caked with dirt and tagged with spray paint.

No one in their right minds came within a hundred feet of this building. Twenty years ago, the area had once been busy, used primarily by cloth merchants, who sold their bolts of fabric out of small store fronts and occasionally from stalls set up on the street corners. When the gangs had moved in—Armenian and Russian families that battled over turf, women, and the right to breathe the air in general—things had become unsettled and the clothiers had moved on to other parts of Brooklyn and Hell's Kitchen. Soon, the buildings were abandoned, losing their value, and Oscar Finch swept in and snapped up The Barrows, or the Barrowman Hotel, as it had once been called. He brought henchmen toting semi-automatic weapons along with him, who terrorized the gangs that remained behind, and soon they were all either dead or had moved on, too.

The four-block radius surrounding The Barrows was a ghost town, the streets deserted and cluttered with garbage. Plenty of parking, though. I pulled up beside the curb on the opposite side of the street from the old hotel, noting a gleaming black muscle car parked fifty feet away, but aside from that, there were no other vehicles in sight. Oscar discouraged people from bringing their cars on nights like tonight. He liked to keep things as quiet as possible and having a fleet of sports cars and souped-up SUVs pulling up out front only served as a pulsing beacon for the cops, who sometimes dared to patrol the area when they were feeling brave.

Tonight, I was breaking Oscar's rules—more than one of them—but I didn't give a fuck. I needed the truck nearby in case I had to make a swift exit. Without it, I'd be vulnerable, and the very last thing I felt like doing this evening was running for my life through the streets. Oscar's sentries were everywhere. Mostly ex-military, they were brutal, and didn't think twice about shooting an unarmed man in the back if they thought he might be running from Oscar.

I checked my wallet, making sure I had the correct amount of cash on hand to buy my way inside the building. A cool grand, all in twenties. The money wasn't just to gain access to The Barrows; it was also my contribution towards tonight's prize money. Everyone who entered was permitted, and expected, to fight. Newbies started in the basement. Crowds gathered there, fight club style, to beat the shit out of each other, until someone either submitted or fell down fucking dead. If a fighter survived the basement, they were admitted to the elevator, where they would be granted access to the next floor up, and the circus would begin all over again. And so on, and so forth, until the sun came up and everybody limped or crawled home. There were fifteen floors. No one ever made it to the rooftop, where Oscar awaited, on their first night. If a fighter found himself on the eighth floor by the time the klaxon sounded at dawn, then the next time he came back, if he chose to come back at all, he would start at the fifth floor. The three-floor rule, they called it. The Oscar Finch Fuck You. No matter who you were or how hard you fought, it didn't matter. You never re-entered The Barrows on the same floor you walked out on. That's just the way it was. The moment a fighter did make it to the fifteenth floor, that was it. They could ride the elevator straight up to the rooftop every weekend without ever having to fight again. But if they *did* fight, they had a chance at winning some seriously big money. Hundreds of thousands of dollars. Guys came to fight at The Barrows to claim status and bragging rights. They came to prove their worth and test their mettle. A tenth-floor graduate was always going to get served before a basement chump at any bar in Hell's Kitchen. But that huge pot of money Oscar presided over was the main reason people came here. They wanted out of their shitty situations. They wanted to clear their debts and start afresh. Sometimes they just wanted to buy their body weight in cocaine and snort themselves to death on the winnings. But it was the money that made people so hungry, and they were merciless in their pursuit of it.

I bared my teeth at the doormen guarding the entrance to the building. These guys were nothing like Rabbit's bouncers. These men were a different species entirely. Their necks had vanished, their traps were so big. Their eyes were blank, lacking any arrogance and bravado. They didn't need such devices. They were fifteenth-floor veterans many times over, and since Oscar had hired them to man his doors, they had proved themselves to be lethal many more times than that. They were brothers. Clinically insane. Probably. When they'd first started coming here, years ago, they'd show up over and over again, battling their way from the twelfth floor to the fifteenth, thanks to the three-floor rule, for what appeared to be the sheer joy of letting blood. And once they had destroyed everyone and everything in sight each time, they had left, never once stepping foot onto the rooftop to celebrate their victories or try their hand at winning the pot.

From what I'd heard, Oscar paid them an average salary, and the boys were happy to stand guard each night, just waiting for the opportunity to beat someone to death with their own dismembered leg.

"Foster. Falco." I greeted one and then the other.

"Marcosa," Foster growled in response. He nodded as if to himself, his mouth turned down at the corners. "We figured you were dead."

"Probably should be by now." I kept my back straight, staring both of them down. They shared the same cold, dead eyes—the eyes of a shark, or some other primitive, small-brained predator.

Falco jerked his head back, gesturing to the heavy reinforced steel door behind him. "You want in?"

"Yeah. I need to speak to him." I hadn't thought about how I was going to get the thumb drive, but I did know where it would be. If it was important—and it sounded like it was—it would be on Oscar's person. He was just as insane as Rabbit, and twice as paranoid. He had an office here somewhere, but he never used it. Even the prize money was kept in a steel lock box on the roof, where Oscar could maintain a visual on it at all times.

"Still gonna cost you," Foster said.

I already had the money in my hand. I thrust it out toward him, slapping the wad of twenty-dollar bills against his chest. "It's all there."

Foster didn't make a show of pretending to check it. He probably couldn't count that high. "All right, then. You gonna take him, brother, or should I?" he asked. He didn't look at Falco. He stared at me some more, like he was casually wondering how much force it would take to rip my head clean off my shoulders.

"You take him, brother," Falco replied. "I'll stay here, just in case."

Foster smiled, and it was hideous. "After you, Father."

I narrowed my eyes, every part of me going cold. "Just Fix. Marcosa, if you have to. But call me Father again, and I'll rip your ball sack off and use it as a motherfucking coin purse." Violence begat violence, it was true. But sometimes it was necessary. It was all these two fucktards understood, and politely presenting them with a request wasn't going to get me anywhere with them. I had to be dominant and forceful. They had to believe I would do something as rash as attacking one of them, and they had to believe, from the stone-cold steel in my eyes, that there was a possibility that I would fucking win. Foster drew himself up to his full height, at least four inches taller than me, and he leered into my face.

"You still got a tongue on you," he snapped. "Maybe *I* should rip *that* out."

"Go ahead and try. But when people start asking you why you're speaking in falsetto, don't be surprised. *Bitch.*"

God. Bitch? That was pushing it. I set my jaw, piercing him through with my gaze, tamping down the nerves that were once again rattling through me.

Foster flared his nostrils. It looked like he was scenting me, like he could actually detect the pheromones and testosterone in the air. For one long second, I thought he was going to pile drive his fist through my face. And then his head rocked back and laughter boomed from his chest, ringing down the deserted street. Falco joined in two seconds later.

"You're funny," Foster said, clearing his throat, after his amusement had waned. "Come on. We're busy tonight. There's a lot of fighters. Some of them are even pretty good." High praise, coming from a man who considered everyone else inferior and weak. He pounded on the thick steel door, and a loud, metal clanging noise reverberated on the other side. The door swung back a second later, and Foster disappeared inside. I followed after him, and I was swallowed by the darkness.

~

Sweat. Bleach. Blood. The air inside The Barrows was just as I remembered it. The place reeked of violence and aggression—the stench was like a slap in the face as Foster lead me through the trashed lobby of the hotel toward the elevator. The ground beneath my feet rumbled, like an earthquake was trying to split the hotel in two. It wasn't an earthquake, though. The vibrations were coming from the basement, where over a hundred people were all trying to kill each other. Their shouts and savage war cries could be heard even through the two-foot thick concrete flooring.

Foster stuck a polished silver key into the lock next to the elevator call button, and he turned it. A light came on, and then the numbers above the doors illuminated in turn as the car came down to meet us. When the doors rolled back, we were met with a smear of blood on the floor along with a dark brown stain that looked suspiciously like shit.

"Probably shouldn't have worn those shoes," Foster crooned, looking down at the white sneakers I was wearing. I didn't bother replying. I entered the car, and I held my breath as they closed behind us; the cramped space smelled like a goddamn slaughter house.

Foster mashed at the buttons, and then we were moving. Not a word was said as we climbed. Not until the elevator dinged and began to slow. Too soon. The elevator was stopping too soon. I checked the number that was lit up as we came to a halt, and I clenched my jaw. Fucking hard.

"I've paid my dues," I snarled. "We don't need to stop here." The twelfth floor. I'd fought my way up and earned my unquestionable right to head straight to the rooftop close to four years ago. Foster knew that, and yet he hadn't taken me directly up to meet with Oscar. He'd punched in a floor that was insulting and downright unnecessary. The huge man smirked.

"Boss's orders. Don't shoot the messenger. He told you never to come back here after that stunt you pulled the last time. Said he wanted to make sure you'd earned the right to see him if you ever dared to step foot back inside The Barrows."

"I don't have time for this bullshit. I need to talk to him. *Now.*"

Foster shrugged—*I don't give a flying fuck.* The doors rolled back, revealing a melee of confusion and blood beyond. "Think yourself lucky," he said. "We said he should toss your ass back in the basement."

Clearly Oscar had vetoed that idea, but even so...to shove me back onto a fight floor, after I'd already bled and broken bones to reach the roof? That was fucking unbelievable. Unprecedented. Foster hadn't fought me downstairs when I'd threatened him, but I could see it in his lifeless eyes: he would fight me now, if I didn't get out of the elevator and accept the work that I had to do.

I stepped out onto the floor, and Foster whistled to the floor boss. "Make sure this one's shown the royal treatment, Jason. He's been here before." The tall guy standing in front of the tally board nodded sternly. The royal treatment was far from pleasant. Foster meant for me to be pitched against the toughest, most blood thirsty opponent available, and Jason was ready to oblige.

"Oh. And make sure you mark him down on the board properly," Foster added. "We have a returning victor in our midst tonight. His name's The Priest."

Where there had been roaring and shouting only a heartbeat

earlier, the floor suddenly fell silent. There must have been at least six or seven fights in play, but the moment Foster yelled that name over the hubbub and the brawling, everything just...stopped.

Bruised and swollen faces turned toward me. Black eyes, split lips, bleeding knuckles halted in midair.

Just. Fucking. Great.

There were people out there in the world who still called me Father. The odd ex-parishioner who recognized me on the street. Friends from seminary, who occasionally reached out to see if I was ready to quit my stubbornness and come back to the church. Monica still slipped up from time to time and used the title, though she knew how much I hated it. But I hadn't been called The Priest since the last time I'd come to The Barrows. The time I'd won my rooftop match and claimed the pot—two hundred and eighty thousand dollars—and then proceeded to try and burn down the building with everyone locked inside it.

"That's him?"

"That's The Priest?"

"Nah. The Priest was way bigger. Weighed two-twenty. He was a fucking monster."

Whispers filled the cavernous space. Twenty or thirty shirtless guys covered in tattoos, skin glistening with sweat, observed me with hard, cold, ravenous eyes, their brains kicking into overdrive. I was an opportunity not to be missed. I was a golden ticket.

"No fucking way," the guy closest to me announced, laughing. He was missing one of his front teeth. "The Priest got to the roof in two tries. No one's ever done that. Not before, and not since. This guy ain't him, Jason."

"He's The Priest," Foster repeated, his voice loud, bouncing off the walls. "Make him feel at home, gentlemen." Then Foster winked at me, his laughter raucous and booming. "And you? Why don't you get comfortable, *Father*. You're gonna be stuck on twelve 'til sun-up."

He disappeared, the doors sliding closed, and the elevator car began its descent down to the ground floor, where Falco had probably been laughing himself stupid since I'd stepped inside The

Barrows. This was fucking bullshit. Bullshit of the highest order. Oscar was expecting me to balk at the fact that I had to fight, expecting me to hit the call button to head back downstairs and leave for good. There would be no coming back here at all if I did that. Fighters who quit before the klaxon sounded were disgraced, never allowed to fight again.

Fuck Oscar, though. Fuck him, and fuck Foster. If I had to fight in order to meet with the boss, then that was what I was going to do. And woe betide the person Jason was about to match me with, because I would prove to these doubters that I *was* the Priest. Just for tonight, anyway. Reaching the rooftop was the only thing that was going to keep Sera safe. And right now, in this instant, keeping her safe was the only thing I fucking cared about.

I discarded my bag of weapons, shrugged off my leather jacket, and I dumped them on the floor by the elevator. My shirt came next, and then my belt. No one breathed as I made my way into the center of the space, stretching my arms out behind my back.

I'd expected there to be trouble when I arrived here. Oscar was undoubtedly still pissed at me for what I'd done. They'd had to shut down the fights for two rotations in order to repair the damage I'd caused when I'd started that fire. I'd assumed there was going to be a lot of bowing and scraping on my part, but I hadn't expected to fight.

I could, though. I would. And I was going to fucking win.

I cracked my neck, casting a disapproving glance around the sweltering room, at the sea of faces that were watching me intently, and then I grinned like the bastard that I was. "Come on then, Jason. Who have you got for me?"

39

FIX

THE PRIEST

The Priest wasn't a fighting title I'd given to myself. Oscar had given it to me after my first night at The Barrows, when I'd made it to the fourteenth floor, and I'd only missed making it to the fifteenth by a hair's breadth. My last opponent had toppled to the ground mere seconds after the klaxon had sounded, and the rules were the rules. Oscar had come down to see me, to praise a combatant for the first time in the history of the fights. He'd researched me. He'd already known about my past. Said he was going to name me The Priest, because I won every fight like I had a guardian angel watching out for me. Like God himself had rigged the matches.

I'd come back the next night, started on eleven, and I'd fought like a motherfucker until I'd hit the rooftop less than two hours later. Oscar had a whiskey waiting for me when I sank down, bloodied and panting, into the chair opposite him.

Tonight, I was going to have to be that man again.

Jason chalked my moniker up onto the board, and everyone watched as he then scrawled the name of my opponent.

Dementor.

Fucking *Dementor.*

Great.

Who the fuck called themselves Dementor? Sounded like a fucking wrestler's name. And not a proper wrestler. The kind of wrestler that wore makeup and a shiny purple thong, prancing around the ring, pretending to smash chairs over people's backs. He probably had a mullet.

Yet another hushed silence fell over the gathered fighters as they parted for the man who was coming forward. My pretentious wrestler theory went flying out of the window when I managed to get a look at him. Dementor was about my height, about the same weight, and his body was much the same as mine, too: muscled, zero fat reserves, and broad shoulders, with arms that likely had a reasonable reach on them. He was covered in tattoos from the neck down, a jumble of color and smudges that barely justified the name artwork. His head was shaved and covered in scars, and his left eye was milky and clouded over.

The guy looked like he raped small children.

Shooting me a smile, displaying a mouthful of broken, crooked teeth, he spat on the floor and ducked down into a low fighting stance that said he knew what he was doing.

Awesome.

There was no bell. No signal that the match had begun. The guy sprung like a coil and leapt, barreling at me with a loud, unhinged howl that sounded more beast than man. I ducked to the side, and he skidded, trying to pitch up in time to land a blow on me, but I was no longer there. Moving quickly, I kicked out, my foot connecting with the side of his right knee, and the guy dropped. Just for a second. Just to his knees. But the crowd roared.

"So it's like that, huh?" the guy, Dementor, said. He was up and circling me in no time. The men gathered around us chanted Dementor's name, punching their fists in the air, shouting at the top of their lungs. It was all coming back to me now—the madness of The Barrows. This kind of aggression seeped into your veins without you

I didn't feel bad as I brought my elbow down on the back of the guy's neck. I didn't feel bad when I dropped to the floor and wrapped my legs around his ribcage, squeezing as hard as I fucking could. I felt a rib crack, and then another, and Dementor's agonized shout filled the room, from floor to ceiling. Out of the corner of my eye, I saw a short, stocky guy with a spider web tattoo on his cheek take a step forward, toward us. The second I turned my attention to him, fixing him with an icy, unforgiving glare, he stopped dead in his tracks. "Don't even think about it, shithead," I growled. "I can kick both your asses at the same time. Don't fucking doubt it."

Spider Tattoo scowled, deep lines contorting his face. He was Dementor's friend, or maybe they'd formed an uneasy alliance tonight in order to whittle down the competition, but he knew better than to take another step toward us. My eyes were promising death, and he must have seen it.

Dementor clawed and scrambled at my legs, trying to free himself, but I wasn't going to let go. No fucking way. I tightened my grip, and he hollered as his ribcage flexed between my thighs.

"This has gotta hurt. Wanna tap out yet?"

"Fuck...you...man!"

"All right. Suit yourself." I spun him around on the floor, winding my arm around his neck, the crook of my elbow right up underneath his jaw, pressing down on him, and Dementor fought every step of the way. I didn't *want* to hurt him. Unlike Foster and Falco, inflicting pain on others didn't make my dick hard. But he wasn't going to give in gracefully, and the more he wrestled and struggled in this position, the more pressure I applied to his ribcage and his throat. If he was stubborn enough to snap his own neck against my hold, then so be it. Survival of the fittest. This was why stupid people were getting killed all the goddamn time. It was a motherfucking epidemic.

"You're...fucking...cheating...man," Dementor gasped.

I leaned down and spoke into his ear. "Why? Because I'm beating you? There are no rules in this place. I do can whatever the fuck I want."

He grabbed at my arms, trying to loosen from around his

neck, and when that didn't work, he started slamming his elbows into my sides, arching his back, trying to squirm his way free.

No dice, asshole.

It wasn't my finest win, but when Dementor finally fell peacefully to sleep in my arms, I didn't give a fuck.

I was moving up to the next floor.

40

FIX

BAD BUSINESS

*T*hirteen.

Lucky number thirteen.

What a fucking nightmare.

Jason shoved me in the elevator, though begrudgingly. He'd obviously wanted the fight to last a little longer, to see a little more blood —mine, preferably—and he'd been disappointed. But the cameras mounted on every wall and on every available surface in this damn place had logged and recorded my win, and he'd received the green light to send me up.

Now I was standing on a new level, in front of an entirely new crowd of crazed, murderous cretins, and I was going to have to do it all over again. And it appeared as though the news had spread, and my identity had already been shared with these fighters. They were all standing in a regimented line, arms across their chests, their faces grim and livid. Some of them must have already progressed two or three floors themselves today, and weariness hung over them. Others were fresher, though, contenders who'd come close to making it to the roof the last time they were here, and now they were hungry to reach their goal. None of them looked like they were going to let *me* stand in their way. The floor boss of thirteen was called Henson, and he'd decided to let the fighters chose amongst themselves who was going to face me.

He watched on, wearing a bored expression, as a huge guy with fists the size of my head lumbered into the rough circle sketched out on the floor in chalk.

"The Priest versus Jackhammer!" Henson yelled, as he wrote the information down on thirteen's board.

"Fuck off," I said, laughing down my nose. "Jackhammer? Are you going to fuck me to death?" Technically, that *was* allowed. Oscar would probably get a kick out of that play-by-play, especially if it was me getting reamed by a seven-foot-tall Goliath. This guy didn't look like he was going to use his dick to murder me though. He looked like he was going to use those gigantic fists of his.

"I'll call you Jack," I said, rocking on the balls of my feet. No way I was ever going to refer to the guy as Jackhammer. Nope.

"Call me whatever you like. I'm gonna take my thweet time with you, thunshine." His voice was unexpected—soft and light... and he had a fucking lisp. I refrained from laughing. It took everything I had, but I did not laugh.

"All right, then, Jack. Let's get this over with. The night's passing us by, and I've still got another floor to go."

Mr. Hammer scowled. I wasn't taking him seriously enough, and he was taking offense. He was far bigger than Dementor (whom I was beginning to wish I'd also renamed) and he was also much slower, too. He was waiting for me to make the first move, so I just stood there with my hands in my pockets, sending him confused glances out of the corner of my eye.

"You weren't kidding when you said you were going to take your sweet time, were you?"

"Fuck you, man."

"That's what the last guy said."

Jack was growing redder and redder by the second. He wasn't used to this. People didn't normally mock him, that much was clear. They were respectful because of his size. Intimidated by his sheer mass. I wasn't shaking in my Stan Smiths, and poor old Jack wasn't taking it too well. "Why don't you come here and thay that?" he fumed.

"What? Come over there to tell you that the last guy said fuck you, man? That makes no sense, Jack."

"I'm going to enjoy peeling your thkin from your body, Priest."

"You sound like a bad movie villain, dude. Just try and fucking hit me already." The last time I'd fought on the thirteenth floor, one of my back teeth was knocked out. The guy I'd been pitted against fought like a goddamn bulldog, and he hadn't given up easily. Seemed as if The Barrows standards had fallen significantly since then. Maybe all of the tough fuckers in New York had already made it up to the roof, and these guys were the only other fighters left. Maybe they never actually progressed from their floors and had been locked in the same circle jerk for months now, using the fights as an opportunity to get together and drink tea and talk about the fucking weather.

I was growing tired of this.

It was a fucking farce. Oscar was playing with me, just as I was guilty of playing with Jack. Time to end it and get on with the real business at hand: finding that thumb drive and getting the fuck out of here. I still had my bag with me. I'd brought the weapons along just in case Oscar tried to pull anything shady, but now I was considering taking out my gun and putting a bullet right between Jack's eyes. That would be bad business, though. There was an understanding here that there would be no gun fights. It was common sense, really. Everyone came here with a gun, but no one used them. If one person fired a gun, the next minute everyone would be firing a gun, and then, shortly after that, everyone would be fucking dead. No more victories. No more glory. No more striving for the roof. Just an old, run down building full of dead idiots.

I left the gun where it was. I left all of the weapons I'd brought with me, and I approached Jack with intent.

It was over quickly.

Jack, to his credit, got a few solid punches in—one to my face, one to my shoulder, and a blazing right hook to my temple that made me see stars. I was too fast for him, though. Once I could see straight again, I took him out at the knees and twisted his giant arm so far behind his back that I could feel the bone flexing, about to break. He slapped his palm against the ground, wheezing asthmatically, and I let him go, strangely disappointed that the fight hadn't been harder.

In the elevator up to fourteen, I scrubbed at my face with my t-shirt, loudly cursing Oscar. "Fucking cunt. Totally fucking stupid. Fucking huge waste of time."

The elevator jerked to a stop.

"Cunt, huh? Such a graphic word to come out of an ex-priest's mouth."

I hadn't noticed the small speaker underneath the camera in the corner of the elevator car. It crackled, Oscar's voice coming out of it, and I pinched the bridge of my nose between fingers. "Do we really need to play this game?" I groaned. "Just call the elevator up."

"You're lucky you're not fucking dead right now, you psycho little fuck-boy. Your unbelievably crazy actions have earned you this little exercise. I'm still not sure I'll grant you an audience if you complete the next floor."

"If I complete the next floor? Those last two fights were ridiculous, Oscar. Let's just be done with this and talk like adults. I have a proposition for you."

I didn't have a proposition for him, but *he* didn't know that. Oscar loved haggling and bartering with people. Loved negotiating, even when there was no need. The very word 'proposition' was like a red flag being waved in front of a bull. Static crackled and hissed out of the speaker.

A knot of worry formed as I waited for Oscar's response. How long had it taken me to reach the Barrows? Half an hour? Forty minutes? And how long had I been participating in this charade of Oscar's? The fights had been over quickly, but I must have spent half an hour on each floor, and now I was suspended somewhere between the thirteenth and fourteenth floors, wasting even more time. What if Sera wasn't alone? What if someone went to the apartment while I was here, fucking around and playing these stupid games? What if she was in danger? I balled my fist and drove it into the side of the elevator car.

"Oscar! If you're not going to let me up to fucking see you, then send me back down, you motherfucker. I swear to god—"

"I didn't think you and God were on speaking terms, Felix."

I scowled at the camera, hoping he could see the rage in my eyes. "I make promises to Him sometimes. Very serious fucking promises. Promises I don't break. If you don't let me the fuck out of this fucking elevator, I'll be making a promise concerning you, Oscar. Your body guards won't matter. Your trip wires and your traps...none of the measures you've put in place will fucking save you, you bastard. Do you understand?"

Oscar laughed. *"Don't get worked up, friend. I just wanted to apologize. That's all. The men you fought this evening weren't up to scratch. You should have been matched against more competent fighters. I'm sending someone down to fourteen now. Someone far more suited to your...*capabilities." As soon as he'd finished speaking, the elevator began to move again.

He wasn't letting me up to the roof. He still expected to fight, and then, *maybe* then, he would see me. It wasn't fucking good enough. I was going to rip the fucker's dick off and shove it down his throat, and then I was going to shove burning coals down there after it. He wasn't going to know a moment's peace. If anything happened to Sera... If she was harmed... If she woke up tonight, alone and scared, Oscar Finch was going to wish he'd never fucking been born.

The elevator jerked to a halt, and the doors moved back.

The fourteenth floor was completely silent. There wasn't a single soul in sight. Countless boot prints marked the dirty floor, and blood, fresh blood, was splattered in great swathes all over the concrete. There had been a match here tonight, but all of the fighters had been moved, relocated somewhere else. I stepped into the eerily quiet space, casting a look around. And then—

There *was* someone. A man, leaning against the fourteenth floor's leader board. Another of Oscar's men. He barely acknowledged me as I walked out onto the floor.

"Well?" I snapped. "Who the fuck am I fighting?"

The guy licked his index finger and dipped his finger in the chalk dust that was gathered in small dunes on the lip of the match board. Slowly, he raised his hand and put his finger to the board. He drew two straight lines, parallel to one another, about three inches apart. And then, carefully, he drew a long diagonal line from the left-hand corner of the bottom line to the right-hand corner of the line sitting on top.

It was the letter Z.

Nothing more.

"Zee?" Zee was more respectable than Dementor. Definitely more respectable than Jackhammer. I searched and found a camera bolted to the wall, then stalked up to it, knowing that Oscar would be watching the feed from his chair up on the roof. "Who the fuck is Zee, Oscar? And why the fuck am I fighting him?"

Behind me, a scraping sound interrupted the silence. I spun around, and a figure appeared from behind one of the pillars close to the windows, on the far side of the space.

A man.

Tall.

Broad.

As he got closer, I saw the packed muscle on him. The tattoo chaining his collar bone that read, "*Such is Life.*" The large, black fleur de lis that marked his chest. The array of angled scars on his stomach that looked like long-healed stab wounds. I saw the amused twist of his mouth. The slight frown that formed a crease between his brows. And I saw the dark, familiar shadow in his eyes. The same dark shadow I saw in my own eyes whenever I looked in the mirror.

"*I'm* Zee," he growled. "But only my friends call me that. You can call me Zeth." He cocked his head to one side, sizing me up, the same way I was sizing him up. A savage, slow smirk spread across his face.

"You must be The Priest. I think I'm supposed to kill you now."

PROLOGUE

CARVER

I had never killed anyone before.

There had been times when the desire had been there, of course. Plenty of times when the rage and the pain inside had demanded justice. This was the first time I'd taken action, though. And once the task was done, once the girl was dead, I was sure the knot of anger that roiled inside me would finally subside. That finally there would be peace, if only a tarnished, impure kind of peace that maybe wouldn't eradicate all of the suffering and the trauma but might bring with it a shadow of rest.

That would be enough. Maybe then, there would be some way forward out of the darkness that had obscured the world for so long.

As I stood in front of the laptop on the otherwise empty desk, the words appeared almost by themselves on the screen. Another email, this time severing the contract that had been put in place. Marcosa had seemed like a solid bet. A man who would carry out the job he'd been hired to do without pause. There'd been no way to know he would fall for the girl. So fucking stupid. Lafferty was beautiful, there was no denying that, but the assassin had come with the highest of recommendations. Had never once quailed at the hardest of jobs. So why, now, had the man allowed his morals and his *dick* to get in the way? It should have been easy. Should have been a quick, clean kill that took up no more than thirty minutes of his day.

My fingers hammered at the keyboard.

M,

*D*isappointment doesn't cover it. I trusted your colleague to be a professional. Now, I've discovered your services to be unreliable. I've entered into an alternative contract to take care of the matter. This new individual's methods are questionable at best, but he will not waiver until the work is complete. Please convey my dissatisfaction to Mr. Marcosa. Tell him, whereas before he could have saved SL considerable pain and misery, he has now guaranteed that she will suffer.

• —Carver

*C*losing the laptop and stowing it away, I considered the stack of drawings sitting in the bag beneath the desk. The images depicted on those countless sheets of paper were as graphic and sexual as could be. They'd been in that bag, carried from pillar to post, from one side of the country to the other, for years now. They'd become a focus of intrigue and hate, a fascination and an obsession, but now they were no longer needed.

Sera Lafferty would soon be dead, and this whole, messy saga would be done with. No more need for sneaking around. No more lies and deception. Tendrils of spite and fury would no longer choke the very air I breathed.

Those drawings wouldn't be carried back home this time. The bag would stay down here to rot, just like the disgusting piece of shit lying on the cot on the other side of the bunker—the same piece of shit who hadn't stopped sniveling and whining since the needle had pierced the crook of his arm fifteen minutes ago and the poison had slowly entered his sluggish bloodstream.

"Don't. Don't just fucking leave me down here. I can help you. I know what to do. I won't mess it up, I swear!"

I sneered. "There *is* one way you can help me."

"How?" Anderson's eyes were already bloodshot and bulging, the toxins getting to work inside him.

"I could really use your sneakers." Kicking the polished leather shoes off was easy; the damn things were three sizes too big. I began unlacing Anderson's dusty, filthy New Balance running shoes, tugging them from his feet, first the left and then the right.

"Why are you doing this?" he moaned. "I ain't done nothing to deserve this."

I almost laughed at that. "You know all too well what you did."

The sneakers stank to high heaven and were trodden down at the back where he'd jammed his feet into them without undoing the laces, as I had just done. I set my jaw and slipped my own feet inside, fastening them up tight. Anderson's car was parked a mile away and it was dark outside—there was little chance of being seen—but still. I'd run back to the car just to be safe, and I didn't want to end up tripping over my own feet. The sneakers were still too big, but better than the dress shoes had been.

I turned, ready to leave this godawful place behind forever, but Anderson grabbed the hem of the shirt I was wearing, fisting the material tightly. "What happened to you?" he whispered.

The man lying on the cot had gone by another name once upon a time. Just as I had, he'd changed his given name in order to build a new life for himself. He'd wasted the opportunity, though. He was old now. Fat. Useless. Another ugly sneer contorted my face; I felt it molding my features, setting there permanently. "I am merely a product of my surroundings." I tilted my head, studying him with utter contempt. "But you, *Anderson*? What happened to *you*?"

His mouth flapped open and closed a couple of times. It must have been getting pretty hard for him to breathe. Hard enough that he couldn't reply.

I didn't think twice as I ripped the shirt from Anderson's hand. There had been a time when I might have felt a twinge of remorse for shooting him up with formaldehyde and leaving him to die. But not now.

No.

There was no guilt left inside of me.

I didn't feel anything anymore.

41

FIX

NEVER GO DOWN

*I*n the beginning God created the heaven and the earth. And the earth was without form, and void; and darkness was on the face of the deep.

A lot of shit had happened since then.

Light. The Aztecs. Pompeii. The Marie Celeste. Hitler. Dunkin' Donuts. Celine Dion. And, now, this Zeth guy...who looked like he was primed to beat the shit out of me.

Unlike the other two guys I'd just fought at the behest of Oscar Finch, the madman who ran The Barrows, this Zeth guy radiated not only violence, but intelligence, too. His dark eyes flashed steel, and his body hummed with power. Here was a true fighter. Here was the *end level boss*, designed to beat me into a bloody pulp and send me packing with my tail between my legs. He was strong. Looked light on his feet. By the way he prowled toward me, his eyes scanning my own stance and build, he was assessing me, getting a measure of me, too.

When he pulled up in front of me, eye-to-eye, we were exactly the same height. I rolled back my shoulders, rocking my head from side to side, cracking my neck. "Zeth? Doesn't sound like a real name," I said.

"And *Fix* does?"

My mouth curled up at the right, lifting into a smirk. "Got me there."

"I got you *everywhere*," he fired back. "I have no idea how the rules in this place work. Don't you just want to hit the elevator and make your way downstairs, though? You get to keep your teeth. I get to finish the really good scotch I have waiting for me on the roof."

He didn't know how this worked? What the actual fuck was that supposed to mean? "You came down from the roof?" I asked.

"What of it?"

"You didn't have to swing a few punches on the way up?"

The guy's smirk was just as twisted as mine. "I climbed up the fire escape."

I just blinked at him. *You have got to be fucking kidding me.* He climbed up the goddamn fire escape. Completely avoided Falco and Foster. Avoided the basement, and all the other floors in between, and headed straight for the roof? Motherfucking *genius*. I attempted to conceal the grudging respect building inside me, right alongside my annoyance. Why the fuck hadn't I thought of that? "How did Oscar take your unorthodox arrival?"

"I believe this fight with you is supposed to be my penance."

Yeah, that sounded about right. Actually, it sounded like he was getting off fucking light. "Well, I hate to break it to you but whatever you came here for, whatever reason had you scaling up the side of The Barrows like Spiderman, you're not getting back up on that roof. I have a damn good reason to get up there to Oscar, and there's nothing like an incentive to make a man swing hard."

"If you say so, Padre," Zeth growled. "Win or lose, I'll be leaving with the thumb drive I came here for. Honestly, you look like you're gonna put up a good fight. I'm looking forward to it."

The soles of my boots felt like they were suddenly glued to the floor. Thumb drive? He just said thumb drive. Had I heard him right? What were the chances that Oscar had two mystery thumb drives? And I just so happened to be here for one of them, and Zeth was here for the other? Basically zero. Fuck. Come *on*. This just wasn't fucking happening.

Even if I won this fight, I was probably going to have to kill the bastard to make sure he didn't try and take the damn thing anyway. He didn't play by the rules—Oscar's or anyone else's by the sounds of things—and I didn't have fucking time for this. I needed to get back to Brooklyn, back to Sera, and the sooner the better.

"What's on the drive?" I demanded. Blunt and to the point.

"You're not supposed to be having a nice chat. Fucking hit each other," the floor boss yelled from over by the board.

My lip curled back. Zeth's lip curled back. We traded identical irritated looks. Both of us ignored the guy. "What do *you* care what's on it?"

"I was hired to come here and collect it for a client. Must be pretty fucking important, if it's garnering this much attention."

Zeth was a wall. No expression. No movement. Nothing but cold, assessing judgement in his dark eyes. I hadn't been back to New York in well over six weeks, but I kept my ear to the ground. I made it my business to track and monitor the rise and fall of power in the city. I would have heard of this guy if he'd been picked up by one of the gangs or the mob. And I definitely would have heard of him if he'd been attempting to build an empire of his own. So, he was from out of town. His accent was clean, no hint of any twang, drawl or lilt that would identify his place of origin. His eyes narrowed a fraction—the only indicator that he wasn't paralyzed from the roots of his hair down. "Trust me," he rumbled. "If you don't have any personal ties to this thumb drive, then you're better off keeping it that way. Whatever your client's paying you, it isn't enough. Walk away."

I didn't have the time to explain to him that I wasn't getting paid at all. That I was locked into a trade with Rabbit—the thumb drive, for the identity and location of the guy who was intent on having Sera killed. Plus, it was none of this fucker's business. "You've said you're going to beat me more than once in the past two minutes. But for someone so sure of victory, you sure do seem to want me to walk away," I observed.

Zeth's flat expression didn't falter. "I fight people when I have to. I fight for exercise, and to protect those I care about. While I don't have a problem with knocking a hole right through your face with my fist, I don't like being told I have to fight someone for the sheer spectacle of it. I'm not a fucking gladiator. And that fat fuck up there on the roof isn't my boss. I don't owe him shit. I tried doing this the nice way. I asked politely. Oscar didn't feel like obliging me. So now, all I want to do is get back up there and beat the fucker to a bloody pulp."

"I'd love to do the same. Sounds like we have more than one common goal."

Nostrils flaring, Zeth stepped forward. "Then perhaps we can work together. We fight. You go down after a couple of hits. We fool that asshole by the board into thinking you're unconscious. When he comes over to check, we lynch him and steal his access card to the elevator."

His mind obviously worked in a similar way to my own. I'd been about to suggest the same thing. "Sounds great. There's only one problem, though, *Zee*."

He just arched his brow questioningly.

"I never go down in a fight."

His response was an earthy, deep rumble of laughter that echoed around floor fourteen. "I suppose I admire that."

"You'll go down, then?"

"*Fuck no.*"

A burst of static ruptured out of a small set of speakers mounted on the closest support column; a crackling, popping sound splintered through the air, followed by a blast of sharp, grating, high pitched feedback. Oscar's aggravated voice followed after it. "If one of you doesn't make the other bleed in the next five seconds, I'm going to send someone down there with an AK47 and enough rounds to kill you both fifty fucking times. Get on with it!"

Zeth shrugged a shoulder, sighing under his breath. "I guess we'll just figure this thing out as we go, then." I'd figured before that he was quick, but I hadn't realized just how quick. The pain hit me first —an explosion of white light that filled my head silently, like the blast starship blowing up in a science fiction movie, the light calmly washing over everything before the chaos of the detonation actually took hold. The annoyance hit me shortly afterward, and for a brief, unpleasant, fucked up moment, I couldn't tell which stung more: the fact that he'd hit me without me seeing it coming, or the fact that it actually just really fucking *hurt*. I allowed myself a single step back. Just one. I bent my leg and braced, stopping myself from reeling. From toppling over like a felled fucking tree. Now that would have been seriously embarrassing.

My vision swayed, colors returning, too bright, bleeding together in a mess of yellows, and oranges, and blues and reds, and then it sharpened, bringing Zeth back into focus; he was fucking close. Closer than he should have been, and his fist was flying toward my face for a second time.

Oh no, sunshine. No, no, no. Not again. Not *ever* again. I ducked to the right, my hips twisting, and the bastard's fist sailed on by, buzzing my nose. The strike would have broken the damn thing if it had connected. I clenched my teeth, hissing between them, and I reacted without a second's thought. I raised my own fist, but I didn't jab directly. I lifted my whole arm, locked my elbow out, and I brought the back of my fist crashing down on his temple. I'd always known how to defend myself. When I was a teenager, I'd enrolled in three different kinds of martial arts, purely because I knew how badly it pissed my father off. After I'd joined the church, there hadn't been much time for training, though. I'd managed body weight work outs in the rectory when I got up each morning, but the sparring? The actual art of defense and attack? I'd grown rusty over the years. I'd become slow and sluggish. It had taken a long time after I walked away from my position to get back to where I was before. But after months and months of training, sweating, bleeding, gasping for every single breath I managed to drag down into my screaming lungs, I finally did it. And then I got better. Better still. Working out, training, fighting, running...it became an obsession.

And now?

Now I was fucking lethal.

The blow landed perfectly. The guy's head rocked to the right, his neck compressing. Had to have fucking hurt. He skipped to the side, distancing himself from me and my now primed fists as he shook his head, obviously trying to quiet the bells that must have been clanging around the inside of his skull.

When he righted himself, angling his body toward me, a slow, strange, slightly deranged smile spread across his face. "Nice," he said. "Looks like that's a point each then."

"Oscar doesn't count points. He counts pints. Of blood. He won't call the match until we've both spilled at least three between us. Or one of us concedes."

Slowly, Zeth touched the side of his head, his temple, where my blow fell. He wiped at his skin and then held up his fingertips for me to see. They were slick and red, glistening under the florescent lights. "Well, we have our first taste right here. I'm not afraid to bleed a little more, Priest. Are you?"

Dementor and old Jackie boy downstairs did their best to put the fear of god into me, but at the end of the day, their taunts and jeers had been pathetic. Zeth wasn't trying to scare me into submission. He simply opened his mouth and said the first thing that came to him, and I was fully willing to admit it; the guy was a little intimidating. There was nothing wrong with recognizing when an opponent was dangerous. It was fucking *smart* to recognize that. What wasn't smart was letting them know you saw them as a threat. Once they knew they had you spooked, the fight was generally over. These vicious, violent bouts weren't just played out with fists; they were played out in your head, too. And I was keeping mine in the motherfucking game.

I didn't flinch as I stalked toward him, raising my fists into guard. "If you're in, then I'm in." I could see why Oscar sent the guy down here to teach me a lesson. He was huge, and he was clearly a highly-trained fighter. But Oscar was forgetting one thing: I was huge, too. I was highly trained. All he'd done was set two meteors hurtling toward each other, sending them on a collision course, and the impact when Zeth and I finally clashed was going to leave a crater in the middle of New York City, a mile wide and a mile deep.

Zeth came at me again. Great knots of muscle shifted like liquid steel under his flesh. Instead of wondering how badly it was going to hurt if he actually, *really* managed to hit me, I made a quick study of him. I watched those muscles. I disregarded the angle of his body and the way he transferred his weight from one foot to the other, and I saw where the power was building in his body. It all happened in a tenth of a second.

He presented his left side to me, as if he were about to lunge and jab with his left fist, but the tension and the way his abs compressed on the other side of his body told a different story. He was going to feint to the left. He was going to try and misdirect me with a half-hearted strike, and then, while I was focused on the weak punch, blocking him, he was going to assault from the right, swinging his right fist up in a hook that would likely take my fucking head off if I allowed it to make contact.

Well, two could play at misdirection.

I looked to the fist he was thrusting out toward my shoulder, pretending that punch was the only worry I had in the world, and I waited. In the space of a heartbeat, Zeth twisted his body, pivoted, and that right hook was sailing toward my jaw with an unbelievable force.

Motherfucker.

I'd anticipated the maneuver, but fuck me running if the man's speed didn't surprise the shit out of me all over again. I had just enough time to twist, spinning to the side and ducking. A microsecond later and that would have been it. I would have been on my ass, eyes rolled back into my skull, counting fucking sheep.

A kernel of irritation itched at me. I'd bitched about the other fights being too easy, but this fight wasn't going to be anything of the sort. It was going to be hard. I'd be lucky to walk away from it unscathed, let alone win, and if I did win, the victory wasn't going to be as sweet as it was earlier. It was going to be tinged with fucking relief, and that bit at my pride.

"Remember, Son. Pride cometh before a fall. After murder, pride is the most heinous sin of all. Do not succumb to it. Do not bow down to your ego.

You'll only ever end up hurt, or hurting those around you who care about you. Do you hear me, Felix? Are you listening to me?"

I shook my head, trying to dislodge the sound of my father's voice as I danced beyond Zeth's reach. Now was not a good time to be reliving life lessons from the Father Marcosa who had preceded me. That was how my father had always operated, though. He was always showing up when I least expected it, when I needed to concentrate, when I needed him sticking his nose in the least. He was a stubborn, obstinate, rigid man who never knew when to back off. Really, I shouldn't have been surprised by the fact that he was still turning up and fucking with me, even though he'd been dead and buried for years. It was just his style.

Zeth huffed down his nose, moving into yet another defensive position designed to confuse and trick me. I witnessed the flare of anger in his eyes, though. He was pissed that he hadn't put me to sleep with that sneaky right hook. Distracted enough that he didn't see my right knee come rocketing up. He didn't manage to step back in time to avoid it. I thrust my hips forward, sending the full force of my body weight into the lunge, and when my kneecap made contact with Zeth's torso, his loud grunt of surprise and pain bounced off the walls of floor fourteen.

There was no time to celebrate. His elbow came out of nowhere, landing a sharp, dazzling blow to the side of my head, and suddenly everything was spinning. Some fighters would have used my momentarily dazed state to recover themselves, but not Zeth. He grabbed hold of me by the back of the neck, pulling me toward him, bringing his own knee up so swiftly that I barely managed to roll and drop out of his grasp in time.

This. Mother. Fucking. Bastard.

He was fucking with me.

He was trying to catch me off guard.

He wasn't going to get away with doing either for long.

I ground my teeth together, swearing colorfully as I straightened and launched myself at him. Not in an uncontrolled attack. No, that would have been a rookie error, and I didn't make those kinds of mistakes. At least not anymore. I threw myself at my opponent, knowing who he was, and knowing all too well how he was going to fucking react. He was going to let me hit him, and then, once he'd taken the blow and absorbed it, he was going to kick my legs out from underneath me and try and get me to the ground. Precisely what I would do in the same boat. I'd trained endlessly in order to counter the move, though, to prevent myself from being dominated in a grappling, wrestling match, and I was ready.

Zeth took the punch I landed to his stomach. My hand exploded with pins and needles, a sharp lance of pain and heat surging up my forearm as my knuckles met a wall of muscle so hard it might as well have been a slab of marble. This guy knew the drill. He knew how to take a hit. Even though he'd tensed to absorb the impact, he grunted, cursing from the impact. He reached for me, grabbed me, wrapped his hand around the back of my neck again, and I saw the moment he lifted his leg, bringing it back, about to sweep my ankles. I prepared to kick out with my own foot, a devastating downward stomp that could shatter bone if I aimed it correctly, but then Zeth was gone. He released me, pulling back, then he was turning, spinning, and the back of his fist was whipping around, about to come down on my temple.

It wasn't a graceful move, but the drop and roll I performed saved me from a guaranteed knock out. Zeth snarled, baring his teeth—the first real show of anger he'd let slip—and he reacted, dropping down, his full weight behind his knee as he brought it crashing down onto my chest.

Oh...

...fuck!

I couldn't...

I couldn't fucking breathe.

That didn't matter, though.

The stabbing, fiery pain that had laced itself around my ribcage and squeezed like crazy didn't matter.

The cold, disconnected, withdrawn look on Zeth's face as he raised his fist didn't matter.

The way my head pitched, my vision seesawing as I turned onto my side and pushed myself back up onto my feet didn't matter.

The only thing that mattered was that fucking thumb drive. If I didn't get it, Rabbit wouldn't find out who Carver was. And if Rabbit didn't help us, it wouldn't matter how many other hackers I tried to pay, threaten or bribe. They were a community of back-stabbing assholes, but they were smart, and Rabbit was the best of them. If Rabbit deemed a job dead in the water, no one else would dream of touching it. They could be running as many protection programs as they wanted, they could be as covert and secretive as they wanted, but he would still find out and he would still punish them. He would take whatever they had. He would destroy everything they'd built for themselves, and once they were ruined in the tech community, he would send someone over to break a few bones, too. Rabbit worked out, but typically hackers weren't gym types. As a rule, they weren't known for being badasses who could defend themselves at all.

I hissed, trying to expel the pain strobing through my body as I righted myself and faced Zeth again. The other man wiped his nose with the back of his hand, sniffing, and I realized with no small amount of satisfaction that he was bleeding from there, too, now. That satisfaction didn't last long. My vision suddenly went blurry, and then it went red, my eyes stinging as my own blood ran into them. Fucking great. I must have cut my head.

"Shame we're not fighting for money," Zeth commented. He was breathing hard, but otherwise he didn't appear to be fazed by the situation at all.

"You'd bet on yourself, I take it?"

He rocked his head from side to side. "I'd have to, you know that as well as I do. But you're a feisty bastard. Seem to know what you're doing. I might have put a couple of bucks on you too, just in case." He grinned, and there was an amused glimmer in his eyes that briefly lifted the stoic, robotic air that cloaked him like a shroud. I returned the smile, a frisson of anticipation sparking and catching light in my veins. Yeah, it sucked being hit. And yeah, it sucked that I wasn't making easy work of wiping the dusty polished concrete floor with the guy. But there was something vaguely exciting about all of this. I hadn't truly had to defend myself in a very long time, and now that I *was* having to, it was as if a part of me that had been slumbering was slowly waking up, coming alive and stretching its legs.

It had been years since I thought I might die, and right here, right now, there was a very real chance I might end up dead. If I lost to Zeth, Oscar could tell the floor boss still keeping score by the elevator to slit my fucking throat. He could also tell Zeth to end me and this evening's earlier transgressions would be forgiven.

That knowledge, the impending nothingness that hovered so close by that I could almost reach out and touch it...it made my heart pump so hard that it felt like it hadn't been beating at all up until now.

"I probably would have dropped a buck or two on you as well," I fired back. "But it wouldn't have mattered in the end. I'd have made a killing when I beat your ass and put you in the ground."

Zeth's eyebrows rose slowly—he looked faintly impressed. "Very confident. I like that." His eyes flickered toward the floor boss, and it looked like he was going to say something else. He didn't, though. He charged me, both fists pulling back, and then he was a whirlwind of arms and legs, his fists and his boots lashing out and striking.

I returned the favor. He wasn't going to beat me. He wasn't going to injure me further than he already had. He wasn't going to gloat over me and goad me into submission, because *I* was going to do that to *him*.

For every blow he landed on me, I landed one on him.

Every time he wheeled, or turned, or struck, I did the same.

Every time he pinned me, or grappled with me, or took things to the floor, I twisted free of his grip and did the exact same thing to him.

We were so evenly matched, I lost count of who was bettering the other.

A fight in The Barrows could last anywhere from five seconds to five minutes. Ten, sometimes, if the fighters were insane and just wouldn't back down. I had no idea how long Zeth and I danced around one another, taking and throwing punches, growling through the hits and refusing to back down, but it was far fucking longer than that.

He was my shadow and I was his. His fury matched my own. He caught me off guard, and seconds later he was on his back when I caught him. I was cut and bleeding, bruised black and blue, and I'd never felt more fucking alive.

The smell of iron and sweat filled the air. We skidded and slipped in the darkening pool of blood that had gathered at our feet, and the whole time neither one of us would call it.

My pulse was a frantic, crazed drum beat, pounding in my ears, as Zeth ducked under my arm and slammed his balled-up fist into my jaw. My vision swayed, white lights flaring and pulsing in my head, but I didn't slow. I skirted around him, feinted to the right, then drove my own fist forward and up into his side, knocking every last molecule of oxygen out of his lungs as he doubled over and groaned. When he rocked back, his teeth were coated in blood and he was laughing like a fucking maniac.

"All right, all right. I get it now," he growled. "You're insane. I'm insane. We'll both kill ourselves before we tap out on this thing."

"Agreed." I tried not to pant. My mouth was full of blood, too. I leaned forward and spat onto the concrete, grimacing at the volley of pain that relayed up and down my side. Felt like something might be broken somewhere, though I couldn't tell what.

"I have a proposition," Zeth offered.

"If you're about to tell me you'll do me a kindness and put me out of my misery, you can go fuck yourself."

He laughed again, drawing in a ragged breath. "I need the information off the thumb drive. You need the information off the thumb drive. I say we bust our way up onto the roof, fuck this Oscar guy up, take the damn thing and get the fuck out of here. We can make copies and we both get what we need. Simple."

I stared him down, narrowing my eyes, which was really fucking easy since both of them were nearly swollen shut at this point. What he was proposing made a lot of sense. But was he lying? Was he going to fuck me over the moment we got our hands on the drive, or was he the type of guy who kept his word? I knew he was a seasoned fighter, and I knew he was pretty quick witted, but beyond that I knew nothing about the fucker. Gears were turning in his head. He could have been plotting ways to bring Oscar down, or he could have been planning on ways to put me down. There was just no knowing. That was the thing about the men who visited The Barrows: typically, they weren't the type of men you could trust. Myself included.

Pacing, circling Zeth, making out as if I was just biding my time, waiting for the perfect moment to hurl myself into another fully-fledged attack, I heaved in a breath and ran my tongue over my teeth, checking to see if any of them were broken. Looked like I'd been spared that misery this time. "All right," I said. "But a word of warning, *Zee*. My life means very fucking little to me. I don't care about pain. I don't care about suffering. I don't care if I have money in my bank account, or a roof over my fucking head. There is only one thing that matters to me in the entire fucking world, and that's the woman currently waiting for me in my apartment. If I don't get that drive, she isn't safe. And if anything happens to her, I will stop at nothing to bring down the fieriest vengeance upon the heads of the people who stood in my way. Do we understand each other?"

Prowling around me, his eyes flashing, a cat-like, calculating smirk pulled at Zeth's mouth. He huffed lightly down his nose—the barest hint of amusement. "Don't worry, Priest. I got it. Now. I'd say it's about time we put an end to this bullshit and move on with our lives, wouldn't you agree?" He held out his hand. An obvious sign of peace, when we were meant to be tearing each other limb from limb.

"Hey!" The floor boss snapped, growling under his breath as he stalked over toward us. "Are you fuckers stupid? Haven't you heard of Oscar Finch? He'll fucking kill you if you don't stop fucking around."

Zeth arched an eyebrow at me, glancing down at his hand.

Sighing, I slapped my own hand into his, briefly shaking it. I'd been a lone wolf for so long now that striking up an accord like this felt alien and unwise. I *did* know one thing, however: there was nothing deadlier than a lone wolf. Unless you had *two* lone wolves, and they were prepared to fight alongside one another. Regardless of whether I had issues with Zeth after we were done here, things were set in stone now. We weren't laying another finger on each other for Oscar Finch's entertainment.

The floor boss's mouth opened, irritation flickering in his weak, watery blue eyes. But before he could say anything, Zeth spun around, faster than lightning, and hit the bastard so hard that I heard his skull crack before it had even had chance to bounce off the dirty concrete.

42

SERA

PULL THE TRIGGER

BEFORE

I waited out on the curb for the black SUV, my back rigid, my chin held high, knowing Sixsmith was watching from the upstairs window. He'd taken to doing that these days—observing me from his bedroom, standing a foot back from the dirt-streaked glass, as if he figured I wouldn't know he was there if he were cloaked in shadows. He didn't realize that I'd spent the better part of my life fine-tuning every sense I owned to detect when his attention was turned to me. My skin was so sensitive to the weight and pressure of his eyes that I could almost feel his gaze burning through the dusty, threadbare carpet that covered the splintered floorboards in my bedroom whenever he suddenly remembered I was up there and not in school.

My jaw was still hurting something fierce from the last time I'd gone visiting with Sam Halloran. I was still bruised from the encounter. A deep, offensive purple shadow marked my jaw, and down my neck four smaller bluish marks chained the column of my throat. *"For the life of me, Seraphim Lafferty, I don't know what gets into you girls at your age. Those ugly things on yo' neck ain't love bites, y'know. They be hickeys, markin' you out as a woman of loose morals."* Mrs. Merrit, our neighbor three houses down, told me when she'd come across me walking home with the groceries yesterday. She'd chosen to frown and tut at me, chastening me for the marks, when she knew full well the bruises weren't fucking love bites. It was plain as day that they were finger prints.

I'd attempted to cover the bruises with makeup before I'd left the house; Sam hated seeing the evidence of his own brutality on me. He liked to pretend he was a kind, caring lover, and I came to him twice a week of my own volition. But covering bruises was tricky, because Sixsmith would tan my hide raw if he ever saw me wearing makeup.

Keeping the two of them happy was impossible. If I made sure Sam was placated, then inevitably Sixsmith ended up laying into me for one thing or another—wearing the skimpy clothes Sam had me parade around in for him, or smelling of the perfume Sam insisted I spritz all over my body. And if I, instead, made sure Sixsmith was as happy as Sixsmith ever was, then Sam would strap that goddamn ball gag into my mouth so tight it felt like the corners of my mouth would rip open. He would punch me so hard it felt like landmines were detonating inside my skull. He would do far, far worse things than that as he shoved my legs apart and forced his way inside me.

I was constantly balancing on a tightrope of hatred and abuse. Every morning when I woke up, I found myself curiously wondering which one of them was going to send me toppling from that rope, plummeting to my death far below. Strangely, I wasn't scared. In point of fact, I was actually kind of looking forward to it.

The sky was hazy and white, a thin layer of clouds stretched thin between horizons like teased out cotton wool. And hot. It was too damned hot. The afternoon air was cloying and thick, threatening to choke me as it shoved its way down my throat. I'd already sweat through my thin, gauzy white shirt by the time the SUV pulled up and hugged the curb. Thankfully Sam didn't bother sitting in the back of the car and making the journey across town to come and get me anymore. He waited for me back at the apartment above the bar, usually throwing back shot after shot of whiskey and singing along to old Frank Sinatra tunes that he blasted from an ancient Sony stack system in the living room.

As always, Peter sat in the driver's seat, drumming his fingers against the wheel. I climbed inside and he didn't even turn around to look at me. He'd played ball in high school, but he'd never been truly athletic. God only knew why Sam had hired him. He was hardly body guard material. I often thought about it: what would Peter do if I reached forward, grabbed the handgun he always wore in a holster, strapped to his side? What would he do if I pressed the muzzle to my temple and I pulled the trigger?

There had been a thousand opportunities for me to grab his gun over the weeks that I'd been taken back and forth to the bar. Weeks that had turned into months. And still, I hadn't done it. Every time I contemplated how heavy the weapon would feel in my hand, I thought of Amy. Every time I daydreamed about the bullet firing from the chamber, exploding down the barrel, meeting my flesh and ripping through me like it was a hot knife through butter, I remembered that I'd be leaving my sister behind.

So, I didn't grab the gun. I didn't kill myself in the back of the SUV, and I didn't kill myself in any one of a hundred other ways I imagined when I was at home or at school, either, because I knew Amy wouldn't survive without me.

That didn't stop me from daydreaming, though. Most teenaged girls fantasized about the boys they liked, becoming famous pop singers, or being the most popular kid in school. I regularly daydreamed about downing a quart of bleach and passing into a blackened abyss that no one would ever be able to wake me from.

But Amy.

Always...

Amy.

I didn't believe in any sort of afterlife. If there was an afterlife, Mom would have come back somehow and told me she was all right. Nothing would have stopped her; she would have found a way. But even though I didn't believe in heaven or hell, I knew I'd never be able to rest easy in my grave if the burden of Sixsmith and Sam's attention fell to Amy once I was gone. She just wasn't strong enough to bear it, and that's what I loved about her most. Her innocence, and her softness, and that sense of oblivious fairytale that lingered over her, as it had since she was seven years old.

"You...you'd better be careful today."

I looked up from my hands—knuckles white, fingernails gouging into my palms—to find Peter glancing nervously at me in the rearview.

I cleared my throat. The air conditioning in the SUV was cranked up as high as it would go, and the frigid air made me want to cough. "What?"

He studied me for a second, then his eyes went back to the road. He didn't look at me again. "Sam. He lost a fuck load of money at poker last night. He's seriously shitty. I'm just sayin.' You oughta be careful when we get there. He's already smacked Julia."

Sam hitting his daughter was nothing new. He banished her to her room every time I came over, and I knew why. Just as he didn't like seeing the bruises, cuts, scrapes and teeth marks on my body, he didn't want anyone else seeing the marks he left on Julia's body either. I didn't doubt for a second that he whaled on her every night until he was so tired he couldn't lift his own arm.

I turned and looked out of the window, leaving Peter hanging. What would I even say to him, anyway?

Thanks for the heads up?

Sure, I'll be very careful.

Sure, I'll obey Sam and give him absolutely everything he demands of me from the moment I step through the door?

I already did that. I was meek, and I was subservient, and no matter how hard the fat bastard slapped or kicked or thrust his cock inside me, I didn't make a goddamn sound. It didn't matter. Sam's fucked up sexual proclivities didn't end at girls forty years his junior. He liked them young, but he also liked them bleeding. He liked them crying. He liked to see the despair in their eyes, and at the end of the day, there was nothing I could do to hide *that*.

The apartment was buzzing with a tense, uncomfortable silence when Peter ushered me through the door and closed it behind me, locking us inside. In the bar downstairs, numerous palms and fists slammed against tables, a chorus of muffled shouts and cries rumbling beneath my feet—the sound that usually accompanied a local sports team losing an important game. The commotion below did nothing to cut through the wall of deafening silence that filled the hallway I now stood in.

Looked like Peter's warning had been legit. Sam definitely was in a bad mood. I could feel it radiating through the dry wall, plaster-board, the insulation, and a couple of layers of cheap matte paint from three rooms away.

Peter's face, usually a deep tan from so much time spent outside running errands for Sam, was ashen. "Listen, Sera—"

Oh, for fuck's sake, Peter. Really? Now? You're going to suddenly develop a conscience now?

I shook my head as I walked away from him, toward the door with the chipped paint on the right, at the end of the hallway. "Don't sweat it, Peter. It's okay. If I need you, I won't shout."

I could have looked back, but I didn't. I already knew what frightened, spineless Peter looked like when he knew something bad was going to happen and he didn't plan on doing anything about it. I knocked on Sam's bedroom door—three small, timid taps.

From the other side of the door, the word, *"Come."*

Sam did that a lot, ordering me to come. When he was inside me, it was his favorite command. *'Do it. Do it, you stupid bitch. And don't fake it. I can tell when you fake it. Your pussy doesn't grip my cock the way it would if you were having an orgasm.'*

I hadn't known it was possible to reach climax through sheer terror alone, but somehow I'd trained myself to do it. Mercifully, once he was ready to fuck me, usually after an hour of 'toying' with me, as he liked to call it, he didn't last very long. His pride was insurmountable. He

404 | CALLIE HART

was a piece of shit rapist who forced himself on me twice a week, but he never wanted to come before I did, as if the orgasm he insisted I endure made whatever messed up bullshit he did to me okay.

It wasn't okay. It was never okay. Before Sam, no one had ever made me climax before, so I had no idea how it was supposed to make you feel, but with him, it brought me no release. It didn't make me feel good. When that searing, tingling surge of pure sensation hit me, I wanted to rip my own skin from my body. I wanted to cauterize my nerve endings and deaden every single one of them, so Sam Halloran could never make me betray myself so heinously again.

When I entered, Sam's room was turned upside down. His bedside lamps were smashed on the floor. The garish piece of modern art he prized so greatly, worth well over thirty thousand dollars according to him, had been slashed, the canvas rent wide open like a yawning mouth, it's frame shattered into pieces. The blue vase that had sat on top of Sam's chest of drawers for the past year, always containing a bouquet of fresh flowers, was now in seven or eight pieces on the floor, and long stemmed red roses, stripped of their petals, had been trodden into the carpet. The glass coffee table, normally positioned in front of the flat screen TV, was upended and destroyed, and large shards of tempered, smoky grey glass glittered maliciously on the carpet, diamond-shaped and dangerous.

All those broken shards of glass needed was someone with enough imagination and grit to come along and transform them into knives.

I looked away.

I knew better than to open my mouth. Instead, I dropped my backpack at my feet and I dropped to my knees, sitting back on my heels and placing my hands on top of my thighs, bowing my head, assuming the position Sam told me I must *always* assume whenever I entered his domain.

I hadn't even looked in Sam's direction, where he perched on the end of his bed, wearing his maroon, silk dressing gown and his slip-on house shoes.

Shit. This wasn't going to be good. I flared my nostrils and drew in a calming breath, closing my eyes.

"Well? Aren't you...going to say...anything?" Sam snapped. His voice came out rough and slurred. He always drank before I arrived, but this was something else. Today, he was drunk, and from the stale, acrid stink that was hanging in the air, he'd also been smoking too. Didn't smell like cigarettes, cigars, or weed. The scent was pungent, chemical-rich, and it bit at the back of my throat.

I shook my head. No, I wasn't going to say anything.

"That's rather rude. A man's in obvious distress, and you're not going to ask him if he's all right?"

Sam wasn't all right. He was fucked up and out of his goddamn mind, and any words that passed my lips right then were going to be wrong. If I asked him what the matter was, he'd strike me for being nosy. If I asked him if I could do anything to help him, he'd punch me in the face for being so stupid. If I told him everything was going to be okay, I'd be beaten within an inch of my life for being an uncaring little shit who didn't take his problems seriously. There was no positive outcome here. I clenched my teeth together, tensed my shoulders, braced myself, and I did not say a single motherfucking word.

Sam's top lip curled back, revealing his stained, jigsaw puzzle teeth. I saw his expression sour out of the corner of my eye, and it sent a frozen chill of panic skittering down my spine.

"Ungrateful little bitch," he snarled. "After everything I've done for you and your family, you'd think I'd receive a little more respect." He kicked out with his slippered foot, and his heel connected with my hip bone, unbalancing me, sending me sprawling onto the carpet. I let myself go limp. No sense in trying to stop myself from falling. That would only make him madder, so I laid there, my face pressing into the weft of the carpet, and I didn't move an inch. I didn't even blink.

"No point playing fucking dead. I already know you know," Sam spat, getting to his feet. "I already know your piece of shit father must have told you."

My father must have told me? My father must have told me what?

Sixsmith had woken me up at two a.m. and informed me I was to come here today, that I was to be downstairs and waiting for Peter at eleven a.m. sharp. Uncharacteristically, he'd left my bedroom without so much as sneering in my general direction. He'd been sober, too, which had come as a shock. Once he'd gone, I'd laid in bed, unable to get back to sleep, thinking about what Sixsmith must have traded for me this time. I'd paid off his original outstanding debts with my pussy about six months ago. Now, he mostly used me as a line of credit on a weekly tab at the bar, but sometimes I was good for the occasional bit of help with the authorities, whenever Sixsmith found himself in trouble with the law and he required Sam's influence to get him out of trouble.

Other times, Sixsmith traded me for cash, so he could fix up his car. The Beretta broke down more often than it ran; I must have blown Sam enough times to pay for an entirely new engine block by now.

Sixsmith hadn't shared what he was getting out of today's visit, though, and I hadn't asked. I'd simply thanked my lucky stars that he hadn't been in a more volatile mood and I'd waited for the dawn.

Grunting with the effort, Sam stooped down beside me, crouching by my head. He brushed my hair back out of my face, and then he cupped my cheek tenderly in his hand. Fear stabbed at me, sending a spasm of electricity through me; when Sam was gentle, it meant he was going to be *extra* rough later. "You come from weak, sullied stock, Sera," he said in a monotone voice. "Your father is bottom feeding scum. A liar, and a cheat. Did you know? Did you know what he was planning to do?"

A thousand thoughts reeled and cartwheeled through my head. What the fuck had Sixsmith done now? How had he upset Sam this badly? The man had *never* liked my father, was always cursing him and calling him every name under the sun, but this level of hatred was new.

Out of nowhere, Sam slipped his hand around the back of my neck and grabbed a fist full of my hair, yanking my head back so hard that I yelped. He shoved his face into mine, his teeth bared, breath reeking of rye as he yelled, *"Did you know he was going to take the bar? Did you know he was going to fucking clean me out? Huh?"* If he wanted an answer from me, I'd never know. My teeth crashed together as he picked up my head and smashed it against the floor. My field of vision shrank, darkening around the edges, like the screen of an old television as it powered down. For a second, I thought I was going to pass out, and relief hit me like a fist in the gut.

Then I realized that, no, I wasn't going to lose consciousness. I was going to remain wide awake. And it wasn't relief hitting me in the stomach. It was Sam. He pulled back his fist and then drove it forward again, putting so much force into his punch that I bowed, curling inward, my body curving itself around the unexpected pain and shock.

"Who was he?" Sam hissed. "Who was that fucker Sixsmith brought to the game last night? Where the fuck did he find him, Sera? He told you, I know he did. That drunk moron can't keep a secret to save his life."

He was right: as a rule, my father couldn't keep anything quiet. But this time, I had no idea what Sam was talking about. I was still fighting to pull in a much-needed breath when he launched himself at me again, this time rearing back so he could lay into me with his feet. He didn't kick me. That would be too kind a term for what he did next. He *stomped* on me—my stomach, my chest, my head. Over and over again, he stomped down as hard as he could while he screamed at me, demanding answers I couldn't supply.

"How did he beat me? How did he fucking do it? How did he get that guy to play for him? I mean it, Sera. Tell me now!" He was gone, lost in a sea of hysteria, and there was nothing I could do but ride it out.

The pain consumed me.

The pain...*became* me.

I was made up of it. Every part of me. Every fiber. Every molecule. Every cell.

Bones broke.

Skin split.

I bled.

I bled.

I bled.

And then...everything stopped.

"He thinks he's a big man now, huh? Thinks he can make me feel small? Gives me a week to get out of my own goddamn house, and he thinks he's going to fucking *get away* with it?" A flat, eerie calm replaced Sam's fury. His words were whispered, and worried me far more than the violence he'd just inflicted upon me.

I needed to get up. I needed to get the fuck out of here. I had no clue what had happened last night, but it sounded like my father had pulled something incredibly dumb and incredibly dangerous at a poker game, and he'd somehow won Sam's bar. If I stayed here, Sam was going to kill me. I was going to end up too broken to crawl my way out of this apartment, and then I would be well and truly screwed. I had t—

A sound stopped me dead in my tracks.

A sound I knew very, *very* well.

The scrape of metal on metal.

The sound of Sam's favorite handcuffs.

Oh god.

I cracked my eyes open, and...*fuck*. Sam had dropped his robe to the floor. He stood naked at my feet, his gut bulging, his cock hanging flaccid between his legs, his eyes filled with pure fire. He scissored the cuffs back and forth in his hand, a brutal smile blossoming on his face.

"Your daddy knew what would happen to you if you came here today. He doesn't care if I cut you up. He doesn't care if I make your ass bleed. He doesn't care if I strangle the last ounce of life out of you while I come inside your bruised cunt. That's the kind of man Sixsmith Lafferty is. I hope you're fucking proud of him, girl."

Even as he talked, his cock was growing harder and harder. He was emasculated and angry as hell, that much was clear, but the idea of causing me so much pain while he fucked me was obviously tempering the sting. I looked into his eyes, and I knew he was going to do it. Every dark, sick, perverse, fucked up thing he'd ever wanted to do to me and had held himself back from…he was going to do them all. Panic hit me, a tidal swell of terror that made the roof of my mouth prickle and tingle.

Move. Move, damnit!

Kicking back, my legs screaming in pain, I shoved myself away from him.

Fuck.

Fuck, fuck, fuck!

Sam lurched forward. I tried to roll, to shift myself out of the way, but every movement was agony. I wasn't quick enough. He landed on top of me, grabbing me, trying to get hold of my wrists. If he pinned me, he'd slap those cuffs on me and my chances of fighting him off would be zero.

I fought.

I kicked.

I screamed.

I bit.

I scrambled through the pain, and my burning lungs, and the shell-shocked silence inside my own head as I wrestled to free myself of Sam's weight. He was a man possessed, strong and determined. My efforts were wasted. He grabbed my left arm, grinning like a lunatic, and held it above my head. His dick was fully erect now. He ground it against my stomach, panting, sweat dripping from his forehead down onto my face.

"This won't be quick," he rasped. "It's not gonna be painless. I'd save my energy if I were you. For fuck's sake, just give up, you stupid bitch. It's over. It's…all…*over*."

His words were a trigger. At the sound of them, something reacted inside me.

Sam was a worthless human being who could only feel good when he was making someone else feel bad. He wasn't smart. He wasn't important. He was nobody and nothing. Who the fuck was *he* to say my time was up? What gave *him* the right?

No…

No, this *wasn't* over.

My admittedly pathetic, miserable existence wasn't much, but the occasional patches of joy I shared with Amy made it worth something. Worth more that Sam Halloran's greasy cock and his pinching handcuffs. Enough was enough. For the first time in my life, as Sam held my arm over my head, preparing to snap one of the cuffs around my wrist, a spark of rage ignited in the pit of my belly. That spark took hold, and within seconds it had ravaged me, the flames of my wrath consuming every fiber of my being. Sam saw that fire raging in my eyes, he must have done, because he peeled his lips away from his teeth in a cruel, warped smile.

"Oh, Sera. *There* you are. Been waiting for you to develop a fucking backbone. Are you gonna fight back? Are you finally going to do something to make this a little more interesting?"

A scream built in the back of my throat, itching and clawing, begging to be released, but I clamped my mouth shut and swallowed it down. I wouldn't give him the pleasure of hearing me cry out, even if it was in anger. I knew him; he wanted me spitting and cursing, calling him every name under the sun, as I fought for my life. He wasn't going to get a word out of me. I wasn't going to make a goddamn sound.

He lowered his face closer to mine, and his rank breath washed over my face, snaking its way up my nostrils, making my gag reflexes come alive. "Don't let me down now, Sera," he growled. "This is your final moment to shine. Make me remember you. I want every second of this etched into my memory. I want to be able to relive it for years to come...late at night, when I'm lying in bed with my hand around my cock...I want to remember that look of defiance as it faded in your dying eyes."

Disgust roiled inside me. He was subhuman. He was the lowest of the low. I wasn't going to give him what he wanted. And more than that... I wasn't going to let him do this to anyone else, ever again.

I was much smaller than Sam. Small enough that I was able to twist my leg up to the side and gradually drive it sideways, into my chest, wedging it between our bodies. Sam didn't even try and stop me. He laughed, looking down as I drove my kneecap into his chest, trying to push him away from me. "Really? That's it? That's the grand plan? That's your move? Honestly, I expected more from Sixsmith Lafferty's daughter. Something far sneakier."

That's right. Keep laughing, you fat fuck.

Tears welled in my eyes, but I left them unshed. There was no time for tears. Later, maybe, when all this was over, I would sink into shock and horror, but not now. Everything hinged on this moment. I had to keep calm. I had to keep a clear head...

I pulled my other leg up to the side, cringing away from the position I'd put myself in by raising both my legs; Sam's erection was now digging greedily into my jeans between my legs, as if it could burrow through the material and inch its way inside me. Sam groaned, his eyes drifting over my head—the promise of what was to come must have been too much for him, because he allowed his focus to wander, just for a moment. It was a mere split-second, but it was enough.

See, I *was* Sixsmith Lafferty's daughter. I *was* sneaky as fuck. Trying to push him away with my legs was a fool's errand. There wasn't enough space between us for me to build momentum and force him away. The struggling, though. The determination in my eyes. Sam fed off the weak and the helpless. Their pathetic efforts fueled him in the most fucked up, depraved ways. Which is why he didn't notice, as I was heaving and battling with his considerable weight, that I had been very busy with my right hand.

Misdirection wasn't a skill I was well versed in, but I knew enough: make someone look to the left, when the magic was happening on the right. Poor Sam never saw it coming. A part of me wished he had. *I* would have liked to commit the moment to memory —the moment he saw the huge, jagged piece of glass coming flying out of nowhere, slashing across the meat of his neck. His look of confusion was going to have to do instead. One minute, he was leering down at me, flicking his coffee stained tongue over his bottom lip, excitement dancing in his eyes, and then the next he was gurgling, choking, coughing, spluttering, dying.

A stream of vibrant crimson blood arced from the hole in his throat where I'd opened up his flesh, as I dug the wickedly sharp shard of glass from the broken coffee table through soft skin and firmer muscle, until I reached sinew and bone.

I gasped as a jet of blood sprayed me in the face—hot, metallic, reeking of iron—but I didn't stop. I didn't stop until I'd dragged the make-shift weapon from his left ear to his right. Sam's eyes bulged out of his head, his tongue protruding, veins straining under his skin at either temple.

He rolled himself sideways, away from me, onto his back, his fingers digging at the tattered edges of his flesh, as if trying to press them back together, but he knew it as well as I did: he was a dead man. His body was simply taking a moment to catch up with the inevitable. He gurgled, making a wet rasping sound as he tried to say something to me, but he couldn't do it. The terrified, accusatory look in his eyes said all he needed to say.

He was cursing me, damning me to hell, and I didn't mind. He could damn me all he liked. I didn't believe in hell. And even if I was wrong and the place *did* exist, then it would be okay. I'd pay my penance and gladly, because at least Sam would be there, too, paying for *his* crimes, which were considerably worse than mine.

The hatred flared and then dimmed on Sam's face as his muscles fell slack, his fingers stilling at his throat. A shudder ran down his body, making his stomach and thighs wobble, and then... nothing. He was gone.

I was too shocked, too numb to feel it right now, but I knew what had just happened would haunt me for the rest of my days. I stood, my legs weak and unstable beneath me. My heart was barely beating, and my ears were ringing, but none of that worried me. A peaceful calm had fallen over me, dulling my senses. I didn't feel the sting of my skin breaking as I brushed tiny fragments of glass from my white shirt, which was now soaked in blood and colored red, as if it had been tie-dyed. I didn't see the slender, dark-haired figure standing in the doorway of Sam's bedroom, covering her mouth with her hands. I didn't hear the strangled sob that came out of Sam's daughter as I made my way down the hallway, my body made of wood. I didn't feel the blazing sun beating down on my tender skin as I walked all the way across town.

I barely even felt the throb of hatred that pulsed through me when I arrived home, walked through the front door, and found Sixsmith sitting on the floor in the living room, his back resting against the couch, surrounded by empty beer bottles. He let out a raucous bark of laughter when he saw the state I was in, and then shrugged. "It was only fair, Sera." Taking a swig from his beer, his thin lips curved into the shape of a smug smile as they formed a seal around the beveled rim of the glass. "I took everything from the bastard. Figured I'd let him have one last fuck for the road." He laughed harder, snorting as his head rocked back. "Looks like old Sammy boy got more than he bargained for, though."

I waited for weeks for the authorities to come and take me away. I waited to hear about the murder in the news or it being gossiped about it in the hallways at school, but no one breathed a word of Sam Halloran's gruesome demise.

In the end, the body had just...disappeared.

Three months later, I ran into Peter Fairley at the convenience store. He told me he'd taken care of the situation and Julia had gone to live with her Aunt in Texas. Turned out he hadn't been completely spineless, after all.

Six months after that, the name Halloran had been forgotten altogether in the town of Montmorenci, as if the old Dutch thug had never even existed in the first place.

43

SERA

STORM

I'd witnessed many dawns.

The way the sun crept up over the horizon, stretching its fingers into the sky, banishing the darkness, was spectacular to watch. The world always seemed to still. As if it had momentarily ceased to turn just for those few minutes, while the first shafts of life-giving light, the very first light of the coming day, washed over the earth and painted everything it touched a shimmering gold. The land, the sea, the sky—everything ached in its sheer perfection during those still, silent minutes.

Not this morning, though. The day broke into a storm. Rain hammered at the huge windows that overlooked the city, the sun barely forcing its way through the heavy, gunmetal grey of the pregnant clouds overhead. All was dark, the air buzzing with electricity and tension, and the crash and rumble of thunder in the distance filled me with a sense of foreboding that made me nervous.

I'd known Fix was going to The Barrows when I'd fallen asleep last night. He'd seemed so confident. So relaxed and at ease. I hadn't questioned him, hadn't given it another thought. But when I'd woken up and found myself alone in his bed, I'd started to worry. Rabbit had wanted Fix to go to this Barrows place instead of accepting a large amount of money. He'd implied that only certain people could go there, would be *able* to go there, which now made the place sound pretty damn dangerous.

I'd never cared where Gareth was. I'd never needed to know where any of my other previous boyfriends were at every hour of the day either, but things were different with Fix. He hadn't just gone to run some errands and was taking longer than expected. He'd gone somewhere unsafe. He'd been gone for hours, and he hadn't reached out to let me know he was alive. That complicated things.

I would have texted him, but I still didn't have his number. How fucking stupid was that? I'd be keying his digits into my cell the moment he got back, that was for damned sure. Until then, there was nothing for me to do but wait, and waiting was *not* something I was very good at. I made myself a coffee, and then I sat at the dining table, stirring a spoon around a mess of sodden, mushy cereal, pretending I might eat it at some point, while I watched the heavens roil and rage out of the window.

Lower Manhattan looked like the backdrop to a sinister dystopian movie—I could imagine civilization descending into chaos and anarchy right before my very eyes. Planes took off and landed on the other side of the city, and ferries risked the choppy waters of the Hudson river, and all the while the rain came down harder and harder, exploding off the glass and rattling the windows with every squall of wind that buffeted the building.

At nine a.m., I decided I needed to distract myself and hunted down my phone, intending to message Sadie. As soon as I scooped the device up in my hand, however, I remembered Fix ordering me to remove the sim card. He'd flushed it, just in case this Carver person had hired someone really tech-capable and they could have used the small chip to track me down. He'd promised we'd get another sim for me later on today, but in the meantime, I was completely without any means of contacting the outside world.

Damn it.

What if Fix ended up dead at The Barrows? What if he didn't fucking come back? My heart was climbing up into my throat as I stood from the table and jogged my way over to the front door. There was a keypad affixed to the wall, just as there was on the entry to the building down in the alleyway. Fix had given me the code, but I was damned if I could remember it now. Still, I tentatively took hold of the handle, turned, and pulled...

The door opened.

It wasn't locked.

Ahh, Jesus. Did that mean it could only be opened from the inside, or would anyone be able to waltz right in if they came up here? I closed the door and pressed my back to it, my heart thrumming like the wings of a caged bird. This was a fucking nightmare. The door probably wouldn't open from the other side if the code wasn't entered. Fix was safety conscious. He would never have left in the middle of the night while I was sleeping and then neglected to make sure the penthouse was secure. I reassured myself of that as I paced up and down, staring out of the floor-to-ceiling windows, chewing at my nails.

An hour passed.

I showered quickly, brushed my teeth and distracted myself by applying a small amount of makeup.

Another hour passed.

I was so jittery by the time I heard someone out in the hallway that I'd already figured out how to operate Fix's M4; I was sitting at the table, and I had the butt of the assault rifle nocked against my shoulder, the muzzle aimed at the entryway, with my finger on the trigger. The door swung open.

The man standing in front of me wasn't Felix. He was nothing like Felix. Just as tall, just as broad, but that was where the similarities ended. His arms were covered in tattoos, and his eyes glinted with a furious kind of malice that made a shiver skip up my spine.

It was him.

The guy Carver paid to murder me.

I hoisted the rifle up, quickly sighting the guy's chest, I inhaled...

And the guy held his hands up.

"Easy, tiger. I've been shot at enough recently. I don't need another orifice," he rumbled.

I jabbed the rifle toward him, baring my teeth. "Who the fuck are you? And where's Fix?"

"My name's Zeth. And Fix is right behind me."

"Bullshit." I scanned him from head to toe, wildly committing him to memory. He was a fucking mess. His t-shirt was drenched in blood, and his face, neck, and arms were covered in cuts, scrapes and darkening bruises. Fix hadn't said anything about a Zeth. There was no way he'd allow someone up here without telling me first. I eyed the black bag at the guy's feet—the one he'd been holding in his hand before he caught sight of the M4 aimed at his chest and he'd dropped it to the floor. "Kick it over to me. Now. And get on the ground."

The guy looked like he'd been beaten half to death, but the smirk that lifted up his left cheek into half a cocky smile made him seem none the worse for it. He hooked his boot behind the duffel bag and shoved it across the floor toward me. When it had skidded to a stop next to the table, he said, "Search through it, by all means. But there's only one way I'm gonna end up on the ground, woman, and that's if you shoot me."

I ground my teeth together so hard it felt like they would crack. "Do it! Now!"

He shrugged. "No."

"I'm serious. I'll fucking shoot you."

His eyelids lowered as he scanned from the crown of my head down to the rifle I held tightly in my hands. "Hmm. I actually believe you. Still. A guy's got to have rules. My number one rule is don't lie down for someone unless you're about to fuck 'em or you're dead."

A cold anger took hold of me, creeping up my neck; I must have been turning redder by the second. This man, whoever he was, was a threat. Fix wasn't here. I had no idea if he really was moments behind this stranger, as he'd claimed he was.

I did the math in my head. I could wait a few seconds and see if Fix did show up. I could hit pause on the situation and play it safe.

But a lot could happen in a few seconds. Everything could turn on its head. I could find myself lying in a pool of my own blood, my life slipping away from me, regretting the moment that I hesitated.

I swore I'd never deal in regret again. I promised myself years ago that I'd never hesitate again.

There was only one thing I could do.

I aimed, took a sip of oxygen, steadily blew it out down my nose...

...and I fired.

44

FIX

I WOULDN'T RECOMMEND IT

*O*scar Finch wasn't going to fuck with me again. It would be a long time before he fucked with *anyone* again, and that was the god's honest truth.

He hadn't sent the elevator down for us. No surprises there; the guy wasn't completely insane. He knew the moment we hit the roof, he'd find himself neck deep in some serious shit. While I'd climbed hand over hand up the service ladder bolted to the wall inside the elevator shaft, Zeth right behind me, the piece of shit had tried to flee down the fire escape. Only, when Zeth had come up it earlier in the evening, Oscar had ordered the metal staircase ripped clean from the wall, and so he'd found himself well and truly, *ironically* trapped.

He'd been spitting teeth and choking on his own blood by the time he reached into his suit pocket and handed over the thumb drive. Zeth had taken it from him, then handed it over to me—a show of good faith? We'd left together, riding the elevator down to the bottom floor, and no one had stopped us. Not even Falco or Foster, who were nowhere to be seen. A hail of gunfire chased after us as we climbed into Zeth's ride—the same pristine, gleaming black Camaro that I'd noticed when I parked up outside The Barrows hours ago.

Zeth had snarled, cursing violently as Oscar's braver men took potshots at the car. He'd seemed really fucking relieved when none of them actually hit the paintwork. Guy obviously liked his car. Understandably. It was a sweet fucking ride.

Besides the odd direction I supplied back to the Gas and Electrical Works—he was going to have to come back with me and wait while I copied the drive—we didn't speak much as Zeth tore through the bleak, stormy dawn toward Brooklyn. Halfway home, the sky split open and a curtain of torrential rain descended, fat droplets of water slamming onto the windshield. By the time I gestured for Zeth to pull down the side alley and park up next to the chain link fence that split the alley, I could barely see three feet in front of my own face.

Zeth kept his thoughts to himself as he climbed out of the Camaro. In the darkened alleyway, I mentally surveyed my body, noting the points where I was stiffest or sorest, cataloguing them and plotting out a contingency plan. If this Zeth Mayfair guy was going to try something, he was gonna do it here, in the alleyway, away from the watchful eye of the public. In his head, he was probably thinking how easy it would be to jump me, take the thumb drive and burn off in his car. I readied myself, prepping to start throwing punches all over again, even though it felt like my arms were barely hanging in their sockets. Zeth simply peered up at the building, running his tongue over his teeth.

"Keyless entry. Smart. What about the windows? They reinforced?"

I didn't miss a beat. He'd never know that I'd been planning on staving his face in with the butt of my gun only seconds ago. "Only three windows on the ground floor haven't been bricked up. All the other windows are reinforced. No one gets in or out unless it's through that door."

He placed a hand against the building, leaning his weight against it, looking up at the brickwork. "Oscar knows you live here?"

"I don't make a secret of it."

"And if he shows up?"

"He dies. He, and anyone else he brings here. There are charges in the stairwells. The roof's covered in trip-wires. And..." I waved my hand at the building. "There are no fire escapes for people to scale, either."

He smirked. "You got all the angles covered. Place is a fortress."

Zeth and I weren't just cut from the same cloth. We'd been cast from the same mold, and that mold had cracked asunder and broken once it had finishing forging the two of us. We were the last of a dying breed—not only strong, not only fiercely loyal, but quick-witted and calculating, too. We were as smart as we were lethal with our fists, and that combination made us a force to be reckoned with. I skirted the vehicle and punched in the access code to the door, every part of me wary, my focus homed in on the man standing behind me as I pulled back the slab of steel and stepped to one side, making way for him.

"We're going all the way up," I said.

"Of course we are." He prowled inside. I was following right behind him when the cell in my back pocket began to buzz. I drew out the device and was seconds away from hitting the 'decline call' button when I saw the image on the screen: Bugs Bunny, holding a half-gnawed carrot up to his grinning mouth as if it were a cigar.

"Take it if you need to. Loony Tunes characters get a little crazy when you ignore them," Zeth jibed.

"Yeah. And this particular rabbit's already fucking insane as it is." I exhaled a hard, displeased sigh down my nose. "Wait for me at the very top floor. I won't be a second."

Zeth's boots made light scraping, scuffing sounds as he climbed ahead without me, the black duffel bag he was carrying in his right hand swinging as he reached the top of the first flight and turned the corner, disappearing out of sight.

I clenched my jaw, stabbing at the green 'accept call' button, and then I held the cell to my ear. "What is it?" I snarled.

Rabbit's irritatingly smug voice buzzed against my ear drum. "That's no way to greet a friend."

"We're not—" I stopped myself, biting back the words. Some-where along the road, Rabbit had gotten it into his head that we were going to be best pals. More than anything, I wanted to burst the guy's bubble, but that would be counterproductive. Once he had the thumb drive and he'd told us who Carver hired to pick up Sera's job, I'd be putting him over my knee and tanning his ass like the little punk ass piece of shit that he was. Until then, I had to play nice.

"As I'm sure you can imagine, it's been a really long night, Rabbit. How can I help you?" It almost caused me physical pain to be polite. He had no idea the trouble he'd caused over at The Barrows. He could have just accepted the money and kept things neat and tidy, but no. He'd had to fuck with me and make absurd demands. See, this was the problem with love. It weakened a man. Made him vulnerable. Had him agreeing to stupid requests he would otherwise normally have laughed at.

"Just wanted to make sure you'd survived the night," Rabbit mused. "Heard reports that there was some crazy shit going down at The Barrows. Apparently, someone riled Oscar Finch so bad, he personally shoved two of his best body guards off the roof. Brothers, I think."

I almost snorted. Oscar *had* been boiling mad when Zeth and I walked away from the rooftop like we owned the damn place. No one had been standing watch by the front door—I'd made a mental note of that when we'd jogged across the road and jumped into the Camaro. Sounded like Falco and Foster had borne the brunt of Finch's notorious wrath. I allowed myself the brief luxury of wondering if their heads had exploded like watermelons as they'd hit the sidewalk. Served 'em right, the bastards.

"I'm just fine. Thanks for checking in," I drawled. The truth was even the roots of my hair were aching, and every time I tried to draw in a deep breath, it felt like someone was stabbing a rusty screwdriver between my ribs, but I wasn't going to tell fucking Rabbit that. As far as he was concerned, I hadn't even broken a sweat while obtaining the thumb drive, and it was staying that way.

"Glad to hear it." There was a repetitive sound in the background, as if Rabbit was clicking a pen. "So, where are you? What are you doing right now?"

I scowled. The kid was like a needy fucking girlfriend. "I'm home. I actually just found out about this revolutionary thing called sleep. Heard of it? I thought I might try it out for a couple of hours, see what happened."

Rabbit's high-pitched, unbalanced rattle of laughter set my teeth on edge. "Ah, yeah. Sleep. I wouldn't recommend it. You know what happens when men sleep, Fix? The world has this annoying habit of continuing to spin on its axis, hurtling around the sun with complete disregard for the fact that us dreamers are no longer paying any attention. Problems develop. Assassins find their marks. People end up getting killed..."

My hand tightened around the cell. "What are you saying? Is Carver's guy close?" I'd figured I'd trade off the drive for the information later in the afternoon, once I'd had time to check in with Sera and make sure she was okay. Weirdly, Rabbit hadn't even asked about the drive. He'd held up his end of the bargain, though. He knew something about Carver. He wouldn't bait me with such poorly veiled comments, otherwise.

"Yeah. I'd say Carver's guy's a lot closer than you think," Rabbit said, his tone a little too high pitched. "I heard you made yourself a friend at the fights last night? Someone...from out of town?"

A powerful, bleak wave of fear slammed into me, pushing against my chest, refusing to let me breathe.

Oh god.

Oh my fucking god.

Was he serious? He sounded fucking serious.

My head whipped around, my eyes moving up the stairs after Zeth. After the man I'd just allowed access into the Eddison Gas and Electrical Works. Who wouldn't have been able to get in here otherwise. No. No fucking way...

My heart stood still, but I did not.

I dropped the phone.

I didn't hear it hit the ground.

I didn't hear my own ragged breath as I threw myself up the stairs after him.

I didn't hear a thing, because it was too late.

My ears were ringing with the sound of shotgun a blast.

45

FIX

M4

She was dead. She was fucking dead, and I'd just let it fucking happen. As I raced upward, around and around, taking the stairs four at a time, my head was turning itself inside out. How was I going to face the sight of her lying on the floor, arms and legs at strange angles, those beautiful eyes of hers staring blankly into nothingness? It was going to break me. Kill me. The universe would cease to exist. Everything would end. Only one thing would matter: my need to exact revenge upon the man who had snatched the sun right out of the sky and blown it out as if it were nothing more than a candle flame.

I could barely see straight as I barreled up the last flight of steps, my throat swelling closed as I raced toward the open door to the penthouse. And then, inside...

I stopped dead.

What...the...*fuck*?

My imagination had painted a horrific picture of Sera's death. It could never have conjured up the image that faced me instead. Sera wasn't lying dead on the floor after all. She was standing in the middle of the living room with my M4 butted up against her shoul-

der, and she was pointing the business end right between Zeth
Mayfair's eyes.

"Aim was a little off with that first shot," she said calmly. "I won't
miss again, though." Her gaze flickered to the right, toward me.
"Jesus, Fix. Are you okay? You look like you're about to drop
down dead."

What in the actual fuck was going on? I'd thought the back of her
skull had just been blown out, but *she* was the one who'd fired the
gun? I glanced around, disbelief slapping me in the face when I saw
the huge, smoking hole in the wall behind me, a foot to the left of the
front door. She must have barely missed his head.

Zeth slowly turned and faced me, holding his hand out in front of
him so I could see them. He should have been afraid, but he wasn't.
His dark eyes were alive with what looked like intrigue. "Wanna call
off your body guard?" he asked.

I squared my shoulders, then strode across the room, slamming
my hands into his chest and grabbing the fucker by the shirt. "You're
not from New York," I snapped, shoving my face into his. "Where did
you come from? And why?"

He didn't flinch. "I came from Seattle. I'm here because my boss
told me to come."

Seattle? Well that was no fucking coincidence. No way in hell a
guy like Zeth, a guy from Seattle, the city where Sera lived, would just
suddenly appear in New York. Not for a goddamn thumb drive. There
was no such thing as chance. If there was one thing I'd learned over
the years, putting people down, cleaning up other people's messes, it
was that everything happened for a reason.

"*Why?*" I pushed him, slamming his back into the wall. It had to
have hurt. Zeth blew down his nose—a wild animal, outraged by the
fact that it had been cornered.

"You already know why," he said sharply. He locked eyes with me,
and I saw into the bottomless depths of his soul. He was a raging
tempest, but then again...so was I. I pulled my arm back, then drove a
savage right hook at his head, intent on forcing my entire fist through
both his skull and the wall behind it. He wasn't having her. He wasn't

fucking taking her life. If he thought for one second that I'd allow him to even disturb a—

A hand clamped around my arm, pulling me away. The force of her grip was nowhere near enough to hold me back, not even close, but her touch alone stopped me in my tracks. I'd *never* risk hurting her. Sera adjusted the assault rifle, hitching it up so she had a better purchase on it. "Brawling isn't going to solve this," she hissed. "You're bleeding everywhere. If he's..." She risked a sidelong glance in Zeth's direction. "If *he's* the one Carver sent, we should just hand him over to the cops. They might be able to find out who paid him. They can arrest Carver and we can fucking move on with our lives."

Zeth began to laugh. In his position, I'd have done the same thing. He rocked his head back, resting it against the wall. "Your boyfriend isn't gonna hand me over to the cops. He's a stone-cold killer. And even if he wasn't, he knows better than to think they'll do anything about this. They'll let me go inside of an hour. I'll be gone. You'll never see me again. Until I'm slitting your throat in your bed," he added. Turning his attention to me, he flared his nostrils, his mouth forming a tight smile. "If I were you, I'd let your girl press that thing up against my head and pull the trigger. Be the easiest way to solve this."

It would. It really would. Sera had tried to do it moments before I charged into the penthouse, too, so it wasn't as if she wasn't capable, but...

If Zeth died, Carver would just send someone else, and someone else, and someone else after that, and Mayfair fucking knew it. There was only one way to end this permanently, and that was to convince Carver that Sera had been taken care of. At least that way, we'd buy ourselves some time. We'd be able to find out who Carver was and where. Then I could roll up on him in the middle of the night and peel his fucking flesh from his goddamn body.

Zeth's eyes flashed as he nodded at me—the motherfucker knew what I was thinking, and he'd already realized I wasn't going to kill him. I closed my hand around his neck, and the man did absolutely nothing to stop me.

428 | CALLIE HART

"Let's start with your boss, shall we?" I growled. "Give me a name."

Zeth didn't hesitate. "I work for a very angry, very mad Englishman. Goes by the name of Charlie Holsan. And whoever this Carver guy is, he paid Charlie directly. I don't have a fucking clue who he is, so I wouldn't waste your breath trying to beat it out of me. It won't get you anywhere. Trust me."

I'd already made the mistake of trusting this asshole and it hadn't ended well. I tightened my grip around his throat. "Did you even need the thumb drive?"

Slowly, Zeth shook his head. "Your little hacker friend told me where you'd be tonight. He's quite the double agent. All bent out of shape about you not meeting him for coffee or some shit."

Sera took a step back, clearing her throat. "Oh my god. I don't know what's going on, but I swear I'm going to kill Rabbit myself."

Ha. She was a fucking spitfire when she was riled. My beautiful, fearless, brave Angel. She'd kill Rabbit, I had no doubt, but I wasn't going to let her. Selfishly, I wanted the honor of that task all to myself, and I didn't plan on sharing. I was going to relish every last second as I destroyed Rabbit piece by piece. He was going to suffer for fucking with me like this, and I didn't care what it did to me. I'd give away the very last gentle, good part of my tattered soul if it meant he paid for endangering Sera's life. He'd known Zeth would come back here with me. He'd known all too well that Zeth would never make it inside the Gas and Electrical Works unless I let him in. So he'd orchestrated this entire night—the fight at The Barrows; Zeth and I having to work together; having to leave together once we'd taken the thumb drive. He'd already planned all of this out as he'd sat in that booth and smiled congenially at Sera, complimenting her on how beautiful she looked.

He was scum. He was a lying, backstabbing fucking monster. But most importantly, he was *so* fucking dead.

"So. Where we going from here?" Zeth asked. He didn't seem remotely bothered by the fact that I had him by the neck. Honestly, we were so evenly matched, he probably could have broken free. He could have tackled me, and we would have found ourselves locked in another fight, trading blow for blow until one of us eventually fucked up and the other took advantage. But he was obviously good at reading people, just like I was, and he'd made a firm judgment where Sera was concerned. He'd taken her measure. He knew she'd fucking shoot him if he so much as sneezed right now, and he was biding his time, waiting to see what would happen.

"*We* don't go anywhere," I snapped. "We're going to figure out our next move, and you...you're going in the bathtub."

A cold, hard light burned in Zeth's pupils. "Better tie me up good, Priest. I'm not known for being a well behaved captive."

"Don't worry. I got you covered." I flashed my teeth at him. "I learned all of my knots at motherfucking church camp."

46

SERA

GUILT

It was two in the afternoon and Fix was making grilled cheese sandwiches in the kitchen. I'd fired an M4 assault rifle just a couple of hours ago, and there was a hitman trussed up in the clawfoot bathtub two rooms away. All in all, it was a perfectly normal Saturday.

Fix faced the stove, his back to me, wearing just his jeans. He'd kicked off his shoes and pulled his shirt over his head the moment he'd walked out of the bathroom, slamming the door closed on the huge, dark-haired guy who'd shown up here to murder me. If I hadn't had that rifle in my hands...

I shivered out of the thought, unwilling to even consider what would have happened.

Fix was angry. I could feel it radiating off him like waves of heat boiling off a stretch of blacktop on a summer's day, and every time I thought about going to him, speaking to him, those waves of anger seemed to intensify to searing levels. He wanted to be alone, I knew it, but every time I tried to slink off back into the living room, he came and took me by the hand, firmly leading me back into the kitchen. He was still covered in blood. His torso was streaked with it, his skin marred with countless cuts and scrapes, and the bruises... fuck, the bruises were beginning to deepen, developing into dark, malevolent stains beneath his skin. It was a miracle he was still standing, and yet somehow he was stomping around the kitchen like a man possessed. His hair was falling into his face, and his brows were banked into one dark, furious straight line, his jaw clenched and set. There was a deep cut underneath his left eye, and his bottom lip was split, but neither appeared to be causing him distress.

His eyes had been swollen and puffy when he'd rushed into the penthouse, but amazingly the swelling was now almost gone. It was as if he'd bullied his body into submission, refusing to allow himself to be hurt through sheer force of will alone.

He slashed at the bread with a butter-loaded knife, greasing it before he thrust it into the hot frying pan.

"I'm sorry about the wall," I said. "You don't need to worry about it. I'll get it fixed."

"I'm not worried about the fucking wall."

"Then I'm sorry about...shit, I'm sorry about *everything*. I'm sorry I brought this crazy bullshit to your doorstep. I'm sorry you had to deal with Rabbit. I'm sorry you have a guy tied up in your bathroom. I'm sorry I—"

I stopped short, my head jerking back as I realized what was happening. What the *fuck*? What was I doing? I was *apologizing*? No. No, no, no. Just hell *no*.

"You know what? None of this would actually be happening if you hadn't agreed to take money from someone to fucking kill me. You wouldn't be dealing with the inconvenience of having to protect me at all if you hadn't accepted forty thousand dollars from a complete stranger in return for ending my life." My cheeks were on fire, flames licking up the skin of my throat. *He* was in a shitty mood with *me*? What the fuck was *wrong* with him?

Without turning around, Fix said, "Twenty thousand."

"Excuse me?"

"I only got paid twenty grand. We take half up front and then the other half once the job is done. So, I only took twenty thousand dollars to kill you."

I let my mouth hang open. "Oh, well *that* changes everything."

Fix stopped what he was doing. The spatula he'd been holding in his hand clattered on the countertop as Fix leaned forward, palms planted on the granite work, and he braced himself. "You're right," he said quietly. "You shouldn't be apologizing to me. You've done nothing wrong."

"So why are you acting like this? Why the fuck are you so damned pissed at me?" I hated that my eyes were stinging. My throat was aching, too. I did not want to be on the verge of tears. I'd been strong so far. I'd withstood so much over the past few weeks. Hell, I'd withstood so much over my entire fucking life, that raising my chin, looking trouble dead in the eye and facing it without balking had become second nature to me.

An ever-present exhaustion tugged at me, though. Relentless, it was constantly demanding that I just lay down and give up. How much easier would it be to simply crumble when things got tough? I knew women who burst into tears when their coffee makers quit working, or they broke a fucking nail. I was nothing like that, but today? Today was really taking the cake. And the guy I'd come to lean on, who I'd secretly allowed myself to believe would be a form of support for me, was now treating me like I'd fucked up his entire year.

Glacially slowly, Fix straightened, pivoting to face me. His expression was a mirror of the weather outside—thunderous, dark and ominous. "I'm not mad at you, Sera. I'm mad at myself."

"Why? You dealt with that guy. You figured out a way to buy us some more time. Things are way better than they were this time yesterday."

His pale silver irises seemed to glow as he stalked toward me. He looked like he was going to eat me alive.

Fuck.

"I brought him back here," he whispered. "I let him inside the fucking building, Sera. I nearly got you killed. Things are *not* better than they were this time yesterday. Yesterday, I hadn't dropped the ball so fucking unbelievably that I nearly cost us everything." When he stopped in front of me, he lifted his hand, touching his fingertips to the waves of hair that fell about my face. His smile was a jagged, mirthless slash that marred his handsome features. "I'm furious with *myself*, not you, Sera. You have no idea... You have no idea what it would have done to me if he'd fucking killed you."

His voice was thick with emotion. Fix was like a dark, glittering diamond; there were so many facets to him, a thousand different aspects, many of which I was still yet to learn. I could spend the rest of my life with him and I'd still discover something new about him every day, I was certain of this. But the very core of him, at the very center of that compounded, brilliantly impenetrable wall he'd formed around himself, there stood one solid, undeniably irrefutable truth that I already knew without a shadow of a doubt: he was a protector.

That might have seemed contradictory, given what he did for a living, but everything Fix did he did for a reason. Franz, back in Liberty Fields, had kidnapped and raped a girl so brutally she nearly died. The very first guy Fix killed in New York had attacked and murdered a defenseless little boy. Right now, he was furious with himself because he cared about me, he'd assumed the role of my protector, and he felt like he had failed me.

"Accountability's a strange thing, Fix. We dread it more than anything else, but we're all so eager to heap it upon ourselves for no fucking reason. Zeth isn't your fault. None of this is really your fault. You don't need to feel guilty."

He gave me a lopsided, sad smile. "I know about guilt. This is *not* guilt." He fastened a loop of my hair around his finger, his eyes shining brightly, beautifully, as he considered it. "This is *fear*, Angel. Bottomless, terrifying, soul-shaking fear. Without you..."

"You'd be just fine. Life would return to normal. You'd accept jobs. Complete them. Move on. You'd find a pretty girl to sleep with every once in a while. Things would be easier. They'd be simple."

"Simple doesn't always mean better."

"For you it would."

He watched me. I counted each of his breaths and the seconds between them. God, he was so fucking spectacular. Completely *other*. So strange, and exciting, and different. I was a firm believer in evolution. I'd never questioned the science of evolution before, but now I kept stumbling across holes in the theory. There was no way Fix had evolved alongside other men like Gareth. Yes, he was human. He was tall, but not abnormally so. He was in possession of the correct number of arms and legs. He was officially a member of the Homo Sapien family, but there was more to him than that. The unearthly feeling that settled over me whenever he studied me in that intense, penetrating manner of his, and the way his eyes seem to dance and spark with understanding and comprehension, even though I often hadn't even opened my mouth—it all made him appear to be so much *more* than human. As if he lived on a higher plane of existence. One that ran parallel to the everyday reality I occupied, and he could see and feel everything I could see and feel, but he was privy to far more from his lofty vantage point over the world.

"Nothing will ever be simple after you, Sera." Unraveling my hair from around his finger, he reached down and took my hand. Thoughtfully, he turned it over and began to trace the lines of my palm. "I'm unwilling to even think about what my life would look like if you decided to turn around and walk away from me."

"You don't need to think about it. It's not going to happen. But if it did," I said, arching an eyebrow at him. "Then you're supposed to tell me you'd never want anyone else. That you wouldn't even *consider* sleeping with another woman."

"My, my. Are you getting a little possessive over my dick, Sera Lafferty?"

"Of course not. It just...*belongs* to me." I tried valiantly to keep a straight face.

Fix lit me up with those devastating silvery eyes of his. I was locked onto his mouth, watching his full lips form the words, when he said, "My dick's like a Porsche, Sera. You just bought it. Paid an insane amount for it. But you've been sitting in the passenger's seat, afraid to get behind the wheel. You've been letting *me* drive it ever since we met. I think it's about time you took control, don't you? See what this thing can really do."

Flushed with heat, heart somersaulting, my pulse galloping, I opened my mouth...and realized I had no clue what to say to that.

Fix hummed. He placed his hands either side of me, trapping me between his arms. "You're blushing."

"Thanks for the notification."

"You're throwing off enough heat to give me sunburn."

"Heat doesn't give people sunburn."

"Touché. I suppose my flawless complexion is safe, then." He rocked his head back and ran his tongue over his teeth, considering me. "You're fucking beautiful, Sera."

"Even when I'm beet red?"

"Yes. Especially then."

He leaned forward, pressing his hips against mine, and I stifled a knowing laugh. "Wow. Really? I cannot believe you're turned on right now."

"What can I say? Tying guys up and dumping them in my bathtub really gets my dick hard." His mood had very plainly shifted from angry to teasing—and teasing me was one of his favorite things to do. It *wasn't* the fact that we were holding someone captive in his bathroom that was turning him on. It was the fact that I'd just told him I owned his dick. And he wasn't going to let me get away with not proving it.

I moved my hand down and placed my palm against him through his jeans. Fix's nostrils flared, the muscles in his jaw popped as he clenched his jaw. I almost crowed with victory as I tightened my grip around his cock and his eyes almost rolled back into his head.

"Should I be making some sort of joke about your stick shift?" I whispered.

"Only if you want me to make one about my engines revving."

"Yeah, let's skip the jokes. How about I just do this..." I unfastened his fly, slowly unzipping his pants. I placed my palm against the washboard, taut flatness of his stomach, trying not to hold my breath like a lovestruck teenager as I began to slide my hand down the front of his boxers. I grasped him firmly, and Fix's head dropped, hanging down, his shoulders tensing as I worked my hand up and down his shaft.

He'd tormented me so many times. Propelled me to the point of insanity with his featherlight touch. It was time for some mother-fucking payback. Swiftly, I moved, spinning us around, so that his back was pressed up against the kitchen counter.

"I don't want to hear a peep out of you," I whispered into his ear. "For the next thirty minutes, you're my plaything. You do what you're told, or I'm going to punish you."

His body seemed to be vibrating with anticipation as he leaned back against the wall, raising his hands in the air. His eyes were burning white fire. "Have the thirty minutes started yet? Beca—"

I pushed myself up onto my tiptoes and I fastened his lower lip—his *split* lip—into my mouth, biting down and pulling hard.

"Argh! *Fuck!*"

I released him. He pressed the back of his hand to his mouth, and when he drew it away, his skin was marked with his blood. The dark look he shot me said a thousand words. Most of them were expletives, but the others were something along the lines of, *'I'm impressed. You're really not fucking around.'*

I fired back a look of my own. *'I know. Now don't let that smart mouth of yours get you in trouble again.'*

Fix shuddered as I tightened my hold around his cock, and a shot of adrenalin fizzed in my blood. This was going to be interesting. His skin was like velvet, the rigid muscle underneath smooth and hard. Working my hand up and down the length of him, I used one hand to reach around my back and undo my bra strap. I only had to release him for quick second as I stripped out of both my shirt and my bra at the same time, but by the look on Fix's face made it seem as though the lack of contact had been far, far too long.

He glanced down at my chest, the hunger in his eyes a living, breathing thing. Instead of pushing my hand back down beneath his boxers, I slowly lowered myself to my knees and pulled his jeans down in one swift movement.

"Put your palms flat against the wall," I ordered.

He did as he was told.

"You're going to want to bury your hands in my hair. You're gonna want to hold my head. You're going to want to touch my breasts. But if you so much as even lift one finger, Mr. Marcosa, you're going to regret it." From my vantage point, kneeling in front of him, Felix looked like some kind of monolith, made out of muscle and smooth, perfectly tanned skin. He was magnificent, and right now, he was my fucking slave.

My pulse racing, I finally looked down at his erect cock, and my own lust threatened to overcome me. I nearly begged him to take back the reins, to spread me out on the kitchen floor and fuck me right here and now. I pinched the end of my tongue between my teeth and held it there until the moment passed. When I knew I was in complete control of myself, I licked my lips and pressed them against the very tip of him.

He was sweet, and salt, and smooth, and hard, and addicting. As I wrapped my mouth around him, I could tell how badly he wanted to use his hands on me. His legs were twitching like crazy. The man with the silver eyes also had a silver tongue; the fact that I'd forbidden him from speaking was probably killing him. He'd have a thousand sarcastic or witty digs, ready and begging to be used, but not being able to open his mouth, not being able to touch me...

He'd made a big deal of giving me control, but how long could he realistically keep this up? How far could I push him before he snatched back the reins and taught me a lesson for torturing him so mercilessly?

I had to make the most of the situation while I could.

I steadied myself, my right hand resting on his tensed thigh, and then I put my other hand to good use. Fix flexed, his body locking up as I cupped his balls. He responded to my touch immediately, and in a way I wasn't expecting. He made fists out of his hands and slammed them into the wall behind him, releasing a strained, jagged groan that echoed around the kitchen.

"Fuuuuuuu—" He didn't complete the curse word. He cut himself off when I dug my fingernails into his leg.

"Careful, now. That came pretty close to an actual word," I purred.

He blew a hard stream of air down his nose, his eyes glimmering with a dangerous level of frustration. He'd challenged me to assume this role, though. He was going to have to deal with it for a little while longer at least.

I placed my mouth over him again, moaning at the back of my throat when I felt him swell and harden even further. Holy fuck, he hadn't been kidding. He really did have a Porsche for a dick. Performing blow jobs on past boyfriends had been uninspiring and underwhelming. Much like going for a joyride in a nineteen ninety Chrysler Lebaron. But having Fix's dick in my mouth for want of a better word, exhilarating.

He grew tenser by the second. If his shoulders and his legs and his stomach muscles continued to tighten like this every time I swept my tongue over the tip of his cock, or I pushed my mouth all the way down his shaft, he was going to fucking pull something.

He couldn't take much more of this.

I couldn't take much more of it, either.

If I continued, I was going to make him come. That would turn me on to the point of distraction, but I was being greedy tonight. I wanted him. I wanted to feel him pulse and throb as he fucking came inside me.

I stopped, getting to my feet, and Fix nearly lost his mind. He was more than frustrated now; he was exasperated, and he wanted to claim me. It was tough fucking luck.

He'd already been shirtless before we'd started out on this little adventure. I took a step back so I could kick out of my jeans, daring him to break my rules as I then shimmied out of my panties and tossed them to one side. "On your back," I told him. "I want you laid out, bare and ready for me."

There was nothing like watching Felix Marcosa simmer as he obeyed a command. It would have been the stuff of legends, but I doubted anybody else had actually ever witnessed it before. He laid down, his dark hair falling about his head in a halo, and I stood back and inspected him—the ripped cut of his abs, the defined line of his pecs, his collar bone, and his traps. Then, further down, the cut vee of his groin that lead down between his legs. He was still hard, rock solid, his erection resting heavily on his belly.

He fidgeted, his fingers curving, digging into the tile beneath him. He was fighting with himself, battling to stay in command of himself...and it looked like he was losing. I threw back my shoulders, lifting my chin, and I stepped over his body, so I was straddling him.

"I'm going to fuck you," I informed him. "And if you're a very good boy, I might just let you come when I'm done with you."

A languorous, downright immoral smile spread across his face. I didn't need his words to tell me what *that* meant. He was going to make me pay for this. He would let me have my fun, but when it was his turn to take back control, he was going to keep me panting and moaning until I fucking wept. And it would all be *so* worth it.

I took him in my hand, guiding him to where I needed him to be. The moment I slid down onto him, Fix's wicked smile disappeared. He locked his jaw, the tendons in his neck bulging as he groaned, his hands curling into fists all over again.

He might not have touched me once yet, but I was more than ready for him. I stretched to take him, his size still enough to make my breath catch in my throat. Fuck, he felt so fucking good. Sitting back, I started to rock, angling my hips, and Fix snarled. I shot him a warning look, then sucked my bottom lip into my mouth, cupping my breasts in my own hands.

My nipples were so sensitive. Peaked and swollen. It felt so fucking good to roll them between my finge—

Fuck!

I was moving. Being hurled through the air.

I let out a scream, and strong, powerful hands caught me just before I hit the ground.

Fix was on top of me, out of nowhere, his mouth crashing down on mine. He shoved my legs apart and settled himself between them, thrusting himself inside me. I couldn't tell which was more savage—

his searing, demanding kiss, or the way he sank himself inside me with such desperate need.

""You ask too much, Angel," he growled in a ragged voice. "I can take a lot of things, but...you can't fucking touch yourself while you fuck me. I can't take that."

I could have stopped him. He'd earned himself some *serious* punishment for this kind of insolence, but I was too stunned by the feeling of his skin on mine, and the way his lips had scorched at my mouth.

"*Fuck*," he groaned. "The moment you slid your pussy down onto my dick, I was a fucking goner. Now I'm going to have to make you scream or I'm going to fucking snap."

His hands were all over me, his fingers gouging into my skin to the point of being painful, but I'd already given myself over to him. He was truly an evil mastermind. He knew there would be no recourse for his actions, because I needed him so fucking badly.

He rocked his hips forward, and I gasped.

"You can take me. Don't worry, Angel. I'm not going to ruin that tight little pussy."

When I'd realized he wasn't going to hold up his end of the bargain, I'd counted on him taking a little longer to cave. But, honestly, I wasn't all that upset that I'd had the keys to the Porsche taken away from me. He sweetened the blow; using a combination of his fingers, and his tongue and his dick, Fix coaxed two mind-bending orgasms out of me.

The third and final time, he came right along with me, and I found myself marveling at the sight of him as he threw his head back and cursed like the sun and the moon had just collided.

47

ZETH

CLAWFOOT

I'd killed people for less than this.

I'd stabbed a guy in the armpit for giving me side-eye in a gas station once. I had been nicer than I should have. Could have shoved the shank into his groin and let him bleed out that way. Would have been pretty fucking quick. Messy, though. Nasty. Wouldn't have been a clean getaway for me. But you know what? You gave me attitude, you reaped the rewards. It was that simple. Fix had given me *nothing* but attitude. Most guys laid eyes on me and they knew what was good for them; they laid down and died, or they walked the fuck away.

This Fix guy had slapped restraints on me and shoved me into a copper bathtub. Did I care that he'd thrown a clean towel at me, and that I'd been using it to cushion my neck? Fuck no. Did I care that I knew I was getting out of here within the next twenty-four hours, give or take a minute or two? Uhhh, that would be a hard no. Felix Marcosa had taken some epic goddamn liberties, and my patience was nowhere near as long as my dick. By the time I unfolded myself out of this bath, there was going to be fucking hell to pay. And guess what? The Prince of the Damned didn't accept Visa or a Diners fucking Club Card, and a Mastercard wasn't gonna get the ex-priest anywhere, either. Fix was screwed.

Officially.

Inevitably.

Unequivocally.

So *fucking screwed.*

I would have laughed if my own thumb knuckle wasn't digging me in the left ass cheek. I'd seen the pathetic, desperate light in his eyes back there in The Barrows; he was in love with the woman, this Sera chick. I almost felt sorry for the poor bastard. Women were wonderful, wonderful creatures, but boy did they complicate the fuck out of things.

The tap dripped on my foot—one large, offensive water droplet after the other. A loud, rhythmic banging started up in the apartment, two rooms away if my calculations were correct. Unmistakable banging sounds. The sound of a guy pile-driving his dick into a pussy. Un-fucking-believable.

They were out there, hooking up, and I was tied up in a fucking bathtub. Originally, I'd planned a little get-together at my place back in Seattle for this weekend. Would have been fucking perfect. A sea of naked, writhing bodies, tangled together, mouths on mouths, hands on skin, so many exquisite bodies on display. I would have had my choice of any of them, but no. I was stuck in fucking New York, one of my least favorite fucking places on earth, tied up in a bathtub while two other people got to fuck each other's brains out within hearing distance. Least they could have done was fuck in front of me or something. I could have enjoyed the sensation of my dick getting hard, even if I wasn't able to touch it.

And they didn't just get the job done and move on with their day. Fix made sure his girl was screaming his name for a good forty minutes before he finally let her come. Hats off to the guy for that, at least. Afterwards, silence fell over the apartment, and I got fucking bored and made a point of falling asleep. The nightmares that plagued me whenever I passed out were goddamn brutal, but still, I could sleep through a fucking hurricane if I wanted to. A neat trick

I'd picked up in prison. It was simple: you either learned to accept physical discomfort, screaming, shouting, and the constant possibility that you were going to get your throat cut while you were unconscious, or you never got any fucking rest.

It amused me greatly when I woke to find a perplexed Fix standing at the end of the tub with his arms crossed over his chest some time later. It had gone dark outside, so I must have been out cold for a while. With sharp, accusing, unnervingly pale eyes narrowed at me, the priest huffed out a sharp breath. "Sweet dreams, princess?"

"Yeah. Thanks for asking. I was fucking your mom."

He didn't skip a beat. "So you like fucking dead people. Stands to reason. Necrophilia's probably the only way you can get laid."

I let the dig slide. "Mmm. I was wondering why she was such a lousy lay. Very unenthusiastic. All makes sense now. Did your father quit fucking her when he became a priest? How'd that even work?"

A flicker of emotion chased across Fix's face—a mixture of anger and expertly concealed pain. Maybe other people didn't see through the façade, but I knew what that kind of pain looked like. I'd had plenty of experience with people shielding their flaws, their faults and their weaknesses over the years, that he might as well have been screaming it from the rooftops. I almost yawned out of disappointment. He was fucking predictable, just like everyone else. He had issues with his parents. Boo fucking hoo. I'd been hoping for something a little more *complex* from him.

"I have no idea," Fix said lightly. "I wasn't very concerned about where my father stuck his cock. I was more worried about getting my own dick sucked at the time."

"Aaaand why is it that I don't believe you? A good little boy like you doesn't follow in Daddy's righteous footsteps if he's chasing pussy every night of the week."

He did a better job of hiding his thoughts this time. His face was a blank mask. My lip curled up to one side as I watched him lean forward and stick his hand inside the bath.

"Plenty of room for two in here," I jabbed. "If that's what you're into. I heard you fucking like a pair of teenagers before. Didn't your pretty little girlfriend get the job done? With a mouth like that, I assumed she'd—"

"I'd stop talking right fucking now if I were you." His words were laden with ice. Dead, cold, unfeeling words. The kind of words that came out of my mouth all the time. He fiddled with something for a second, and then he straightened, placing a hand on the cold water tap. He cranked it all the way to the left. Water roared out of the faucet, drenching my socked feet first, then quickly pooling in the bottom of the tub, hitting my thighs, my ass, my back. It was fucking freezing.

I didn't say a word.

Fix stood, detached gaze scanning over me, and I imagined what was taking place inside his head. It was so, so easy to imagine, too, because I'd watching him recede into that dark, quiet place—the same dark, still, quiet place I withdrew into whenever I was about to do something seriously fucked up. He was going to fill the tub up with cold water, dump a couple of bags of ice in here with me, and then he was going to leave me for a couple of hours. Let me freeze for a while. Nothing made a person more malleable than a brutal case of hypothermia.

Or maybe he was going to try and waterboard me. Cover my face with a cloth, hold a funnel over my mouth, and start pouring. Being stuck in a full bathtub would make the process even shittier for me, but it would make *his* life easier. Plenty of precious H_2O on hand to partially drown me with, until I gave him whatever it was he wanted.

Of course, he could just be planning on straight up drowning me. My hands were trussed behind my back, and my ankles were bound so tight I couldn't even feel my toes anymore. If he'd left it at that, I would have been able to launch myself out of the fucking tub and free myself pretty easily, even if it meant dislocating a shoulder, but no. The fucker had been far too smart for that. He'd connected my restraints together behind my back via a rigid, thick piece of reinforced steel cabling. I'd already nearly flayed the skin from my wrists trying to wrestle myself free, and I hadn't gotten anywhere. So, I was stuck in the fucking bath, and I was about to die. However Fix decided to end me, it wasn't going to be fucking pleasant.

I watched him with detached curiosity as he paced to a cupboard on the other side of the bathroom, opened it up and began pulling clean towels out of it and dumping them unceremoniously onto the floor.

This day had been coming for a very long time. You didn't do what I did for a living, or work for the kind of man I worked for, without expecting to die a horrible, painful, terrible death at some point in the future yourself. I'd wondered often enough how it was going to happen and when, and now that we were here I couldn't muster any sort of emotion beyond a slight sense of annoyance as the icy water inched its way up the sides of the bath, filling the tub quicker and quicker, covering more and more of me as the surface rose.

"Back in a minute," Fix said casually. He stalked out of the bathroom, leaving the door yawning wide open. That's when I saw the girl standing in the hallway, leaning against the wall with her head resting against a framed picture of Trinity Church. The straight edge of her dark hair barely grazed the tops of her shoulders.

"Come to watch the show? I'm impressed," I ground out. "Most women wouldn't want to witness a man being tortured to death."

"I'm not most women," she replied stiffly. "I don't relish the sight of someone suffering. But I'm a pragmatist. You came here to hurt me. I need to make sure you're not going to be able to do that, which means I have to watch. I have to *see* what he does to you with my own two eyes, so I know you're not a threat anymore."

"You think that way you won't see me lurking in the shadows every time you walk down a dark alleyway?" I bit back the laughter burning at the back of my throat. "You think if you watch me die, you won't still see my face every time you're lying in bed at night and you can't get to sleep?"

A slight wrinkle formed in the center of her forehead. "Something like that."

The water continued to spew from the faucet; it had nearly filled the tub all the way to the rim. I allowed myself to feel the cold instead of shivering against it. I embraced it, letting it seep into my bones, forming shards of ice within the blood that was slowly pumping through my veins. "Then you're fooling yourself, Sera. I will be the only thing you see for a long time to come."

She shifted, moving her weight from one foot to the other. "You flatter yourself. I'm sure I'll have forgotten all about you by the time Fix drags your carcass out of this penthouse and dumps it down the garbage chute."

"Hmm." The water rose up over my shoulders, hitting the back of my neck. I tipped my head to one side, resting my temple against the side of the bath. "How long did it take you to forget that other guy's face? The guy you killed back in Montmorenci when you were sixteen?"

Her face lost what little color it had as she fidgeted, her eyes rounding, doubling in size. She pulled the sleeves of her oversized shirt down over her hands. Unnerved. Shaken.

Bingo. You're not as strong as you think you are, little girl.

Still, she didn't run away. "If you think I'll talk Fix out of this, you're wrong, asshole. You can't appeal to my conscience. You can't stop this."

Rolling my head so that I was staring up at the high ceilings above, I admired the intricate crown molding around the light fitting. "Never said anything about you stopping it. I'm just reminding you of the bad taste I'm gonna leave in your mouth. You can scrub and scrub and scrub all you like, Lady Macbeth, but this damn spot won't be coming out. At least for a while anyway. Until you've killed a bunch more people and *nothing* matters anymore."

I returned my gaze to her, peering past her caution and her hesitation. How long would it be before she picked up a gun or a knife and she used it? She'd been willing to shoot me with that assault rifle; she'd fucking tried to. It had only been her shitty aim that had saved my head from being blown off my shoulders. I didn't lift my chin to avoid the water as it finally reached the lip of the bath and began to spill over the sides. I remained still, the surface of the water lapping at my top lip as I looked at her. No, it wasn't going to be long before Sera Lafferty became the monster this Carver guy was trying to sell her as.

Not very long at all.

Fix appeared behind her, then, carrying something in his arms. Small. Cube-shaped. Black. A set of black leads with clamps attached to either end was slung over his shoulder.

Jumper cables. Jumper cables, and a brand-new car battery.

So *that* was how I was going to die: he was going to electrocute me.

Fix didn't look at me as he stepped into the bathroom, unfazed by the water that was all over the floor. He turned the tap off, movements measured and unhurried, and then he kicked at the towels he'd dumped on the floor, arranging them haphazardly around the bathtub with the toe of his boot.

"Make sure you mop up good." Opening my mouth, I let the water rush inside. I swirled it around my teeth. Swallowed. "Electricity doesn't discriminate. One little spark, one little pool of water touches your foot, and boom. You're one crispy padre."

Pulling the jumper cables from over his shoulder, Fix shot me a winning smile. Perfect white teeth. Motherfucker. "The soles on these boots are an inch thick. Rubber. I'm sure I'll be just fine. Thanks, though."

I shrugged. "Just doing my civic duty. Wouldn't want you getting hurt now." Somewhere, deep within the cavernous black space where my heart would have been located (if I'd had one) something fluttered, coughed...and then died. Nope. I really couldn't muster up a single fuck to give right now. How depressing. It wasn't as if working for Charlie was very rewarding on a day to day basis. My right hand guy, Michael, would notice if I was suddenly no longer around and I stopped sending him lists of tasks to complete and people to hurt, but apart from that...

I was hardly going to be missed. And I was okay with it.

Against my will, an image flashed into my mind: a woman with long, dark hair. Tall, with fire in her eyes. A white jacket. A stethoscope looped around the back of her neck. A heavy, stifling mantle of sadness weighing her down as she stood in front of an elevator, waiting for the doors to roll back.

Oh no. No fucking way. Not happening.

I shoved the image out of my head so fast, I left myself reeling. *She* wasn't welcome here. She had been a stupid mistake. A lapse in judgement. A moment of weakness that I was never going to revisit again, not even here, inside my own head, seconds before my death. The woman in the white jacket was trouble with a capital T, and she'd follow me into the damned afterlife if I didn't keep her out.

Fix clamped the ends of the jumper cables to the lip of the copper tub. He was methodical and intent on what he was doing, a calm resolve settled over him, giving him an eerie sense of peace as he worked. When that was done, he set the car battery down on a wooden stool that he placed at the other end of the tub by the taps, and then he held the other end of the jumper cables in either of his hands, raising them up.

"Try not to shit yourself," he growled. "You've made enough of a mess of today as it is."

I bared my teeth, snarling at him like a wild dog. I wasn't going to beg for my life. I wasn't going to plead, and he was going to show no mercy. Men like us never broke, one way or another.

"Just fucking do it," I snapped. "Do your fucking worst."

Determination, grim and lethal, flared in Fix's too-pale eyes. He connected the other ends of the jumper cables. And when the current hit, the savage roar that ripped from my throat felt like it would be my fucking last.

48

FIX

CAMP

*A*t the age of nine, my father spirited me away to church camp during summer break. It had fucking sucked, not only because all my friends from school had gone to baseball camp and I missed out on all the associated fun, but because, on the very last day of said church camp, I nearly fucking died.

Camp clean-up had been well underway. We were all supposed to be preparing for the journey home. My father had told me to get all of my shit together and to help the younger boys pack up their stuff, but it was sweltering and sticky, the air close, almost unbreathable it was so humid, and I'd decided to go swimming instead—one of the very first times I'd dared to actively disobey the great, intimidating and thoroughly imposing Father Marcosa after he'd issued a direct order.

The camp lake was long and thin, the size of four full football fields strung end to end. On our side of the lake: the Sunday meeting house; the kitchen block; eight small cabins which housed the camp attendees; and a store house where the canoes and the other sporting equipment was kept. On the opposite side of the lake: farmland, for as far as the eye could see. Dairy farms, mostly. The stench of manure had hung in the air, a thick cloud of sulphur that refused to budge, no matter how strong the breeze.

A group of boys, a couple of years older than my unimpressive nine years, had decided at the beginning of the break that swimming from one side of the lake to the other without the aid of any floatation devices was the best way to prove you were one of the cool kids. I hadn't even tried. I fucking hated swimming. Hated the water in general. One by one, though, the other kids had completed the trial, and by the second to last day, I was one of the only camp-goers who hadn't undertaken the swim.

So.

The day I disobeyed my father, stripped down to my underwear and stepped into the lake, pigeon chested, gangly limbed, knock-kneed, covered in sweat and determined, it had been my last opportunity to prove my worth. I'd paced myself, making sure not to power too hard for the line of the other shore too quickly. I'd known I needed to conserve my energy in case I got tired, so I'd doggedly plowed my arms through the water, daring every three or four strokes to duck my head below the surface into the murky green soup below.

I was fine until I reached the halfway mark, and that's when I'd begun to wonder: did I have enough energy to go as far as I had already come? My heart was thrumming inside my chest, my blood thundering in my ears. I felt okay, muscles warmed and relaxed, but panic had a way of twisting things. Very quickly, my side was cramping, my chest tight, and my head felt lighter than air. Rush after rush of adrenalin washed through me, urging my body to react, to get itself out of the uncertain situation it found itself in. Before I knew it I was floundering.

I couldn't breathe.

Couldn't keep myself afloat.

Couldn't quiet the deafening alarms screaming inside my head.

Couldn't calm the burning fear that had sunk its claws into my back and was trying to drag me down, down, down.

I'd swallowed half the lake and I was more afraid than I ever had been by the time I dragged myself, coughing and spluttering, out of the water. The exhaustion I'd felt was like nothing I'd ever experienced before. I hurt everywhere, and my lungs burned like they'd been branded from the inside by a hot poker.

Sleep claimed me.

It was dark by the time I woke up and realized to my horror that I was still on the other side of the lake with no means of getting back. And I was in my underwear. I'd heard people say the word 'fuck' before, but I'd never uttered it myself before that moment. I said it quite a few times as I trudged along the muddy shore of the lake, trying to avoid the piles of cow shit that had been deposited at the edge of the water. Cutting across the farm land, higher up, along the edge of the grassed fields soon seemed like a preferable option, and so I altered my course.

I tried not to think about what my father was going to say when I finally found my way back to camp—the punishment for this transgression would be severe to say the least—but I couldn't help it. His wrath was *all* I could think about. I wasn't paying attention, which was why I didn't notice the fence up ahead. I didn't notice it until I'd plowed right into it, and—

Fire.

I was on fire.

I was—

I couldn't—

I—

My brain had wildly shuttered on and off like a light switch being flicked up and down at speed. My thoughts were fractured, broken apart...

Made absolutely no sense.

My heart skipped and slipped and tripped and back flipped, and then...

It stuttered to a dead stop.

I didn't hear the shouting from further up the field. I didn't see the figure come charging out of the night toward me. I saw nothing, not even the darkness as it engulfed me, folding me into its soft embrace.

Later, in the tiny, ill-equipped hospital close to the camp that I'd been rushed to, my father had told me I'd stumbled right into an electric fence. I'd played chicken with my friends before, grabbing hold of charged fences to see who could hold on the longest, but I'd experienced nothing like the lightning bolt of pure power that had forced its way inside my body in that field, though. Turned out the field I'd been trudging through was home to a highly-strung bull; the farmer who owned the bull had amped up the voltage to insanely high levels—levels high enough to deter an eighteen-hundred-pound bull...and to stop a nine-year-old boy's heart dead in his chest. I wouldn't have survived if the farmer hadn't been out feeding the animals that night.

Now, at the age of thirty-seven, I still remembered both the sensation of drowning and the sensation of being electrocuted, but the experiences had somehow melded together into one, horrific event. I knew what the panic felt like as your synapses fired like crazy below the water. I knew what it felt like to be unable to move, your muscles rigid and taut, straining as your heart labored to beat.

I *knew* what Zeth Mayfair was feeling right now. I held onto the plastic grips of the jumper cables, watching smoke rise off the edge of the copper tub in my bathroom as he flailed and thrashed, his body locked up, and water sloshed out onto the floor.

I took a step back, aware of the spreading pool that was forming around the tub. Zeth had been right: the soles of my boots were rubber, but it really wouldn't take much. If a stream of water hit me, I'd be fucked.

I counted in my head.

Five...

...six...

...seven...

...eight...

My heart was the slow, rhythmic beat of a lazy metronome.

"Fix."

I looked up, almost surprised that Sera was still standing there in the doorway. Her eyes were alight with worry.

"Fix, I don't think…I don't think this is the best way. Please stop," she whispered.

Distancing myself from what I was doing often helped get the job done. Made things clinical. A series of tasks that needed completing. Sera, on the other hand, hadn't developed that skill. I prayed she didn't have to as I looked down at Mayfair, still bucking and thrashing, and I slammed back into my body, back into the reality of the situation. Ripping the jumper cables from the battery, I grimaced down at the guy in the tub, watching as his body relaxed and his head slipped below the surface of the water.

The fucker deserved to drown for what he'd been planning to do to Sera. He'd caused nothing but trouble since the second I'd laid eyes on him in The Barrows less than twenty-four hours ago. Letting the fucker drown would have been the easiest, smartest thing to do, but…

Sera had asked me to stop.

That was the end of it.

And we still needed him. A cruel voice in the back of my head insisted otherwise, that I'd be able to figure this out on my own, that we *didn't* need him, and his death was justified. That fucking voice had been niggling at me for years, trying to lead me down many a dangerous path, but I'd always managed to ignore it with relative ease. Today, though… Shit, today, that voice was practically all I could fucking hear.

Fisting the front of Zeth's t-shirt, I reluctantly dragged him upward out of the water, grabbed him by the arm, hooked him partially over my shoulder, and then I heaved him out of the tub and dumped his limp body onto the tiles at my feet. "I'm not giving him mouth to mouth," I said. "I won't kill him, but there's no way I'm fucking resuscitating him."

Sera rolled her eyes. Stepping into the room, she seemed relieved as she skirted around the tub, studying the huge form on the ground. "He doesn't need mouth to mouth. Look. He's still breathing."

"Bummer. I was hoping he'd have the decency to die anyway."

Sera nearly jumped out of her skin when Zeth's body bowed, his boots scrambling against the tiles as he regained consciousness. He drew in a strangled, gurgling breath, and then proceeded to cough and choke as he spat up a lungful of bathwater. He was pale, the blood absent from his face as he turned furious brown eyes on me.

"Thought you had more backbone," he wheezed. "Couldn't follow through, Father?"

I ignored his hacking and sputtering, along with his frustrating use of that damned name, and I crouched down beside his head. I would unfasten his restraints soon, because I had to. Because Sera would be upset with me if I didn't. In the meantime...

Zeth's eyes sparked with rage. I saw the death he was planning for me, shining out of his bottomless pupils, and it didn't look like fun. "Don't expect me to thank you for stopping," he growled.

I looked around the bathroom, sighing heavily. The place was a fucking mess. This entire situation was a fucking mess; cleaning any of it up was going to be a fucking nightmare. "I don't care if you thank me or not, asshole," I said. "If it were up to me, I would have let you die. It's Sera you should be thanking." I looked up at her, feeling the weight of her gaze on my shoulders, her judgement more precious and terrifying than my father's ever was. "I call her my angel, because she brings me back from the edge. She reminds me I'm not *entirely* lost. That there might be a way back for me, one day, when all of this bullshit is over. She spoke up for you just now. I've no idea why, but turns out she was your guardian angel today, too."

49

SERA

PROOF OF DEATH

I'd imagined how I was going to die, and it was nothing like this.

I'd always figured I'd die alone, in my bed, of a stress-related heart attack in my sixties, much earlier than I should have, and that my body wouldn't be found for days.

Lying on the cold concrete in the stairwell of the Eddison Gas and Electrical Works, my head twisted at a migraine-inducing angle, my hands bound behind my back, the rope digging into my skin so deep I knew it was going to fucking bruise, I felt as though I was somehow inviting a much more horrific end with this charade.

None of this was real, but it had to look real. That meant the restraints had to break the skin. That meant I had to bleed. That meant my body had to be tangled up and twisted in as unnatural a position as possible, and, according to *Zeth*, it meant that I had to be scared. I wasn't having any trouble with that part, at least; I really *was* scared.

The last time someone had tried to tie me up, I'd slit their throat with a blade made out of glass. I hadn't felt this vulnerable since then, and that was saying something. My troubles had far from ended the moment Sam Halloran died. No, there had been plenty more fucked up, damaging scenarios I'd had to endure after that day. Sixsmith had made sure of that.

"You okay?" Fix asked, as he finished binding my ankles together. He'd refused to let Zeth anywhere near me when he'd set him free, let alone help him. He'd given Zeth his freedom on the condition that he sent his boss, Charlie, evidence of my death, and then he leave New York immediately. Zeth had agreed, but even I'd seen the cold, wicked look in his eyes as Fix let him go. The man was not happy. Personally, I thought it was insane that Fix had released him at all, but Zeth had grudgingly given his word that he wouldn't do anything once he was free, and Fix had chosen to believe him.

"Yeah. I'm okay," I muttered. "My back feels like it's about to break in two and my hip's bruised, but I'm fine." I wasn't just lying in the stairwell of Fix's building. I was sprawled down a flight of stairs, head first, my entire body weight resting on my left shoulder and my jaw. To say I was uncomfortable was a serious fucking understatement.

"Just need a little blood and then I'll be able to get you out of here," Fix said quietly under his breath.

I hadn't even thought about that. Of course there'd be blood if I'd been shot in the back and tossed down a stairwell. But where was he going to ge—

A thick, cloying, metallic, highly unpleasant odor hit the back of my nose as Fix began to pour something over my back. "You ever see the movie, Carrie?" he asked.

"No," I answered through my teeth. "Why? Is it important?"

"Nope. Not in the slightest."

I tried not to jerk away when he began to pour a thick, viscous, almost black liquid around my head onto the steps

"That stinks. What is it?" I hissed.

"Really. You don't wanna know."

"All right. Just hurry up. I hate this." It was all a little too real for my liking. There was a chance I was going to end up this way for real, broken and bleeding, vulnerable and dying, tilted upside down as my vital lifeblood spilled out onto a flight of concrete steps. I almost laughed.

"What's so funny?" Fix brushed his hand through my hair, and stupidly I thought he was being sweet, trying to reassure me. Then I realized his hand was covered in that vile, crimson-black fluid and he was rubbing it through my hair. Charming. "It just occurred to me. If Carver doesn't buy this, we'll be right back where we started, with yet *another* mystery hitman out to hunt us down."

From the corner of my eye, I watched as a wan, almost sad smile twitched at the corner of Fix's mouth. Earlier, standing over the bathtub with those jumper cables in his hands, he'd been terrifying —a shade of the man now crouched next to me, trying to make me look convincingly dead. He'd been a different person altogether.

The words he'd said to Zeth, that he called me his angel because I brought him back to himself, reminded him he wasn't entirely lost, had been surprising. Did he really feel that way? How the hell had I managed to become such an important anchor to him, when I constantly felt like I was drifting toward ruin and destruction myself?

"I wouldn't worry about it," Fix murmured. "You're the woman no assassin could kill. One look at you and we're all fucking helpless, useless morons."

From the top of the stairs, a very bored voice said, "Speak for yourself."

Fix glowed with annoyance. "You ended up in a bathtub with twenty thousand volts flowing through you, if you'll recall."

"Didn't happen because I'm useless. That happened 'cause she pointed a fucking assault rifle at my head."

Fix's top lip curled back. I couldn't reach out to touch him—my hands were otherwise occupied, turning numb and probably blue behind my back—so I nudged his knee with the end of my nose. "You're like oil and water. And the oil is on fire, and the water is boiling. Just ignore him, get him to take the damn photo, and let's get out of here."

He grunted in response. Standing quickly, he jogged back up to the top step where Zeth was waiting and said, "You heard the girl. Take the photo and send it."

Silence flooded the stairwell. After an incredibly long minute,

Zeth's gravelly voice echoed off the walls. "Done. It might have been in your job description once upon a time, but *I* don't forgive people, Priest. And I sure as fuck don't forget. If I ever see or hear from you again, I won't leave you alive. You feel me?"

Fix didn't say a word. I knew the look he was giving the other man —a defiant, challenge-laden glare that was bound to be making things even worse. Still, Zeth didn't cause trouble. I heard the slow, scraping approach of boots on the concrete steps, and then he stepped over me. Pausing a moment, he twisted and looked down at me. "Let me give you a piece of advice for the road, little girl," he rumbled. "The man standing at the top of those stairs? There's no such thing as a *life* with him. There's excitement, there's danger, and there's adrenalin. But there isn't much of anything else."

"Is that supposed to be your ironic attempt at looking out for me, after you came here to kill me?"

Zeth huffed—maybe the suggestion of laughter. "No, not even close. If I cared, I'd probably be warning *him* away from *you*."

My cheeks burned with...with...I didn't know *what* I was feeling as Zeth Mayfair walked away. After Fix untied me and we went back up to the penthouse, I stood at the window, leaning my forehead against the glass, looking out over the sprawling city while my mind raced.

Fix hovered behind me, close enough for his scent and the warmth of his body to affect me in the most dizzying of ways, but not close enough to touch. He was a looming presence, intense and ominous, just like the storm that still warred over the skyscrapers and the flashing gunmetal grey of the river that wound like a serpent across the vista before me.

"Tell me what you're thinking, Sera."

The hairs on the back of my neck stood on end. If anyone else had demanded information from me so bluntly, I would have told them to go fuck themselves. Fix had certain privileges, though. He could command anything he liked of me, because I could do the same to him. We'd reached an equilibrium. For everything he took, I took something. For everything he gave, I gave something. Without even

trying, we'd reached this perfect balance of submission and dominance that I knew I'd never achieve with another human being.

I turned around, leaning my back against the window. "What's to
stop him? Zeth? What's to stop him from telling his boss he didn't
complete the job as soon as he gets back to Seattle? Or worse, what's
to say he's not going to wait for us to leave tonight and blow up the
damn truck?"

"He definitely isn't going to blow up the truck."

"How do you know?"

"Because I left it outside The Barrows. Oscar probably had it
torched."

"Jesus! Can you be any more infuriating? I'm looking for some
reassurance here, you jerk."

Fix ran his tongue over his bottom lip, which was split and a little
swollen. I couldn't tear my eyes from his mouth as he approached.
The color of his eyes had darkened to oxidized silver. "He won't say
anything to Charlie," he said. "He won't turn back and kill either of
us. I *know* he won't, because he and I..." He shook his head, his dark
brows drawing together. "He and I might be like oil and water, but
we're also exactly the same. He gave me his word he wouldn't touch a
hair on your head, and I know he won't. He won't break his word,
because *I* wouldn't break mine."

It made sense. Barely, but it made sense. If Fix felt strongly
enough that Zeth would honor his promise, then I was willing to put
my trust in that, at least.

"We'll wait for the rain to stop, and then we'll go," Fix told me.

Was he as sad as I was to leave the penthouse? I'd hardly spent
any real time here, to be fair, and I'd hardly had a peaceful, restful
experience at that, but...this was Fix's home. I read his personality in
each and every little touch, every book that sat dog-eared on the
shelves, and every piece of art that hung on the walls. I'd even gotten
a kick out of opening the top drawer in his chest of drawers and
seeing the numerous pairs of neatly folded socks and boxer shorts
that lay within.

Every item inside the penthouse had been picked out, chosen and put there by Fix. This was his world. Until recently, I would have fought tooth and nail to avoid finding myself here, trapped amongst his things, everything smelling of him and reminding me of him, but things were changing rapidly, faster than I would have thought possible. I wanted to see his world, to explore it and lose myself amongst it. More than that, however, I wanted to be a *part* of it. What a terrifying thought. In a weird, unexpected way, I was optimistic. If things worked out the way I hoped—with me *living*—then perhaps we could come back here, to New York. Go out for dinner in the evenings. Do touristy things. Go to museums. Visit the Empire State Building. Gawk at all the lights in Time Square. Go and see The Lion King on Broadway at Christmas.

But, shit. Christmas felt very far away. A life where we might enjoy the luxury of such simple things felt very, *very* far away. "Where are we going now?" I sighed.

"Somewhere we can breathe for a little while. Where we can figure out how all of these pieces fit together. That is...if that's what you want, Sera. I'll take you wherever you want to go."

I considered it for a moment. Could I really just go back to Seattle and pick up where I left off? Aside from the most salient question— was it even *safe* to go back?—was my old life something I even *wanted* anymore? When I'd fled Montmorenci, I'd talked myself into studying business because it had seemed like a smart, safe, reliable thing to do. I enjoyed the security of my job, and I enjoyed being my own boss, but was I really bouncing out of my bed, raring to get to my office every morning, challenged and excited by what I was doing? Fuck no.

I could sell everything. I could give it all up. But then what?

"*Sera.*" Fix said my name quietly, but the word contained a well of emotion within it. "The fact that you're having to think about this so hard says enough. Just decide where you want to be, and I'll make it happen." He about-faced and walked away, his back drawn straight, his shoulders stiff. I stood there, mouth open, not quite believing that he was bailing on the conversation. Stupid, idiotic, overly dramatic man.

"Hey! Where the hell are you going? I wasn't deciding if I wanted to be with *you*. I was trying to figure out if there was anything left for me back home, that's all."

He stopped. He wanted to turn around, I could tell, but for some reason he didn't. The tension in his shoulders grew.

"Why does that make you mad?" Exasperation colored my voice. "I thought you wanted me. I thought you wanted *us*."

"God," he whispered. "I'm not mad. I'm *relieved*, Sera. So fucking relieved. I feel like my chest is about to burst open. It's not fair of me to want this, though. I'm not proud of how fucking selfish I'm being. Better men would pretend. They'd make sure you were safe, and they would leave you the fuck alone. I'm the very worst kind of creature, the fucking worst, because I can't do that. I can't fucking let you go. I'm in love with you, Angel. And it will be the death of us both."

Oh.

Well.

Shit.

I swallowed. Hard.

If emotions could have been identified by color, I'd have been swimming in a rainbow of confusion right now. Shock. Surprise. Panic. Excitement. Elation. But mostly, I was angry. "Don't you dare tell me you love me for the first time with your back turned to me, Felix Marcosa. Don't you fucking *dare* do that to me."

His head dropped. A pained, desolate sound came out of him as he slowly turned around. My breath caught in the back of my throat when I saw his expression. He was on fire. Made of it. Consumed by it. Devoured by it and yet constructed from it at the same time. His eyes bore down deep into me as he stepped forward.

"You want to see inside me when I tell you that?" he asked. His stance was menacing, his profile stiff and uncompromising, but I could see that he wasn't doing it to frighten me. He was trying to hold himself together. His handsome face was bruised from brawling at The Barrows, and the stubble at his jaw was now the beginnings of a beard, not to mention that his dark, thick hair was wild and out of control, but somehow his unkempt, disheveled appearance made him even *more* attractive.

I stood up straighter. "Yes. I do."

"Then come here."

The four steps required to bring me in front of him were the hardest four steps I'd ever taken. I wanted to stay rooted to the spot, feet firmly planted on the ground, a safe distance from the man who had the ability to turn my world so radically upside down. He was throwing down the gauntlet, though, it was obvious. He wanted to know if I really *did* want this. He wanted to know if I could stare down the barrel of the gun, look hell right in the eye, face down the storm, climb the mountain, stand at the edge of the cliff face, and...

...leap.

I refused to look away as he fixed his blistering attention on me. The intensity of his gaze could have reduced another to cinders, but I wasn't the weak, vulnerable, frightened girl I could have easily been. I'd forced myself to face my fears head-on at an early age, and I'd never stopped. I was used to accepting my fear. I knew how to shape it, learn from it, and, eventually, overcome it. I wasn't going to back down, no matter how hard he tried to scare me with the truth.

"Say it again," I whispered.

Fix placed his hands on my hips, his eyelids lowering as he glanced down at my mouth. When he looked up, I watched, awed, as everything came crashing down. I hadn't realized how high and how thick Fix's walls were, kept in place every waking second of every waking day, in order to keep the world out...and himself *in*.

Now, those walls were gone. It was all there, plain as day for me to see. His pain, his own fear, the anger and the undeniable violence that lived inside him. His extreme need for me that bordered on obsession. But then, the deep, penetrating love that promised heady oblivion. He wanted me more than anything else on earth. He would protect me. He would care for me until he drew his last breath. All of it warred openly on his face, each aspect of him battling for supremacy over the other.

Slowly, he lifted his hands from my hips and cupped my face with them instead. "I love you, Sera. I have for a while now. I'm sorry if that frightens you." His words were a caress that ran along the length of my spine; I shivered, unable to stop myself.

"It doesn't frighten me," I whispered.

"It fucking should. This isn't a let's-date-and-see-where-life-takes-us deal, Sera. This is all or nothing. This is to the ends of the fucking earth and back. This is giving all, giving everything, total fucking surrender. Total victory, and total defeat. There is no going back from it. Not ever. So, I want you to really think this through. Really fucking understand. Don't you dare tell me you love *me* unless—"

"I do." The words were out before I could do anything, to barricade them behind my teeth. "I *do* love you."

His hands dropped to his sides, his eyes widening. He looked astonished. "Sera..."

"You're not the only one who doesn't do half measures, Fix," I said. "You don't have to be the only one who feels too much all the time. I had to feel so little for so long that I swore to myself I would never allow that to happen again. So, I'll love you as fiercely as the sun fucking burns, and you'll have to fucking like it, because you did this, Felix. You made me love you just as much as you love me, and it's never going to go away now. *I'm* never going to go away. This is it."

When his mouth met mine, his kiss branded me, down into my soul. It marked the end of anything that had come before. My shitty childhood. The fear that I'd conquered, but that had left a dirty smear on my soul. The days and nights I'd spent alone, wondering if life was ever going to catch up with me, or if death was going to find me first. All of it was brushed away with the touch of his lips and his arms crushing me to him. I'd done it. For better or for worse, we were more than just Fix and Sera, now. We were far more than that, unbreakable and indestructible, and heaven help anyone who tried to fuck with us.

Fix's chest was rock solid as he held me against him; he was the embodiment of strength and safety. He was a fortress made out of bone and muscle, and against all the odds I'd found myself a home within that fortress. He made a rumbling, vibrating sound deep in his chest as he pulled back to take me in, his quicksilver eyes evaluating and assessing.

"There's something I have to do," he said. "Something you're not going to like. I want you to come with me, though. I don't want to let you out of my sight. It's not going to be easy. Think you can handle it?"

I stole myself, taking a deep breath. If Fix said something wasn't going to be easy, then it was going to be *insanely* difficult, but I nodded anyway. "If you think I can, then I don't see why not."

His pulse hammered under his skin against my fingertips as he sighed, the muscles jumping in his clenched jaw. "I would have said no a couple of weeks ago, but you continue to surprise me, Angel. I don't think there's a thing you couldn't handle if you set your stubborn mind to it."

50

FIX

JUST GET TO THE FUCKING POINT

*C*ommitting a crime was much easier when you were accompanied by a woman. People didn't look at you with suspicion clouding their eyes. They saw what they wanted to see: a young couple in love, holding hands, walking down rain-soaked streets, whispering in each other's ears as they made their way home from a bar or a romantic dinner.

That wasn't actually too far from the truth. Sera and I had grabbed a bite to eat at the penthouse and I'd poured us a shot of tequila each—hopefully the liquor was going to calm Sera's jangling nerves—and now we *were* a love-struck couple, leaning into each other and whispering conspiratorially as we hurried our way through the streets of Brooklyn. We weren't heading home though, back to our beds, where we'd lazily make love and fall asleep in each other's arms.

We were looking for a car to boost.

I found the perfect vehicle five blocks from the Gas and Electrical Works—an average looking sedan with a scuffed bumper and tags that were in date. The Ford was at least eight years old, too, and didn't have the keyless entry most new cars were fitted out with. I popped the lock within seconds, pocketing the short length of wire and the rounded metal hook I'd brought along specifically for this purpose, and Sera hummed.

"Is it wrong that I find that incredibly hot?" she asked.

I tried not to smirk like an asshole, but it was tough. Mostly because I *was* an asshole. "Which part?"

She shrugged. "Most guys don't even know how to change a light-bulb these days. You made that look far too easy. Not that I'm condoning grand theft auto, but it's pretty damn sexy watching you work, Mr. Marcosa."

My smug attitude curdled a little when I realized what she would be watching me do very soon. She probably wasn't going to admire how easy I made *that* look. I opened the driver's door for her and gestured her inside. Her perfectly arched eyebrow rose upward toward her hairline.

"You want me to drive?"

"The cops aren't likely to pull over a couple in a shitty four-door. They're even *less* likely to pull over a couple in a shitty four-door if a woman's driving. Statistically, anyway. This time of night, they're gonna assume I've had too many beers and my girlfriend's pulling designated driver duty..."

"Pretty sexist if you ask me. I could be a getaway driver."

"Sorry, Angel. I don't create the stereotypes. I just use them to my advantage."

"Hmm." She didn't look impressed, but she got into the car. I got in on the passenger's side and bit my tongue while Sera fidgeted with the mirrors and adjusted the seat.

"You *can* drive, right?"

She stopped what she was doing. "After all the shit that's happened recently, you really want to die because *I* killed *you* for being a jerk?"

I held my hands up in mock surrender. "Pretend I didn't say anything."

"That might be for the best."

New Yorkers were used to driving in the rain. Traffic didn't normally ease up just because the heavens opened, but tonight it seemed as if people were keeping off the streets. Definitely worked in our favor. I directed Sera which lane to take, which left or right, and at some point she figured out where we were going.

"Won't he be expecting you?" she asked under her breath, as she swung the car through a right-hand turn.

I grunted, thumbing the small plastic object in my pocket. "Probably. But I can't stay away. There has to be a price, Sera."

She didn't say anything, but a vein pulsed in her temple. If it were up to her, we wouldn't be doing this. We'd be headed somewhere quiet and out of the way, and we'd stay there for the rest of our lives. She wasn't a part of this world, though. She didn't know how it worked.

People assumed the criminal underworld was an anarchic, lawless place, and maybe it looked that way from the outside. Truth was, the circles I moved in, the same circles Rabbit moved in, were bound by very strict laws, and they were policed far more stringently than the rules and regulations of regular society.

If you broke your word, you were blackballed. If you cheated, backstabbed, or stole, you were gonna end up in the hospital. No way of avoiding it. And, in my world, if you betrayed someone and tried to get them killed, you'd better hope you were successful, otherwise you were gonna end up in the fucking ground yourself. There *was* an honor amongst the thieves, gangsters and assassins of New York City, and Rabbit had sacrificed his honor.

About a mile out from Rabbit's place, I asked Sera to pull into a parking lot and I got out of the car, dodging the persistent rain as I ran into Starbucks. Only took me a couple of minutes to pick up a couple of regular black coffees. I got back in the car, and Sera gave me a *look* out of the corner of her eye; she knew the second coffee I'd bought wasn't for her.

Unlike the night of Rabbit's party, there were no body guards standing sentry outside the church when we arrived. The pillar candles that had all been lit, perched on the broken headstones in the graveyard, were now all guttered out, their waxy hollows overflowing with rain water. No lights shone from within the building itself.

Sera followed close behind me, quiet and watchful as I strode up the broken flagstones toward the entryway. She looked relieved when I tried the handle and it was locked. She'd obviously forgotten how quickly I could pick a lock. The door was open in no time. She still carried the coffees I'd asked her to hold. The wet soles of our shoes squeaked against the stone floor; the only other sound that broke the deathly silence inside the church was the electric buzz and whir of a security camera, following us as we made our way down the aisle, and past the pews.

"How are we going to get past the security door," Sera hissed. "There was a keypad, remember."

Oh, I remembered all right. I might not have been able to hack a computer, but I was fucking smart. Smarter than Rabbit, any day of the week. I was the kind of guy who paid very close attention to the smallest of details. Often, those ended up being the most important details. The last time we'd come here, Rabbit had walked ahead of us and he'd plugged the code into the keypad, opening up the security door. And I'd been standing right behind the fucker.

Opening up the door to the rectory, I stabbed a series of numbers into the keypad, fighting the urge to roll my eyes.

"You've got to be kidding me," Sera groaned. "Sixty-nine, sixty-nine?"

"I can guarantee that piece of shit's never had a girl sit on his face his entire life," I added, as I hit the pound key and, soundlessly, the security door swung back. "Probably never fucking occurred to him to pleasure a woman while she had his cock in her mouth." Rabbit was a good enough looking dude, but he thought paying for sex was some kind of badge of honor, preferred to pay for it over getting laid the good old-fashioned way. And because it was a business transaction, he boasted constantly about the lack of effort he put in between the sheets. The women were there to make him feel good, so why the hell should he go to any great lengths to make it a pleasant experience for them? I'd never understand his warped, fucked up logic. Not that I particularly wanted to. I'd never fucking paid for sex. And the most erotic part of fucking a woman, as far as I was concerned, was watching her fall apart as she came.

Down we went into hell. The lights might not have been on upstairs in the main body of the church, but they were certainly lit up down here. The same obnoxious sign glared bright red in the narrow stairway as we descended into the church crypts. Music, much quieter than it had been at the party but still thumping and driving, bounced around the low-ceilinged space. A group of guys dressed in black suits stopped talking when they saw Sera and I appear at the foot of the stairs.

A guy with a shitty man-bun squared his shoulders. "Who the fuck are you?"

"The guy you shouldn't have." I walked past him, making sure to keep Sera on the other side of my body. The guy grimaced, his face contorting in anger. He reached out and grabbed the top of my arm.

"The guy I shouldn't have what?" he snapped.

"The guy you shouldn't have laid your fucking hands on." A second later, my left fist was buzzing with pain and the asshole was on the floor, lying on his back, nursing his broken nose with both hands.

Sera cleared her throat disapprovingly.

"*Motherfucker! You broke my damn nose!*" the guy roared.

"I did warn you." None of the guy's friends intervened as I stepped over the asshole, holding out my hand to Sera, firing a lethal warning gaze around the group just in case they got any ideas about touching her. None of them were that fucking stupid apparently.

"We paid for this entire space tonight, man," one of them spat. "This is a private party."

"Five guys standing around a bottle of Cuervo with your dicks in your hands? Not much of a party if you ask me." I didn't stop to argue with them further. I knew where Rabbit was, and by the whirring of that security camera up on ground level, he knew where we were, too. Right now, he was either armoring up or he was trying to flee the fucking building, and neither of those were good options. I didn't bring Sera here for her to get blasted in the stomach by a shot gun, and I wasn't wearing the right kind of footwear to go chasing after someone through a network of winding catacombs, either.

We left the black suits behind, and I lead the way to Rabbit's private booth, keeping an ear out for anything that sounded like a weapon being primed. My ears pricked just before we reached the velvet rope that had cordoned off Rabbit's booth. The sound that snagged so aggressively at my attention wasn't that of a gun being cocked. It was a voice. A voice I knew really fucking well.

"Seriously. Just let me do the talking. He won't get mad at me."

I stopped a couple of footsteps away from the arched entrance to the booth. "What...the...*fuck?*"

Sera paused right behind me; obviously she'd heard the same voice. "Why would she be here?" she asked.

I had no idea. I literally had *no* fucking idea, but it complicated matters. I ground my teeth together, stepping into the room, already horrified and prepared for what I knew I would find. Rabbit sat at the same booth he'd occupied when he asked me to go to The Barrows, and next to him sat a woman wearing a pair of blue nurse's scrubs. Last time I'd seen her, she'd been wearing a nun's habit, eating a slice of pizza.

She looked at me, defiance shining in her eyes, her blonde hair wound up in a messy knot on the crown of her head. "Monica," I said tightly, flaring my nostrils. "Guess I should have expected something like this. You two seem to have grown close of late." I'd overlooked it until now—she'd had my invite to Rabbit's party in her possession the other day. She'd known he was angry with me back in her apartment. And Rabbit had let slip that she'd told him of the predicament Sera and I faced, too. These separate pieces of information had been clues, clear indicators that Monica had been spending an unusual amount of time with Rabbit, and I was only putting those pieces together now. How fucking stupid of me.

I hadn't been paying attention to her. I'd dropped the ball as far as she was concerned. I'd taken my eye off her, and this is where she'd ended up.

Monica shifted awkwardly in her seat. She lifted her chin, angling her jaw, preparing for war. "I know why you're here, Felix, and—"

"You *do*?" I couldn't hide my incredulity. "You know he sent someone to worm his way in with me, to get inside my home? To fucking kill the woman I'm in love with?"

Pain flickered in her eyes, a brief shadow, there one second, gone the next. "I did what I thought was right," she said quietly. "This girl's been screwing you up from day one. You *don't* love her. She's manipulating you. You read that file. She is not the innocent party. She saw a way to bargain for her life and she took it. Don't be stupid enough to think—"

"You have no fucking idea what you're talking about," I hissed. Sera had been standing behind me since we entered the room, but now she stepped around me, her expression transformed from wariness to outright fury.

"Who the fuck do you think you are? You don't know me. You know nothing about me. You read a bunch of fabricated bullshit some psycho *emailed* to you, and you decided it was enough to sign my death warrant. This is the biggest pile of horse shit I've ever heard!"

It didn't take much to send Monica spiraling into the depths of a complete breakdown on a normal day; Sera's verbal assault was like pouring gasoline onto an already out of control forest fire. Monica picked up the empty glass in front of her, swung back her arm and launched it at Sera, screaming at the top of her lungs. "You've ruined everything! He's supposed to be helping *me*, not you!"

I'd considered Monica might worry that I was no longer going to try and find the son of a bitch who attacked her, but I'd summarily dismissed the thought out of hand. We'd spent the better part of five years trying to hunt the fucker down. It made no sense to me that she'd think I'd stop looking now, for *any* reason. I hadn't taken into account the fact that Monica wasn't exactly rational most of the time, and didn't think rationally either, though.

The glass sailed passed Sera's head, shattering against the wall by the bar. Sera surveyed the broken glass on the ground, then slowly began to walk toward the table where Monica and Rabbit were sitting.

Oh shit.

If there was one thing I generally tried to avoid, it was watching a woman getting her hair ripped out at the fucking root. I placed a hand on Sera's elbow, but she shot me a look that could have stripped paint. "I'm not going to hurt her," she said.

I believed her. I couldn't say that Monica wasn't going to try and hurt, Sera, though. I took the cups of coffee from her, moving beside her until we reached the table, where I placed them down in front of Rabbit. Sera folded her arms across her chest, glaring at Monica with the intensity of a thousand burning suns. "I would never take him away from you," she said harshly. "I'd help you, too, Monica, if you gave me the fucking opportunity. But you've been rude, aggressive and shitty to me since the moment we met. I'm *not* evil. I didn't do the things it said I did in that dossier. When my mother died, I lost everything. *Everything*," she said, her voice cracking. "And I would never hurt my sister. She's the only true family I have left. I love her more than you will ever know. I've done some terrible things, and I've had equally terrible things done to me. I understand the living, breathing pain that exists inside you more than you realize. But if you ever throw anything at me again, I will make you fucking regret it. Do you understand me?"

The fight evaporated from Monica's eyes. She looked at me, and then back at Sera, her chin wobbling.

"Jesus Christ," Rabbit spat. "What is this, a fucking Hallmark Special? Mentally damaged girls learn to love and trust one another? Get the fuck out of my house, Fix, and take both of your bitches with you. I think they're menstruating or something."

A cold, steely fist clenched in my stomach. Now was *not* the fucking time to be ironing out relationship kinks with Monica and Sera, I was well aware of that, but Rabbit had run out of hall passes with me. If he'd known any better, he would have kept his fat mouth shut and prayed to whatever deity he held dear that I'd forget he even fucking existed. His arrogance knew no bounds, though. He had friends in high places, had more money than god. In short, he thought he was fucking invincible.

I smiled at him tightly, and Monica's face turned the color of ash. "I came to have coffee with you, though, Rabbit. You wanted it so fucking badly. You put me through hell to punish me for forgetting, right? Now you don't want it?" Pulling out a chair for Sera, I sat myself down in front of Rabbit, then I slid one of the coffee cups across the table toward the hacker. He blinked at it, as if trying to process what was really happening here. Taking hold of the coffee cup, he lifted one of his shoulders in a blasé, off the cuff shrug.

"Might be a little too late now, don't you think?" He took a sip and wrinkled his nose. "It's fucking cold, man."

"Just drink it," I snarled. I took a sip myself and made a show of enjoying it a little too much. "Mmm, that's a fucking delicious beverage. While I'm here, Rabbit, you'll be happy to know I procured that item you were looking for." Reaching into my pocket, I pulled out the thumb drive and slapped it onto the table. I laughed, the sound tinged with a hysteria that even I recognized as borderline insane. "Care to tell me what's on this, now that we've dispensed with the subterfuge?"

Rabbit looked at me closely, narrowing his eyes. "My guys aren't far, yknow. All I have to do is shout for them, and they'll come running."

"I doubt either of those fat pieces of shit can run," I said airily. "Go ahead, though. Call them if you think you need their protection. I'm just sitting here, enjoying a coffee and a conversation with a friend."

Sera shifted in the chair next to me. She was close enough to feel the baleful energy pouring from my body like a waterfall of hate, but Rabbit...he clearly didn't feel it. He took a second longer to stare me down, and then he inhaled, straightening his back, clapping his hands together in front of him. "Okay. Fair enough. You caught me." Picking up the thumb drive, he got to his feet and stepped around Monica, heading for the bar. I watched the fucker like a hawk as he took out a laptop from underneath the counter and plugged the thumb drive into one of the USB ports.

Monica kicked me under the table. "Fix, please..." she whispered. "I know you're angry, but—"

"Not even close. *Angry does not even come close.*" If she thought she was going to bargain for mercy on Rabbit's behalf, she was sorely fucking mistaken. I used to be merciful. Empathetic. Trouble was, my empathy had caused me way too many sleepless nights. The faces of all the men I'd killed would come to me at night, invading my dreams, until in the end I hadn't known a moment's peace. I'd faced a decision: either I quit trying to avenge victims of hate, rape, violence and abuse by murdering their attackers, or I hunted down the part of my brain that dealt in empathy and guilt and I figured out how to turn it all off.

The first option had been a clear no-go. I'd spent some time learning how my own brain worked, and I'd found that fucking switch. I'd thrown it without a moment's thought, and ever since then I'd slept like a baby. No way I was turning that switch back on now for Rabbit's sake. He could have sold me out, put me in serious danger, caused me to lose everything I owned, my money, my apartment, my fucking *freedom*, and there still would have been a chance I'd have found it in my heart to forgive what he'd done. A slim chance, but still, a chance all the same. But Rabbit had made a fatal fucking error. His actions had endangered Sera's safety. The stunt he'd pulled could have ended *her* life, and no matter how sorry he was, how hard he fucking begged, there was nothing he could do to save himself now. Not that that was even an issue, because the bastard clearly wasn't sorry.

Monica whimpered, tapping her fingertip against the tabletop. Her tapping matched Rabbit's as he hammered away at the laptop keyboard by the bar. "It was kinda genius really," he said. "Oscar's been sending his guys to this dipshit on the Upper East Side, some rich momma's boy who's been undercutting my services for months. I wanted to teach him a lesson about customer loyalty and punish that asshole at the same time, so I whispered a couple of mistruths into a few select ears. Said I had some insider trading info on a thumb drive in my office. Data worth millions to anyone who had a little money to invest. I knew it would get back to Oscar, and whaddya know? Two days later, a guy in a ski mask breaks into my office during a party and steals the drive from my desk."

"Just get to the fucking point, Rabbit. What's on it?"

He was unbearably smug as he looked up from the screen in front of him. "An insanely clever trojan. Encrypted so heavily, I knew Oscar's posh-boy motherfucker wouldn't be able to resist trying to crack it. And when he did..." He stabbed at a series of keys, hitting the final one with an ostentatious flourish.

Music blared into the booth; sounded like the laptop was connected to the audio system. I knew the song, but it took until the lyrics kicked in for me to place it.

"As I walked through the valley of the shadow of death, I took a look at my life and realized there's nothing left..."

Gangster's Paradise, by Coolio.

For fuck's sake.

Rabbit grinned, spinning the laptop around to reveal a series of spinning numbers and characters that cascaded from the top of the screen to the bottom like something out of the fucking matrix. "The second he bypassed the encryption, the trojan would have taken hold. The virus was designed to crack Oscar's financial establishments, to drain every single last penny from his accounts. The funds would have been automatically sent to an anonymous holding company in the Caymans. Obviously mine," he said with a wink. "And the most beautiful part?" He had to raise his voice over the blaring song. "The trojan is unstoppable. It buries itself deeper and deeper into a mainframe as soon as it has access. It would have destroyed that cunt's entire system in less than a minute. He would have known about it, would have watched it as it happened, and there wouldn't have been a single thing he could have done about it. It was a beautiful plan."

I couldn't care less about his plan. Would have been great to know that Oscar was ruined and penniless, but it didn't really matter. "You sacrificed that beautiful plan by telling me to go get the drive back. And all because you were pissed at me." I struggled to keep my voice even.

Rabbit's expression turned rueful. "Mayfair did pay me a lot of money to orchestrate that complicated little ruse. He badly wanted an in with you so he could take care of your pretty friend and get home as quickly as possible."

Don't kill him yet. Don't fucking kill him yet.

It took every ounce of strength I possessed to listen to the voice in my head. I drew in a steady stream of oxygen through my nose, trying to push down the rage that was burning like bile in the back of my throat. "But you searched him out. Hunted him down and told him we were in New York. He never would have found us otherwise."

Rabbit came back to the table and slumped down into his seat. An impish light shone in his eyes. "Oh, no. That wasn't me. Fuck. As if I've got time for that shit. It was Monica who—" His eyes went wide.

I couldn't decide if his sudden hesitation was real or expertly faked. Twin spots of color burned in his cheeks, which made me think that maybe he really was worried about what he'd just let slip.

Slowly, I turned to Monica. She sunk away from the table, her back pressed up against her chair, trying to make herself as small as possible. She had every right to be afraid. Rabbit had fucked me on an unbelievable level, but what she had done was so much worse. She'd reached out to Carver? Told him where we were? She'd done everything in her power to make sure Sera died. The high-pitched whine in my head drowned out all logical thought. I just—I didn't even know how to wrap my head about the treachery...

"I'm sorry, Fix," she whispered. The apology burnt in her eyes, but I couldn't bear to see it. The hurt was more than I could comprehend.

"Don't speak," I seethed. "Don't breathe another fucking word."

Rabbit drummed his hands against the table, running the tip of his tongue over his teeth. "I, for one, regret sending you to The Barrows. My therapist's been telling me I need to be a better communicator, and I'm beginning to see that he might be right. In future—"

I reached behind me, into the small of my back. I took hold of the gun that had been sitting there, waiting for its moment to shine. I drew it, my finger hovering over the trigger. With furious calm, I faced Rabbit and said, "*What future?*"

The crack of the gunshot was deafening.

Monica screamed.

Sera jumped up, her chair toppling to the ground as she pushed away from the table.

And Rabbit's skull exploded into a cloud of blood, and bone, and brain matter.

"*Been spending most our lives living in a gangster's paradise. Been spending most our lives living in a gangster's paradise.*"

My heart pumped evenly in my chest.

It didn't even skip a beat.

51

SERA

UNSHAKEABLE

"*Let* me go! Fix, *please*. I swear...I didn't know he was going to send you to Oscar. *Please!*"

Monica was losing her shit, but I barely registered her frantic pleading. My ears were still ringing from the gunshot that had claimed Rabbit's life. I was never going to stop hearing that sound. I was never going to be able to eradicate the sight of the guy's head bursting like an over-ripe watermelon that someone had struck with a sledgehammer.

The blood...

There had been so much blood...

At a respectable distance, that shot would have created a neat little hole in the center of Rabbit's forehead, but at the distance we'd been sitting—point blank range—things had gone a little differently. Rabbit's cheekbone had caved under the pressure of the impact, and his jaw bone had been all but severed from the rest of his skull, leaving it hanging by a bloody rope of sinew. What had once been his mouth had transformed into a gruesome, yawning maw that I was going to be reliving whenever I closed my eyes for the foreseeable future.

No one had come running. The guards Rabbit had warned of hadn't shown their faces—probably a calculated move on their part, if they'd known Fix was on site—and the guys dressed in black had been nowhere to be found when we'd made our exit. Fix had been grim and forbidding, his hand clamped like a vise around Monica's arm as he'd dragged her out of the place. He'd growled like a rabid wolf when Monica had kicked and screamed, trying to free herself, and when she hadn't calmed down, he'd thrown her over his shoulder and carried her out of the church.

We were almost back in Brooklyn now, and her anxious wailing had increased instead of tapered off. "Fix, please," she sobbed. "I'm sorry. I'm so sorry. I had no idea he would do that, I swear. Just...*please!*"

Finally, the deadly calm that had fallen over him after he pulled that trigger shattered. Slamming his fist into the steering wheel of our stolen sedan, he bared his teeth at the rear-view mirror, a brilliant silver storm flashing in his eyes. "Fuck, Monica! *Really*? You really think I'm going to fucking *hurt* you?"

"I—I don't..." she whimpered. "You're angry. I don't know."

"Then you don't know *me*," he hissed at her reflection. "I promised I'd find the guy who hurt you. I promised I'd protect you. But fuck," he said, grinding his teeth together. "I never thought *I'd* need protecting from *you*."

A miserable silence fell over the car.

I watched the city whip by in a stream of orange and red lights, and I tried to formulate something to say. I felt Fix's eyes on me a number of times, but I couldn't return the eye contact. I needed to unpack everything that was going on in my head before the pressure became too much and I ended up screaming at the top of my lungs like a lunatic.

Was I angry?

Was I horrified?

Was I scared?

Was I going crazy?

I couldn't answer a single one of the questions that were furiously demanding my attention. All I could do was sit in the seat next to Fix and stare out of the window, replaying the moment when Rabbit's head exploded on an endless, terrible loop.

Exhaustion gnawed at me, but I wasn't going to sleep tonight. No chance of that. My thoughts were going to fester until I was mentally raw from their constant chaffing, and even then I wasn't going to be able to pass out.

I didn't know where we were going, and I didn't even bother to ask. The tides of influence that affected my life were so far out of control now that trying to rein them in would be much like sticking my hand into a blender to try and catch hold of the spinning blades.

I realized Monica had stopped crying.

A cop car hurtled by, lights and sirens cutting into the night, but no one inside the car flinched. We were a group of friends on our way home from a night out. Fix was studiously observing every road traffic law there was, so there was no reason we should be noticed. The blood that spattered our skin couldn't be seen; the gun tucked into Fix's waistband was hidden from view. It was beyond strange, but I wasn't worried we were going to get caught.

It seemed as if the events of the evening had taken place outside the realms of normal life, in some other place unreachable to anyone who might cause trouble for us. In my head, Rabbit's body was going to rot and eventually turn to dust back there in the crypt, undisturbed for the rest of time.

At some point soon, someone was going to come across him, of course. Rabbit's parties were frequent and popular, and by the sounds of things his client list was extensive. The question was, what was going to happen when he was discovered? I kept trying to picture someone calling the cops and reporting his death, and I just couldn't do it.

Fix had located Rabbit's office and destroyed all of the security camera footage before we'd left the church, so there was no direct evidence that we'd been there. There were so many fingerprints all over those crypts that it would be near impossible to separate one from the other.

Another cop car burned past us, heading in the opposite direction, and I finally twisted to look ahead out of the windshield. Fix didn't even look at me, but I could sense his thoughts searching, reaching out to me, as if I were inside his head and I were able to read them as if they were my own. He had a thousand questions, I knew, but mostly he wanted to know if I was afraid of him.

Once upon a time, a set of rules had governed him. Ten non-negotiable commandments that provided a set guideline as to how he was supposed to live his life. Since he'd left the church, Fix had broken so many of those commandments. Theft. Adultery. Murder. But lying? Dishonesty wasn't something Fix undertook lightly. As far as I knew, he'd only lied to me once, and that was a lie of omission. He hadn't told me he'd been hired to kill me when we'd first met. He *had* told me he was a paid assassin, however, and he hadn't pulled any punches with me since then, even when the truth had been a hard thing to hear. So, if he asked me if I was frightened of him right now, putting his fears into words, I was going to have to tell him the truth.

Yes.

I was afraid of him.

I was fucking terrified of him.

But...

I was also in love with him, more than I'd have ever believed possible, and I trusted him with my life. I knew he would die before he ever let anything bad happen to me. The lengths he'd already gone to in order to keep me safe had gone a long way to proving that. The beating he'd taken at The Barrows simply so he could try and find out what the fuck was actually going on had made me sick to my stomach.

Yeah, he'd been pissed, but I knew he hadn't killed Rabbit out of anger. He hadn't done it for the sheer fun of it, either. He'd done it out of fear, because of what had almost happened to me, and he wanted to make sure Rabbit could never pose a threat to me again.

Where did that leave me?

There were so many sides to Fix. He was so damn mercurial. One second he could be making a joke out of something that, nine times out of ten, was definitely *not* funny. The next, he was bending me over a table and fucking me senseless. And the next moment, he was drawing a gun and firing it into the face of a twenty-something-year-old hacker.

I knew what Sadie would be telling me right now if she were here. My friend would tell me to leave, to get the fuck out of dodge before something really awful happened.

She wouldn't understand, though. This pull that I felt whenever I was around Fix wasn't something that could be ignored. I would feel it no matter which state I ran to. I could flee to another country altogether and that same tugging in my chest would still be there, calling me to him.

I'd meant it before: when I'd lived under Sixsmith's rule back in Montmorenci, I'd fabricated this small, limited world for myself. Fear, anxiety and pain had been an ever-present constant within that world, and for a very long time they had been the only things I had felt. Months into the arrangement Sixsmith had made with Sam Halloran, I'd realized that I needed to feel something else or I was going to end up slitting my own wrists. I decided I wasn't going to feel the fear, or the anxiety or the pain anymore. I was going to blot out the negative by purposefully seeking out and fixating on the positive. Small, brief moments of happiness that I treasured and secreted away inside, so I could close my eyes and draw on them, disappear into them whenever Sam laid his hands on me. Making milkshakes with Amy in the kitchen while our father was at work. The quiet moments after school, where we'd venture out into the back fields to soak our feet in the creek. Stolen minutes in the middle of the night, where I adventured inside the pages of a book, becoming someone else entirely.

I'd only allowed myself to really feel anything inside those moments. I'd carried that practice forward even after I'd escaped out from underneath Sixsmith's tyranny, and I hadn't even noticed. For years in Seattle, I'd been numb, only experiencing flashes of emotion whenever something truly unexpected and wonderful happened.

And then something changed.

I hung up a phone in the lobby of a shitty motel in Liberty Fields, Wyoming, and a tall, broad, incredibly sexy, arrogant man had spoken to me. His words had rankled at me from the get-go; he'd provoked such strong emotion in me from the moment our eyes had met, and that had only gotten worse. Or better, depending on how I thought about it.

It was as if I'd been living my life in black and white, and suddenly along came Fix and my world was suddenly painted in startling, vibrant technicolor. I felt the fear I'd become so well-versed at blocking out again with such an intensity that it was almost paralyzing, but I also felt a happiness I hadn't known before. Wild stirrings in my soul that I'd frankly thought other people were making up before now. Everything was electric, and perilous, and wonderful...

And I wasn't going to give that up.

Not for Monica, not for the malignant specter that was Carver, and certainly not for the dead man we'd left behind in those crypts.

I made up my mind.

I cast away the image of Rabbit's ruined face, banishing it from my head. The memory of it was never going to go away, but I would be able to breathe around it now, fucked up though that was. Fix was right; there had to be consequences. The unshakable bond we shared was paramount above anything else. He would go to extraordinary lengths to defend it—defend me—and I would do the same. Other than Amy and Sadie, there wasn't a person on earth I wouldn't shoot to save him. No crime was too heinous, if it ensured his safety.

Maybe I *was* fucking crazy for feeling that way, but Fix hadn't just gotten under my skin. He was a part of my soul, and I wouldn't willingly part with that. Swallowing, I reached out and found his hand tightly gripping the stick shift. I rested my palm on the back of his hand, loosening his fingers so I could thread my own between them. He glanced at me out of the corner of his eye, and a rush of adrenalin surged through my veins.

Fix exhaled, a long, ragged blast of air leaving his body, and it was only then that I realized he'd been holding his breath. His shoulders relaxed. His features remained strained, his brows banked together, his mouth still pressed into a flat line, but the light in his eyes had changed. Where he'd looked cold and hollow inside a moment ago, now he looked relieved.

52

SERA

FAITH LOST

*W*e didn't head back to Brooklyn, after all. Instead, we doubled back on ourselves and headed north. The night grew darker as we left behind the tall buildings and the lights of the city, and the hustle and bustle of New York began to fade to indeterminable stretches of highway that whipped past suburbs and eventually small towns with names like Elmsford, and Sleepy Hollow, and Archville.

I'd never heard of half the places we passed, but still I didn't ask where we were going. I wasn't one to bury my head in the sand. When I'd left home with Amy, I'd made sure to enter into unknown situations armed with the facts. Made it easier to know what to expect, how to react, and how to handle whatever came my way. But right now, not knowing seemed better than having to face whatever shit storm was about to land in my lap. I needed a break. I *deserved* a damn break, even if it was only a temporary one.

We continued to head north.

Soon, the towns we passed grew more and more infrequent and the landscape changed, tall trees looming up on either side of the road like sentinels. Maple. Redwoods. Beech. Oak. Mountain Ash. In autumn, the canopy of the forest we had entered must have put on the most vivid, striking display of color, but now, with little more than the hint of moonlight piercing through the thick cloud cover overhead, everything was painted in black, greys, a deep, depthless shade of royal blue, and shimmering silver.

Monica was so quiet, I swung around to check on her—I didn't know the girl, but during my brief encounters with her, the last thing she'd ever been was quiet. Her forehead was pressed up against the window, her face relaxed in sleep, the panic and the fear of the night's events gone from her face. How the fuck was she *sleeping*?

"She was so wrong to do what she did," Fix murmured. His eyes were practically glowing incandescent, reflecting the blue glow of the sedan's dashboard. Normally so angular and sharp, his features were much softer than usual. The bruises that marked his jaw and beneath his right eye were darkening to an angry violet, but I barely noticed them. He was tired. So much driving. So much worrying. So much running. It was finally beginning to take its toll on him. I'd begun to think the man was impervious to the body's need for sleep, but looking at him now I realized I'd been wrong. Fix had his limits, just like the rest of us. Granted, those limits were beyond those of anyone else I knew, but they did exist.

"She's from Canada," he said, his voice a soft lull against the rhythmic rumble of the tires on the road. "She was fragile before she even came to America. Her mother was schizophrenic. Dad left when she was a kid. Sometimes things were okay with her mom, but whenever she had an episode or stopped taking her meds, Monica was put into foster care. Spent a lot of time being passed from one home to the next. Her mom killed herself when Monica was fourteen. The care workers couldn't find her a permanent place to stay at that age, no one would take a teenager with a tricky background who was likely to cause trouble, so she ended up in a church funded facility. The nuns were good to her. Things became a little more consistent. I think she found comfort in the rules and the routine. So when she finished high school, she stayed on. Became a novice. Decided to help out. When they sent her to the States on exchange, it was meant to be a learning experience for her. Supposed to give her confidence. Help her interact with strangers without flipping her shit."

His chest rose as he took a breath that never seemed to end. "I knew none of that when she came to St. Luke's to serve. Her file was sitting on the desk in my office. I'd expected her, but that morning I'd been trying to write my homily, and people just kept walking through the fucking door, needing something from me. If I'd taken a moment to flip through her paperwork, I might have chosen to spend some time with her, making her feel comfortable. Safe. As it was, I was listening to the most pointless fucking confession ever when that bastard came into the church and took her. He raped her while I was trying to stem my own boredom in the confessional. He beat her. He broke her body so badly, it didn't look like she was going to live."

A cold, unwelcome sweat broke out across the back of my neck. The shit Monica had been through was the stuff of nightmares. I was intimately familiar with the terrors that plagued her when she passed out each night, and that were probably tormenting her even right now. A tendon strained in Fix's throat as he rubbed his thumbs against the steering wheel. "The shit she pulled with Rabbit was really fucking bad, and I'm fucking furious with her, Sera, believe me. She could have cost both of us everything. But I owe her. I owe her so fucking much. If I'd been a little more diligent in my responsibilities, she never would have been attacked."

This was hard for him. He spent so much time presenting a grave, stony, impenetrable front, occasionally diverting those around him with a level of sarcasm and dry humor that even I couldn't match, that this kind of open communication was unfamiliar and uncomfortable. I fucking *knew* it was hard for him; his uneasiness was carved into the lines of his face and radiated off him like heat from a dying fire. Still, he continued with a dogged determination.

"I lost my faith so gradually that I hadn't even noticed. People were relying on me at St. Luke's to help them. I was supposed to be a solid foundation they could lean on in times of need, and I wasn't. I couldn't help them in the way they needed me to. I was lying to them. I still wanted to help, though. The path I chose to walk with Monica...

it was the only way I knew how to do that. But I should have walked that path alone. I should have refused to let her tangle herself up in this fucking life. I thought it'd give her some kind of peace to know that the evil in the world was being dealt with, one way or the other, but she wasn't strong enough. She never has been. I should have fucking *known* that.

"I didn't just let her down once, Sera. Every day I've permitted her to live this kind of life, I've been letting her down all over again." He growled at the back of his throat, an angry frown forming two deep lines between his eyebrows. "I need to forgive her for what happened tonight, because it's my fucking fault. I don't expect *you* to be able to. If I were you, I'd fucking hate her for what she did. So, I get it."

I hadn't allowed myself the time to think about Monica's duplicity. Just as I'd screamed at her back in the crypts, she didn't fucking know me. She didn't know the first thing about me. Her actions hadn't surprised me in the least. If I'd been in her position, left to my own devices, not knowing what was going on, worrying about the safety of someone I cared deeply about...would I have done the same thing? I couldn't say for sure.

Part of me wanted to say no. I would have listened to Fix. I would have waited. I would have given the unknown woman in the file the benefit of the doubt before doing everything in my power to make sure she wound up dead.

But I was stronger than Monica. Whatever made one person more capable of handling traumatic experiences than another was a mystery to me, but obviously I was better equipped to handle my past than she was. She was as fragile as a butterfly with broken wings, extraordinarily afraid of the huge, terrifying world that surrounded her, with no way of dealing with her own vulnerability.

Well... she had one way of dealing with her vulnerabilities, and that was to lean on Fix. I'd threatened that crutch. I'd essentially taken it away from her, and that must have been petrifying for her.

The thing about anger was this: you could argue and reason with it all you liked, but it was like a drug coursing through your veins. It was almost impossible to relinquish. It made you feel righteous, and it made you feel strong, and at the end of the day there was nothing worse than feeling unjustified and weak instead.

I looked over my shoulder at the girl sleeping on the back seat, and I did my best to bundle up all of the fury and the resentment I felt toward her. When I turned back, I cautiously slid my hand onto Fix's leg; beneath the material of his jeans, his muscled thigh tensed.

"My father sold me to his friends when I was fifteen. For two years, he let one of his friends *use me* as he saw fit. Sixsmith was in a lot of debt, and Sam, his friend, agreed to settle that debt by...by *fucking* me twice a week." I nearly choked on the words. They were like poison, bitter and terrible tasting on the end of my tongue. "Each time Sam fucked me, eighty-six dollars and seventy-three cents was deducted from the amount Sixsmith owed."

I risked a sidelong look at Fix. He wasn't looking at me, though. He was staring ahead out of the car, his jaw locked, his shoulders rigid, his back ramrod straight. His body was taut as a bowstring, drawn to the point of snapping.

"Sam wasn't kind to me. He wasn't...*gentle*." God, this was so fucking hard to say. Fix hadn't pushed for the information, not once. He'd made passing comments which had made it clear he knew something had happened to me when I was a kid, but he'd never tried to force the details out of me. His patience and his trust that I would tell him when I felt the time was right had been one of the very first things I'd loved about the man. I would keep my secrets inside me until the end of time if I waited for the right moment to share them with him, though, and I couldn't keep on holding things back from him anymore. Not now.

"Things would get bad. And then they would get worse...and I did my best to keep myself together. Then, Sixsmith did something really fucking stupid. He hired someone to bet Sam for his business. Sam owned a bar in Montmorenci. Sixsmith tricked him in a game of poker, and he won the bar from him."

I was shaking as I told the rest of the story. There was a wild animal inside me, trapped in a snare, trying to free itself from the inevitable, wrestling to run and hide itself from reliving that day in

Sam's apartment, when I'd taken hold of that piece of glass and I'd buried it into Sam's flesh. That wild, scared animal was me. I wasn't going to give into myself. I was going to grind the words out, and I was going to be rid of them once and for all, because once I'd said them, I knew I wasn't going to have to clench them so tightly inside my chest anymore.

I parted with every last one of them, not sparing the details, and once it was over...I really did feel *free*.

"If you can forgive Monica for selling you out, and for selling *me* out, then I can forgive her, too. It might not be easy, but I'll do it, because I have a long-lasting relationship with hatred, and it's eaten me alive for too long. I refuse to be a shelter to it anymore."

He growled—a sound filled with pain, and regret, and an unquenchable need for violence. I twisted in my chair, digging my fingers into his leg. When he looked at me, his torment was so obvious and painful that it nearly broke me. I knew him well enough to know exactly what he was thinking: he hadn't been there to protect me when I'd needed him. He hadn't been able to swoop in and kill Sam for me, to save me the horror of having to protect myself. His self-recrimination was futile, and he must have known that. It didn't stop him from feeling it all the same, however. It was just the type of person he was.

"Don't you dare feel sorry for me, Felix Marcosa," I whispered. "And you didn't know me back then. You can't be responsible for every single wounded person's pain. I didn't tell you any of that to make you feel bad for me. I told you because you deserved to know, and because I..." How did I word what I needed to say? How did I give meaning to the thoughts and emotions that were cutting me to the quick? "Because I want you to know that I'm not like Monica. I walked the road to hell, and I lived there for a time, but I'm not going to be another broken girl you have to take care of. You're a fixer. But you don't need to fix *me*. I mean it, Felix. I already fixed myself a long time ago."

53

FIX

CONSEQUENCES

*a*n eight-year-old girl told me she was being molested once. I was tired as fuck and I was ready for the day to be over. The line for the confessional had felt like it would never end, and I'd been relieved when the short, narrow frame of the child had entered into the booth and sat herself down on the stool on the other side of the grill. Children were bad at confession as a rule. They didn't like punishment, even if it was just a few Hail Mary's and a promise never to sass their parents again; typically, they confessed a few arbitrary sins, and typically I let them off light, making the experience as short and sweet as possible. I was a terrifying authority figure to most kids. A direct line to God, who I knew seemed like a pretty fucking frightening overlord, ready to smite them for their crimes if they were disobedient. So, I was soft with them. Tried to relax them. Make them feel as comfortable as I could during a time that normally scared the shit out of them.

I'd spoken to the little girl before. She was a collector of shiny trinkets. Thief would have been the wrong word to describe her, though she frequently delved into women's purses on the hunt for glossy lipsticks and compact mirrors, and had been known to relieve department stores of candy on the odd occasion when she thought she wasn't being watched. She'd grown out of her compulsion for the most part, but there were still times when she took something she wasn't supposed to, and I would gently chastise her and send her on her way.

On this particular Sunday, she'd sobbed quietly on the other side of the booth, holding back her hiccups and her misery, and told me that she was scared. She'd said she didn't want her mother to hear her crying, because her daddy would punish her for it when she got home.

Her father was an upstanding member of the congregation. Directed the church choir. I'd gone for beers with him a couple of times after charity drives, when I'd needed to blow off a little steam. He was funny and down to earth, seemed like a real family guy, and I couldn't imagine him punishing the girl for being upset. I asked her why she thought she'd get into trouble.

After a little coaxing, she'd begun to tell a disturbing story of abuse and assault that had me gripping the side of the booth until my fingernails had gouged deep holes in the wood. If she didn't eat her food, he touched her between her legs. If she broke something in the house, he put his fingers inside her. If she made her mother angry, he made her open wide, and he put the thing between his legs inside her mouth until she couldn't breathe and she was sick.

I'd erupted out of the confessional like a raging storm. My blood had boiled. My vision had swum, tinged crimson by my rage. The little girl's father had already gone home ahead of his wife and child. Her mother had begged and pleaded with me not to call the police. She'd asked me to wait until she'd had chance to ask her husband about the little girl's claims, and said she was sure her daughter was just confused and didn't know what she was saying.

I'd considered holding back. For a split second, I'd thought about letting the girl's mother handle the situation, but I saw how it was going to play out in my head. The guy would deny everything. He'd be disbelieving and hurt that the little girl would say such things. He'd make a show of trying to comfort the child and would ask her why she was so afraid of him. His wife would believe him—nine times out of ten, they always did, preferring to believe their kid was making shit up instead of wrapping their minds around the possibility that the man they married was capable of abusing their own child—and then the girl would pay. She'd be branded a liar.

Of course, there was a chance she *was* lying. I hadn't been about to check the girl's body for signs of assault. But I also hadn't been willing to risk the chance that she was telling the truth, and I was sending her back into a dangerous household. I wasn't going to teach the child that speaking out led to angering the adults around her, and that her bravery would be rewarded with punishment. I wasn't going to leave her fucking alone in her fear.

I'd called the cops. They'd arrested the guy, and when the little girl had undergone a medical exam, it turned out she *had* been telling the truth. The guy had gone to prison, but every day after that I'd regretted my actions. Yeah, I'd done the right thing. The little girl was no longer being abused by a person who was supposed to be her most staunch defender against the worst kinds of evil that existed in the world. But I'd never been able to shake the feeling that I hadn't done enough. I'd wanted to hurt the guy who'd ruined that little girl's childhood. I'd wanted to break every single one of the fingers he'd used on her. I'd wanted to zip tie the bastard's hands behind his back and cut off the dick he'd forced into her mouth. Slowly. As painfully as possible, while I'd made him watch.

I'd wanted to fucking kill him for what he'd done.

I'd regretted not doing so ever since.

I wasn't going to make that mistake again.

One day, and one day soon, Sixsmith Lafferty and I were going to have a little fucking chat.

54

SERA

OBNOXIOUS

*T*he house was grand on a Victorian scale, but Colonial in design. Six white columns braced the front of the building, supporting the deep overhanging eaves that wrapped around the property. There was no porch swing here, but rather an expensive set of garden furniture, three and four-seater rattan sofas and armchairs complete with tasteful floral cushions that created a vibrant slash of color against the stark, bright white paintwork of the house itself. The tall, arched windows on the upper floor were all in darkness, but three of the six ground floor picture windows glowed a warm yellow, lit up against the night.

Fix grunted in displeasure as we pulled up outside the vast mansion. "No one's supposed to be here," he muttered under his breath. Silencing the engine, he got out of the car, a stony expression marring his features. I got out after him, my legs complaining as I stretched them.

"Are you going to tell me where *here* is?" I asked.

Fix displayed an uncharacteristic level of discomfort as he faced the house, shoving his hands into his pockets. "This," he said tightly, "is my parent's house. Or rather it was. It's mine now."

Ho-ly fuck.

I didn't want to be that girl, gawking in shock over someone's surprise wealth, but this was just fucking ridiculous. In a city where space was at a premium, the penthouse back in Brooklyn was huge, so I'd known he had money. But this wasn't money. This was *rich. My-ancestors-were-founding-members-of-the-country-and-made-billions-during-the-oilrush-of-eighteen-sixty-seven* kind of rich.

I tried not to react, but my surprise must have been all too obvious.

"You can say it." Fix's eyes were hard as flint. "It's fucking obnoxious."

"It's not obnoxious. It's just... it's..."

"*Obnoxious*. It's bigger than a department store." He began walking to toward the front door.

"Shouldn't we wake Monica?"

Fix bent down and looked through the window at the sleeping woman, the bridge of his nose crinkled. "She's dead to the world. I'll send Richard out for her in a little while."

"Richard?"

Sighing, Fix rubbed at the back of his neck. "My father's man."

I must have been pulling a face, because Fix clarified. "His butler. My father had a butler. Before he went into the church, we lived here, and he had a butler called Richard."

He was snappy, but I gave him a pass. He was exhausted, and something about coming here made Fix very edgy. If we hadn't had our backs to a wall, I suspected he would never have brought us here, to this sprawling pile of brick and stone in Upstate New York. Following after him, my eyes caught on a flash of wicked metal at the base of Fix's back—the gun he'd pulled on Rabbit.

This was so surreal.

This was so fucking surreal that I was beginning to question my own sanity now. How the fuck had any of this happened?

I'd left Seattle over a month ago now, with only a small suitcase containing a week's worth of clothes. I was supposed to have an interesting cross-country adventure on my road trip, celebrate Amy's over-the-top wedding, and then I was supposed to get back to work.

Instead, I was walking up the sweeping staircase of a twelve-room mansion behind a man who'd just committed murder, and—

A bar of light fell across my face, and I looked up. The monstrous double doors to the house swung inward, and the silhouetted, dark shape of a man appeared.

"Master Felix," a voice called down to us. "I didn't know you were coming. I nearly called the police."

"You're meant to be at home," Fix growled.

As I climbed the final step, I found myself standing in front of a tall, reedy-looking man with eyes that might once have been brown but were now clouded and milky with cataracts. His wrinkled skin looked paper-thin and was a beautiful dark bronze color, and his top lip was capped with a snowy white moustache. His hair was short, salt and pepper curls. It was just after four in the morning, which explained the red, worn dressing gown hanging over his shoulders, but not the crisp white button-down shirt he was wearing beneath it, or the neat black dress pants. The old man's hands shook a little as he gestured to Fix, beckoning him to step into the light.

"This *is* my home," he replied churlishly.

"Your home's four miles away. Remember? That three-bedroom villa by the water? With its own private dock?"

The man, Richard, gave a dismissive wave of his hand. "Psshhaaw. That place? *Haunted. As. Fuck.*" He hefted his considerable, bushy eye brows up toward his hairline. "Told you not to buy it. Told you I wan't gon' live in it. Might as well sell it again, you brat."

The very last thing I expected to be doing at this end of the car ride we'd just taken was laughing, but I couldn't help it. Fix? A brat? If anyone else had called him that, they'd have been nursing a broken jaw. Fix just scowled at the old man, and then he scowled at me for good measure.

"I done told you plain and simple I wan't gon' retire. I looked after this house since I was twenty-nine years old, an' I'm gon' look after it 'til I'm dead. That's all there is to it."

"Great," Fix replied. "So you're gonna die here and make *this* place haunted."

Richard turned around, hobbling a little, and went back inside the house, crooking a bent finger behind him over his shoulder, clearly expecting us to follow. "Damn straight, I am. I'm gon' haunt the shit outta *you*, boy. 'Sides, I wouldn't be the first shade to walk these halls."

Fix loosed a weary sigh. "If this place is haunted, then what's the big deal about the old Fallbrook villa?"

Richard made an angry sound at the back of his throat. "I *know* these ghosts. I don't know none o' they ghosts. I am eighty-nine years old. I shouldn't have to be learnin' no new ghosts. Have you forgotten all your damn manners, boy, or are you working up to an introduction?"

Richard's gaze flittered pointedly to me.

"Richard, this is my friend Sera. Sera, this is Richard Montrose Jnr."

"The third," the old man emphasized, holding up three gnarled fingers for me to see. His hand then swooped down and snatched hold of mine, lifting it up to his face. He didn't kiss the back of my hand. I thought he was about to, but he didn't. He bowed his head in a show of deference and dipped a little arthritically at the knees, then he turned a broad smile on me, his skin creasing at the corners of his eyes.

"You are a *very* pretty woman, Sera," he informed me. "I am honored to make your esteemed acquaintance."

I sought out Fix's attention, unsure what to do.

"Don't be asking him no questions with those fancy eyes o' yours. That boy knows nothin,'" Richard chided. "You come on inside with Old Richard. You both look frightful, and I got a nice bottle of whiskey I been thinkin' 'bout openin.'"

∾

The interior of the house was much like the outside: sumptuous, grand and breathtakingly beautiful. For starters, the foyer was larger than my entire apartment back in Seattle. The polished floors were old fashioned parquet, but the wood-work looked brand new, as if it had just been laid yesterday. People didn't make this kind of flooring anymore, though. It was a lost art, replaced by quick and easy solutions like the polished cement in Fix's penthouse.

An imposing staircase arced around in a circle up to the first floor, at the foot of which a stunning grand piano sat with the fallboard open, as if it someone had been playing it moments ago and had only just stepped away. Antique sideboards, bookshelves, and sleek mahogany cabinets. Vases filled with sprays of colorful flowers, and cut crystal decanters resting on silver service trays. Massive, heavily gilded frames, and stately oil paintings. Everything inside the house screamed of money, decadence and luxury, but that wasn't what I noticed first. The atmosphere was nothing like I would have expected it to be—austere and stiff. There was a worn quality to the place that made it feel lived in: the slightly worn pathway on the narrow rug that ran from the foyer into what looked like a formal sitting room; the stack of papers balanced behind a gold cast figurine of a slender woman holding a baby in her arms; the tasseled lamp on by the entranceway that looked like it belonged in a great-grandmother's parlor; the large umbrella propped up against the wall, half fallen open where the fastener hadn't been closed around it after its last use.

Strangely, despite the cost of such a residence, its contents weren't wrapped in cotton wool and preserved like museum pieces. This was a home. It felt like a place that might have been a sanctuary to a happy family once upon a time.

Fix was watching me as I took everything in. He stood like a statue in the foyer, hands still stuffed into his pockets, his demeanor calm and still, but I could tell there was a tempest of emotion roiling under his unruffled façade. He most certainly *was* ruffled.

"You want ice in your whiskey, Lady Sera?" Richard called from the sitting room.

I couldn't tear my eyes away from Fix. He was at war with himself, but why? What was troubling him so badly that he looked like he was going to turn on his heel and march right back down those stairs again? I had absolutely no idea what was going on in his head. "No. Thank you."

When Richard came back, he handed me a tumbler containing a healthy pour of amber liquid. Fix was given the same. "Since you *are* here, Richard, Monica's in the car outside. She's asleep. Can you make sure she gets to bed, please? Her usual room will be just fine."

So, Monica had been here before. She had a usual room. I didn't know why I found that surprising; the two of them had been through a lot together—Monica's attack and subsequent recovery, Fix leaving the church, Monica leaving the church, not to mention their burgeoning assassin-for-hire business. "Sera and I are going upstairs. We'll see you in the morning."

Richard gave him a mock salute, winked at me, then trundled outside, presumably to show Monica to bed. Fix took me by the hand and started to lead me up the wide, carpeted staircase.

"I'm assuming you're too tired for the nickel tour," he said stiffly.

"Yeah," I confirmed. "But maybe tomorrow...?"

"Yes. Tomorrow." There was a frosty edge to his tone that I found less than heartening. What the hell was wrong with him?

At the top of the stairs, a broad hallway stretched to the left and right; Fix turned to the right and led me after him. After passing a number of closed doors, he stopped at the second door from the end and opened it. The room inside was nothing like his bedroom at the penthouse. Where that room was fairly sterile and spare, this room was overflowing with stuff. Baseball gear. A basketball, wedged between a row of books on a wall-mounted shelf. CDs and DVDs. A lovely brass telescope beneath the window, the lens pointed up toward the sky. This was the room he had grown up in, and, while all signs of his adolescence was gone, I could easily imagine the walls covered in posters of sports cars and woman in bikinis leaning over motorcycles as if they knew how to ride them.

Then again, maybe the original Father Marcosa hadn't allowed such suggestive images on the walls of his home.

Fix dropped my hand and raised the tumbler to his lips, taking a sip as his eyes traveled around the room, as if seeing everything for the first time. "Maybe we'd be better off in one of the other rooms," he said.

"What's wrong with this one?"

He stepped toward the large double bed and swiped something from its surface, stuffing it into his back pocket.

I canted my head to one side. "You trying to hide something from me, Mr. Marcosa?"

Leveling me in a pitiless stare, Fix shifted his weight from his right foot to the left, raised his glass to his lips again and drained its contents in one mouthful. "Yes," he said.

Oh.

He was being honest, at least. But fuck that. After the past month and everything that had happened, he figured hiding things from me now would be okay? "Why?" I demanded.

"I'd have thought that was obvious. Because I didn't want to see it."

"I just watched you kill a man. Before that, I watched you electrocute a man in a bathtub. What could you possibly not want me to see *now*?"

A hard, unyielding light flared in his eyes. He thought for a moment, and then he shrugged his shoulders. "All right. Fine. Here." He reached into his back pocket and produced the mystery object he'd secreted away out of sight. He slapped it into my outstretched hand, and I stared down at the piece of stiff white fabric with a morbid kind of fascination.

It was a Roman collar.

A priest's collar.

His.

"Richard must have forgotten to throw it out," he said.

"Why would you want to hide this from me?" I asked slowly. "I know about your past. I know who you were before you started all of this." I held up the collar, frowning at it, and then turning that frown on him. "This is nothing to be ashamed of, Fix. Just because I don't believe in a higher power doesn't mean I've judged you because you used to be a priest. Is that what you think?"

"No."

"Then what? You've been acting weird since the moment we arrived. I don't think either of us have the energy to be dancing around whatever it is that's clearly bothering you."

He sucked his teeth, his lips forming a pinched line as he looked down at his feet. "This place...a lot happened here. There are a lot of...*memories*."

"I can imagine."

"Most of them are difficult for me. My father was a hard man, Sera. And my mother was a bitter, unhappy woman. Being here reminds me of all the shitty, harsh words that were traded here. I don't feel comfortable in my own skin within the walls. I don't know myself here. And that," he said, jerking his chin at the collar, "only goes to prove that point further. The man who wore that thing is a stranger to me. And I don't particularly want to be reminded of him."

A selfish thought occurred to me. A thought that would have dramatic implications for me if I were right. "Do you regret walking away from that life? Do you wish you were still a priest?" I'd asked that question in my head before. Wondered if he still talked to the god he devoted so much of his life to before that fateful day when he found Monica, lying broken and bleeding on the floor of that rectory.

"Of course not. But I—I miss *aspects* of that life. The..."

"Innocence?"

He gave a hard laugh. "Being a priest doesn't afford a man any kind of innocence. Death. Deceit. Betrayal. Guilt. Lies. Every day it's something new. People get to be their very worst when they sit down on a church pew. They know, when they walk out of the building an hour later, they've been forgiven for every terrible thing they've done, and all because they've taken a few moments out of their week to soothe their consciences and say they're fucking sorry."

"Then what?"

"I miss the idea of freedom. I miss being able to make plans. I miss the simplicity of it all. Knowing what my day is going to look like. I miss meeting people and seeing hope and kindness in their eyes, instead of hurt and anger. You spend so much time around hate, and greed, and people's lust for revenge, and it begins to change you in irreversible ways. I—" He sounded like he was being strangled by the words he was trying to force out of his mouth. He sighed, frustrated, running a hand through his hair. Putting down his glass, he began to pace up and down at the foot of the bed.

There was more that he wanted to say. More that he felt he *couldn't* say.

I stepped in front of him, holding out my glass of whiskey to him. "Looks like you need this more than I do." He gave me a thankful look as he accepted the glass and drained it in one go.

"I miss the idea that I might be able to have a family one day," he said quietly. "I used to hate coming back here. Fucking *hate* it. My mother told me that would change at some point in my life. One day I'd bring a woman here and I would feel differently. I wouldn't see a cage with high walls and bars at the windows. I'd see a place where I could build a life with someone. Where I could raise a family. She knew I'd end up leaving the church at some point, even before I did." His smile was sour and strained. "And when I turned around and saw you standing there in the entranceway, Sera, that's exactly what happened. I imagined a life here, for us, and...*fuck*. I wasn't afraid of it. I always thought I would be, but I wasn't."

A heavy weight settled over me. Heavier than a ten-ton elephant sitting on my chest. I'd never given any thought to kids. I'd done everything in my power to not think about kids. My childhood had been so messed up and damaging that I couldn't even begin to comprehend how I would care for a child and give it the life it deserved.

If I were smart and possessed a single ounce of common sense, I would have turned around and told Fix I was never going to have children with him. It was one thing to accept this kind of life for myself; I was old enough and tough enough to make my own calls, to weigh the risks, to assess what a life with him looked like, the dangers and the complications that came with it, and to take them on with a full knowledge of what the decision could mean. But a child couldn't choose for themselves. They couldn't weigh the pros and cons of a life with us as parents and sign up for it willingly. It wouldn't be fair.

But then again, if things were to change. If there was any chance things were ever going to be more stable for us, would that make a difference? The question was too big for me to even begin picking apart.

"No need to look like you're gonna shit yourself," Fix said, smirking. "I'm not making plans, Sera. Just talking out loud. For the time being, I'm focusing on one thing, and that's extricating us from the current clusterfuck of a situation we find ourselves in. Once that's all said and done..."

"Yes. Once that's said and done, we can start to think about the bigger picture," I agreed. Relief soaked into my bones.

Time.

Once this was over and I wasn't in danger of losing my life, we would have time to think about things like that. In the meantime, all we had to do was stay one step ahead of the game.

"I've freaked you out. I'm sorry for that," Fix said, stepping closer to me. "I'm not sorry for the sentiment, though. This place will always be here, waiting for us, if you decide you want to take a run at a big, bold, beautiful, *relatively* normal life with me. Now let's forget all about it. I have something I want to ask you." He seemed lighter. More his usual, cocky, easy self. He smirked as he leaned in close, his lips brushing the shell of my ear. "I'm wondering if you'll hear my confession, Sera Lafferty."

The apples of my cheeks ached as I tried not to smile. "That might be a monumental task. How long has it been since your last confession, child?" I asked in a mocking tone.

Fix was often so stoic, his facial features so well restrained that it must have been difficult for anyone who didn't know him intimately to tell what he was feeling. I knew his secret, though. He expressed himself with those brilliant silver eyes of his, and right now they were filled with a wicked mirth.

"That was far too convincing," he murmured. "You sure you haven't done this before?"

"First time. But I've watched a lot of movies. I know how this stuff goes."

"Well, my lady. In answer to your question, it's been five years since my last confession. And I have been an *unbelievably* bad boy," he whispered.

Holy shit. This man was going to be the death of me. "Is there something in particular that's playing on your mind?"

"Actually, there is. I've been spending a lot of time with someone new recently. She's brilliant, and beautiful, and she makes me feel alive. I've been having impure thoughts about her. Very, *very* impure thoughts."

A shiver danced down my spine, sending out a wave of anticipation that made my nerve endings prickle. "I see. And this woman. She's aware that you harbor feelings for her?"

"Oh yes. She's very aware."

"And do you think she feels the same way about you?"

"I *know* she does." The low, deep rasp of his voice was tinged with the beginnings of desire. "I see the way she looks at me. The way her body reacts whenever she's around me. Her pupils dilate. Her cheeks turn bright red. Her lips..." He turned his head, angling himself so his mouth was hovering over mine. "She wets her lips, as if she wants me to kiss her."

"Do you think she'd let you?" I fought to keep my voice level. Unaffected. It was impossible. Fix's mouth lifted up at the corner— one half of a salacious grin. "Oh, yeah. She'd let me do whatever the fuck I wanted to her."

I tutted disapprovingly. "Language, my child."

"My girl *likes* when I say bad words," he breathed. "She likes when I talk dirty to her."

A scorching heat rose up my neck. "How can you be so sure?"

"Because her breathing changes," he said casually. "Her back arches. I can *smell* how badly she wants me."

"And what...what..." His close proximity was messing with my body. My mind. My thoughts. They were fractured, spinning around like drunken moths around a flame. "What do you tell her?"

"I tell her how hard my dick is. I tell her how badly I want to unzip my pants and take it out, so I can show her how fucking hard she makes me." He moved as he spoke, doing exact that—unfastening his fly, his hand sliding inside his pants. He shuddered as he took hold of himself. My eyes flickered down between our bodies, but Fix used his index finger to lift my head, so that my gaze moved back to his. "I tell her when she is and isn't allowed to look, though. I tell her that she has to play the game, or she doesn't get to see anything."

"That sounds like a cruel punishment to me."

"Mmmm. But I *am* cruel. I make her wait. By the time I give her permission to give in to her needs, she's panting for me. Begging for me. Whispering all of the things she wants and needs from me."

"You like it when she begs?" My breath hitched in the back of my throat. This was pure torture, and he knew exactly what he was doing to me. He smiled, his mouth returning to whisper in my ear.

"The sound of her begging makes me want to hold her down and pin her to the ground. It makes me want to use my tongue to lick and taste every inch of her. Makes me want to slide my fingers between the folds of her wet pussy, so I can feel how badly I've caused her to lose control. When she begs and pleads for me to take her, I feel like a fucking king."

My palms were slick with sweat. I wanted to touch him. I wanted to take hold of the hem of his shirt, and I wanted to lift it up over his head, so I could feast my eyes upon the hard, packed muscle of his chest. "You enjoy feeling like a king? Does that mean you want to rule her?"

"Yes. I want to rule her. I want to own her. I want to dominate every part of her body and her mind. But that's the thing about this woman. She's my queen, and she has her own desires. Sometimes she wants to be ruled. Other times, she demands I obey *her* commands down to the letter. For every dirty, filthy thing I do to her, she's free to do the same to me."

Slowly, he reached around and placed his hand at the small of my back, drawing me to him. The negligible space between us disap-peared, and his body lined up with mine, his chest pressing up against me. His hand worked between us, still down his pants, stroking himself as he sighed his dark entreaties to me. I wanted to watch what he was doing more than I wanted sleep. More than I wanted food, or light, or the air in my lungs. He could have demanded anything from me at this point, *anything*, and I wouldn't have been able to stop myself from giving him exactly what he wanted.

"If you were with this woman right now, what would you ask her to do?" I panted.

Fix didn't hesitate. "I'd tell her to get down on her knees. I'd tell her to open her mouth and stick out her pretty, pink little tongue for me."

I didn't even think about it. If I thought about it, I was going to end up thinking *too* much. Less than a second later, I was on my knees, my heart surging, throbbing so hard that I felt like I was about to pass out. I opened my mouth and stuck out my tongue, battling against the urge to close my eyes.

"Don't do it," Fix warned. "Don't you dare, Angel. You already boarded the ride. The safety announcements have already been read. There's no getting off now."

A frisson of electricity zipped down, between my shoulder blades —a cascade of lust and need, colored red with fear. Fix dipped his thumbs below his waistband and teased his jeans down over his hips. His cock sprang free, swollen and rigid, the tip glistening with a bead of pre-cum. I loosed a strained breath down my nose, waiting for what was about to happen next. "My girl loves the taste of my come," he growled. "She'd never admit to it, but when I come in her mouth, she loses her fucking mind. Watching her break apart as I climax for her is the most beautiful thing in the world."

With slow, measured movements, he rubbed the pad of his thumb against the end of his erection, smearing the pre-cum onto it. I couldn't hold back the moan that clawed its way up and out of my throat when he touched his thumb to the end of my tongue, depositing the evidence of his arousal there for me to taste.

Fix's matching, breathless groan had me closing my lips around his thumb, sucking it into my mouth. "Fuuuck, Sera. Oh my god."

With his free hand, he caressed his fingers down the side of my face, along the line of my jaw. His eyes flashed with a savage hunger when I looked up at him, and I gently bit down against his skin, sending him a savage look of my own. He withdrew his thumb, running the slick wetness of my own saliva along my bottom lip.

"I confess," Fix said, his chest laboring. "There are things I want to do to my queen. Things that would make her quake down to the roots of her soul. She inspires the most twisted, dark, fucked up fantasies in me."

Oh my god. I *needed* to hear his confession, but I was scared. Beyond scared. The boundaries he'd already pushed with me had been exhilarating and confronting beyond measure. If there was more...I had no idea if I could handle more from him. I'd been brave enough until now, though. I could be brave again. And I knew that even though this ride *had* started, Fix would apply the brakes and carry me away from it the moment I told him I wasn't enjoying it anymore.

"Say it," I whispered. "Tell me."

"I want her on her stomach. I want to tie her down. I want to gag her. I want to lie my body over hers, and I want to slide myself inside her tight little asshole. I want to feel her break out in a sweat as I thrust myself inside her. I want to fuck her pussy with my fingers at the same time. I want to dig my fucking nails into her beautiful, round ass cheeks as I watch my cock drive into her."

Each statement was ground out between his clenched teeth. I didn't move as he bent over me and fisted my shirt, ripping it over my head. I stayed exactly where I was as he tugged the straps of my bra down over my shoulders, pulling the lacy cups down to reveal my breasts. He kneaded them roughly with his hands, and my body responded, my back arching. I fastened my lip between my teeth, biting down so hard I could taste blood. I was awake. I was humming with expectation. I was *alive.*

"I want to mark her body with my teeth," he continued. "I want to bite her nipples so hard that she can't take it anymore. I want to spread my come all over her body and rub her clit with it until she comes all over *me.* I want her to give herself completely to me. I confess. I don't just want her body. I want her trust. I want her—"

"Fuck, Fix," I panted. "God. *Please.* I can't...I need...Fuck, just...*please!*"

"Are you begging, Angel? Are you *begging* me to fuck you?"

"*Yes. Fuck, yes, I am.*"

"I told you how it makes me feel when you beg." His hands were on me, taking hold of me, the contact of his skin on my skin setting me ablaze. "Up," he commanded. "On your feet, Angel."

I had hoped he was going to slide himself into my mouth. Giving Fix head was a dizzying experience. The way he tangled his fingers into my hair, and the way his head tipped back, his eyes closed as he lost himself to his longing, filled me with such an intense high. I really did love making him come with my mouth, feeling him getting impossibly hard as I slid my lips down over him. There wasn't time for any of that tonight, apparently.

His hands were quick but precise; my jeans were around my ankles seconds later, and he was crouched at my feet, pulling the material from my body. My panties were the last things to go. Our positions now reversed, Fix looked up at me, his lips parted, and a strange, heavenly look of fascination strewn across his remarkable face. It was written all over him: he was *stunned* by me, surprised that I even existed, which was ironic given that I felt exactly the same way about him.

Did fate exist? And if so, how the hell did it work? How was it decided that Felix and I should cross paths?? How did two broken, scarred, and damaged people end up in the same motel room in the middle of the same storm? And which interweaving threads of the universe decided we should fall in love? I couldn't even pretend to know the answers to those questions. All I knew was that I was grateful for the providence of our situation, however it came to be. Even if we had been brought together by the most frightening of circumstances.

Fix was plagued by the most inconvenient attribute any assassin could possess: a conscience. He was complicated. He was constantly being pulled in so many directions at once, but he somehow managed to navigate the treacherous waters that surrounded him without appearing to flounder.

He was undeniably handsome. His full mouth, so often curled into the most infuriating smirk, haunted my thoughts all damn day. The angular cut of his high cheek bones, and the stubborn, defined line of his jaw were all I could seem to think about sometimes. And his eyes. Fuck, those eyes. I'd never seen anything like them before. So startling. He could penetrate the depths deep down into my soul with those burnished, quicksilver eyes of his. He had the face of an angel, the body of a god, and a mouth that could make the devil blush.

"Your body's the most incredible thing I've ever fucking seen," he growled. "I'm not greedy. I'm not fucking jealous. I don't care about money, or cars, or any other material possession. I don't crave things. But you, Sera...I crave *you*. I covet your perfect fucking body. I won't allow anyone else to touch it. To look at it. To even imagine what it would be like to revel in it. Your tits and your ass are mine, Sera. Your beautiful pink pussy is mine. Your mouth. Your hands. The sexy arch of your back when you're riding my cock. Mine. All of it is mine. Do you understand?"

His possessive streak really was a mile wide. If Gareth had ever tried to tell me he owned me, I would have kneed him in the balls so hard he would have been spitting up blood. Being owned by Gareth would have meant I no longer had a voice. I wouldn't have been entitled to an opinion. Would no longer have been free to do and say as I pleased. I would have been under his control every waking moment of every day, his play thing to be used and abused as he saw fit.

It was different with Fix. Being his didn't mean I lost a part of myself. He treasured my opinions. He encouraged me to use my voice. He might have wrestled with me for control, but he never forcefully took it from me. If I handed over the reins to him at any point, it was because I wanted to experience the rush and the freedom that being vulnerable with him invoked. Being Felix Marcosa's queen was a title I cherished more than any other title I could ever possess.

"I understand," I said softly. "I *want* to be yours."

He snarled as he unfurled to his feet, running the palms of his hands along the sides of my body as he rose. "My blood's on fire, Sera. I'm completely fucking losing myself to this. If I ask too much..."

"I'll tell you. I'll stop you. But I know you won't." I wanted him so fucking badly. He'd already told me exactly what he wanted to do to me, and I hadn't flinched. I'd surprised myself, but it was true. A deep rumble emanated from Fix's chest, vibrating against my sensitive skin. Taking hold of me, he swept me into his arms and threw me onto the mattress.

He rained down kisses all over my legs, my hips, my stomach, and the swell of my breasts as he climbed up the bed, hovering over my body. Mesmerized, I watched the muscles in his shoulders and his chest flex and contract as he shifted, reaching into a drawer next to the bed, and he pulled out a long length of cord.

No, it wasn't cord.

Small, polished beads of obsidian shone in the dim light. Something dangled from the loop of the beads, undistinguishable at first, and then forming the shape of a carved, stone cross. A crucifix. Fix was holding a rosary.

Taking my right hand in his, he looped the rosary around my wrist, once, and then again, and then he took my other hand and slide the heavy, cool rope of beads around that wrist, too, repeating the process until the small, hard orbs of stone were pressing firmly into my skin. My fingers tingled, the blood flow to my hands immediately restricted.

Fix took hold of beads and looped them over the wrought iron bedpost to my right. There was nothing stopping the loop of beads from sliding down the post, all the way down to the mattress, where my bound wrists came to rest on top of the crisp white sheets.

"Spin over, Angel. You know what's coming."

My heart stuttered, climbing up my throat, but I swallowed it back down. I obeyed. With my bare back to him, and my buttocks on show, I felt suddenly very exposed. Fix climbed off the bed, was gone for a split second, and then he was back, his body bracing mine, arms and legs either side of me.

His skin didn't touch me anywhere, but I could feel the blazing heat coming off him in waves. He reached around and his hand came into view. In it: something white, bundled in his fist. "Open your mouth." The order was low and brooked no argument.

The white material he slid into my mouth was rough and rigid and tasted faintly of chemicals. What the fuck was it? What the fuck was *on* it? My mind cartwheeled out of control for a moment, but then...I knew what the piece of material was. The chemical taste on the fabric was starch; it was the Roman collar he'd tried to hide from me.

Holy fuck.

Flames licked at my face, down the skin of my neck, across my chest. There was probably a crimson blush covering half my body. A rosary and a Roman collar. His choice of restraints said a lot. Once, these items had been a sign of his faith. *Tools* of that faith. Now, he was using them to tie me up and gag me while he fucked me. I got the feeling that he was making a point. Here, in his father's house, who had been cruel and harsh with him his entire life, who had forced him into a life he wouldn't have chosen for himself otherwise.

His actions were a fuck you to a man long dead, but I didn't mind. These were relics of a religion I didn't believe in. Fix could use them as he saw fit, especially if that use brought him some kind of closure.

He rocked his body over the top of me, grazing his chest along the skin of my back. Over my buttocks, I could feel the long, hard length of his cock, pressing insistently against me. He was so fucking big. So fucking hard. How the hell was he going to fit himself inside me?

"Shhhh. Don't tense up. I'm going to look after you, Angel." Fix could read my mind, or perhaps he was just really fucking good at reading my body. Either way, he knew I was wondering how badly this was going to hurt, and he was doing his best to put my mind at ease. Kissing the nape of my neck, his rough stubble caused goosebumps to spread down the backs of my arms and my legs. *Shit.* The sensation was devastating. I whimpered around the collar in my mouth, my muscles softening like butter beneath him.

I couldn't move. If I moved, the rosary strained against my skin, making my hands throb like crazy, so I stayed as still as I could while Fix slipped his fingers down between my legs.

"Fuck me, Sera. You've drenched the fucking sheets." I could hear the hunger in his voice. It coated his words like thick, warm honey. "I'm going to make you feel so fucking good," he swore.

He'd already begun. My thoughts were splintered all over the place. As he slowly inserted his fingers inside me, and a string of colorful expletives formed on my tongue; mercifully they were muffled by the collar, otherwise Fix would have heard me call him something rather offensive. He was teasing me, moving too slowly. I needed him inside me right fucking now.

He chuckled darkly under his breath. "It's okay. Don't worry. You can take it." The timbre of the statement suggested I was going to have to figure out how, one way or another, because he wasn't going to give in to my screaming desire before he was good and ready.

I closed my eyes, breathing heavily down my nose, bracing for whatever was coming next. I didn't have to wait long. With fingers slick from my pussy, Fix slowly began to rub between my ass cheeks. The tips of his fingers worked over me, moving in small circles, working me until I relaxed against the contact. It was going to hurt. I knew it was going to hurt, but when he slipped one of his fingers inside me, he did it gently, carefully, moving a millimeter at a time.

His prediction came true; I began to sweat like crazy, beads of perspiration breaking out across my brow and down the center of my back. The feeling was so intense, the pressure so great, almost *too* great, but Fix took his time, moving at a snail's pace, until gradually I began to feel myself sinking into the mattress. It was starting to feel good.

Soon, Fix replaced his finger with the tip of his cock. I locked up all over again when he started to work himself into me, bit by bit. I had to bite down on the collar to stop myself from grinding out an uncomfortable growl between my teeth, but soon even that discomfort waned, and I was left with a pleasant, burning hot sense of pleasure instead.

"I'm so fucking deep," Fix panted. "Can you feel me all the way inside you?"

I could. His touch was agony, and I was addicted to the pain. I couldn't separate myself from it, even if I'd wanted to.

I rocked my hips back against him as he drove himself forward, and a carnal, desperate pleasure spread through me, taking over. I was so close...

So close.

And so was Fix.

We both summited the peak of our climaxes together, and Fix roared as he came. I stumbled, tumbled and fell, soaring and falling all at once, and the pressure at my wrists increased as I strained to feel more of him, to take more of him.

The rope of beads that held my hands together strained, and then...*snapped*. Suddenly the pressure was gone, and a shower of obsidian beads exploded all over the bed, rolling off the mattress and scattering to the floor, each of them a prayer.

Fix curved over my body, his breath ragged as he stroked his hands over my prickling skin. "Now you've heard my confession," he whispered in a hoarse voice. "What will be my penance?"

I pressed a kiss against the arm he'd wrapped around me as I closed my eyes. He was still inside me, and he still would be, even after he'd withdrawn and I'd washed the evidence of our sins away. "No penance required, Mr. Marcosa. You and I are square."

55

SERA

SHUT DOWN

I woke alone. Bars of warm, honeyed light slanted through the open windows to the bedroom, and a gentle breeze tugged at the cream, floor-length curtains. When I turned over, I noticed the small beads stuck to my skin. The rosary beads from last night. A warm flush of horror washed over me, but then quickly dissipated. How was I supposed to feel bad for last night? It seemed as though Fix needed the release of the defiant act to dispel all the other memories that echoed at him from his bedroom walls.

I listened, straining to hear some sort of sound that might indicate where the man himself was, but I heard nothing. I was a stranger here. Fix had told me he'd give me the nickel tour today, but in the meantime I would have to locate him by myself. I got out of bed, dressing quickly, and I walked out onto the landing, once again listening for any sort of voice or indication as to where Fix might be.

I came across Richard first. The old man was standing at the foot of the wide sweeping stairs, as if he was waiting for me to appear. He was wearing the same crisp white shirt and black trousers as last night, except now the red tattered robe that had been slung over his shoulders had vanished. At his throat, a smart black bow tie had been tied, and a white linen cloth was draped over his left arm, as if he were waiting to accept an empty champagne flute from me.

"Well, good morning Ms. Sera," he said. "Been waiting on you. Not surprised you slept in late, I heard the pair of you caterwauling until the dawn."

Oh, perfect. Juuuuust fucking great. I probably wouldn't have given a shit if Fix's parents had heard us, but somehow, knowing the poor old man had been kept awake by us, especially in a house this big, embarrassed the crap out of me. "Yeah. Well, I'm sorry about that." I said, smiling awkwardly. The old man returned my smile, an impish light glimmering in his eyes.

"He be waiting for you in the dining room with Ms. Monica," he told me. "They already had breakfast, but I saved some for you. I'll go and warm it up now."

My stomach tightened and twisted at the mention of food. I hadn't even realized I was hungry, but the thought of eating now made me realize just how ravenous I was. Richard threw the white linen cloth over his shoulder and beckoned for me to follow after him. I would never have found the formal dining room if he hadn't found me at the bottom of the stairs. Guiding me through a series of wide, well-lit hallways, we passed a number of beautiful oil paintings and many more side tables bearing vases full of beautiful flowers. Knick-knacks, keepsakes and all kinds of treasures rested on shelves and bookcases, along with tome after tome. Fictional works, autobiographies, books on philosophy and theology. Countless works that covered the natural world. The sciences. Economics and politics.

Underfoot, plush rugs covered the parquet, and then the marble flooring, which was the color of freshly poured milk, flecked with hints of gray and gold that shone in the early morning light.

Eventually Richard led me through a right-hand turn, and I found myself within the formal dining room he had mentioned. A long, heavy, worn oak table dominated the room, with chairs enough for twelve people. At the far end of the table, Monica sat in front of an empty plate, and Fix sat beside her, rotating a coffee cup around and around on top of a coaster by its handle.

Monica's nurse's scrubs were gone. She was wearing a dressing gown, a lot like the one Richard had been wearing last night, and a pair of oversized navy-blue pajamas, shot through with a white pinstripe. She looked up when she noticed we'd arrived, and her entire demeanor changed. She'd been at ease and very still, and now she was like a startled deer, fidgeting in her seat.

Fix, on the other hand, seemed just fine. Better than fine. A secret, devious smile played over his lips when he glanced up from the coffee cup. Patting the seat next to him, he motioned for me to join him. Richard grumbled as he turned about-face and left the room, grousing about fetching my food.

There was something very Victorian about the whole affair, as if, when we'd driven upstate and entered this house, we'd stepped back in time to a more genteel era, where servants were still a thing, and luxury was expected. Where the lord and lady of the manor were waited on hand and foot.

My body ached as I sat down. My wrists were banded by a chain of small red marks, too—more evidence of last night's encounter; I'd be remembering and replaying the way Fix had masterfully manipulated my body long after the physical signs had faded away, though. I was probably never going to forget.

There was a light, unburdened air to Fix as he poured me a cup of coffee and placed it in front of me. The razor-sharp tension that normally hung over him was gone this morning, leaving behind a side of Fix I was unacquainted with. Happy-go-lucky Fix. Wonders would never cease.

The coffee was acerbic and slightly bitter, but as soon as the caffeine hit my lips I suddenly felt very, very awake.

"Monica has good news," Fix said.

The woman squirmed, tugging at the bottom of her navy-blue pajamas. She didn't say anything until Fix gave her an encouraging sidelong glance. "Carver emailed," she said. "He wanted to thank me for helping him locate you. He thinks..." She paused. "He believes that you're dead."

So, it had worked then. Staging my own death, lying in that stairwell, my body twisted like a pretzel, had paid off. Despite my misgivings, Zeth had done as he'd promised. He'd convinced his boss, who, in turn, had convinced Carver. I didn't even know how to react.

Monica rose from the table, quickly getting to her feet. "I just wanted to say that I was sorry, Sera," she said. "I didn't mean...I didn't mean to cause so much trouble. If I'd known how strongly Fix felt about you, I would never have..." She trailed off, her eyes cast down at her feet.

"It's okay." I tried to scrub the hard edge from my voice. "I understand why you did it. You don't need to say another word about it."

Fix gave my knee a thankful squeeze under the table. I raised the coffee mug to my mouth, hiding behind it as I took a deep swig. Apologies were difficult things. It was my experience that they were hard for the person who owed them, but just as hard for the person who had to accept them. A few words, even if they were heartfelt, didn't necessarily banish the consequences of someone's actions.

"Monica's going to stay here with Richard for a while," Fix said. "The old bastard's so intent on keeping the place tidy, but he's breaking more shit than he's cleaning. She'll be able to help him. Make sure he doesn't end up having a heart attack while he's polishing the silverware." His words were more for Monica's benefit than mine. He wanted her to feel useful, like she had a purpose.

But did that mean...?

I put my coffee cup down, just as Richard reappeared with a plate piled with eggs and bacon. I thanked him with a smile as he set it down in front of me. I waited until he left before I asked the question burning in my mind. "What about the *business*?" There was nothing else I could call it. Essentially, the operation Fix and Monica had been running for the past five years *was* a business. They provided a service, and they got paid for it. Or Monica did. And just because the service they were providing was highly illegal and would almost certainly earn Fix a one-way trip to death row, didn't mean there was no industry involved with it.

"Shut down," Fix answered. "At least for now. I think we need a break from all the..."

Murder.

"...*stress*," Fix finished carefully. Richard probably didn't know how Fix had been occupying his days these last five years; he clearly didn't want the old butler finding out now, because of a few errant words.

"I'm going to need a uniform," Monica said quietly. "A black and white one. Like in the movies." Black and white, like the very first uniform she put on back in Canada. The nun's habit.

"I'll order one for you," Fix said. His shoulders tensed as he glanced down at the ring of faint bruising around my wrist; he mustn't have noticed it until now. Tracing his finger along the mark, he hummed softly under his breath. "And I am finally going to take *you* back to Seattle," he informed me. His focus had drifted, his eyes a little glazed over. I knew exactly where he'd traveled to: last night, to his bedroom, to that Roman collar gripped between my teeth, and my hands bound over my head. To the outrageous, deviant things he'd whispered in my ear. I sucked my bottom lip into my mouth, trying not to turn red.

"And who said I wanted to go back there?"

"Your apartment's there. Your business. Your friends. You at least need to go back and tidy up some loose ends. See Sadie. Pack up your place. Assign someone to take care of your company."

He was right. And I'd already come to that decision myself; to have someone step in as temporary caretaker for the business, until I figured out what I wanted to do in the long term. Jasmine would be thrilled to be appointed temporary CEO. She was good at her job and deserved the opportunity to prove herself. She'd been holding down the fort for a long time already. She'd be more than capable of doing so indefinitely, or at least until I decided if I wanted to sell or not.

I did need to go back to my apartment, too, if only to pick up some extra clothes and some of my personal items. And Sadie. God, I really fucking missed Sadie. I hadn't had chance to check my own emails in days, and I didn't have a cell phone anymore. I'd told my friend I'd meet her for lunch at the beginning of the week, and I hadn't called or messaged to let her know I wasn't going to be able to make it. She was probably going out of her fucking mind, bombarding the Seattle police department with countless missing person's reports.

Monica excused herself, wrapping her dressing gown tightly around herself as she hurried out of the dining room. I dug the tines of my fork into the food Richard had scrounged up for me, sighing. "Fine. We'll go back to Seattle. But on one condition. I know how much you love driving, but I am so fucking sick of sitting in cars. We either fly across country, or we don't go at all."

He turned a devilishly smug smile on me. "Do I get to fuck you while we're in the air?"

"Of course."

"In that case, anything for my queen."

56

SERA

HOME SWEET HOME

The city looked like it was on fire as the plane touched down. The sky was burning gold, orange, and scarlet, bruised a deep purple on the horizon where the night was drawing in. How long had it been since I was here? A month? Five weeks at most. It felt like I'd been gone for a lifetime. So much had happened. So many hurdles and obstacles thrown in my way. Everything had changed the night of that storm, where I'd found myself trapped in that dingy motel room with a man I did not know.

Now I felt like I didn't know myself anymore. Something had changed so irrevocably inside me since that night in Liberty Fields that I knew I'd never be the same version of myself again. And the truth was, I didn't even know if I would ever *want* to be that person again. I'd been so set in my ways, following a routine day in and day out. Coming to work, meeting with clients. Attending meetings, then coming home, eating dinner, hanging out with Sadie. Years had passed, and nothing had changed. It would be safe to fall back into that life, but if the past month with Felix had taught me anything, it was that safe didn't always mean happy.

I'd slept some on the plane, drifting into a state of dreamless unconsciousness, but Felix had sat alert and rigid next to me the entire time, refusing to close his eyes. I got the impression he hadn't been on a plane in a very, very long time, which made sense given that traveling by air wasn't exactly easy for him. He'd used a fake ID to board the plane, one of many I'm sure he kept on his person at all times, but I could see by the sharp, irritated flashing in his eyes that the experience had been a troubling one.

We left the airport, collected our bags and headed out to find a cab. I was plagued by nerves as we approached the city center, nearing my apartment. Technically, I was going home. But home was no longer a collection of rooms, filled with books and clothes. It was the man sitting next to me, holding my hand. I was anxious as we climbed the stairs up to the third floor.

My building was so old it didn't even have an elevator, which made me feel weirdly embarrassed. Felix's penthouse in New York was beautiful. Everything was new, everything was shiny, everything was so distinctly *him*. When I'd left to attend Amy's wedding, I'd been in a hurry. I'd left the place in a state, my shoes strewn all over the entryway, papers left stacked all over the dining table. I was pretty sure I'd left dirty dishes in the sink and by now the jungle of plants dotted around the place were probably all dead. Not ideal.

What would my life here look like to him? Small? Average? So very underwhelming? I couldn't help but feel like he was going to judge me the moment he saw the place in such disarray. That was stupid, I *knew* I was being stupid, but I still couldn't shake it. Felix had put up with me rotating through the same seven sets of clothes for the last month and he hadn't blinked an eyelid. Why would he care that I hadn't been able to tidy up before I'd thrown my bags into my rental and fled the city?

I braced myself as I slid the key into the lock and opened the front door, cringing at the prospect of the mess we were about to face. Fix caught me up, wrapping his arms around my waist and holding me to him before I had the chance to step inside.

"Just fucking relax," he said, breathing into my ear. "You're wound up so fucking tight, you're gonna snap any second now." I could literally hear him smirking from behind me. "You got a weird china cat collection in there or something?"

"I hate cats," I replied.

"Creepy dolls then? Stuffed toys? Are there posters of Hanson all over your bedroom walls?"

I laughed despite myself. "The most embarrassing thing you'll find in here is a bunch of dead Peace Lilies and a half-eaten bowl of cereal on the kitchen counter."

"Well, then. Quit freaking out. Take a deep fucking breath and let's get inside. There's a weird old man staring at me right now and he's making me fucking nervous."

I glanced down the hallway to find Mr. Conroy in 12B peering through his cracked doorway. I waved to him, and the grumpy old bastard scowled so deeply it looked like he was sucking on a lemon. "Been strange people hovering outside that door for weeks, Sera Lafferty," he groused. "This is s'posed to be a quiet building." Giving Fix a pointed glare, he shook his head, his tufty white hair bobbing comically. "And no guests after nine," he sniped.

"That's not a rule, Julian. We can have guests whenever we like, and you know it. Now go back inside before I tell Rhonda you were being a dick."

"Who the fuck's Rhonda?" Fix hissed.

I tried not to smirk as I hurried inside the apartment, pulling Fix along behind me. "Rhonda's his nurse. He's kind of terrified of her, but she's the sweetest."

"She probably beats him with a paddle behind closed doors. Poor fucker."

I stifled a laugh as I wormed my way out of his arms, trying to scoot through the apartment before him so I could assess the damage. There were no shoes in the hallway, though. The throws had been straightened on the couch, the TV remotes placed carefully side by side on the arm. In the kitchen, the bowl I could have sworn I'd left sitting out was nowhere to be seen, and as for the house plants...

They were all alive and, frankly, looking better than they had when I'd left them.

Weird, but whatever. Obviously, my memory was playing tricks on me. I dumped my bag on the dining table. My hair had grown long enough to tie back over the past few weeks. I undid it, releasing it from the small ponytail I could now manage, shaking it out, sighing with relief.

"You'll feel even better if you take your bra off, too," Fix rumbled. "And if you're planning on taking that off, I don't see why you shouldn't just take everything else off, too."

"You just want to see my boobs."

"And?"

"And we've been on the road all day. I feel gross. I need a shower."

Fix shook his head. "You're not gross. You're sexy as fuck. I want to bury my head between your legs right fucking now. You're telling me you don't want that?"

The prospect was mighty appealing, but I had plane all over me, and I was pretty certain I smelled fucking disgusting. "I am showering," I insisted. "I didn't say you weren't allowed to join me, though."

"Now *that* sounds amazing."

Sex in the shower with Fix. Holy shit, sex in the shower with Fix would be a whole new experience that would likely cause bathing to become an addiction. He stalked toward me, looking up at me from beneath his brows, a salacious tilt to his mouth. "I'm going to soap up your tits. I'm going to wash every inch of you. Your chest, your back, your thighs. Between your legs..." He lowered his mouth, so that it was hovering over mine, little more than hair's breadth away. "And when you're all soapy, and you're whimpering and pleading in my ear, pleading for my fingers, and my tongue, and my cock, I'm going to bend you over, and I'm going to sli—"

He stopped, his sentence hanging in the air. His head picked up, his eyes glinting like chips of ice under the light cast off from the lamp by the table.

"What is it?"

"There's someone outside the front door."

"How the hell can you possibly know that? We're two rooms away from the—"

He held up his hand, cutting me off. He'd gone from turned on to on guard in less time than it would have taken me to blink. "Go to the kitchen. Get a knife. Wait there until I tell you it's safe," he commanded.

"Fix, you're being crazy." Man, being on the run since Wyoming had made him paranoid. But...then I heard it, too. A rustling, rummaging sound and then another sound, like metal scraping on metal. "*Fuck.*"

Fix hadn't been able to fly with a gun. He didn't have a single weapon on him, but he bolted toward the front door regardless, silent as a ghost, a deadly look on his face. My pulse began to thunder, pounding in my ears. I'd been so fucking stupid. I'd wanted to believe that this was all over so badly, that I'd managed to convince myself of it. I'd dreamed of being safe so much that I'd allowed myself to become complacent. Running into the kitchen, I did what Fix had told me to do, grabbing a knife from the block on the counter.

The front door opened.

A series of loud bangs rang out, echoing through the hallway. I waited for the sounds of a struggle.

Waited...

And waited...

They never came. My head was spinning so hard. I was going to throw up. Oh god, I really was. What the fuck was happening?

I resisted the urge to step out into the hallway to find out for myself. Fix had said he'd call when it was safe, and he hadn't called...

Stay put, Sera. Do not fucking move. Do not *fucking move.* I clutched the knife to my chest.

And then—

A loud thumping sound and a string of violent curse words. "What the fuck are you doing here?" a female voice cried.

Oh shit! I dropped the knife back on the counter, and I ran from the kitchen out into the hall, my legs threatening to go out from underneath me. God, I hoped he hadn't hurt her. "Fix, it's okay! It's okay! It's Sadie! She has a key!"

How could I have been so stupid?

In front of the open doorway, Fix was standing in front of my friend, fist raised, ready to punch her squarely in the face. I threw myself at him, grabbing his arm, relief singing through me when I realized she was okay.

Sadie's mouth fell open. Her eyes doubled in size, and she promptly dropped the bottle she was holding. It shattered on the hardwood flooring, a pool of ruby red wine spraying all over the place.

"Oh—oh my *god*," she said, holding her hand to her chest. "You guys...you fucking *scared* me." I stepped over the mess at her feet and threw my arms around her neck, hugging the shit out of her. She hugged me back, laughing nervously into my hair. "Shit, I'm sorry, Ser. I made a mess."

"It's totally fine. I'm just so happy to see you. I had no idea you were coming over."

"I didn't know you were going to be here, either. I just...I figured I'd bring over a bottle of wine for you, so you could have a glass whenever you finally got back." She untangled herself from me, holding me at arm's length so she could get a proper look at me. "I didn't hear from you. I was worried out of my mind. You look great, though," she said, shaking her head as she smiled. "Really, really great. That extended vacation obviously did you the world of good."

"Ha! Something like that. Sadie, this is Felix," I said, stepping to one side so he could meet her. "Felix, this is Sadie."

"Nice to finally meet you." He offered her his hand. "Sorry about the...y'know. For nearly knocking your front teeth out."

She'd turned a brilliant shade of scarlet. "That's okay. It's fine. Really." Her arm pumped up and down as Fix shook it. Sadie volleyed a confused look back and forth between me and Fix. The shock of being faced with a deranged six-foot-four man, ready to launch himself at her, was obviously still having an effect on her. "I'm afraid I haven't heard a word about you, Felix. Sera, you've been keeping secrets," she chided.

"I'm sorry. I—" Where did I even begin? The events that had taken place since I left for Amy's wedding were so monumentally huge that I didn't know which point to start at. And then I realized...I couldn't tell her most of it. I couldn't. If she knew how I'd come to be traveling with Fix, if she knew what he did for work, it would not end well. She was a fiercely logical, straight forward person. Telling her Fix was a hitman would only land him in jail. She'd call the cops immediately, if only because she thought she was doing the right thing to keep me safe.

"I kind of disappeared off the map there. I'm so fucking sorry. I'll tell you all about it over a glass of wine, though."

Fix cleared his throat, giving me a subtle *that's-really-not-a-good-idea* look. I returned one that clearly told him I knew what I was doing. We were getting pretty good at the whole communicating without talking thing. "All right," he said. "Well, I'm going to the store to grab some essentials. You guys probably need a good catch up. I'm assuming there's nothing in your fridge. Looks like you need a new bottle of wine, too. I won't be long."

I wanted to keep him here with me, to not let him out of my sight. He hadn't left me alone for days. Felt weird for him to be going somewhere without me now. *Good god, girl. Get a fucking grip. He's going to the store, not outer space.*

Besides, he looked uncomfortable as all get-out, probably unnerved by the prospect of two women giggling and chatting together like school girls, which explained his desire to make a sharp exit. "Thanks. Maybe make it two bottles." I winked at him, and he winked back.

A part of me swooned and died.

God, he was so fucking hot.

Fix patted his jeans pockets, checking to make sure he had his wallet, and then he left, giving me a lopsided smile as he closed the apartment door behind himself. I was still staring at the closed door when Sadie clicked her fingers in front of my face, trying to get my attention.

"Okay," she said, a wide grin taking up most of her face. "You have got some serious explaining to do, young lady. Who..." She shook her head, screwing her eyes shut, holding up an index finger. "No. *What* was that? I have no idea how you managed to convince that walking sex god to come home with you."

"Geez, thanks!"

"I'm serious," she said, laughing. "When I turned around just now and saw him coming at me like a fucking MMA fighter on crack, I sent up a prayer and thanked the universe that the angel of death was the sexiest thing I had ever seen. I swear, if he had just killed me, I really wouldn't have even been that mad about it."

I kept my laughter light and happy, but boy was it hard. Sadie's joke was ridiculously close to the truth; Fix kind of *was* the angel of death. I poked my tongue out at her. "Personally, I think he's lucky to have scored *me*."

She wrapped her arm around my shoulders, leaning her head against mine as we walked into the kitchen. "I know, babe. You're a hottie, too. But Jesus fucking Christ. Those *eyes*..."

~

I told her as much as I could without telling her the truth, which felt terrible and so, so wrong. I made up some bullshit story about meeting Fix at Amy's wedding instead of at the motel from hell, and when I explained to her that I'd extended my trip and stayed on, traveling through Virginia, Pennsylvania, and then to New York with him, she teased me, prodding me in the side, making fun of how I apparently 'went all starry eyed' whenever I said his name.

Did mentioning Fix's name put stars in my eyes? It was weird to hear things like that. I'd had no real time to process the fact that I'd, against all the odds, fallen in love with someone. It felt wrong to even acknowledge that I had fallen at all.

Fix had been gone for twenty minutes when I got up from the dining table and told Sadie I needed a moment to freshen up. "I was about to jump in the shower when you got here. I feel so nasty. I'm just gonna wash my face and my hands real quick."

"Please. I don't mind at all. Take a shower. I'm sure lover boy'll be back with the booze by the time you get out."

Lover boy.

Ha.

I made sure the water was piping hot before I climbed into the shower. The pressure was super high, striping layers of skin from my body as I stood under the powerful stream. So freaking good. I felt like a new born baby by the time I climbed out and wrapped a towel around me.

Shit. I should have brought clean clothes into the bathroom with me. I leaned over the bathtub, squeezing the excess water out of my hair, and then I brushed my teeth until I didn't feel like something had crawled into my mouth and died anymore. The blast of air that hit me when I stepped out into the hallway was cool and refreshing. "Just gonna get dressed, Sads," I called out.

No answer. She was probably rifling through the cupboards, hunting for something to eat; the girl was always hungry. I paused in the hallway to pick up her bag. The loud thumping sound I'd heard when I was stupidly clutching that knife in my hand, waiting for Fix's all-clear must have been her dropping it to the ground. The large, tan, leather record bag was beaten and worn from years of heavy use. Sadie had been carrying the thing around with her since the day I'd met her, which was to say a very long time. A notebook and a sheaf of papers had half-slid out of the bag and onto the floor. I gathered them up, about to push them back inside, when something caught my eye.

Strange...

It was a foot. The bridge of a foot, drawn in startling detail. I pinched the paper that was poking out of Sadie's notebook and carefully tugged on it, my forehead creasing with confusion as more and more of the drawing became visible. It was Sadie, but a younger version of herself. She was sitting on the floor, legs bent, knees drawn up to her chest, her arms folded and stacked, her chin nestled into the crook of her left arm, as if she were trying to hide. And, most worryingly of all, she was naked.

The curve of her breasts had been drawn with exaggerated care, and between her bent legs, the dark fuzz of pubic hair had been drawn in, disguising the outline of her vagina. How old would she have been in this picture? Thirteen? Fourteen? Way too young to have posed in a such a strangely sexual, vulnerable position. I frowned, my throat closing up by the second as I stared at the drawing, trying not to jump to conclusions. But it was hard. So fucking hard. Because I recognized the use of crosshatching in the figure's shadow. I'd seen the loose, messy stroke technique that made up Sadie's hair once before.

Whoever had drawn this...was the same person who had drawn those incredibly graphic images of me. The ones Fix had found in the bunker back in Centralia.

My hand began to shake.

Surely Sadie...

Fuck. There was no way Sadie had drawn them. She would never have drawn a picture of herself like this. There was just no way. Sadie was so straight-laced, it was hard to imagine her even making out with a guy, let alone going further with him. She was not a hyper sexual person. She wouldn't have even commissioned someone to do a portrait of her like this.

It wasn't as though I'd asked anyone to do those drawings of me back in Centralia, though. And I hadn't posed for them, either. Maybe the sick fuck who drew them drew this picture, too, and sent it to Sadie as a way of fucking with me. Of infiltrating my life.

God, if that were true, I was going to have to tell her the truth. I was going to have to tell her *something*. If she'd been dragged into this nightmare and she'd been sent such graphic, vile, personal artwork, then I owed her the apology of a lifetime.

I kept hold of the drawing as I padded barefoot down the hallway and opened my bedroom door. I'd get dressed, and then I'd have to speak to her. I didn't know what I was going to say, but—

The scream left my lips before I even really registered the sight before me.

Blood.

On the bed sheets.

On the window panes.

On the walls.

On the rug.

There was blood *everywhere*.

I couldn't fucking breathe. My bed was soaked with the stuff. I took a step into the room, and that's when I found the source of the blood. Dead eyes stared up at me, black and lifeless. Matted fur—brown, white, and now red—lay in clumps all over the sheets, torn from the...

I tried not to gag.

...torn from the body, as if someone had grabbed handfuls of skin and *ripped*...

It was no good.

I dropped to my knees, crumpling forward, and I retched, vomiting so hard it felt like I was never going to stop.

It was Archie, my dog.

Archie?

It made no sense. Archie was with the dog sitter. Colby would never have brought him back here and left him if I wasn't here. He loved Arch more than life itself. They were best fucking friends. Most of the time, I felt like Archie loved Colby more than he even loved me. So this...this was not sinking in properly. Who would have done this? Who would have hurt him so badly? Cut him open and pulled out his intes—

"I wasn't joking when I said I'd made a mess, Ser. I really am sorry about all of this."

I blinked, staring at the crimson stained rug beneath my palms, trying to focus my eyes, but they weren't cooperating. Slowly, I turned, and Sadie was leaning against my bedroom door, holding a mug in her hands. Hot steam rose from the mug—she must have made herself a coffee. "I see you found Daddy's drawing, too. Quite the little sneak, aren't you?"

"Daddy's...?" My whisper barely made a sound as it slipped past my lips. What the fuck was going on? What was she saying? I couldn't fit any of the pieces back together now. I couldn't comprehend even the simplest, most obvious of things.

Archie was...dead?

Sadie walked into the bedroom, the Cuban heels of her boots making dull thudding sounds against the rug; she pulled a face as she gingerly stepped over a red, twisted mound of what looked like internal organs that had been piled to the right of the bed. With her back to me, she faced the window, clasping the mug in both hands as she looked out over the city. "He didn't like people to know he could draw. He was always so dead-set on people being afraid of him. Drawing seemed like too romantic a pastime for a man supposed to strike fear into the hearts of anyone who had dealings with him. Funny, really. If he'd shown anyone his drawings, they'd have seen right away that there was nothing romantic about them at all."

"Sadie. What the...fuck is going on?" I was breathless. Couldn't fucking speak.

She came to me, squatting down so she could pick up the drawing I'd dropped. Our eyes met, and for the first time in years, I felt like I was looking into the face of a complete stranger. The warmth in her eyes was gone. Her usual, sunny disposition was gone, vanished, as if it had never been there at all. Her mouth was drawn down at the corners into a grimace of displeasure.

"What d'you think's going on, Sera? Come on," she said, tutting quietly. "I thought you were the clever one. The girl who had it all figured out. You certainly pulled the wool over my eyes, that's for sure. Do you have any idea what it was like to stand in that hallway before and see you hurtling around the corner toward me? Hmm? I thought I was about to have a fucking heart attack. See, I thought you were dead." She stroked her hand down the side of my face, her eyes sharp as daggers. "I brought that lovely bottle of wine here to celebrate your untimely demise, *finally*, and then boom. There you were, alive and well. I shouldn't have been surprised. You have this way of manipulating people. Bending them to your will and getting them to do whatever the fuck you want. I've watched you do it for years. If you could convince one hitman to spare you, why would I have assumed you wouldn't do the same with the second. Tell me. Did you fuck him, too?"

"*What are you talking about?*" No. No, no, no. This wasn't happening. Couldn't be. Something ugly, and cold, and evil squirmed in the pit of my stomach. This was a joke. A really cruel joke. A tear streaked down my cheek and dripped off the end of my chin. "You're *not* Carver," I whispered.

Sadie canted her head to the side, arching an eyebrow. She laughed, and the sound was brittle in my ears. "I'm not?" she asked in a mocking tone. "You sound so sure."

"You're my friend. We've known each other for years. You wouldn't do anything to hurt me." I didn't know who I was trying to convince, now—myself or her.

"Yes, we have been friends for years," she conceded. "And even I found myself falling for your bullshit charms. You made it so hard to hate you some days. Mostly, I've been quietly despising you, though. Waiting for the perfect time to teach you a fucking lesson."

"For what? What have I done to you?"

Sadie's face was a mask of pure hatred. "What's the worst thing you've ever done, Sera Lafferty? The thing that cripples you with guilt whenever you're alone?" She used such a measured tone and spoke so quietly that I knew this was a serious question. She really wanted to hear the answer. I wracked my brain, searching through my memories, bracing myself for the fall when I finally tripped over the answer.

"I didn't protect Amy as well as I should have," I said. "I didn't take her away from my father. I should have put her in the back of the fucking car and driven away from that place way sooner than I did."

Sadie's eyes narrowed into furious slits. Suddenly there was a knife in her hand. The same knife I'd pulled out of the block in the kitchen and then left on the counter. God knows where she'd been hiding it. "*Wrong,*" she snapped. "Wrong, wrong, wrong. That isn't the worst thing you've ever done. Try again."

I eyed the knife, flinching at the five-inch blade as she held it up in front of my face. The thing was wickedly sharp, its serrated edge a row of jagged teeth, primed to bite.

"I don't know. I have no idea."

She turned the knife and pressed the tip of it against my cheek. "*Think*," she hissed.

"I—I—fuck! I don't know!"

"You are *such* a piece of work. Let me help you out, since your conscience seems to have taken a permanent leave of absence. You used to live in Montmorenci. Your father, Sixsmith Lafferty, was a gambling, womanizing, alcoholic scumbag who didn't like to pay his bar tabs. One day, Sixsmith made an agreement with a local business owner he owed money to, and low and behold, you started to pay that local business owner weekly visits. You'd go to his apartment above his bar, and you'd disappear into his bedroom. You'd be in there with him for hours, crying and moaning, begging for him to stop, *pretending* you weren't enjoying his attentions, and all the while the local business owner's daughter sat in her bedroom with her hands clapped over her ears, trying not to listen."

Oh...

Oh my god.

She was...

"*Julia*?" I didn't want to believe it. I didn't want to process the information, but it was written all over Sadie's face: she was Sam Halloran's daughter. I would never, *ever* have known. She looked nothing like him. There was nothing of that fat, disgusting pedophile in her at all.

Her lip curled back into a sneer. "Before you started going to Sam's bar, he used to worship the ground his daughter walked on. He venerated her. Treated her like she was a princess. But all of that changed the moment you walked through their door. You warped something inside his head. You liked to pant and groan. You said no, you told him you didn't want him, begged him not to hurt you, but you *made* him do all of those things. You enjoyed it when he was inside you. You twisted everything, turned everything upside down. You taught Sam that a girl meant yes when she said no.

"And then, one day, Sam was furious. Sixsmith kept you home, told Sam you were sick, but the old man had been anticipating your visit all day. He'd paced the floor for hours, waiting for you to show up. He was disappointed. He turned to his daughter with a dead, hollow expression on his face and he told her to go into his bedroom. And there, inside the four walls of his bedroom, his daughter begged and pleaded for him to stop. But he didn't. He did terrible, awful, painful things to her. From that moment forward, Sam fucked you twice a week, but the other *five* days of the week, he dragged his own daughter into his room by the roots of her hair...and he did *unspeakable* things to her."

I didn't know how to process any of this. The shock was just too much. "He told me he never touched you," I said numbly.

"Maybe at first, he didn't. But you gave him a taste for the taboo. And what's more taboo than raping your own kid?"

"You really think I went in there willingly? You really think I fucking chose to go visit your father?"

"I didn't see anyone walking behind you with a gun to your head. Yeah, that's right. I used to watch you coming and going all the time."

"Peter would never have let me run."

"Pssshhhh. Are you kidding me?" She was tinged with madness: the wild, unbalanced excitement in her eyes; the way her fingertips drummed against the handle of the knife; the way she kept lifting the coffee mug to her mouth, only to lower it a second later. She'd been so calm and together when she'd walked in here. Now, she was anything but. She'd completely lost her cool. "Peter was a weak, mindless idiot. He wouldn't have done a fucking thing if you'd tried to bolt."

God, perhaps she was right. Peter had been a bit of a soft touch even back in high school. Still, there were other reasons why I'd had to comply with Sixsmith and Sam's fucked up arrangement. "If I didn't give them what they wanted, my sister would have paid for it. I could take them hurting me, but I couldn't let them hurt her. And I never encouraged Sam. I wasn't saying one thing and meaning another. I meant no. He *raped* me. Every week, twice a week, for a solid year, he fucking raped me."

Sadie rolled her eyes.

I couldn't believe any of this. For the longest time, I'd been meeting her for lunch. Brunch every Sunday. Yoga classes. Margaritas and tacos whenever either one of us was celebrating a big win. And all along, she'd been putting on a front. For fucking *years*. She'd been pretending to be my friend, pretending to be there for me, tolerating me when I came to comfort her, when all along her skin must have been crawling at my very presence and she'd been plotting *this* in the back of her mind.

"I need to put clothes on," I said. "You need to let me stand up."

"Does it really matter if you're naked or fully dressed when you die?"

"Sadie, please. Just let me get dressed and we can talk. You can tell me what happened with Sam. Explain everything. Just let me put some clothes on first."

She looked at me pityingly. "You're in no position to bargain. You don't get to negotiate terms here. If you think you're gonna be able to talk your way out of this, then you clearly don't know me at all."

"I *don't* know you, Sadie! You've been lying to me since the day we met."

An arrogant pride flashed across her face. "Of course I did. There's something quite intoxicating about holding the balance of power in one's hand. At any moment, I could have brought everything crashing down around your ears. You thought you were so smart, that you had everything under control, but you had no idea how much danger you were in. How out of your control your life was. Even with Gareth, you were so fucking blind. You caught him fucking his secretary in the end, but you had no idea I was fucking him *for months* before that."

What? Sadie and Gareth? I rocked back on my heels, the hairs on the backs of my arms standing up. I'd had no idea. Literally none, whatsoever. Gareth had let me down and hurt me, but that was old news. It hurt beyond belief to know that *she* had betrayed me with my ex-boyfriend. Stung more than I knew what to do with.

"Get up, then," she said, poking the end of the knife at me. "Get dressed if it'll make you feel better. Hurry, though. I plan on being far,

far away from this place by the time your treacherous moron of a boyfriend returns."

I didn't take my eyes off her, didn't turn my back to her as I quickly donned a sports bra, panties, an over-sized t-shirt and a pair of running shorts. Could I get away with putting shoes and socks on? I doubted it. She'd know I was trying to figure out how to run, and she'd never let that happen. My stomach tied itself into a knot of sorrow as I moved back to stand by the blood-soaked bed.

"You didn't need to kill Archie. He was a fucking dog. He didn't do anything wrong." I wanted to close his eyes, to try and give him some kind of peace, even though he'd obviously died in agony, but Sadie stepped in front of me, brandishing the knife in my face.

"I *did* have to kill him. You loved him, and he loved you. I need to destroy everything and everyone who cares about you. That includes your sister, and Marcosa."

"You really think you're going to outsmart Fix?" A chill ran up the length of my spine, though. She'd managed to fool us all until now. She was an expert liar, and an even better actress. If she put her mind to it, she'd probably be able to concoct some sort of scenario whereby Fix found himself alone with her, vulnerable and taken by surprise. Sadie would revel in the chance to prove he wasn't as smart as he thought he was, too.

She was a complete sociopath. Were sociopaths capable of feeling alone? If I were her, living a lie every day, putting a fake smile on every time she saw or spoke to me, feigning our entire friendship, then I would have felt like the loneliest person in the world. It was all pretty sad, for me *and* for her. She'd wormed her way into my life out of hate. And it turned out the woman I'd called my best friend for a long time had been secretly planning my violent demise since day one.

"My father drew you from memory, y'know?" Sadie said, kicking at the drawing on the floor with the toe of her shoe. "He never wanted to ask you to pose for him, so he'd sit there for hours, scribbling, trying over and over to capture an accurate likeness of you in his sketch book. He'd get so frustrated when he got something wrong that he'd beat me. That wasn't the worst of it, though. It was when he got it right that I'd be truly scared. When he was pleased with what he'd done, he'd get turned on. He'd bind my hands behind my back, then bind my wrists to my ankles, so I was stuck in a kneeling position, then he'd cut my clothes from my body with a knife. He'd fuck my mouth until he came, and all the while he'd be staring at the picture he'd drawn of you, grinding out your name between his teeth as he thrust himself as far as he could down my throat. Didn't care if he made me gag. Didn't care if I threw up all over him. He actually seemed to like it when I did that," Sadie clarified in a bitter tone. "So long as his imagination could whisk him away to you, it didn't matter if I was hurt, or sick, or bleeding. All he fucking cared about was you."

I was sick to my stomach. Peter had never said anything about Sam interfering with Sadie. With *Julia.* Why would he have said anything, though? It wasn't like he'd ever told anyone about Sam raping *me.* He'd kept his mouth shut, and he hadn't breathed a word to anybody about anything. Sadie blamed me for what happened to her back then, but it wasn't my fault. It was difficult to purge myself of the guilt, though. I supposed, in a small, fucked up way, she *was* right. If I'd railed against Sam a little harder in the beginning, his sense of shame might have gotten the better of him. He might have stopped. And then, later, if I'd quit beseeching him to end the assaults, if I'd just laid there, limp like a ragdoll, glassy-eyed and staring at the ceiling while he took what he wanted from me, maybe he would have grown bored. I'd known how excited it made him when I cried and whimpered. I was all too aware of how hard it made him when I told him he was hurting me, and I wanted him to stop.

He'd become obsessed with the power he had over me, and that obsession had bled over into his relationship with Sadie, until even her misery and fear didn't matter to him anymore.

"I'm sorry," I whispered. "Truly, I am. I can imagine what he put you through, because he put me through the same thing. But I'm telling you, if I'd known..."

Sadie sobbed, lunging forward with the knife. Her eyes shone brightly, but she wasn't crying. It was as if she was refusing to let her tears fall. "If you'd known, you would have killed him sooner?" she spat.

"Yes. Maybe. I don't know. I never intended t—" She lashed out with the knife. The polished steel sang toward me, making contact before I could dart out of the way. Blood blossomed from the burning three-inch long laceration on my forearm, and Sadie froze, eyes locked on the sight of my blood, as if transfixed by it.

"Don't make excuses, Sera. Excuses are only going to make me angry."

I hugged my arm to my chest, covering the shallow wound with my hand. If I didn't hide the damage she'd done, I could guess what was going to happen: one cut wouldn't be enough. She'd want to do it again, and again, and again. She'd want my blood to flow freely, and once we'd reached that stage, I was fucked. She had a knife. I had nothing to defend myself with at all. I knew how to relieve an attacker of a weapon, but I needed to wait for the perfect moment. Act too soon, and I'd end up on the floor, staring up into Sadie's crazed eyes as she stabbed me to death.

How long had Fix been gone? If I kept Sadie talking long enough, he'd come back and knock her the fuck out for real this time. I couldn't rely on him, though. It was too dangerous to play a waiting game like that. I had to handle the situation as quickly as possible. "Aren't you happy that I killed him?"

She jerked her head back. "What?"

"Aren't you at least glad that I *did* kill him in the end. I stopped him from hurting the both of us."

A vein pulsed angrily at her temple. "Are you insane? He was my father. I loved him. Even when he—even when he did those things to me, I knew he didn't really want to. You turned him into that monster. He just needed to get away from you. If you'd only left us alone, he would have stopped. He wouldn't have touched me anymore. But you fucking carved him up like a piece of meat." She was fire and vitriol— a spark, waiting to ignite. Leaning close to me, she shoved her face into mine, brandishing the knife underneath my throat. "You were the carver once, but not anymore. I didn't think I'd have the strength to face you like this. I hired Marcosa to do my dirty work, because I didn't want to sink to *your* level. Now, I'm glad things have worked out this way. Now, I really *do* get to become the carver. Marcosa won't even be able to recognize that pretty face of yours by the time I'm satisfied, Sera. I'm going to cut you into ribbons."

I was running out of time. She was losing her grip on reality. She was delusional if she believed her father would have stopped abusing her. *Ever.* Men like him never stopped until they were forced to. I didn't waste my breath trying to make her realize the truth, though. She'd never listen to me, no matter what I said. All that was left to do now was to get the fuck away from her before she had chance to follow through on her threats. I had to arm myself, and quickly.

"Peter paid for his crimes, too, y'know," Sadie said. "Took me a while to find him. Just like me, he'd changed his name. Moved to some fucking nowhere town in the middle of Pennsylvania. I hired him to work for me for a while, just like Daddy did, and then, when I was done with him, I shot him up with formaldehyde and left him to die slowly. Painfully. It must have been an awful death for poor old fat, useless Peter. I know you found him down there in that hole. I made him sit in front of a computer for hours, tracking you, monitoring your card transactions, figuring out where you were at all times.

"I waited for Marcosa to kill you for two fucking weeks in Seattle, but he didn't carry out the job. I figured the setting hadn't been right. Too crowded. Too busy. So, I tried to speed the process up. I hired him to take out that mechanic in Liberty Fields. I put him directly in your path again. Right in front of it, so he'd have no excuse. Next thing I know, he's in the background of three separate photos at your sister's fucking wedding!"

So Fix's job in Liberty Fields hadn't been a coincidence after all? He'd picked up the job to buy himself some more time, but Sadie had been the one to drop the work in his lap. She'd been pulling the strings behind the scenes this whole time, and I hadn't suspected a thing. She'd been the one to murder the guy in the bunker in

Centralia, too. Peter. I still couldn't believe that guy, Anderson, had been *Peter*.

He'd looked nothing like he used to, but then again, I hadn't hung around to get a proper look at him. His swollen, purple face and his bulging eyes had scared the shit out of me.

"Fix saw right through that ridiculous bullshit you said about me," I growled. "He watched me. He knew that file you sent through was complete and utter bullshit. You really expected him to believe I murdered my mom? That I was poisoning my sister? Come on, Sadie."

She shrugged. "I gave him the ammunition he needed to satisfy his bizarre moral code. I didn't expect him to try and verify any of it. Besides, you might not have been responsible for your mom's death, but you're very much responsible for Amy's. As soon as I'm done with you, I'm getting on a plane and I'm going to pay your little sister a visit. I'm going to slip a needle in her arm. I'm going to poison her, just like I poisoned Peter. And that *will* be your fault, Sera. She will settle the final debt between you and I. It's not enough that you'll be dead. You need to die filled with despair. You need to know that the people you love are going to suffer for your sins, even after you're gone. Amy. Marcosa. I'm going to—"

I saw my opportunity and I took it.

Sadie was ranting, lost in her rage. Her words struck fear into me, paralyzing me, but I couldn't afford to give in. If I quailed now, I'd be dead. Fix and Amy would be in danger. That simply wasn't an option. Reaching out, I grabbed hold of Sadie's wrist and twisted as hard as I could.

Her shriek of pain echoed around the bedroom. I yanked her entire arm around, gritting my teeth together as I pulled, forcing her arm up behind her back. She wailed, fury cutting through her pain; I was seconds away from ripping her arm out of the socket, but still she didn't drop the knife.

"Give it to me, Sadie!" I roared. "It's fucking over. Just drop it!"

"So you can stab *me* with it? I don't think so." With inhuman strength, she lurched forward, tearing herself from my grip. She spun, ducking low, dropping into a fighting stance—a whirlwind of malevolence, dressed in Lululemon yoga gear. If the situation hadn't been so dire, I might have fucking laughed at the madness of it all. The knife cut through the air as she slashed it toward my stomach. "Move, Sera. Out into the hallway. Go!"

I began walking backwards; there was no way I was turning around. I was going to see the crazy bitch coming if she decided to attack. "You're not going to do it," I told her. "You *aren't* strong enough. If you were, you would have killed me years ago, when we first met." Goading her was definitely not a smart move, but it was the only option available to me. If I riled her up enough, she might slip up. React before thinking, leaving herself wide open for my own assault.

"Shut up. Just shut your lying, manipulative little mouth, Sera. Go on. Into the bathroom."

Bad, *bad* idea. The bathroom was the smallest space in the apartment. At such close quarters, I'd almost certainly wind up dead. *Fuck.* What was in there? What could I use to defend myself. The sharpest thing I could think of was a razor, and against the huge knife in Sadie's hand a razor would be fucking useless.

"I'm not fucking around. Move it!" Sadie charged, jabbing the knife out in front of her. I twisted to one side, trying to avoid the sharpened steel, but I wasn't quick enough. The bite of pain seared across my flesh, digging its teeth in deep. She'd slashed my side open. Quickly, the fabric of my white t-shirt turned bright red as my blood began to soak through it.

Oh... *fuck.*

My head swam as I clasped my hands to my side, trying to stem the bleeding. I had no idea how deep the cut was, but it felt bad. It felt like she'd almost gutted me.

Sadie's entire face was lit up with excitement as she prowled toward me, backing me into the bathroom. "You're wrong. I'm *am* strong enough. I'm not weak anymore," she said. "I'm going to enjoy inflicting pain on you. I won't stop until every last inch of your skin is in ruins."

With that, she snatched up a ceramic candle holder from the shelf above the toilet and hurled it at the shower screen with all her might. I watched, my body slowly turning numb, as the glass screen shattered into a thousand pieces.

She grinned with menacing delight as she stooped, picking up the largest, sharpest piece of the glass, and took a step forward.

57

FIX

OH. SHIT.

"Thirty-eight fifty, please."

The male cashier smiled at me as I handed over two twenties; people were a hell of a lot friendlier here than they were in New York, that was for damned sure. I took my change and the bag of groceries from him and made my way outside, not caring about the fact that it looked like it was about to rain. I'd walked past four different stores before I'd stopped at this one, wanting to give Sera plenty of time to catch up with her friend. She undoubtedly had a lot to talk about with the woman after the long weeks spent apart, and the night air seemed fresher here. Crisper. Less muggy and humid than the sweltering, sticky streets of Brooklyn after the sun had gone down. The walk had actually been great after being cooped up on the plane for so long.

Didn't matter what Sera said. Driving here would have been better. We could have broken up the trip. Stayed in nice hotels. Enjoyed ourselves a little. Fucked each other's brains out at every rest stop along the way. Being stuck in that cramped tin can for six hours, unable to get up and move around, unable to take a breath of clean air, had been fucking torture. Next time I was going to put my foot down. No more planes for me.

My dick was still hard from earlier. We'd been seconds away from doing very dirty, degrading things to each other in the shower when Sadie had turned up unannounced. Seriously fucking inconvenient. Would have been better if she'd shown up tomorrow afternoon. Or even better, tomorrow evening. By then, my need for Sera might have been slaked a little, and we'd have been fit for polite company. As it stood, I was going to be itching to get the woman out of the door the moment I walked back into the apartment.

I needed Sera's perfect mouth on me. I needed her hands on my skin. I had some pretty elaborate plans that involved my tongue and her pussy, but they were going to have to wait until we'd made it out of the shower and into the bedroom.

I slowed my gait, grumbling to myself under my breath. If I came back sporting a raging hard on, snapping like an enraged bear at a woman I'd already nearly scared half to death, Sera would probably die of embarrassment. She'd wanted me really badly before her friend had shown up. I knew she had. But that didn't mean she'd want me acting like a fucking caveman, tearing her clothes from her body and demanding she get on all fours in front of Sadie.

So, I dragged my feet.

This was why I didn't have friends. They only complicated things and showed up without being invited. Sadie hadn't even known we were going to be there and she'd still let herself into the apartment. The girls must have been really damn close if Sadie was used to showing up without permission and taking advantage of Sera's place when she wasn't there. Sure, she'd spun some story about swinging by to drop off that bottle of wine for Sera to enjoy when she got back from her trip, but I could smell the lie on her. She'd come there to drink that bottle of wine herself. Lord knows why, when she could easily have stayed at home and drunk it there, but whatever.

When she'd turned around in the hallway and seen me, it had been the weirdest thing: she hadn't even flinched. Instead of surprise, her eyes had been filled with another emotion—something that had looked an awful lot like irritation.

The words she'd spoken had been a little off, too. At the time, I hadn't had the opportunity to pick them apart, what with Sera screaming toward me, yelling at me not to hurt her friend, but now my mind kept pulling me back toward that moment, as if trying to show me something I hadn't noticed yet.

What the fuck are you doing here?

What the fuck are you doing here?

What the fuck are you *doing here?*

Not, "Who the fuck are *you?*"

Not only had she asked the wrong question, but her inflection had stressed the wrong word, too. The way she'd emphasized the word *you*, as if she'd recognized me, as if she knew my face and she wanted to know why the hell—

The bag of groceries almost slipped from my hands.

Oh.

God.

No.

No, I was being crazy. Sera had only spoken highly of her friend. She'd only had great things to say about her. There hadn't seemed to be any sort of animosity between them back at the apartment. Sadie has seemed genuinely happy to see Sera, after she'd gotten over the initial shock of—

Unbidden, a thought occurred to me, giving life to a dark and terrible suspicion inside my mind. Sadie hadn't been shocked when she laid eyes on me. Why not? The hypothetical answer to that question: she knew perfectly well who I was...because she had hired me to put an end to Sera.

Sadie *had* been incredibly shocked to see Sera. Why? The hypothetical answer to *that* question: because Zeth Mayfair's boss had forwarded a photo of Sera's contorted, bleeding body to Carver, informing him that his mark had been taken care of.

Except in this hypothetical world, Carver was not a man. He was a woman.

Sadie *was* Carver.

And as far as she'd been concerned, Sera was fucking dead.

The night pressed in from all sides as I postulated a series of further questions to myself:

Why would Sadie want Sera dead?

Did she have the means to set something like that in motion?

If she were Carver, why wouldn't she have dealt with Sera personally, if she'd had so many opportunities in the past?

Any answer I formulated in response to those questions was mere speculation, weak at best. But there was this festering feeling, sinking down into my bones. This feeling I just couldn't shake. I'd gotten good at reading people in my previous line of work, and there was just something off about this whole thing. Something that suddenly refused to sit right...

I was running before I'd even really made the decision to move. The bag of groceries crashed to the floor, another wine bottle exploding on the ground, but I didn't care. If I was wrong here, if Sadie and Sera were gossiping like old housewives at the dining table when I arrived, then I'd happily go back out and get another fucking bottle of wine.

But if they weren't...

If I was right...

Hot, acidic bile rose up the back of my throat, making it hard to breathe as I pumped my arms, pushing myself, forcing one foot in front of the other.

Fuck, fuck, fuck.

I'd purposefully taken my time. I'd gone way further than I'd needed to. I'd stretched out the walk back, moving at a snail's pace, thinking I was doing Sera a favor, and yet there was a chance...

Fuck, I couldn't even think it.

I dodged pedestrians on the sidewalk, roaring at them to get the fuck out of the way as I barreled back toward Sera's building. I ran on the road, dodging the traffic, ignoring the angry car horns, when my path wasn't clear.

I faltered when I reached the lobby. Where was the elevator?

Where the fu—

Shit. That's right. There wasn't one.

My heart was bursting out of my chest as I launched myself up the stairs, taking them three and four at a time. I was used to running, but I'd never moved this fast in my entire fucking life. Adrenalin spiked, lighting up my bloodstream, making the lights burn brighter overhead, my ears picking up every sound as I sped toward Sera's apartment. The door to 12B swung open and the old man who'd been staring at me when we first arrived stepped out, a newspaper gripped tightly in his hand.

"Not now, Julian," I growled as I sailed past him.

"You tell those girls to quit screamin' and hollerin' at one another. I'm tryin' to watch my shows, and all anyone can hear is them bickerin' at the top of their voices.

Shit!

It took everything in my power not to slam the sole of my booted foot into the front door. If I busted my way in, my presence would be known immediately. Likewise, if I knocked, that would tip Sadie off. Instead, I moved quickly, fishing a card out of my wallet and sliding it between the doorjamb and the actual door itself, wedging it between the wood, giving it a hard, solid shove down, and then...

The lock popped open.

"That's illegal," Julian grumbled. "I'm afraid I'm gonna have to call the police."

"Damn it, Julian. I'll get Rhonda over here in a minute if you don't mind your own damn business." I left him standing out in the hallway, hoping and praying that he went back inside his own apartment and he didn't call the cops. Cops were the last thing we needed right now.

The door to the bedroom was wide open. When I saw the scene of destruction and old, dried blood beyond, my vision nearly faded to black. What the *fuck*? Where was Sera? Was she fucking hurt? If that bitch had harmed one hair on her head...

"*...inflicting pain on you. I won't stop until every last inch of your skin is in ruins,*" a voice hissed. By the way it echoed, its owner was somewhere small, somewhere cramped, somewhere tiled. They were in the bathroom. I rushed down the hallway, already planning the glorious revenge I was going to enact on Sadie for creating this mess.

When I saw the small pool of blood on the floor outside the bathroom, my rage, my fear, and my panic all just...ground to a halt.

This was not old blood, like in the bedroom. Was it Sera's? The sight of the vibrant, bright red fluid against the floorboards kindled the most reckless, cruelty in me. Of all the times I'd killed over the past five years, I hadn't enjoyed the experience once. If Sadie really had made Sera bleed, however, that was all going to change. I was going to do more than enjoy it. I was going to savor every last second of it as I strangled the life from her wretched body.

A crashing sound cut through the silence. The nerve endings in my body fired, pulsing through me like an electric current.

"Sadie, no! Just *stop!*"

I had no idea what was going on in that room, but I wasn't going to wait any longer. Sera was in danger. Her life was being threatened. I threw my weight behind my shoulder, crashing into the bathroom, and an explosion of broken glass went skittering across the tiled floor. Sera stood by the wash basin, wearing a white shirt that was stained red with blood. There were small cuts and scrapes all over her feet. Her eyes were vacant, staring numbly down at her hands, which were...

Which were...

I released an uneven breath, my finger nails digging into my palms as I stared down at her stomach. She was holding something in her hands. Something jagged and sharp.

To the side of her, Sadie smiled smugly down at the huge piece of glass she'd obviously just driven into Sera's stomach.

"This is how she did it to my father," she said, addressing me. "I could have used the knife, but this seemed more fitting. A shard of glass for a shard of glass."

Sera's eyes found mine. Her lips were parted and flecked with blood. She licked them, and the blood transferred to her tongue. She was so, so still, but she was panicking, I could tell. "Do *not* pull that out," I told her. "Look at me. Sera, look at me. Everything's going to be all right. I promise."

"Tut tut, Father Marcosa. You really shouldn't make promises you can't keep," Sadie said in a sing-song voice. "Little Sera Lafferty only has about half an hour to live. Stomach wounds aren't very practical if you want someone to die quickly. I don't mind waiting a while, though."

What the fuck did the woman think was going to happen right now? Did she really think I was going to let her live long enough to see Sera draw her last breath? *No fucking way.* A ruthless growl built at the back of my throat as I crossed the small bathroom and I took hold of the woman by the throat. "You're insane," I snarled. "You've accomplished nothing here. You're going to fucking die, and we're going to forget all about you."

I slammed her into the tiled wall. Her feet were five inches off the ground, the heels of her boots kicking and scraping at the patterned ceramic tile as she fought for purchase. I wasn't going to let her have it. She'd dared to hurt Sera. She'd been hurting her for weeks, and I wasn't going to fucking let her do it anymore. Sadie's face turned a brilliant shade of red as I closed my fist tighter around her neck, digging my fingers into her throat.

"*Fix.*"

I immediately responded to the sound of Sera's voice, turning my attention to her. The bloodlust that had taken hold of me was powerful, but it wasn't powerful enough to drown her out. Nothing would ever be *that* powerful. "Please," she said. "Just let her go. Take me to the hospital."

"I *can't*. After everything she's done to you..."

Sera's face was sheet-white as she reached out and placed her hand on my bicep. "All of those people who hired you came to you, begging for you to deliver them vengeance. I'm begging for you to have *mercy*. She's already suffered enough. We should let the police deal with her. I just... I just want this to be over."

I stared into her eyes, wondering how I'd ever come across anyone capable of such compassion. I'd forgotten what compassion was altogether. Had no clue what it even fucking looked like.

Just fucking kill her. Snap her neck. Get it over with.

The voice inside my head, urging me to handle the situation with swift, brutal precision, was very persuasive. But when I looked at Sera and saw the resolved angle of her shoulders and the fiery determination in her eyes, I knew I would lose her. If I squeezed just that little bit harder, if I twisted my wrist, snapping the column of bone in Sadie's neck, I wouldn't just be breaking bone. I'd be breaking Sera's trust. Showing her what to expect of me for the rest of our days together. Her entreaties would go unheard. I would always be cruel, hard, and brutal, leaving no room inside myself for anything that might resemble peace.

She deserved more than that. Our life together *had* to be more than that. Slowly, I loosened my grip around Sadie's neck, ignoring the twinge of frustration I felt when her rasping, spluttering gasps for breath eased. Oxygen was too precious to waste on her. She didn't deserve one sip of the same air that Sera breathed.

I dropped her, and she slumped to the ground, hacking and spluttering, rubbing at her neck. Her esophagus was going to be real fucking bruised, and I couldn't muster up a single fuck to give. "You can't hide behind your anonymity anymore, you deranged bitch. I swear to god and all things fucking holy, if you so much as think the name Sera Lafferty, I will fucking know about it, and I will come for you. I'll find a hundred and one ways to cause you pain before I'm done with you, and she won't be able to stop me next time."

I wrapped an arm around Sera. There wasn't going to be a second to waste here. She was pale as death, her skin waxy, her brow beaded with sweat, and the pool of blood on the tile at her feet had grown uncomfortably large. I knew exactly where the nearest hospital was. I'd seen one in the cab on the way over here, about six or seven blocks away.

"My car keys are on the hook in the kitchen," Sera said. There was a worrying wet rattle in her lungs. The glass couldn't have hit them, it was too far down for that, but whatever was happening in her chest didn't sound good. I began to guide her out of the apartment. I couldn't carry her. Lifting her would compress the wound, potentially causing untold damage. We'd almost made it to the front door, when the skin at the back of my neck prickled.

Sadie was still weeping in the bathroom, right?

Wrong.

I pushed Sera out of the way as Sadie hurled herself down the hallway. In her hand was a knife, now—a seriously fucking sharp one. She swung her arm down, trying to dig the blade into Sera's back. I reacted, ducking low, then brought my body up as I tackled her, lifting her off her feet and then slamming her down onto the floor.

"*You* don't get to show *me* mercy," she screamed. "You think you have everyone so convinced. Sera, the little fucking goody two shoes. Sera, the benevolent. Sera, the kind. I know the fucking truth, you whore! You're a fucking monster! I'll never stop!" She kicked and spat as she fought, trying to rid herself of me as I pinned her to the floor. She clawed at my arms like a rabid dog, snarling and baring her teeth. "I will *never* stop, Sera. I won't rest until you're dead and rotting in the ground. You won't know a moment's peace. I will always find you, no matter where you go!"

This was pure fucking madness. I understood Sera's need to show compassion, but this woman wasn't capable of appreciating it. She was mentally incapable of letting this thing go, whatever it was. "This can't go on, Sera. She's crazy," I reasoned. "The only way to end this is to end *her*. If not, you'll always be looking over your shoulder. We both will. I can live like that. I'll tolerate it, if it makes you happy. But can you?"

Sera swallowed as she looked down at her friend. A wave of unfettered emotion rolled across her pale face. "I need... Fuck, Felix, I need a moment to think."

58

ZETH

THE WOMAN IN THE BLUE SCRUBS

*S*o far, three ambulances had screeched up to the emergency entrance of St. Peter's of Mercy Hospital, unloading their critical patients as I sat in my car staring at the building like it was the very gates of hell itself. Michael had been calling for the last hour, had left a number of messages for me on my burner, but I hadn't picked up, hadn't wanted to speak to the man directly. I'd gotten dressed at the warehouse. Put on my best tuxedo. Had even taken the time to polish my fucking shoes. But when I'd gotten into the Camaro, I hadn't headed towards the apartment where the party was being held.

I'd somehow ended up here, parked outside the hospital. That seemed to be happening more and more recently. I liked to lie to myself. To tell myself that I didn't know why it happened, but I knew perfectly fucking well why I found myself parked here all the time. The woman I'd met in the downtown Marriott eighteen months ago had been on my mind ever since. Every goddamn day, she'd haunted my thoughts and my dreams like a goddamned ghost. Try as I might, I couldn't fucking shake her and I had really, *really* fucking tried.

The cellphone I'd been using for the past two weeks lit up on the dashboard, letting me know that Michael was calling me yet again. I glared at the device with a kind of malevolence that sank down deep into my bones. He wasn't going to stop. Not until I picked up and answered him. The party that was taking place at the apartment on the other side of town was my party after all. I'd carefully handpicked and invited each and every guest. They were all waiting for me there. Expecting me to show my face at any moment. I knew how these things went, though. The Moet would already be flowing. Silver trays, filled with party favors, were already being passed from hand to hand as the nights revelers sank into their debauchery. Usually I lived for these gatherings. They were an outlet for my pent-up aggression. A place for me to blow off some serious fucking steam. But ever since that night in the hotel with Sloane, my deviant little get-togethers were less and less appealing to me.

The woman was a plague. A curse I had willingly invited upon myself. And now there was nothing I could do to break that damn curse. I'd tried everything. Blonde women. Redheads. Brunettes. Short girls. Fat girls. Tall girls. Three girls at the same fucking time. No matter what I did, no matter *who* I did, Sloane was always there, lurking at the back of my mind.

I already knew I was going to go inside the hospital. The past three times I'd come here, I'd given in to my own weakness and stepped foot inside the building, pretending to be the loved one of a sick patient, or a delivery man. Once, I'd even impersonated a fucking doctor. I had watched her from the waiting room, from the hallway and from the canteen, always observing her from afar. I didn't know when I'd turned into the type of creepy motherfucker who would stalk a woman around the hallways of a hospital, but that's where I'd somehow ended up.

As I climbed out of the Camaro, leaving my phone on the dashboard, a light rain began to fall. I hardly noticed the fine mist as it fell and clung to the material of the Tom Ford tux I'd donned for the evening's frivolities. It rained so often in Seattle that the weather hardly registered with me at all anyway, but tonight sheet lightening could have been splintering the skies apart and I wouldn't have noticed the storm.

I recognized the woman at the nurses' station when I walked into the building. Her name was Gracie. She was a powerhouse. A force to be reckoned with, and Sloane seemed to rely on her whenever she was on shift to make sure her patients were being well cared for. Gracie looked up, her face a mask of professionalism as she picked up a tablet, ready to record whatever injury I had come to report.

Most women flinched when they made eye contact with me. It wasn't their fault. It was a natural reaction. Some innate sense of self-preservation within them, screaming at them to run away and hide. Gracie didn't flinch. "How can I help you this evening, sir?" she asked. Her index finger hovered over the tablet, ready to take down my details.

"Got a serious headache," I told her gruffly. "Had it for three days now."

I'd learned a long time ago that I couldn't report anything more serious than a minor injury. If I said I had chest pain, I'd be bumped to the top of her list and a doctor would be with me within ten minutes. I didn't want that. I wanted to sit in the waiting room. I *wanted* to sit here for hours. I wanted to be forgotten about, until I became a piece of the furniture, and the nurses', and the doctors', and the porters' gazes skipped over me. That was the key. If I wanted to go unnoticed as I wandered the halls of St. Peter's, I had to be seriously fucking unimportant.

Gracie gave me a tight-lipped smile, raising her eyebrows. "Do you get headaches often?"

"Sometimes."

"And have you taken any pain relief?"

I gave her a bored, lazy smile. "Just some Advil."

Two small lines formed between her brows. Gracie fucking *hated* me. Tonight was a busy night at St. Peter's of Mercy. With the three triage patients that had been rushed in here earlier, all of the doctors were busy. All of the nurses, too. She didn't have time to deal with some idiot dressed in a tux, complaining of a fucking headache.

"Okay, sir. If you can fill out your information here and then take a seat, I'll have someone with you as soon as I can." As soon as she could meant about two to three hours, given my past experiences here, and that was just fine by me. I took the tablet from her and began to fill out my information, providing my name and my address —all bullshit—and then I supplied a very bland medical history and family background at the bottom. Handing back the tablet, I went and took a seat.

Mothers bounced screaming, red-faced children on their knees in every direction I looked. A guy with a pretty serious looking gash on his shin argued with someone on his phone. In the corner, by the vending machine, an old woman sat in a wheelchair, staring blankly at the opposite wall. Of all the people gathered in the waiting room I was probably the least significant. Perfect. An hour slipped by. Occasionally, the double doors would open and a doctor would appear, calling somebody's name. A name that was never mine. Every time I caught sight of blue scrubs, my heart seized in my chest, the oxygen burning in my lungs, but it was never *her*. It was never Sloane.

They didn't change the codes on the security key pads here at St. Peter's. Michael had given me a list of them after I'd tasked him with obtaining the information, and he hadn't asked why. I knew the layout of the hospital like the back of my hand now. The blue prints were online, a matter of public record, but I'd also spent plenty of time hovering outside the labs, or X-ray, or the CT department. I knew precisely where a patient would be sent if they needed an MRI, and I knew how to get to the ICU. I knew where the fucking morgue was, for that matter.

At ten-thirty, an hour and a half after I'd arrived at the hospital, Gracie took her break. I used the change in staff to my advantage, getting to my feet, pretending to head toward the bathroom. Yeah, like anyone would actually, willingly use the bathroom in an E.R. waiting room. If you weren't fucking sick before you used the john in a place like this, you were going to be violently ill by the time you had.

I breathed through my mouth as I cut across the waiting room. Everything smelled like bleach and disinfectant here.

Bleach.

Disinfectant.

And death.

No one made a peep as I made my way over to the double doors, entered the code, and opened them. In the hallway beyond, I ducked my head, walking with purpose past a row of examination cubicles. There were people everywhere. I sidestepped around a woman with a tear-streaked face, clutching a small, red jacket to her chest. A child's jacket. While millions of people were going about their lives in the city of Seattle tonight, this woman was stuck here in this cold, sterile place, praying to god that her son or daughter would make it to see the dawn.

Pretty fucked up.

Working for Charlie had equipped me with a set of skills that I put to good use as I wound my way through the rabbit warren of hallways and corridors. My body was a weapon, a finely tuned instrument, primed to detect one thing, and one thing alone: Sloane Romera. I constantly scanned my surroundings, using my peripherals, searching for any sign of the woman. She wasn't tending to patients in any of the triage bays. She wasn't updating patient records at any of the computer stations. She wasn't in x-ray, and she wasn't outside the labs waiting for results, either. Maybe I'd remembered her schedule wrong. Maybe she'd taken the night off.

Maybe she was sick.

I railed against the unease that settled over me at that thought. If Sloane was sick and she was at home laid up in her bed... If we hadn't met under such strange circumstances... If I were any kind of *normal* man, and I had pursued her in any kind of *normal* way, I would've been able to go to her, take care of her, make sure she was okay. I knew perfectly fucking well where she lived. Her pretty little house perched up on the side of the mountain overlooking the city was out of the way, though. I couldn't just drive by pretending to be lost or visiting another property. If she heard a vehicle winding its way up the road towards her place, she'd be ready and waiting for it by the time it reached the driveway.

I broke into a cold fucking sweat whenever thoughts like this occurred to me. I shouldn't be fucking thinking them. If Sloane was sick, the very best thing I could do was stay the fuck away from her. Her life was complicated enough, and my life didn't exactly allow for personal connections of any kind. If Charlie knew I occupied my days and nights with thoughts of a woman, he'd use the information to his advantage. She would become collateral in a twisted game he and I had been playing for many years. And that I could *not* allow.

By the time I'd scoured the lower floor of the hospital, I'd given up on the hope that I was going to see her tonight. Wherever she was, she wasn't here. But then—

I paused.

Stopped altogether.

My stomach slowly twisted itself into a knot. There she was, standing next to a public payphone, leaning against a wall, talking to another doctor. Her long brown hair was intricately braided around the side of her head and twisted at the nape of her neck. Her cheeks were marked with a high flush of color, and her dark eyes were bright, and shone with excitement as she talked to the man standing opposite her. I knew the guy. I'd done my research on the fucker when I realized how much time he spent with Sloane. Dr. Oliver Massey was a walking advertisement for clean living. A spoiled rich boy whose father had invented some sort of cardiovascular surgical equipment that had made his family millions. With the allowance his parents gave him every month, the arrogant bastard certain didn't need to work. And yet here he was every day, hanging around Sloane like a bad smell.

After so many years working for Charlie, I'd lost the capability to really feel anything strongly. It was better that way. No guilt, no remorse, no shame. But when I looked at Oliver Massey's smiling face as he chatted so casually with a woman I couldn't even fucking say hello to, I was filled with a very strong emotion indeed. I hated Oliver Massey. I seriously, *seriously* fucking hated the man.

Sloane grinned, and then took a sip from a takeaway coffee cup in her hand. "I can't believe he made it," she said. "When he tanked for the third time, I was sure we'd lost him."

"Just goes to show, you never can tell," he said. "Makes you wonder how many more flatlines would survive if we kept working on them. A couple more minutes of compressions. Another shot of Epi. Maybe more people would revive if we didn't have to call time of death so soon. Twelve minutes is nothing. I read in a journal last week about a guy who was brought back after forty-eight minutes. *Forty-eight*."

I looked around, found a seat to park myself on, and I let my head rock back against chair, staring at the ceiling as I listened to their conversation. God, this prick was such a fucking do-gooder. Probably participated in human rights marches. Probably totted his handmade signs baring slogans like, 'Meat Is Murder' outside steak houses, feeling pretty damn pleased with himself. I made a note to stop by Rosaria's on the way over to the apartment later on. I was going to eat a fucking steak the size of a goddamn dinner plate. Extra bloody. I was going to make sure I fucking enjoyed it, too.

Sloane drank the rest of her coffee, crumpling the takeaway cup and tossing it into the trash can beside her. "Alright. I got three more patients I have to see before I can go and get some food. I'll meet you when I'm done," she said.

"Sure thing." Oliver flashed his pearly whites as he held up his hand, waiting for Sloane to give him a high five. Who the fuck gave high fives anymore? This wasn't nineteen eighty-five, for fuck's sake. Sloane slapped her palm to his, giving him a rye look out of the corner of her eye, as if she were mirroring my own thoughts, and then she turned and walked away.

Once Massey had gone, I got to my feet and followed after her, maintaining a safe distance. I knew how to do this. Knew how it worked. I'd tailed her successfully many times before while she was on shift, and it'd been all too fucking easy. As we approached the ground floor elevators, I crossed my fingers in my pocket.

Don't go upstairs. Don't go upstairs. Don't go upstairs.

I had a rule. One that couldn't be broken. I could follow her. I could watch her. But the moment she stepped foot on an elevator, it was game over.

Elevators were strange places. People would stand in line in the canteen. They'd sit next to one another in the waiting rooms. They'd stand side by side in the pharmacy, but the moment you put them in an elevator everyone turned into a chatty fucking Cathy. The closed, confined space made people sufficiently awkward that they ended up shooting tight-lipped smiles at one another, eyebrows raised, as they rocked back and forth on the balls of their feet, ready to make polite conversation about the fucking weather.

The one and only encounter Sloane and I had shared had taken place in the dark. She hadn't seen my face, didn't know what I looked like, but she'd certainly heard my voice. She could have forgotten what I sounded like, or she could have blotted the timbre and the rolling pitch of my deep tenor from her mind on purpose. But it was far more likely that she remembered it with a crystal clarity that would get me into serious fucking trouble the moment I opened my mouth.

Thankfully Sloane sailed right past the elevators, bypassing them and taking a right hand turn back towards the triage bays.

"Dr. Romera. Just in time. I have a present for you."

Shit, shit, shit.

Gracie, the nurse who had checked me into the waiting room nearly two hours ago, had stopped right in front of Sloane, wielding a clipboard. If Gracie noticed me, she'd know I wasn't meant to be here. She was good at her job. A hard ass. She'd have no qualms about approaching me and forcing me back out into the waiting room.

I casually slowed my pace and came to a stop in front of a notice board that was plastered with leaflets and flyers. Women's health leaflets and flyers. I glared at a very detailed diagram instructing women how to perform thorough breast exams, tilted my chin down to my chest, angled my face away, and hoped Gracie wouldn't see me.

"Woman in four's got a stab wound," Gracie told Sloane. "Deep but hasn't hit anything major. Could be some glass in there, though. They already removed most of it and she's had an ultrasound."

"Got it." Sloane took the clipboard from Gracie and scanned the details. "Wow. This chick got lucky. All right. I'll take care of this and come back out front when I'm done."

"Thanks. Oh, and...be warned." She motioned toward the exam room. "Patient's boyfriend's a little uptight. Just a head's up." Gracie winked—way cooler than trying to instigate an awkward high five—and spun on her heel, heading back toward the nurse's station. Sloane entered exam room four, pulling back the curtain and disappearing inside.

Well, well. There weren't many guys wondering around the hospital in a five-thousand-dollar tux, I was willing to bet, but somehow I'd managed to go unseen. My lucky fucking day. Strolling slowly down the hall, I came to a stop outside exam four, positioning myself opposite the drawn privacy curtain, slipping my hands inside my pockets. Should have brought my cell after all. Michael's incessant calling had been driving me to the point of insanity but having it on me now would have been useful. A prop I could have used to make myself look busy as I hovered in the bustling corridor.

Instead, I picked up a pamphlet from a rack fixed to the wall and pretended to read it as I listened carefully to what was taking place in the cubicle ahead. The stab wound Gracie had described didn't sound particularly dangerous, or even that fucking interesting, but that didn't matter. I just wanted to hear the sound of Sloane's voice; the woman could read from an encyclopedia and I'd still have found myself enthralled.

Jesus fucking Christ.

I was fucking crazy.

I'd lost my goddamn mind.

Sloane was the epitome of professionalism when she spoke: cool, calm, and collected. "Looks like you've had quite an evening. How on earth did you end up with a shard of glass stuck in your abdomen, Ms. Lafferty?"

My hand made a fist, crushing the pamphlet inside it. *What? What did she just say?*

Lafferty?

The world was not that small.

The world was not that fucking unbelievable.

It couldn't be her.

"It's a long story," a tired female voice said. *Sera's voice.*

No fucking way.

I'd shown Charlie the staged picture of the woman, laying in a jumbled, bloody mess at the foot of those stairs as I'd promised I would. I'd gotten into the Camaro and driven at breakneck speeds back to Seattle, and I hadn't given the priest and his girlfriend another fucking thought. Actually, that wasn't strictly true. I had thought about *her*. I'd figured she'd wind up dead sooner rather than later, even if I wasn't the one to complete the task. These things were inevitable in the end. And now, here she was at St. Peter's, being treated for a stab wound by Sloane fucking Romera.

Of all the hospitals in all the world...

Of all the doctors...

I didn't believe in fate, kismet or karma. They were made up concepts designed to control people or give them false hope, but even I had to admit that this was seriously fucking strange. Gracie said the patient's boyfriend was up-tight, which meant that, not only was Sera here, but so was Fix.

I had better things to do than tangle with the likes of him tonight. Be better if I just left. Went to the party and forgot about Sloane for the night. Better yet, it would be fortuitous for all concerned if I forgot about Sloane once and for all. Banished her from my mind for good. I needed to go to the apartment and pick out a girl. The prettiest, sexiest, wildest girl, wearing the least amount of clothes. If I fucked the living daylights out of that kind of woman, I'd be able to finally let this thing go. The lie jarred me down to the sockets of my teeth. It was an outright lie that I'd told to myself—the stupidest kind of lie there was. I wasn't going to be able to let this thing go. Never in a million years.

I dropped the screwed-up pamphlet onto the ground, my blood hot and irritated in my veins. There would still be plenty of booze left by the time I reached the party, and I was going to fucking need it. I would drown myself in whiskey, glass after glass of the burning liquid, until I couldn't remember my own name anymore, and it would be a fucking relief.

Sera sighed heavily and began to explain how she'd come to find herself in the emergency room: her friend had lost her temper and attacked her in her home. She'd smashed the shower screen in her bathroom and had stabbed her with one of the pieces.

Sometimes, the explanations people gave to doctors were the unfortunate truth, but ninety-nine point nine percent of the time, they were falsehoods, made up to protect the person who'd hurt them. Didn't sound like Sera was making shit up right now, though.

I set my jaw as I slowly turned away. I'd taken one step when the curtain snapped back, and suddenly Sloane was standing in front of me, scribbling something down on Sera's chart, the tip of her pen flying over the paper, leaving a string of indecipherable black scrawl in its wake.

"Oh. You must be Sera's boyfriend," she said stiffly. She didn't look up at me. "You can go in and wait with her, but she's on a lot of pain meds. She might be a little out of it. I'm just going to find some instruments so I can investigate the wound. Be back in a moment." She rushed off, head down, concentrating on her clipboard. I hadn't even needed to speak to her.

"You have *got* to be fucking kidding me." Sera was propped up on the bed, wearing a surgical gown. Her face was pale and spattered with blood, hair all over the place. Her lips were a little blue, but other than that she seemed fine. Aside from the gaping hole in her stomach, that was. "What the fuck," she hissed. "I knew Fix shouldn't have trusted you."

"Calm down. I'm not here for you." I stepped into the cubicle, rocking my head from side to side, trying to crack my neck in order to rid myself of the inexplicable knot of pain that had developed there during the past twenty seconds.

Sera's pupils were blown and dilated so wide, her entire iris was almost obscured by the black. "Carver's been taken care of," she informed me. "We dealt with her before she..." She visibly battled with the word 'her', struggling to say it without shaking.

"A *woman* hired half the hitmen in the country to ex you out?"

Slowly, Sera nodded her head. Her eyes were laced with a penetrating, deep kind of pain that told a tale of its own. Likely, she'd known this woman all along. Carver had been close to her. Someone she hadn't suspected.

"Yes. And there's no point in hurting me now. You won't get paid for it,"

"I already *got* paid for it, if you'll remember. And I gave the priest my word," I snarled. "I wouldn't break that."

Sera huffed out a rattle of disbelieving laughter. "What is it with you guys and the whole, 'my word is my bond' thing? You're hardly upstanding members of the community."

"No. We're criminals. The worst fucking kind. We rob, and we cheat, and we steal people's lives. But when we promise we will or we won't do something, you can bet your ass we'll keep that promise. Every single time. Our word is our only currency in trust."

Sera stared, her gaze skipping over me, as if she couldn't really focus properly; Sloane must have dosed her with the really good stuff. "If you're not here for me, then why *are* you here, Zeth Mayfair?"

I pouted, running my tongue over my teeth. "Is Fix taking care of the body?"

"What?"

"Is the priest taking care of Carver's body right now? Is that why he's not here?" That would be the only reason good enough for me to leave the woman I loved alone in a hospital bed.

She blinked, looking down as she tugged at the sheet covering her legs. "He's...dealing with the situation. But that's none of your concern. You still haven't answered my question."

"I don't have to answer your question," I said sharply. The glare she sent my way could have flayed a man alive. "But since you asked so nicely...I'm here because of a woman."

"Have you been paid to kill her, too?"

"No." My history with Sloane was far more complicated than that. I didn't want her dead. Far from it. But I *had* wronged her. Wronged her in a way that kept me up at night, pacing the warehouse, running my hands through my hair like a fucking guilty teenager.

Sera let her head fall back against the pillows. She was plainly exhausted. If Charlie hadn't bought the text I'd sent him, proving that the woman was dead, I would easily have been able to rectify the situation now. Ending her life would have been a moment's work, with her laid here, half out of her mind on morphine, incapacitated by a serious injury. "Somehow, I can't imagine a man like you knows what it is to love another human being," she said.

"I never said I was in love with her," I fired back. God, the very fucking idea of something so preposterous. It was laughable. But still...the fact that she'd made such a statement irked me. "That's interesting, though. You can imagine that Fix is in love with you?"

She didn't hesitate. "I *know* he loves me."

"What makes you think he and I are so very different? We're both in the same line of work. We both have blood on our hands."

She stared at me. Stared through me. Her mouth remained firmly closed.

"He and I share many similar attributes," I continued. "If you know he's capable of love, then it stands to reason that I would be, too."

"Fix keeps saying the same thing. He keeps saying you're both so alike, but I see a world of difference. He isn't shut down. He hasn't shut the world out. His heart..." She paused. "He *has* a heart. Maybe you do, too, but you'll never allow anyone to touch it. To find a home within it." She squinted, her eyes distant and glazed over as she searched my face.

My mouth twisted into an unpleasant smile. No one spoke to me the way she was speaking to me. No one fucking dared. She was pretty fucking observant for someone in her position, though. I didn't want to admit that she was right, but her words struck something inside me that I didn't want to deal with right now. "I think I should probably be on my way, Sera Lafferty."

"Yes," she agreed. "But first...why did you say that to me? Back in that stairwell. You told me I was the one who was no good for Fix."

I thought about leaving this particular question to eat away at her, but then I changed my mind. What would be the point? I smirked, placing my hands on the railing at the end of the gurney, leaning my weight against it. "Women like you are dangerous to men like us. Fix's heart was probably just as dysfunctional as mine before he laid eyes on you. He was probably just as angry as me. And then you came along and took all of that away from him. You made him weak. You made him mortal again. Now, he's no longer untouchable."

She processed the words—I could see her doing it. She appeared to consider her response carefully before she answered me. "And do you honestly think he would have it any other way? You think he would choose to go back to the way he was before he knew me, if he could?"

The smile froze on my face. "I know he wouldn't. And *that* is precisely why you're dangerous. Because, once men like us fall into bed with women like you, the world could set alight and burn for the rest of time. Society could crumble and fall into ruin, we wouldn't care, so long as *you* were safe."

Sera's expression softened. She closed her eyes, breathing out steadily down her nose. "Then I apologize. I was wrong about you just now, Zeth Mayfair. You *do* know what love is. I can hear it in your voice. The only difference between you and Felix is that you're just not ready for it yet."

59

SERA

TRADITION

THREE WEEKS LATER

I was healing up nicely, though I still ached from time to time. My stomach throbbed, reminding me to take it easy if I tried to take on too much, but other than that I felt stronger and stronger every day.

I hadn't told Fix about Zeth appearing at the hospital the night of Sadie's...or rather *Julia's* attack. On one hand, I couldn't be sure that Zeth *had* actually been there. I'd been drugged up to my eyeballs, and everything had seemed so surreal and strange that I couldn't have been sure I hadn't imagined the conversation. Then there was the possibility that Fix might try to go after Zeth. If he knew the guy was aware of our presence here in Seattle, he might see him as a threat to my safety and hunt him down. I'd had enough violence and bloodshed recently to last me a lifetime. I'd tell him one day, when we'd figured out what we were going to do with ourselves now that Sadie was out of the picture and there were no more contracts out on my life. Until then, I was going to enjoy the comfortable albeit weird existence we had now fallen into.

Things were never going to be what anyone else might call normal for us.

The foundations of our relationship had been formed during a time of intense unrest and fear, and now our existence together felt strange, as if we were holding our breath, waiting for the other shoe to drop. Could things be this calm for us now? Could they ever be simple? I'd be a fool to believe they would be.

There were going to be bumps in the road. Obstacles we had to overcome in order to move forward. There were probably going to be days when Fix behaved so egregiously that I wanted to murder him for his actions. And there were definitely going to be days when I wanted to be alone, to run away and hide from the world, and I was going to try and push him away. I wasn't afraid, though. We'd get through it.

See, easy and simple weren't concepts I was used to. I'd had to fight for everything in my life, and I didn't regret that for a moment. The fight had shown me how strong I was. It had shown me the true value of happiness, and it had shown me the lengths I was willing to go to in order to protect it. It would be okay if I had to fight for a life with Fix from time to time. After all, he'd been fighting for me since the moment he set eyes on me, and it didn't look like he was planning on stopping any time soon.

"I've been meaning to ask. Why did you rent a car for your trip across country when you had this beauty sitting in the garage the entire time?" Fix asked, slapping the steering wheel as he headed north east, up toward Redmond.

The Chevy Beretta I'd stolen from Sixsmith had gotten us as far as Washington State. I'd walked into a Walmart in some town I couldn't even remember the name of anymore, with the purpose of buying Amy and I a few items of clothing. At the checkout, the woman in front of me was struggling to wrangle two tiny children while she'd counted out the change to pay for the diapers and baby food that sat on the conveyor belt. She'd looked tired and harassed and had nearly burst into tears when the guy waiting behind me had told her to hurry the fuck up. Outside, once I'd paid for the clothes I'd picked up, the same woman was waiting at a bus stop in the rain, her children quiet and round eyed, and I hadn't even thought about it. I'd pulled the car over, told Amy to get her bag, and we'd gotten out.

The sheer disbelief on the woman's face when I'd handed her the keys and told her the car was hers...I was never going to forget that. The mother had taken some convincing, but in the end she'd taken it. I advised her to exchange it for another car and soon, or sell it outright and keep the money, and she hadn't asked why. Essentially, the car had been mine to give away. I'd paid for it three times over with my twice weekly trips to see Sam. Sixsmith was a fucker of the highest order, though, and had no doubt reported the Chevy stolen, so I figured it was better to be safe than sorry.

Five years later, after I was done with college and had been working for a while, I'd picked up the Fastback. She was a thing of beauty. With the gleaming, slick, paint job in midnight black and the matte black rims to match, the thing was almost murdered out.

"Didn't wanna put the miles on the engine," I mumbled around my mouth full of sandwich.

Fix gave me a sidelong look, smiling, the corners of his eyes crinkling.

I'd been about to take another bite of my sandwich. I lowered it. "What?"

"Nothing. I just never realized I'd fallen in love with a greaser is all. This is a badass car, Sera."

"I know. But I'm a badass. I deserve a badass ride. Count your lucky stars I'm even letting you drive it."

Fix smile wavered. "You *are* a badass. You've been a badass since that night at the motel."

I angled my head, wondering at the odd tone to his voice. "Does my badass status worry you or something?"

"Quite the opposite. Your badass status compliments my totally-fucking-awesome-smart-and-sexy-as-fuck status quite nicely."

Asshole. I stuck my tongue out at him.

"I'm just wondering if you've thought this through, that's all. You don't have to be so strong all the time. You're allowed to be affected by things from time to time. You don't owe her anything, Sera. Not one thing."

I cringed, my appetite evaporating into smoke. Silly, really. We were less than thirty minutes away from the facility where Sadie was...*living*? I'd been lying on a gurney, getting my stomach stitched back together, while Fix had left me to take Sadie upstairs to the psych ward at the hospital. Of course, he'd had to use a fake name when he'd dealt with the care staff. He'd become Daniel Whitechurch—the same Daniel Whitechurch who'd accompanied me on a plane back from New York City only a few hours earlier. The cops hadn't suspected a thing when we'd both had to give our account of what had happened.

After a thorough examination, the doctors put Sadie on a seventy-two-hour hold, deciding that she was, indeed, suffering from some sort of mental illness. Since we weren't family, they wouldn't tell us exactly what their diagnosis was, but they seemed appropriately concerned by the fact that she'd stabbed me in the fucking stomach with a nine-inch-long piece of glass. Once the psychiatric hold had expired, they'd deemed her a risk to herself and others and had moved her to Gateway House.

Today was the first and last time I'd be paying her a visit.

"I've thought it through. I've done nothing but think it through," I said. "Part of me thinks I'm being selfish. That I just want to see her in there with my own two eyes, so I know she's not getting out any time soon. And if that's the case, then I should just walk away and not step foot inside the place, because me going there is only going to rile her up and completely unbalance her again."

"I wouldn't worry about that. Unbalanced is Sadie's *permanent* state. If you need to see her for some reason before you can move on, then just fucking do it. I know she's sick, but really. *Fuck her.* She tried to fucking kill you. Came pretty close to succeeding, too. Let's not forget that."

He was right.

Some nights, I laid awake in bed, sweating, panicking, questioning if I'd done the right thing. If I'd just let Fix kill her, I wouldn't be feeling like this now. More than likely, I would feel free. She would never have posed a threat to us again. Sadie would have been yet another life Fix had taken, though, and, although he never said it, I knew the weight of the dead pressed down on him every day.

"I don't expect this to make any sense to you," I said weakly. "But we *were* close. For years. Maybe she was only pretending, and she *really* fucking hated me the entire time, but I believed she was my friend. She was so important to me. I leaned on her. I trusted her. I relied on her for so much. And we *laughed*. We had some amazing times, Fix. It all sounds so fucked up and crazy when I say it out loud, but in a way it doesn't matter if none of it was real to her. It was real to *me*, and I feel... God. I feel..."

"Like you want to say goodbye to your friend," Fix murmured.

Staring straight ahead, I wrapped my sandwich up with numb hands, putting it back into the plastic bag at my feet. He was so astute. He saw absolutely everything with those beautiful, fierce, moonlit eyes. "Yeah. I guess you could put it like that."

Forty minutes later, we'd found Gateway House, parked and signed in at the front desk. But when we were getting ready to be shown through to the common area where Sadie was reportedly watching television, a short woman in her forties with a high blonde ponytail and very businesslike horn-rimmed glasses intercepted us, calling us into her office.

"I'm Doctor Sandra Hewitt," she said, vigorously shaking my hand. "I'm very glad to meet you, Sera, although I am a little surprised that you're here. Most victims of violent physical assault choose to avoid seeing their attackers for quite some time. And you must be Daniel?" She smiled brightly up at him.

Fix smiled tightly as he also shook her hand. He was really, really hating this, and I couldn't blame him. I was hating it, too. The place wasn't bad at all. Everything was very relaxed, the décor plush, and none of the (super friendly) staff were wearing scrubs. It didn't feel like a medical facility at all, but there was just something unsettling about the place.

"Listen, I'm sorry to have stopped you in the corridor there, but unfortunately I don't think it would be wise for you to see Julia at this time. She's really struggling to come to terms with reality at the moment. In fact..." She squinted at me, her eyes flitting sideways, taking in Fix for a second. "She's made some very concerning accusations about you, Daniel. Can I ask what line of work you're in?"

A good-natured frown of concern creased his brow. "I'm a hitman. I murder people for money."

"Oh! Oh, goodness!" Sandra said, laughing. "So you're aware of Julia's manic delusions."

Fix laughed, though I couldn't quite manage to do the same. I was still reeling from the shock of what he'd just said to a professional health care worker. He'd been true to form, though. The night of the storm, when I'd asked him the very same question, he'd given me the very same answer: the disarming truth.

"Yes, sadly Julia didn't like me spending time with Sera. Over the past few months, she began to invent this bizarre story that I was a priest or something. That she'd tried to pay me to kill Sera, and..." He shook his head, incredulity written all over him. He may have been a firm advocate for honesty, but it turned out he was a very convincing liar when he needed to be. "I just don't know where any of it came from. She'd be fine one minute, then sending weird, random emails the next. None of it made any sense."

"No, well I'm sure it wouldn't. Hyperreligiosity is quite common amongst our patients here. We have no idea why, but the Church, religion, God...all seem to be triggers for people who suffer from bipolar disorder and a number of other disorders, too. It's not surprising that Julia assigned you this role, Daniel. The role of a negative figure head, who has power over her." She turned to Sera. "Julia's admitted a number of times that she wishes to kill you, Sera. She also admitted to killing your dog, though sometimes these violent fantasies bleed through into a patient's mind, and we can never really tell—"

I cleared my throat. "Ahh, yeah. She did actually kill him."

Sandra gave me doleful, sympathetic eyes from behind the thick rims of her glasses. "I'm terribly sorry to hear that." She scribbled something down on a notepad. "As I was saying, I don't think it would be advantageous to you or to Julia if you were to see one another today. Her emotional state's currently very erratic. I'm sorry to say I think she might try to harm you if you were to sit in a room together."

"Right. Okay. If you think it isn't a good idea..." Relief. Holy fuck, the relief. I'd forced myself to come, it had felt like the right thing to do, but the relief that came over me now felt like warm sunlight thawing out the ice that had formed in my veins.

Sandra smiled in a benevolent, saintly way. "You know, you don't need to feel bad about Julia being here, Sera. This is the best place for her. This is one hundred percent where she needs to be."

I drove us home. About ten miles from the apartment, Fix began toying with the back of my neck, stroking his fingers up and down, weaving them through my hair. His touch was like live electricity, but instead of causing me pain, as it had Zeth when he'd run that current through him in the bathtub back in New York, the electricity that sparked from his fingertips now made my head dance and spin with pleasure. I still couldn't believe that he was mine, and I was his. That the constant fear of death was no longer hanging over our heads, and we could simply...*be.*

"I've been thinking about what that shrink said," Fix rumbled. His voice was so ridiculously sexy—deep but carrying a playful warmth that made me want to blush.

"And?"

"And Julia's where she needs to be now. But...what about us? Where should *we* be?"

That was a monumentally huge question. I'd been trying to figure that out myself, but I hadn't wanted to ask him. I hadn't wanted to assume...

"I don't believe in the church anymore. I'm never going to go to Mass, or Confession again. But I would like to go back to church one last time, if you'll come with me."

"What for?"

Fix untangled his hand from my hair. He used it to rub at his stubble, his gaze pointed out of the window—I sensed that he wasn't actually seeing any of the buildings or the houses that streaked by as we grew closer and closer to my place. After a moment's thought, he shifted in his seat, repositioning his whole body so that he was facing me. He rubbed at his jaw again, wincing as if he were in pain.

"Jesus," I laughed. "If whatever you want to say is causing you this much trouble, then might I suggest you don't say it?"

"It's not causing me trouble. I'm just...I'm gonna ask you something, and I'm weighing up how badly I'm going to want to hurl myself off a bridge if you say no."

Oh fuck.

Nooooooo.

He wasn't. He was not going to ask me what I thought he was going to ask me. I shot him a wide-eyed look, daring to take my gaze off the road for a split second in order to deliver it properly. "Don't do it," I whispered.

He looked very serious. The joking twitch at the corner of his mouth was nowhere to be seen. "Why not?"

"Because. If you ask, I'm going to say yes. And if I say yes, then everything will change."

"Like what?"

I wrung my hands over the steering wheel, trying to settle the jittering bounce in my right knee that had just started up. "We'll have to make plans. We'll have to decide where to live. We'll have to figure out if I'm going to sell my business. You'll have to stop killing people—"

"I've already stopped killing people." He winked.

"No, you haven't!"

"I didn't kill Julia. And Monica's shut down all of our accounts on the dark web. We're officially offline."

"Until you need money."

"Tisk, tisk. You know I don't take the money. You know I don't need it, either. I'd be hurt if you weren't so obviously shitting yourself right now."

"I—" I gaped, opening my mouth and then closing it again. "I am *not* shitting myself."

"You are. You're being a coward."

I reached for a blistering retort, but none came to hand. "*You're* the one too scared of my answer to even ask the question in the first place."

His full mouth curved up into an amused smile, and his lone dimple appeared in his right cheek. "Fine. Sera Lafferty. Since the very first moment I aimed my sniper rifle at you and targeted you down its sights, I knew—"

"Stop! Oh my god, please, Fix, you need to stop!"

"See. You're the coward, not me."

"I just really don't think this is something we should be doing in a car on the way back from a psychiatric hospital."

"Any other excuses you want to fling out there for good measure? What about the fact that we've only known each other for two months?"

I nodded my head up and down like crazy. "Yes! That! That is a very good point!"

"And kids. We haven't even talked about kids. Do you want them?"

I eyed him nervously. "Do *you*?"

"You can't ask me what *I* want, wait for me to answer, and then give the opposite answer just to prove how bad we are for each other, Sera."

Goddamnit! How the fuck was I that obvious to him? I scowled deeply as I took the exit and then a left, heading back toward the apartment. We were almost home. So fucking close. If I didn't shut this down now, he was going to take me upstairs and he was going to start kissing me, I would be fucking doomed. "This is completely the wrong way to go about this," I said firmly. "You don't even have a ring, Felix Marcosa."

The silver in his eyes sparked as a wide, shit-eating grin took over his entire countenance. "All right. Okay. Whatever you say, Sera Lafferty."

"Jesus. You have a ring, don't you?"

He shrugged, laughing softly under his breath as he turned to look out of his window.

"Fix! You're joking. You have *not* got a ring."

"What? I didn't say anything!" He held up his hands as I repeatedly tried to swat him to death. "Sera! Sera, fuck! Watch the road. You're going to run Julian over."

He was right; poor old Julian was standing right in the middle of the entryway to the underground parking lot beneath my building, looking lost. We'd arrived home and I hadn't even noticed, I was that distracted by the conversation. I swerved around Julian and parked, then got out of the car before Fix could lock the doors and trap me inside the vehicle with him; I knew his fucking game. He got out right behind me. "You're running away from me now. Very cowardly."

"I'm not running away. I just have to help Julian inside. It's my civic duty."

My heart felt like it was skipping backwards the entire time I helped the old man inside the building and up flight after flight of stairs; Fix was right behind me, smirking like the Cheshire fucking Cat. "Some people might say that using an eighty-nine-year-old as a human shield to protect yourself from the man you love might be a little unnecessary," he observed.

"He's ninety actually. It was your birthday last week, right, Julian?"

"Who, me?" The old man's head whipped back and forth between me and Fix. Poor bastard. I totally *was* using him as a human shield, and it was pathetic. The door to apartment 12B was wide open. I really was going to have to call Rhonda and get her to come over today. Julian seemed to be even more out of it than usual. I settled him in front of the TV, reheated some food for him, and fussed around the old man's apartment, straightening things up, and all the while, Fix leaned against the wall with his arms across his chest, the same broad smirk plastered all over his face, and that damned dimple cutting into his cheek, watching me intently.

Fucker.

He didn't belong here. He was larger than life. His presence was so huge, it felt like he sucked all the air out of a room simply by walking into it. The black t-shirt and the ripped black jeans. The way the muscles in his arms and his chest flexed whenever he laughed under his breath. His shock of devastatingly thick, dark hair, that was now a little wavy, falling into his eyes.

I was *so* in love with him.

I was *so* fucking screwed.

Eventually, there was nothing left to do but vacate Julian's apartment and go home. My ears were on fire, burning red hot as I opened up the door and let us in. Fix hummed quietly as he slipped past me and went into the kitchen. I heard him opening up the fridge.

For real? He was going to play it cool now? Uhhh, no way. He was biding his time, waiting for the perfect moment to strike. I stalked after him, index finger raised, ready to give him a piece of my mind, but Fix was one step ahead. Leaning against the kitchen counter, now facing me, he unscrewed the top off a beer and handed it to me, raising his eyebrows. "Look like you've got something you want to say there, Angel."

"You're unbelievable, you know that?"

"Why? Because I love you? Or because I want you to participate in an archaic tradition that doesn't really mean anything anymore, just so I get to see you in a really fancy dress?"

"I hate wearing fancy dresses. Especially white ones."

"Liar. You wear white all the time. And you looked like you enjoyed that fancy dress you wore to Rabbit's party."

"That was different, Felix!"

"Okay. So don't wear the fancy white dress. Wouldn't be the end of the world." He raised his own beer and pressed it to his still-smiling lips, drinking down the amber liquid while I openly snarled at him. His laughter nearly caused him to choke. "Fuck, Angel. If you really don't want to, then I'm not gonna make you."

"Why does it even matter? Like you said, it's an archaic tradition that doesn't even mean anything anymore."

Fix sighed as he put down his beer on the counter. Slowly, his smile faded. He took a deep breath as he crossed the kitchen and placed his hands in the small of my back. He smelled like fresh cut grass, and the dusk, and the back field where Amy and I used to play when we were kids. He smelled like happiness.

"I used to see really dark, heavy, fucked up shit every day of the week back when I worked for the church. But not on Saturdays. Saturdays were fucking beautiful. They made me not hate the human race. I used to stand up there at the front of the church, and I used to look into the eyes of these two people who'd come to stand opposite me, and I would see the hope in their eyes. I would feel their love as it filled the building, and my fucking soul would *ache* because I knew *you* were out there. The other fucking half of me. And it seemed like the biggest tragedy of all time that we were never going to stand in front of a priest and knock him the fuck out with the brass-knuckled love we felt for each other. That we were never gonna look each other in the eye and fucking swear we were gonna protect each other and put each other first for the rest of time.

"I'm not bound by the restrictions that denied me that possibility back then, so yeah. It matters to me. It matters to me, now *you've* given me hope. *You* make me not hate the human race. You've made me believe that there are still reasons to try and be good. I want our Saturday, Sera, because I know it will be fucking beautiful."

Well. *Fuck.*

The raw intensity in his eyes made me want to hide, but I couldn't. I was never going to hide from this man. Walking forward with him was terrifying, but...I was going to find a way to do it. Because he was right. A future with him really would be fucking beautiful. It'd be complicated and messy, and we were going to fight like cat and dog, but in the end, we were going to climb mountains together. We were going to face down the darkness together. We were going to set the world on fire.

I tilted my face up to his, offering him a shy smile; my hands shook as I reached up to wind my arms around his neck. "Okay, then. Fine," I whispered. "I give in. Ask me your question."

He bit down on his bottom lip, tugging it between his teeth. I knew there was some caustic comment on the tip of his tongue, begging to be set free, but he masterfully reined himself in. The very first time in history, I imagined. His grin nearly split his face apart. "First. Spoiler alert. Is the answer going to be yes?"

He already knew, though. He already knew it would be.

"Yes, you unbearable asshole. Of course it will be. Now get on with it. I want to see that ring."

ALSO BY CALLIE HART…

The Blood & Roses Series (more Zeth!)

The Dead Man's Ink Series

Violent Things

Savage Things

Wicked Things

Vice

Rooke

Mr. North

Calico

Between Here and the Horizon

Written as Frankie Rose:

Halo

Radicals

Winter

Summer

Black Moon Rising

Made in United States
North Haven, CT
28 September 2022

24688288R00320